PRAISE FOR JANE JENSEN'S
JUDGMENT DAY

"A THRILLING READ . . . HARD TO RESIST."

—USA Today

"[A] NEAR-FUTURE SCI-FI THRILLER . . . An exciting debut . . . Imaginative, snappy, and incident-packed."

—Kirkus Reviews (starred review)

"RECOMMENDED . . . [Jensen] turns her talents to storytelling on a grand scale, skillfully building suspense."

—Library Journal

"VIVID . . . Lovers of tales full of conspiracy theories, technology run amok, and ancient prophecies will relish Jensen's first novel."

—Booklist

By Jane Jensen

Novels:
Judgment Day (originally titled *Millennium Rising*)

Gabriel Knight novels:
The Beast Within
Gabriel Knight: Sins of the Fathers

Computer Games:
Gray Matter
Blood of the Sacred, Blood of the Damned
The Beast Within
Gabriel Knight: Sins of the Fathers

Dante's Equation

Jane Jensen

DEL
REY

BALLANTINE BOOKS • NEW YORK

A Del Rey® Book
Published by The Random House Publishing Group

www.delreydigital.com

Library of Congress Cataloging-in-Publication Data is available from the publisher upon request.
ISBN 0-345-43037-9

First Edition: August 2003

146122990

DEDICATION

————— ✳ —————

For my husband, Robert Holmes

ACKNOWLEDGMENTS

————— ✳ —————

Writing *Dante's Equation* was a long and challenging task and I had many sources of help and inspiration along the way. I was turned on to kabbalah by the work of Rabbi David A. Cooper, whose *Mystical Kabbalah* was a major inspiration for the dualistic view of kabbalah in this book. My favorite book on the Bible code is *Cracking the Bible Code* by Jeffrey Satinover. He writes about the scientific side of the code and of the link between code scholars and physics. It is not my intention with this book to argue either for or against the legitimacy of the code but merely to share the inspiration and flights of possibility that such books as Satinover's made me experience. I'd also like to thank Robert M. Haralick of the University of Washington, a code scholar that indulged me with a gracious interview on the subject. In the realm of science the ideas in this book owe a huge a debt to *The Seven Mysteries of Life* by Guy Murchie and *The Holographic Universe* by Michael Talbot and also to David Bohm and David Peat.

I had my own reviewers who dealt with *Dante's Equation* in the early stages and helped me understand what worked and what didn't both factually and from a dramatic point of view. I'd like to warmly thank Marcia Adams, Julia Wilson, Lois and Jim Gholson, Tom Stolz and Assaf Monsa. My husband, Robert, is subjected to hours of plot and character debate during any of my projects and Dante was three years worth—the man deserves a medal. Finally, thanks for the warm enthusiasm of my agent, Shawna McCarthy, and the hard work of my editor, Shelly Shapiro, and also Eric Miranda and Betsy Mitchell at Del Rey.

One finds, through a study of the implications of the quantum theory, that the analysis of a total system into a set of independently existent but interacting particles breaks down . . . the various particles [of physical matter] have to be taken literally as projections of a higher-dimensional reality which cannot be accounted for in terms of any force of interaction between them.

—David Bohm,
Wholeness and the Implicate Order, 1980

By looking into the microscope we peer at G-d. Science *is* the face of the Ein Sof.

—Yosef Kobinski, *The Book of Mercy,* 1935

Kabbalah Tree of Life

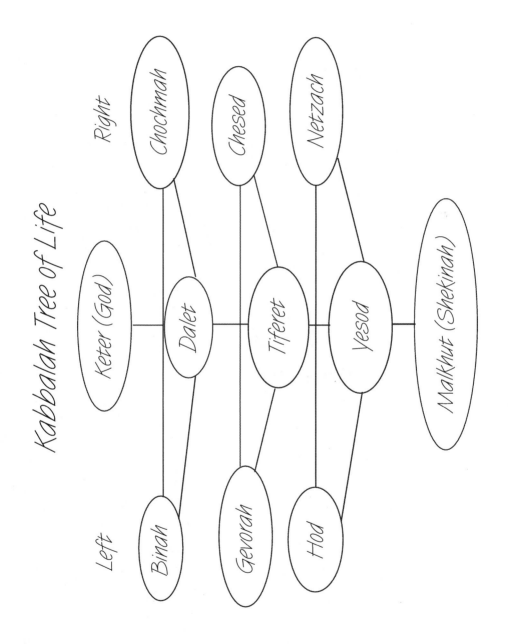

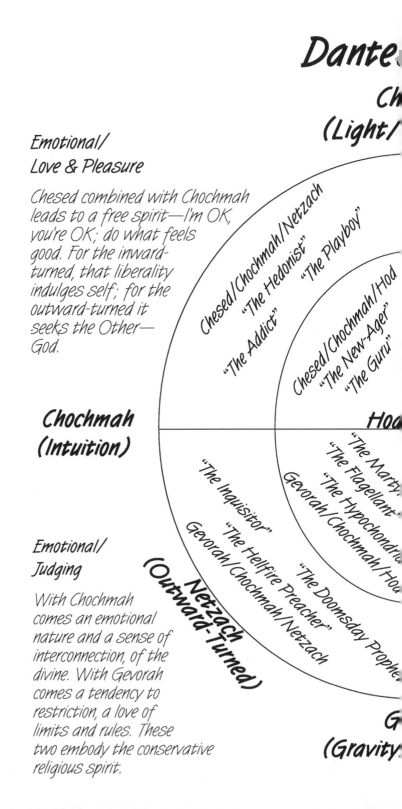

Dante[...]
Ch[...]
(Light/[...]

Emotional/
Love & Pleasure

Chesed combined with Chochmah leads to a free spirit—I'm OK, you're OK; do what feels good. For the inward-turned, that liberality indulges self; for the outward-turned it seeks the Other—God.

Chochmah
(Intuition)

Emotional/
Judging

With Chochmah comes an emotional nature and a sense of interconnection, of the divine. With Gevorah comes a tendency to restriction, a love of limits and rules. These two embody the conservative religious spirit.

Chesed/Chochmah/Netzach
"The Hedonist"
"The Playboy"
"The Addict"

Chesed/Chochmah/Hod
"The New-Ager"
"The Guru"

Hod

"The Marty[...]
"The Flagellant[...]
"The Hypochondri[...]
Gevorah/Chochmah/Hod

"The Inquisitor"
"The Hellfire Preacher"
Gevorah/Chochmah/Netzach

"The Doomsday Prophe[...]
Gevorah/Chochmah/Ho[...]

Netzach
(Outward-Turned)

G[...]
(Gravity[...]

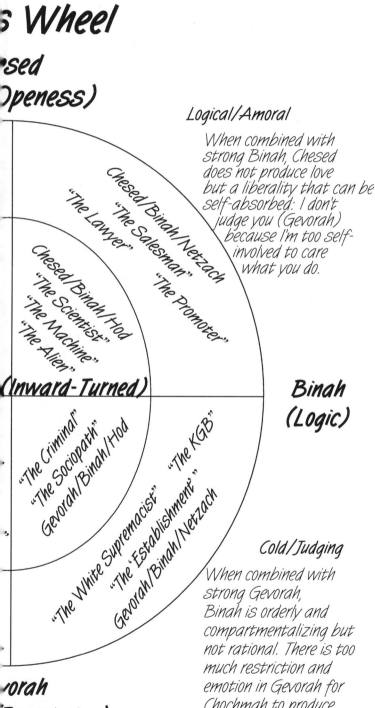

s Wheel

*sed
(Openess)*

Logical/Amoral

When combined with
strong Binah, Chesed
does not produce love
but a liberality that can be
self-absorbed: I don't
judge you (Gevorah)
because I'm too self-
involved to care
what you do.

Chesed/Binah/Netzach
"The Salesman"
"The Lawyer"
"The Promoter"

Chesed/Binah/Hod
"The Scientist"
"The Machine"
"The Alien"

(Inward-Turned)

**Binah
(Logic)**

"The Criminal"
"The Sociopath"
Gevorah/Binah/Hod

"The KGB"
"The White Supremacist"
"The Establishment"
Gevorah/Binah/Netzach

Cold/Judging

When combined with
strong Gevorah,
Binah is orderly and
compartmentalizing but
not rational. There is too
much restriction and
emotion in Gevorah for
Chochmah to produce
great scientific minds.

*orah
(Restriction)*

BOOK ONE

THE ONE-minus-ONE

I

We are like Midas ... Humans can never experience the true texture of quantum reality because
everything we touch turns to matter.

—Physicist Nick Herbert

I.I. Denton Wyle

March
Aboard the Coast Guard MLB Invincible II,
off the coast of Florida

Denton Wyle was seriously reexamining his choices. His fingers were wrapped
like living clamps around a pole, his blond hair dribbled water down his patrician nose, and his back pressed hard against the cabin of the rescue ship as sea
spray slapped him on the cheeks like an outraged Englishman and the deck
beneath his feet pitched like a bucking bronco.

He was on a ship, in a storm, smack dab in the Bermuda Triangle.

The Coast Guard crewmen, bright orange specks in a wet, gray world,
moved about the tilting slippery deck with ease. They were on a mission to locate a yacht, the *Why Knot Now*, in distress off the Florida Keys. A sailing advisory was in effect and the yacht, manned by a couple and their teenage
daughter, had radioed that their compass appeared to be in error, because they
were lost and didn't know which way to go to find land.

It was the call Denton had been waiting for, hanging out in the Coast
Guard station for weeks now, schmoozing with men who had sea salt in their
eyebrows. A bad compass? A lost vessel? Denton Wyle, intrepid reporter for
Mysterious World, was all over it.

Only now he realized, as his fingers spasmed from being clenched so
tightly around the pole, that the two key words in this entire scenario were not
bad compass or even *Bermuda Triangle* but *sailing advisory*. *Sailing advisory*
meaning: "our advice is, don't go out on a freaking ship."

"Wyle?" A rain-soaked face in a blue hard hat appeared. It was Frank, a
burly New Yorker. Denton had spent an afternoon watching him hose down
nylon netting.

"Yeah?"

"Get. Inside. The cabin." The words were shouted over the howl of the wind and symphonic crash of waves. Frank hung lightly with one hand to the pole just above Denton's white knuckles. With the other he jabbed an index finger at the cabin behind them.

"I'm fine," Denton shouted back, because moving anywhere meant letting go of the pole.

But Frank had been trained in dealing with the hapless. He grabbed Denton's upper arm and pulled. Behind Frank the side of the rescue boat was tilted at a forty-five-degree angle, and its thin, insubstantial metal rail kept dipping in and out of churning water. Denton could so clearly imagine sliding into that maw if he let go, just like the scene from *Jaws* where the fishing boat captain slides down the deck into the shark's mouth.

"Come *on!*" Frank yelled.

Denton let go. There was a panicked moment of sliding feet; then the cabin door was in his hand and Frank shoved him through, slamming the door behind him.

Inside, Denton stood panting, trying to get a firmer grip on his breakfast. He made no pretensions of bravery. The right stuff had been left out of his genetic code; he could admit that. But he was also not a boat person. Even growing up on the shores of Massachusetts, where yachting clubs got better attendance on Sundays than churches, he had not liked boats. What on earth had he been thinking?

He hadn't been thinking about the Bermuda Triangle or the sea. He'd been thinking about woods, about a little girl and flashes of light.

The rain lashed the windows so hard you couldn't see a thing on deck from inside the cabin, only great watery swells as they blocked out the sky.

"They keep fading in and out of radar," one of the crewmen reported.

Captain Dodd looked from the window to the radar screen and back again, peering out with squinting eyes. "How far?"

"About five hundred meters."

"Move closer. Slowly." Dodd never took his eyes off that window.

Denton found this conversation curious enough to nudge awake his reporter's instincts. He remembered the camera that had been flopping around on his chest for the past hour. He dried it with his sleeve and took some snapshots. It made him feel a little better.

"Damn it, we should have a visual by now!" Dodd stomped to a rack of gear and grabbed a rain poncho. "I'm goin' out. I'll send Johnson in to watch for my signal."

The wind intensified as the door opened and closed. Denton moved in to get a tight shot of the radar screen. He didn't recognize the operator, a baby-faced kid, no more than nineteen. He seemed amazingly unafraid, unfazed by the heaving deck beneath them or the towering waves above. He was intent on trying to tune in a better signal.

"Which blip is theirs?" Denton asked, teeth chattering.

The operator pointed to a faint ping, barely there. For a few seconds it went away; then it reappeared.

"We're not sure that's them, but we're close to their last recorded position." The kid looked up. "You okay?"

"Fine."

"You look chalky."

"I'm . . ." Denton glanced up and saw a gigantic wall of water. The wave slipped beneath them with a pitch and roll. ". . . fine. Look, does the radar usually do that? Fade in and out?"

The operator looked around, as if someone else could answer for him. "It's not supposed to, but this is pretty bad weather."

The wind blasted again as Johnson came in and took up a position by the window. Denton watched the blip disappear. This time, it didn't come back.

And it didn't come back.

He felt a rising sense of excitement at the sight of that dead screen. A headline was taking shape in his head: *Coast Guard Witnesses Disappearance of Vessel on Radar in Bermuda Triangle.* He took more pictures, struggled to see out the window.

Johnson held up a hand. "Starboard! Thirty degrees!"

The atmosphere in the cabin changed instantly from one of grim worry to confidence and competency. It was amazing what the willpower of man could do, Denton reflected, even in the face of something as elemental as this storm. The ship turned, the men shouting instructions, working as one. Their energy was so intense that for a moment he glimpsed what it would be like to be one of these boatmen, mastering the great watery tide.

There was a flash of another vessel in the window, but it disappeared in the rain and waves. Denton couldn't see a damn thing in here. He had to go outside.

Now that the ship had turned, the deck was tilting the other way and Denton had no problem grabbing the pole from the cabin door. He clung to it, wrapping his legs around it like a pogo stick, and managed to bring up his camera. They were indeed approaching another ship.

Captain Dodd was at the bow with the other crewmen. He was motioning the helm operator into position as they approached the smaller vessel through the heaving sea. It was a small yacht. Denton struggled to make out the name on the side.

Why Knot Now.

Crap.

Denton's excitement faded along with the headlines in his mind. They'd found the boat. There was no story. He'd come out here for nothing.

The crew secured a line to the *Why Knot Now*, and two of them, like Day-Glo monkeys, made a death-defying cross to the deck.

And Denton realized that something was wrong.

He snapped another photograph as the two men went inside the cabin of the yacht. The two men came out. One scrambled back over to confer with the captain while the other moved around the side of the yacht, his face turned out to sea, searching. And Denton knew: the *Why Knot Now* was empty.

*   *   *

"So what happened to them?" Jack demanded.

Denton had made the mistake of calling his editor on his cell phone before he'd gone out on the rescue, and there were three messages waiting when he returned to the hotel. By the time he'd gotten out of a hot shower, Jack had rung again.

Denton rubbed his eyes with both hands, the receiver crooked in his neck.

"The official report says they went overboard and drowned. But they didn't, Jack, I swear. There were two life preservers untouched on the rail. It's unlikely they all three would have gone in at once, and if they'd gone in one at a time they would have used the preservers, right? We searched for two hours—there was *nothing*."

Jack didn't answer. No answer was possible. They'd both been in this business long enough to know a dead end when they saw it. "Did you get pictures inside the yacht?"

"No." Denton sighed. "Dodd wouldn't let me on board. But one of the guardsmen told me nothing was out of place over there. Not so much as a cushion."

"Well . . . write up what you've got. See if you can make it work."

Jack didn't sound very enthusiastic. There was no reason that he should be. And the real frustration was that it might well have been a legitimate case. And he'd been there. *He'd been right the hell there.* And he still had squat.

The series of articles on vanishings had been Jack's idea, but Denton had been all over it. There were some interesting historical cases. In 1809 an Englishman named Benjamin Bathurst stopped at an inn. He went around the coach to check the horses and was never seen again. In 1900 Sherman Church went into a cotton mill in Michigan and never came out. Ever. In 1880 a farmer named David Lang was walking across his pasture when he simply *winked out* according to five eyewitnesses. The grass where he disappeared was said to have died and never grown back.

And there was one even Jack didn't know about. In 1975 a little girl named Molly Brad vanished in a flash of light while playing in the woods.

Over two hundred thousand people were reported missing in the United States each year. And while most of those were probably runaways, deadbeats, or undiscovered homicides, Denton didn't think it beyond the realm of possibility that some of them, just a *couple*, were like David Lang.

But he was never going to prove it here.

"I'm ready to come home. The Bermuda Triangle angle isn't happening. I mean, I believe there are places where vanishings are more likely to happen, and that this is one of them. But if someone disappears out here there's no way to prove they didn't go into the sea. We need . . . I don't know, more of a 'locked room' scenario. And call me a freaking idealist, but an eyewitness or two wouldn't hurt." Denton heard the whine in his voice. He was tired.

"Funny you should say that. Did you get that package I sent?"

Denton looked at the red, white, and blue mailer by the door. "Yeah. What is it?"

"Take a look. But don't get distracted. I need you to finish the *Triangle* article. It's due Tuesday."

"I know. It's almost done." Mostly.

"Good. You sound bushed. I'll let you get some sleep. 'Night, Dent."

" 'Night."

He almost didn't open the package. His legs were the consistency of pâté from trying to brace himself on the ship for five hours, and the volume of adrenaline that had passed through his veins had left him with a hangover. But Jack's hints had taken hold. He couldn't go to sleep without knowing.

He ripped open the pull tab and looked inside. It was a book: *Tales from the Holocaust.*

It made no sense, because the Holocaust had nothing to do with the article he was working on. And yet that good old Wyle instinct roiled in his gut like the turning of some gigantic subterranean worm.

He opened to the earmarked page and began to read.

1.2. Aharon Handalman

JERUSALEM

Such a city. Rabbi Aharon Handalman had lived in Jerusalem for twelve years, and he was still amazed by it. He always left home before the crack of dawn so he could watch the sunlight warm the stones. There was a cold bite to the air this morning. His black wool coat and hat absorbed it like a sponge.

Aharon, along with his wife, Hannah, and their three children, lived in the new Orthodox housing near the Valley of Ben-Hinnom. At this time of the day, without the squeal and clamor of little ones, the plain, square apartments felt as hollow as cardboard boxes. They fell away behind him as he walked, the ancient walls appearing on his right like the edge of a woman's skirts.

He drew close to the Jaffa gate. Before it rose the Tower of David, a thin and pointed shadow in the darkness. He turned into the city, the stone rising above his head. His fingers trailed along the arch as he passed, the *Shma Yisroel* on his lips.

Down the ancient avenue he went, into the heart of Yerushalayim. The roads outside these walls—especially Jaffa Road—were too modern for his tastes. Advertisements for Camel cigarettes and doughnuts marred shop fronts. But once you were inside, the twenty-first century fell away. Now he only had to deal with the indignities of the Christian Quarter on the left and the Armenian on the right. He walked quickly past these invaders, his lip curling. He could continue straight ahead, but it was his habit to turn into the heart of the Jewish Quarter, choosing alleys and courtyards for their aroma of antiquity. Later today, they would be crowded with kaftans and T-shirts, with cheap madonnas and stars of David. But now they were only dim stone chutes that might have existed a thousand years ago, two thousand, more.

He, Rabbi Aharon Handalman, might have been from a different time as well: forty years old, of average height and weight, still handsome, brown eyes glittering, brown beard free from gray as it hung long and untrimmed, his black clothes roughly twentieth-century. If the clock were rolled back twenty years he would not be out of place; two hundred years and the cut of his clothing might be a bit odd; two thousand years, put him in a different outfit and call it good. He liked to think that at heart, *at heart,* he was unchanged from his ancestors, unchanged from an Israelite who trod this very path on his way to the Temple in the days of Jeremiah. Reading the Scriptures Aharon identified exactly with the feelings of the prophets: that Jerusalem was storing up sins for some divine retribution thanks to the unholy ways of her people. In the days of Jeremiah that had meant harlots and drunkards and Jews with no sense of their past. In the days of Aharon Handalman that meant cut-off shorts and Uzis and Jews with no sense of their past. Even Moses had voiced the same frustration: *You are a hard-necked people.* More than stones never changed.

Aharon went past the Dung Gate, down a set of stairs, and through a security checkpoint. The soldiers knew him but insisted on patting him down. Orthodox rabbis drew as much suspicion as Palestinians these days, but with the crazy state of the world, who could blame them? Then he was through and in front of *HaKotel,* the Western Wall, the only remnant of the Second Temple.

The light was rosy, pinkening the cream-colored edifice. As always, he approached with a sense of privilege, of excitement, like a bridegroom. He crossed to the wall, lowering his hands gently to the cold stone, then his forehead, with the tender sigh of a lover.

Around him were several dozen others saying their morning prayers at this sacred spot. Some were *haredim* with beards, side-locks, and fur hats. Aharon, who was Orthodox but not *haredim,* had a beard but no side-locks, and his hat was a simple black wool fedora with a *kippa,* a skullcap, underneath.

He joined a minyan of early risers from his synagogue and opened his briefcase. He took out his *tallith* and *tefillin,* kissing them. He wrapped himself in the prayer shawl and put on the ancient leather straps with their boxes of Scripture on first his left arm, then his forehead. And he began to pray, rocking in front of the wall.

Even though there was no pretense in it, he was not unaware of the picture he made: stately, paternal, rabbinical. He was proud to be making it. Someone had to show the world what being a Jew was all about.

An hour later, Aharon was in his office at *Aish HaTorah*. *Aish HaTorah* was a "master of the return" school, designed to teach Unorthodox Jews the ways of Orthodoxy. The Jews in question were usually young Americans whose parents were nonpracticing or (which was maybe worse) Conservative or Reformed. Aharon taught Talmud and Midrash. It wasn't much money, but it placed him across from the wall all day, and his class schedule left him plenty of time to pursue his *real* passion—Torah code.

The code was the flame in Aharon's heart. The greatest rabbis had always known there were messages hidden in the Torah, but the sages, may they rest in peace, didn't have microchips. Now you could run a program, give it a keyword like *heaven*, and the search routine would scan the Hebrew letters of the Torah looking for the keyword hidden in the text. A "hidden" word appeared via Equidistant Letter Spacing—the ELS or skip. For example, the plaintext phrase "The Rabbis hoped and prayed for God to lead the people over land and over sea to the kingdom of their being, Eretz Yisrael" contained the hidden word *heaven* at a skip of eleven: "The Rabbis **h**oped and pray**e**d for God to le**a**d the people o**v**er land and ov**e**r sea to the ki**n**gdom of their being, Eretz Yisrael."

What had really stunned the world was the presence of arrays of *related* words and phrases in the Hebrew Bible. Arrays were arrangements of the plaintext letters into columns the width of the skip. These arrays made it easier to find related words or phrases near the original keyword.

```
T h e r a b b i s h
o p e d a n d p r a y e
d f o r g o d t o l e a
d t h e p e o p l e o v
e r l a n d a n d o v e
r s e a t o t h e k i n
g d o m o f t h e i r b
e i n g e r e t z y i s
r a e l
```

The fact that such arrays were sought in the *Hebrew* version of the text made the task both easier and harder.

But . . . the scientific community was outraged, naturally. What good could atheists have to say about divinely implanted messages? Their most damning rebuttal showed that similar "themed word arrays" could be found in any text—*War and Peace,* for example. Hence Aharon's current line of research.

He was still puzzling over the latest stack of printouts when Binyamin Yoriv came in.

"Good!" Aharon grunted. "I have a riddle for you."

"Is that from last night's test?" Binyamin crossed to the desk.

Aharon shrank back. The boy had halitosis and a skin problem that left scales in his wake. It was written that God gave everyone a mix of assets and flaws, but Binyamin's assets, like the Torah code itself, were extremely well hidden.

"What happened?" Binyamin asked. "Was there a bug in the program?"

"No."

"But there are too many pages."

"Nothing is lost on you, Binyamin."

Aharon waited for the boy to catch on as he scanned the three-inch stack. His scaly eyebrows went up. "Hey, one of our search phrases, 'Yosef Kobinski,' is really *in* all these arrays. That's strange."

"Strange? Three hundred arrays for one little rabbi. As usual, you understate the case."

Aharon wheeled his chair to the left, not only to get away from Binyamin's exhalation zone but also to pick up Chachik's *Encyclopedia*—a Who's Who of Jewish scholars. "I would say my theory has been disproven, wouldn't you?"

"What *was* your theory?"

Aharon felt a spark of aggravation. He had explained this three or four times already. "Witzum, Rips, and Rosenberg, in their *Statistical Science* article, took the names of the thirty *greatest* rabbis from this very encyclopedia. They found code arrays for each rabbi where his name appeared close to his birth and death dates, *nu?*"

"I know."

"That's good that you know. I know, too."

"So—"

"So *they* took the rabbis with the longest entries in this encyclopedia. I took the *shortest.*"

"What for?"

"Think!"

Binyamin appeared to give it a legitimate effort. He shrugged.

"Someday you're going to learn how to use that brain of yours. Then again, someday the dead will rise, so it is written."

"Rabbi—"

"So we run the same test they did with a new set of data; that is point one. If we find arrays for all these rabbis also, it is further proof of the code. As for my own theory, I had a little idea that the 'lesser' rabbis would appear in the code less often than the 'greater' rabbis. If we could show *that* it would be very difficult to explain with *War and Peace!*"

Binyamin pointed to the open encyclopedia. "But Rabbi Kobinski has only one paragraph, yet he appears in three hundred arrays. That's even more than the Ba'al Shem Tov, the most famous rabbi ever."

Aharon tapped his temple, looking pained. "Didn't I *say* it disproved my theory?"

"So how come—"

"That's the question, Binyamin, *how come,* as you so eloquently put it."

"Must be a characteristic of the name—common letters or something."

Aharon stroked his beard. "Yosef—perhaps. But the phrase we searched for was 'Yosef Kobinski.' How common could it be?" Aharon picked up Chachik's and began reading the Kobinski entry out loud: " 'Yosef Kobinski, Brezeziny, Poland. Born, Tish'ah b'Av 5660.' "

"Nineteen hundred," Binyamin calculated quickly.

" 'Died Kislev 5704.' "

"November 1943."

Aharon rolled his eyes. The boy had failed a test on dates last month. As usual, he had learned it only after the rest of the class had moved on.

" 'Rabbi Kobinski was a student of Rabbi Eleazar Zaks, the famous kabbalist of Brezeziny. He studied physics at the University of Warsaw and later taught there before leaving to pursue kabbalah. Rabbi Kobinski was considered by many to be a genius of kabbalah. His first and only book, *The Book of Mercy,* was a prelude to great things. Unfortunately, he was lost in the Holocaust when he died at Auschwitz.' "

Aharon leaned back, the chair groaning with his weight. Yes, this certainly killed his theory. Who had even heard of Kobinski-of-the-300-arrays? Nobody. A burning in his chest bothered him enough that he popped antacids from his linty pocket. He noticed that his fingers were puffy. (*Salt,* Hannah would say, *heart,* she'd remind him, and he'd ignore her.)

"Maybe he *is* important. Or will be." Binyamin poked his glasses up with an extended middle finger.

"He's dead. Somehow I don't think he has any more tricks up his sleeve."

"So whaddya wanna do?"

Aharon frowned at the boy from under bushy eyebrows. "What do I want to do? Is that what you're trying to ask, with your fine language? I'll tell you. We're going to see if there's something special about our new friend. We'll take a few other words from the biography. Let's see." He scrabbled for a pencil and notepad. "Brezeziny. Eleazar Zaks. *The Book of Mercy.* Auschwitz." He tore off the page and handed it to Binyamin.

"All together?" Binyamin regarded the list with a squint.

"No," Aharon said, with a martyr's sigh. "No, no, no. Run each of them *separately* as keywords. See if you can find any of *those* words in *these* three hundred arrays." He fanned the stack on the desk.

Binyamin shoved up his glasses again, his mouth open in an "oh." "That will take a while."

"*Nu?* You have better things to do?"

Aharon went to the hook on the back of the door and took up his prayer shawl. It was time for his first class of the day. He opened the door, waited. Binyamin just stood there lumpishly.

"*After* class?" Aharon reminded him.

As they walked down the hall, Aharon felt a new lift in his step. He had the distinct feeling he had just had a stroke of luck. That in itself was not so amazing. The sages say, "Even a fool has luck." What you *did* with the luck, that was the tricky part.

Fortunately for him, and perhaps for the cause of Torah code also, Rabbi Aharon Handalman was no fool.

I.3. CALDER FARRIS

ORLANDO, FLORIDA

The Doubletree hotel where the convention was being held was large and generic and smelled of suntan oil. Calder Farris made his way to the registration desk, where he would use his own name but not his rank. No one would take him for a soldier in his civvies.

He kept his sunglasses on.

He didn't expect a lot from the convention. Its title, Holism and the New Physics, was typically lame. Still, it was his job and he had other reasons to visit Orlando. Dear old Dad.

The woman at Registration had long gray hair and a gauzy skirt-and-top ensemble. People like her were into ESP or auras or some such shit, but she obviously couldn't have read vibes with a manual, because she made the mistake of flirting with him. She tittered on about the sessions, laying her pink hand on Calder's black-sweatered arm.

"My goodness!" she gasped, squeezing the unyielding muscle. She gave him a predatory gleam, her eyes telling him that she liked the iron hardness of his arm and that she'd love to explore other hard things of his as well.

Calder had an overpowered urge to smack her. Instead, he removed his dark sunglasses and inspected them casually.

The woman's hand fell to her side. For a second he got the satisfaction of her queasy face as she stared into his eyes, mesmerized; then she busied herself with someone else. He put the glasses back on and walked away, registration packet in hand.

There was nothing wrong with Calder Farris's face—it was a tad lumpy, a result of teenage acne, but it had improved with age. At thirty-two it looked more rugged than pockmarked. He was six-foot-three and he ran and pumped weights obsessively. With his sunglasses on he could be mistaken for the tall, dark, and handsome type. But sooner or later he had to take them off.

It was his eyes. His irises were a blue so light they were nearly white. People didn't like that. It was as if they made a window where the cold inside him seeped through. He couldn't hide his essential nature when people looked into his eyes. The demon peered out. It was fucking inconvenient.

But, like everything else, it had its uses.

He sat down in the hotel bar and ordered a coffee. He went through the list of sessions, slashing with a felt-tipped pen.

Healing and Synchronicity. Slash.

Wormholes and Frank Herbert's Folding Space. Slash.

Quantum Leaps: Leapfrogging the Laws of Physics.

He'd been to so many of these things, he could practically give the lectures himself. But there was always the remote possibility something useful would turn up someday, the proverbial pearl among the swine. This topic had potential. He flipped to the credentials of the speaker. He recognized the name; the guy was a hack. He slashed out the session.

The bartender refilled his coffee. A few stools away sat two young men engaged in casual conversation. They were obviously a couple. That was nothing out of the ordinary for Florida or for weird science conventions like this one, wherever they might be. That was the fucking state of the fucking country he'd vowed his life to serve and protect.

Calder's body tightened. A feral smile bared his teeth.

He wished the faggots would approach *him.* He'd take them out to the parking lot and teach them the true meaning of male–male penetration—his fist down their throats.

The rage inside him flared momentarily, like a black sun. He tamped it down. Of course, he wouldn't *really* do anything, not even if provoked. He wouldn't touch the young men if they stuck their hands down his pants and said howdy-do. Beating up civilians of whatever proclivity did not look good on a service record, and Calder cared very much about his service record.

Besides, he was a trained professional. He didn't kick ass pro bono.

A flicker of humor assuaged his anger. He refocused on the schedule of events.

A Symphony of Strings and the Theory of Everything.

Calder glanced at his watch. It had started ten minutes ago. He gathered up his papers and went to find the room. He didn't leave a tip.

*   *   *

The conference room held about sixty chairs and most of them were full. Calder settled down in the back and looked up the lecturer's bio. Dr. Larch was a young professor at Florida State. Probably half the listeners were his students, brownnosing. Calder sized him up. Intelligent-looking. Showy. The guy had the style of a talk show host. Calder hated that. He folded his arms over his chest and settled in to listen.

Forty-five minutes later, Calder watched the rabble stream out and kept his seat. As usual, there were three or four supergeeks hanging around the lecturer chatting him up. Calder doodled on his pad—guns, stark faces, dark slashes on white paper. Once or twice Larch glanced at him curiously.

The professor finally walked by, heading for the exit. Calder unfolded himself from the chair with a deliberate display of strength.

"Dr. Larch? I'm Calder Farris."

Calder held out his hand. Larch shook it. His grip was damp but not completely mealy.

"Hello." Larch's greeting had the lilt of a question. *And you want . . . ?*

"I'd like to speak with you about your lecture. Can I buy you lunch?"

"I'm . . . rather busy."

Calder smiled. "How about a drink then? And it's *Lieutenant* Calder Farris. United States Marines."

Half an hour later, Calder sat across from Larch at an Italian restaurant down the street. Getting out of the hotel had been Farris's idea. The Italian place, Larch's. He'd decided to get a free meal for his trouble after all. The Marines bit had done it. Larch probably didn't meet a lot of Marines. Not a lot of Marines would be caught dead anywhere in his orbit.

"So, Lieutenant Farris, what exactly do you do for the military?"

Farris poked at his salad. "I'm in Intelligence."

"Oh?"

"I really can't say anything more than that."

Larch smirked, so Calder pulled out his wallet and showed him ID. The identification was official United States Marine Corps, had "Intelligence Division" written on it and a tough-looking picture of himself in uniform.

"So what does the Intelligence Division of the Marines do exactly?" Larch asked, leaning forward. "Reconnaissance mostly? Isn't that what you guys do? What's your interest in physics?"

"*Dr. Larch.*" Calder had been perfectly civil so far. He'd even kept on his glasses, though he'd switched to a darkly tinted pair that was not prescription but looked it. Now he let a thread of something heavier enter his voice. "We have limited time. I'd like to discuss *your* work, if you don't mind."

Larch studied him. "Can I ask in exactly what capacity you're conducting this interview?"

"It's not an interview; it's lunch," Calder explained in a reasonable tone. "And you *could* ask, but, well, you know . . ."

"Then you'd have to kill me." Larch snorted. Calder didn't. He sat and looked at Larch from behind those glasses, cold as stone. Larch's amusement faded into an awkward uncertainty with just a touch—yes, Calder could smell it—just the smallest trace of fear.

It was the perfect moment and Calder didn't waste it. He began firing questions, calmly but insistently. The lecture had been on string theory and there were a couple of points he wanted to explore, a few unexpected threads that had interested him. He pressed in those directions, one by one.

Larch talked. Calder was pretty sure he held nothing back. There was no reason that he should. This stuff was probably regurgitated in front of several hundred students every day, most of them too brain-dead to pay the slightest fucking attention. And here was a golden opportunity—a guy who actually wanted to hear him yak.

There was nothing earth-shattering, but there were a few ideas that were new to Calder, and he stored them in his memory mechanically.

When he was done with the conversation he let the waiter clear their plates. Calder was ready to leave, but Larch ordered spumoni. Calder watched him poison his body with sugar and saturated fat and felt his muscles flex in response as if itching to work out. In ten years, Larch was going to look like a sack of potatoes and have the use of about 30 percent of his arterial capacity. Fucking desk jockey.

Calder glanced at his watch. He felt as if he'd just gotten laid. He had gotten what he wanted from Larch. The man no longer interested him.

"So," Larch said, "maybe now you can tell me about *your* work. Nothing classified, just . . . what's it like? Do you travel a lot?"

"Sometimes."

"Married?" Larch eyed Calder's bare hands speculatively.

"No."

Larch licked his spoon. "You're good at physics. Did the Marines train you for that?"

Larch was only making conversation. It was what normal people did, Calder knew that, but still the demon inside him reached out its hand and squeezed his heart until it was full and tight. Larch wanted to poke behind the shutters, lay his soul bare. Calder was tempted to let him.

Then he realized that he was done with Larch; he didn't have to play nice anymore. Slowly, he removed his glasses and smiled.

"Check?" Larch called, signaling the waiter.

＊　　　＊　　　＊

Lt. Calder Farris's ID was a lie. He was, in fact, not with the Intelligence Division of the Marines. He had been a Marine, still was, but when he got his break into Intelligence it had not been a position in the MCIA. His particular skill set, most particularly his aptitude in science, had him on permanent loan to the Department of Defense.

But not officially. If you ran your finger down all but the most classified versions of the DoD org chart, you would not find him there. You would find DARPA—the Defense Advanced Research Projects Agency. One of the branches of DARPA was the DSO—the Defense Sciences Office. You would find the director of the DSO, Dr. Alan Rickman, one of the men Calder reported to. You would not find Calder Farris.

The DSO's mission was "to identify and pursue the most promising technologies within the science and engineering research community and develop them into new DoD capabilities." In other words, to find Shit to confiscate, rework, and adapt into Big Bad Shit that could make the enemies of the United States turn green, shed their skin, or otherwise go away in a hurry.

The DSO was mostly made up of civilian scientists. They schmoozed, gave grants, and recruited other civilian scientists with lucrative offers. They followed the work of people such as Hawking and Feynman, subscribed to journals such as *Nature* and *Science* and *Cell*. They had contacts at Bell Labs and Intel and all the best universities.

That wasn't Calder Farris's world. His mission was to locate the people who *weren't* in the journals: the blackballed physician in South America trying to perfect human cloning, the lone genius trying to invent smaller, more lethal bombs, the embarrassing kooks of academia who just might be onto something after all. He stalked his prey outside the bounds of scientific credibility where technology went on all the same, often in wacky directions, sometimes with frightening results. To the government these people were just slightly better than full-blown terrorists. If possible and if there was time, et cetera, et cetera, they would be won over in a friendly fashion. If not . . .

Fortunately for Dr. Larch, his ideas were not substantial enough to be of any further interest to the DoD.

Back at the hotel, Calder took the plastic wrapper off a glass in the bathroom and filled it up with water from the tap. Drank it. Filled it again and drank another. The spaghetti marinara sloshed in his stomach.

He went to his black bag, government issue, and unpacked his Blue Dress uniform. He used the hotel iron to remove a few suitcase wrinkles. He showered and dressed, putting on every article as carefully as if he were heading for an inspection. He spent several minutes in the mirror adjusting his hat and checking the alignment and shine on his medals and ribbons. In the mirror the pale, lumpy face and white-blue eyes looked ghostly, dead, against his short black hair. He stood to attention, his eyes on the figure in the glass.

He was pleased at how hard he looked. He looked like one deadly bastard. No one would ever cross him lightly. Never again.

It was dark when he drove up to the Florida National Cemetery in Bushnell and parked on the long driveway through endless white headstones. His father had been retired when he'd kicked it, but he'd chosen this place. His whole pathetic life had been the Army.

All the markers looked alike and there were hundreds of them, but Calder made his way easily in the moonlight. He found his father's grave without hesitation.

He stood for a minute in front of the headstone, his father's decomposing flesh five or six feet beneath his shoes. The letters on the stone read: "Captain John Macum Farris II."

The second. But Calder, only son, was not John and not number three. He hadn't been good enough, even on the day of his naming.

Calder looked around. He was alone. A warm Florida breeze tickled his clean-shaven face. He unzipped his trousers. His piss, hot and steamy, hit the stone and trickled down into the grass. Calder stepped to one side so he could soak the old man head to foot.

He shook himself off when he was done and zipped up. Then he saluted the grave, ending the gesture with an upturned middle finger and a sneer. "Hope you're enjoying Hell, you fucking son of a bitch."

1.4. Jill Talcott

University of Washington
Seattle

Dr. Jill Talcott was not going to take no for an answer. She stopped in the bathroom and ran a brush through her shoulder-length dirty blond hair, applied Chap Stick, and smoothed out her navy gabardine slacks and sweater-vest. She ran through her speech, muttering to herself in the mirror, then headed for the Shrine.

The Shrine housed the physics department's holy grail—a quantum computer. The beast itself, Quey by name, was as large and unsightly as an industrial trash bin. On its metal cover was a Huey, Louie, and Dewey comic book page with a fourth duckling penciled in, a computer in the place of its head. That was Dr. Grover's idea of humor. Nerd. He could afford to laugh. Rumor had it that Grover and his computer had cost Udub over 5 million to steal from Berkeley. Rumor had it that Udub president Paul Reardon would have given his firstborn son if it had come to that.

Grover was putzing at a monitor. In his shorts and Birkenstocks he gave the impression of an aging beach bum. A full beard added to the disguise. The university brass ate it up.

"Jill Talcott," he said, as though naming an inkblot in a routine psych exam.

Jill forced a pleasant look. "How are you, Dr. Grover? How's the baby?"

"Blew some chunks the other day, but she's back up. Whaddya need? I'm superbusy."

"Well, you see, Dr. Grover—"

"Chuck."

"Chuck, I need some time on Quey. You may remember from staff meetings that I'm working on wave mechanics. I've worked out an equation and I'm ready to crunch some numbers."

"So file a request with the Committee."

"I'd rather not. I only need a few hours. Two slots, two hours each, would be fine. I'm willing to do them in the middle of the night."

Her voice was crisp, no-nonsense. He glanced up at her, amused. "You'd 'rather not'? *You've* got balls. Jill the Chill." This last was muttered, almost too low for her to hear.

"What was that?"

"Nothin'. Sorry, but we're already scheduled twenty-four seven." He typed in something at the keyboard and a diagnostic screen appeared.

Jill was prepared for rejection. Even the insult of that ridiculous nickname only made her more resolute. Her chin came up. "This work is incredibly important, Chuck. If my equation works—and it *will* work—it'll be groundbreaking. Particularly the way I've . . . that is . . ."

"It's up to the Committee to decide if your work has merit."

The Committee: Grover himself, Dick Chalmers, the physics department head, and President Reardon. The three heads of Cerberus.

"I'm not ready to show my work to the Committee," Jill said impatiently. "There's got to be something we can work out."

Grover swiveled away from the keyboard and eyed her appraisingly as if considering menu items on a cold buffet. Jill thought it was the first time he'd ever *really* looked at her. She knew what he'd see: an associate professor, low on the radar, a thirty-four-year-old pixie-sized southern woman with boring taste in clothes, no makeup, no glamour. He'd see all that, but what she hoped he'd *also* see was the ambition in her eyes. Jill the Chill. Maybe. But a man like Chuck Grover ought to know the value of being tough.

"Look, Chuck, no wave mechanics equation has ever been proven, because they can't be run on a conventional computer—there's way too much data to crunch. You beat everyone with your technology, but in ten years, there'll be another two dozen quantum computers at *least*. Sooner or later someone is going to solve wave mechanics and it's going to be a major event. It's either going to be *your* quantum computer or it'll be someone else's. I want to make it yours."

It was the speech she'd prepared, and she thought it was a good one.

He patted his pocket, found his cigarettes. "Lemme show you somethin', Jill."

He led her out of the Shrine and up a floor to his office. It was Grand Central Station compared to hers. Stacked along the front of his desk were dozens of wire baskets filled with files. At the sight of them, Jill began chewing on a fingernail.

"Do you know what those are?" he asked, lighting up.

She nodded, hopes sinking.

"That's right. Official requests for Quey's time from all over the world. And do you know how many of them are about wave mechanics?"

She had a moment of sheer terror. "How many?"

Grover made her wait for it. He plopped down in his chair and tapped his ashes in a coffee cup. "Well . . . only two that I can remember. But I get more every day, and I haven't looked through the new requests in a couple of weeks."

"Chuck! Whoever else is working on this, they can't be as close as I am. And besides, I'm right here at Udub, not halfway around the world! Isn't that why the university pays you through the nose? So that *our* department, *our* staff, can become world leaders in physics research? Isn't that the deal?"

"Bottom line, some of the people who want Quey—and that means they want *me*—are big names, Jill. *Big names.* So if I give you time instead of them there has to be something in it for me."

He waited, obviously expecting something. What? Not her body; his eyes told her that. Shit. Normally, she didn't give a good goddamn what anybody thought, so she was lousy at reading people. She took a shot.

"If my equation works, I'll be able to publish in the best journals. There might even be a book in it. Naturally, I'll credit your work. Quey's an important part of the process."

"I'm glad you see it like that. The thing is, I can't tell if you're full of shinola or not, can I, since you refuse to file your theory?"

"But—"

"Forget it. I wouldn't have time to review your work if you printed it in fifty-point font and hung it over my bed." He smirked at his own cleverness. "The point is, if I let you use Quey it's a risk—there's got to be an upside for me. I want co-authorship."

He said it so casually. For a moment Jill was sure he was joking. She waited for him to crack a smile or say "gotcha." He didn't.

"But . . . you don't know anything about my work."

"And you know about Quey? Face it—without her you can't crunch the numbers. Without the numbers your theory is one of thousands, not even interesting to the lowliest publication. So much TP in other words. Isn't that right?"

He looked so infuriatingly indifferent. Whether she took his offer or not or did a striptease in front of his desk, it was all the same to Chuck Grover.

"But Quey is a *tool*! Like a particle accelerator or a telescope. You can't claim credit for my work just because I use a tool you built!"

"That's harsh, Jill." Grover stubbed out his cigarette, looking deeply disappointed. "I prefer to think of us as a team. But if that's not how you see it I guess you'd better just go through the channels like everybody else." He walked to the door.

Jill was not naive. She prided herself on knowing the score, particularly when the score in question was hardball as played in academia. But even she was stunned at Grover's cojones. He thought he could glom onto the work of others, those without the clout to kick up a fuss, because he held the keys to Heaven. And he was absolutely right.

"Fine," she blurted. "I agree. But in return you've got to give me a little flexibility. I may need a couple of run-throughs."

"Three slots," Grover said crisply. "Three hours each, between midnight and three A.M."

Jill nodded her assent, biting her lips over what she really wanted to say.

Grover grinned, his happy self once more. "Cool. Send me an E-mail. We'll work out the schedule."

As he walked away, Jill heard the mocking voices of the faculty saying that to get Quey, Reardon would have given his firstborn son.

*   *   *

Jill slipped into her office and leaned against the door, grateful for the privacy to vent.

Only she was not alone and couldn't vent. Her grad student, Nate Andros, was in early. The office was so tiny that accommodating his desk and hers left barely enough room to open the door and an aisle so narrow even Jill, a size 4, had to turn sideways to get through it. In this small space Nate was a startling apparition, with wild black curly hair, olive skin, and large dark eyes. He was saved from being outright gorgeous by his unkempt mop and a slovenly dress code. Any myth of exotic origins was killed by a flat Boston accent.

"Morning. You look like you're being chased by the undead."

"Close." Jill made herself pull it together. Nate was still a pup; she didn't want to be the one to clue him in on the cannibalism of university peers.

"Did we get our time on Quey?"

"Yup." Jill scooted past his chair.

"Cool!" Nate smiled happily.

She poured herself a cup of coffee from the community pot. "You haven't told anyone about our work, have you? Any of the other students?"

"Only Susie Forester and Gretchen Mach. Traded it for sexual favors." Nate took a sip of his coffee.

"Very funny."

"Why are we keeping this so secret, Dr. Talcott?" He widened those big dark eyes, the look in them a little more astute than she liked.

Her first instinct was to evade the issue, as usual. But if things progressed, and it looked now as though they actually might, he should know the risks.

She perched on the edge of her desk, the cup warming her cold hands. "Okay. It's like this: The theory I'm playing with is extremely unpopular. In fact, it could probably get me fired."

"Um . . . I know it's not exactly standard, but . . . isn't that what science is about? Experimentation? Thinking outside the box?"

"*No*," she huffed a laugh. "Science is about what's sexy. You play with the sexiest theories because that's where the grants and prestige are. What you *don't* do is play with theories everyone else thinks are laughable. And *we're* working on a real howler."

"It would be particularly funny if we were right," Nate said dryly.

Jill's chest constricted with longing. It was all she had ever wanted in life, to have this career, to be famous. Grover. What a jerk. He already had the grants, the kowtowing university brass, the sidebars in scientific textbooks. But he wasn't content with all that; he had to have *her* work as well.

What was *really* funny was that he probably played that little game with every peon who came into his office on the off chance that he might get lucky someday. He had no idea.

If she was *right* it would change physics forever. And damn if she didn't think she had a good shot.

She took a drink of coffee, her legs bouncing against the desk with nervous energy. "Did I ever tell you about Dr. Ansel?"

Nate shook his head, face curious.

"I was *his* graduate student. The energy pool theory was his pet obsession."

"Was this at the University of Tennessee? That's where you graduated from, right?"

She nodded, surprised he knew her alma mater. It certainly was not a name she ever dropped.

"Ansel was brilliant. He *had* been at Harvard before he started to talk about 'energy pools.' "

She made a face. Then she noticed that Nate wasn't looking at her face. He was watching her legs—*way* too closely. He had a knack for reminding her that he was male and she was not. She stopped bouncing and pushed her way to the front of her desk, putting distance, and a good chunk of wood, between them. Annoying. When Nate first came to her she'd assumed he was gay. It was that soft, moony edge to him and the fact that he lived on Capitol Hill—the artsiest, and gayest, Seattle neighborhood. Which just went to show how little she knew, or cared, about men.

"Um, is the energy pool model in your equation the same one Ansel was working with?" Nate asked, pretending he hadn't just been caught watching her legs.

"Basically. Ansel's energy pool theory was that all matter exists as energy waves in a higher dimension. What looks solid and three-dimensional to us—objects, people—is really nothing but pure energy. Something in our brains translates these energy waves to 3-D, like the projection of a hologram.

"In Ansel's model subatomic particles are energy waves. Space-time is like a huge pond and particles are like pebbles being thrown into the pond. Imagine the smooth surface of a pond being inundated by billions of pebbles. Each pebble creates ripples—that's the energy waves. And all of those ripples intersect with each other and create interference patterns."

"Interference patterns," Nate intoned. "When two waves merge they create a third wave pattern. Where crest meets crest it creates a bigger crest, where trough meets trough you get a deeper trough, and when crest meets trough they subtract from one another."

"Yes, and that process is repeated over and over as the waves ripple out and interfere with *other* waves. The entire pond is one huge, chaotic pattern. But it *isn't* chaotic. That's the key. Each wave is generated in a very mathematical way. What Ansel never got around to was the idea of mapping these altered waves *back* onto matter. That's what my wave mechanics equation attempts to do: predict the behavior of subatomic particles based on the interaction of wave patterns in the higher dimension."

Jill sipped at her coffee. It was bitter. She preferred lattes but was always too consumed to walk outside to one of the ubiquitous coffee stands and get one. Even now, as her tongue registered the bitterness, her mind went back to its intellectual acrobatics. The enormity of it was staggering. The idea that all changes in the physical world—the growth and decay of cells, the firing of synapses in the brain, germination of seeds, everything—could be traced back to the interaction of energy patterns and, therefore, someday be *predictable*, maybe even *artificially manipulated* . . . Christ. It was bigger than the discovery of DNA. It *was*.

"I always liked your energy pool theory." Nate pushed his chair upright with a bang. "It reminds me of Heraclitus. Ever heard of him? He said the universe is both 'the many' and 'the one' and that 'the one' consists of the integrated movement of 'the many.' "

Nate's undergrad had been in philosophy, explaining why such a bright boy hadn't gotten snatched up by a professor higher in rank than Jill Talcott.

She scowled. "That's exactly the kind of thinking that makes this theory unpopular! It's a perfectly logical scientific model, and any attempts to connect it to psuedomystical, wacko ideas can only hurt it!"

"So you don't like the comparison, then," Nate said, with a straight face.

Jill hmphed.

"What interests me is how *you* hooked up with Ansel. You're pretty conventional, Dr. Talcott."

Damn. He *was* a bright boy. "The important thing," Jill countered, with a tone that firmly closed *that* topic, "is to get ready for our time on Quey. We're only going to get a few hours, so the test run has to be perfect."

Nate hoisted himself to his feet and stretched, forcing Jill to look away from the tightening expanse of T-shirt material.

"I'm up for whatever. But what numbers are you gonna feed Quey? Your equation is reiterative. In an ideal world it could account for all the particles in the universe interfering with all other particles all the time. Not even Quey could crunch *that* kind of data."

Jill took a diskette from her briefcase, barely able to suppress a self-congratulatory chortle. She laid it on her desk with an exaggerated *twump*.

"What's that?"

"Data from the particle accelerator at CERN. They took snapshots of a carbon atom once a nanosecond for a full second. It's accurate enough to test my equation—we plug in the state of all the particles at time x and see if my equation can predict what they'll do from there. But best of all . . ." she could barely restrain herself, ". . . the carbon atom was *in a vacuum*."

Nate had a half-pleased smile on his face, but he didn't quite get it.

"*So,* we only have to calculate the interference that would occur *between the particles of the carbon atom itself.* In other words, we have a pond with a limited number of pebbles in it. Quey ought to be able to calculate *that.*"

Nate's face grew serious. He looked at the data, looked back up at her. "Shit, Jill . . . I mean . . . dang, Dr. Talcott, we can really test your equation. *Really test it.*"

Jill the Chill permitted herself a moment of unrestrained triumph. Insoluble equations were about to be solved, and she was going to be the one to do it. She had been very quietly setting up this hand for years. Ace #1, her elegant equation based on Ansel's theory and a lot of her own damned hard work. Ace #2, her access to a quantum computer. Ace #3, the carbon atom data, attained using technology so cutting-edge it drew blood.

Genius was all well and good, but timing, luck, and access to the newest toys played a role in scientific discovery, too. She was pretty sure there wasn't another scientist in the world who could match the cards she held at this moment.

Jill Talcott, Tennessee long shot, was about to move into the lead.

2

Isaac Luria said that before creation the emanations of divine light, the Sephirot, were stored in vessels. One day the vessels shattered and the light escaped in tiny fragments. This "shattering of the vessels" is the same thing as Lemaître's "big bang." Before creation all the Sephirot were separate, all "in their own vessels," because in the spiritual dimensions "closeness" and "distance" are the very same thing as "similar" and "dissimilar." In the spiritual world, things are near each other only to the degree that they are exactly alike. So when G-d wanted to mingle his rainbow-like Sephirot together, he had to create physical space and time, a place where opposites can meet.

—Yosef Kobinski, *"The Book of Mercy,"* 1935

2.1. Denton Wyle

April
Upstate New York

Denton pulled the rental car into the gravel parking lot and peered at the white stone edifice. HEBREW ACADEMY OF SYRACUSE, the sign said. It wasn't particularly exotic-looking, just a turn-of-the-century Greek revival surrounded by woods, but the granite played nicely against the maples and aspens. He got out of the car and took a couple of pictures.

A fifteen-year-old boy with a yarmulke and black pants made a dash up the drive and pulled open the heavy wooden door. Not exactly the cloistered, monklike atmosphere Denton had expected—modified with side-locks and Torah scrolls, of course—but that was all right. A little poetic license was always a possibility.

Inside, there was no receptionist. A man walking through the foyer took notice of Denton. The man had a beard growing untrimmed and white fringes showing under his black vest. Better.

"Can I help you?"

Denton smiled. "That'd be great. I have an appointment with Rabbi Schwartz."

He was led down a broad corridor. He paused to take in a library, visible through an impressive arch. A few young students sat reading at a long table. Beyond them, in a smaller niche, were two older men, middle-aged and bearded like his guide. They were poring over fragments of paper laid flat on the table, shifting a scrap delicately with tweezers. There was an air of intense focus about them, of Serious Work. Denton couldn't resist popping off a few shots with his digital camera.

"This way, please," his guide prompted, coming back for him with a disapproving air.

"Sure thing."

Rabbi Schwartz was a plump man who gave off waves of authority. He looked to be around fifty, with shimmering strands of silver in a black, curly beard. He was pale and carried at least thirty unnecessary pounds, giving the impression of a man who seldom rose from his desk.

"Come in, Mr. Wyle. You phoned with a recommendation from Roger Steiner in New York?"

"That's me." Denton gave his best smile and smoothed the lapels of his sports coat. He knew he made a good impression. His blond hair was fashionably trimmed, his nails manicured, his clothes expensive yet casual. He looked Ivy League. Slap a tennis sweater on him and he'd be ready for a casting call for a *National Lampoon* movie. He worked hard to dispel that image in his personal life, but he used it when he thought it would buy him something. He extended his hand and the rabbi pressed it.

"I've heard so much about you," Denton said. "Everyone says you're one of the few experts left in the field of kabbalah."

Schwartz motioned to a chair. "Have a seat, Mr. Wyle. As I understand it you wanted to interview me? And this is, I presume, *about* kabbalah?"

The way he said it, kabba*lah*, in a rich, smooth rush, with a curious tweak of the syllables, brought goose bumps up on Denton's arm. "That's right. And I really appreciate your taking the time."

He put his brown leather backpack on his lap and opened it to dig out *Tales from the Holocaust* and his mini tape recorder.

"Can I ask what publication you're with? My secretary didn't get that on the phone."

"Um . . ." Damn. He should have had something prepared. He didn't think Rabbi Schwartz would approve of *Mysterious World*. Sometimes Denton told people he worked for a history magazine, but only when he was sure they wouldn't check him out. Schwartz looked like the sort who might.

"Mr. Wyle?"

"Sorry. I was trying to remember if I'd put new batteries in this thing." He held up the mini tape recorder. "I work for a magazine called *Mysterious*

World. We cover religious mysteries, miracles, things like that." It was remotely true, if you considered things like Atlantis and tarot to be religious.

"Are you associated with any particular denomination? Roman Catholic?"

"No. Not really." Denton held up the book *Tales of the Holocaust*. "Have you ever read this?"

It could have been his imagination, but he swore Schwartz looked at the book too briefly before answering. "No."

"It's, um, true stories from Holocaust survivors. I'm interested in one of the stories in particular, about a man named Rabbi Yosef Kobinski. Ever heard of him?"

Schwartz wiped his long beard with his hand thoughtfully. "Could be."

Denton was not getting the best vibes in this room. Schwartz was stiffening up, his face thickening like a time-lapse film of growing mold. Denton turned the charm up a notch, fixing a smile to his face. His muscles, used to smiling, held it effortlessly, like an Olympic gymnast standing on one leg.

"According to a supposedly true account by an eyewitness, Yosef Kobinski disappeared from Auschwitz in 1943."

Schwartz's lip curled. "Mr. Wyle, over six million were lost during the Holocaust."

"No. He *disappeared*. From Auschwitz."

Schwartz didn't ask him what he meant, which Denton found odd. He just looked extremely disinterested.

"So I talked to the editor of *Tales*. He said the old man who told this story was very reliable and not senile at all. Unfortunately, he's passed on since the book was written, so I couldn't interview him directly. But the editor did recall something he'd left out of the book because he thought it would make the story less credible."

Schwartz was positively having a field day with that bored expression.

"What he didn't write was that Kobinski was a kabbalist. And the eyewitness was convinced that Kobinski used some kind of kabbalah magic that caused him to just . . . vanish."

"*Mr.* Wyle . . ." Schwartz shook his head in a tut-tutting gesture. His voice, to Denton's ears, did not ring true. He was now looking down at his hand, which had creepy longish fingernails and was carefully realigning papers on his desk.

Denton flipped open his notebook. "So I dug into a bit of research . . ." Actually, he'd paid his research assistant, Loretta, to do it for him. ". . . and came up with some other interesting cases. Moses ascended to Heaven in a cloud. Ezekiel vanished on a 'fiery wheel.' And there are lots of folktales about medieval rabbis and kabbalists pulling all kinds of, um, crazy stunts."

He laughed, but with a touch of respect, "*heh-heh*." He'd swerved into this later lightheartedness in an effort to get Schwartz to smile. He could sense which way the ball was rolling and was trying his darnedest to get on the other side of it.

But Schwartz rolled right over him. "Is there a *question* in there, Mr. Wyle? Or just foolishness?"

"You think the Ezekiel story is foolishness, Rabbi?"

"What's foolish is that I still don't know why you're here."

"I, um, hoped to get a little background on kabbalah. Speak to someone who really knew it. The real thing."

Schwartz steepled his fingers together on his belly thoughtfully, then shook his head. "You want background on kabbalah? No. I think you want foolishness—floating rabbis, mud golems, descending clouds. And I think this *Mysterious World* of yours is a foolish publication."

In all his days as a reporter Denton had run into plenty of naysayers and skeptics. But never had anyone been so unabashedly rude. "Uh. Well . . ."

"*Kabbalah* is sacred. Can you understand that? It is *deep, sacred work.*" Schwartz leaned forward, glaring. "There are things in it so sacred they mustn't be said out loud even."

"Well, I don't mean any—"

"Kabbalah is, in fact, a privilege so rare, an elixir so potent, that even a Jewish *rabbi* may never earn it."

Denton sat frozen, his mouth still more or less in the outline of an understanding, patient smile.

"Well, I'm really just looking for a little sidebar material. Maybe I should ask some questions. Is there *anything* in kabbalah which could explain a disappearance? Someone vanishing into thin air? Or maybe some old stories about incidents like that? Because this eyewitness account seems really . . ."

Schwartz was holding up a hand, had been for some time. Denton trailed off, his words thudding to the ground like overripe tomatoes.

For a moment there was silence. Schwartz pressed his lips. "This is what I will give you. I will give you a story for your 'sidebar.' Ready?"

Denton nodded. He crossed his legs and tried to look grateful.

"Four sages entered Paradise. One was so enamored with what he saw that he could not bear to return to his life on earth and he died. One looked and became so immersed in the contemplation of the mysteries that he went mad. One thought the glory of the angels rivaled God Himself, and he gave up his religion in confusion and became an apostate. Only one had the maturity to handle what he saw. He survived to become a great teacher."

"That's nice. Thank you."

"Mr. Wyle, it is not *nice*. It is a warning to those who would thoughtlessly approach the gates of Heaven! I hope you will heed it."

Schwartz's eyes were piercing. Denton sat for a moment, trying to find something to say and failing.

Schwartz stood up, his tone lightening. "Done. I hope you enjoyed your visit upstate. It's beautiful countryside." He held out a hand. Denton stood slowly and took it. "*Shalom,* Mr. Wyle. God go with you."

Denton stood outside the yeshiva, rerunning the scene in his head. The moody clouds of spring opened above him and it began to rain. It sprinkled for about half a second; then it poured.

Water running down his face, still rooted to the driveway, the comic value of the deluge was not lost on him. He might even have laughed, were he not so humiliated. What! What on earth had just happened—besides the fact that he had walked in there completely unprepared? Why hadn't someone warned him that Schwartz was a kabbalah nazi? Why had he not *bothered* to seek out some of Schwartz's scholarly writing and figure out his agenda ahead of time? But no, that would have been too much trouble. He'd gone in there like a complete moron, "Oh, please, let me interview you!," assuming that like all *decent* religions—Christianity, for example—Judaism would not be able to resist a little free PR and a chance to sink its teeth into fresh meat. It was like an Ethiopian Jewish homosexual walking up to Goebbels and saying, "Hey, can I get your autograph?" *ahuh ahuh ahuh.*

Denton, you ass!

And he'd gone to so much trouble to interview a real kabbalist, too. They weren't exactly listed in the phone book.

The Kobinski story described in *Tales* was the most legitimate disappearance case Denton had ever run across. Real, live, historical people were involved. It hadn't happened in a locked room, not exactly, but it *had* happened on perfectly dry land in the midst of a group—as in *eyewitnesses.* And the kabbalah spin had been too rich! He'd *so* been able to envision his article given the weight of legitimacy by fuzzy black wool vests, long beards, mysterious tomes, and fringes and freaking tweezers!

He plodded morosely to his car, shoes squishing, got in. He was angry at Schwartz, angry with himself. But overtaking that, like some tardy but determined tortoise, was a squeezing in his chest, a sense of doom and danger—a panic attack.

He leaned against the steering wheel and took deep breaths. He hadn't been able to get Rabbi Schwartz on his side. Why, Rabbi Schwartz had never even smiled at him; he'd seen through Wyle's shtick as easily as if Denton were a housewife wrapped in Saran—hadn't liked him, hadn't engaged with him, hadn't given him the *slightest freaking break.*

Denton had a very hard time with rejection. When he was a boy and he'd felt this panic, he'd had visions of a rabbit: a rabbit sitting in a cage in the children's playroom, knowing that the kids had stopped being charmed by its cute fluffiness, had stopped coming around at all, and that the cook had a strange glint in his eyes these days. For when you were a rabbit, cute and fluffy was all you had.

But he wasn't that needy little boy anymore. Many, *many* people liked him now. Women, for example, he always had, and male friends, too, a lot of them. Some of them didn't even know about the money. He usually didn't tell the women he slept with, just to avoid problems. And mostly he got any woman he wanted—and many he didn't. Yes, people liked him very much as a rule. He was a goer.

But not Schwartz.

A movement caught Denton's eye, making him sit up straight in the seat and paste on a pleasant face. It was a kid walking a bicycle down the driveway. Denton had seen the boy in the library earlier, with his red curly hair and big glasses splattered, now, by rain. The bicycle had a large wicker basket strapped down on the rear guard. The kid paused at the end of the driveway, looked up the hilly road with an unmistakable "do I really have to do this?" set to his shoulders, and mounted up. Town, as Denton had recently found out, was five hilly miles away. He started the car.

"Hey!" He rolled smoothly up to the bike. "Can I give you a lift? It's raining pretty hard out here and I was just leaving."

The boy looked at Denton's clean-cut face, then glanced up the road. He brought the bike to a stop, balancing it between his two legs, and took off his glasses to wipe. They smeared wetly. "You going to town?"

"Can you get anywhere else from here?" Denton gave a phony laugh.

"I can't get my bike in there."

"You have a point." Denton looked behind him at the backseat of the sedan he'd rented. The kid was getting wetter by the minute.

"I'll just go. I only have to take in the mail."

"Is that all? Why don't I just drop it off for you? I pass the post office on my way out of town."

The boy's face struggled between the sheer appeal of the offer and his sense of duty. "But how would I get the basket back?"

"No problem." Denton put the car in park and got out. He unstrapped the wicker basket from the boy's bike and dumped the contents onto the passenger seat of his car—a few dozen letters and a small package. He put the basket back on the bike. "There. Now you can get back to the library. It looked pretty cozy in there." He smiled, holding a hand over his head to keep off the rain.

And that was how it happened that Denton found himself driving up the lonely road from the Hebrew Academy of Syracuse—in the presence of maples and aspens and nothing else—with Rabbi Schwartz's mail on his passenger seat.

To his credit, it did not occur to him to look at the mail until he was halfway back to town. And then it was only after a glance to see if the mail had gotten wet (it had) and another glance, curiously, to see the address on the topmost letter, and then, looking around guiltily in his rearview mirror to confirm that no one was there, he sidled off the road and began to look at the mail in earnest.

So it wasn't as though he had planned and plotted. He hadn't had the idea in his mind, even, when he'd offered to help the boy. How could he? He hadn't known what was in the basket. And he certainly hadn't known that among the bills and personal letters of the students he would find a letter from Rabbi Schwartz himself, a letter addressed to an antique dealer in Zurich, which piqued Denton, stirred visions of tweezers and tomes, a letter that, as fate would have it, had been dampened by the rain and had a corner on the back flap that was puffed up enough to insert a finger and that, with minimal tugging, opened without any ripping at all.

> *Yes, I am interested in the manuscript pages of Yosef Kobinski that you describe and will meet your price of $15,000 for the nonexclusive rights and the physical document.*

Why was it that for Denton Wyle, the important forks in his life were never consciously chosen? That fate was always a brick wall he ran into while drifting about aimlessly like a leaf in the wind? He was a seat-of-the-pantser, a blind pup rooting around for the teat, rooting and rooting.

And somehow he always found it.

2.2. Aharon Handalman

JERUSALEM

Aharon Handalman kicked off his slippers and pulled the heavy binder into bed with him. Hannah was reading something, hopefully (he gave her the benefit of the doubt) some novel of the uplifting sort appropriate for a rabbi's wife.

"Look at you," she said. "You're worse than Yehuda with his homework."

Aharon grunted and settled in, fluffing the pillows behind him. He cracked open the binder, pencil at the ready in his pajama pocket.

The binder contained printouts of all the Kobinski arrays, keywords circled. There were nearly four hundred of them now. Some of the words circled were from the encyclopedia entry—*Eleazar Zaks, Brezeziny, The Book of Mercy, Auschwitz*. But none of them told Aharon *why* Kobinski was there, why he should be sprawled like "Kilroy was here" all over the holy Torah.

Also, it was unfortunate, but the computer could only look for the words you *told* it to. And since he still didn't know much about Kobinski, the only thing left was to eyeball the array like a word search. This was not a skill a Torah scholar had much need for, as things normally went.

Hannah leaned toward him. "What is this?"

"It's my work, Hannah."

"It's Torah code, yes?" She lay against his shoulder.

He moved the binder a little to the right, away from her. "Hannah, *please.*"

She stayed where she was, gazing up at him with a slight crease between her eyebrows. "Why is it you never want to talk about your work?"

Her tone—a little hurt, a little too serious—surprised him. He turned his head on the pillow to look at her more closely.

When he'd married Hannah, she'd been very young, eighteen, the pretty daughter of an Orthodox rabbi. Aharon didn't know all the details, but there had been some danger; she had met the wrong kinds of friends, *shiksah* friends. Her father had seen in Aharon the makings of a proper son-in-law, and the marriage had been arranged quickly.

That was not to say they'd forced Hannah. In those days Aharon drew more than his share of feminine glances, and he'd been passionate in his courtship. How many hours of Torah study he'd wasted daydreaming about her then! He'd said to her, "You're going to be my wife and that's it." She was a satisfactory wife, except, perhaps, for a little rebellious streak—nothing to get excited about, certainly, but it could be a nuisance.

"Hannah, this is *Torah study*," he said, with great forbearance.

"You can't tell me *a little*? How is your work going, Aharon? You never tell me anything."

He sighed a complaint. He didn't want to have this conversation. He wanted to look at the Kobinski arrays. He had so little time with them as it was.

"How are things at the yeshiva?"

"Everything's fine. Everything's good." His eyes were wide, his tone satirical. "They still have young men there, you know. And how are things at home, Hannah? How's the oven—working well?"

"So what is this? New research? It looks interesting."

He looked at the ceiling in a mock pleading gesture.

"*Please,* Aharon. I see no one but the children all day. I need something else to talk about. I feel I hardly know you anymore. You always shut me out."

"Shut you out? What is this 'shutting you out'? You have your work and I have mine, and that's it."

But it was an automatic response. It was actually tempting to speak of it, to tell someone about the Kobinski arrays. For some reason, he'd never had a friend among other rabbis at the yeshiva. And Binyamin was the only student with an interest in the codes, his only confidant. Also, maybe telling her a little would get her off his back so he could get back to work. Yes, this was also true. It certainly was not because in her eye there was a look that meant business.

He filled her in, briefly, on their discovery of the Kobinski arrays and what the encyclopedia had to say about him. "So now we have to analyze the arrays, see if we can learn why they're in the Torah. And that's what I'm doing, Hannah. So now you know. Congratulations."

He pulled the heavy binder back up on his stomach, but he snuck a glance at her to gauge her reaction.

There was a smile on her lips that was rarely there these days. She lay back on her pillows with an air of contemplation. "That's very interesting."

"I'm glad you approve."

"You should learn more about Kobinski, as much as you can."

"Naturally."

"Since he died in Auschwitz, you should visit Yad Vashem."

Aharon grunted. "I have better things to do than *that*."

"Where will you start then?" She turned on her side to face him.

"I start by studying these arrays, which is what I'm trying to do." He focused again on the second page, a frown between his brows.

"What do you do with the arrays?" she asked, more tentative now. She sat up to look over his shoulder again.

"Hannah!"

Her face darkened into her rebellious pout. "So looking at some Hebrew on a page, only a man can do this?"

"Do we need to have this discussion right now?"

This discussion, the one in which Hannah pointed out that some Orthodox now embraced women studying Torah. Aharon knew this. He knew there were no *mitzvah* that specifically prohibited it. But to him, this was simply not his idea of women—nor of Torah study.

"You're searching for words, aren't you? I could help."

"No."

"But I'm much better at crosswords and word searches than you."

"This isn't an amusement; this is worship!"

They knew each other well. His tone meant that this was final and she was not to question it. She didn't. She slipped back onto the pillow.

"How about I do a little background research for you? Try to find out more about Rabbi Kobinski?"

He closed his book, glowered at her. "Three children, one still in diapers, and you don't have enough to do? You want some suggestions? Because this place is not exactly the Palace of Solomon."

She had rolled away from him; now she rolled back, dark eyes flashing. "No, Rabbi Handalman, it is *not* the Palace of Solomon! You want to know what it is? It's a tiny two-bedroom apartment filled with three children—half the size of the house we had in New York, when it was just you and I! I would like to see *you* keep it perfect all the time." Tears threatened, but she was too angry for them. "You know, I have a brain, Aharon. Maybe even as fine a brain as you. In school they thought I would be somebody!"

"A rabbi's wife, the mother of three beautiful children, is a nobody?"

They glared at each other. Aharon had more bitter words at the ready, like poison arrows strung in a bow. He could see on her face, too, that she had things to say on her part. But they had been married long enough—they knew better.

Then, unexpectedly, he thought of his mother. His anger evaporated, replaced by a stab of worry. But Hannah was not his mother. She was not depressed, only a little restless, surely. He sighed and put his binder on the floor.

"*Hannaleh.*" He put his hand over hers on her stomach. They looked at each other for some time, as wrestlers might gauge an opponent. Then he kissed her. He had been too inattentive of late. He was always caught up in his work, staying late at the office to avoid the worst noise of the children in the evenings and tired or distracted after they were in bed. *This,* this was all she was asking for, a little attention. Hannah clung to him as if she could claim his spirit by sheer force of will. And for a few minutes, she did.

*   *   *

It was a shame, but Hannah was not alone in her advice. Aharon called on one of the synagogues that catered to Eastern European Jews, but the rabbi had never heard of Kobinski. "If he died in Auschwitz, why don't you try Yad Vashem? They have a better contact list of Eastern European survivors than I do."

"It's a *memorial,*" Aharon said dismissively.

"They've been collecting a lot of data. So try it. You'll see."

He had looked for Kobinski's book, *The Book of Mercy,* but no one had ever heard of it, not even the rare bookseller in the Jewish Quarter. Aharon's contact at the Hebrew University lectured on Jewish history and occasionally on kabbalah. He'd never heard of Kobinski, either, but he had a brainstorm: "Why don't you go visit Yad Vashem? You might get a lot out of it." It was all Aharon could do not to conk the man on the head with the briefcase he held in his hand.

Now, alone in his office, Aharon stared at the open binder on his desk. The word *Auschwitz,* so consistent in most of the Kobinski arrays, lay hidden among the words like bits of barbed wire.

Get a lot out of it! As if the Holocaust weren't already so deep in his blood that his very corpuscles cringed at the word? Did he need to see those things? Those pictures? Those heaps of shoes and eyeglasses? Did he need to have it pounded into him any more?

He had once left in the middle of a *Beit Midrash* at his synagogue—a visiting rabbi from the States, of course; they always knew how to say exactly what nobody wanted to hear. He'd walked out because the rabbi was talking about the Question of the Holocaust. "The Question of the Holocaust"! A poor excuse for a lack of faith! Did a man stand in front of the Originator of all the universe and say, "Excuse me, but I don't think I can approve of what you did"? Did God need *our* permission to arrange history the way He thought best?

Aharon was getting upset. His stomach was spreading burning fingers up into his esophagus, a clear warning sign. He chewed chalky antacid tablets and, when they didn't help, put on his coat. He would go out for a walk, anything to avoid thinking about *her*.

The old city was crowded with rush hour in Jerusalem, 6:00 P.M. and everyone in the streets. Synagogues, mosques, and churches held early-evening services and the wall was thick with men saying prayers. He would pray also, but not while he was in this mood. The walk did him little good. As his shoes clicked on the ancient stones his mind wandered to her anyway.

Rosa had been her name, and sometimes he could still hear her morbid liturgy—*my brothers, my sisters, my papa, Mama, Uncle Sol and Aunt Rivka, the blond baby next door . . .* and on and on and on, as if she had to say the names out of some macabre duty, as if handing crumbs of bread to ghosts.

His father saying, "It's over! Let it go, for the love of Heaven!"

And Rosa, his mother, for the millionth time, "We should have brought *somebody* out."

His father, who hadn't trusted so much as the auto mechanic down the street up until the day he died, had certainly never trusted the Germans. Way back in Berlin in 1929 he'd said, "That's it; I'm leaving." He had given his young bride a choice: "Come with me or stay here and be a widow—I'm never coming back." She had gone with him.

They had not, as Aharon's mother so often reminded his father, taken anyone with them—not her four younger siblings, not her aging grandmother, no one. "Well," said Father, "on a hunch you upset everyone's life? Did I know for certain what was going to happen? Was I a rich man, I could afford to take your entire family to America? Did I not scrimp and save a month for *your* passage?"

Mother: "I wish you hadn't! I wish I had taken my place with the rest of them!"

During the war years, Aharon's father made a living as a kosher butcher in New York. Rosa had to be hospitalized several times during those years as reports of the worst trickled in. They'd sent money to her family; it disappeared into a black hole. When the war ended and they saw the newsreels . . .

In 1952, Father moved them to upstate New York. He told Aharon often enough, "I thought a change of pace would be good for your mother." The way he said it, with that let-down tone, showed he had been mistaken. But it must have worked, for a time. In 1965, Aharon, only son, only child, was born, fruit of a soured womb.

In 1978, Rosa succeeded in killing herself.

His parents had never even *seen* the Holocaust, yet it ruined their lives.

This was what happened when you couldn't forget. And here was Kobinski, threatening to drag that all up again.

Why couldn't the man have died somewhere else, anywhere but Auschwitz?

2.3. Jill Talcott

May
Seattle

There was a video camera rigged up on a tripod nearby. It was a grandiose gesture and Jill tried to underplay it. But Nate had seen enough of her ambitious streak to smell a Historical Moment a mile away. He dropped his hands from the keyboard and rubbed them against his thighs like an athlete shaking out his legs between sprints. "I finished downloading the results from Quey. Wanna wait until morning to see how we did?"

He might have been a lover deep into heavy foreplay, pausing to ask his girl, "Should we wait?" It was tempting in its sheer masochism.

Jill looked at her watch. It was 3:00 a.m. "No, I'd never be able to get to sleep. Besides, it's kind of dramatic—middle of the night." Jill felt uncharacteristically girlish. Her small fingers kept twisting themselves together and she had to keep pulling them apart.

"Well . . . if you're sure." He was teasing now.

"Everything's in? No numbers transposed? No dropped data?"

"Just that power surge when I was transferring the files."

Her heart stopped beating. "What!"

"Kidding."

She glared at him.

Nate nibbled away a smile. "Seriously, all I have to do is push this wee button here and my program will compare the numbers your equation generated on Quey with the carbon atom data. We'll know if your equation was able to predict real-life behavior in about ten seconds."

Ten seconds. That's what it boiled down to after seven years of plotting and effort. She was hyperventilating.

She paced around behind the camera and checked it again. She messed with her hair, put on some Chap Stick. At the sight of the clear balm, Nate made a shocked face, as if to say, *This must be important if you deign to put on any cosmetic whatsoever.* She ignored him.

"Ready?" she asked.

Nate raised one eyebrow warily, moved the cursor over the button on the screen that would run the comparison. "Ready."

"Wait!"

She turned on the camera, squared her shoulders. Stepping in front of the lens, she gave a short introduction: date, time, and the nature of the experiment. She adjusted the camera to look at the computer screen, taking her time to focus it in for a good close-up. Then she sat primly in the chair beside Nate.

"Proceed, Mr. Andros," she said, for the record.

Nate clicked the button. After a few seconds, two columns of data appeared on the screen with a box that said:

Correlation in data above the error factor by 31%

With the uncaring blink of those spiteful words, Jill's heart sank through her legs to puddle somewhere on the floor. Her equation hadn't worked. She couldn't believe it. She had been convinced—*convinced* . . .

She cursed vibrantly, then remembered the camera and turned it off. She stood in the narrow aisle, looking at her shoes and breathing hard. *A scientist observed results coolly, impersonally,* she reminded herself. *You don't get angry at data.*

"Damn!" Nate exclaimed. "I really thought it was gonna fly."

Jill was too wrapped up in her own frustration to care about his. She sat down at the computer again. "Bring up the grisly remains."

He expanded the boxes that contained the complete set of numbers.

"Your velocity predictions are off by thirty percent," he commented. "Position, twenty-eight percent."

"I see it," Jill muttered.

After several minutes she sat back, pressing icy fingers to her forehead. It would take a long time to pore over the results, not a task to be undertaken tonight. And she could already see that it wouldn't tell them what they *really* needed to know. It wouldn't tell them where she'd gone wrong.

She felt like crying. Stupid, stupid data.

Nate glanced at her sympathetically. "Even a small error in the equation could cause this, if it was in the right place."

"No. Position, velocity—those are in completely different ends of the equation. The whole underlying theory has to be wrong. I don't know why I should be surprised. We knew the energy pool model was *crap.*"

Nate looked uncomfortable. "But that's what an interference pattern *does,* Jill. I mean, Dr. Talcott. It makes everything completely interconnected. One little change in a ripple over here means a cascading response on the other side of the—"

"Just . . . *leave* it."

She was angry and disappointed and snappish. Nate started to say something, then closed his mouth. He looked hurt at her taking it out on him.

"It's late," Jill said. "I'm going home."

*   *   *

The next morning she couldn't face a day of classes or Nate, so she called in sick. Seven years of work were down the tube, and she had no idea how to start again. She lounged around at home for half the day, her mind a miserable blank. She tried to do some stretching exercises, but her body was so used to being utterly ignored that it wouldn't cooperate.

Jill Talcott's physique was small but not particularly fit. The same could be said of her house. The tiny 1920s bungalow was situated in an urban Seattle neighborhood called Wallingford that had once been low-income housing but now came with heavy mortgages as well as no closet space. Her neighbors were high-salaried technocrats, couples, and young families. Jill lived alone. Not even pets disturbed the domestic order. The great scientists filled one narrow bookcase in the living room, and a ten-inch TV gave her the national news if she became conscious enough to show an interest, which was roughly never. The house was orderly, if not cozy; functional, unadorned, like its owner. And thanks to flawed insulation, it was frequently cold.

After lunch she drove to a beach on Lake Washington. It was a weekday, and she had the place to herself. Looking at the water, she thought about the energy pool model of the universe, all those particles making ripples in the gigantic pond of space-time. Dr. Ansel used to say that the refusal to accept the theory represented fear in the scientific community. Physicists knew that if it were taken seriously they'd never be able to pin anything down again. All their wonderful divisions and categorizations would dissolve like ice cubes in warm water. Chaos theory mathematicians might nod their heads in sympathy at the thought, but physicists turned green in the gills.

She had rejected Ansel, too. She'd resigned as his graduate student once she'd figured out how off the beaten track his work was. He and his wife had been kind to her, a rube from the sticks, but ultimately Jill had considered him a hindrance to her career, didn't want the sly looks and chuckles of his peers to rub off on her. Bye-bye, Dr. Ansel. So why, then, had she returned to his theory, like Oedipus, who ran away from his fate only to fall right into its lap? She didn't miss the irony. What would Ansel think if he knew of her equation? Would he laugh? Would he think her a two-faced bitch?

He wouldn't be the first.

Jill Talcott had been born and raised in the South—not the South of the Clintons or of Thomas Wolfe but of Loretta Lynn and black lung disease. Her childhood in the seventies had boasted dirty, puffy polyester clothing that never wore out, making the most lurid hand-me-downs live forever.

Her mother's family had not been wealthy, but they'd had a piano, new clothes for school, pot roast on Sundays. That was the story Jill's mother told. She talked wistfully about that world. No white picket fences for Jill's mother, not even chipped ones. Her downfall had been a man, what else? Jill's father, slim and wiry. He'd aged to old leather, but he'd been irresistible when young, so the story went, with a pencil-thin mustache, slicked back blond hair, and flashy clothes. He was a gambler, always out for the easy buck. He had a great deal of charm, but Jill learned early on to discount it, for his promises were pretty puffs of air and nothing more. Jill's mother worked as a waitress, worked harder at home trying to hide the money from his grasp. They lived in a rented shack. There was no pot roast, no new clothes for school, only what Jill's mother pulled from the charity box. And there never was, never would be, a piano.

As a child, Jill had no outward gifts to balance this deficit of poverty. She was a runt with an unremarkable face and mousy hair badly cut. Early on she decided that the best way to deal with the mockery of her peers was not to care what anyone thought. Then she learned she was gifted in certain subjects—math, for instance, and chemistry. Her teacher cautiously suggested that Jill *might* be able to earn a college scholarship. She grasped that lifeline and never looked back, hadn't seen her parents since she started college, never answered her mother's letters—tales of woe every one.

Two things Jill vowed never to do: place money on a bet and let a man into her life. Because once you hooked up with someone, by definition you could no longer call your life your own. By definition his liabilities became your liabilities. And once you'd taken a wrong turn like that you paid dearly. Even in this age of divorce, you would pay.

All her energy was focused on her career. Perhaps it was because the very idea—that Jill Talcott from Pittsville, Tennessee, might *be somebody*—was so absurd. Like her father, she always did have a soft spot for the long shot.

Are the people and events in our lives like pebbles? Jill wondered, watching the lake. *Do they spread out the ripples of their impact, changing us in ways we could not even guess?* It was not a happy thought and certainly, she admonished herself, not a very scientific one.

Frowning, she gathered pebbles on the beach and began tossing them into the water. On the surface of the lake they left rippling patterns. She toyed around idly for a few minutes, then got absorbed by it. She made piles, arranging the pebbles by size. She watched the ripples her pebbles made with ardent interest, watched multiple ripples intersect.

Crest, trough, crest, trough. Where two waves meet they form an interference pattern: crest + crest = higher crest, trough + trough = deeper trough, crest + trough canceled each other out, creating a shorter crest or shallower trough. And that new pattern went out to intersect and merge with the next and the next and the next and the next.

Two hours later, Jill was still at the beach. The wind had picked up, and the lake was getting choppy. Jill, grimy with sand and dirt, her piles of pebbles denuded, stood on the beach with very small pebbles in her hand. She tossed them in, then got down on all fours to look across the surface of the water, watched the waves intersect, ripple out, fade away.

It was getting difficult to see the ripples because of the water's rising chop. She squinted—had the queerest sense that there was something she was not quite grasping.

Then she *did* see it, so obvious it blindsided her. *The lake has a wave pattern of its own.*

The idea floored her: the simplicity of it, the beauty of it, the way it shifted her entire worldview. It was one of those moments that a scientist might get, at best, once or twice in a lifetime, and her eyes teared up with the power of it.

The lake's surface was a repeating choppy wave. Yes, the pebble waves interfered with one another, but they were *also interfered with by the stronger wave of the lake itself.*

She sat back on her heels, hands clutching at the sand beneath her. They'd been counting on the fact that the carbon atom data had been run *in a vacuum*. But of course, the particle accelerator was a "vacuum" only in the sense that there were no other *particles* in the accelerator—in other words, *no other pebbles*. But there was *space* in the accelerator, space-time, the stuff of the universe. In other words, the *lake* had been there.

Was space-time a mirror-smooth surface, as she'd unwittingly assumed? Or did it have a wave of its own, like the surface of Lake Washington?

What was the wave pattern of space-time itself?

3

"Listen to me," cried Syme with extraordinary emphasis. "Shall I tell you the secret of the whole world? It is that we have only known the back of the world. We see everything from behind, and it looks brutal. That is not a tree, but the back of a tree. That is not a cloud, but the back of a cloud. Cannot you see that everything is stooping and hiding a face? If we could only get round in front—"
—G. K. Chesterton,
The Man Who Was Thursday, 1908

3.1. CALDER FARRIS

Mark Avery left four phone messages before Calder finally made himself respond. He didn't want to visit Avery, a man rotting away with cancer, a man who'd once been the closest thing to a friend that Calder Farris had ever had. A nine-hour sigmoidoscopy would have been more inviting than a visit with old Mark now. But on the last message Avery had sounded like he was at death's door and said he had things, important things, to pass on.

Hell and goddamn. Calder phoned and arranged a time with Avery's wife, Cherry, to come visit.

He pulled up outside the small officer's bungalow where Captain Avery and his family lived, dread turning to resentment, resentment sparking anger so black he ground his teeth. He made his way up the walkway, kicking a plastic PlaySkool scooter out of the way. At the door he smoothed his black trench coat in an effort to gain control before he rang the bell.

Cherry answered. Calder eyed her warily. He took his glasses off, but she didn't even blink. Cherry had never been intimidated by his eyes, funnily enough. In fact, she seemed to know he used them deliberately and to find that pathetically amusing.

Calder couldn't stand her.

Years ago, Mark Avery had been a bachelor. Mark had trained Calder when he'd come to the DoD, worked as his partner for about a year. They'd developed an understanding that was rare for Calder. They'd believed in the same things: in the United States of America, in military power and order, in dedicating their lives to keeping their country number one. Or so he'd thought. Maybe it had even been more than that. Maybe there had been something paternal in the older man's affection—or maybe Calder had just imagined it.

Screw it.

Anyway, they'd spotted each other at the gym, watched games together on TV in this very house, pizza and beer, card games sometimes, shit like that.

But then Calder's training had been over and he'd traveled a lot. He and Avery got together once in a blue moon. And one day Avery said he was getting married. Calder couldn't fucking believe it. The man was nearly fifty and had known the girl all of three months. She was younger than Calder, ferchristssake.

Calder had tried to talk him out of it. He'd told Avery exactly what he thought, that he didn't need a ball and chain, that he had no business marrying someone her age. Calder had only met Cherry once, but he hadn't liked her but figured she was marrying Avery for free housing and a military pension package, and said so.

In the end, Mark had married Cherry and Calder had hardly seen him since. And Cherry must have known some of it, because she treated him pretty cool.

Yup, as far as Calder was concerned, Mark Avery's life was over long before he'd been diagnosed with the big "C."

Today, though, Cherry didn't give him the Popsicle imitation. She invited him in as if he were her old pal. Her too-pretty face, the face Calder had once found such an affront to his good opinion of Mark Avery, was thin and pale and wore no makeup. A kerchief held back unwashed red hair. She looked exhausted. She looked like something you'd scrape off the bottom of your shoe.

"He'll be so glad you came." Cherry smiled, gratefully. Great. If Cherry was happy to see him it had to be pretty damn intolerable.

A small body came charging out of the kitchen and smashed into her legs. Avery's son. Calder couldn't remember his name. He stared at the kid uneasily—red corduroy overalls and a striped T-shirt, red baby hair, sticky face.

"Mama!"

Cherry smiled and picked up the kid.

Calder couldn't get over the baby smell—fleshy and sickly sweet and faintly uriney. Man. The one time he'd visited since the kid was born it had taken hours at the shooting range for the acrid gunpowder to burn away that smell. He held his breath, wondering how Avery could stand it.

"Go on back to the den, Calder. I'll make you boys some coffee."

Avery was sitting on a couch that was made up as a bed. He had on clean pajamas and Calder could swear his hair had been washed. Cherry must have done that, in honor of Calder's visit. It made him feel guilty as hell.

He sat in a chair and Mark acted like they were two buds on some average, ordinary visit. For a while they chatted, Calder not having a whole lot of news because he'd been working, mostly, and Avery going on about Cherry and the kid—Jason, that was his name. "Jace." The way Avery said it made Calder's teeth hurt.

Jesus, it was as bad as Calder figured it would be. Avery was wasted away to nothing, his face like a skull, his remaining hair dry and dead-looking, as if it had passed on a couple of months ahead of Avery himself.

"You said on the phone you had some things to tell me," Calder reminded Mark, to get the show on the road.

"Yeah." Avery tried to sit up straighter and looked so damned pathetic that Calder stared out the window at the backyard. There was a play set back there. A *play set*.

"I taught you how to do your damned job." Avery grinned—a rictus. "But that doesn't mean I told you everything I knew."

Calder wasn't surprised. He knew exactly what was going down. Avery wanted to do a mind dump before he kicked it. And whatever had happened between them, Calder was his dumpee of choice.

"So what is it?"

"It's waves, Farris. It's all about waves."

"Sound waves?"

There were a couple of top-secret projects going on in the DoD revolving around the lethal use of sound waves. Calder wasn't supposed to know about it, but he did. Avery and he had always known these things.

Avery shook his head. "What if you could point a device at someone that would disrupt the particles of their bodies? Scramble their atoms? Neutralize their electrons? What if you could make a bomb that would do that to an entire city? And do it clean, not leave a couple of millenniums' worth of radioaction behind?"

Calder was interested. "You have something solid?"

"Some good leads . . . The subatomic level, that's the future. I'm talking about the fundamental nature of matter here."

Calder slowly smiled, despite himself. It was like old times. They used to go on about this shit for hours.

For a moment, he remembered how much he owed Avery. Calder had always loved weapons, even as a kid—toy guns, soldiers, stone "grenades" . . . But Avery had taught him a deeper truth. Since early man picked up that first stick and conked a rival over the head with it, technology had always been about one thing: power. He who has the biggest toys rules. And power was *everything*.

"I'm serious," Avery insisted. "The Next Big Thing is not going to be explosives. The future is going to be about undoing life from the ground level up, from the *inside*. And, Calder, matter *is* waves. You want to know who really has their hands in some nasty-assed science, you find someone who knows that."

"What kind of leads do you have?"

"Some names. Some ideas. It's all in the file." Avery motioned his hand toward a thick envelope on the coffee table. Calder picked it up and looked inside—a big manila envelope, papers. Mark Avery's legacy. It gave him a momentary stab of pain. He swallowed it.

"Thanks."

"Hell." Avery dismissed the word with a blink. He sank back, looking so tired suddenly, Calder thought he was going to red-line right there. "Everything's kind of a mess. I didn't really have the . . . energy to neaten it up for you."

"No problem."

The moment stretched out awkwardly. Mark coughed, doing it weakly, as though it hurt. Calder clenched his jaw.

"The thing is, the DoD—that whole institution—it's gotten to be about sucking down tax money and producing jack-all. And the academics, hell, they've gotten themselves so tied up in knots they can't see their way out of a cardboard box. The Big One, when it comes, is gonna be some undiscovered Einstein out there who isn't a part of any of that. It'll be someone from Podunk, New Jersey, and he's gonna belong to *you*." Mark turned his eyes on him. For once *his* eyes looked spooky. "He would have been *mine*, but I guess that's unlikely now. You should thank me, you lucky bastard."

"Yeah, right." Calder tried for a jokey tone and missed. He just sounded pissed off.

Cherry brought them coffee. It gave them something to do. Calder could barely stand the taste. Between the smell of the kid that pervaded the house and the stench of Mark's sickness, he had to gag it down. As they drank he sat with the envelope on his lap like a freaking job applicant. And Avery lay there, hardly able to hold the cup. Neither one of them could bear to look at each other.

As soon as he was done with the coffee, Calder thought, he could go.

Out the window, he saw something red flash by—the kid. Cherry came into view, chasing the baby, picking him up, swinging him in the air. Fucking Hallmark moment.

There was a muffled noise from Avery, and Calder looked at him. His eyes were on the backyard, too, his face so *regretful* it made Calder want to hit something. Avery glanced at him, guiltily. His face twitched.

"I . . ." He hesitated. Calder thought, *Whatever it is, spare me, please God.* Avery didn't. "I almost didn't give that to you, you know." He met Calder's eyes in a challenge, then looked back out at the kid. "I dedicated my whole life to weapons technology. Jace's birth . . . sometimes I wonder if what we do . . . if it's the right thing."

Calder saw red as a hand reached up from his gut, squeezing. "What is *that* supposed to mean? We have the freedom we do in this country because we have the meanest, most kick-ass weapons, end of story. What the fuck's the matter with you, Mark?"

Avery's eyes were unapologetic. "I wonder if you'll be as sure of that when you're a father."

Calder snorted. *I'd have my balls chewed off by alligators before I'd let that happen.* He kept it to himself.

"Calder, if you *do* find him . . ." Avery paused. Calder didn't need to ask who the "him" was; it was the next Oppenheimer, the inventor of the new Big One. "When you do . . ."

"What?" Calder said impatiently.

Avery licked his cracked lips. "Ever heard that whole thing about what you'd do if you had the chance to go back and meet Hitler in 1925?"

"Stop talking this crap!" Calder's tone said he meant it. It was a tone that would have made most men stick a horn up their butt and blow taps if he'd told them to.

Avery smiled sadly. "I guess when you're dying you get some funny ideas." He looked out at the backyard again where Cherry was swinging the baby around and around. "I don't s'pose . . . if I asked you to keep an eye on them for me . . ."

"Jesus, Mark! Are you drugged or what?"

"Forget it." Avery sounded resigned, like he'd known Calder would refuse and that it was stupid to ask him in the first place.

Well, it was stupid. Damned stupid. He *must* be stoned to have even thought such a thing. Then Calder recalled that Avery didn't have any family. He'd been as much a loner as Calder himself until Cherry came along. *God*, he hated this.

"I'll make sure they don't starve, if that's what you're asking." Calder spit it out like shards of glass. Fucking Cherry, she knew what she'd been doing when she married Avery. She'd get a pension. She and the kid would do just fine. And he'd bet anything she was remarried within a year anyway. But he had to say *something*.

"Thanks," Avery said.

He sounded like he believed it about as much as Calder meant it.

3.2. Denton Wyle

Zurich

Denton beat the letter to Zurich by a whole week. Thank God Schwartz was too cheap or too old-fashioned to spring for FedEx. *Why* Denton went to Zurich—that was something he didn't examine too closely. He was moving on pure intuition. Schwartz had lied. He had *big-time* lied.

Kobinski. Ever heard of him?

Could be.

All that feigned disinterest and hypocritical scolding! And for what? What was Schwartz trying to hide? Denton couldn't wait to find out.

Denton's stubbornness, once awakened, wasn't like other people's: it wasn't a brick wall; it was more like water, flowing around or through or under all obstacles, seeking its instinctual resting point.

He'd never been fond of Zurich. It was a city of unbridled materialism, more his mother's style than his. He walked through street after street of glitzy stores, entire shops that sold nothing but gold pens, furs, or crystal stemware. Zurich's good taste weighed on him like a thumb.

The address he had was in an area that looked older, the stores even posher, if only because they didn't scream their message. Some of the shops were so discreet you couldn't even tell what they sold. The address he had was like that. He found himself the only customer in a small room filled with polished, translucent antiques. Sophisticated hand-printed cards rested on each object. He began to question, for the first time, and rather belatedly, what he was doing here.

An elegant elderly man approached him. The man began the formalities in German, moving smoothly into English on hearing Denton's reply. His name was Gretz and he had a highbrow British accent. Denton buttered him up by admiring the pieces in the shop before sidling, nonchalantly, into his real business.

"Do you work with rare manuscripts, papers, things like that?"

Gretz reappraised him. "As a matter of fact, we do. But you must have heard this from someone, no? Are you looking for anything in particular, sir?"

"As a matter of fact, yes. I'm looking for anything written by Yosef Kobinski."

Gretz blinked. "That's quite remarkable."

"You have something in that line?"

"I do indeed, sir."

The man waited, his soft, long-fingered hands pressed together. *And?* Did he want a secret password or something?

"I'd love to see what you have if that's at all possible."

"This way, please."

He led Denton through a curtain to a part of the shop that was—Denton saw at once—the real heart of the place. There were smooth mahogany tables. Bookcases lined two walls and cut-glass display cases held ancient manuscripts. There was a reverent, hushed tone to the room.

"Please be seated." Gretz donned plastic gloves and retrieved a transparent folder from one of the cases. He carried it over to Denton, drew up a chair opposite him, and, like a jeweler, took a pair of long flat-pronged tweezers and a magnifying glass from a nearby shelf, adjusted a small desk lamp with a protective filter, and turned it on.

With these elaborate preparations met, Gretz carefully turned the folder around, maneuvering it gently by its edges. He handed Denton the magnifying glass. Under the plastic, Denton could see a piece of dirty brown paper marked with characters he didn't recognize.

"Five pages, written in Hebrew," Gretz said melodiously. "They were found in 1962 in a metal cylinder buried on the grounds of Auschwitz. Since then they've been in private hands. I obtained them three months ago."

Auschwitz! This had been written *in* the camp.

"The papers date from approximately 1943. Every page bears the mark 'YK' in Hebrew." He pointed to said mark at the bottom of the page with his tweezers. "The author is a Polish rabbi, Yosef Kobinski, about whom you appear to know."

Denton studied the identifying mark with an escalating sense of nervous wonder. Maybe it was just the old-world surroundings, or seeing an actual relic of Auschwitz, or the mysterious tinge of secrets that pervaded the room, but he half expected Gretz to say, *"Eez eet safe?"* like Olivier in *Marathon Man*.

"Um, yeah, I know something about him. But I'd like to know more."

"I don't have a great deal of background on the man myself except that his work was based on kabbalah. He published one book before the war, *The Book of Mercy*. It had a very small run and is extremely rare. Fragments of his Auschwitz manuscript, titled *The Book of Torment*, are rarer still. He went to a great deal of effort to hide individual pages."

Denton nodded, as if he knew all about it.

"As I'm sure you know, prisoners in the concentration camps were not allowed personal property, nor did they have access to writing materials as a rule. Still, the human mind is quite ingenious, yes? These things appear now and then. That's not to say that they aren't extremely valuable."

"Valuable," Denton echoed. "Are all five pages in this condition?" He asked it because it was something a serious customer *would* ask.

"Yes. But I must tell you, I have an offer pending for the papers."

"Ah!"

Denton pretended to study the page, but he wasn't really seeing it. He was trying to sense the dealer's attitude, and he decided that there was definitely an open door here somewhere. So the sale wasn't completely final or perhaps Gretz had something else in mind.

"I'm new to the area of rare manuscripts. I hear there's a difference between an exclusive and a nonexclusive purchase. Is that right?"

Gretz looked at Denton as if he were being coy, like maybe he was a riverboat gambler asking how many cards to deal. "In the antique business a rare manuscript is considered to be a *physical* object—an antique—quite a separate thing from the text on the page. Most dealers will photograph any object before selling it and, in the case of written materials, may copy or transcribe the text. You see, the text is usually not what's important but rather the document itself which has value."

Had he sensed a door? This was a freaking *canyon*. "Interesting."

"And when a buyer purchases an unpublished manuscript such as this, he may opt to buy the physical document only, or he may choose to also purchase all rights to the text. Naturally, purchasing all rights is the more expensive option."

"In other words, a nonexclusive purchase means someone else could buy a *copy* of the text?"

"That is the arrangement, yes."

"Say the pending sale for this document turned out to be a nonexclusive agreement. How much would you want for a copy of it?"

"Five thousand U.S.," Gretz said, without a moment's hesitation.

Not to be gauche, Denton didn't reveal his delight. Five thousand was well below his guilt level. He'd paid nearly as much for the plane tickets.

What was he thinking? He didn't even know what the pages said.

"Is there a lot of demand for, um, Kobinski's work?"

The dealer smiled. "Documents from the camps are always in demand, Mr. Wyle, especially documents written by camp prisoners. Though I must say, I've only encountered two people who were looking for Kobinski's writing specifically, and you are one of them."

That smile glittered with a question that Denton could not have answered even if he wanted to: *Why Kobinski?*

When he left the shop, Denton had more or less an unspoken agreement with Gretz. Even so, he told himself he'd never return. He didn't know what was in the manuscript. It probably had nothing to do with the disappearance of Kobinski or anything else of interest to him or the readers of *Mysterious World*. And it was a *fragment*. What could anyone say in five pages that would be worth five grand?

He debated with himself like this for three whole days. He stayed at a decent, but not exorbitant, hotel. He toured the city with, and made love to, a blond Scandinavian backpacker he met on the street. She had a face so pretty it belonged on a dairy ad, thighs like silk, and a mouth sweet and tight, even if she was only nineteen, immature in her giggling eagerness. She and her friend camped out in his room and invited him to meet them in Munich. He said he might, knowing he wouldn't. He walked them to the train station, and all the while, even as he kissed her good-bye, he was arguing with himself about the fragment.

But when the days had passed and he knew Schwartz's letter had arrived, he found himself heading back to the shop, as if his feet knew full well what his brain didn't. He would buy the copy just because he wanted it, had wanted it from the first moment he'd laid eyes on those scratchy markings under plastic in that half-lit inner sanctum, from the instant he'd seen those tweezers. His gut was just about his only compass in life, and it said that this was more than just *a* story; this might well be *the* story.

Had there ever been any real doubt?

*   *   *

FROM THE BOOK OF TORMENT BY YOSEF KOBINSKI, AUSCHWITZ, 1943

Last time I discussed how physics, the physical laws of space and time, are not only hospitable to the mysteries of faith; they are exactly the same *thing. A scientist is a blind man probing the face of G-d.*

Did I already write that? Yes, that must have been the pages I gave to Georg Bruzek. The important thing is that all must be preserved. The gifts of knowledge the Lord has given to me . . . I don't care so much for my own life, but to have this knowledge die with me is unacceptable.

One of the keys to deep wisdom is that there are only a few patterns in all of creation, and they are repeated over and over. The planets revolve around the sun just as the electrons in an atom revolve around the nucleus. The whorls of a seashell mirror those of galaxies. "As above, so below." The Micro is a mirror image of the Macro.

. . .

The physical world is made up of dualities: male/female, hot/cold, day/night, birth/death. There is no "itness," no "beingness," which does not have an opposite. Science has proven this true at every level of life: there is no particle without a corresponding antiparticle, no force without a counterbalance.

Why is this so? Because to have physical space you must have a "here" and also an "other there." Before creation, everything was the same and there was only one place. To create distance and volume and expanse, opposites were necessary: poles between which life itself could be stretched.

The importance and meaning of dualities is one of the greatest secrets of kabbalah.

All dualities are mere echoes of the four great dualities. They are the sephirot, *the opposing arms of the kabbalistic Tree of Life:* Binah/chochmah, gevorah/chesed, hod/nezach, *and* keter/malkhut. *These four great opposites form the lower four dimensions of space and time.*

Keter *and* malkhut *are the highest duality.* Keter *is the spiritual realm and* malkhut *the physical.* Keter *is the "Heaven" to* malkhut's *"earth." It is "God" to* malkhut's *"man." Some believe only in what they can see, feel, and hear (*malkhut*). Others suspect there is a teeming pool of meaning and energy that resides beyond or outside or throughout the physical world.* Keter *is that fifth dimension.*

The next great duality is binah *and* chochmah. Binah *is our logical, rational mind.* Chochmah *is intuition, creativity. In the beginning, before the "big bang," everything was one thing—that "oneness" is* chochmah, *a spiritual state that mystics and artists strive to recapture.* Binah *separates, categorizes, labels. It is the great sieve. In human psychology they call these traits left-brain and right-brain. In our physical world,* binah *is solid and rigid and* chochmah *is pure and flowing—they are land and sea, earth and water.*

The third great duality is gevorah *(judgment) and* chesed *(mercy).* Gevorah's *language is black and white, good and evil, right and wrong. As the Greeks said, it is blind.* Gevorah *lays down rigid laws and does not care about an offender's background, excuses, or motivations.*

Chesed, *loving-kindness or mercy, is the opposite of judgment. It is empathy, expansiveness, generosity of spirit, love. Of all the* sephirot, chesed *appears to be the most purely good. Could there ever be too much loving-kindness? Yes! Anything taken to its extremes creates evil. Think of a child or a society with* no *laws or restrictions—chaos results. Without boundaries there is no definition, no form.*

The final great duality is hod *and* netzach. Hod *is inward-turned, contemplative.* Netzach *is outward-facing, social.* Hod *is the introvert and* netzach *the extrovert instinct. At its best,* netzach *is the teacher, the benevolent leader, the mediator. At its extreme it is the bully, the manipulator—those who get a sense of self only by controlling others.* Hod, *in its most favorable light, is the scholar, the independent thinker. At its worst it is antisocial, cut off from the world.*

There is a connection between these great elements. Binah, gevorah, *and* hod *are "left-hand" traits.* Binah *(logic) separates "I" from "them." When we separate our own identity from that of others it becomes easier to judge them (*gevorah*). Your judgments can become so rigid that no one else is deemed acceptable but you yourself. This is a hell of* hod's *making.*

Chochmah, chesed, *and* netzach *are "right-hand" traits.* Chochmah *(intuition) says: "We are all one." Chesed (mercy) responds with love and acceptance. Netzach, therefore, thrives in relation to other people.*

The thing to remember about dualities is that they are not two dots on opposing horizons. They are continuums. *You might be more merciful than judgmental or more judgmental than merciful. But it is very unlikely you are so merciful you contain not the tiniest drop of judgment or so judgmental you lack the merest wisp of mercy!*

If you picture the great dualities like pegs between which you *are stretched—*gevorah *and* chesed *at your head and feet,* binah *and* chochmah *at your left and right hands,* hod *and* netzach *at your chest and back, and time as the last force,* malkhut *and* keter, *pulling you between birth and death, Heaven and earth. . . . This is really what the forces in our lives are like. How can you escape such torture?*

By finding the middle. In each of these dualities there is an absolute perfect middle point. On the continuum between judgment and mercy there is a point of perfect balance: judgment tempered perfectly by mercy, loving-kindness with healthy boundaries. There is a similar perfect point between logic and intuition. It is the scientist-mystic, East-meets-West. The perfect balance between the internal and external exists also—a place where we can enjoy loving relationships but retain a strong sense of self.

All of these perfect points of balance meet where? The center of all these continuums is the same *center. Where is this magical place? As you lie there, stretched between these poles, there is a place in the exact center of you—your heart, body, and mind—where all these points meet. If you find that place, tension and struggle disappear.*

This is also the point where keter *and* malkhut *meet. God and man. God-in-you.*

. . .

I have not slept for four nights. My heart has been filled up with ground glass. I have tried to think of some way, any way, out of here. My mind has grasped something, though it may be madness.

Years ago, while listing correspondences between heavenly bodies and their earthly counterparts, I came across a curiosity. Schwartzschild's "ergospheres" or "black holes" are massive stars that have been condensed down by gravity so completely they form dimensionless objects of infinite density. These black holes are literally holes in the fabric of space-time. And since my correspondence theory states that everything that exists in the heavens (macro) has an equivalent in the subatomic world (micro) then there would have to exist such

Forgive me. There must exist such an entity as a "microscopic black hole."

It was idle musing at the time. An innocent time! Now I am forced to revisit the idea in a much more desperate frame of mind. Do these gateways exist? And might they be our salvation?

It sounds absurd, yet the more aggressively I attack the mathematics the more I am convinced the idea is sound. If they exist, they must not be obvious in their behavior for good reason. Although a macro black hole would pull into it anything that crosses its horizon, it would not be as easy to engage the operation of a micro black hole. One must take into account the difference in mass between

I can barely write for shaking. The mass differential is a problem. I have been working intensely on pinning down the play of forces.

Beyond these difficulties there is also the question of where such a thing would lead. I have my theories, but there is no knowing absolutely until the deed is done. Like Moses, I must believe there is a promised land.

Nothing could be worse than what Isaac

No. These gateways cannot be common—no more than black holes are common in the heavens. I would have little hope that one would chance to be nearby if it were not for one factor: In the vicinity of such holes one might expect to see extraordinary good or evil. The influence from the fifth dimension and from other universes might seep through as cold seeps through a crack in the window. And surely, if there was one place on earth that could be defined as evil beyond the pale of mortal experience, it is this place, Auschwitz.

LOS ANGELES

"So what do you think? Huh?" Denton was too impatient to wait for Dave to speak on his own.

Dave Banks didn't answer. He was still glued to the pages of the Kobinski translation. Dave was an electrical engineer, sci-fi fanatic, and Denton's ex–college roommate. Until today, Denton hadn't seen him since graduation even though they'd both ended up in LA years ago. Dave had never quite forgiven Denton for sleeping with his girlfriend.

Which was totally unfair. Dave hadn't even been serious about that girl, and anyway, it wasn't as if Denton had set out to seduce her; it just happened. Some people held a grudge. Others nursed it until it grew up, graduated from college, and retired.

Unfortunately, Denton's researcher, Loretta, had zero ability at science and all his current friends were wanna-be actors and models who thought *black hole* was either a psychedelic or sexual term. So Dave Banks was Denton's only alternative to reading a book. And Denton was a social animal. He learned by picking brains and soaking up atmosphere, not by any activity as numbingly solitary as reading.

Dave looked up from the Kobinski pages, his small eyes glittering. "Interesting."

"How so?"

Dave tilted his head thoughtfully. "Got another beer?"

Denton wanted to scream with impatience. Instead, he went to the kitchen of his condo to fetch a Corona.

The dining room was open to the living room, and beyond the tastefully decorated "conversational space" (he'd used his mother's decorator—a real flamer) Denton could see that the sun was setting. The skyscrapers of Century City glowed all around them.

He still appreciated the million-dollar view. He appreciated it more knowing Dave was right on his heels and lived in a crappy apartment in West Hollywood.

It was like old times, the two of them leaning against the kitchen cabinets tossing back longnecks. The déjà vu was strong because Dave had never quite left 1989. He still wore the same ragged jeans and tacky sloganed T-shirts. His thin red hair was still in a long braid down his back, ever ready for his beloved medieval fairs.

"What, exactly, do you want from me?"

"I want your opinion on this black hole thing."

"I'm not a physicist."

"Yeah, I know, Dave." Denton rolled his eyes. "But you took a couple semesters of physics. Aced them, if I recall."

Dave raised his eyebrows as if to say, *Yeah, so what?*, but the geek in him was pleased. He had a vain streak when it came to his intellectual prowess. Which, Denton was willing to admit, was considerably greater than his own. But then, he didn't run around with a hairstyle that had gone out in the year 1500, either.

Dave pinched his nostrils with two fingers. "What *I* want to know is how you got into this?"

"I told you. I'm working on a series of articles about vanishings."

"Yeah, but how did you *find* this?" Dave had brought the stapled pages into the kitchen and he waved them with something like awe. "I mean, this is, like, a relic. How come no one's ever found this before?"

"Someone has."

Denton told him about Schwartz. Naturally, he modified the bit about how he'd seen the letter to Zurich, said he'd eyed it on the rabbi's desk instead of opening his mail. He didn't need Dave to give him that *look*, that "I've got your number" look.

Denton hated that look.

When he was done explaining, Dave flipped to the translation. "Well, if you're asking me about the math, forget it. Those equations and stuff in the margins? *Way* beyond me."

"But what do you think of the *idea*, though? See, the thing is," Denton's voice got higher with excitement, "what if people *do* disappear? And what if these black holes are the reason why? The 'smoking gun,' as it were. Right? Because it does seem that there are places where disappearances are more likely to happen, like the Bermuda Triangle or Stonehenge or something. So—"

"Stonehenge? I never heard anything about people disappearing at Stonehenge."

"*Whatever*. You know what I mean. So what if that's because these *places*, these *vortexes*, are where the black holes are?"

Dave was giving him a blank look.

"Okay, never mind. Just . . . what do you think of the idea of miniature black holes? From a physics point of view?"

Dave leaned back against the counter, taking his sweet time. "There are all sorts of bizarro things at the subatomic level, and they're still finding new stuff all the time. I mean it's not like, you know, expecting to find Bigfoot in LA. Quite the contrary."

Denton's grin widened. "Great! So let's say these things exist; what—"

"I didn't say that. I said it was *possible*."

Well, *yeah*. But that was about as credible as anything ever got in Denton's line of work. He found himself thinking that Dave was annoyingly *binah*—all logic, no creativity. The thought surprised him. He'd picked up more from Kobinski than he'd thought.

"Okay. It's *possible*. But what I still don't get is how a person could go through a black hole if it's the size of, say, an atom."

Dave shrugged. "A particle at a time would be my guess. Pretty messy."

"Kobinski didn't think so! He talked about using it as an escape route."

"Um, yeah, and he was in *Auschwitz*. I'd say he was probably a little stressed; wouldn't you?" Dave sounded peeved. He hated to be contradicted.

"There were eyewitnesses!"

"So? Even if there was a hole, and even if he did go through it, that doesn't mean he wasn't a string of platelets when he got to the other side."

Denton supposed that was true. But like the official report of the *Why Knot Now* incident, it didn't feel right. And it wasn't very satisfying, either. Talk about a bad ending.

So Denton went around the problem. "Let's just say for grins that you *could* go through a teensy-tiny black hole and survive. Where would you end up? Kobinski says he has a theory, but he doesn't say what it is."

Dave sighed a god-give-him-patience sigh. "This is totally cliché sci-fi. Don't you watch *Star Trek*?"

Denton shook his head, feeling pop-culturally challenged.

"See, the theory is that a black hole has such a tremendous amount of gravity that it actually *punctures a hole* in the fabric of space-time. So the question really is, 'If you found yourself outside space-time where would you be?' For that matter, *when* would you be? Some figure that black holes are just, like, shortcuts to some other part of the universe." Dave appraised him critically. "You've really never watched *Star Trek*? Like *ever*? That's amazing."

"I've seen *Star Wars*."

Dave sighed. "All right. Hypothetically, a 'hole' in space-time could pop you out somewhere else in the universe, possibly a gazillion miles away. So you can use 'em for space travel. And they can be used as time travel devices, too, because essentially they could pop you back up any*when* as well as any-where. But there's also a chance they're *not* shortcuts to someplace else in our own universe. Maybe they go to some *other* universe or just, like, outside of space-time. Which is not a place physical beings like you and me wanna be.

"Assuming," Dave continued sarcastically, "you aren't completely ripped apart when you go through a black hole, which is what most *real* scientists think would be the case."

Denton didn't think any of those explanations were likely to be Kobinski's theory. He may not have understood Kobinski's science, but he was pretty good at soaking up the general tenor of things. And it had sure sounded to him as if Kobinski had a good idea where they would go, and he hadn't thought they'd end up dead in the process. It was possible Kobinski had been just plain wrong, but somehow, Denton believed him. Then again, Denton had never had much resistance to believing just about anything—which was why he worked for *Mysterious World*.

"Any more beer?" Dave fished.

Denton opened the fridge and stared into it, lost in thought. He felt like he was on the verge of a major insight. It was just lurking below the surface like a gigantic sea monster. He waited for it to swim up a little higher so he could see exactly how big it was, count its teeth.

In the next room the phone rang. Denton didn't answer it. It was probably a woman. He listened vaguely to the voice on the answering machine as he popped the tops off a couple of beers, still trying to bring up that idea. The person on the phone wasn't a woman; it was Jack at *Mysterious World*. He was wondering where the Kobinski article was—sounded a little anxious. Jack rang off.

Denton handed a bottle to Dave. Dave was giving him that look. "What are you up to?"

"Who, me? Nothing," Denton said, aggrieved.

Dave continued to frown suspiciously. "So where are you going to go with this, Dent?"

"I don't know," Denton said, and it was true. Only he had the feeling he *did* know. He had the feeling it was part of that lumbering sea monster—already formed and just waiting to pop up. Dave was still giving him that look.

"*What?*"

"You're shafting your magazine, aren't you? That you've worked at for how long?" Dave snorted his disbelief.

Denton felt himself grow pink. "I am not! What . . . ! Why would you say that?"

No change in the Davester.

"I paid for the Kobinski pages with my own money!"

Dave gave him that look in spades.

He was making Denton feel guilty, and Denton didn't like feeling guilty. He mustered as much dignity as he could. "I didn't *say* I was going to blow them off. Jeez. I'm just . . . thinking, you know, what would be the best thing to do. You have to admit, this manuscript of Kobinski's is a lot more legit than the stuff that typically goes in *Mysterious World*. I mean, I love 'em to death, but . . . I wouldn't want to do Kobinski a disservice."

Dave pinched his nose. "You have a point there."

Denton glowed. He loved having a point.

"But . . . this manuscript . . . it's not really *yours*, is it?"

Dave! He was still pissed off about that girl, that ancient history. "It's not anybody's! The copyright ran out years ago."

"Yeah? What about this Rabbi Schwartz guy? He's not gonna be too happy about you sticking your nose into this."

That was true enough. Denton's subconscious already knew it was a problem, maybe because, deep down, he already knew what he was going to do. He'd dreamed about Schwartz. In the dream Schwartz had been a wild-eyed, black-bearded maniac chasing after him (chasing after a rabbit) with knives waving. Oddly, Schwartz had on a chef's white uniform and Pillsbury-Dough-Boy hat.

"Well . . . what do *you* think I should do with it?"

Dave looked away coolly and chugged his beer. "I think you'll find a way to do exactly what you want to do, Dent. You always do."

3.3. Aharon Handalman

JERUSALEM

Aharon could not believe how many cars were in the Yad Vashem parking lot—even in the middle of a workday. He'd thought it would be easier coming on a Wednesday: not so many families, maybe not so many tourists. But Israel's biggest Holocaust memorial was packed.

He scowled as he walked down the Avenue of the Righteous among Nations (or so it was marked on the map the attendant forced upon him), scowling. He passed a statue to Oskar Schindler, huffed at it. In the distance he could see a six-branched candelabra and, in another direction, a large stone monument, the Pillar of Heroism. Such an enormous campus, such expensive buildings and artwork, all wasted on the dead. It made him sick.

The entrance to the main cluster of museums was a round red curve with black glass doors. He paused before he went in, preparing his defenses. His lips drew back like a horse chafing at the bit. A group of schoolchildren passed him, filing through the door with excited solemnity. A secular group. The beautiful Jewish boys had disposable paper *kippas* on their heads. Disposable! It was a shame.

He couldn't help himself. "Torah is more important than *this*," he told the teacher. The teacher smiled falteringly and hurried the children inside.

"Straight to the Hall of Names," he told himself, and pulled open the door.

It was a fine strategy, but not practical. In order to reach the Hall of Names, he had to pass all the way through the long expanse of the Historical Museum. Arrows directed him to choose one of five halls, and he took the first: Anti-Jewish Policy in Germany, figuring that the years leading up to the war had to be the least depressing. He could hear the different guides on each side of him fading in and out as he passed the aisles. Large posterboards hung from the ceiling or were mounted on stands, photographs of the world of the Jews in Europe in the years leading up to 1939. This had been his parents' world. He felt that finger of fire poking up from his nether regions and tried to focus on the reason he was here: Kobinski.

With some relief, he reached the Hall of Names.

The Hall of Names was part library, part mausoleum, with thick dark woods and embedded lighting. He dodged into the stacks, more hopeful of actually finding something now that he had conquered his resistance and made it here.

It wasn't so simple. The bookcases contained binders—millions of them, all neat and similar. The binders contained "Pages of Testimony," brief biographies of those who had been in the Holocaust. The binders were organized alphabetically by the victims' names. As Aharon searched for Kobinski the sheer number of binders weighed heavier and heavier on his shoulders. He passed entire rows of bookcases only to move up one letter in the alphabet.

"Kobinski," he muttered, "Yosef Kobinski," to hear himself talk.

He narrowed in on the relevant section and found the one he wanted. His fingers trembled as he touched the first page of Kobinski's entry. There was a photo. Without looking further, he took the binder across the room to a group of study tables and arranged himself, taking out a notepad and pencil.

He was disappointed with the first page—only what he already knew; name, profession, dates of birth and death, hometown. But it did include the name of Kobinski's parents and of his wife and son. There was a photograph, encased in plastic. The label said: "Yosef and Anna Kobinski and their son, Isaac, Lodz ghetto, early 1940."

In Jerusalem, a lot of judging was done based on a man or woman's dress. There was nothing but piety here—Anna in a long dress and soft hat, Yosef in a dark suit and hat, beard long. Isaac wore a *kippa*. Anna's face was in the shade, but she looked too thin, not well. They were all younger than Aharon expected; the boy looked seven or eight. His eyes were dark and serious, as though the responsibility lay on *his* shoulders. And Yosef—his face was pale and sensitive in the photograph, almost glowing. It was a real Torah scholar's face. He had a dreamy look, like he was "counting mansions in Heaven."

Aharon turned the page. There were appended pages here, old-fashioned paper hyperlinks. Kobinski was mentioned in a survivor testimony by Abram Solarz and in one by Haskiel Malloh. Also there was a reference to an article 378881 in the Collections department. The reference only said it was "a document."

Aharon wrote all this down in his little notepad. It seemed this trip would not be as in-and-out as he had hoped. He didn't go to look for these items right away but turned in the binder and found the entries for Anna and Isaac Kobinski. Anna died in the Lodz ghetto in 1941; Isaac, in Auschwitz in 1943.

Aharon worried his bottom lip, felt the rough edge of his beard there. Well, it had happened, hadn't it? Everyone knew it had. Millions had died, so why should he feel surprised about these three? What, other people hadn't suffered? His jaw tightened against the gaze of the boy's eyes. Aharon looked on his little map, businesslike, to see where he could find the survivors' testimonies.

The testimonies were in another building, naturally. He made his way over there and had to wait for a spot at a computer. After fifteen minutes, a middle-aged woman with a large purse left a station and he snatched the seat. On the entry screen you could browse by year, subject, or location or enter a search word. He entered "Abram Solarz."

Solarz's testimony was twenty pages long. Aharon scanned it looking for Kobinski's name. Solarz had been in the Lodz ghetto, had managed to stay there until the entire thing was liquidated. He'd survived Auschwitz. But his mention of Kobinski came during his description of the day, in 1942, when there had been a *Selektion* for the remaining children.

> It was the 4th of September. Rumkowski gathered together everyone. He said, "I can't bear to tell you this, but they want us to give up all the children and the elderly."
>
> At that time, we did not know that eventually everybody would be taken.

We were only trying to hang on to the ghetto by digging in our fingernails as hard as we could. As bad as it was there, we knew it could be worse.

Rumkowski said, "I never imagined I would be forced to deliver this sacrifice to the altar with my own hands. In my old age I must stretch out my hands and beg: 'Brothers and sisters, hand them over to me! Fathers and mothers, give me your children!' "

Such a terrible speech. Such wailing! Some said, "Do not take an only child, only take children from families who have many." Others said, "We should defend to the death the children." But Rumkowski shouted over all of them. "They have demanded twenty thousand," he said, "all the children under age ten and all the elderly. And even that will only be thirteen thousand, and we must take the rest from the sickest and weakest who would not survive long anyway."

He said we had to cut off limbs to save the body. At that time, there were still one hundred thousand Jews in Lodz, so you can do for yourself the numbers.

After this speech, everyone was in a panic, running around, trying to hide . . .

Aharon skipped ahead, feeling sick to his stomach. He scanned down the text quickly. Where was Kobinski? Was he mentioned in here or not?

The deportation of the twenty thousand was to begin that Monday, but already Saturday the Jewish officials—policemen, doctors, firemen—began to collect them. They went into every building, every room, and when they found the elderly or sick or children, they took them to hospitals to wait. You could not believe the cries, the screams, the pleading of the parents! People were out of their minds.

At last they came to our building. They had a list of names and addresses, but they searched everywhere because parents were moving around the children, trying to hide them. In our flat, there was only my wife and I, both young enough and healthy enough to be safe.

After they left, we heard a commotion in the hall. She insisted, my wife, so I cracked the door to look. Down the hall lived Rabbi Kobinski and his son, Isaac. This man, he worked all the time, you never saw him except maybe on Shabbes he would walk to shul with his son. His wife, Anna, had died some nine months past, sick from pneumonia and weak from no food. Now they were taking Isaac. Kobinski had him by the shoulders, saying to the Jewish doctor, "He's eleven, he's eleven, you can't take him." Because they were not supposed to take ten years and over of age.

It would be a miracle if the boy looked eight. Of course, the children were all small, with nothing to eat. But I knew that he was younger anyway. I could have said to the doctor, "Yes, he's eleven," even though he wasn't, but I said nothing.

The doctor looked at his form. "It says here he was born on such-and-such a date. We must take him."

Kobinski kept saying, "He's eleven." He told the boy to recite something in Hebrew and Isaac did. "You see, he's preparing for his bar mitzvah." But the doctor didn't care. Two policemen took hold of the boy and pulled him from Kobinski's hands.

Kobinski's face—such a look of resignation, so heavy! He said, "All right. In that case, I'll go with him." The doctor tried to talk him out of it, but he insisted he was sick—pneumonia, like his wife. He coughed into his hand.

They waited while he packed a bag and they all left the building together. I heard stories later—Kobinski was not the only parent to do this. Many gave themselves up to die with their children.

Aharon could not stop his imagination, could not help but think—what would he do if they came to his door and tried to take Yehuda? Any of his children? The baby? It made him feel terrible, so he pushed it from his mind. Thinking like that was no use to anyone, and certainly not to God. Look, if things happened then there was a good reason and that was that.

He returned to the main screen, entered the search words *Haskiel Malloh*.

Malloh had been in Auschwitz with Kobinski. Aharon had to scan several pages before finding a mention of him.

Whenever I could, I would line up against the fence to see a new transport arrive. Many of the men couldn't stand it—to see the selection—but I was searching for my daughter, Tanya. Several times I saw people that I knew, but never Tanya. I saw the rabbi's wife from my old hometown sent to the gas chambers. She was alone. I don't know what happened to her family. I saw once this beautiful blond Jewish girl, maybe nineteen. Mengele told her to strip right there. He could see that she was shy and this was only meant to torment her. She refused so they carried her away and put her in the ovens alive and screaming. I have never forgotten that girl.

I saw the arrival of Rabbi Kobinski and his son, Isaac. I didn't know who he was then, but he drew everybody's attention. When they tried to take his things, he put up a fuss. He was protecting his books, of course, only a rabbi would be shot over books. And they would have shot him, but his son pleaded and he relented. "Okay, only let me keep my notebook," he said to the guard. Bitte nur mein Notizheft, bitte nur mein Notizheft. *The guard watched him take it from his bag, like he was going to let him keep it. But once he had it out, the guard snatched the notebook from his hand and flung it onto a fire they had burning in a barrel to keep the guards warm.*

This was Wallick, the guard who did this. After that, these two had something else between them, you would not believe. Kobinski was yelling, "My manuscript! My manuscript!" in Polish, and his son was dragging him away. Only nine years old that boy, and always such a presence of mind.

I was not happy later, when I saw they were in my barrack. I thought Kobinski was trouble. Sometimes men come in and you can see right away they don't get it. They are dreamers. Such men are dangerous. Men like that, they can get you to believe anything, risk stupid things for stupid reasons. Many people risked things for Kobinski. They thought he had magic, you know, because he was a kabbalist. And he had to keep writing, rewrite everything that had been in that notebook. So people risked their lives to get him paper, to do other crazy things for him.

Kobinski never did get it. No, I take that back. In the end he did, after his son was killed. But still he dreamed. I was out of the barrack by then. I had been moved across camp, but I heard about it. Kobinski talked many in his barrack into risking a crazy escape attempt. Of course, everyone died who went. You see what I mean? Such men were more dangerous, almost, than the guards.

There was a young man at the Collections desk—bookish-looking, with a beard and *kippa*, but he wore an earring. An earring! As if he couldn't make up his mind, was he religious or not. What a *nebbish*. He glanced up, looking startled, as Aharon approached. He reached a steadying hand across the desk.

"Are you all right?"

Aharon did feel strange, but he brushed off the young man's hand. "How could I be all right? Such an uplifting place you have here!" He waved his hand at the room. He needed to go lie down somewhere, but first he had to get out of this place. He wanted to get out so much, suddenly, that he could feel the sweat break out on his brow.

"It can be overwhelming. Is this your first time?" the *nebbish*-whose-name-tag-said-HERSHEL asked sympathetically.

Aharon had a tightening sensation in his chest. He pointed a finger. "The Torah says you mourn for a year and that's it!"

Hershel shifted his eyes away, his sympathy fading. "Did you need something from Collections, sir?"

"Rabbi."

"Do you need something, Rabbi?"

"Yes, I need. Thank you." Aharon tried to be a little nicer. After all, not everything was Hershel's fault, earring or no. Aharon wiped his brow, showed the number from Kobinski's file.

Hershel went to retrieve the item. He returned with small stack of plastic sleeves. "Here it is. You can look at it over there. Please don't take the documents out of the sleeves." He pointed to yet another row of anonymous cubicles, their backs open to face the Collections counter.

Aharon grunted and went to sit down.

The pages were handwritten in Hebrew. There were six of them, and several were embellished with complex-looking mathematical notations in the margins. The pages were old, irregular, of different shapes and sizes and colors. With a chill, Aharon realized that these were some of the pages Haskiel Malloh had talked about; they'd been written in the camp.

Aharon went back to the *nebbish* at the counter. "Do I have to look at these here? Can't I take them out, bring them back later?" He waved his hand at the cubicle. "How can anyone study in such a space?" Though it was not the cubicle but the entire weight of Yad Vashem that smothered him.

"You can't take it out, but you can have it Xeroxed if you like. There's a fee."

Of course there was. "How much?"

As it turned out, the fee was manageable. Aharon paid it and had to wait another twenty minutes while Hershel took the sleeves away. The wait was less manageable. Finally Hershel returned with the pages in a neat little paper folder, but he did not hand them over. "You have to sign," he said, bringing a logbook from under the counter.

Aharon felt as though he'd been wrapped in red tape and deep-fried. He took the pen Hershel offered. The logbook had a page with the historical artifact number and a brief description at the top. There were three names on the page with corresponding dates. One was a Rabbi Schwartz in New York; one was a woman, Loretta Wilson, in Los Angeles. The last of the three names was his wife's.

The hand holding the pen went up to his lips to catch a gasp. He stared at the name, then the date. Last Thursday.

"This woman," he said, pointing to the entry, "Handalman—were you here then?"

A spontaneous smile crossed the *nebbish*'s face. "Yes. Very pretty. She had a baby with her. Do you know her?"

Aharon sucked in his cheeks and signed his name quickly. He was walking away before the pen hit the counter.

*   *   *

Hannah was feeding the baby at the kitchen table when he arrived. It was only three in the afternoon and she was shocked to see him. "Aharon! Is everything all right? Are you ill?" She hurried to him, searching for signs of debilitating injury.

He pushed past her and threw the paper folder on the table with a dramatic gesture. She saw what it was immediately, that name on the front, Yad

Vashem. She blanched but held her ground. "So? You went to Yad Vashem. Congratulations."

"Hannah, did I not *expressly* forbid you to go?"

The baby started crying. Hannah picked her up, spoke calmly. "What are you talking? You never once forbade me to visit Yad Vashem. Only a crazy person would do such a thing."

"I said you were not to meddle in my work!"

"I didn't meddle. Now keep your voice down. Can't you see you're upsetting Layah?"

Aharon ground his teeth. That such a thing as a man's anger, his dominion in the household, should be controlled by women and babies! But he couldn't stand to hear Layah cry, either. He spoke quietly. "You went deliberately to Yad Vashem to look into Kobinski. That is *my* work, and I told you I did not want your help."

Her dark eyes flashed angrily. "I went to Yad Vashem with Yehuda's class, as a chaperone."

Aharon's eyes narrowed. He was stumped for a reply momentarily, a gap Hannah had no problem filling.

"*So*, I thought while I was there, waiting for the children to be done with their tour, I would look him up. What else did I have to do?"

"You don't tell me? You don't tell me you and my son are going to Yad Vashem? You don't tell me *after* you went? You went last Thursday. When were you going to tell me, Hannah?"

He had gotten loud again. The baby, whose head had been bobbing tiredly at her mother's chest, straightened up with a yowl. Hannah shot him a look and went to put Layah down. Aharon waited in the kitchen, strutting like an angry bird. He could hear the baby's cries sputter out with weariness in the next room. Hannah returned to the kitchen, began wiping down the baby's high chair.

"Hannah, I asked you a question."

"I didn't tell you because you don't care what the children and I do."

"That's not true!"

"It is. You couldn't care less that we went to Yad Vashem except for this Kobinski business. Whenever I try to tell you about something we did or something we're going to do, you barely listen."

"I do listen!"

"You think the children are my business. So? I don't waste your time with it. But don't complain if you don't know everything there is to know."

Aharon, a yeshiva boy, could easily deduce that this was not the original argument. "This is nonsense, and also besides the point. Even if what you say is true—and it isn't—you knew, didn't you, that *this* time I would want to know you were going to Yad Vashem!"

Hannah said nothing. She went to the double sink and rinsed out the sponge.

"So you go, you do work there that you know I didn't want you to do, then you come home and you don't even tell me *then*? When were you planning to give me the notebook pages, Hannah?"

Hannah drew herself a glass of water. She motioned to him, *Want some?* "Tea," he replied. She put the kettle on to boil. Then she sank down into one of the kitchen chairs, her face a misery.

"It's true. I didn't tell you I was going to Yad Vashem with Yehuda's class because I normally don't bother you with such things, but *also* because I knew you wouldn't like it. And when I was there, I did a little checking into Rabbi Kobinski. I was going to tell you what I found out." She stared down at her work-reddened hands. "But I chickened out. There was no way to show you what I found without having a scene. Like this one."

A heavy sigh caught on a sob. Her face reddened. "Oh, Aharon! You can be so hard!"

Aharon's anger had turned into something heavy and sour. It weighed down his stomach, his soul. He was thinking that she always did have that rebellious streak. Her father had married her off when it first showed itself. Smart man.

He went to the table so that he was standing right in front of her. He placed his fingertips on the wood, looked down at her with a stony face.

"Am I hard? Because I ask for a little respect? Because I think a man is a man and a woman is a woman?"

"But . . . many feel that . . ."

"Who is your husband, Hannah? The 'many' or me? Am I the head of this household? Am I to be listened to in my own home?" His voice sounded terrible, even to himself, but he would not feel guilty. The sages say, "A firm hand in the beginning will save a horse in the end."

"All right, Aharon. I'm sorry."

He grunted his acknowledgment of her apology. The teakettle began to whistle. He motioned to it with his hand and sank down into one of the kitchen chairs. Her repentance gave him the first relief of the entire miserable day. His anger drained away into weariness. That horrible place, now this fight with his wife. Such a waste!

When she brought him the tea she was biting her lip. She gave him a pregnant look from under her lashes. She *was* pretty. And that was another reason that she shouldn't be traipsing all over town unescorted, so that young men like that *nebbish* at the Collections desk could ogle over a respectable *rebbetzin*, a wife and mother.

"What is it? What now?" he sighed, pulling the mug toward him.

"Well . . . I found something else at Yad Vashem that day. If you won't be angry. I can just throw it away if you want."

He stared at her, astonished. Now she was toying with him. And after he'd thought he'd succeeded in chastising her! But he had already spent his anger and, like a lover, could not dredge it up again so quickly. He settled for long-suffering, and rolled his eyes to Heaven. "Just say what you have to say."

"I'll show you." She padded into the hallway and opened the folding closet door to get her purse. She brought back a few sheets of paper, sat down across from him, her face proud. "I looked up Rabbi Kobinski's barrack. You see, they have a database with the names of all of the Holocaust victims and survivors, and many of them have barrack numbers and dates and—"

"The point, Hannah?"

"This is a list of the men who were in the same barrack as Rabbi Kobinski at the same time." She smoothed out her pages proudly.

Aharon grunted, his eyes half-lidded in disinterest.

"I cross-checked every name on the list with the lists of survivors, and I found three names."

She revealed the second page. "These three men lived with Rabbi Kobinski in the barrack—*and* they're still alive."

Aharon got up, added some cold water from the tap to his tea, and sipped it at the sink.

"*Aharon,* one lives in Tel Aviv. Maybe you could go see him. He might remember something about Rabbi Kobinski."

Aharon rubbed his brow where a headache was beginning to stab with tentative thrusts of the knife. "I already wasted the whole day at Yad Vashem. I've heard all I want to hear about Auschwitz!" He dumped the tea into the sink. He felt so tired, completely drained. Perhaps he'd take a nap.

"But he might know something important. How can you know unless you talk to him?"

"*Hannah,*" he warned. He pointed toward the pages. "Now is this it?"

"Yes," Hannah said, frowning.

"Are you sure? There's nothing else you did at Yad Vashem? Rearrange their filing system maybe?"

"No."

"Did you already call these three survivors? Get their life stories on tape?"

Hannah made a face. "I didn't call them."

"You're sure?"

"Of course I'm sure!"

"So there's *nothing* else?"

"That's everything, Aharon," Hannah's lips were heading into that pout of hers.

"Thank Heaven for small miracles. Now I think I'll lie down for a while."

"Are you feeling bad?"

He gave her a look that said, *After all this, you can ask if I feel bad? Of course I feel bad!* and headed down the hall.

In their bedroom he shut the door and kicked off his shoes. He would sleep, dreamlessly he hoped, just like his baby lying in the children's room next door. He was exhausted, and he was still worried about Hannah. What was he to do with her? Well, she would have to learn not to question his authority, and that was that. Then everything would be the way it should be.

*   *   *

ARTICLE 378881-A KOBINSKI, YOSEF, AUSCHWITZ, 1943.
DONATED BY MR. AND MRS. IRA ROSENBAUM, NEW YORK, USA, 1972

Why does evil exist? Reb Zaks, may his name be blessed forever, says that evil is what happens when the sephirot *are out of balance. I look at these monsters, these Nazis, who are my tormentors. What are they made of? I come up with* gevorah. *Restriction, judgment. How can it be otherwise? Is there any* chesed *in them? Mercy? Loving-kindness? No. You could argue that at home, with their families, there is* chesed. *But I don't believe this. Can a snake turn into a rabbit at night?*

There are only two possibilities. One: they are really snakes—on top of the mask and beneath it. Two: they are not really snakes but only act like snakes because they are surrounded by snakes and they try to pass. Perhaps there were a few of these, in the beginning. How can a whole nation be born snakes? But my mother used to say if you make a face it will stick that way! These snakes-who-are-not-snakes experience pain, regret, at first. But maybe they soon find that they become snakes period. In the ghetto, I saw pity in the eyes of a few of our tormentors. Now there is nothing in the eyes, ever.

This is important to know: you can change your sephirot. *Oh, yes, you can change it completely! This in itself is* chesed/gevorah—*a great mercy and a terrible judgment. The great mercy is: you don't have to remain what you are. The great judgment is: you will become what you deserve.*

ARTICLE 378881-B KOBINSKI, YOSEF, AUSCHWITZ, 1943.
DONATION FROM THE HOLOCAUST MUSEUM & RESOURCE CENTER,
SCRANTON, PENNSYLVANIA, USA, 1995

Here is a question I have been wrestling with: Is the gevorah *of the guards the same as the* gevorah *of Rabbi Donel, the Hasid who gave my beloved teacher such a hard time, a strict YHWHist if ever there was one?*

Yes. Judgment is judgment. Rabbi Donel says so-and-so is a sinner for doing such-and-such on the Sabbath. Mitigating circumstance? What mitigating circumstances? The Torah says, right here, that you are not to do thus-and-so on the Sabbath. The only exception is to save a life. Was he saving a life? No! So he was wrong! What does Rabbi Donel feel in his heart for this man? Pity? Empathy? Is he thinking: what would I have done in his shoes? He is not because such things are chesed *and in this he is lacking.*

Now the Nazis. The guard says: You are a Jew. It says right here in this Nazi handbook that all Jews are filth, vermin, parasites. You say you are a human being? That you suffer pain? Nonsense! It says right here in my Nazi handbook that you are not human at all! What does the guard feel in his heart as he strikes a Jew? Pity? Empathy? Is he thinking: how would I like to be on the other end of this stick? No.

Gevorah does not dictate what *you believe, only that you will be blind in the belief of it.*

And what else are the guards? Are they completely like Rabbi Donel? No. Rabbi Donel is gevorah/chochmah. *There is* no *chochmah here—no intuition, no sense of G-d, no sense of the whole. There is efficiency, there is automation, there is clinical, detached hierarchy—in other words, pure* binah.

The Fascists are gevorah/binah/netzach: *judgment, logic, domination. They have a desire to annihilate anyone who does not fit their perfect schematic, whose very existence threatens their logical criteria of a perfect world.*

How did an entire nation become gevorah/binah/netzach? *Become snakes? Where is the other sweep of the pendulum? Where is the good that balances the evil?*

Where is G-d?

ARTICLE 378881-C KOBINSKI, YOSEF, AUSCHWITZ, 1943.
DONATION FROM OTTO BURKE, GERMANY, 1983

I have written out all of my equations neatly and carefully on two pages. These equations are my life's work. They must survive if nothing else does. I have asked Anatoli to use his safest container and his safest hiding place for them. Please, Lord, may the Nazis not destroy this also!

4

Betazel knew how to permute the letters with which heaven and earth were made.
—*The Talmud,* 1000–1499

If one knows how to manipulate the letters correctly, one can also manipulate the most elemental forces of creation.
—*Sefer Yetzirah,* pre–sixth century, translation by Aryeh Kaplan, 1990

4.1. JILL TALCOTT

JUNE
SEATTLE

Jill was in the middle of a lecture when Nate burst through the door at the back of the hall. The look on his face made the words disintegrate in her mouth like salted slugs. She dimly finished up what she'd been saying and dismissed class early.

"What is it?" she asked, following him down the hall.

"You'll have to see for yourself." Nate's tone said he wouldn't know where to begin.

They passed Dr. Grover, who must have smelled something was up. He made a U-turn and attached himself to Jill's heels. "Morning, Jill. I haven't seen you in a while."

She slowed down her gait, pushed back her hair. "Chuck."

"I never heard how your data panned out." Grover glanced sharp-eyed at Nate, who had paused a few paces down the hall and was waiting for her with all the subtlety of a child at the door of a candy shop.

"Um, we haven't completed our analysis."

Nate moved on, turning into the corridor to her office. Jill went after him and, to her horror, Grover came after her. By a flash of luck their department head, Dick Chalmers, was passing by. His face lit up with a Grinch-like smile at the sight of his star professor. He pulled Grover into a conversation, allowing Jill to slip away.

"What is it?" she asked Nate when they were safely locked in her office.

He was breathing hard. It took him a moment to get the words out.

"I finished that program we talked about. It was a lot simpler than I thought. All I did was take the data we got by running your equation on Quey, *subtract* the real-life carbon atom data from CERN, and map the difference onto a wave pattern."

Jill had already moved to his computer. A screen saver had come up while he'd gone to fetch her. All she had to do was move the mouse to get it to go away, but she didn't. Her fingers twisted together at her waist.

"I assume there was an interesting result or you wouldn't look like that."

Nate pointed toward the computer as if it were a ghost. "Go ahead."

"It's on the screen? Now?"

Nate nodded dumbly.

Jill reached toward the computer. Her hand paused in mid-air, almost afraid to end the suspense. "Should I . . . Should I get the camera?"

He shrugged, wide-eyed. *Don't ask me.*

She was being a ninny. She took a deep breath and pushed the mouse.

On the screen was a moving wave pattern. It was pulsing like a heart monitor—running steadily over and over and over. It was unlike any wave she had ever seen. It was not gently rolling crests and troughs of varying heights, like a normal sine wave. Instead, it was a blunt, castellated pattern, the crests and troughs formed by absolutely perpendicular lines in a perfectly even, repeating up-and-down pattern, crest–trough–crest–trough.

"Is this a joke?" Jill asked weakly, sinking into Nate's chair.

"Um, *no.*" He squatted beside her and stared at the wave.

"Well, what exactly is *producing* it?"

"Just what I said. *That wave* is the difference between what your equation *predicted* the particles of the carbon atom would do and what the particles actually did. I caused it to loop so we could see it in motion, but that's all I did to it."

Jill felt her skin turn cold as the blood drained south. It *had* to be a joke, but a sidelong glance at Nate's face confirmed that a cheap jolly was the last thing on his mind.

"But . . . but . . . that's not possible."

He waved a hand at the screen as if to say, *Don't blame me. Damn thing just showed up.*

"Could it be some kind of data fluke?"

"How? The *math* is producing that wave, nothing else. And it's perfect. I mean, look at that. You can't just pull random numbers out of the air and make something like that. Whatever it is . . . ," Nate swallowed, "it was in the particle accelerator with that atom."

Jill was light-headed. She might just slip out of the chair. She felt as though her reality had shifted.

No, not just my reality. Maybe everyone's reality.

Was she misrepresenting it? Overdramatizing? She tried to grasp the concept that was being displayed on the monitor. What *did* it mean?

It means that:

A. My equation was correct after all, which means we've *proven* the energy pool model of the universe.

B. What was in the particle accelerator with that carbon atom? Nothing. Nothing but space. We've just discovered an energy wave pattern in the very fabric of space-time, the "chop" of the universal "sea"?

How huge was *that*?

"Dr. Talcott?"

She must have gone somewhere, because Nate was looking at her with concern. He had a hand on her shoulder. She moved away from his touch instinctively. She wished she could be alone to truly savor this moment, really let herself go, do a few leaps in the air with glee. Instead, she heard herself speak briskly from very, very far away.

"We'll have to double-check it. Go over and over the data."

She went to the video camera and turned it on. She gave a brief rundown of the situation, sounding nearly rational, and focused the camera on the computer. The wave was duly recorded. As Jill spoke about it she paused, blanking out.

"I . . . guess we should name it."

Nate made a face, like he couldn't believe this was happening. He peered at the screen.

"It's so regular," he offered. "Like a binary message or something: one, negative one, one, negative one, one, negative one. Like Morse. Only it's not saying anything."

Jill touched the screen lightly with outspread fingertips. "Oh, it's saying *something* all right. We just don't know what yet."

She turned back to the camera with a dazzling sense of the monumental. She felt like man taking his first step on the moon.

"The wave is called the Talcott-Andros one-minus-one."

*   *   *

Nate entered Jill's office three days later to find her on the phone. She was scribbling furiously on a pad.

"Right. I saw the schematics on the Web actually. So you're running at about three-point-oh megawatts right now?"

Nate raised his eyebrows at her curiously and poured himself a cup of coffee.

The person on the other end of the phone was obviously going on in great detail, but Jill looked only partially interested. She was perfecting her type A worried look. She tapped her pen on her collarbone. Her rust-colored scoop-necked top emphasized her lightly freckled skin, fragile collarbones, and the gentle swell of her small, high breasts. Nate watched the pen *tap tap* and a tendril of heat bloomed in his stomach. He looked away.

He had the hots for his professor. How pitiful was that? On the Bill Clinton scale of 1 to 10: 10. He couldn't help it. Jill was so . . . *intense,* so sharp and focused, her mind like a supernova at times, bursting in all directions at once and at a million miles an hour. All of the other women he met seemed dull as dirty socks in comparison. And physically . . . she had that tiny southern Holly Hunter look. He'd had way too many fantasies about how her small body would feel fitted to his. How perv was that? It wasn't as if she *asked* to be cast in his lustful fantasies. The only signal she projected was *NO TRESPASSING.* But that only made it worse. She had that librarian thing, the thing that made a man want to rip off her glasses (metaphorically, in this case), unpin her hair (also metaphorically), and make her howl (literally).

Yeah. And someday he wanted to climb Mount Everest, too.

"That sounds fascinating. I was wondering . . . have you detected any unusual results when you're running at full peak? Any side effects of the broadcast—visual abnormalities, audio abnormalities? A high number of equipment breakdowns, anything like that?" Pause. "No, Dr. Serin, I can assure you I have nothing to do with environmentalists."

Jill wrote some more on her pad and motioned Nate to fill up her cup. He brought the pot over and poured some for her. He was definitely curious now.

"Okay. Well, thank you *very* much. I do appreciate—what? Oh . . . of course. It's Dr. Alkin, University of Washington. Yes, thank you."

She put down the receiver and picked up her cup.

"Careful, it's hot . . . Dr. *Alkin.*" Nate peaked an eyebrow at her.

"You must have heard me wrong. What a shame." Jill took a delicate sip. She had the superior look of a woman with a secret.

Nate dropped into his chair and spun to face her. He had to do it carefully, because otherwise his knees would bang into the base of her desk. He knew because his knees had been black-and-blue for the first six weeks he'd been in this rat cage.

"You gonna tell me?"

"Mmmm. That was the HAARP program in Alaska. HAARP uses high-energy radio pulses to manipulate the ionosphere. Something to do with improving radar signals."

"HAARP? They're military, aren't they? Do you think it's smart giving a false name?"

"Are you my mother?" Jill quipped, face blank.

"Um, is that a trick question?"

"I asked him a couple of things on the phone. I didn't go in and steal government secrets or anything, god!"

"Okay. So why *did* you call the HAARP program?"

In the back of his mind it occurred to him, with more than a tinge of disappointment, that she must have heard about someone else who was on to the one-minus-one, like, say, HAARP. Since he'd first seen the wave on his computer three days ago, he'd been waiting for the other shoe to drop. It blew his mind to think that they honestly could have discovered—well, her more than him, really—that she could have discovered what they *thought* she'd discovered. In fact, he hadn't completely bought it, though he knew she'd bought it, decorated it, and taken out a second mortgage.

Jill was slow in answering. She had a storm-clouds-gathering look on her face that told him he'd better get his thinking cap on.

"I've decided not to publish on my equation. Not right away."

"Why not?"

She tapped her chin with the pen. "Because they'd line up to refute me. They'd say there must have been some other factor in the carbon atom data that made the one-minus-one—interference from the walls of the accelerator or hum in the machinery, anything but admit that we might have stumbled onto something this big." Jill tossed down her pen, looking very determined. "We need more proof."

"But they can't argue with the equation itself—it worked. The numbers prove it worked."

"I know. There is that. My wave mechanics equation is news in its own right, but . . ."

She hesitated and Nate knew exactly what she was thinking. Up until a few weeks ago, they had both thought solving wave mechanics would be the biggest thing since sliced bread. *But.*

"The one-minus-one is bigger," Nate said.

Jill nodded, biting her lip. "Yes. And I don't want to go out of the gate with anything less than that."

He could have argued with her, debated the pros and cons just for the heck of it. But she was inspirational when she got like this. She saw heights of glory he'd never dare, and sometimes she made him see them, too.

"So what do we need to publish the one-minus-one?"

"Independent confirmation."

"How can we get independent confirmation when no one else has even heard of it?"

"We look for things that were perhaps unexplained in other experiments—indicators that make no sense if you don't know about the one-minus-one, but if you do . . ."

Nate smiled. "So *that's* why you were calling HAARP?"

Jill shook her head impatiently. No, it appeared they weren't at the actual point yet. Nate leaned back in his chair, happily content to follow the thread through to its end. He loved the labyrinthine twists of her mind, how you could go down and down her line of reasoning, like climbing down a rope into darkness, and every time you thought you had reached the end it turned out there was always more down there.

"Go on, Herr Professor."

Jill got up and shifted into the aisle where she could pace a foot or two in either direction, a tight little bundle of energy. Nate had to move his legs farther out of the way to avoid getting trampled. Not that he would mind.

"I've been wracking my brain trying to think of experiments we could do to measure the one-minus-one—to prove it exists. Anything that would show a quantifiable result." She tapped her chin with one finger as she paced. "So I was thinking: what if we could *alter* the one-minus-one?"

"Alter it? How could we alter the pattern of space-time?"

Jill waved in the air as if scattering his remark. "We couldn't alter it *permanently*, no. But think about it. The one-minus-one is a wave like any other wave. Say you drop a wrecking ball in the ocean," she said, smashing a fist into her palm. "It *would* affect the wave pattern of the sea, right? It would disturb the waves, creating all kinds of new interference patterns. It's just that it would only affect the sea in a limited area and for a short period of time. Pretty soon the pattern of the sea waves would return to normal. See what I mean?"

Nate's red tennis shoes bounced nervously as he visualized it. "Yeah. But that would take a ton of energy, right? Is that what that phone call was about?"

Her eyes widened at him appreciatively. "Not bad for a philosophy major."

Nate sniffed. "Aristotle was no slouch. So if anyone *has* ever altered the one-minus-one, even accidentally, it would be someone like HAARP."

Jill smiled. *Damn.* Her smiles were so rare they always broke his heart. And it looked like they'd finally reached the point.

"Yup. HAARP uses high-energy radio pulses. The highest."

"But . . . didn't I hear you say on the phone that they *hadn't* noticed any weird effects? Does that mean they haven't altered the one-minus-one?"

"That's right," Jill agreed. "But I'm not really surprised."

Big news flash: they hadn't reached the end of the ladder after all. "I'm sure you'll explain that to me."

"Even at high energy, I don't think radio waves *would* affect the one-minus-one much. Except maybe randomly, as a fluke. Do you know why?"

Nate sighed and tilted back his head, concentrating. His legs extended thoughtlessly, tangling momentarily with Jill's. They both jumped as if shocked. Nate gave her a sheepish look in apology and struggled to pull his mind out of the gutter.

He remembered Socrates' analogy about how man's soul was like a chariot pulled by two horses. One of the horses was a noble sort, representing man's higher nature. The other was a wild, unruly beast that represented man's animal lusts. Man's rational mind was the charioteer whose duty it was to keep the wild horse in check. But Socrates failed to mention how damn *fun* it was to just let that bad boy rip.

"Nate?"

"Huh? Oh. Radio waves. Well, they're sine waves which have a gentle rolling pattern. So there'd probably only be random instances where a sine would collide in just the right way with the one-minus-one to alter it by much. And you'd *have* to alter it quite a bit to notice anything unusual out here in the material world, because matter waves are interacting with the one-minus-one in subtle ways all the time."

"Exactly!" Jill looked at him with such a triumphant, resolved expression that he was sure he was supposed to have gotten more out of what he'd just said than he actually did.

"So . . ."

"So I know how we can conduct our experiment!"

Nate waited, squinting at her.

"If we used a wave pulse that *wasn't* a rolling sine wave," she explained energetically, "but was instead a steady *pulse*—a full *one* pulse or a full *minus one* pulse—"

Nate whistled in appreciation. "It would have the maximum possible impact on the one-minus-one!"

"Exactly!"

She smiled at him, looking about as happy as Jill Talcott ever looked, which meant to say that she looked unpreoccupied, present in the moment, and enormously pleased with herself.

"Yeah, but . . . do you think that's smart?" Nate asked.

Jill's smile vanished. Her eyes sparked with annoyance. "You said yourself, there's no way we can *permanently* alter anything."

Nate wasn't sure that made him feel any better. "What do you think it would do, Dr. Talcott? I mean, say we figured out the power requirements, set up our equipment, sent out our pulse . . . what would the results of altering the one-minus-one *be* out here in the physical world?"

Jill went around her desk and sank back in her chair, a curl of anticipation on her lips. "Well, that's exactly what we're going to find out, isn't it?"

4.2. Aharon Handalman

Jerusalem

A month after his visit to Yad Vashem, Aharon had mostly recovered. It was like digesting a bad meal—when enough time has passed you get an occasional belch, which brings with it a puff of bad air and a smell that reminds you of things you would rather forget, but other than that you don't feel so sick.

But Yad Vashem had left a dis-ease that transferred itself from the Holocaust museum to the Kobinski array project in general. Aharon could shake the dust of Yad Vashem from his shoes, but from his heart? Not so easy. Besides, he didn't know what to make of the pages he had copied from Yad Vashem. He didn't care for Kobinski's ideas, period, but especially he didn't care for that business about a rabbi being like Nazis. Ridiculous! What could Kobinski mean by making such a comparison? Still, he was willing to admit that what he'd read was brief and that Kobinski could not have been at his best when he wrote it. As for all the mathematical notations in the margins? Aharon neither knew nor cared.

If that wasn't enough, if you had to be greedy about it, as Rosa used to say, the whole Yad Vashem excursion had not even *bought* him anything. Aharon had made a list of new keywords: *Isaac Kobinski, Anna Kobinski, gevorah, binah, Nazi,* and so on. The results? Precious little. He found a number of instances of *gevorah* in the Kobinski arrays, but it wasn't such a rare word in Hebrew ELS, and in any case, what did it mean? Nothing.

On the other hand . . . There were still 400 Torah arrays with the name Yosef Kobinski in them. Like an overbearing mother-in-law, this fact could not be avoided. So he and Binyamin continued to pore over them. Only Aharon had begun to think of other things again, his students (god forbid). If they were lackluster, if they were behind in their studies, whose fault was that? They say, "If the baby is ugly, don't expect a beautiful mother." It was time to knock a few heads together, get the brains working in a few young men, get them filled with fire about Torah.

And perhaps because he no longer cared so much, he finally had a breakthrough.

*   *   *

It was an unusually rainy June morning in Jerusalem. The soft drops on his face as he said his morning prayers at the wall were like God's own tears. Afterward, comfortable and dry in his office, he picked up the binder and flipped to a random array . . . and saw it.

He had stared at this sequence over many months, and it had not clicked in his brain. This morning it did: נשק

It was such a small word. Perhaps that's why his eye had always skimmed over it: נשק. *Weapon.*

He stroked his beard, made a clicking noise with his tongue that was the equivalent of a cat switching its tail. He turned the page. The thing about it was he thought . . . yes, it was in the array on the next page also, the same word. He began to search in earnest, circling each instance with a pencil as he found it. When Binyamin knocked, an hour later, Aharon had gone through five arrays—and had found the word right next to the name Yosef Kobinski in every single one.

"Do you believe in miracles?" was what he greeted the boy with. "Because wonder of wonders, I found something."

"What is it?"

"Look for yourself."

Binyamin looked at the binder, blinked at him blearily. "Weapon?"

"I found it in four other arrays also." Aharon showed the boy his circled words with growing authority. "Listen, we'll do a computer search later. For now have a seat and start from the front; I've already started from the back."

It seemed appropriate that they should dig this treasure by hand. It was a communion with the text, the way Aharon might put his fingers on the Scripture as he read it, as if his touch would earn him additional insight and blessings. Binyamin was not so readily harnessed.

"What do you think it means, 'weapon'? Why would that be in Rabbi Kobinski's arrays?"

"It's obvious. He was a physics professor in Warsaw in the early nineteen-twenties. Maybe he did some work which led to nuclear fission; did you ever think of that?"

Binyamin admitted that he hadn't.

"So?" Aharon continued, eyes alight. "Who invented atomic bombs? Wasn't it Eastern European scientists? Born when?"

"I don't know."

"Think! The bomb was invented near the end of World War Two, so the scientists who invented it must have been born around 1900, same as Kobinski. Maybe they *knew* Kobinski. *Maybe* he had something to do with it."

Aharon went back to his array, but he was feeling infinitely self-admiring.

Binyamin scratched at himself. "So that might be why he's in the Torah so many times?"

Aharon held up both hands in an "of course" gesture. "If he had something to do with the discovery of atomic bombs, what could be more important than that?"

"Cool."

Aharon was in too good a mood to correct the boy's lingo. He had an urge to share the discovery with someone else, but who? The yeshiva's dean? No, Dean Horowitz and he were oil and water; the man was too liberal. Besides which, Horowitz had never been a true advocate of the code. Someone else then. There was his contact at the Mossad—so often he'd avoided Aharon's phone calls. This would change his tune.

"Um . . . Rabbi Handalman?"

"Eh?"

"Found something."

Binyamin marked the find lightly with a pencil underline, as Aharon had taught him to do, and passed the binder. Aharon looked at it. The boy had found the word *weapon* on a diagonal, but it didn't end there. The encoded phrase continued:

נשק להתרת שדים

Weapon loosing demons.

The flesh on Aharon's arms stood up in ridges. Seeing it hidden in the text that way, text he had stared at for so long, was like seeing an evil face appear outside your bedroom window.

"Is that talking about the atomic bomb, do you think, Rabbi?"

"It must be," Aharon answered gruffly. "Yes, it could be. I could see that. Keep looking."

But as he went back to search, Rabbi Handalman was no longer quite so sure.

*   *   *

Aharon used the school's phone to place a long-distance call to a synagogue in Warsaw. The rabbi put Aharon in contact with a synagogue member who taught at the university, a man named Lestchinsky. Lestchinsky was pleased to help. A week later, he e-mailed Aharon the details.

Kobinski had enrolled at the University of Warsaw in 1918. His hometown was listed as a small *shetl* near Brezeziny. In 1924 he'd earned his degree and begun to teach. He was employed by the university only a few short years, leaving unexpectedly in 1927. Aharon assumed that was when he decided to study kabbalah with Eleazar Zaks.

From the records, it appeared that Yosef Kobinski was an exceptionally brilliant student. Certainly he was the best of his class, though a Christian won top honors the year Kobinski graduated, naturally. After 1924, he taught in the physics department. Kobinski was listed in the annual reports as specializing in the "quantum theory of atoms." As far as Lestchinsky could tell, there was no research related to atomic fission going on in Warsaw during those years. None at all.

Aharon was disappointed, but the news didn't come as a big shock. While waiting for the professor's reply, he and Binyamin had searched on the keywords *nuclear, atomic, fission*, and *bomb*. They found no hits within the Kobinski arrays. So Aharon had checked some history books. Fermi's work did not begin in earnest on atomics until the mid-1930s. Uranium fission was not discovered until 1939, over ten years after Kobinski had left the University of Warsaw, and then it was discovered by Germans. That was not to say that a smart Jew in Warsaw couldn't have been ten years ahead of German scientists or even that they might not have stolen his work. But the news from Lestchinsky combined with a lack of confirmation in the arrays . . . Aharon had to admit, it didn't look good.

But. But. If Kobinski had *not* contributed to the invention of the atomic bomb, then what weapon *were* the arrays talking about? It came down to that; that was the thing. *What weapon?*

4.3. DENTON WYLE

CAPE COD, MASSACHUSETTS

Denton's mother met him in the foyer and air-kissed his cheeks. He had a compulsion, as he always did, to shift, force her lips to make actual contact with his actual skin. But she'd ignore it, and he'd look childish. He refrained.

"Denton, it's so lovely to see you."

His mother looked more plastic than usual. She must have had another face-lift and/or eye job. Her expensive black pantsuit couldn't hide her anorexic dimensions. Her patrician blond beauty, so like his own, had not aged well. It was depressing.

She led the way to the white-and-gold reception room and called Carter to serve tea.

"How are you, sir?" Carter asked Denton, pausing before leaving the room.

"Great! It's nice to see you."

Carter returned the sentiment with genuine feeling.

Jeez, his mother should get the number of Carter's plastic surgeon. The man hadn't changed in twenty years. It really was a kick seeing him. When

Denton was young he'd been convinced Carter was a cat burglar. It was the silent, fluid way he had of moving, never making so much as a footfall. Denton had followed him for months around the house while his parents were gone, sneaking behind him with Carter patiently ignoring him. It all made so much sense at the time. Denton smiled.

"Will you stay for lunch?" his mother asked. "I'll be out, I'm afraid. I have an appointment at noon; then I'm luncheoning with friends. But I'm sure Carter can whip something up."

Denton felt a grinding resentment, fleeting and futile. "If you're not going to be here, Mother, why invite me to stay?"

"I thought you might be hungry."

"I can feed myself. They taught me that at NYU."

Denton liked mentioning NYU because his mother was disappointed he hadn't gotten into one of the *better* schools. Well, his grades hadn't cut it—his parents' fault for traveling so much.

"As you wish." Mother used her polite, put-upon voice.

Denton's anger soured. "*Why* can't you stay?"

"I have a fitting. You wouldn't believe how difficult they are to get."

"Well, I appreciate you having Carter send me your itinerary so that if I decide to take the trouble to fly across the country to see you, I can get half an hour of your time!"

"Don't be dramatic. If you don't give me notice, what do you expect? Besides, I've visited you in LA."

"During layovers. I appreciate it."

Mother fiddled with her teacup, her face distant. She was no fun to fight with. She just refused to engage. And the worst part was, in a half hour she'd be off again and he'd not see her for the rest of the year, and he would have wasted what little time they had.

Denton's resentment shifted into clutching anxiety. "I'm sorry."

Her face lightened. "So . . . are you still writing for that magazine?"

He was pathetically eager to tell her. "Wait till you hear—something very big has come up. I was working on an article, and I came across a Polish rabbi who died at Auschwitz, right? He was writing a book called *The Book of Torment*, and he had to *hide* the pages around the camp. Isn't that cool? I got a section of it through this antique dealer in Zurich, and it's this amazing thing. . . ."

Denton babbled on like an agitated sports commentator. His mother's expression was slightly puzzled or slightly disapproving or slightly troubled, or she thought there was something wrong with tea—he couldn't tell which. He hardly ever knew what she was thinking.

". . . It's *so* major. I'm thinking I might . . ." He bit his lip slyly, like a naughty boy. His vision of what he wanted to do with the Kobinski material had come to him slowly, but it was indeed monstrously huge. "I might try to gather the complete manuscript and publish it—publish *The Book of Torment*. You know, give it a 'lost treasure of the Holocaust' spin. Isn't that great? There might even be a movie deal in it. It's got a lot more human interest than *Schindler's List*. Don't you think so? Huh? I think so."

"Oh, Denton," his mother sighed. "The Holocaust! How depressing."

Denton's enthusiasm withered, instantly. He swallowed and a hot, aching feeling coursed down his body, as if someone had poured molten lead over his head. He drank some tea, blinking rapidly.

"That's, um, why I came to see you, Mother. I need the name and number of that agent you used when you were collecting those antique filigree things. If I'm going to track down the rest of the manuscript I need someone good."

He'd meant it cruelly, paying her back in kind. He waited for her to look hurt that he'd only come to see her to get a name. It didn't even register.

"Fleck, I think. Carter has the information somewhere. He's *very* good, but expensive. I don't suppose your precious magazine is paying for any of this? Of course not. What they pay you in salary wouldn't buy a decent meal, and you don't have to tell me you cover all your own expenses. Why bother? Or if you *must* do this journalism business, why don't you find a legitimate publication? Maria Shriver works for CNN. Or is it NBC?"

"What does this have to do with Maria freaking *Shriver*?" he shouted.

"Don't curse at me. And don't use that tone of voice!"

"I *didn't* curse! 'Freaking' is not a curse."

His mother only looked put upon and dropped the subject. "Well . . . if it makes you happy."

Mother poured herself more tea, dosed it with milk. She mainlined tea—always had. It was what she did instead of putting food, like, *in* her body. Meanwhile, she had dismissed the conversation and Denton sat in his exquisite chair trampled into the dust, his eyes ground into bloody sockets by her high heels.

He wanted to defend the Kobinski project . . . but he couldn't. His obsessions come and went too frequently for him to claim special deference for this one. He knew it, and he had enough crumbs of objectivity besides to admit that the Kobinski project might sound, to any rational human being, a little unfeasible.

Of course, his gut told him it *was* feasible. And even if it wasn't, he didn't give a rat's ass.

"This is important to me, Mother. I wish you could be more—"

"Important! How could it be important? You're not Jewish! Really, Denton, I don't understand your predilection for morbid things. Is it because your childhood was too easy? Do you have to seek out ugliness and . . . and craziness because we didn't give you any? There are *such* nicer things you could do with your time."

She shook her head in incomprehension. Denton was silent for a minute, his anger and self-pity gathering like clouds.

"Kobinski disappeared, Mother. In a flash of light. There were *eyewitnesses.*"

It was out of his mouth and there was no taking it back. His mother stilled, going motionless in her chair, her elegant legs closed and canted to one side like Nancy Reagan.

"Why don't you tell me about the young women you're seeing? Anyone I would know?" she asked brightly.

As a redirect it was excruciatingly lame. Mother hadn't asked him about girls for years because that was much too, oh, *involved.* It would invite details about his life she didn't really give a crap about. So Denton knew he had gotten to her. He felt a low, sick thrill.

"See, I'm doing this series of articles on disappearances. I didn't tell you that, did I? I should really interview *you*, Mother. After all, you were involved in a disappearance case yourself once, weren't you?"

She tsked and picked up her teacup.

"Though you weren't exactly an eyewitness."

She didn't answer and suddenly the conversation wasn't just a jab at her anymore. It had been so long since they'd talked about it. Heck . . . no . . . they had *never* talked about it. And suddenly Denton wanted very badly to talk. He *needed* to. The neediness, when it overcame him like this, was like an aching hollow in his stomach, a void that felt like it would grow and grow and grow until it swallowed him whole if he didn't find a way to feed it.

"What happened back then, Mother? I mean with the police and everything. I don't know much about that part."

"For god's sake! I hope you're not going to drag family laundry into your sordid little magazine."

"I remember taking a lie detector test. I remember the wires and everything. But I don't really know how it turned out. What happened, Mother?"

She pressed her lips tight, staring over his shoulder.

"Please. I won't write about *us*; I swear. I just . . . need to know, for myself."

"I would *hope* you wouldn't be so dim."

"I *promise.* Please. Tell me about the lie detector test."

"There's nothing to tell! You were only eight years old. What did they expect?"

Denton stared at her numbly. His heart turned over in his chest, a burning, squiggling lump. "What . . . it showed . . ."

"It was inconclusive. That's what the detective said. You appeared to be very upset."

"I *appeared* to be upset?"

Mother didn't answer.

Denton's skin felt clammy. His mouth tasted unbearably of rancid tea and sour milk. "What about specific questions? I remember they asked me very specific questions like 'Did you push Molly in the river?' What—"

"Denton!" Mother stood up. "It's water under the bridge. Leave it."

She rang the bell. Carter came in on his cat burglar feet. "Yes, ma'am?"

"You may clear."

Carter picked up the tray, waiting, stooped, for Denton to put his own cup on it. He did so, his hand shaking. He couldn't look Carter in the eye.

His mother was fixing her hair in front of the mirror over the fireplace as Carter left. Denton struggled to pull it together. He knew how to approach her, damn it. At least, he knew how *not* to approach her. She wouldn't respond to badgering; he had to get a grip. And in a minute she'd be gone and this would be all he'd have to remember of this day, this bad feeling. But he *couldn't* drop it. The pain inside him was too great. He went to her.

"No wonder you always thought I did it." He huffed, tried to make it sound like it didn't matter. "If that's what the test said. Do you know that right after it happened you and Father went to Europe and didn't come home for a *year?*"

She kept her eyes on the mirror. "Those are two completely separate things, Denton. My god. Anyway, we put it behind us a long time ago." Her voice was blank, final. She produced lipstick out of a small black pouch from her pocket, reapplied what didn't need reapplying. "Accidents happen. You were very young."

It wasn't an accident! he shouted in his head. *Molly vanished in a bright light! I did not push her in the river, even accidentally. I did not see her fall in on her own. We weren't even near the river when it happened. Do you want me to take a lie detector test* again?

Only he didn't say any of that. His mother finally looked at him, a rare sternness in her features.

"What do you want from me? Have I ever punished you for this? Is there something I've failed to give you? You have a trust fund which is more than adequate. I've offered to pay for any education you care to pursue. It's over, forgotten."

But it wasn't over and it had never been forgotten. How could he explain that she, and his father before he'd died, had never looked at him the same after that day? That there was a remoteness down deep in their eyes that said that, while he was still their son, they believed him capable of pushing a little girl in a river or even just seeing her fall in and then lying himself blue in the face about it to escape punishment and that such a person was really not a nice person, not cute and fluffy at all.

"I didn't do it," Denton whispered, blinking back tears.

"Oh, for heaven's sake!" Mother spoke with exasperation, then composed herself, smoothing her features to her polished, pleasant look. "I *must* go. But do think about Switzerland for Christmas. And next time, give me at least two weeks' notice, won't you, dear?"

She air-kissed him and called for Carter to bring around the car.

5

When a child is conceived, a million sperm compete for one egg. What mysterious process is it that closes the gates once one sperm has achieved penetration? This same process insures that only one sentient species arises on a planet. I have heard rabbis question the theory of evolution asking, if apes are our relatives, why did they never get the spark of consciousness that is a soul? It is this: as evolution burgeons, a million species are competing, progressing faster and faster to achieve that spark. And once one species has achieved the gift of consciousness, the gates are shut to the others forever.

The mysteries of the universe can be found in eggshells, if we know how to look.

—Yosef Kobinski, *The Book of Torment,* 1943

5.1. CALDER FARRIS

JULY
KNOXVILLE, TENNESSEE

Calder was parked down the street from the house. He checked his watch again: 10:15. On cue, an expensive-looking black van appeared in his rearview mirror. The van glided smoothly to a stop and shut off its lights.

The street was residential, an upper-class neighborhood littered with Southern Colonials. Other than a few stray lights in windows, the inhabitants were already asleep. Farris got out of his car and into the van.

"Lieutenant Farris," the largest of the three men saluted him. "Nice to work with you again."

"Lieutenant Hinkle."

Hinkle was a slab of meat who looked like he ought to speak like Lennie in *Of Mice and Men,* so his rich, formal voice was always incongruous. Hinkle and his companions were dressed, like Farris, in black civilian clothes.

"These are Sergeants Troy and Owen," Hinkle made the introductions.

The men saluted him and Calder made a preemptory return. They looked fine: both Caucasian, buzz cuts, square jaws, eyes that showed nothing. Hinkle was dependable that way.

Hinkle motioned for Troy and Owen to get out, and Calder slid into the abandoned driver's seat. His face was lit by the fluorescent streetlights outside. Hinkle looked away, his expression uneasy. Fucking Hinkle. Even *he* couldn't look Calder in the eye. For a moment, Calder had a tightening sensation that threatened an oncoming rage. Hinkle spoke.

"So what's the story?"

"B and E, document recovery." Calder's words were tight and hard. "It's an old man, a professor, widower, lives alone. I've met with him several times. He refused to cooperate." Calder looked at the house down the street, his temper cooling slowly. "I followed him home from the university at about fifteen hundred. He hasn't left, but the lights never came on."

"Maybe he's napping."

"Maybe. There's a study at the back of the house. Clean out his files, hard drive, everything. If he is home, tell him his work is being confiscated. Don't tell him who you are—he'll know. Give him a few bruises if he tries to stop you, but go easy; he's an old man. On your way out, advise him to reconsider his options."

Hinkle absorbed his orders, not looking into Calder's eyes. He watched Hinkle's meaty face and wished again that he hadn't had to bring him in. Information was better when willingly conferred. But there were people in this world determined to make life difficult, people who refused to do their patriotic duty.

Calder could have strong-armed the subject himself, but that would make it difficult to go back in later and play good cop, and Calder wanted very much to be the one to whom the old man capitulated. Hence Hinkle.

"Questions?" Calder asked.

"What's the subject's name? Or is that classified?"

"It's Ansel, Dr. Henry Ansel."

Calder waited in the van. While he waited he couldn't stop thinking about Mark Avery. His ex-partner had been very interested in Dr. Ansel. Avery's funeral had been last week. Calder managed to be out of town.

He'd been in Oklahoma and had spent three hours at a shooting range that day, the hours Mark was buried. That night he hadn't slept at all. He'd had nightmares about his father, first time in years. Avery's death had stirred all of that up again. Calder was not a happy camper.

He and his father . . . shit, they were mortal enemies even when Calder was small. It took Calder a while to figure it out is all. His mother, so he was told, was a whore who ran away, leaving him in his father's care. They lived on Army bases where his father hired the least appropriate people he could find to take care of Calder during the day—from a schizophrenic German lady, to a chain-smoking teenage pothead, to a woman who could barely get out of a chair.

When Capt. John Farris II came home at night he would wring every last detail of his son's misbehavior from the caretaker du jour and mete out Calder's punishment like an appetizer before supper. He had a strict and precise set of rules. A cussword got three strikes with the belt; a broken dish, four; talking back, five. Sexual misconduct, such as touching himself, however briefly, brought down the almighty wrath of God. And always, always, the fucking bitches who watched him during the day would chat up every single thing he'd done, even after Calder told them he'd be beaten for it. *Even when they knew.*

No. That wasn't a hundred percent true. The pothead wouldn't tell. She didn't rat him out. But after a couple of weeks John Farris got wise and replaced her with a woman with loose lips. There were *plenty* of those. It was in the breed.

When Calder got a bit older he found he had a talent for dishing it out as well as taking it. Hell, he was a prodigy at intimidating other kids, even ones larger than himself. It gave him a sense of power and triumph when they cringed and sobbed and ran away, a sense of control when *he* hit and *they* cowered.

Didn't solve his problem with his old man, though. When Calder was seventeen he bought a derelict car with money he'd earned at a fast-food place. *His own fucking money.* John Farris hated that car, hated that Calder could get into it and escape anytime he goddamn well pleased. So when Calder got a speeding ticket, it was a no-brainer that John Farris was going to make it an issue and take the car away.

That night, that argument, was lividly burned into Calder's memory, every corrosive word. Calder wasn't going to let his father take the keys, would have died before he'd allowed it—just lain down in front of a steamroller if that had been the only alternative. So when his father had taken off his belt something inside Calder snapped.

He'd almost beaten his father to death that night. And then he ran—never saw the old man again. Years later, Capt. John Farris II had died and there had been one less prick in the world. End of story. Except for some reason Mark Avery's death had made those memories come rising to the top like a bloated corpse in a lake. Fuck if he knew why. Calder had gotten over his old man *years* ago.

And as soon as he discovered the Next Big Thing and got promoted to major, he would have bested John Farris II at the only thing he ever cared about—the military—and exorcised the jerk-off completely.

There was a knock on the window—it was Troy. Calder rolled it down an inch.

"Lieutenant Farris, you'd better come inside."

Inside the house, the sergeant motioned toward the stairs. Calder took them two at a time. He found Hinkle in the master bedroom, standing over a figure on the bed. It was Ansel—a very dead Ansel.

"Suicide." Hinkle held up a prescription bottle. "No label. Not sure what it was."

Calder put his hands on his hips. The feel of the gun holstered beneath his jacket gave him a sense of command he badly needed at the moment. "How long ago?"

Hinkle had gloves on and he tried turning Ansel's head—it was stiff with rigor mortis. He picked up an arm, which was stiff, but not very. "Anywhere from two to six hours."

Calder had seen him alive at three. "God*damn* it!"

It was as much emotional expression as he would permit himself. He took a few deep breaths. "Get everything out of the study. We'll go over to the university tonight. His office—"

Hinkle was looking at him with a tight-lipped expression. The words died in Calder's throat. He ran downstairs. He knew where the study was. He'd been inside it once, before Ansel learned he was military and threw him out. He burst into it now to find Troy standing with a black plastic sack, looking around uncertainly. Owen was bent over the fireplace.

The file cabinets stood open and empty. Ansel's desk was clear. In the fireplace was a smoldering log—and a *lot* of ashes.

The demon towered up inside Calder like a roaring savage. For a moment he was in danger of losing it. He wanted to punch the wall, the door, something. But the Army had taught him discipline and Owen and Troy were watching.

"Bag the ashes," Calder ordered, with a voice like curdled milk. He turned on his heel and left the room.

In the foyer he paced from wall to wall, driven by strangled fury, trying to get clear enough to think. He breathed deeply, counted to ten, counted a dozen more.

They would go over to the university, but if Ansel had gone to this much trouble over his home files, he'd probably already trashed his office. Calder had been too slow or too lenient. He had missed the signals that his target was going south. He should have . . .

Fuck that. He had to focus on what he could salvage.

Mark Avery's file had been full of Henry Ansel. There were clippings of the old man's obscure articles and lecture notes as well as Avery's own thoughts on the possible uses of Ansel's ideas. Calder had begun to see what had interested his ex-partner. He'd gotten a hard-on for it himself.

But when he'd approached Ansel, the man had been vague—*purposefully* vague. It wasn't the hedging of a clueless geek who was full of shit (Calder had plenty of experience with that type). No, it was the hedging of a liberal geek who was scared of what Big Bad Mr. Government might do with what he knew. If Calder had needed confirmation of that, it lay up there in the bedroom. But the fact that he'd been right about Ansel, that he did, indeed, have something he thought was dangerous enough to die for, was of little comfort to Calder Farris and none to the US of A.

Salvage? How? What? The professor's brain would not reveal its secrets under the knife. And there was no one besides Ansel who *could* talk. There were no children, his wife had been dead for years, and Ansel had worked alone. He had worked alone for a very long time.

5.2. Jill Talcott

Seattle

THE ONE PULSE, 50 PERCENT POWER

Jill Talcott checked her E-mail and pulled some overhead slides from a filing cabinet. She'd hoped to spend the entire summer in the lab she and Nate had set up in the basement of Smith Hall. But she'd been playing her cards so close to her chest that Dick Chalmers, thinking she had nothing better to do, had given her not one, but two summer sessions, the worm. Meanwhile, Nate had gotten a job as a waiter on Capitol Hill working the dinner rush and could spend all morning and afternoon in the lab while she lectured to sleepy window-watching students. Double worm.

She was contemplating her revenge, which, as usual, had to do with her imminent success and glory, when a knock startled her. The slides spilled onto the floor. Red trajectory arcs and blue equations suggested themselves over dirty linoleum. The knock came again.

"Damn it, come in!" Jill bent to the scattered sheaves.

She was not in the mood to see anyone this morning, but of all the people she was not in the mood to see, Chuck Grover topped the list. He shut the door deliberately behind him and looked at her with a calculated challenge in his eye. "I wanted to chat, Jill." He loped over to Nate's chair, swung it closer to her desk, and sat in it backward.

"I have a class in ten minutes, Chuck. But if you can make it quick . . ." She plopped the slides on her desk and began to shuffle through them to avoid looking at him.

Grover's appearance was even more horrifyingly Californian than usual, thanks to the July weather. His open sandals displayed hoary feet, and a baggy pair of shorts provided even more unwelcomed information as he sat, legs spread. The neck of Nate's office chair was uncharitably thin, and Jill, who had not seen that portion of the male anatomy by choice for some years, was not happy to be subjected to it now, at ten in the morning in this claustrophobic office.

"I wanted to touch base about our agreement."

"What agreement is that, Chuck?" Her small fingers tapped at the salvaged file.

"The agreement we made when you came crawling to me six months ago for time on Quey, time I did not by any means have to give you."

He kept his tone light, but Jill was shocked at his blatant choice of words. Apparently, he was through pretending theirs was a civil relationship. She answered equally lightly.

"Believe me, I haven't forgotten that day. Nor will I."

"Good. Then perhaps you'll take a few minutes to bring your partner up-to-date."

Chuck leaned forward in the chair, folding his arms over the top. Despite the Coppertone pose, his eyes were angry. It was true Jill had brushed him off in the hallways more than once in the past months. But she wondered when, exactly, Grover had decided she had something worth bothering over.

"Certainly!" she said brightly. "I was fortunate enough to get data on a carbon atom from the accelerator at CERN. . . ." She told him, in more detail than he obviously wanted to know, how they had set up the original experiment. It was all true, as far as it went.

Grover's eyes narrowed, not trusting her sudden forthcomingness.

"So we crunched through it all using Quey—which was really remarkably fast—you must be congratulated."

"Thank you."

"And then we compared the two sets of data. . . ." She sighed, trying to look discouraged. It was hard. "And found out that they were off from one another by over thirty percent. I'm afraid my equation was a failure."

It hurt her to say it. Really, it bugged the crap out of her. Grover would have the news all over the department within hours. Yet something within her felt confident enough today to take the inevitable heat. In fact, she was almost enjoying this confrontation. She felt strong, invincible.

"Can I *see* your results, Jill?"

"Of course, Chuck." She went over to Nate's computer, feigning calm. Was the old data still in place? Could she remember how to run the program that showed the original error? She booted up Nate's machine and looked around his C Drive.

While she was searching, Chuck picked up something off Nate's desk. It was an operations manual for their new radio generator. He stared at it with a frown, flicked its cover with his fingers thoughtfully.

Her mouth went dry. "Here we go." She double-clicked on the program she thought was the right one and stood back. She glanced at her watch as though this were routine and she had better things to do. Inside, she was screaming.

The two columns of data and the box that read: DATA OFF BY 31% came up. Hot damn.

"There you go, Chuck. Just like I said. Now I'm very sorry, but I do have a class starting in five minutes."

Grover would not be rushed. He put the generator manual down and looked at the screen for a good long time, like it might change in front of him from a pile of garbage to a pot of gold. Jill folded her arms, tapped her fingers on her collarbone, and bit her cheeks to keep back an evil smile.

"Why didn't you tell me this two months ago? And what've you been doing since then? I *know* you're working on something. I gave you two more slots on Quey and you never—"

"I realized we needed to do a lot more groundwork before we bothered you again. Then . . . well, to be honest, we're on a completely different track now. But I do appreciate your interest, Chuck." She turned off Nate's machine. "Can I walk you out?"

Walk him out. Yeah, all one and a half steps to the door.

Grover stood up slowly, his face uncertain. "Even if the equation *was* wrong, you couldn't have known that without Quey, so whatever—"

"Excuse me?" She had a flash of temper. "Yes, Quey showed me that my approach was in error, and for that I'm grateful. But now I'm on to new things. Are you seriously going to claim my work for the rest of my life? How many people have you done this to, Chuck?"

Grover paled to the color of Swiss cheese. He pointed a finger at her chest. "You'd better hope you never need anything from me again . . . *Jill*. Because I don't like being jerked around. If I see *anything* in your work which points to Quey being even a factor, *anything*, I *will* have what we agreed on."

Jill's confidence faltered. Grover had a lot of weight in the department. Hell, he had a lot of weight just about everywhere. And she *had* agreed to a partnership, even if he'd had no right to ask her in the first place.

But the sun was streaming in through the window and she felt remarkably buoyant, like, well, like he couldn't touch her. "Gosh, I'm sorry you feel that way. As for me, it's been a pleasure working with you, and I hope someday we can work together again."

She held out her hand. He stared at it wordlessly and walked out.

After her morning class, Jill hurried down to the basement lab and donned their protective gear—lead aprons of the sort X-ray technicians used. She didn't know if the aprons did anything or not, but the precaution soothed her conscience. Nate was seated at the radio transmitter table where they had a computer set up. He was wrangling data.

"How's it going?" Jill went over to the test subjects and eyeballed them for any change.

Their experiment was quite silly. Silly enough that she would feel idiotic should anyone—Chalmers, for example—get wind of it. Then again, playing with mold must have seemed equally silly in its time. Besides, she'd be damned if it wasn't working.

Nate joined her. "They still look really good." He peered at a plate of fruit.

The experiment: bombard the room with a solid one pulse. They didn't need the power of a HAARP station because they weren't trying to reach the ionosphere. In fact, they worked very hard to keep the waves right inside this room. They'd chosen the basement room because it was unused, but more important, it was underground. A heavy rubber curtain hung in front of the door, and they'd covered the walls and ceiling with soundproofing. On a few of the walls Nate had hung up vast sheets of papers, charts of equation matrices they'd worked on months ago. She thought he meant the charts for inspiration—or perhaps he just wanted to clear them out of their crowded office in the physics building.

Jill had purchased a transmitter with her own money and had scavenged the rest of their equipment. They could produce a total of three kilowatts of power, which was modest. But even now, running at 50 percent of their capacity, *something* was happening.

"Ready to record today's numbers?" Jill asked.

"Sure."

Nate went over to a grid on an enormous old white board. Down the left side of the grid was a detailed list of their three subject groups; each banana, apple, mouse, and virus culture was listed. Along the top of the board were three months' worth of days. Only the first weeks had been filled in.

"Go ahead."

Jill began, with infinite care, to study each of their subjects. "Banana one gets a four. Banana two: four."

Nate recorded the numbers in the grid.

"Apple one: three; apple two: three."

Fruit was judged on the amount of its surface area that was bruised, sunken, or dried; the virus dishes, by the amount of growth and activity in the culture. The mice were harder, but the amount of food they ate was measured; their general appearance, health, and activity were also quantified on a 1–10 scale.

Jill found her excitement kindling as she went through each group. Silly or not, they were seeing results. The control group was at her house in Wallingford. She and Nate made trips to the market, taking care to put together pairs of fruit in exactly the same condition, bringing one of each pair to the lab and placing the other in Jill's spare bedroom. They had mice from the same litters at her house also and virus dishes carefully prepared to match their twins in the basement lab. The basic idea: to determine if altering the one-minus-one in the lab made any discernible difference in their subjects.

"Remarkable," she said, straightening up from the fruit. "All the fruit at my house are in stages six or seven at least. They're lasting much longer here."

Nate came over and squatted down, peering at a banana. "It's cooler here than at your place. That might slow the decay."

Jill shrugged, knowing it was a valid point and knowing, also, that there wasn't much they could do about it—not on their budget. But that was why they had a variety of subjects. None of them would respond favorably or negatively to exactly the same conditions.

"Virus one-point-one gets a six," she reported, peering down at the culture through a microscope.

The virus cultures, too, were doing noticeably better here than at Jill's house. The growth rate was up almost a third over the control group. And the mice were distinctly more active, waiting in line for a turn at the wheel and the males sniffing aggressively around the females, copulating often.

When they were done, Jill poured herself a cup of coffee and sat down. Nate got a glass of water from the sink.

"No coffee?"

"Nah. I'm already on full pilot. Don't wanna blow a fuse."

Jill watched him surreptitiously. Before, she might spend entire days with Nate in the office and not have the faintest idea what he was wearing or if he'd been tired or ill or what. But it had dawned on her recently that he was as much a subject as the mice in the room, as *she* was herself. It had given her a whole new interest in him. At the moment, for example, he looked jumpy. She felt that way, too, energized and hyper. She was filled with such eager anticipation, such optimism about their work, that she could hardly sleep at night. Analyzing, hypothesizing, planning—she couldn't shut her brain off. And today she'd even had the nerve to face down Chuck Grover.

"I wish we could make it less subjective," she said. "I think the virus will be our best bet, don't you?"

"Yeah."

"What we need are incubators so we can keep the virus at the same temperature, same light conditions, same humidity, here and at my place. I'll visit the biology department later, see what they have to spare."

"Good idea." Nate was beating his fingers against the lip of the table like a kid mimicking drums. He grabbed a pen and wrote that down.

Her freckled brow scowled at a sudden thought. "Damn! I wish we could keep our control group close by. We ought to be taking our readings simultaneously. The time of day might have an effect, particularly on the mice. We never get over to my place until after three with my class schedule." Chalmers. The worm.

"But we *can't* have the control group anywhere near the pulse, and we're not sure how pervasive the pulse is." Nate waved at the ceiling, "Or if any of this stuff keeps it in. We agreed: the control group shouldn't even be on campus."

"I know. I'm just saying—if we *did* know exactly what would contain the pulse . . ." She chewed on a fingernail. "We know so little about the one-minus-one."

She felt Nate looking at her and met his gaze. He had his pensive philosopher's face on. "I'm not even sure it's smart to have the control group at your house."

"Why not?"

"Well . . . you're down here quite a bit. So am I, actually. Anyway, the change in the one-minus-one affects waves, right? See what I mean? *You and I* are made up of particles, just like the fruit and the virus cultures. *More* particles maybe. But that could even make it worse. Because *you* are connected to *your house* and the objects in it. We both are in a way, since I go over there, too. It's not my *place*, but I'm *there.*"

He was talking with his hands, his words rapid.

"Nate—"

"So if the interference model is correct, wouldn't *your own personal waves* have some effect on the waves over in the control lab? If we *really* wanted to be safe, our control group should be run by someone we don't even know over in Siberia or something. And maybe we shouldn't even talk to that lab on the phone. We could pass the information through a router which—"

"Nate!"

"Huh?"

"You're babbling."

Nate blinked, as if he couldn't remotely see her point. "Me? I'm cool. I'm just *saying.*"

Jill went over to check on the radio transmitter. It was broadcasting steadily. "Which reminds me, I think we both should start journals." She hesitated, not eager to bring this up, to verbally admit to the chances they were taking. "How are you feeling? You're down here even more than I am. If you start to feel bad, Nate, I want you to tell me."

"Bad?" Nate's eyes grew big and bright. His fingers bounced on the desk, *rat-a-tat-tat.* "No way. I feel great. Great. Really. Really, I feel great. It's totally fun."

"I feel good, too," Jill admitted. A smile of sheer unfettered optimism teased her lips. She gazed lovingly at the white board across the room.

Nate cleared his throat. "It's kind of strange, actually."

"What?"

He didn't answer and the silence grew . . . pointed. She glanced at him curiously. He was blushing. "What, Nate?"

"Never mind."

"*What?*"

Nate tried to make light of it, joked, "Well, you know, I'm feeling about as . . . as, um, reproduction-oriented as the mice. *Big*-time. Big-, big-time."

He gave her a look that was so smoky it punched her in the gut like a fist. She turned away, looked at some dials. Her face burned like a goddamn schoolgirl's. She hated herself for reacting so virginally, hated it even more that it had to be visible a mile away. Then she was irritated at him for bringing up something so . . . personal. And inappropriate, damn it. Then she thought that she *had* asked.

She said, in the coolest voice she could muster, "That's the sort of thing you should write in your journal. Of course, anything we feel *may* be purely psychological. You know that expectations often—"

"This is *not* psychological. Trust me. So you're not feeling anything like . . ."

"*No.*" The machinery below her was really quite interesting, though she was beginning to feel that if she didn't get out of here soon, she'd make a complete ass of herself. And now that he mentioned it . . . she had been particularly enjoying her hot baths recently, her skin especially sensitive. And this sudden interest she had in studying him—was it really just because he was a subject in the experiment? The thought made her hyperventilate.

"Jill the Chill," Nate muttered, almost too soft for her to hear.

She spun to look at him, but he was typing at his keyboard, face stolid, and somehow . . . It was easier to pretend she hadn't heard. She went to the sink, poured her coffee down the drain, then rinsed the cup with a thoroughness that would have made Martha Stewart sweat.

"The important thing," she said firmly, "is our subjects. I think we have to make *some* assumptions. We have to assume that the further we get from this room, the weaker and more inconsequential any effect of the pulse will be. As long as we recognize what our assumptions are, and document them, we're ahead of the game."

"I guess so."

Satisfied that she'd made her point, or at least sidestepped his, Jill glanced at his screen. "Where are we at now? Can you run the numbers?"

Nate punched some keys, brought up an Excel spreadsheet that matched their white board. "I haven't finished entering today's data yet."

"So finish."

She waited while he typed in the numbers. When he was done he ran the total. "Twenty-one percent differential between the subjects here and the control group."

That put her in a better mood. Her shoulders relaxed. "Good. It's still in‐creasing. But I'd like to see at least a fifty percent differential. I think we're ready to bump up the power; don't you?"

Nate grimaced. "To what—sixty percent of power? Sixty-five?"

Jill drummed her fingers against her collarbone, considering. "Why not seventy-five? We're not seeing anything all *that* spectacular. I don't think there's any danger. We can always lower it if . . ." *If something happens.* ". . . if we want."

Nate stood, shakily, like he'd been drinking a lot of caffeine after all. He went to the transmitter and pumped up the power level to 75 percent.

Neither of them said anything. They both stood there, *feeling* the room, feeling that additional 25 percent, as if the one-minus-one were a living crea‐ture and if they listened hard enough, felt deeply enough, they would be able to detect its now-panting breath brushing up against their very cells.

5.3. Aharon Handalman

JERUSALEM

Rabbi Aharon Handalman was becoming very frightened. Over the past month it had come upon him gradually. At first, his stomach terrorized his esophagus and he was reduced to living on yogurt and saltines. Then, as their discoveries accumulated, the acidic fingers were superseded by a deadening numbness at his breastplate, which was maybe worse. Emotionally, he was a wreck, as if a divine finger were stirring up the stuff of his soul.

Using *weapon* as a secondary keyword, they had found *200 instances* in the Kobinski arrays. And in marking those finds down in their binders he and Binyamin had checked for phrases on either side of the word *weapon* and had found the following:

"weapon of obliteration"—5 instances
"from him the weapon"—3 instances
"weapon of torment"—5 instances
"weapon of terror"—4 instances
"weapon of evil"—4 instances
"the great weapon"—5 instances
"weapon loosing demons"—4 instances

And the biggest discovery: in three separate places where the word *weapon* ran horizontally one of its letters was shared by a phrase running vertically, which, as far as Aharon could tell, read: "the law of good and evil."

That single word—*weapon*—had opened up the door on a deeper, more sinister dimension of the arrays, like the key that Bluebeard's wife wielded. They searched on *good, evil, demons, angels, heaven,* and *hell* and found them again and again in the arrays. Looking up *torment* they found a phrase, *book of torment,* that appeared in the arrays thirty times!

Aharon neglected his classes again. Dean Horowitz noticed. He called Aharon into his office and had a long talk with him. Aharon was going to tell him about the arrays, but as soon as Horowitz heard the word *code,* he shut Aharon down, talking about his duty to the students. If the man chose to remain ignorant, was it Aharon's fault? As for life at home, what home! He hardly saw it. Normally, Hannah would rattle his cage to get his attention. But lately she'd grown cool and distant. The other day his six-year-old, Devorah, had asked, "How come you never come home anymore?" and the baby, Layah, had cried when he'd walked in—as if her own father were a stranger!

He felt an increasing pressure to tell someone, and he knew who he *must* tell. After several days of leaving urgent messages (he plagued the answering machine with the determination of Jacob setting his sights on Rachel), the man finally returned his call. Aharon would not describe the situation on the phone: "For this, the eyes must see for themselves," he insisted. Shimon Norowitz agreed to meet him in Jerusalem at a particularly good kosher deli.

Shimon Norowitz was not the excitable type. He was in his fifties, a onetime military officer, secular (no facial hair), but perhaps not completely irreligious. Aharon, because he needed the man, gave him the benefit of the doubt. Also, God works in mysterious ways: Norowitz truly loved Haman's Deli on Jaffa Road, so it was excuse enough to drive all the way over from Tel Aviv. Even corned beef could have a greater purpose.

Aharon had sought a Mossad contact several years ago when he'd made his first big discovery in the code. He'd had no luck finding one until he learned that one of the boys in *Aish HaTorah* had a father in the government. Aharon had finagled an invitation to meet the father, and that was how he'd been put in touch with Shimon Norowitz, a man who might or might not head up the Mossad's encryption department. Aharon was never able to get a straight answer on that point.

Over corned beef, Norowitz broached the topic: "So what do you have for me this time, Rabbi? Last time you were convinced Israel would come under nuclear attack from Syria. I believe the dates you pinpointed came and went last year, didn't they?"

"The code *also* includes might-have-beens. That doesn't mean that when a revelation falls into our lap we should not take the proper precautions or we should not pay attention."

Shimon savored his corned beef, unmoved by this profundity. "And this time?"

Aharon looked stern so the man would take this seriously. "What I'm about to show you is the most important code discovery ever."

"Good. Is that it?" Norowitz nodded at the binder. Corned beef juice dripped from his pinkie.

"What would you say if I told you that I have found *four hundred* arrays, all about the same subject?"

"I suppose it would depend on what the subject was. Four hundred arrays containing the name Moses wouldn't be so remarkable. Those letters can be found in ELS a thousand times over."

"Oh, yes," Aharon scoffed, "if the name were *Moses* and if the other words in the arrays were made up of equally common letters. Would I bother you if that were the case?"

"So are you going to show me, Rabbi Handalman?"

"You must be prepared."

"Believe me, I'm prepared."

Aharon gave him a warning look: *You only* think *you're prepared.* But he opened the binder and held it out. Norowitz released his sandwich to take the thing with both hands, but Aharon didn't let him have it.

"Your hands," he said. "This is Scripture."

Norowitz, reddening, wiped his hands clear of corned beef juice and took the binder.

Aharon had planned to explain the whole thing. Who could resist such an opportunity? But his instinct now told him to let the binder tell its own tale. "If a word is worth one shekel, silence is worth two," as the Talmud says.

Shimon turned pages, studying the arrays and their circled words intently. The binder was heavy. He pulled it onto his lap, moved back in his chair, propped the binder up against the edge of the deli table, and turned pages. Once or twice he wiped at his indecently clean upper lip. Aharon smiled smugly; he didn't have to feel that finger to know it was as cold as ice.

After ten minutes, Shimon sat upright and closed the binder carefully on his lap. "*Who* is Yosef Kobinski?"

"You can see the dates for yourself in the arrays. He was a Polish rabbi, caught up in the Holocaust. He was also a physicist at the University of Warsaw from 1918 to 1927. He was *also* a kabbalist."

Shimon looked quizzical, said nothing.

"But that's a good question," Aharon said emphatically. "*Who* is Yosef Kobinski? What weapon did he develop, Shimon Norowitz? Whatever it is, I think it is something the state of Israel should know about, *lo*?"

Shimon looked through the arrays some more, face pensive. "Do you know what he did at the University of Warsaw?"

"Exactly! I looked into it, but there was nothing. No atomic research at that time in Warsaw, and nothing about it in the *arrays*, either."

"Is there anything else I should know about this?"

"That depends on what you plan to do."

Norowitz sucked his teeth, thinking or maybe just collecting corned beef fragments. "If you get me a copy of these arrays, I'll have one of my people take a look."

"That's it?"

"There's not much to go on, Rabbi. And this word *weapon*—it must appear all over the Torah. It's only three letters long."

" 'Weapon of obliteration'—you think this is a fluke?"

"Don't misunderstand me; I'm interested. You'll continue to work on it, I hope. And keep us informed of your progress." He hesitated a moment, then took out a notepad. "I'll give you my direct line. If you find something *important*," he looked up, emphasizing the word, "call me."

Aharon took the proffered bit of paper, knowing this was not an inconsiderable concession. Before, he'd always had to go through the switchboard and was easily put off that way. A direct line: so now he was somebody? Still he wasn't satisfied. He'd come feeling almost giddy with his discovery's importance. Now anxiety was creeping back in.

"Listen," he said, more confidentially. "I would appreciate some help on this. I—I'm not sure what else to do and I'm . . ." Norowitz was looking at him curiously. "So I'm a little frightened. This weapon, it has to *mean* something, and God has seen fit for me to find it and—"

"What is it you'd like me to do?" Norowitz handed back the binder and reclaimed his sandwich.

Aharon thought about it as he watched the beardless man gobble his food. *His* appetite, at least, was not disturbed by the arrays. Yes, he would *like* to advise Norowitz on what he should do, but he found he didn't know. All this effort to get the man here and *that* he forgot to prepare.

"So I'll keep working," Aharon said.

5.4. Denton Wyle

Frankfurt

"The copy," the German said, "is nine pages long."

Denton nodded, trying to keep himself from salivating. This was the first piece of manuscript Mother's agent, Mr. Fleck, had uncovered. He'd promised that if any more of the manuscript was available for sale anywhere, he would find it. And he would, too. He would run it to ground like a terrier, because Denton had paid him a big fat retainer and he got a nice commission on everything Denton bought. Visions of *The Book of Torment* on bestseller lists danced in Denton's head like sugar plum fairies.

Except the Frankfurt antiquities dealer, Uberstühl, had an expression that could only be described as sneaky. Denton didn't care for it at all. He removed his coat, hoping it was just a vibe he was getting from the dingy, mothball-smelling shop.

"So you told my agent on the phone. May I see them?"

"This way, please."

Uberstühl took Denton back to his private office where a computer sat on a plain wooden desk. Denton looked around, still smiling, wondering if he was about to be felt up or something. Uberstühl had a constipated expression.

"You know what it is we speak of, yes? You understand what the piece is?"

"Yes," Denton said carefully. "A Xerox copy of nine pages of a Hebrew manuscript written in Auschwitz by Yosef Kobinski."

"*Richtig.* Exactly." Uberstühl glanced at his computer. Denton followed his gaze and saw that the man's E-mail in-box was up on the screen.

"So . . ." Uberstühl said, clearing his throat. "Let me give you a price to think about while I go get the item. Twenty thousand U.S."

Denton squeaked out a laugh and gasp simultaneously. "I've, um, gotten similar pieces for around five."

"That would be a bit low in the best of circumstances. But in *this* circumstance . . ."

"What about this circumstance?" Denton asked, then sensed that this was where the rotten stink was coming from.

"Allow me to get the document, Mr. Wyle." The dealer gave another meaningful and lengthy gaze at his computer before exiting the room and leaving Denton alone.

Denton didn't need the man to call out the fire department to give him a clue. There were only a few messages in the in-box. It had no doubt been cleaned out for his benefit. The one he was supposed to notice was at the top. The return E-mail address was SSchwartz. Uttering a curse, Denton double-clicked on it to read the text.

> *Two years ago I purchased part of an Auschwitz manuscript from you. It was written by Yosef Kobinski in 1943. I would like to upgrade to an exclusive arrangement on this document. Please respond with the necessary details of the transaction as soon as you can.*
>
> S. Schwartz

Denton gasped in outrage. The *bastard!* Schwartz had called Mr. Fleck a few weeks ago, wanting to know who was on to Kobinski and why. Apparently, Fleck had placed an ad in several international antiquities magazines and Schwartz had seen it. Mr. Fleck didn't tell him, of course (having money was really quite nice at times). And it seemed Schwartz had not connected the reporter who'd come into his office months ago with this mysterious new buyer.

What Schwartz *had* done was utter dire warnings, something about how it was "dangerous" to publish Kobinski, yada, yada, yada. He'd even threatened to sic the Jewish League on them. Still, Denton was aghast that Schwartz would go to this length. Where was the man coming up with the additional cash? Some rich kabbalah Nazi donor? Who did he think he was?

Thank god Uberstühl was one greedy son of a bitch.

Denton heard the door open and got up quickly, forcing a smile. The German had a small flexible black binder with a neat label on the cover: "Kobinski manuscript, Auschwitz, 1943." Denton grew light-headed at the sight.

"Have you been thinking about the price, Mr. Wyle?"

"Yes. Yes, I have."

"And?"

Denton kept his smile fixed. "I'll have to see the manuscript first."

"Naturally."

Uberstühl sat down at the desk and motioned Denton to pull up a chair. He didn't hand Denton the manuscript but kept hold of it himself. He opened it delicately to the first page.

The Xerox was not perfect by any means. There was something dark about the surface, as if it had been copied from many generations before or, more likely, from a very poor original. But the Hebrew characters and even the notations in the margins were legible. Where they weren't someone had gone over them with a fine-tipped pen. All said, it was an exacting, professional job. It ought to be, for twenty grand. It ought to be written on gold tablets by the finger of God.

"And the other pages?"

Uberstühl showed them briefly, only a few seconds per page. Long enough to confirm that the material was all there but not long enough to read. As if Denton could.

A full-fledged presidential debate was going on in Denton's head. He shouldn't buy it. Even his trust fund wasn't limitless. Did he really want to pursue this thing if the price was going to jack up like this? There was no *guarantee* he'd see a return. And Schwartz, Schwartz had threatened him. He was rather afraid of Schwartz.

"Um, what kind of paper was the original on?"

Uberstühl flipped to the front inside cover. There was a photo of the original and a thick label giving all the details. "Two of the pages were heavy dark butcher paper. One was a waxed wrapper, and the rest were paper toweling used in the officers' toilets."

Denton leaned forward to peer at the label. Was that . . . Did he read there that some of the ink was identified as a mixture made with *human feces*? He could see the shock on Barbara Walters's face as he mentioned it.

"I'll take it," Denton said.

While Uberstühl went to check Denton's platinum card, Denton looked again at the E-mail. This time, he was no longer surprised and the weight of it sank in a little deeper. It was such a profoundly warlike thing to do—unfriendly, unfair. It struck Denton that he had a nemesis. Denton Wyle, easy-going rich guy and the best little brownnoser you'd ever care to meet, had his very own Moriarty. In a yarmulke. It was enough to make a bunny very ill indeed.

And he also saw what he had not seen the first time, sitting right in front of his eyes. First, that S. Schwartz was all the identification given. There was no hint that S. Schwartz was a rabbi. Fleck had warned Denton about the Holocaust artifact market. The last person a non-Jew seeking good money for an artifact would want to deal with was a rabbi. Rabbis and Holocaust museums and the like had a habit of trying to claim moral rights to such property and get out of paying at all. The fact that Schwartz was buying "incognito" might be turned to Denton's advantage someday.

The other thing was the TO line. Uberstühl was not the only addressee on the E-mail. There were, in fact, three others. *Denton had just found the sources of three more fragments.*

Denton grinned. "Take that, Moriarty!"

*　　*　　*

FROM *THE BOOK OF TORMENT* BY YOSEF KOBINSKI, 1943

Consider: A star is nothing if not a war between the strong nuclear force and gravity. The intense fuel of the star wants to explode, expand outward. But gravity is working in exactly the opposite direction, forcing the star's energy down into itself.

Gevorah (restriction, judgment) is the gravitational force. Gravity is its embodiment. And chesed *(love, expansion) is the nuclear force—light. So there is a lesson for us in the stars, you see? Gravity and light must dance together, expansion and contraction, in balance, just like judgment and mercy. This is the dance of the spheres, of life.*

If gevorah *and* chesed *have an equivalent in the physical realm, then so do good and evil. This is where the most critical aspect of my work has been done. I have found the physical correspondences of good and evil. The energy patterns of matter in the higher dimension, the fifth dimension, cannot be understood without them.*

The Midrash says that for every blade of grass there is an angel who has the sole task of leaning over it and whispering, "Grow, grow." This is not far from the truth, although it would be more accurate to say that there is also a demon leaning over it saying, "Die, die." The life impulse and the death impulse: both exist in equal measure.

It is all there in my equation, the equation. Indeed, when my work becomes public there will be a revolution in the sciences such has not been seen since Galileo first trained a telescope at the stars. This is why the work must not be allowed to perish in this place.

But back to the point. At the subatomic level we can get close to a glimpse of the true nature of physical matter—energy. It is at this level that we find

[Notation: Further pages of this entry missing]

. . .

Nearly all of my work for the past ten years has been concerned in some way with the fifth dimension. By exploring the three dimensions of space scientists can only learn what *and* where. *The fourth dimension of time allows us to learn* when. *But the fifth dimension . . . the fifth dimension will tell us* why.

To visualize the fifth dimension first visualize one dimension by itself, North–South, a line one atom wide. By adding a second dimension, East–West, every atom on the North–South line is repeated again and again for every atom in the East–West dimension, forming a flat plane. The entire flat plane of North–South and East–West is multiplied again and again for every atom of Up–Down, making a cube. And when you add the dimension of time, every atom of three-dimensional space in that cube exists anew for each microsecond of time. This room I am sitting in, this chair— it is not the same room and the same chair as it was a second ago, and it will not be the same a second from now. Thus it stands to reason that in the fifth dimension every atom of three-dimensional space in each microsecond of time exists over and over and over again—but repeated in what? What is the fifth axis?

According to kabbalists, the fifth dimension is the dimension of good and evil. To me it is the spiritual dimension, the dimension of meaning. The fifth dimension is: every atom of three-dimensional space in each microsecond of time connected to *every other atom of three-dimensional space in each microsecond of time. In other words, the fifth dimension is the living pattern. It is the dimension of* interconnection, of relationships, *a tapestry of cause and effect.*

If we could read the fifth dimension we would be able to see the pattern that leads up to every action. And if we could trace back every thread of that pattern, back and back, we would be able to identify every cause of that effect, and the causes of the causes, and the causes of the causes of the causes, back and back until all causes merge into a single cause at the start of time.

We would be able to answer the question "Why?"—not only for every individual action, but for the start of life itself.

. . .

While deep in meditation, on a night just before things changed forever in Brezeziny, I had a vision. I saw a ladder, Jacob's ladder. From the rungs of the ladder hung entire universes. To the right, the ladder grew increasingly bright until the end of the continuum was pure light. To the left, the ladder grew darker and darker until the end was so black it could only be described as the utter absence of light. Our own universe was exactly in the middle of the ladder, hanging from the middle rung. An angel pointed to it and said, "Only from here may souls escape."

Then I saw the ladder reshape itself until it was a wheel, a wheel of fire that was round like a globe and divided into four segments. Then it changed again, this time into the figure of a man, a man made of stars, of universes. The head of the man was bathed in solid light and his feet vanished into darkness. At the center of the man was the navel and an umbilicus of light and energy grew there, shooting up, up, into someplace beyond the material, even beyond the fifth dimension.

When I came back to myself, I knew I had been given a gift. Even in science, there is an iron veil between what we can learn—the facts of our own cage of space-time—and what lies beyond. We are utterly cut off from knowing the Other except, perhaps, in such dreams.

But now that I have experienced Auschwitz I can only wonder, my Lord G-d, if this is the middle of the ladder, if our own world is in the center and to one side lie heavens and to the other lie hells, then how bad must Hell be?

6

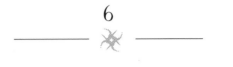

Distance is not in heaven as it is here. Here is a limited distance and therefore measurable. There is it limitless and therefore immeasurable.
—Emanuel Swedenborg, *Heaven & Hell*, 1756

6.1. JILL TALCOTT

SEATTLE

THE ONE PULSE, 75 PERCENT POWER

Jill wasn't sleeping anymore. Nate wasn't, either. He had bruised circles under his eyes. On his olive-colored skin the circles were purple and sage, which she found herself staring at sometimes, marveling over the way the desert colors contrasted against his thick black lashes, like a midnight sunset.

Things could not be better. Most of the staff were on summer vacation and the physics department had received a large grant from Microsoft. Everyone was congratulating Grover and Chalmers: Grover because the quantum computer was the reason for Microsoft's generosity, Chalmers because he held the check. This kept both of them off her back. There was lots of talk about the Udub's physics program becoming world-class. Jill smirked to herself and continued her subterranean journeys to the basement lab. If they only knew.

Knew this: that the one-minus-one was the most important thing that had happened to science, ever. And it was hers, all hers.

She and Nate went over to her house, late every afternoon, to check and log the control group. It amused her that they would pull up to the curb in that unassuming neighborhood, where programmers in jeans or marketing types in Dockers were arriving home for the day. And she and Nate, toting her briefcase and his laptop, getting out like normal people and opening up the door to her little house, no one giving them the slightest glance. Some days she laughed out loud.

She tried to remain objective, tried not to allow herself to project too much on the subjects or anticipate results. But there was no denying that altering the one-minus-one had an effect on the subjects in the basement lab. Their mates in the control group at home, the mice and the virus and fruit, appeared normal when considered in their own right, but in comparison with their twins in the lab they were . . . dimmer somehow, as if existing in slow motion or with great apathy.

The lab mice were glossy and racing around, rising up on their hind legs and sniffing, copulating almost continually, even male on male when she and Nate separated the sexes to give the poor females a break. The virus was flourishing so rampantly they'd added more dishes. The original cultures in the lab were now in three dishes each, compared to the single dish at Jill's house. The fruit *refused* to decay.

And then there were the human subjects. Her period had become heavier and about a day longer. She'd always had fine hair, but a thick new row of down on the edge of her forehead indicated abundant new growth. She had continual copious energy even without food or rest. Her mind calculated, organized, but often got fuzzy out of sheer overload. Emotionally, she was ecstatic but fragile, easily broke into tears of frustration at traffic jams or whining students, and was just as instantly elated when they made the slightest progress. All this she noted, too.

July 20. The takeout on the counter in the kitchen went unpacked. Neither she nor Nate had an appetite these days, a fact Jill noted in her journal. She had begun stopping at a little teriyaki shop every night. And every night, after Nate went home, she'd dig out his take-out container from the trash and log just how much he'd eaten. For the past three days he'd barely touched it.

They finished logging the numbers on the subjects in her spare room at four o'clock. Jill should have been tired, because she hadn't slept in days, but she was still bursting with energy.

"What's the new total?" she asked Nate when she'd finished her last examination. She was hoping for a half a percent up from yesterday, at least. Only three more percentage points to go and they'd be at a 50 percent differential between the control and test groups.

When he didn't answer right away, she turned to look at him. Nate was panting, perched on the edge of a folding chair, the only place to sit in the crowded guest room. It was a warm night, and he had fine sweat on his face. "Think I'll . . . " he muttered weakly, and headed for the doorway.

Jill followed. "What's wrong?"

His laptop hung heavily from one hand, and when he landed on the sofa he let it drop to the floor beside him. He fell back against the cushions, partially reclined. He looked like he couldn't move to either sit up or lie all the way down.

He looked seriously ill. That sparked fear and guilt in Jill about what she was doing, exposing him—exposing them both—to the altered one-minus-one. She mumbled something extraneous and went to the kitchen, wet a dish towel with cool water from the tap. His face was so white . . . her heart pounded violently, another overreaction. Knowing that didn't make it go away.

When she came back, he was weakly pulling off his T-shirt, which was damp with sweat. He collapsed back on her couch, his skin clammy and slick, looking exhausted, looking green. He appeared to have come close to losing consciousness—perhaps still might. "Hot," he panted. "Fan?"

"No, I'm sorry."

She ran to open the windows in the living room and kitchen, hoping for a cross-breeze. And although it *was* a warm day, it did not seem unbearably hot to her. This thought scared her further and she ran into the bathroom and rifled for a thermometer. She took it back to the living room and knelt down by the couch. Nate's eyes were closed.

"We should take your temperature," she said, feeling awkward. She stuck the thermometer in his mouth and began wiping the pale skin on his face and arms with the cold cloth, the way her mother used to when she had a fever. His skin was radiating heat. He opened his eyes.

"Do you think you need to go to the hospital?"

"Just hot," he managed around the thermometer.

"No talking. You didn't touch your dinner. You haven't been eating at all, Nate! You're going to make yourself sick, and then how would we know if the experiment had anything to do with it or not?"

She spoke with annoyance to cover her fear, puttered nervously with the cloth, wiping and wiping at the long inside length of his right arm. It was so pale it glowed, skin taut against muscle. She wiped at his hand, which she held open for access, half noting its wide, creamy surface and dark rivulets of lines, the incredibly soft texture of his fingertips.

Why was time crawling all of a sudden, and how soon could she check the thermometer so she could get away? She reached up with her free hand to feel his forehead, but moving seemed to take an exorbitant amount of effort, and the distance to his forehead seemed endless. His forehead felt cold and wet. Hadn't he just been burning up? No, it was her own hand that was damp and cold. How could she tell anything?

She should feel relieved that he appeared to be recovering, lying there looking up at her with a gaze as pressing as a stone. But a heavy, nauseous, foreboding feeling was gathering in her groin. She was the one who was sick; she was sick.

He was staring, sunk into the dark couch as though he were floating on a velvet sea. With his black curly hair and bare chest he looked like some Greek boy nymph or something, and she could not get off her knees. She suddenly thought of a million things she should go check in the house while the thermometer did its thing and the seconds crawled by. A breeze from the windows stirred the hair at her neck. She witnessed the skin on his smooth chest attenuating into a field of tiny bumps in that same breeze, and it seemed to have more clarity, more intensity of light, than anything she had ever seen. The cloth was leaden. Her hand lay heavily on his arm, immobilized.

He took the thermometer from his mouth, reached up to cup the back of her neck, pulled her down, kissed her.

At the first touch of his lips, an electric tide washed through her body. It was like being hit by a truck, the force of it; it was like being injected with hot and cold fluids at the same time. She could feel the chemicals rush madly through every part of her, from her tingling crown to the tips of her fingers and toes (suddenly numb), to her constricted chest, her trembling legs, her utter core of awareness, which was now located deep and low in her abdomen.

He surged up against her, urgent yet impossibly soft and fluid at the same time. It was as if she were melting into him, as if he were a river current sucking her down, his lips, tongue, soft and dangerous as the rushing tides. She could *feel* his passion, so dense the heat of it burned in her mouth like a glowing sun. Or was that her own passion? Her mouth was responding with a will of its own, seeking out every bit of him as if he were the air and she was dying with need of it. His fingertips grasped her arms, pulling her down and down even while his body arched up to meet her. It was a moment with a relentless, inescapable drive, a forward surge with only one possible end.

But. But. Her mind was strong. Her fear was stronger. She did what every human cell in her body was screaming at her *not* to do: she pushed him away, fell awkwardly back on her rear, scrambled to her feet, ran to her bedroom, and locked the door, choking on a sob.

She did not hear him leave, but when she finally summoned the courage to check, perhaps an hour later, he had gone.

The next day she could not, would not, avoid the lab on Nate's account, though she'd rather have faced a firing squad. She had a speech prepared in her head and gave it, clumsily, about student–teacher relationships, about age differences, about how they both knew that certain . . . physical propensities . . . seemed to be exacerbated by the experiment and that while she didn't blame him exactly, the important thing was to remain objective and *observe* the effects and not contaminate this incredibly important work with even a whiff of impropriety, and blah de blah de blah.

He didn't look at her through most of it, held his shoulders stiff as a shield against her words. But when she was done, he turned and gave her a look of such regret and . . . *pity* that she felt herself break into a million pieces, as if her very identity were fragmenting into nothingness.

Then he began to comment on the mice and it was over.

*   *   *

A week later, Jill was in her office going over her mail and feeling particularly pleased by an expected and late tax rebate check. She got a cramp of genuine hunger, the first in days. She was suddenly voracious.

She crossed the campus, heading for the restaurants on University Street . . .

and saw Nate. He was under a tree on the lawn with a girl, a student by the look of it, and they were lying side by side. He was kissing her, with great care, their bodies not touching. But the whole world existed where their lips met; anyone could see that: infinitely deep, infinitely sweet.

A gasp of pain and longing stabbed through her. She steadied herself, as if she'd been physically struck, then turned around and went back to her office, where she sat for an hour, arms wrapped around her stomach, trying to subdue the physical and emotional rampage wreaking havoc inside her body.

After that she saw less of Nate in the lab. He was always there when it was time to go over the day's results, but at other times, when she'd normally find him just hacking around or watching the subjects, he was gone.

After a while, she was able to look back on the situation with relief. She'd avoided a nasty and highly unprofessional entanglement. She even called it courage. And when they reached the 50 percent differential in their experiment, Jill, who should have stopped there, did not. She felt reckless and a little wild. She wanted . . . needed . . . *more*.

She told Nate to turn it up.

6.2. AHARON HANDALMAN

TEL AVIV

It was only a sixty-two-kilometer drive from Jerusalem to Tel Aviv, but Aharon came here as little as possible. Tel Aviv was a beach town, a secular city. Here one saw few, if any, *haredim* in the streets, but there was an abundance of bikini tops and torn-off shorts. In Aharon's opinion, which he would happily relay should anyone ask, it was a modern-day Sodom. He'd chosen a Sunday to make the trip. He did not tell Hannah where he was going. Wasn't today going to be bad enough without his wife making a fuss?

It was with a very glum face that he approached the apartments for the elderly on Ben-Gurion Street. It was not a cheap place, these apartments. Someone must be doing well. As he took the elevator up to the third floor, the sight of an old woman shuffling along with a mangy cat and the distinctive odor of the elderly did little to cheer him up. From dismal to more dismal—and he hadn't even spoken to the man yet!

Steeling himself, like Joshua going into battle, Aharon knocked on the door. He had to look down on the man who answered. He was under five feet tall and frail-looking. What was left of his hair was so thin you could see the mottled scalp beneath. The face was pale between the discolorations, the lips slackened into a watery consistency.

The man blinked looking up at him, as if trying to place his face. "Rabbi Kaufman?"

"No. This is Rabbi Handalman. I called about coming today. Is it Karl Biederer?"

The old man held out a trembling hand. "Yes. I forgot a little, that's all." Then, "It's not a crime."

"May I come in?"

"Yes. Come in; come in."

Biederer shuffled back into the interior and Aharon followed. He watched as Biederer looked out into the hallway—both ways—then shut and locked the door, putting on two dead bolts.

Biederer headed to what Aharon assumed was the kitchen. "Tea?"

"Herbal?"

"Of course, herbal."

"Then, yes, I would like some. Thank you."

While Biederer puttered in the next room, Aharon removed his coat and outdoor hat, placing them carefully on a chair. He put an automatic hand to the wool *kippa* still on his head, to check that it was in place. He looked around.

The room was a plain but modern apartment with white textured walls. The furniture was old, dusty, out of place in this architecture. The sofa looked continental, with faded silk brocade and ornate carved wood that was chipped and dull. Nothing else matched this eyesore, and the general air was one of clutter. The air was rancid.

The closed, smelly apartment did nothing to inspire comfort in an anxious soul. There was a large window on the far wall and the day outside was sunny, but Biederer had the blinds drawn tight as a fist against the light.

"Here." Biederer brought in two cups of tea on a metal cookie sheet and put them ungracefully on the American West wagon-wheel coffee table.

"So sit," he offered, lowering himself into a Biederer-shaped hollow on the sofa.

Aharon was at the blinds. "Would it be a bother if I . . ." He motioned to the window.

"No," Biederer said in a reasonable tone. "If you don't mind killing me."

Aharon smiled faintly and took a seat. The tea smelled all right, but some crusted bits on the side of the cup put him off. He sighed. *Just get it over with.*

"Mr. Biederer, I wanted to speak with you about Yosef Kobinski. You were in the same barrack at Auschwitz."

"So you said on the phone. See, I remember."

"Yes. I'm looking for information about his work."

Biederer studied Aharon with a pained expression. "What's so important that I should dredge that all up again? What do you want with Kobinski?"

Aharon hadn't expected the question, but he was a truthful man. Telling a *little* truth, however, as opposed to spilling one's guts, was also perfectly acceptable. "I teach at the *Aish HaTorah* in Jerusalem. I also do Torah code research. You have heard of the Torah code?"

Biederer made a dismissive "of course" gesture.

"As it happens, I found some references to Rabbi Kobinski in the code, so I want to learn more about him."

Biederer was plundering his lower lip with his tongue. Aharon resigned himself to a long list of questions about Kobinski and the code, but the old man only shrugged, "Nu," as if he was not surprised, and began to talk.

"I was entombed in Auschwitz on September 18, 1942. That's what I call it—entombed. My family was from Nuremberg. My father was a banker, a rich man, but even this couldn't save us. Now, my son is also a banker." Biederer waved a hand at the room. "He pays for all this."

"I'm sorry, who?" Aharon had brought a tape recorder, in case the man said anything important about Kobinski, and he was fumbling to get it started.

"My *son*."

"Oh. Yes. He must be a comfort."

Biederer shrugged, but his eyes were warm. The warmth didn't last. "I was only fifteen when I arrived at Auschwitz. You would not believe how old you can be at fifteen."

The tape recorder safely churning on the wagon wheel, Aharon sat back a bit, breathing hard from the effort or from stress. He hoped Biederer wouldn't go on too much about his own experiences.

"Didn't Rabbi Kobinski also arrive at Auschwitz around that time?"

"He was in the barrack when I arrived. He and his son, Isaac." Biederer had a distant look in his eye, his lips turned down. "Well, if it's going to be like this . . ." He got up from the sofa, with clever positioning of strengthless limbs, and went to a little table. From a drawer he took a pack of cigarettes, a lighter, and an ashtray.

"So open the window," he said to Aharon as he crossed back to the couch. "But just crack it at the bottom; don't open the shades."

Aharon cracked it as much as he thought he'd get away with and pulled the closed blinds up an inch to free them from the draft. The room was a little lighter as a result, and there was a tiny bit of fresh air. The effect was soon ruined by the pall of cigarette smoke.

"Want one?" Biederer offered.

"No thank you," Aharon said, stiffly enough to show his disapproval.

"Now. Kobinski." Biederer pulled hard on his cigarette. "I was only fifteen and my family was not so religious. But even I knew that he was a great *tzaddik*—a saint. You should have seen the man. . . ." He rolled the tip of his cigarette in the ashtray. "He looked different from the rest, like there was a kind of peace over him, you know? Like he was strolling down the nicest street you could imagine, as if there weren't bedbugs the size of grapes infesting the urine-stained mattresses we had to sleep on, all crammed together, as if . . . "

Biederer's voice shook. He stopped himself, was quiet for a moment. "*Everything*, everything, he took in stride. It helped. You cannot imagine how it helped. You could look at that man, and while you saw his face, you could pretend there was still a God."

Aharon shifted in the chair. He was warm in his long sleeves and black vest, and the apartment was getting warmer as the sun grew in strength in the sky. He was sweating. The mental effort of keeping his brain like a fortress, only letting in the information he wanted to hear, didn't help. "Is there anything specific you remember about his background, maybe something he said about his work? Did he ever mention . . . Did he say anything about a weapon?"

"Who's telling the story here?"

Aharon frowned. "I do understand the general conditions of Auschwitz. I'm only interested in Kobinski."

Biederer squinted at him appraisingly, the way a father does, trying to figure out what his son has done that gives him such a guilty look.

"Uh-huh." Biederer's face melted into a knowing and not particularly friendly look. "In our barrack we had something like two hundred to two hundred fifty prisoners. We slept three in a bunk, with bunks three stories high."

"Yes, I know," Aharon said futilely. The old fool was going to insist; what could he do?

"We had lice, we had bedbugs, and we had typhus. Food we didn't have. Water we didn't have. A place even to wash ourselves—soap, just plain soap—we didn't have. You think I didn't mind because I was fifteen? Had I ever had as dirty a day in my life before that? Never!"

Aharon felt a burning swatch on his back where the light from the bottom of the window struck him, scorching like a brand. "Rabbi Kobinski's work . . ."

"Some thought he was mad, you know. There were two kinds: the kind who thought he was mad and the kind who thought he was a saint. Myself, I went for the saint. Why not? What else did we have to hope for? In the evenings, he would pray and people would gather to hear him. The *capo* got tired of beating him for it—he never seemed to mind being beaten. He scared the *capo*—a nasty *Schwein* named Gröding. The rebbe scared a lot of people."

"Scared them? What do you mean?"

"Walking around immune to it all. You cannot imagine how frightening this is. Because the reality," Biederer held his fingers together in a strong gesture, "the *reality* . . ." He bounced that hand, looking for words. "It was like walking on a tightrope. You had to be alert every second. You let down your guard for an instant, and you're dead. And here was someone who was oblivious! It was a miracle or a terrible danger; no one knew which. And he did this chanting. The first time I noticed Kobinski he was chanting under his breath and making signs all around the room—first on the wooden posts of the bunk where he and Isaac slept, then in all four corners of the room, in the center, on the doorways leading out."

Biederer stopped deliberately and took drag after drag on that stinking cigarette.

"The *capo* barks at him, 'What are you doing there! Stop it at once!' and Kobinski ignores him. Gröding tries to pull his arm, to pull him away, but Kobinski is a *tree*. He doesn't budge, not even his arm, not even *a little*. And Gröding was not a weak man! So everyone whispers—'the rebbe has magic,' 'he's got supernatural strength,' 'God won't let Gröding disturb him.' Gröding gets red in the face, says loudly to everyone that the man is insane—a simpleton—and then he leaves like he can't be bothered.

"After that, you couldn't see those letters Kobinski had written with his bare finger, but everyone knew they were there. People rubbed the posts of his bunk, the doorways, anyplace he'd marked." Biederer smiled. It was a brittle, miserly thing. "I'm telling you, it didn't *always* go so easy with Kobinski as that bit with Gröding, but many people believed he had magic."

"He was a kabbalist," Aharon said, clearing his throat.

"Yes, a kabbalist. Of course, typical Jews, some of the men pooh-poohed kabbalah, even some of the religious. But not to his *face* they didn't!"

"What did he say to people? Did he just make marks in the air or what?"

"Say?" Biederer looked at him as if the concept were foreign. "He talked to his followers, but I never dared go over. I was afraid of being noticed. But I did hear him say—and people would quote him—he'd say, 'The world is a balance of good and evil. It is a physical *law*. So it can only get so bad before things have to get better.' Of course, *they* made sure to teach him otherwise."

Aharon wiped his forehead. So hot! "What about his work? Did he ever mention a weapon? Or talk about physics?"

Biederer glared at him dully. He finished his cigarette and lit another. "He was writing a book. His followers would bring him anything they could find: toilet paper, butcher's paper, even dry leaves he would write on. This, too, the men in the barrack fought about. Some thought he endangered all of us with such things. But his followers would always defend! There was one—Anatoli, a Russian Jew. The man was a fanatic. He followed Kobinski around like a dog.

"As for myself, I thought they should leave him alone, let him write. Even though he didn't have the strength, who did? He worked all day, and in the evening he would write, always, like a madman, as if all day he had been writing in his head and this was his only chance to put it down on paper. If there was moonlight, he would go sit by a window or the crack of a door after lights-out, long after I fell asleep. I don't know why, but Gröding always turned a blind eye to this."

"What happened to the book?"

Biederer shrugged. "Anatoli was in charge of that. I think he buried it; I don't know. Only he and the boy knew where it went."

"The boy?"

"Kobinski's son, Isaac."

Aharon took a breath, wanting to get it over with. "Isaac died in Auschwitz, too."

Biederer nodded. For some reason this, specifically, brought tears to his eyes, incapacitated his voice. Aharon waited. Biederer dragged on his cigarette.

"In the end," Biederer said at last, "not magic, not kabbalah, not the greatest rabbi in Europe meant *this* against the Nazis." He snapped his fingers.

"Well," said Aharon weakly. "If there's nothing you can remember about his work . . ." He got up.

"Siddown." Biederer's voice was menacing. "You started this." He pointed at Aharon with his cigarette. "Now you *listen*."

"But if there's nothing more specific about—"

"You don't know what I know," Biederer said, tapping his temple. The frail old man had suddenly become very hard, dark with anger and other undefined emotions. Aharon found himself shaking, not out any real fear, of course, but from a sense of impending ruin that hovered over him, as it had at Yad Vashem. He felt confined, harried, like a turtle being poked with sticks. Weakly he sat.

"You think this is bad, this little nothing?" Biederer's watery lips hardened in disdain. "You people! You've heard *makkes*, my friend, *nothing*! *This* story . . ." he trailed off, as if not able to find an expletive large enough. "You wait." He pointed again at Aharon with his cigarette. "You wait."

Biederer stubbed out the half-smoked cigarette, lit another. By now the room was not only hot but also hazy with smoke. The six-inch gap in the window was not letting the smoke out fast enough. He had a fuzzy cast to him, as if viewed through Vaseline. This only added to the impression that time was becoming thinner, that the past was closer. Even the taste of smoke in Aharon's mouth could have been any smoke, even that of the ovens.

"There was this guard; Wallick was his name. He and Kobinski . . . it was a battle between them, a battle to the death."

"Why?"

"Why? Because Wallick took it as a challenge to break Kobinski, that's why—to bring him down into the dirt and horror with the rest of us *pishers*. If Kobinski's saintliness intimidated Gröding, it only made him the special target of Wallick. And let me tell you—you didn't want to be a special target of any of those demons, but particularly not Wallick."

"Wallick killed Kobinski?" Aharon asked, glimpsing an end to this story.

"Killed him? He wanted to *break* him. Can you break a dead man?"

"I really don't need to—"

"He beat him, often. Every time he saw him. With a stick he beat him—sometimes just a little, sometimes a *lot*, till there was blood covering his face. Even in a place like Auschwitz, where you saw *everything*, it was still upsetting to see such a great rebbe covered with blood like this."

"I think I—"

"Then there was mealtime. Wallick would come through after we'd been served our nothing soup of water and potato peelings, and he'd always time it just so. Anyone else in the same situation would have gobbled the soup in line, as soon as they got it, but Kobinski never did. Can you imagine it? Day after day he stands in line, gets his soup, smiles at the inmates handing it out, waits for his son, walks calmly to find a place to sit—never hurries, never acts as if anything were wrong. Then as soon as he sits—bam—Wallick comes along and knocks the bowl from his hands. And Kobinski just sits there, looking at the spilled soup while everyone else goes after it on hands and knees, eating the wet *dirt* trying to get a little nutrition."

Biederer sighed. "I'll tell you who it hurt—his son, Isaac. Sometimes I saw tears running down his face as they walked away from the line with their pitiful bowls. Once I heard him urge his father as they walked past me, 'Eat, Papa; eat now,' and his father said, 'We must first find a seat,' in a pleasant voice. Oh, the poor boy—what a curse, to have such a great rebbe for a father!"

Something trembled on the tip of Biederer's tongue, trembled like the moisture on the edges of his eyelids. But he shook his head. "One thing at a time." He took an enormous breath. "What else did Wallick do to Kobinski? Latrine duty, all the time. Horrible. Truly horrible, such a great scholar crawling around in absolute filth. Disgusting! Wallick wouldn't allow him any help during the day, but when his followers got back from their own labor sometimes he would still be at it and they'd finish for him."

Biederer pointed those smoking fingers at Aharon. White streamers drifted around his face like premonitions of his shroud. "I'm telling you, the stink of such a place—you can take it maybe two minutes without vomiting. Buckets and buckets of the worst . . . ! It's not just normal slops, see. Everyone was sick with diarrhea, typhus, every illness known to man. And the smell starvation gives a man's guts . . . ! This is hell, I'm telling you."

"Please," Aharon said weakly. He *could* smell it. A distinct scent of urine and feces was in his nostrils. He stood up and went over to the window, no longer caring about Biederer. He opened it fully, pulling up the blinds. He leaned out and gulped in fresh air. But the air outside was so hot by now that it did little to clear his head, only sat in his lungs like wet towels.

"But none of this—*none* of it broke Kobinski."

Biederer's voice came from behind his head, like the voice of the dead. There was that heavy weight in the old man's voice again, something large unsaid. But this time, Aharon had the feeling he *would* say it. Aharon couldn't stop him. He couldn't even open his mouth to talk.

"Not . . ." Biederer said with a thick tongue, "not until Wallick began to mess with his *son*."

"*Please, Lord.*" Hot tears of pain and frustration filled Aharon's eyes. He pushed against the sill to stand. He went over to the chair and picked up his coat. "*Shalom,* Mr. Biederer."

"Okay, Rabbi Handalman," Biederer said, his hands out and down in surrender.

"No, I'm sorry, but—"

"So I'll *stop*," Biederer said firmly.

Aharon stood still, coat and hat in hand. The sweat tickled as it ran down his cheeks into his beard. Biederer made a gesture upward with his outstretched hands—*nu?*

"I don't need to hear any more." Aharon put on his hat.

"There's *more.* So we'll skip the son. I can't say I blame you there. But I have something you want. It's about the rebbe's work. So sit."

Aharon fingered his coat for a moment. He slowly removed his hat and returned to his seat. He was beginning to hate Biederer. The old sadist, he had some kind of perverted desire to pass along that black chip in his heart, poisonous and festering.

"It was after Wallick had . . . well, Isaac was no longer in our barrack."

"He was dead," Aharon said with a resigned sigh.

"No," Biederer said, eyes bright and terrible. He took another cigarette. "But you don't want to hear about that, so you won't hear. Since you're so delicate, Rabbi Handalman. I know your type. Yes, I know your type."

Aharon clenched his fists on his hat brim. "Say what you have to say."

"After Isaac left the barrack Kobinski finally began to wake up to reality—you know what I'm saying? He became obsessed with finding a way out of Auschwitz. Somehow Anatoli managed to smuggle in a map of the area. Kobinski pored over that map, drawing lines and numbers. Some said he was using astrology; others said it was devils' work."

Aharon sat forward on his chair rigidly. What was this?

"He told us he had found a gateway." Biederer looked sheepish, as if knowing it sounded crazy. "A gateway to . . . to Heaven. It was out in the woods, about a mile from camp. If we could only get *to* it."

Aharon felt a surge of disappointment. This was what he had come here for? Sat through all this horrible sewage of the past? "That's ludicrous!"

Biederer shrugged. He leaned back, tapped his foot, but there was a stubborn look in his eye, the look of a true believer. "Maybe. And maybe some people even back then didn't believe him—maybe *most* people. But some *did*," pointing his cigarette/fingers at Aharon. "Some said he was a great kabbalist, that he could call down a heavenly chariot like Ezekiel. And maybe some just thought they had nothing to lose."

"This is the escape attempt?" Aharon said, connecting this with what he'd read at Yad Vashem. Biederer nodded.

Aharon huffed. "But everyone was killed that night! Rabbi Kobinski—may he rest in peace—he must have been driven over the edge. I'm sorry for it, but it's true."

Biederer leaned forward and took his cup, drank from it. He shook his head. "No, Rabbi Handalman."

"How do you know?"

"Because it worked."

Aharon stared at him, astonished. There was something so calm and triumphant on Biederer's face that Aharon was intimidated to stillness.

"You can think what you like—who can stop you? But what happened, happened. I didn't go. I was afraid; that's God's truth. About ten men from our barrack went. Only two returned—Anatoli was one of them. They managed to slip away from the others in the darkness and made it back to camp. They told us."

"Yes?"

Biederer's wizened face was practically glowing. "That night they got out of the camp and reached the place where Kobinski said they would find the gateway. The guards caught up with them there. They rounded up the prisoners, were going to bring them back to camp to be executed. But Kobinski challenged Wallick, and they struggled—hand to hand, *hand to hand* . . . like Jacob wrestling with the angel!"

Biederer closed his eyes, his face triumphant, as though he was viewing in his mind's eye a scene he had imagined many times before. He took one last drag on his cigarette, holding the moment on his tongue. "Then the chariot *did* come, in a flash of light, and took them both."

"What?"

"*They disappeared*, Rabbi Handalman. Kobinski and Wallick together— vanished! And no one ever saw either one of them again."

*   *   *

The older children were playing quietly in the apartment courtyard with the neighbor children. The baby was asleep in her crib. Hannah Handalman sat at the kitchen table, looking out the window.

She knew Aharon had gone to Tel Aviv to see one of the survivors on her list, Biederer. He didn't tell her. He was going for a drive alone, he said. But he didn't go for drives, her husband. Jerusalem was all the world to him. Where else would he go on a whim? And then there was the look on his face, the look of a man going to a dentist for a root canal.

Hannah was fighting temptation. She'd had the misfortune to notice that

Aharon had left his bags in the hall last night and that one of them, a large black bag, was the bag that contained the Kobinski array binder. When Aharon left this morning, he did not take it with him.

Unfortunately, that left her in a predicament. She told herself her husband had been very clear about not wanting her interference. But then, she thought perversely, *she* had been very clear about wanting him to spend more time with her and the children. And did *she* get *that*? No.

The more she contemplated the situation, the more hotly rebellion burned in her breast; it was like a clawed little mammal with a mind of its own. If Aharon had been a loving husband, if he'd been warm and tender and asked her nicely, there was nothing she wouldn't do for him. Their marriage itself proved that.

There had been a time when she had considered a life other than this. There had been a time when she had friends who wore blue jeans and mocked tradition. When she married Aharon, she understood that she was signing up for the life of her parents. But he had been so handsome and fiery, standing at their dinner table speaking passionately about the Torah, he'd made her believe in it all again. The dramatic young Torah scholar! A jewel of Jewish manhood! She'd thought he was the rock upon which she could anchor her belief, that the world of the *frum* made sense as long as their love was in the center of it. What she hadn't understood was that the lifestyle she'd chosen would go on and on, but his ardor for her would not. What she had taken for a rock had been no more substantial than passion's first blush. What bride understood this?

She had already disobeyed him a little. Her parents, bless them, had moved to Israel to be close to their grandchildren shortly after Yehuda was born. The last time she'd visited them with the children she'd seen her younger brother, Samuel, surfing on the Internet. Would there be—she'd asked him— an on-line network of Holocaust survivors? With a little searching, Samuel found a newsgroup. He posted a message there under her direction:

> *Looking for anyone who knew Rabbi Yosef Kobinski, Lodz ghetto and Auschwitz.*

She was almost relieved they hadn't heard anything back yet. Of course, she hadn't told Aharon. It had been a whim. Nothing would come of it.

The children were playing quietly below; the baby was sleeping.

The binder was heavy. She got it onto the kitchen table, where she could still watch the children. But after a while she forgot to watch, and when they came in an hour later she plopped them down in the living room with new coloring books she'd been saving for a rainy day and continued searching.

*   *   *

All the way back to Jerusalem, Aharon could not stop seeing the scene Biederer had painted: the frail camp prisoner, Kobinski, dressed in filthy stripes, and the sharply dressed Nazi guard, Wallick, struggling hand to hand, the one hopelessly outmatched but determined, the other toying, cruelly, and then the two of them vanishing to the astonishment of the onlookers.

Ezekiel's chariot. Even he could see that stank of mythmaking. *A flash of light.* Could it have been the weapon? Could Kobinski have managed to make the weapon, somehow? Had it been on him that night? Had the two of them been vaporized? Or was there something else going on entirely?

By the time Aharon reached home it was late. He dragged himself in the door with the weariness of the walking dead.

"It's about time," Hannah said to him, coming from the kitchen. Her cheeks were pink. "I started supper. It's chicken."

"I'm not hungry. So where are the children?" he called out, louder. "My son and daughter don't have a kiss for their papa?"

The children used to run to him when he entered, but they hadn't for months now. Devorah and Yehuda peeked cautiously from the living room. Aharon knelt down, held out his arms.

"Come here, Devehleh."

The little girl ran to him with restrained eagerness. Then Yehuda. Aharon found himself clinging to the boy. Yehuda, his eldest, his son, was nine years old—the same age as Isaac Kobinski in that picture. He turned his wooly face to the boy's small shoulder when he felt tears.

"Papa, what's the matter?"

Aharon let him go, pushed himself upright. "Nothing. Everything's fine; why shouldn't it be?" He wiped his eyes. His son and daughter stared up at him in shock until he shooed them back to their games. He felt weighted with grief, as if he'd been sitting *shivah.*

"*Aharon,*" Hannah said, tenderly, but she didn't come to him.

He wanted to reach out for her, but the gap felt so wide. He rubbed his lips with trembling fingers. "I'm not hungry, but maybe I should eat."

"Come into the kitchen while I cook. Come on."

The baby was in the kitchen high chair, happily munching on a sliced apple. Aharon kissed the warm and scented top of her head before slumping into a seat. Hannah used tongs to turn the pieces of chicken in a hot pan, then came to sit with him. "Was it so bad?"

He looked at her. Of course she had guessed where he'd been. "Oh, Hannah. I don't know what I'm doing anymore. Am I tracking a madman? Am I crazy myself? What?"

"Shhhh." She patted his hand.

"God has given this to me, and I'm failing Him. I'm not capable. Nothing is fitting together. Nothing makes any sense!"

He knew this dark emotional tide was temporary. It was the images Biederer had tried to poison him with, not just that last battle in the woods but all of the terrible atrocities. And he had never, *never* wanted this.

"God knows what He's doing!" he said fiercely. "If He punishes, there must be a good reason. Who are we to question?"

Hannah regarded him with wary concern. "You had a bad day. Tomorrow you'll feel better."

"*Lo.*"

"Stop then," Hannah said impulsively. "Aharon, please. Sometimes you have such a look . . . I'm afraid for you."

"God wants what He wants. Jonah tried to run away. Look where it got him." The words, and all they brought with them of the simple, straight-forward God of the Torah, made him feel better. He sat up a bit straighter and searched in his pocket for a handkerchief.

"What?" he asked, because the fact that his wife had something to tell him was written all over her face.

"Nothing."

"There's something, *what*?"

"I . . ." She shook her head and leaned forward in her chair, burying her face against his vest. "I love you, Aharon Handalman. I still love you."

"Of course," he said, but he heard the doubt in her voice and gripped her tightly.

7

───────── ⁂ ─────────

When it was taken seriously, Copernicus' proposal raised many gigantic problems for the believing Christian. If, for example, the earth were merely one of six planets, how were the stories of the Fall and of the Salvation, with their immense bearing on Christian life, to be preserved? If there were other bodies essentially like the earth, God's goodness would surely necessitate that they, too, be inhabited. But if there were men on other planets, how could they be descendants of Adam and Eve, and how could they have inherited the original sin, which explains man's otherwise incomprehensible travail on an earth made for him by a good and omnipotent deity?
—Thomas Kuhn, *The Copernican Revolution,* 1957

Failure to adjust early in evolution may be just what is needed for success later on, that stress and strife are ingredients of long-range harmony, that pain is vital to birth and creation.
—Guy Murchie, *Seven Mysteries of Life,* 1978

7.1. Jill Talcott

August
Seattle

THE ONE PULSE, 90 PERCENT POWER

She probably should have stopped at 75 percent power. But Jill Talcott had too much at stake to play it safe. And since no one except Nate knew what she was doing, there was no one to advise her otherwise.

She did *try* to get advice. The thought of Dr. Ansel had been more and more on her mind. She wanted very much to talk to him about her discovery and what it might mean. He was practically the only person she *could* speak to. But there was the business of the bad parting holding her back.

When she finally gathered her courage to call, a secretary answered and she was transferred to Tom Cheever, the head of the department.

"Jill Talcott? You were Dr. Ansel's graduate student? I guess that was before my time. I've been here five years."

"Yes," Jill agreed, feeling guiltily relieved. Cheever didn't know her, which was good. Not that Ansel had made a big deal out of her transferring to another professor. It probably hadn't been a big deal to anyone but her, but—

"What is it that you're working on now?" Cheever asked.

"Work? Um . . . wave mechanics. I'm at the University of Washington."

"Wave mechanics," Cheever repeated faintly.

"I don't understand. I called to speak to Dr. Ansel. Is he on sabbatical, or—"

"I'm sorry you hadn't heard. Henry . . . Dr. Ansel passed away last month."

Jill was floored. He'd been in his late fifties when she worked with him and far from decrepit. She felt a grief that was genuine, if self-interested. "Jesus. What happened?"

"He . . . took some pills."

He took some pills? Ansel had committed suicide. A terrible coldness sluiced through her. How far down he must have sunk into the cesspool of shame and dishonor to do such a thing. How hopeless he must have felt. It was awful, terrible. She felt bad for Ansel, but the worst part was that she could practically taste that fate as her own. The horror she felt was as much for herself as for him.

It took a moment for logic to override emotion. That *wasn't* going to happen to her. That would never happen to her. Because she had *proven* her theories. And when she finally spoke out she would have so much evidence that no one would be able to refute her.

"Dr. Talcott?"

"I'm here. Thank you for—"

"We were friends. I know many people here didn't believe in Henry's work, but I did. I knew quite a bit about his work. Things other people didn't know."

Jill was starting to feel uneasy. Something wasn't adding up. Ansel had been a nice man, a very nice man, but he'd also been pretty stubborn. It was hard enough to imagine that he'd gotten so battered down that he'd committed suicide. But if he'd had the support of his department head . . . ?

Things other people didn't know.

Cheever's voice lowered. "If you're working on anything *close* to what Henry was working on, then I really think we should—"

"God, I'm sorry; look at the time. I have to go."

Jill hung up. She stared at the phone for a minute, her mouth dry. She would give anything—yes, she wished very, very much that she hadn't made that phone call.

Her mind raced through the possibilities. Ansel hadn't had access to a quantum computer. Therefore, even if he had turned to wave mechanics after she'd left, even if he'd come up with her exact equation, he would never have been able to test it. Therefore, it was unlikely he even suspected the existence of the one-minus-one. And even if he did, he couldn't have had more than a vague idea about it. She went over it several more times, but she was certain her logic was correct.

She put her head in her hands and sighed deeply. Her work was safe. And even if Ansel *had* been close to some of her theories, as long as she didn't know the details no one could accuse her of plagiarism. Part of her knew that she was being paranoid. Cheever had just wanted to talk; he'd sounded perfectly nice.

But she wasn't going to let him steal her work.

August 15. The morning was warm and sunny. The newspapers proclaimed it had been one of the driest, hottest summers on record in Seattle. Jill, to whom the sun was merely an eye-blinding annoyance on her forays from class to basement lab to her house, wished for rain. She was finishing up some journal entries regarding her students' grades. She had begun to notice some weeks back that the papers and tests were quite a bit better than normal, so she had dug out files from last summer and compared them. The scores *were* much higher this year, sending the bell curve lofting in the middle like a cat's arching spine. But since they were different students, there was no *verifiable* correlation. . . .

She heard the door open with that sucking sound the rubberized curtain gave off, and Nate entered the lab. A black leather motorcycle jacket was slung over one tanned arm. The rest of him was clad in blue jeans and a black T-shirt. She found it annoying that he was looking less like a frumpy science student and more and more like his funky co-residents on Capitol Hill. He'd purchased a motorcycle this summer with some financial windfall or other and the black leather gear had triggered a chain reaction. First his hair had been cropped to a thick nubby cut; then he'd colored it with a fluorescent blond on top that made the olive in his skin shine like gold. He'd had a hoop punched into one earlobe where it glittered against his dark neck, and he'd lost a good fifteen pounds. He looked amazing, even younger now than his twenty-eight years. It made Jill feel pathetically old and unhip by comparison.

"I thought you'd be late today. The 520 bridge is closed, isn't it?" Perhaps, Jill thought, he hadn't gone over to Linda's last night, hadn't had to take the bridge back this morning. He'd made such a point of telling her about his staying with his girlfriend in Bellevue, so she'd know why he was late in the mornings, he said, though she suspected a bit of face rubbing was involved. Her face had stung afterward, at any rate.

Nate tossed his jacket and helmet on the coatrack and put on a protective apron. "They finished up two days early. God bless the highway department."

"Hmmm."

"It was beautiful driving over the lake this morning. The water was like *glass* and it had this deep greenish-blue color. The sky was *flawless.*"

"Huh." Jill moved over to the objects on the table. *Here's a topic of conversation,* she thought, *the experiment.* "The growth rate is still slowing down on the virus, and the mice aren't as hyper."

He came over and squatted down beside the mice, his face focused in that utterly dedicated way of his. "They look healthy, just not as active as they were."

"Should we risk putting the males and females back together?"

" 'Kay."

They were up to six cages of mice now, so quickly had the reproduction proceeded before they'd separated the sexes. The homosexual "humping" activity in the male cage had not been noticed for about a week. Perhaps the mice had been shamed to abstinence by some homophobic moralist in their midst. Then again, perhaps they'd lost the drive. Nathan took three male mice out of cage A and three female mice out of cage D and switched them.

Jill and Nate knelt opposite cage A and watched. There was a flurry of mutual sniffing as the mice reacquainted themselves; then the three girl mice settled down near the food, unmolested.

"Being back together might set them off again," Nate suggested.

"Hmmm. Keep logging sexual activity. Every day."

"Mine or theirs?"

If looks could kill, the one she shot him would have been the equivalent of a coronary thrombosis.

"Right." He went over to his computer and opened the mouse file, began taking notes.

"The virus has slowed, too," she said, then remembered she'd already said it. They'd noted all this yesterday afternoon, on their daily rounds, but it seemed from moment to moment she could not help wanting to check it all again. "The fruit just *won't* rot. These bananas are still yellow and it's been a month. The produce industry applications alone could make us rich."

"I know," Nate said, still typing.

She was not kidding. It had occurred to her that they might one day be able to use this technology to delay the decay of food on a large scale. As in ending starvation. Nobel prize, anyone?

She moved over to the equipment table, freshened her cup of coffee. "You want some?"

"Yeah, thanks."

She got him a cup and came over and sat down next to him, yawning a bit. "Are you still keeping that journal?"

"Yes."

"I'd like to see it."

He snorted as if she'd just said she wanted to dissect his liver.

"I *have* to, Nate. It's part of the experiment."

"Does that mean I get to see yours?" he asked dryly, going back to his typing.

"If you'd like." The mere thought made her hyperventilate.

Priority one: Rewrite her journal. Take out the personal bits.

As if reading her mind, Nate said, "I'll rewrite it for you. It'll take a while."

Jill started to protest, knew it would be not only pointless but also hypocritical. "So how *are* you feeling?"

He stopped typing, took a drink of coffee. "Good. Calm." There was a bit of hedging in his voice.

"But not as good as before?"

"Not as *maniacally* good. I'm sleeping better."

"Yes," Jill agreed. "Me, too. Appetite?"

"Functional. I'm still not excited about food, but I'm handling it better than I was. My stomach's calmer. I'm calmer in general. Too calm, almost."

She allowed herself to really look at him, since it was her job. He was so gorgeous, the swine, definitely healthy-looking. And with that half-lidded look of complacency he did seem remarkably relaxed and untroubled. Damn it.

"Yes. And, um . . ." She couldn't say it, no matter how scientific her motivations.

"It's . . . less," he said tightly, then added, more cruelly, "I'm not surprised. I probably *broke* something with Linda."

Jill got up and went over to the mice. They were still there, still not interested in one another. "That's not it," she forced herself to say. "The subjects are showing the same thing. That's very curious. So at seventy-five percent of power on the one pulse, sexual activity and overall stimulation peaks. At ninety percent there appears to be a more mellow kind of well-being. What would be your hypothesis on that one, Nate?"

"Maybe the mice have broken hearts," he muttered.

7.2. DENTON WYLE

OUTSIDE STUTTGART, GERMANY

For a while, things had not looked too good for everyone's pal, Denton Wyle. Of the three names he'd gotten off the E-mail to Uberstühl, two of them had resulted in the purchase of Kobinski pages, negotiated by Mr. Fleck. Unfortunately, neither set of pages contained anything more about black holes or the night of the escape. And the third dealer, a gentleman in Charleston, had taken Schwartz's exclusive, wouldn't talk to Fleck at all.

It might not be a big deal. But it might. Those pages might be *exactly* the ones Denton needed, and now they were gone forever. And Fleck, in his capacity as "adviser," had warned him that Rabbi Schwartz might have been collecting Kobinski for years, might have other pages he'd gotten from private parties or whatnot. Fleck felt it was his "duty" to point that out.

Yeah, thanks. Thanks *a lot.* If it was meant to bother Denton, it worked. It was bothersome the way pins stuck in one's corneas would be bothersome. If Denton really thought about it, which he tried not to, it made him weak-kneed with frustration.

But as Kobinski might say, the pendulum finally swung the other way. Fleck had located a new manuscript fragment. Apparently, when World War Two artifacts were sold among the German community—that is, among those who had been on the non-PC side of the war—they were advertised in certain German small-press magazines, things unlikely to be read by any outsider. The advertisements were discreet and inquiries were responded to with the utmost caution. That's where this nibble had turned up, and Fleck had confirmed that it was, indeed, a Kobinski fragment, one that even Schwartz probably didn't know about.

Denton was on the plane that same afternoon, Fleck's words of warning and instruction glowing in his ear: *Take cash. Don't ask questions. And whatever you do, don't get into politics.*

Denton understood perfectly. He was prepared to kiss some Nazi butt if that was what it took: *You guys lost the war? Bummer, man. I hate when that happens.* But as he drew closer to his destination—a farm in the Schwäbischer area east of Stuttgart—and found himself in a rural landscape where there was about one house per hundred sheep, he felt a leaden reluctance settle in the seat of his pants. His foot eased from the rental car's pedal until he fell far below the speed limit.

Excuse me, his foot was saying, *but are we going to a* Nazi's *house? Out on a farm in the middle of absolutely nowhere? Where the nearest neighbor is good ol' Hans, ten miles down the road? Are you out of your freaking* mind?

"It's okay," he said aloud. "The guy's gotta be pushing eighty. Besides, he has no reason to dislike me. I'm the blond white guy with the bag of money."

He cracked himself up with this and forced his foot down on the pedal. He wanted this *bad.*

His first Kobinski article—which he'd written to get Jack off his ass and start some PR for the book—had been a background piece only. It had talked about the manuscript but hadn't actually printed any of it. Still, it had been a big hit with their audience. He'd laid the groundwork for his black hole theory of vanishings by discussing stories from various religious traditions of mystics visiting other planes of existence, usually called heavens and hells. Heck, the entire Tibetan Book of the Dead was a description of the various worlds one passes through after death. And the Swedish mystic Swedenborg? He claimed to have visited Heaven and Hell on many occasions. He was, you might say, "a regular."

Of course, the leap from mystical visions to believing that a man had used kabbalah magic to physically disappear from Auschwitz was a big one. Then again, the readers of *Mysterious World* were leapin' fools.

But the real meat of the article was courtesy of Loretta. She'd found an almost-eyewitness, a survivor named Biederer in Tel Aviv. Denton had interviewed him over the phone. Biederer's story was amazing—two enemies wrestling, a flash of light . . . But Beiderer had also said something not too cool. He'd mentioned that "other people" had been talking to him recently about Kobinski.

Denton knew very well who those "other people" were: Schwartz!

Denton hadn't seen or heard from the man, not directly. Yet he was convinced that Schwartz knew what he was up to, was doing everything in his power to work against him, was dogging his every move.

The more Denton thought about this whole kabbalah magic thing, the more he'd become convinced that there was some seriously heavy-duty power there. What if Schwartz was the head of some secret fraternity of kabbalist magicians? After all, Schwartz was reputed to be one of the greatest living kabbalists, wasn't he? And the man was so damned secretive. He'd totally lied about his familiarity with Kobinski, tried to put Denton off the scent, tried to block his getting any of Kobinski's work.

Why? Because Kobinski had written big-time kabbalah secrets, that's why. Maybe it wasn't all that clear in the pages Denton had seen so far, but he just knew there were pages out there that contained powerful spells and formulas or whatever of kabbalah. That's why Schwartz didn't want them found.

Which was a little bit scary. Denton's latest imaginings of Schwartz included candlelit rooms in that nice stone building and clusters of chanting bearded-and-fringed men swearing blood oaths and mumbling Hebraic incantations. It included ritual knives intended for Those Who Revealed the Secrets. He wished to God he hadn't seen the movie π.

Denton tried to put the problem of Schwartz from his mind. Because the alternative was to give up, and he couldn't do that. Molly Brad was just the kernel of it; he knew that now. He didn't bother to analyze his motives. He just *wanted it*. And Denton always got what he wanted.

Fortunately he, and not Schwartz, had the services of Mr. Fleck.

When Denton found the address he was able to convince himself to pull into the driveway.

The farm was of medium size. It was late August and the corn was high. The house was large and typically German: white and rectangular with brown beams and window boxes. But the paint was chipped and the only car in the driveway was a small, older economy car. It appeared the German junk police never made it out this far, because a pile of rusting trash sprawled behind the barn. The place was strangely quiet.

Denton got out. He stood for a moment next to his car, certain he was being watched. The house windows were dark and curtained. He had a brief image of a butchery in there, with dripping flanks of meat hanging on hooks in the kitchen. Lovely.

He plastered a smile on his face and crossed on wooden legs to the door. Then he did see a face, a woman's face, studying him and the car from the kitchen window. He turned up the wattage on his smile for her. She came to the door.

"*Ja?*" she asked, opening the door a crack.

"Frau Kroll? I'm Denton Wyle, the buyer Mr. Fleck contacted you about."

She scrutinized him and the car, with the face of someone drinking arsenic, and then she let him in.

"Sit, please, Mr. Wyle," she told him in heavily accented English.

He sat at a pine kitchen table, old but sturdy, with what looked like handmade looped yarn place mats in blue and white. German kitsch. The rest of the kitchen was at least fifty years old, with cabinetry that had not been all that grand to begin with. A rusting long-necked tap stuck out of a cracked basin filled with dishes. The wood floor was sticky and warped under his soles. Denton put his briefcase awkwardly between his feet, still smiling. Without asking, Frau Kroll brought him a cup of coffee. It was hot and thick as sludge.

"Well . . ." he said, not sure how to lead in. *So! Someone in your family was a Nazi?*

It was obviously not Frau Kroll herself. She was in her mid-forties, with a worn, bruised look and a pasty face. The skin around her eyes was brown in raccoonlike rings. Her hair was a thin blond-gray that hung limply on either side of her hard face. Her clothes were old and poorly made. She looked like she could chew nails, and if her chipped teeth were any evidence, she did.

"It's beautiful country," Denton tried. He forced down another sip of coffee, grimacing at the taste.

A man entered the room, making Denton flinch. He was large, ugly, and gangly, as weathered as the woman and around the same age. He wore filthy jeans and a field jacket.

"This is my husband," Frau Kroll told Denton.

"Guten Tag, Herr Kroll." Denton considered rising for a moment and shaking hands, but the man shifted his gaze out the window.

"You have some manuscript pages for sale?" Denton asked Frau Kroll, still smiling.

She went into the next room and returned with an old file folder, very old, it appeared from the faded green color and the thick, they-knew-how-to-make-stuff-back-then cardboard. She placed it on the table and motioned to Denton. "You look."

Denton was definitely getting the sense that these people were as anxious and uncomfortable as he was. He cleared his throat and opened the folder.

Inside, without any further protection whatsoever, were pages of Kobinski's manuscript. Denton knew them at once. The top page was written on a heavy toweling, brown all around the edges, with a bug squashed among the text. It was unexpected to suddenly be right there within finger's reach of an *original*—not in plastic, not under glass, not a Xerox. He drew in a hissing breath.

He looked up. The Krolls were watching him with painful hope and greed.

He wished for tweezers. If he'd been prepared, been professional, he would have brought some. There were more pages under the first, a lot more. In lieu of the proper tools, he carefully closed the folder and, propping it on its fold, tried to open it to the second page, then the third. The first three pages were written on the same toweling—it looked like the same session to him. Beyond this was a page of a faded brown postal wrap, then a short piece on a half sheet of wax paper (ink light and hard to read on that one), then more toweling.

There were *ten pages*. The last two contained nothing but mathematical equations, very neatly and carefully transcribed. Those must be the pages the Yad Vashem entry had mentioned.

Denton must have lingered too long, because Frau Kroll reached for the folder. "Enough," she said, snatching it from him. He wanted to scream at her to be careful, but she placed the folder safely in front of her on the table. He smiled weakly. His dumbfoundedness was misread.

"It's real," the woman insisted, fiddling nervously at the folder's edge. "From my father. He died, eh, few months . . ."

"A few months ago?"

"Yes. He was only a *worker*." She said it fiercely, eyes darting to her husband. "Only cleaning things in the camps. He sleep outside camp."

"Of course." Denton nodded sympathetically. *Yeah, cleaning up things like, oh, Jews.*

"And a few things from the camp he keep." Her eyes darted back to Denton. "This," she poked at the folder, "is from Auschwitz."

"I know it is. I can tell it's genuine."

"Yes, genuine," she said, latching on to the word. A trickle of sweat ran down the side of her face. "You make offer?"

Herr Kroll turned from the window and leaned back against the cracked sink, arms folded over his chest.

"Hmmm. . . ." Denton put his finger to his chin in a pleasant *"well, let's see"* gesture, but inside he was kicking himself around. The Krolls obviously were on their own, didn't even want to pay a commission to an agent. They probably had no idea what the manuscript was worth, and he was getting the distinct impression they were desperate for money. On the other hand, he didn't want to risk offending them. Whatever he started with, they were likely to bid him up.

"Four thousand dollars, U.S.?" he offered, with a lilt to his voice and raised eyebrows to show that he wasn't completely firm on that.

Frau Kroll glanced at her husband, her face neutral. They spoke for some time in German, their voices low and tense.

"You have hotel phone number?" she asked. "We call, yes? Another man comes also today."

No.

"We talk to him first; then we call."

Oh god, no.

"Well, that's not a final offer," Denton stammered. "If you—"

Herr Kroll turned at the sink to look out the window, hearing it the same instant Denton did. Tires. In the driveway.

Oh dear Lord and his host of angels.

Denton got up and peeked out the curtain of the kitchen door. His entire bloodstream turned to antifreeze. Moving up the driveway was a small car, a rental like his. There was a man in the driver's seat wearing a hat, but Denton couldn't see the face. He knew perfectly well who it was, though. He knew perfectly well!

For a moment Denton was frozen, like a rabbit in headlights. Then he turned to his hosts with frantic energy.

"You can't—! I know this guy! He's a rabbi, for god's sake! A complete asshole! He's *a rabbi*!"

The Krolls looked at him in alarm. They conferred in German. They looked upset, but more at his outburst than at the new arrival. Denton realized they didn't know what he was talking about.

"A rabbi! A Jewish priest!"

That the woman comprehended. Her face grew dark and she went over to her husband to look out the window. She gave him the news, which he answered with a louder voice, hand gestures. They began arguing. A car door slammed outside.

Oh dear Jesus Christ.

In his mind Denton saw a bunny cowering in a corner, the wild-eyed, knife-waving chef-Schwartz approaching. He moved as far as he could from the kitchen door.

The Krolls were arguing, but Denton got the feeling the topic was the laxity (H. Kroll) or thoroughness (F. Kroll) of her background checks on her buyers. They didn't seem very focused on the fact that a rabbi was approaching their door. Weren't they going to do something? Chase him away? Grab a gun? Footsteps on the gravel outside.

"I'm telling you," Denton all but screamed, "the guy's a Nazi hunter!"

They both stared at him in shock. There was a knock on the door.

7.3. AHARON HANDALMAN

JERUSALEM

Having Shimon Norowitz's private phone number was some big deal, as it turned out. There was still an answering machine, and Norowitz still didn't call back. Aharon had almost given up when finally, on a hot summer morning, the phone rang and Mr. Big Shot himself was on the line.

"So what have you made of it?" Aharon asked, skipping the preliminaries. "Did your code people come up with statistics?"

"We haven't had time. It's in the queue."

In the queue! Aharon found words in his mouth it could do no good to utter. He scowled at thin air, stumped for a more moderate reply.

"Say, have you got any more of those notebook pages?" Norowitz asked casually. "The ones written by Kobinski in Auschwitz?"

"Why do you ask?"

"Why? Because I want to know."

"I don't have any more."

"So now I know. Do you know of anyone who does?"

Aharon thought this over, his hand tightening on the receiver. "Was there something in the pages? In the math maybe?"

"Not especially."

"But you had someone look at the doodling? Some mathematician?"

There was a pause. "Rabbi Handalman, if I had something to tell you, I'd tell you."

"If you had someone look at it, the least you could do is say so. Out of respect only. Because, remember, I didn't have to bring this to you."

There was a pause. Aharon heard the shuffling of papers. "All right. If you give me a straight answer, I'll give you a straight answer."

"When have I not been straight?"

"Rabbi! Do you know of anyone who has any more material written by Kobinski?"

"No."

"Very well."

"Is that straight enough for you?"

" 'No' is good. Thank you."

"You're very welcome. Now you: Did you have some scientist look at those pages?"

"Yes. Several."

"And they said what?"

Norowitz hesitated. "They said they didn't know what to make of it. That's straight."

Aharon picked at his beard. Straight as a crooked pin, maybe. "Didn't know what to make of it *good* or didn't know what to make of it *bad*?"

Norowitz sighed in exasperation. "Look, I have a very important call coming in. We'll talk in a few weeks."

"Bu—"

Norowitz hung up. Aharon sucked his teeth with his tongue. Kobinski's manuscript. He had dismissed the pages because he hadn't liked them. Maybe, so just maybe, he had dismissed them too soon.

After his last class of the day Aharon took a bus over to Yad Vashem. He felt different about it this time. He didn't realize how different until one of the handles of the curved red doors was in his hand; then he remembered the abhorrence and anger he'd felt that first day. Today he had walked all the way up the drive from the bus stop and had not thought twice. He looked down at the handle in pained surprise, but it was a momentary remembrance. A second later, he was inside and heading for the Hall of Names with other things on his mind.

Anatoli Nikiel. He was Kobinski's most devoted follower, according to Biederer, and his name appeared on Hannah's list of barrack mates still alive. Aharon found the binder and stood in the stacks to read the two-page entry. Anatoli was a Russian Jew, prisoner of Auschwitz, number 173056. His hometown had been Rovno in eastern Russia. He'd been nineteen when sent to Auschwitz in 1943 and was still alive for the liberation in 1944. There was a snippet of camp records, his arrival on such-and-such transport. His name was on a list of those treated by the Americans after the war. There was no current address, nothing about relatives or friends.

Aharon went to the computers where the survivors' testimonies were kept, even though nothing in Anatoli's binder mentioned such a testimony. He searched on Anatoli's name and found *makkes,* zip. Aharon did the numbers in his head. The man would be in his early eighties now, if still alive. *If* alive. He was probably dead.

Aharon sat at the computer until the hostile throat clearings of a young woman broke his reverie. He scowled at her. Her shirt covered her navel, thank god, at least she had that much respect for this place, but fit entirely too tightly at the bosom. In his contemplation of this immodesty his eyes lingered too long on the area, earning him another dirty look as the girl took his seat.

He wiped his hands on his vest. No Anatoli. What did he expect? Yad Vashem, as good as it was, wasn't going to hand him everything on a silver platter.

Now to the other thing he'd come for. He'd been chewing it over since that last phone call with Norowitz. Hannah was listed on the register of people who'd copied Kobinski's manuscript pages. Just thinking about it made his heartburn flare up. He didn't want a man like Norowitz to even know his wife's *name*, much less to have her on some . . . Well, any list of the Mossad's was not a fit place for his wife.

He could go *look* at the ledger. How hard would it be to change her name to his? His own name could be there twice; that made perfect sense. He only had to worry about the *nebbish* at the counter.

The *nebbish* was not at the counter. At the counter instead was a young woman. Aharon gave her the file number he had written down in his little notebook. She looked on her computer.

"I'm sorry. That document has been removed from the collection."

"What are you talking? I saw it myself a few months ago."

"It's listed as unavailable now."

So Aharon went over the number with her again, a digit at a time. He made her turn the computer to face him so he could see she wasn't typing it wrong.

"Why was it removed?" His exasperation was turning to anger.

"I have no idea."

"What genius made such a decision?"

The girl's spine was growing stiffer by the minute. "You can speak with the manager, Mr. Falstein, if you'd like."

"Of course. Yes. If that's what it takes. Go get Mr. Falstein."

She went.

Falstein was not so easily intimidated. His face was already set into a no-nonsense grimace as he approached. "That document has been removed from the public collection."

"For what reason? By whose authority?"

"The document has been removed from the public collection," Falstein said more firmly still. "That's all the information I have."

Aharon was still fuming as he left the document department and began to make his way back through the historical wing. Leave it to a place like this! The one thing of interest in the entire collection, and they took it away from the public. It just went to show that you could have all the money in the world and still be incompetent.

He was halfway through the hall when it occurred to him, like a flash of lightning.

Norowitz. Mossad.

He sank down onto a bench, a smile quivering about his lips. Could it be? Could it be *really*? Yes, it could, and oh-ho! Ah-ha! So Shimon Norowitz, Mr. It's-in-the-queue, was interested after all! Interested *enough*, let's put it that way, that he didn't want anyone else seeing those pages. And he had asked Aharon over the phone if he had any more. Of course Norowitz wanted more! It is written: "A handful does not satisfy a lion."

After a few moments of feeling gratified that he was neither crazy nor useless, it began to dawn on Aharon that maybe . . . maybe the Mossad being interested wasn't such a blessing.

He sat contemplating this turn of events for some time, reasoning through the pros and cons, projecting possibilities, as if he were writing Midrash on the subject. And perhaps it was some of the darker turns in his reasoning that caused him to notice the large photograph right in front of his eyes, or perhaps the photograph subconsciously infused some of his darker thoughts. At length, he found himself staring at the picture.

It was a photograph blown-up and printed on a large posterboard and hung from the ceiling. In the black-and-white image three young Nazis were beating an old Jewish man with the butts of their rifles. He had a long white beard and fedora. The side of his head was bloody. In his hands he clutched a small carpetbag as if it contained all that was important in the world.

Aharon stared at the image for a long, long time. As it settled into him his mind became blank, not thinking, only looking, only *seeing*, really seeing. Then words crossed that blank space like a funeral procession:

The manuscript. What if the danger isn't something that's already occurred, something Kobinski did in the past? What if it's something that hasn't happened yet? Some weapon that will maybe come about through the discovery of his manuscript?

Then: *And I'm the one who told them about it!*

*   *   *

Evil. What is evil? I come back to it again and again. I think I know, and then I realize I know nothing. My equation tells me it is a natural force in the very fabric of space-time. Kabbalah says evil is what happens when the sephirot *are out of balance. I once believed both those things were true at the same time. But what does that explain? Is a little imbalance in the* sephirot *all there is to it? To this hell? To this stinking carnage of pain and piss and death? To our complete abandonment by G-d? To the torment of a beautiful, innocent, precious ten-year-old boy?*

And what about the law of good and evil? Where is the good here? Where is the balance? If one place, one time on earth could convince a placid, lifeless, scholarly Jew that such a theory was complete nonsense, that all his work meant nothing, it would be this time and this place.

Wake up, Kobinski! Here are the questions you should be asking yourself: Who is *responsible? Who made these snakes?*

7.4. DENTON WYLE

OUTSIDE STUTTGART, GERMANY

If Denton could have run past Herr Kroll into the living room of the farmhouse he would have. But he was still debating how weird that would seem when Frau Kroll opened the door.

Denton's eyes rolled in anguish toward the opening and saw a tiny, frail old man in small wire glasses and a huge overcoat. The coat's style was thirty years old and it was way too large. It looked like it would bend the man beneath its weight. Black gloves and a hat completed the picture. He might have been dressed for December, and it was a warm August day outside.

The man opened his mouth to introduce himself, but replacing his voice, as though he were a ventriloquist's dummy, was Frau Kroll, screaming in German. Denton didn't speak German well enough to know what she was saying, but his mind readily filled in the blanks. "You pig-sucking Nazi hunter," would probably be high on her agenda and, "You didn't tell me you were a Jew," along with variations on the theme. The old man shut his mouth and gazed at her calmly as she roared, but he shuddered inside his coat, like a well-rooted tree in the wind.

"Frau Kroll," Denton said sheepishly. He had to touch her arm to get her attention. She turned to glare at him. Appropriately shamefaced, he shook his head. "I apologize. This isn't the . . . who I thought it was. It was a mistake."

Frau Kroll's mouth worked speechlessly.

"I'm, uh, very sorry. There's this other man who's been following me. But this isn't him. I'm really sorry. I'm sorry I upset you."

Frau Kroll went off some more in German, mostly to her husband. Denton guessed that the main thread this time was his status as a form of life lower than that in the bottom of their cesspool. Meanwhile, the old man waited patiently on the stoop.

The husband argued back, reminded the woman of, oh, *the money*. She went back to the door.

"Herr Neumann," the old man introduced himself with a nod of his head.

The Krolls both glanced into the driveway again, confirming that there was only this one old man and not a troop of reporters or Israeli soldiers.

Then Frau Kroll took the man's coat. Herr Neumann gratefully accepted a seat at the kitchen table. Denton wasn't asked to leave, but the woman's eyes compelled him to keep quiet. The old man was given the file folder to peruse as Denton had been.

Herr Neumann opened the cover. Denton's breath caught in his throat. He crossed his leg and jiggled it, put a hand up to press his smiling mouth to keep from screaming.

The old man looked the pages over carefully, his lips pursing with emotion. Denton's leg jiggled more ferociously. He was thinking about how much cash he had with him and wondering if the Krolls would take a check. He had made a freaking ass of himself, but he *would* walk out of here with those pages.

It occurred to him that this old man might be an *agent* of Schwartz, even if he wasn't Schwartz himself. A moment later, he was convinced of it. Behind his hand his smile slunk away. How much cash did this old fart have? Denton felt a wave of nausea at the thought.

After an unbearable time the old man closed the folder. He took off his glasses, brought a white handkerchief from one pocket, and began to clean them. He looked up at Frau Kroll with tears in his eyes. "Thank you for letting me see it," Denton understood him to say in German.

Frau Kroll and her husband exchanged a look.

"Do you speak English?" she asked Herr Neumann.

"Yes," he switched at once, offering Denton a small smile.

"We do business in English, yes? Herr Wyle gave me a price for the papers. Now you please."

Denton uncrossed his leg and crossed the other one. He had to pee all of a sudden, probably because his insides were gripped so tightly there was no room for any fluids.

Herr Neumann continued to clean his glasses, calmly and serenely unaware of the tension in the room. The Krolls were trying to look businesslike, but her hands gripped and regripped her apron and he was licking his lips like a dog with peanut butter.

"What was the current bid, might I ask?" Herr Neumann said, looking up as though this had just occurred to him.

The Krolls discussed this briefly, in hushed tones. He seemed to be in favor of telling; she was not.

"Four thousand," she said hesitantly. "In American dollars."

"It was five thousand," Denton rushed in, "wasn't it? I thought . . . And that was just an *opening* bid."

Frau Kroll and her husband exchanged a smirk. Denton didn't care. He had flinched; he'd admit it. Whatever. Let them milk him dry. Let them retire to the Bahamas.

"I see." Herr Neumann put his glasses back on.

Denton forced his mouth to stay shut. They waited.

"Very well," the old man said with a sigh. "I have no objection to this young American owning the papers. Perhaps he and I can reach an agreement later, if he would be so kind." He smiled distractedly at Denton.

Frau Kroll exploded. She must have been holding her breath, because what came out of her mouth was ejected on a fury of air and spit. She was ranting in a mixture of German and English, *"You can't do that! You can't make a deal with him later! You have to pay me now! You swine, son of a swine, swine's ass, nose of a swine that's in another swine's ass . . ."* Her husband joined in. Clearly they had wanted a bidding war and were a little put out that they hadn't gotten one.

Herr Neumann sat looking down at the closed folder in front of him with an expression so tranquil it was almost a smile. Denton thought he was plumb nutty.

It was clear the old man wasn't going to do anything, and Denton hated, *hated*, arguments. He stood abruptly, knocking over the kitchen chair. He righted it, clumsily, while the Krolls turned their expletives at him.

Denton held up his hands, pleading surrender. "Ten thousand," he said, and when it got no response he repeated it at the top of his lungs: *"Ten thousand!"*

The Krolls fell silent.

"Ten thousand U.S. In cash," Denton added, taking a heaving breath.

Herr Kroll pulled his wife into the other room to consult. Denton waited, glancing out the window nervously. No one else was showing up, thank god. He glanced at the old man, who smiled at him politely. Denton tried to look unfriendly to show his suspicion. It was so unlike him that it took him a minute to remember that a frown went down instead of up.

The Krolls returned. Denton had just bought himself a chunk of Kobinski's manuscript.

Outside in the driveway, Denton's feet followed the old man to his car. In one hand was the manuscript folder (god, he had to get it hermetically sealed or something, and soon). Herr Neumann opened his car door, then turned to acknowledge Denton's hovering.

"Mr. Wyle, I hope you won't mind if I ask you what you intend to do with the manuscript?"

Denton didn't answer. "Who are you?" he demanded, the old man's passivity giving him a semblance of courage. "Did Schwartz send you?"

"No. You see, I would have offered any price, but I'm afraid I have no money. None at all." His eyes were a fading brown. The sincere smile on the old man's face trembled. "If you would please answer my question. I hope . . . I hope you have no intentions of publishing it."

Denton's suspicions were renewed. But there was a sincerity and dignity to Neumann that he found hard to dislike. And he was so frail: the skin on his face, now that they were outside in the daylight, was thin and spotted with age. Beneath were veins so lightly blue and thin that it appeared no blood at all could move through them anymore, like the veins of a dried-up leaf.

"Please tell me. I can offer you something in return."

"Like what?" Denton asked, with a huff.

"Information. I knew Kobinski well."

Denton experienced a surge of greed so powerful it made him wobble. If only! But he shook his head. "You couldn't!"

Neumann reached a small hand into the large sleeve of his overcoat and pulled down the top of his glove. In the warm daylight, the numbers, blue and faded as his veins, were delineated against the thin white skin of his arm: 173056. Denton sucked in his breath.

"Oh my god, you really knew him?" He felt an absurd urge to fall on his knees, as if the Virgin Mary, and not a Holocaust survivor, had suddenly materialized in front of him. He reached out his fingers to touch the numbers that, maybe, Kobinski himself had seen, touched. Words tumbled from his lips: "Did he talk to you about the gateways? Do you know what happened during the escape attempt? Were you there?"

"Reb Kobinski was taken up to Heaven." Neumann nodded, eyes glowing. "But he'll be coming ba—"

Neumann frowned, his head pivoting. In the distance, coming down the dirt road from the main rural highway, was a gray sedan.

"Schwartz!" Denton exclaimed. He'd already bought the manuscript, true, but he still had no desire to see or be seen by that man, that threatening bunny killer, that Jewish Aleister Crowley.

"Not Schwartz," Neumann said in a dead voice. Then, before Denton could react or even *think*, Neumann snatched the folder neatly from his hand, got into the car, shut the door, and locked it.

"*Hey!*" Denton screamed. He tried to open the door and failed. But he was still not really comprehending what was going on—not this nice old man, a Holocaust survivor, not after he, Denton, had spent *ten freaking grand. . . .*

Neumann started the car and rolled down the window a crack. "I'll be in touch."

"Are you crazy?"

But the car was reversing now. It pulled out and drove toward the gray sedan and the main road with what looked to Denton like ironic slowness. Denton might even have chased it on foot, if he hadn't been too stunned to move. The other car, still a half mile from the house, rolled to a stop as Neumann's car cruised gently by. Denton thought he saw Neumann wave to the other driver.

"Hey!" Denton shouted again.

The sedan made its choice and continued on toward Denton and the farmhouse. Denton kicked at the dirt and sobbed in frustration.

*   *   *

Denton had just figured out that he had at least a couple of good reasons to get into his car instead of standing there furious (follow Neumann, get away from whoever was coming, which still might be Schwartz, whatever the old guy said) when the sedan pulled into the driveway. Too late.

He moved for his car anyway, though the sedan appeared to be purposefully blocking the drive.

Two men got out. Big men. They looked like casually dressed businessmen, casual in a flashy, somewhat overdone European style. One wore Armani loafers and a sports coat; the other, a black leather jacket in a froufrou style (as Denton thought of it) that Middle Easterners and Italians favored. They looked at the house, then at Denton.

Denton, still furious and upset, put his hands on his hips with untypical defiance. "Um, could you move your car, please?"

They came over to him at once. Both had dark hair, dark eyes. The taller man, the one in the sports coat, spoke English with a slight accent.

"Who are you?"

He debated telling them the truth. "The people you want are inside the farmhouse. Now if you'd just move your car . . ."

The man in the sports coat motioned toward the farmhouse with his head, and black leather coat man went to the door.

"I really have to be somewhere," Denton said, looking at his watch. He was trying to place these guys in his head. Antique dealers? Thugs hired by Schwartz? Cops? He cleared his throat. The man in the sports coat stared blankly.

Frau Kroll, who'd been peeking from the kitchen window, answered the door and had a brief exchange with the man. She pointed several times at Denton, waved her hand as though asking them to be gone. The man in black returned.

"This is Mr. Wyle. He purchased the manuscript."

"Ah! Mr. Wyle, I'm Mr. Edwards and this is Mr. Smith. Would you be so kind as to speak with us? We can offer you a lift back to Stuttgart."

Denton looked at them incredulously. "I do have a *car*."

"Mr. Smith can drive your car. That will give us more time to chat."

"But . . . !" Denton was growing deeply confused. First that freak Neumann— he was still in shock over that one—now these two men were standing in his way like an unmovable wall. It began to dawn on him that something was very wrong. "Look, guys," he said, sighing now more with fear than exasperation. "If you're after the manuscript, I don't even have it anymore."

They stared.

"Really! The old guy took it—Neumann. The one who just drove off." He gestured down the road. "You saw him. He just grabbed it out of my hand and took off."

The two men exchanged unreadable glances.

"So why don't you go after him? Do us *both* a favor." Denton put his hands back on his hips in an angry gesture, but those hands were shaking.

"I think we should look into this together," Mr. Edwards suggested. He took Denton's arm. "We'd hate to see you get cheated, Mr. Wyle. And of course, we'd all benefit from a discussion about the manuscript."

"But . . ."

Mr. Edwards had a relentless grip. He was pulling Denton without real violence yet inexorably toward their sedan. "It won't take long—an hour at the most." Edwards's sincerity stank like rotten meat.

This, bizarrely, was really happening. Denton shot a panicked look at the farmhouse. The Krolls, who were peeking out the kitchen window again, disappeared at his glance. *They* wouldn't help. These thugs could burn him alive in the driveway and the Krolls would probably come out with marshmallows on sticks and Hefeweizen.

"Come on! *Neumann* has it—why don't you go after him?"

Mr. Smith opened the front passenger door of the sedan and stood there waiting, like a chauffeur. Mr. Edwards, Denton in tow, paused at the door and put out his palm. "Mr. Smith will need your keys, Mr. Wyle."

It was all too fast. Denton wanted to stop it, but he didn't know how. He looked at the interior of that car and drew back hard, like a man resisting his coffin.

"Why can't I drive my own car, you guys? Come on! What is this?"

The smile on Mr. Edwards's face slipped away. "Mr. Wyle, get in the car. *Now.* We only want to talk to you. You have my word."

Denton looked from Mr. Edwards to Mr. Smith, standing implacably a few feet away.

"We only want to talk," Mr. Smith agreed, in a warmer tone. Denton gave him the keys.

As he settled into his seat, Denton turned to them, eyes tearing up. "You guys are from the Jewish League, aren't you?"

Mr. Edwards and Mr. Smith looked at each other and laughed out loud.

"That's right, Mr. Wyle," said Mr. Edwards. "We're from the Jewish League."

8

The universe has two tendencies: a reality which is making itself in a reality which is unmaking itself. The one is life. The other is matter which is opposed to life.
—Henri Bergson, philosopher, 1859–1941

8.1. Calder Farris

Early October
HAARP facility, Gakona, Alaska

The black Lincoln Towncar slid smoothly through military security at the gate and pulled up in front of the main entrance. The driver got out and opened the rear door for Calder Farris. Calder stood still for a moment, his uniform crisping in the chill. It was a clear day in Alaska, but he could smell snow in the air the way he could smell war, even when it was dozens of miles away. He breathed in the scent, his senses on full alert.

A private emerged from the main building. He saluted. "Lieutenant Farris?"

Calder gave a single nod of confirmation. "Take me to it, Private."

Calder was led through the building and out the back, speaking to no one. He had seen the antennae while driving up, but his view here was closer and unobstructed. A long, wide field of dipole antennae made up the Planar Array. The antennae looked like aluminum crosses—long vertical poles with a horizontal tube and wire mesh at the top. There were 180 towers, spaced out in a grid on a thirty-three-acre gravel pad, and each tower held four antennae. A fence surrounded the entire pad, to prevent animals from wandering into the array, animals being plentiful here in Alaska.

Calder had read through the specifications on his flight. Now his eyes focused narrowly on the scene, trying to find the salient. . . .

There. As they walked closer to the gated array, Calder began to see them, brown lumps on the gravel ground. His gaze swept along the scene. There were more dark shapes here and there in the grass outside the fence's perimeter. And now he could see a few of the bodies skewered on the tops of antennae and on the fence.

"Who's in charge here?"

"Colonel Ingram, sir. He's the site supervisor."

They passed through the open gate and into the array. There were a dozen or so men standing around, most of them civilian. They had softer faces and the occasional beard or glasses. Their dress was pure *Northern Exposure*: jeans, flannel shirts or sweatshirts, and bomber jackets. The HAARP scientists, Calder surmised. He decided they could wait and turned his focus on the brown lumps. He could make out the forms now. They were dead birds, hundreds of them. *A murder of crows.* He felt a kick as his adrenaline level went up a notch.

The private made the introductions. Colonel Ingram was Air Force. He looked at Calder's ID carefully. This particular ID had his name and *Department of Defense, United States* on it, the DoD seal, and nothing else; did not, for example, give a job title or branch. Ingram shook Calder's hand after a moment's hesitation. "I was told you were coming, Lieutenant Farris, but I'm not sure why you're here. Perhaps you can fill me in."

"I'm here to observe, Colonel. Just that."

Ingram seemed to be debating the wisdom of probing more deeply. He clearly was the kind of man who liked to know everything, and he did outrank Calder. But the DoD owned this land, not to mention Ingram. And he would have been telephoned by someone mysteriously high up in DARPA. Ingram decided against further questions.

"As you can see, we've had a little problem with a flock of migrating birds."

"When did it begin?"

"In the night. It was first noticed at about oh five hundred this morning."

"You were told not to touch them. Have you?"

"No, sir," Ingram said coolly.

"How many birds are there?"

"We're not sure. There're a lot of 'em out in those fields." Ingram waved his hand beyond the confines of the fence where tall wild grasses awaited the first snowfall of the year. "There are about four dozen within the array itself."

Calder felt a flash of irritation. Sloppy, very sloppy. "I want you to send personnel into the fields. Sweep the area. I want a *full count*. They're to put flag markers next to the bodies so we can see them from here. I want to define a solid perimeter around the effect."

Ingram's mouth tightened. "If you think the situation warrants it."

Calder didn't bother to answer that. He changed his tone. "Any theories on the cause?"

"No. This is a HAARP facility. We don't work with gas or chemical weapons of any kind. There's nothing like that within a hundred miles. There were no accidents in Gakona, Guikana, or Chistochina, nothing. We've swept the area for radiation; it's clean. We checked with civilian and military flight command: there was no traffic through this airspace last night except for a few small civilian craft, none of them carrying any kind of chemicals or reporting anything usual. There's been some mild stomach upset among our personnel, but nothing you can put your finger on. No ill effects reported in the neighboring towns. The birds were migrating, so something might have happened further up the line. We're checking on it."

Calder nodded, deciding Ingram wasn't a slouch after all. He wasn't surprised by anything Ingram said. If it had been a matter of gas or radiation, he wouldn't be here. They wouldn't discover anything farther up the line, either. A flock of birds wouldn't fly a hundred miles while poisoned before all collapsing simultaneously . . . at a HAARP facility.

Calder felt excitement stirring in his groin. Fuck. Avery would have loved this.

"I want ten of the bodies packed on ice and shipped to D.C. Here's the address." He took a card almost as plain as his own from a pocket and handed it to the colonel. "I want them there by tomorrow morning."

"We do have some medical personnel here, if you'd like us to—"

"*No.* Thank you. The rest should be collected and buried. And if you don't mind, I'd like to go over the details of your HAARP transmissions for the past few days."

"That can be arranged." Colonel Ingram hesitated. "But, begging your pardon, the HAARP broadcasts wouldn't have anything to do with this. They're just radio signals."

Calder pretended to think it over, turning his head to survey the scene once more. In reality, he was buying time to swallow the anticipation he knew would be audible in his voice.

"Quite right, Colonel," he said flatly. "Could you introduce me to your head physicist now please?"

Ingram hesitated, trying again to read him, but Calder gave back nothing. Ingram nodded and took Calder over to the *Northern Exposure* clones. They stopped in front of a man with John Lennon glasses and longish gray hair pulled back in a ponytail. The man looked at Calder with bored, disrespectful eyes, as if thinking, *Oh, great, a jarhead.*

Calder smiled.

"Lieutenant Farris, this is Dr. Serin," Ingram said.

8.2. Jɪʟʟ Tᴀʟᴄᴏᴛᴛ

SEATTLE

THE NEGATIVE ONE PULSE, 50 PERCENT POWER

Things started going bad in October. The summer had been blissfully un-eventful, with no one disturbing them and so much work getting accomplished. Of course, the campus was mostly dormant during the summer months. It couldn't last.

They had finished with the one pulse in mid-September, just before the start of the new quarter. Jill had a bet going with Nate that the effects of the negative one pulse would mirror the effects of the one pulse, that the one-minus-one's crests and troughs were two ends of energy in the same force. Nate disagreed; he thought the negative one pulse would have the opposite effect.

It looked like he'd win that bet. They reset the transmitter for the negative one pulse at 50 percent power. After only six days they started to see a definite decline in their daily "health and well-being" numbers. The virus stopped growing, then began to shrink, dying off around the edges. The mice were lethargic. The fruit rotted.

Deep in her own little world, Jill hadn't bothered to read departmental memos lately, including one requesting research plans for the quarter. On a cold and rainy autumn Wednesday, Dick Chalmers called her into his office.

"Shut the door, Jill."

She was vexed to see Chuck Grover. He was seated in a cross-legged Alan Alda kind of pose, not unlike a probation officer at a hearing. She frowned at him and he met her gaze with eyes as remote and cold as a Himalayan spring.

Chalmers motioned her to take a seat. He was not sitting behind his desk but on a padded chair in front of the desk, like Grover. A third, empty chair had been arranged so that the three roughly formed a circle. Jill's hackles were up at once.

"What are you working on, Jill?" Chalmers asked.

"What is this, Dick?"

"*This* is a civilized discussion." Chalmers spoke in that heavy, paternal, Marcus Welby way of his. "I haven't had a research plan from you in six months. I want to know what you're doing."

"What's *he* doing here?" Jill looked daggers at Grover.

Chalmers neatly picked some lint off his slacks, giving her time to fully comprehend the seriousness of his expression.

"Chuck would also like to know what you're doing. He asked me, which made me realize I haven't a clue. I don't like not having a clue about my staff, Jill."

Her hands found each other in her lap and began entwining. "You do know what my work is about."

"I know what it *was* about, but no, I haven't the foggiest idea what you're working on now."

"Well . . ." She was going to say she was still working on the same old wave mechanics equation; that's what she'd led Chalmers to believe. But she'd told Grover she'd abandoned that. It takes social dexterity to be a very good liar, and Jill didn't have a prayer. "Um, well, I'm still working on wave mechanics, but we've had to go back to scratch and try a new angle on it. And . . . uh . . . well, it's just a different approach."

Chalmers and Grover were both looking at her with slack faces. Chalmers shook his fleshy head. "I'm sorry, but that simply doesn't cut it. What about this lab you've requisitioned down in Smith Hall?"

"Yeah. What, exactly, are you doing down there?" Grover added.

She swallowed, not knowing what to say.

"I had a call from the HAARP program in Alaska," Chalmers remarked. "Apparently, someone calling herself Dr. Alkin and claiming to be from our department contacted them last summer about high-energy wave experiments. I've asked around, but none of the other professors know anything about it."

"Well, I certainly don't," Jill lied. She could feel her face heating up and got irritated. She might as well have a nose that grew, for god's sake.

Grover's eyes narrowed. He leaned forward, practically sniffing her. "What about that book on radio generators I saw in your office?"

"That was . . . Nate's. My grad student's. Hobby."

"Dr. Talcott . . ." Chalmers shook his head again and took off his glasses. Jill knew she was in trouble then. He never called her Dr. Talcott. "I'm mystified as to why anyone needs to waste a single second speculating about what you might or might not be doing. You told Chuck you'd keep him up-to-date on your progress after using Quey, but he says you've refused to even be civil."

That pissed Jill off, big-time. Not civil! She'd been perfectly civil to the creep the day she showed him the sim program. She'd lied her head off, but she'd been civil.

"That's absolutely not true," she said in an icy voice.

Grover started to argue, but Chalmers held up a mediating hand.

"What concerns me is your secrecy. We are a *team* in this department, and that includes every single person. I know that I've been busy the past six months and I haven't pressed you as hard as I should have, but you *have* been damned illusive, Jill."

"That's not my intention. I just get focused." Jill's hands were wrenching each other like wrestlers in her lap. She noticed it and made them unclench, placing them loosely on her thighs.

"If it's not your intention, then you won't object to showing Chuck and me around your lab." Chalmers rose to his feet as if to say that settled that.

"Next week I have some time—" Jill looked at her watch helplessly.

"Right now."

"Right now? But I have to prepare for—"

"Right *now*."

Grover stood up, smiling nastily, as if to say, *Boy, are you going to get it.*

As they left Chalmers's office, Jill wracked her brains for some way out. Passing by the corridor to her office, she said, "Just a second. I need my briefcase," and ditched in there, closing the door behind her. She raced to the phone, picked it up, and dialed the lab. She was relieved when Nate answered on the first ring. "Nate," she hissed, "Chalmers is on his way down. Hide *everything!*"

She put the receiver down just as Chalmers cautiously opened her office door, scrutinizing her suspiciously. Thank god she was a female. Worries about indelicacies had probably given her one moment of privacy at least. She picked up her briefcase from beside her desk. "Coming."

She led them over to Smith as slowly and circuitously as she could. Even so, it only took about five minutes. While they walked she thought over her options. As much as she bristled under the scolding, she knew Chalmers was right. She *did* have an obligation to the university to keep them informed. But the memory of Ansel inhibited her, and beneath that were memories of her own, older scars. She would not be laughed at. Besides, she didn't want to spill it under the gun like this; it ought to be a planned, triumphant moment. And she wasn't at her best, had felt muddled and tired all week, with the sharp edge of a headache pressing into her brain. No, she needed time to write up her findings professionally, the breathing room to present them with clarity and confidence. And she certainly didn't want to try to explain her work to Chalmers in front of Chuck Grover. Her only hope of saving the one-minus-one from his clutches was to publish her findings before he heard anything about it. Then again, she might not have a choice.

"Here we are," Jill said lightly. She opened the door.

The rubber curtain sucked toward them as they pushed through. Nate was seated at the long table with his computer. He looked up at them casually. "Oh, hey, Dr. Chalmers, Dr. Grover." Was Jill the only one who could see that he was breathing hard?

Chalmers squinted at him, confused by the hair. "Um . . . Good morning, uh . . ."

"Nate Andros."

"Ah! Yes, of course, Mr. Andros."

Jill couldn't believe what she was seeing—or rather, not seeing. The middle of the room was entirely bare except for the subject table. On top of it was one of their old charts that Nate had taken down from the wall. It was laid flat, pencils on top of it as though in recent use. The white board (and the grid) was covered up by another of the huge charts. On the folding table where the mice had been there was only their old coffeepot, dying a slow death. The radio equipment was gone; the subjects were nowhere to be seen. Jill was caught in a surprised smile when she saw several of the platters of fruit near Nate on the equipment table, as though they were for eating. She lifted her eyes to Nate, who was sipping a cup of coffee and looking doggedly at his computer screen. His collarbone rose and fell and his nostrils flared as he tried to catch his breath without being obvious about it. He looked up. Their eyes met.

"What on earth *are* you doing down here, Jill?" Chalmers sounded perplexed. Grover was stalking the room's perimeters like a drug-sniffing dog at an airport.

Jill waved an unsteady hand at the charts. "We needed room to spread out. You know how tiny my office is."

"Well, this is a ridiculous waste of space!"

"No one was using this room, Dick. It was full of old junk. We cleaned it ourselves."

"It's still a waste! I'm sure there's *someone* who could put it to better use."

Grover had reached the equipment table. He looked over the top of it, paused where the transmitter had been, looking at the oh, so vacant tabletop. Jill watched him, wondering if there were dust outlines there. She glanced at Nate. He looked worried, too.

"Dr. Grover, how's it hanging?" he asked.

Grover ignored Nate utterly. His face was a blank. He moved toward Jill and Chalmers at the door.

"Well, Chuck?" Chalmers asked.

Grover fingered the rubber curtain. "What about all this insulation?" He looked up toward the ceiling, pulled the rubber curtain toward her. "Jill? Could you explain why you'd need all this if you're doodling equations? This looks like sound insulation to me—for radio waves, perhaps?"

"Radio waves!" She huffed, as if this were the silliest thing she'd ever heard. "No, of course not. It was here when we moved in." She couldn't meet Grover's eyes, so she looked at Chalmers instead. She tried to act normal, but "normal" for her meant hardly any facial expression at all and that didn't seem quite right. She smiled.

"Really? That can be verified, you know. Who had the room before you?"

"I just said; it was empty."

"Ah! Still. Someone would know. A janitor. Acquisitions."

She could have socked good old Chuck. He was right. The acquisition of the insulation could easily be traced to her, but she couldn't back down now. She bit her lips.

Grover turned to Chalmers, his face hard. "You must see this is bullshit, Dick."

Chalmers grunted. "Jill, I want a full—and I mean *full*—report of everything you've done for the past six months, and I want it on my desk by Friday."

"But that's only two days!"

"Five P.M. Friday. And I think you should consider the kind of unproductivity your reclusiveness provokes. Really, this is untenable! From now on I want everyone in the department to know *clearly* what you're doing, even if they don't care. And that goes double for Chuck. When someone in my department makes a commitment to a fellow faculty member, I expect her to keep it."

Chalmers put a hand on Grover's arm supportively. "Let's go, Chuck."

They left, but not before Grover shot her a venomous look, a look that said, *I know you're lying, bitch.*

Jill locked the door behind them and collapsed into a chair. She hid her face in her hands. "Oh god! What an *ass*hole!"

"Are you okay?"

"I *think* we survived. Thank god for you, Nate. How'd you do it? Where is everything?"

Nate didn't look relieved. His dark eyes were full of concern. "There's a storage closet across the hall. Jill, this is not good. They're going to find out sooner or later and Chalmers is going to be *pissed*. I really don't get what you're afraid of. This is great work. Brilliant, actually."

Jill couldn't help feeling a rush of pleasure at the compliment. And he was absolutely right. She'd just outright lied to her department head. She felt sick about it for a moment, a swimmy light-headedness like she was looking over the edge of a precipice. She could visualize getting fired, being thrown out of university life forever.

But surely all would be forgiven if she pulled this off. It would be so huge they'd have no choice. And she could explain to Chalmers about Ansel, about Chuck's blackmail, about how she'd wanted to be *sure* before she spoke out. He might understand.

She still had her eye on the prize.

She smoothed her wool slacks. "You're right, Nate. It's time to start writing our first major article. We can include everything we've done so far. By the time we're done, the negative one pulse tests should be finished, too."

"And you want this by Friday?"

"God, no! We *might* be ready by January, if we bust tail through the holidays."

"But Chalmers said he wanted it by Friday."

Jill rattled her fingertips on her collarbone. Yes, he'd been very clear on that. "Damn it," she muttered. "I'll have to waste at least two precious days."

"You're going to write a bogus report." Nate sounded really upset. He moved his hand to touch her knee but withdrew it under her frowning gaze. It was a gesture of concern, and she realized it at the same instant she realized why he withdrew it. She'd been looking downward and frowning, and she wanted to say, *No, I was just frowning about the situation, not at you.* But what would *that* mean? That she was asking him to touch her knee? And then would he feel like he had to? And would it be awkward because the moment had passed?

She avoided the issue by standing up. "It's all in the timing, Nate," she heard herself say, and she sounded so frighteningly like her father that she had a startling moment of self-doubt.

But it was only a moment. January wasn't all that far away, she reasoned. And with Thanksgiving, then Christmas, Chalmers would be too busy to worry about her. It was ideal, really, because while everyone was absorbed in turkey and caroling, she'd have extra time to get her ducks in a row. It was, as her father might say, an advantage, and even a small advantage could matter if you were smart enough to utilize it just right. And even if Chalmers never would forgive her for lying now, for submitting a phony report, she wouldn't need Udub after she'd published, not with Harvard and Oxford knocking. But Chalmers *would* forgive her—look at Chuck: *he* was an asshole and they kissed his shorts-wearing butt because he was valuable. That's the way things were in the fast lane, and if you couldn't play hardball you'd just get crushed by the people who could.

"We'll have to rush the negative one pulse work a little is all. We'll take a few more days' worth of observations at fifty percent, then bump it up to seventy-five. We really ought to have more time, but . . ."

Nate rose slowly to his feet, his face grim. "Jill, we need to talk."

* * *

Jill knew what Nate was going to say, and her defenses went up at once, like a castle pulling up the gate at the first sign of attackers. She gave him a cool and level *whatever* gaze and walked away. She began taking the chart off the white board.

He was going to tell her he couldn't work with her anymore. Between the risks she knew she'd taken in their research—exposing both of them to the altered one-minus-one—and now the evidence, right in front of his eyes, that Chalmers and Grover were against her, what else could she expect? The kid wasn't stupid. He had his own future to worry about.

Nate went over to his backpack and pulled out a newspaper. She glanced at him and did not see what she expected to see in his eyes: guilt. Instead, his eyes had a lot of deep questions in them. She noticed that they were puffy and those bruised circles were back.

"You look sick," she said stiffly.

"I feel like shit, especially after reading this."

He held out the newspaper. When she didn't cross to take it, he sighed and came to her, held it out.

"What is it?"

He took a deep breath. "I'm concerned about continuing with the negative one pulse experiment. You're moving it up to seventy-five percent—that scares me."

Because of what she'd expected to hear from him and because she really did care about whether he left her, she was uncharacteristically receptive to his body language. She saw that he didn't like what he just said, that he felt cowardly about it, about saying, *"That scares me."* But he had enough conviction to say it anyway, and that made her recall that he'd been expressing doubt for some time now and she'd completely filtered it out.

Her fingers tripped over her collarbone. "Nate, if you want to take a break, focus on your class work . . ."

"It's been raining for three solid weeks."

"It's *October*. In *Seattle*."

"Usually some nice weather in October."

"What are you trying to say?" She looked down at the newspaper, more confused than agitated.

He sighed. "In the past three weeks I've broken up with my girlfriend, gotten two parking tickets, narrowly escaped a semi making a hubcap out of me and my bike, had an altercation in a video store, and a friend of mine at the restaurant nearly cut a finger off slicing vegetables. The guy's a professional chef. Now there's this stuff with Chalmers and Grover."

Despite wanting to understand, a deep stain of irritation blossomed inside Jill. She didn't have time for this nonsense, with the stupid report she had to write and everyone breathing down her back. On the other hand, he'd broken up with his girlfriend.

"Nate . . ." she began slowly. "I'm sorry you've been having problems, but if you think—"

He tapped an article on the front page. She scanned it briefly. Four Udub students were killed the night before when a pickup truck plowed over the rail on the nearby 520 bridge and plunged into Lake Washington.

Jill grabbed the paper, looking for names. The University of Washington was a huge campus, and she didn't recognize any of the victims. Drinking was thought to be involved. "That's terrible."

Nate was staring at her.

"*What?* You can't seriously think this has anything to do with the negative one pulse."

Nate looked down at his black leather boots, hands on his hips. His face was determined. "I think we should stop."

Jill tossed the paper down and strode across the room, surged into motion by a wave of anger. Everyone was against her! The gate on the castle went back up.

"That is totally unfair! You're creating phantoms, Nate. I expect more from you. I expect *science*." She stalked back to the grid on the white board and jabbed a finger at it. "We're only at, what, thirty percent differential between our lab group and our control group on the negative one pulse? *Mice, bananas,* and *virus,* all *right next* to the wave transmitter? Think about it! Even if the negative one pulse *does* have a detrimental effect, how could it have only a thirty percent impact *here*, on small objects with few cells, while across campus at the 520 bridge . . . God, that doesn't even make sense!"

She was breathing hard, felt a stress headache pounding. She told herself to calm down. There was no reason that this couldn't be a rational, scientific discussion, if Nate would only get his head out of his ass.

Nate raked a hand through his blond-tipped hair. "Look. I know I'm not thinking straight. That's part of the *problem*. But just listen for a second, okay? How *is* it that these pulses affect our fruit and mice and virus? Have you really thought about that?"

"Of course." Jill was too worked up to keep still. She marched back and forth in front of the grid like an ant on guard duty. "Our hypothesis is that the full one and full negative one pulses impact the one-minus-one wave, which is the underlying energy pattern of space-time. In turn, matter is affected."

"How?"

"Well, the particles of the banana, for instance . . ."

"Go on."

She *had* thought about this, a lot, though it was all just theory for now. "Well, the one pulse merges with the one-minus-one the way any two waves merge and create an intelligence pattern. It doesn't have any effect on the 'crests' of the one-minus-one since they're already at peak 'one' value. But it *does* affect the 'troughs,' the negative one side of the wave. The net result is fewer or gentler troughs. The particles of the banana, which have their own energy waves, intersect with the altered one-minus-one and end up having fewer or gentler troughs also."

Nate nodded, his eyes shining. "Right. And we've seen that when there are fewer troughs things thrive, burgeon forth, feel good, hump like bunnies."

Jill smirked but nodded, granting her assent.

"And now it seems we've proven the flip side of the coin. The negative one pulse affects the *one* side of the one-minus-one wave. In other words, it *lowers the crests*, right? And it appears that when there are fewer crests things slow down, even die, like the virus."

"We're a long way from proving that."

Nate made a face. "I'm not worried about the damned fruit, Jill. I'm not even worried about myself. Though you're really the worse for wear. You do know that, don't you?"

She stopped pacing to glare at him. "I'm fine!"

"You're very irritable."

"Uh! How would you feel with Chalmers and Grover on your case! Besides which, there's no proof that the one-minus-one affects a person's moods or chemistry or whatever."

Nate challenged her with a raised eyebrow. "Why not? Our brains are matter. So are the chemicals in them. Of course the one-minus-one affects our moods—we've both felt it. Just look at the mice."

"I can't," she pointed out dryly.

Nate went into the hall and came back with the two cages. She locked the door again behind him. He put the cages on the table. One white male sniffed halfheartedly at the treadmill. The others lay and watched him lethargically.

Jill growled a *hmmm*. She needed so badly to justify what she was doing that she argued almost without thought. Only later, lying in bed, would she contemplate the possibility that Nate might have a glimmer of a point. Now she went up to him and put a tired hand on his sleeve as if touching him were a kind of consolation prize for what she was about to say.

"Nate, you know we've got a very modest radio transmitter. We've been seeing results here, yes, but nothing catastrophic or particularly dangerous-looking. You *know* this has nothing to do with that car accident or any other of those other things you mentioned. That's just dumb."

"I'm not saying our experiments pushed that truck off the bridge." Nate closed his eyes, concentrating. "But I also think we're dreaming if we expect to keep the results of our experiment localized to this room. The insulation keeps in the pulse *we're* generating, but that's about it. We're manipulating the fabric of *space-time*, Jill. Besides, that's not how the energy pool theory works." There was a tremor in his lips that made her feel emotionally shaky herself. Her hand fell back to her side.

She was weary of the argument, weary in general. She *hadn't* been feeling at all well. And she still had another class today; then they had to go over to her place this afternoon to check the control group.

"What if . . ." Nate began, "what if there are *probabilities*?"

Jill shook her head. "Totally lost."

"What if there is free will? But what if 'free will' or 'no predestiny' only means that there's some kind of probability curve that one thing will happen versus another? Say this kid who was driving the truck, for example." He waved his hand toward the newspaper. "Say his lifetime is fifty percent determined by pure genetics and maybe another thirty percent by environmental conditioning. Then there's this last twenty percent that's dumb luck. Maybe he could die at five from diving off a swing set because he's got a recklessness gene, or at nineteen from an overdose because he's predisposed to addiction. Or maybe there was always a chance he would have an accident while driving drunk."

Jill rubbed her forehead tiredly.

"I'm not saying the pulse *pushed* him off. But what if it *upped the probability* of that particular event coming to pass? What if some random lucky thing, like a favorite song coming on the radio to keep him alert, *could* have happened last night—if a full crest had been there in his wave pattern—and *didn't*, because that crest wasn't there?"

She stared at him dumbly. "Nate, how do I respond to something like that?"

Nate shrugged sadly. "I don't expect you to. I'm not even sure I believe it. I just think—I think we have no idea what we're playing with."

She leaned back against a table and hugged herself, feeling cold. She studied him for a moment. "You should take some time off."

"No."

"Just a few weeks. You can work on the data over in my office. For the report."

From having been afraid of losing him a few minutes ago Jill realized that she was now pushing him out. She wanted him to go. Because there was something she was even more afraid of losing than Nate Andros: her own faith in the work or even the work itself.

But Nate slumped in surrender. He went back over to his computer and picked up his coffee cup. "Christ, I don't want time off. I just want to talk about it, for god's sake. I mean, sometimes this thing blows my *mind*."

She heard a quiver in his voice and watched his face darken as he stared down into his cup. She felt a lump in her own throat in response but quelled it. A heartbeat later, she was mentally logging his increase of instability, of emotionalism, of paranoia for her journal entry later that night.

"That's all the more reason to finish quickly," she said crisply. "Let's try to get the data up to fifty percent differential between our lab group and our control group on the negative one pulse. That's good enough for publication. We can stop there."

Nate didn't answer or even glance at her.

"So . . . what happened with Linda?"

The words were out before she realized they were coming, and she immediately felt as though she'd just done something particularly humiliating. She compensated by looking supremely uninterested in the answer, checking her fingernails. She could feel him watching her.

"We didn't have much in common when it came right down to it."

"Huh." She turned away, perversely pleased. "Are you sure you don't want some time off? I *would* like to bump it up. But if you're not comfortable with that you don't have to be down here. Just say the word."

His mouth twisted wryly. "No." Then, harder, "And leave you to hog all the glory? Not unless you have a team of wild horses I don't know about."

Jill smiled.

8.3. Aharon Handalman

JERUSALEM

It was Friday afternoon, and Hannah was rushing to get everything ready for the Sabbath. In the oven a brisket baked on a timer. The two younger children had had baths that morning and Yehuda was in there now, his clothes laid out on the bed. She set the table with silver candlesticks that had belonged to her grandmother, stirred the vegetable soup, and put the large skillet on the range for an unusual treat—*latkes*. She looked at the extra place at the table anxiously.

It was growing dark when Aharon arrived, their guest in tow. Hannah had already lit the candles and blessed them. The men had walked from the yeshiva, and the exercise made the recent paleness of Aharon's face, the looseness of his skin, more apparent. Hannah glanced at him worriedly and welcomed Binyamin, taking his coat, trying not to wince at the smell that wafted from the folds of wool.

"It's, um, nice of you to invite me," Binyamin said. "Rabbi Handalman said it was your idea."

"You're very welcome." Hannah glanced guiltily at Aharon. "I hope you both brought good appetites."

She had coached the children to be especially nice, yet Devorah wrinkled her nose as she sat at the table. "It smells!" she said, which Hannah hastily covered by talking about the brisket.

When the food was on the table, Aharon said the blessing: "*Baruch atah Adonai . . .*"

From under her lashes Hannah watched him, her heart weighted with concern. The change in him had been happening for some time, but a few weeks ago there was a sharp demarcation. Sometimes there was an expression on his face that made him a stranger.

It used to be if you were charitable you called Aharon assured, and if not so charitable pompous. When he'd prayed he'd had a solidness about him, as if to say, *This is who I am and who my father was and my father's father,* as if he had a shortcut to God's ear. That man was gone. Aharon went through the motions, mouthed the syllables. He might have been reading a grocery list. The worst thing was, she didn't even think he was aware of the change, didn't think he had any clue about the distracted blankness in his eyes or the fact that at times he had a look there that was pure panicky fear. He slept badly, had nightmares, rose so late she knew he would have little time for his morning prayers, and he didn't even seem to care.

The mealtime crawled under the weight of forced conversation. Binyamin, who would never be any girl's idea of a prince, was also no chatterbox. Fortunately, he was a quick eater. He finished two platefuls in record time, and no one else was hungry. Hannah cleared and served dessert: halvah and herbal tea.

The older two children were excused. Hannah put the baby to bed. When she came out, Aharon and Binyamin were not in the house. In the shadows outside she spotted them sitting in the children's playground. She checked on Devorah and Yehuda, both reading (Devorah pretending to) in the living room. Hannah put on her coat and slipped outside.

The playground was small, only swings and a slide that even Devorah had nearly outgrown. Hannah did not approach it on the path but went around the building instead, hoping the dark would shield her from prying eyes—not Aharon's so much as the neighbors'. What would they say about a woman spying on her own husband?

She came around the side of the building, paused against the wall. She could barely hear the men's voices. Aharon's usually carried well, god knew, but he was speaking without much energy.

"Last night I dreamed I was trying to hide Yehuda at the yeshiva because the Nazis were plundering in the streets. They were knocking down the Wall, and if I didn't hide Yehuda they would find him. I had him by the hand, and I was racing through the school when suddenly there was a brilliant flash in the windows. It was the weapon. I knew it, in the dream; I thought: *The Nazis got the weapon, somehow, and they've destroyed Jerusalem!*"

"It was just a dream, Rabbi." Binyamin's boyish voice was uneasy but also unexpectedly kind.

"Yes, yes, of course. Pray to God it stays that way. We must find Anatoli Nikiel. We must get our hands on the rest of the manuscript before they do." Then the men got up and began to stroll.

Hannah's heart was in her throat, but she didn't dare follow. She went back to the apartment, wrote her note, and waited. Devorah went to bed. The men returned. One more cup of tea, then Binyamin rose to leave. His coat was threadbare and old—like, perhaps, something that had belonged to his grandfather or someone else's grandfather, salvaged from a bargain bin in the marketplace. His parents, who were not poor, must tear their hair out, god help them.

Hannah followed the men to the door and when Binyamin mumbled good-bye he stuck his hand in his coat pocket. Hannah held her breath for a moment, fearing in his simplicity he would give her away, would pull out the note and say, *What is this?*

But he didn't. He frowned at her, clenching something tightly in his pocket, and said good night.

∗   ∗   ∗

Ever since the moment Aharon had decided he didn't want to communicate with Shimon Norowitz anymore, Shimon Norowitz had become his best friend. *"What else have you found in the arrays? What have you learned in your research? Have you spoken to anyone? Who?"* And always, like clockwork, *"Of course, you'll keep in touch?"*

Whenever Norowitz called, Aharon's lips felt pressed shut, too heavy to move, as though an angel were putting a finger there—*shhhhh.* He did not tell Norowitz about his interview with Biederer. He did not tell him about Anatoli Nikiel. And he certainly did not mention the disappearance of two men outside of Auschwitz in a flash of light.

On a Monday after Binyamin had taken Shabbes with them, the boy was already in Aharon's office when he arrived. Binyamin rose with an odd expression, his Kobinski binder in his hands. He looked like a dog that had dug something up and wasn't sure whether to look pleased or guilty about it.

"What? What did you find?"

"I found something," Binyamin mumbled. His cheeks were spotted with red.

"Yes, I know that. I know because I can read minds, Binyamin, and because you're standing there holding the binder with such a look. What is it?"

Binyamin held it out. "Here."

Aharon was disappointed when he saw what Binyamin had circled. "That? That's not a word!"

Binyamin's tapered hands with their chipped fingernails reached for the binder hesitatingly. "Okay, but . . ."

"Don't say 'okay.' 'Okay'—what does that *mean*?"

Binyamin put the binder down on the desk, poked his glasses higher on his nose, and turned pages. Now Aharon could see that there were new Post-it notes adhered to the pages, fresh pink-colored ones showing brightly against all the dull, fading yellows. Binyamin turned to one of the flagged pages, holding the binder open for Aharon expectantly.

"These?" Aharon asked, pointing to the pink flags.

Binyamin nodded. Aharon bent over the binder and looked. The same five-letter sequence, ההקלה, was on this page again, and on the next pink-flagged page, and the next.

"How many?" Aharon asked, his voice small.

"Forty-five occurrences."

Forty-five! "But . . . 'TLCTT'—it doesn't mean anything." But this time Aharon wasn't so sure.

"Maybe . . . um . . . could it be a name? With the vowels, I mean?"

"How did you find this?"

Binyamin shrugged. "Just saw it," he muttered, looking down at the page.

"Hmmm." Aharon stroked his beard. "It *might* be a name. What else? Acronym? Something scientific? A chemical ingredient? A formula?" He rocked back and forth on his toes.

"Could be," Binyamin said doubtfully. "Or it could be a name."

Aharon had a Jewish encyclopedia CD-ROM—something Hannah had gotten him for a birthday. He tried several combinations of vowels added to the Hebrew consonants but found no matches. He did a search for the letters in the Torah and Talmud also, but that sequence of letters did not appear in plaintext of either one.

He sat back, stroking his beard. "At the university, I can find someone in physics. Maybe they'll recognize it. Some kind of scientific term? Roman numerals? Dates?"

"Maybe," said Binyamin. "But it could be a name."

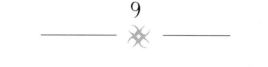

9

I became obsessed with good and evil. When we act or speak or even think, we create energy. In the brain, synapses fire; in speech, we create sound waves; with physical action the impact on matter is even more obvious.

I wondered: Could the energy of these events, in and of itself, be positive or negative, good or evil? Does a hateful thought have a different kind of energy than a benevolent one? Are there laws that govern such energy? How far can evil go—how strong is it at its limit? Does "good" travel at the speed of light?

—Yosef Kobinski, *The Book of Torment,* 1943

9.1. CALDER FARRIS

HAARP FACILITY
GAKONA, ALASKA

Calder had been in Alaska for four days. They'd been running the HAARP facility through frequency tests when the birds fell, so he'd had them run those same frequency tests again—and again and again, much to the perturbation of Dr. Serin. Calder was delaying their research, Serin said; ten Ph.D.'s were sitting on their hands. Fucking whining little shit. Calder gave him a look, said, *"This has priority,"* and nothing more. Serin wasn't stupid. He started to be curious about what Calder was looking for. Calder responded, or didn't respond, to all of it with the same steady chill.

So they ran the tests. And nothing happened.

Serin asked Calder, "What are you looking for? What's all this about?"

Calder said, "Standard procedure."

Serin reminded Calder a lot of the scientists who worked for the DoD. Over the years, he'd developed a particular hatred for the type—liberal science geeks who worked for the government but were so goddamn privileged they forgot who held the silver spoon in their mouths. Sure, Serin was happy to lap up the money Uncle Sam offered, the free housing, early retirement, and great benefits. But when he got home at night, he'd have dinner parties with his liberal geek friends where he'd make fun of the military personnel who ran the facility. He'd make a big deal of the fact that HAARP was not, technically, a weapon. As if he didn't owe every single one of his privileges, not to mention his life and that of his entire liberal geek family, to the A-bomb. At the very least, he'd be speaking Russian and scribbling math equations for fifty cents an hour if that bad boy had not come along when it had. And then there were the stealth bombs and smart bombs and all the other things that kept the man hip deep in opera tickets and Nordstrom's instead of wallowing in a third-world hellhole like the other 80 percent of the world's population who had the sole misfortune of being born in a country without bad-ass technology.

But . . . Serin was not Calder's problem. The man had no clue what had caused those birds to drop from the sky, and he couldn't reproduce it.

Since the death of Dr. Henry Ansel, Calder had gathered every scrap of information he could find, had interviewed Ansel's colleagues at the University of Tennessee and talked to his students. He'd picked up some tidbits, pieces of a puzzle that still had no definite shape in Calder's mind. What he did know with certainty was that Ansel had been working on something that was extremely relevant to Calder and that he'd been closed-lipped about it.

Except, perhaps, with the dean of his physics department. The man had known *something*. But he'd denied it, and he'd been a little too well connected for Calder to sit on him. Though he reserved it as an option for a future date.

The thing that Ansel and Avery had agreed upon was that matter equals waves and that therefore, ergo, and consequently it followed that waves of some specific type, intensity, structure, et cetera, et cetera, *ought* to be able to affect matter. The trick was: what kind of waves? Calder had gone through boatloads of documentation, old journal articles, anything he could find on experiments conducted with waves, but so far he'd not found the red marker: physical matter majorly screwed up by wave transmission.

Until the birds. The autopsies showed nothing. *Nothing.* The birds hadn't died of poisoning or radiation, diabetes or depression. It was as if suddenly, in mid-flight, their impulse for life, some vital spark in their brain, had simply been turned off. Crash and burn.

Calder's biggest fear—and it was coming true—was that it had been a fluke, some rare conflux of random factors he'd never be able to trace, not without knowing . . . something.

Had Ansel known? Had he held the power of life and death in his hands? If he hadn't, he'd killed himself for no good reason, and Calder found that extremely unlikely. Serin sure as shit didn't know. But according to Serin, there was someone else out there who might.

On Thursday, Calder asked, "Did you ever hear back from the University of Washington? About that phone call you had from a Dr. Alkin?"

"Not yet," Serin replied, with zero interest. "I told you it's nothing. I don't

know why I even remembered it except the person had been asking about unusual effects of our wave transmission and the birds reminded me—"

"Maybe you should call them back."

Serin gave him an exasperated look. "I spoke to the department head. He
would have called if he'd learned anything."

Calder removed his glasses and fixed Serin with those cold blue eyes.

"I'll call him now," Serin said.

9.2. Deптоп Ѡyle

UPSTATE NEW YORK

Denton sat watching the yeshiva from a group of tangled honeysuckle bushes
behind the building. In the woods. In the dark. With the freaking maple trees.
Schwartz had made a bad mistake. Denton Wyle no longer had anything
to lose.

He might have bartered with the rabbi, if he'd had the Kroll manuscript.
But Denton didn't have the Kroll manuscript. It had been *stolen* right out of
his hands. Then there were those two thugs who'd taken a copy of every other
scrap of material he'd had in his hotel room in Stuttgart—without asking, despite his furious protest. So Schwartz had everything Denton had anyway. So
it was Schwartz, really, who'd chosen this path. Denton was not responsible.
Furious, yes, petrified, yes, but not responsible.

The lights in the large dining room were on. He saw the boys filing in at
last. He waited until they were all seated, until the blessing had been said.
Then he made his way through the woods to the front door.

He remembered seeing a coat closet in the foyer on his first visit to the
yeshiva. He hoped it might serve his purposes. He tried the main door: open.
He smiled nervously to himself. As he thought, the place was not guarded.
Schwartz might be the head of some secret Jewish cult, but he'd never expect
trouble here, on his home turf. Not with this elaborate facade he'd created,
this innocent "boys' school" act. Huh-uh.

The foyer, as Denton slipped inside, was dimly lit and empty. It was tempting to go to the library now—it was just down the hall, and no one was around.
But he needed time, plenty of time. He opened the closet door and scoped it
out. It was long and deep. The back was nested with boxes. It couldn't *be* more
ideal; luck was smiling on Denton Wyle. He made his way through the coats,
nudged a place among the cartons, hidden from view. His watch had a lighted
face and he read it: 6:30.

He slept a little. By midnight he could no longer wait. His legs were cramped
and he had to pee, plus the dark was getting to him. He was starting to imagine Schwartz (in the chef outfit, his butcher knife raised) creeping toward the

closet door. With a bit more haste than was called for, Denton worked his way out of the boxes and into the foyer.

The foyer was dark but not nearly as dark as the closet. He listened, heart pounding, for distant chanting from some underground temple, like something from *Indiana Jones*. The school was completely silent. Freed from the constricted space, his limbs tingled from disuse and his nerves threatened to fail him. He could still back out. It wasn't too late to run. But . . . no. It would be simple and painless, and no one would ever know it had been him.

He wanted it *so badly*!

The library doors were closed, but they weren't locked. He slipped inside and shut himself in.

Where was it? He was sure Schwartz had a complete or nearly complete copy of *The Book of Torment*. Denton had pictured the whole thing in a drawer, bound in blue ribbon, somewhere in this library. Or it might be on a shelf in a place of honor, like a trophy. And he, Denton, would help himself. Of course he would take it. Schwartz would never be able to prove it was him. It could be any student, for example, or one of the cult members stealing it for his own nefarious purposes. Why not? Schwartz would have other copies, just as Denton had had copies of what had been taken in Stuttgart. Tit for tat. Tat for tit. I tawght I taw a titty tat.

Denton giggled hysterically. He turned on his flashlight and swung it around the room.

Most of the bookshelves he could dismiss out of hand. They were full of standard-looking texts, and Kobinski's work would not be in such lowly company. The long library tables were clean and shone in the beam of his flashlight. He was surprised to find that the library was different than he'd remembered it—smaller. The area he thought he'd remembered the men standing in was not some secret niche, as it turned out, or any kind of niche at all. On that side of the room there was only another long table by the window. Denton scanned the walls and furniture nearby.

There was an old-fashioned writing desk, the kind that had a fold-down lid. It was huge, as such things went. Dozens of drawers, small and large, surrounded the lid. Denton knew in his gut that if the Kobinski material was in the library, that was where it would be. He began to search the drawers, pausing every few moments to listen, head lifted, ears perked. He could picture Schwartz (in slippers and house robe now), silently approaching down the hall, gliding like Nosferatu. No, he wouldn't think about that.

He wanted that moment, that exquisite moment, of laying his fingers on the manuscript. He wanted to get the hell out of here. The thought of being in his car, on the freeway to New York, with the manuscript in the passenger seat, made him continue no matter how badly he was quaking.

In the drawers he found: paper, ink, pens, twine, rubber bands, Post-its, staples, a Hebrew-English pocket dictionary. In one small drawer he found several pairs of long, flat-pronged tweezers and a magnifying glass. He did not find the manuscript or any fragments thereof.

He searched twice, growing more frantic and feeling a leaden knowing descend. When he was done, he wiped his face. There was sweat on his brow and Denton Wyle never sweated. He was sweating now all right, because he knew where it was. He knew exactly where! It was inside the desk, under that lid. And the closed lid's most prominent feature was a large, ornate keyhole.

That, of course, didn't mean it was locked.

But it is! You know it is, because that's just freaking like him!

Denton put the flashlight down on a nearby shelf, beam pointed toward the desk, and tried the lid, pulling wherever he could grasp with gloved fingers. Yup. It was locked.

"Crap!"

He was on the verge of losing it. He tried to slow his breathing using a technique he'd learned from his psychoanalyst. Slow inhale, one-two-three-four, exhale in a *ha ha ha ha* pattern, jerking his lungs like fish on a line. Repeat. Again. Repeat. Again.

Now. Key. Where would the key be kept? Schwartz's office at best, on the man himself at worst. Denton knew where the office was, though it meant possible exposure. Still, the school was asleep, right? And he would be very, *very* careful. He turned off his flashlight, tucked it into his belt, and went back into the hall.

The door to Schwartz's office was easy to recognize. It was at the end of the hall and had a sunken curved arch. It was closed. It was locked.

Denton pounded the stone wall impotently, sobbing under his breath. There was no point in breaking in *here*. The key might not even be *in* the office, and the whole point of the key was to avoid breaking into something. Why the hell were they buttoned down so tight? Didn't that paranoid bastard trust his own people?

"Of course not," Denton said hatefully. "Not that megalomaniac."

None of this got him anywhere. Even while he indulged in a momentary pity party, in his gut he knew what he had to do. He would have to break the damn desk. No choice. It wouldn't be easy. It wouldn't be quiet. He'd need tools. He hadn't brought a crowbar or anything, hadn't wanted to admit to himself that it might come to that.

In the hall he listened. It was absolutely quiet and dark. He went back to the coat closet.

Predictably, he did not find a crowbar in there, or even a screwdriver. What he did find was a massive old umbrella, of the kind built before World

War Two. It was large, with a narrow tip, and it looked like a steamroller couldn't bend it.

Umbrella in hand like Mary-freaking-Poppins, Denton crept back to the library. He checked his watch: 12:45.

He began to work at the desk lid. By 1:00 he had pushed, pried, and prodded enough of a gap in the wood near the lock to fully insert the umbrella's tip. He knew what came next. He paused, shaking out his aching hands and doing the *ha-ha* breath again, rolled his neck, considered strategy. Strategy, however, was not his thing.

He inserted the umbrella into the divot and pulled back hard. For a long suspended moment, nothing happened. Then he felt something give, ever so slightly, and with an enormous *crack* the desk lid opened about an inch and then stopped. Denton grabbed his flashlight and examined it quickly. The wood that held the lock had splintered but not completely. He shoved the flashlight between his legs and rammed the umbrella in deeper, pulled back with all his might. There was another groaning, splintery sound and the desk lid flew open. Denton went reeling. The flashlight slipped from between his thighs and rolled away. He dived after it. The noise from the breakage was still loud in his ears, but he thought he heard other sounds as well, footsteps upstairs. Frantic, he trained the light on the open desk.

There were loose papers in Hebrew, a few books, and a large black binder. He flipped the binder open. Inside, he recognized Xerox copies of Kobinski pages. There were several hundred pages in there. He grabbed the binder and ran for the library doors.

Now there were definite footsteps overhead, at least two sets, and deep voices. He sprinted down the hall and into the foyer, seeing no one, heart tripping like a jackhammer. He hit the front doors at full tilt, only realizing now that they might be locked. He had a flash of himself banging at the doors while Schwartz entered the foyer with his clan of side-locked, black-garbed cultists, all of them stumbling toward him, arms out in front of them, eyes glassy, like a bunch of Jewish zombies and . . .

But the doors were institutional doors, with a large horizontal push bar at waist level. As he hit the bar, the heavy door swung open and the night air was on his face. He barely had time to feel relief when an alarm bell blared. He fled across the wide driveway, across the lawn, onto the main road. He opted for the trees, sure they were right behind him. He crashed through the woods, heading north toward his parked car. He hazarded a glance back.

Lights were blazing from one downstairs window and—now—the lights in the foyer went on. But no one was after him, not yet.

Denton ran. He had done it! *He had the manuscript!*

9.3. Jill Talcott

THE NEGATIVE ONE PULSE, 75 PERCENT POWER

Jill Talcott was home with the flu. She'd been up twice in the night vomiting. Between heaves, she'd thought about Nate's warning. They were at 75 percent power on the negative one pulse. Was it making her ill? But no, a lot of people were down with the flu—most of the people in their department. It didn't necessarily mean anything.

She had planned to call the lab, let Nate know she wasn't coming in, but she had finally fallen asleep around seven. The phone jarred her awake an hour later.

"Hello?" she answered groggily.

"Are you okay?"

Nate's voice. With her head raised off the pillow to answer the phone, Jill felt a wave of dizziness that nearly undid her. "Flu. I was going to call—"

"Oh god."

" 's all right."

"No, it's not. Someone broke into the lab."

Jill dragged on a pair of sweats and drove over to the university. She was feeling a little better by the time she got there, if only because she was so panicked that it distracted her from what her body was feeling. When she got to the basement, Nate was busy on the computer. Her eyes swept around the room but didn't see any signs of disturbance.

"The door," he said grimly.

He followed her back out into the hall and they examined the dead bolt together. They'd had it installed when they first moved down here—it had been bright and shiny new. Now there were scratch marks on the surface of it, near the key slot, and there were heavy marks, too, on the wooden doorjamb, where the dead bolt went in.

"Are you sure they actually got in?"

"Stuff's been moved around."

"Show me."

Back in the room, Jill turned the lock behind her, feeling violated. Nate went to his chair. "I had a bunch of papers near my keyboard. Someone moved them into a stack. I think there might be some missing."

"What! What's missing? What was in them?"

"Just my notes. I'm not sure." He rubbed his forehead with two fingers. The circles under his eyes were grape-colored. She realized he was muddled and that pissed her off.

"Nate! This is important!"

"I'm not sure what pages!"

"Well, what else did they get?" She looked around the room anxiously and went over to their lab subjects. It didn't appear as though any of the cages or specimens had been touched. The white board was intact, but the sight of it, the realization that someone—and she thought she knew who—*knew* all that, had *seen* it . . .

"And maybe stuff on the computer," Nate said dourly.

"The computer!" She stomped over to the machine.

"I think the papers were moved around so that they could get at the keyboard."

"Nate!"

His face darkened with anger. "How exactly is this *my* fault?"

She moved around the desk and looked at the screen. It was running Windows, and right at the bottom of the shortcut list was the little happy-face icon Nate used for their wave simulator. She moaned. "Someone could have gotten the *sim*? Doesn't it have all the Quey data in it? And the differential routine, the one that discovered the one-minus-one wave?"

Nate clenched his jaw. "Yes."

"Could they have copied the program?"

"The directory's too big to fit on disk, but they could have downloaded it to the university network and copied it anywhere they liked."

"Damn it!" Talcott smacked the keyboard in frustration. For a moment she had an urge to beat it senseless, which was really inane, since it was already senseless.

When they'd first moved down here Nate had insisted on hooking the computer up to the campus net, said it would make it easy to transfer files between the lab and their office. And she'd thought him resourceful!

"You didn't even have a Windows password on that thing!"

"No one's ever in here but you and me." He looked guilty and angry about being made to feel guilty.

Jill sank into a chair. She had to think. The thief had possibly gotten the sim and some of Nate's papers. What else? Her notes for the article and her journals were all in her briefcase. She'd gotten paranoid enough to keep them with her at all times, so that was all right. But the Excel data had been on this computer and possibly other things, too, like the early statistics Nate had accumulated.

"What about the equation?" she asked, her tongue thick. "Was my equation on the computer?"

Nate thought about it, then shook his head. "No."

"Not in the sim? Isn't it in the sim? I thought—"

"*No.* The sim just uses two sets of data—the Quey results and the carbon atom data. This computer can't even crunch your equation, remember?"

Yes, that was true, and it gave her some relief. She was pretty sure her equation was in her briefcase and nowhere else. She'd been very careful not to throw it around. It was far too precious for that.

"You're *sure* it wasn't in your papers?" she said carefully.

"*Yes.* I'm sure."

Well, that was something. "Is there any way to find out if someone *did* move the sim from this computer over the net?"

Nate sank into the chair in front of the treacherous machine and played with the mouse. "Dunno. I can call the computer department, see if they'd have a log."

"Call them."

"Fuck it," Nate said coldly. "I'll go over there." He put on his motorcycle jacket with stiff jerks and left.

He'd barely made it out the door when Talcott felt a wave of nausea hit her. She grabbed the closest waste can and held it between her knees, panting. Hot tears stung her eyes.

Someone had gotten, *stolen*, her work. *Her work.* Had he gotten enough to put it all together? To publish *her* work, claim it as his own? Or just enough to get her fired? Of all the questions she asked herself, there was one that never occurred to her, and that was *who did it*. She knew damned well who. Chuck Grover.

Now the sense of pressure, of urgency, grabbed her as never before. It seemed to merge with her nausea. She retched weakly, but nothing came up; she'd had nothing but water for days. She looked up at the white board, at the data, breathing in deep shaky breaths. With less than a week running the negative one pulse at 75 percent power, they only had a 35 percent differential between the control group and the lab subjects. Thirty-five percent. She needed at least 50. She needed it to end.

She went over to the transmitter and put the power up to 90 percent. She locked the lab, put a note on the door.

Nate, take some time off. Don't go back in the lab. That's an order. Jill

9.4. CALDER FARRIS

GAKONA, ALASKA

When Dr. Serin was paged and went to his office to answer it, Calder followed. And when Serin covered the receiver and said softly, "Someone from the University of Washington," Calder hit the speaker button, ignoring the resentful daggers thrown his way.

"Uh . . . hello?" The man on the other end paused in his spiel when he heard his voice echo.

Calder motioned to Serin.

"Go ahead, Dr. Grover," Serin said.

"Call me Chuck." The man on the phone went on to explain that he'd heard about the call that had been placed to HAARP from the University of Washington and that he had an idea who had done it. It was, in fact, his partner. The basis of her research was work done on his quantum computer, for which reason he was a fundamental part, actually co-author—

"That's very interesting," Serin interrupted. "So what's this partner of yours doing exactly?"

Calder sat on the edge of Serin's desk, ready at any moment to pick up the receiver if that became necessary.

"She's doing research with particle waves. The equation she crunched on Quey had to do with particle wave mechanics."

Grover sounded suspiciously like he was reading. Calder's expression showed nothing, but his blood pressure had just headed for the north pole and, mentally, he already had his hand around the caller's throat. Ansel had been working on wave mechanics.

"She put the equation together, but, you know, it would have been impossible to crunch on a conventional computer, but with Quey . . ."

Nearly endless detail about the value of quantum computing. Calder took it all in, expressionless. He was patient. Oh, yes. Patient as a snake outside the burrow of a mouse.

It was Serin who began to fidget. "Is she just running equations or what? Because I got the impression the caller was doing something with wave *transmission*. I'm confused."

"You'd be surprised," Grover said enigmatically. "Actually, I'd like you to take a look at some stuff. I've been pretty focused on Quey lately, and I haven't had time to stay as on top of this as I'd like. I'd love to get your opinion on our work."

"Well, I'm kind of busy myself, *Chuck*." Serin had an academic's loathing of reviewing anyone else's material.

Calder rapped Serin hard on the noggin to get his attention. He nodded a strong affirmative.

"Steve?" Grover asked. "It is Steve, isn't it? The man at the switchboard said—"

"Uh . . . hold on." Serin put Grover on hold and ran the situation through his little gray cells. He rubbed his pate, eyeing Calder with sullen resentment.

"This isn't anything," he said. "I told you before, and I don't have time to go over a bunch of—"

"*You* don't have to go over anything."

Serin frowned, but he did as he was told—typical candyass. He put Grover back on. "Uh, Chuck, go ahead and e-mail it to me."

"You got a big limit on your E-mail? 'Cause I have about twenty meg."

"Uh—we're on the *DARPA* net, Chuck."

"Oh. Right. I'll send it then. You have a fax? I've got some pages, too; I don't wanna scan 'em."

Calder nodded.

"S-sure." Serin gave the fax number and his E-mail address.

"Okay. I'll send it now. Call me back ASAP, okay?"

"Will do."

Grover hung up. Calder stood, stretched his legs. "Bring up your E-mail," he commanded. Whatever restraint he'd displayed in the past few days was gone.

Serin blinked up at him. "Well, *yeah*," as if he hadn't had to be asked, particularly not in a tone like that. He brought it up. The fax machine on the table behind him buzzed.

Calder stepped behind Serin's chair and yanked it out, forcing the scientist to stand or fall. He stood. Calder put a hand on his shoulder. "Okay, Dr. Serin. Time to go."

Serin gaped wordlessly, going apoplectic. That narrow fem face wanted so badly to protest, wanted *so badly to*. But the fax behind him was printing and Calder didn't have time to let him work it out. He placed a widely splayed hand on Serin's chest and pushed lightly, but ever so painfully, with his fingertips. He let the demon creep into his voice.

"Get. Out."

Serin left the room.

Calder Farris locked the door and sat down at the desk, waiting for the new E-mail. The fax machine went on and on. He glanced at the pages but didn't get into them. Mostly scribbles, notes. It would take time to review them.

A *ding* informed him that he had 1 unread E-mail. It was from cgrover at the University of Washington. He opened it, saved the attached executable to his hard drive, ran it.

A minute later he was looking at the one-minus-one.

10

Although not all suffering in human life is wholly
evil, a great deal of it is, and the ultimate source of
all evil is the biological capacity for suffering. The
biological capacity for suffering, in turn, exists because it has evolved. It has evolved because it often
served an adaptive function . . . It was adaptive because it contributed to the reproductive success of
its possessors. Because it contributed to the reproductive success of its possessors, it was favored by
natural selection.
     —Timothy Anders, *The Evolution of Evil,* 1994

All diseases of Christians are to be ascribed to
demons.
     —Saint Augustine, fifth century

10.1. CALDER FARRIS

SEATTLE

The parking garage was vast. The light, at 7:00 P.M., was flat, ugly, and artifi-
cial. Chuck Grover had parked on floor C. Most of the cars in faculty parking
were gone, leaving a space next to his BMW convertible for a large sedan to
slip in and wait.

Grover was just getting into his car when a hand fell on his shoulder. He
jumped.

"Dr. Grover?" Calder removed his sunglasses. "Lieutenant Calder Farris,
United States Marines. We'd like to talk to you."

Grover seemed reluctant to look away from Calder's eyes, the way a man
might fear turning his back on a hooded and hissing cobra. But he did tear
them away, took in Calder's military uniform and that of Ed Hinkle, hulking
behind him. For a moment Grover looked confused; then a self-congratulatory
smugness crept over his face. "This about Quey, right?"

Calder held up a zip disk. On the label was written "wavesim.exe."

"No, Dr. Grover, it's not."

It took twenty minutes to shake Grover down. Unlike a lot of geeks, he
had a healthy and realistic fear of authority (a drug bust way back when,

Calder guessed). But even so, the bastard was cagey. He tried to probe to see how interested the government was and what was in it for him. Calder got tired of it, sensed a snow job a mile high, and began to turn the screws. Grover crumbled like blue cheese.

To be honest, and he was leveling now, he knew absolutely nothing about the simulator. He'd been hoping Serin could tell *him*. He told a story about a Dr. Jill Talcott and how she'd promised him she'd share her work with him if he (a bunch of shit Calder didn't care about), but then she reneged and kept it all under wraps. She was a loner, a hermit. Nobody liked her. Nobody had the first clue what she was doing. *Nobody.*

Calder might not have believed him, might have made sure with what Hinkle referred to as some "serious work," if he hadn't already expected Grover to be clueless from that enigmatic phone call to Alaska. So, like a fisherman being careful to remove his hook before throwing back a fish too small to eat, Calder spun a brief cover story involving HAARP confidentiality and a missing-documents investigation.

But the whole thing, the whole pointless, shitty thing, took thirty minutes. Thirty minutes were lost, all because some marijuana-smoking, self-serving geek would not give Dr. Talcott's name over the phone. It was thirty minutes Calder would deeply regret.

The sedan nudged out a car trying to park in a space on Forty-fifth Street, across from the campus. Calder smiled tightly as Grover tried to make his excuses and slip away. He gripped the physicist's elbow.

"No, I'd like you to escort me to Dr. Talcott's lab."

"It's in the basement of Smith Hall. If you go—"

"I appreciate your help, Dr. Grover."

They crossed the street. The rain had finally let up, but it was colder than a witch's tit, and the cement walkways were turning icy. They passed bundled students. *Might as well be in Alaska,* thought Calder. It wasn't supposed to be like this in Seattle, was it? But he forgot the cold as he walked at Grover's side because he was close now. He could smell it. Close to the Big One, close to congratulations and recognition and a promotion or three or four. Close to being Maj. Calder Farris or, hell, even general, a man personally responsible for his country's continued superiority and invulnerability to the chaotic hordes, maybe for the next several hundred years. Close, after all this time.

They rounded a corner at the library and faced a quad lined with buildings. After a few faltering steps, Grover stopped and stared, perplexed. Calder followed his gaze. At first he took it for a plume of steam from a heating duct. Then he saw it was smoke. It was coming from the basement windows of a Gothic brick-and-cement building. A few students passing in front of it looked at it curiously, but no one seemed unduly alarmed.

Then the ground thudded beneath his feet. There was a cacophony in his ears and a force slammed against his chest. It was like hitting a concrete wall in a car, only he hadn't been moving—the wall had come to *him*. All three of them went down, Grover flying backward into Ed Hinkle and Calder slamming onto slick pavement. He must have blacked out momentarily. The next thing he was conscious of was a ringing in his ears and then, coming muffled through that, distant sirens.

He lifted his head, wobbling, and saw the brick building in front of them blackened from the ground up, flames rising to the upper levels. The basement had just exploded.

Calder's reactions were a tiny bit slow. It took him a moment to grasp the significant point here. Then he grabbed the lapels of Grover's coat, noting dully that his hands were scratched and bleeding. He shook the physicist until his yellow teeth rattled. He shouted, and his voice came from very, very far away.

"Where's Talcott's lab?"

Grover pointed—to the conflagration.

10.2. AHARON HANDALMAN

JERUSALEM

Aharon Handalman did not watch television. He did not even allow it in the house. Yet it just so happened that lately he had varied his route to work. Instead of seeking out the most ancient pathways, he had, once or twice, cut straight from the Jaffa gate to the temple wall, down *Hashhalshelet*, where the modern world was no stranger.

And if he stopped, on his way to and from work, at a little corner store that had television sets in the window? If he watched the news for a few minutes at a time? Was that such a crime?

He didn't know what he was looking for. They say, "He doesn't know what he's looking for, but he'll know it when he sees it," and this was the case. When he walked up to the store this morning, it was there on the screens, all twenty of them. CNN international news, Hebrew edition. A newswoman's voice was being piped from inside the store. To her right was an imposed video of a burning building. The heading said: "Seattle, Washington." The video was replaced by a photograph of a slight, intelligent-looking woman. Underneath the photograph was a name: Dr. Jill Talcott.

Aharon stared at the name for a moment, feeling he had seen it somewhere.

". . . so far missing. The fire is believed to have started in the physicist's lab, where Dr. Talcott was conducting experiments of an unspecified nature. Police . . ."

Aharon turned and began running toward home.

*   *   *

When he arrived, Hannah was just getting up. She stood in the hallway in her robe as he opened the door.

"Aharon?"

He hesitated, the enormity of what he was doing striking him for the first time. He gulped a breath. "Hannah . . . if I had to go to America . . . We have some savings. Half of that is yours, Hannah."

She studied him, her pretty face serious. "This has to do with Kobinski?"

He nodded.

"What about your work, your classes?"

His classes? The thought gave Aharon pause. He had been "talked to" twice more by Dean Horowitz. But what could he do? Horowitz would do what he had to do, Aharon also.

"Tell them . . . there was a family emergency." He colored at how easily the lie came.

She said nothing.

"It's only for a day or two."

She gave him a measured look, long and sad. It was a look he would carry with him to America and far beyond. It said, *And maybe you'll never come back at all. And maybe you've already been gone so long this is only a formality.*

"I'll pack your bag." She headed for their room.

Hannah put the sleepy children in the car and drove him to the airport. When he got out he kissed each of the little ones on the head. Devorah asked, "Where are you going, Papa?" and he said, "I have some business. I'll be back soon." Yehuda turned his head away when Aharon kissed him.

Hannah managed both worry and coldness as she hugged Aharon good-bye. She took a paper from her pocket and pressed it on him.

"Samuel got this through a chat room for survivors. The address and phone number are there."

Aharon took it, frowning, and put it in a pocket for later. He stood, awkwardly, knowing he should say something more, much, much more, but not knowing where to start.

"You've tried so hard to shut me out, Aharon," Hannah said. "So I guess I have no right to know where you're going."

"I never shut you out."

"I hope you can find something that will let you put all this behind you."

He did not like what he saw in her face. He patted her arm reassuringly. "I'm going to Seattle, Hannah. Why wouldn't I tell you? And it will only be for a few days. You're my wife, the mother of my children. You don't have to worry."

She pecked him on the cheek and drove away. Aharon opened the note.

Hannah had found Anatoli Nikiel.

10.3. JILL TALCOTT

SEATTLE

There was a loud battering in her head that Jill took for just another new and fun-filled phase of her massive headache. She had been so sick all night. Now she was in a place that wasn't so very bad. The pain was still there, but she felt detached, as though it were happening to someone else, as though she were in a cage and there was a tiger prowling around outside, but he couldn't get in. She floated in this space, slept. She thought the phone might have rung, several times. She could ignore that, but the battering noise disturbed her. And it gradually dawned on her that someone was calling her name.

Nate.

She managed to get her head off the pillow and look at the clock. It was almost ten. She'd slept in. Lifting her head was a major effort and she would have gone back to sleep, but the banging continued. She wanted to tell him to knock it the hell off, but she'd have to get to the door first.

Her feet perhaps hit the floor by the bed. She couldn't feel them and she wasn't quite sure. She stumbled forward. When she finally pulled the front door open, Nate was on the doorstep, his face wild.

"My god! I saw your car and I hoped . . . ! Christ!"

He assaulted her, black leather arms wrapping her in a child's hug. He squeezed and it felt like she was a tube of toothpaste—all the blood rushed from her middle to her head, making the dull pain scream.

"*S-stop!*" she gasped, pushing him away. She lurched to the couch and collapsed there. He came and knelt beside her, provoking a dim, heart-thudding memory of that day their positions were reversed.

"You're burning up!" he claimed, though she barely felt his hand on her head. "Oh my god. You turned it up, didn't you?"

She didn't answer.

"You didn't call in sick today. Everyone thinks you were in the lab."

" 'sonly ten o'clock," she said crankily. Then she recalled that when she'd opened the door it had been night. Ten o'clock at night? She must have gone to bed leaving all the lights burning. She'd slept through an entire day.

"Jill . . ." The look on his face was scaring her.

"What?"

He turned on the TV, flipped to the local news.

"*. . . terrible scene. The explosion occurred at approximately seven o'clock this evening. Fortunately, no classes were in session at the time.*"

Despite the sense of floating detachment and her pounding headache, this brought Jill to as much consciousness as she was capable of.

"Nate?"

"Smith Hall."

"No."

Tears were on his face. "There was a massive explosion."

"The police will not comment, but sources at the university have estimated that there were at least twenty to thirty people in the building."

"Ohmigod." It was too much to grasp—that she might have been in there, that those poor people *were* in there, that her lab was gone.

"I was at the restaurant," Nate panted, his cheeks wet. "I came over as soon as I heard. We always do the control group here in the afternoons, so I hoped . . ."

On the screen her building was burning, and she couldn't quite make herself believe it. Their computer. Their data. When was the last time she'd made a backup? Their research subjects, which she was hoping to postmortem—gone.

"Jill . . ." There was something on his face, a high color at the tops of his olive cheeks, a weird shininess in his eyes. He took one of her hands.

"At this time we know that there was a lab down in the basement of the building, run by Dr. Jill Talcott. Officials think this was the source of the explosion but have not revealed the nature of the experiments."

It was like a slap in the face, hard, stinging. This wasn't just *any* explosion. This wasn't going to work and finding something had happened to her building, her lab, something terrible and inconvenient as hell but not her fault. This was *her* explosion.

She sucked in air. She was still floating, still remote, still held at arm's length from life by the fever's grip. But this thing came through all that like a speeding bullet.

Dead. My fault.

She heard sirens from the distance, growing louder.

"Jill?" Nate's face, streaming with tears, floated in front of her eyes. She pushed off it, like a swimmer pushing off a raft, and willed herself back into unconsciousness.

II

You thought in your own mind, I will scale the heavens; I will set my throne high above the stars of God, I will sit on the mountain where the gods meet in the far recesses of the north. I will rise above the cloud banks and make myself like the Most High. Yet shall you be brought down to Sheol, to the depths of the abyss.

—Isaiah 14:12

II.I. Calder Farris

SEATTLE

The first thing Calder did after the explosion was find a bathroom and clean the blood off his face. Flying debris and glass had assaulted his exposed skin like shrapnel. Little dark spots showed where particles had embedded themselves. He left them; he didn't have time to dick with that now.

The second thing he did was call Dr. Rickman, his superior at the DoD. This was no longer a solo mission, Calder said; this was a possible XL3.

The XLs were codewords they used in the field when there was something definite to report. An XL1 was the discovery of a new weapon, typically something on the order of a bomb. An XL2 was a really *big* bomb. An XL3 was an unknown weapon of mass destruction.

In retrospect, it might have been overdoing it. But there were two ways to play it safe here. The first way to play it safe was by assuming the worst in order to get the situation under control as hard and fast as possible. The second was to be leery of calling an XL3 until he had proof positive that's what it was. It all came down to his faith in the powers of devastation of the thing he was chasing.

By dawn, Calder had everything the DoD could give him.

7:00 A.M.

Lieutenant Farris, Lieutenant Hinkle, and six other men in long black trench coats and dark glasses walked into Swedish Hospital in Seattle. They had a hardened, regimental look and the gait of a death squad. They knew where she was being kept: the second floor. According to their information, the detective in charge of the investigation was up there now. Calder didn't bother with anyone less than that. When they emerged from the elevator and were questioned by a young officer, Calder flipped his ID and kept walking.

By the time they reached Seattle Police Department's Detective Mathers, they were expected. Mathers stood in the hall, hands on his hips, his officers around him. Calder's eye flickered to Mathers's badge, verifying the name.

"Detective Mathers? Calder Farris, FBI. We're authorized to take over here, as I think you'll find if you contact your—"

"He already called." Mathers looked wary and excited. He jerked his head down the hall, signaling Calder to a private conversation. Calder followed.

"What's the FBI's interest?" Mathers asked when they were alone. He was a lean man, trying to look younger than his forty-odd years. He had a conspiratorial air, chewing his gum in an anxious rhythm. Calder, whose dark glasses were still in place, treated him to a stony, blank face. Mathers lost a little of his bonhomie.

"We're investigating the possibility of terrorist activity."

"Thought so. Is it because of this lab run by Dr. Talcott? You got a tip on her or somethin'? Some reason to think she's in league with Al-Qaeda or someone like that?"

Calder said nothing, letting Mathers draw his own conclusions. The FBI on a terrorist investigation was a common-enough story. It would hold for a while, keep this thing from attracting the interest of the wrong people.

"We have the fire department and an arson expert on-site," Mathers said.

"We just sent in our own. They'll be taking over. For now, we're on media blackout."

Mathers frowned at this, scratched his chin. "You want me to stick around? Go over—"

"I want you to clear out. You and your men. You have notes? Photographs? Information on Dr. Talcott? You will have interviewed her. I'd like a transcript."

"She's unconscious. Been asleep since we brought her in. Doctors advised that we let her. She's had a fever over a hundred and two. Viral, they think."

Calder felt relieved but didn't show it. These past few hours had been frustrating, waiting for everything to be put into place, thinking about what Talcott might be telling the Seattle police inside this very building while he waited outside like a cuckolded husband.

"Fine. Just hand over whatever you have. If I have questions, I'll call you."

Mathers was getting pissed at the brush-off. "I thought the FBI worked in conjunction with local authorities. This is *our* university, *our* kids."

"This is a national security issue, Detective Mathers, and no longer your responsibility."

Within five minutes, Calder's men had the entire floor cleared of Seattle's finest. Objective achieved: contain the situation; eliminate outsiders. Mathers would probably hold up his reports for hours to make a point. Let him. Calder had Talcott, and he'd already done his own background check on her.

He accepted a paper cup of cold water from one of his associates and drank it in a gulp. He removed his coat and went in, alone, to see her.

There, in the hospital bed, making barely a mound under the sheets, was a woman. Calder walked to the foot of the bed and took off his glasses, stared. Her arms stuck out of the hospital gown, thin and pale and freckled. Her hair was a nondescript shade of dirty blond and was unwashed (probably sick for a few days at least, Calder noted). Her face was narrow, aquiline, unexceptional, but not unattractive and not without character. It reminded him of the faces of plainswomen he'd seen in photographs: hard, not with denigration, the way hookers' faces are hard, but with a rocklike determination to take whatever life threw their way. She might prove stubborn, but she was female, after all, and looked too physically insignificant to be a real problem.

As if feeling his eyes like cold spots on her flesh, the woman shivered in her sleep and turned over.

He could wake her now. But he had other things to take care of—making sure the on-site team at the university had cleared out the local workers, for example, and seeing if she had any confidantes, despite Grover's remark that she was a loner. She could wait. She wasn't going anywhere.

Calder picked up her chart and smiled: Jill Talcott, doctorate in physics from the University of Tennessee, onetime graduate student of Dr. Henry Ansel.

II.2. Nate Andros

Nate was serving Saturday brunch at the Coastal Kitchen when the guy came in. Huge, hamhanded, with a face like a pork loin. He didn't exactly fit in on Capitol Hill, where the men were less macho as a rule: students, artists, musicians, gays. Nate was too distracted this morning to notice, not until someone pointed him out.

"Rambo at ten o'clock," said Michél as he spun by carrying twin platters, his hips swinging.

Nate looked and saw that Pork-Loin-Face—Rambo—was looking at a menu. He'd been seated in Nate's section.

"Great," Nate said, to no one in particular.

He was exhausted. He'd been at the hospital until 2:00 A.M., hovering around the waiting room. The police had finally asked who he was, and he'd said, "A friend." He would have told them more, if they'd pressed. They didn't. They seemed disorganized. And the longer he'd sat there *without* being questioned, the more nervous he became about what he would say, so he'd ditched.

Maybe he shouldn't have come in to work today. He wasn't thinking too clearly. This morning it had seemed like a good excuse in case the cops asked why he hadn't come to the station to volunteer what he knew: *I was working.* But he could barely make himself go through the paces. He was frantic about Jill, wishing he could be at her bedside to hold her hand—as if she'd want him to—or at least be there to see for himself that she was going to be okay. And he couldn't stop thinking, too, about the deep, deep, *deep* shit they were in. Atlantic Ocean deep.

What the hell was he going to tell the police? What *could* he tell them without making Jill look guilty as hell? Or himself, for that matter? He was as much a party to everything that had happened as she was.

"What is the *matter* with you today, boy?" Michél asked. Nate was staring down at an undelivered omelet as if the clues to the universe had to do with eggs, caramelized onions, and Havarti.

"Nothing."

Michél put his empty plates in the back room and returned, put a hand on Nate's arm. "Are you sick? You look like Death, and I don't mean Brad Pitt."

Nate collected himself. "I was thinking about something, that's all."

He took the coffeepot and filled up a few of his tables. He was running out of ways to avoid taking Rambo's order, so he headed over there.

Rambo stared at him as he approached. There was a curled-up sneer on his face—the look a cat gets when it's smelled something particularly piquant. Nate could guess what that smell was: he was the only straight waiter in the place and the clientele was pretty much fifty-fifty.

"What can I get you?"

"Steak and eggs. Coffee."

"Sure." Paleolithic. Big surprise. Nate reached for the menu. Rambo clamped a fist over his wrist.

It hurt, as it was meant to, but it was more of a shock, that someone would do that in the first place and do it here, on Nate's own turf. He guffed a laugh, stared at the man indignantly.

"Nate Andros, right?"

Nate nodded, his view of the man shifting instantly. *Cop.* He should have guessed.

Rambo used his nonsqueezing hand to show a badge, making sure Nate had plenty of time to read it. ᴇᴅ ʜɪɴᴋʟᴇ. ꜰʙɪ. "I'm going to eat my steak; then you and I are going to chat. So go tell your boss you're leaving early."

Nate was still nodding; his neck had, in fact, grown springs, so he didn't have to make a special nod for this occasion. Rambo released him.

The kitchen grill was open to the restaurant, the chefs and diners face-to-face. But behind the grill was a back room where they did dishes and yakked. Nate grabbed some dirty plates and went back there, wanting to get out of the man's sight.

Nate stood breathing heavily and looking around the long room. There were boxes of food, the dishwashing machine, and a walk-in fridge. There was no back door. This was an urban neighborhood, and the only doors in the whole place were the front door, in the restaurant itself, and a door at the tail end of the restaurant that led to a small balcony two stories up with no stairs.

FBI! Shit!

He had an order up. He delivered a salmon salad and a scramble. He could feel Rambo's eyes boring into him.

"Boy, you are hyperventi*latin*'! What's *up*?" Michél was at the waiters' counter, along with Justin, a blue-eyed Iowan who had all the other waiters drooling. Nate muttered something indiscernible and went into the back. They followed.

"You're driving me crazy, and I *hate* that." Michél blocked the doorway, hands on his size 21 waist.

"That guy out there," Nate said, scared and sounding it. "He's FBI."

"Rambo? No shit?" Michél looked back over his shoulder, delighted.

"What's goin' on?" Justin asked with cowboy sincerity.

"I think he wants to talk to me about that explosion on campus last night." Nate gripped his abdomen and bent over. Just saying it made his stomach ache.

"You had something to do with that?" Michél was no longer goofing, his face worried. "Oh, *jesu*, are you in trouble. Mannie works over at Swedish. He called me this morning, says the FBI are all *over* the place, man. They've got that scientist from the news, what's her name, Dr. Talbot or something?"

Mannie was Michél's partner, a male nurse. Nate was startled at this news. When had the FBI taken over? And *why*?

"Talcott. I've been her grad student for the past two years."

Michél went maternal and put his arm around Nate. "Oh my *god*! What were you guys *do*ing? Did she really cause that explosion?"

Nate shook his head mutely. *I don't know.* But his face burned. Yeah, she did. He did. *They* did. Michél and Justin exchanged a look.

"Listen, you don't want to talk to this guy, just say the word."

"No problem." Justin nodded.

Nate looked at their resolute faces. "I'll have to talk to them eventually."

"Yeah, but do you want to talk to them *now*, that's the question." Michél held out his hand, expression Cuban cocky, as if to say, *You don't have to do shit while I'm around.*

Nate breathed deeply and raked a hand through his cropped hair. He went to the doorway and peeked out. Rambo was staring right at him. Someone had taken him his order and he chewed steak, looking back at Nate with eyes that had a little too much . . . anticipation in them.

Nate drew back, confused. This didn't feel right. Why was the guy alone? Why couldn't Nate just talk to the police instead of this goon? And there was this whole gay thing mixed up in it, that look of disdain. Was Rambo a homophobe? Would he take the opportunity to beat the crap out of him?

Nate nodded quickly at Justin and Michél before he could change his mind. "Yeah. Get me out of here."

Michél unfurled a smile the devil couldn't have matched. "You got it, sweetcheeks."

Five minutes later, the entire Coastal Kitchen crew was huddled over a piece of chocolate mousse. Michél lit the candle and winked at Nate.

"Happy birthday to you! Happy birthday to you!"

The rousing chorus line descended on Rambo with felicitations, blocking his view and his path. Nate beat it out the front door.

*   *   *

He was heading toward his apartment when he realized that wouldn't be smart. If the FBI knew where he worked they had to know where he lived. And his bike was there, damn it, and therefore irretrievable.

He was standing on one of the residential streets that stretched off Fifteenth. Old brick apartment buildings lined the narrow street. He sank down to sit beside a car to get out of sight, put a piece of gum in his mouth, which was drier than dust, and tried to think it through.

You'd rather talk to the police? So go to the police department. Turn yourself in.

It was a good idea, but he had no idea what he'd say. He'd been gestating that all morning and still didn't have an answer. Did he confess everything about their experiment? Or did he deny up the wazoo and hope no one knew otherwise? After all, the lab was gone, burnt to a crisp. No one knew what they'd been doing.

But there was something else, something that had been bugging him and he couldn't quite grasp. He sat there thinking about the FBI, about how their involvement seemed to really change things, and about ham-hock man, until it came to him.

There was the accident, and that was one thing. But there was also *the technology*.

It came with a shiver and a dawning horror. He remembered the day he'd gotten his first real whiff, complete with major goose bumps, about the nature of the one-minus-one. He'd thought then that if their experiment was really doing what he *thought* it was doing, then this could be some seriously screwed up technology in the wrong hands. Whether or not the FBI was here *looking* for the one-minus-one, they would find it in the course of their investigation. And if they found it, they would pass it on to . . . who? The U.S. government, of course, maybe the military.

Was the U.S. military the wrong hands?

Nate jumped to his feet.

He felt an urgent need to act. The lab was torched and what else was there? Stuff in Jill's office: his papers, the sim, and other files. At Jill's house there was the control group, probably her briefcase. God, her *briefcase*! She kept everything in there. He headed for the bus stop.

*   *   *

When Nate got to Jill's place it was nearly 2:00 P.M. He paused at the end of the street, studying the scene warily. Her street was always lined with cars, especially on a Saturday morning, but he didn't see anything particularly ominous—no black sedans, patrol cars, or men wearing suits. The house itself looked quiet.

Well, he told himself, *I'll either get away with it or I won't.*

He walked to her car and glanced in the windows casually. Her briefcase wasn't in the front or backseats, though it wouldn't have surprised him if she'd forgotten it there, as sick as she'd been lately. He knew it wouldn't be in the trunk; he'd never even seen her open the trunk. Hands in his pockets, he headed for the house. The front door was locked, but he had a key Jill had given him months ago. He let himself in.

He shut the front door slowly, trying not to make a sound. His ears strained for any noise. He heard nothing.

He sighed with relief. Still being quiet, but pretty confident now that he was alone, he surveyed the living room for Jill's briefcase. He didn't see it. He went into the small kitchen—nada. He rummaged around and found a large plastic garbage bag. He'd laid this all out in his head on the way over here like a criminal planning a heist—in and out in five minutes. He would collect the control specimens as well as any papers or records in the house and put them in the bag.

He went down the hall to the guest room where the control subjects were kept and opened the door. The room was empty. He gaped, then blinked hard, several times, as if to change the message being transmitted to his brain. Every piece of fruit, every virus dish, every mouse was gone. Only the barren card tables remained. It reminded him of the time he'd pulled the wool over Chalmers's eyes, hiding all their stuff in the next room. Now someone had pulled that switcharoo on him.

He went and checked the next room—Jill's bedroom. Her closet and bedside table had been rifled through, but they hadn't taken her clothes or even, he noticed, the passport or small collection of family photographs in the open drawer of her bedside table. He paused, unable to resist looking at these pictures. Jill never mentioned family, ever. They looked poor, her mother washed out and old. Jill was younger but just as feisty-looking. She took after her dad.

Nate put the pictures back and checked the bath and hall closet. There was nothing in them but a few towels, shampoo, toothbrush—the basics. Everything related to the experiment had been taken from the house. The briefcase, if it had been here, was now in the custody of the FBI. He was too late.

Nate slumped to the floor in the hallway, garbage bag useless at his side. So his intuition hadn't been wrong. This wasn't just about the explosion; they wanted information. And what were the two most important sources of information? He and Jill. They'd already be grilling her, and it was just a matter of time before they caught up with him.

He had a bad feeling about this. He had a very bad feeling.

He heard the front door creaking open, slowly, as though moved by the wind. He'd left it unlocked. *Damn!* Cautious footsteps. It was no wind.

Nate panicked. The thought of him and Rambo alone was enough to make him gag in terror. But before he could do more than push himself to his feet, a figure stepped into the hallway. Nate screamed. He looked at the man; the man looked at him.

My god, Nate thought, with a hysterical giggle, *I'm hallucinating.* Maybe he'd wake up to find this whole thing was some bizarre lucid dream caused by the negative one pulse. Because the funny thing was, the intruder looked exactly like an Orthodox Jew. There was the long beard, the black fedora and long black coat, black pants, black shoes. He could have walked out of Mr. Broadway's deli in New York. The man was studying him suspiciously.

"Who are you?" the man asked, as if this were his house and Nate had broken in.

"Who am *I*? Who are *you*?"

"I'm looking for Dr. Talcott."

"She's at the hospital."

"I know that." The man put a finger to his lips, thinking. "So who are *you*?"

"Who are *you*?" Nate asked again, frowning.

The man rolled his eyes. "This could go on all day. I'm tired, so I give up first. My name is Rabbi Aharon Handalman. I need to know what Dr. Talcott was experimenting with."

Nate slumped against the wall. He'd accepted the idea that the government might be interested. That the *Orthodox Jewish community* might be interested—that was too bizarre. "How do *you* know about Dr. Talcott?"

"I have information. She'll want to talk; trust me. And who are *you*?"

"I'm . . ." Nate hesitated but figured what the hell. It was all over anyway. "Her graduate student, Nate Andros."

Rabbi Handalman sighed and closed his eyes. "Thank the Lord for that."

11.3. SHIMON NOROWITZ

Aharon Handalman had flown to Seattle.

Shimon Norowitz had not been having the rabbi followed, hadn't given him that much credit. But he had put Handalman's name into the database of "people of interest," a list that would raise flags when processed by airlines, railways, and police departments or if they cropped up in the media.

Norowitz had his secretary call and inquire at the yeshiva. They told her Rabbi Handalman had a family emergency in America—a sick relative. Norowitz called Aharon's wife himself. She wanted to know who he was and sounded nervous. She told him the same thing—a sick relative. She was lying.

The Mossad subscribed to a service that gave them a daily summary of news throughout the world. He brought up the summary for the day Handalman left. There were more than fifty items. He saved it to a text file and brought it up in another window, did a search on "Seattle." He found an article about an explosion on campus at the University of Washington.

He clicked on a hyperlink under the heading. It took him on-line to the *Seattle Times* site. It was suspected that the lab of a physicist named Dr. Jill Talcott was the cause of the explosion, and the FBI was trying to rule out any possible terrorist connection.

Norowitz sucked on his mustache, considering it. He reread all the coverage carefully. There wasn't much there, really. He sucked on his mustache some more.

He picked up the phone and called one of his analysts. Assaf was a gifted mathematician and one of Norowitz's best cryptologists.

"Assaf, listen; bring up your search routine for the Kobinski codes. I want to try some keywords."

Norowitz heard typing in the background.

"Go ahead."

" 'Seattle.' "

Typing. "Nothing."

" 'University of Washington' and 'Washington.' "

"No."

" 'Explosion'?"

"Emm . . . no."

" 'Smith Hall.' "

"No."

Norowitz could still taste hummus on his mustache from lunch. " 'Jill Talcott' or just 'Talcott.' "

"Umm . . ." More typing. "Hit."

"Yes?"

"Hit." Assaf's voice was perking up. "I'm trying the . . . hit. Hit, hit, hit!"

Norowitz hung up the phone. He sat there for a moment, staring at the CNN article. Then he picked up the phone and called the chief of the Mossad.

11.4. Denton Wyle

Los Angeles

From The Book of Torment by Yosef Kobinski

In my being, I represent the essence of opposites. I have striven for perfect balance and nearly achieved it. I have seen the greatest mysteries imaginable and wept for them. Now I struggle against a desire to pick up Hate like a cloak and put it on, sinking down into the depths of darkness like a stone. I could take up Hate like a harlot, brought home to shame my parents. I could wed Hate like a bridegroom. I could wrap my hand around it like a bottle of poison and drink it out of sheer perversity. Oh, Life, you are my enemy now. You have taken the heart from me and stomped it into the ground, and for this, I abandon you!

The Schwartz manuscript. Denton sat in the living room of his condo, the binder in his lap, trying to digest what he'd just read. It was at once wonderful and horrible and disappointing.

There were thirty-two pages of Kobinski material that Denton had never seen, and that was wonderful. There were several long entries going into detail about Kobinski's theory of "balance"—religious stuff. And there were new entries, quite shattering ones, about the camps and Kobinski's son, Isaac. Denton knew these had been written later than any entries he'd yet seen. They seemed to represent a rock-bottom point for Kobinski, a giving up or giving in. Denton got the feeling Kobinski had planned the escape attempt for Isaac's sake, but apparently it hadn't happened fast enough to save the boy. The kabbalist had written very little at the end.

It was exciting to read the new pages for the first time. But now the excitement faded and Denton was stuck facing the sum total of the manuscript as it now stood.

And he was disappointed. The new entries had a lot of emotional impact, but they did nothing for his whole kabbalah magic angle. Not one darn thing. There was nothing more about gateways or black holes or other universes, nothing about the last days of Kobinki's life or his disappearance, nothing that would give him the explanations he had been looking for this entire freaking time. *How* had Kobinski vanished? Where was the charm, the incantation, or at least a detailed scientific explanation? And where did he think he would go? An alternate universe? Heaven? William Shatner Land? *Where,* for god's sake?

All of that was echoingly absent. And Denton had to admit, now, that it had probably never been written and he would never find it. He wanted to sob, scream, run with scissors. How could Kobinski lead him on like this?

The worst part, though, the down-deep unsettling part, was that Schwartz's version of the manuscript was not the complete, cohesive package he'd envisioned. It didn't even include the pages from the Kroll manuscript, the pages stolen from Denton by that old man. What *was* in Schwartz's version, between the Xeroxed pages of originals, was commentary, Schwartz's own commentary—that's what had made the binder so thick. There was lots of thoughtfully scribbled commentary, most of it tediously Orthodox and self-referentially Jewish and—snooze—totally unmagical and completely and utterly and spectacularly without interest to Denton Wyle or the readers of *Mysterious World.* Or, for that matter, anyone who might give him a movie deal or a book contract.

And that scared him. Because reading Schwartz's commentary made him suspect . . . It made him suspect that maybe Schwartz wasn't a Jewish Aleister Crowley after all. Maybe he was just an old fart conservative religious guy—not grand master of a cult, not a devious kabbalist magician, not any of those things he'd imagined.

It was even probable that Schwartz hadn't been behind the guy who stole the Kroll manuscript. Or even, and this was grim, behind the thugs who'd practically kidnapped him from the Kroll farmyard. Maybe Denton had let his imagination run a little too far ahead. Like Siberia.

Which was bad. Because if Schwartz was not the Evil Empire, that meant he, Denton Wyle, was not Luke Skywalker—just a thief.

You'll find a way to get what you want, Dent. You always do.

The phone rang, some woman probably. The machine picked it up. It was a woman—some friend of a friend he'd slept with last week. Nice hair. Big thighs. He didn't answer.

It all sank in, deeper and deeper, taking his spirits lower and lower. One by one, his illusions burst under the weight. There wasn't going to *be* a book or a movie. This was just like all those other stupid cases he'd worked on, cases where no one ever actually *proved* there was a Loch Ness monster or UFOs or ESP.

And lower. He was never going to prove that people really did vanish in flashes of light. He was never going to prove that *could* have happened to Molly Brad. He was never going to know what had happened to her. His mother was never going to know. *She was never going to believe him.*

There was a knock on the door.

For once Denton was not in the mood for company. Then it occurred to him that company might help him forget, forget about Kobinski and Schwartz and his mother and all the rest of it. At the mere idea, in fact, he could already feel the faintest hint of a gust of wind, preparing to lift him off to some other mood, some other obsession, leaving all this angst and disappointment blessedly behind. When the going got tough, bunnies hopped elsewhere.

He opened the door, a smile on his face. A hand clamped over his mouth and he was pushed inside. The door thudded shut. Two men immediately began pillaging the living room. The charts and books, all of the stuff Loretta had sent him, got shoved into piles. His papers, his Kobinski work, including Schwartz's manuscript, were grabbed and stacked by the door.

He watched this, wide-eyed. It took him a moment to register the fact that he was observing this over someone's hand, the hand that was covering the lower half of his face, and the someone who stood behind him gripping his shoulder tightly with the digits not currently sealing his lips.

Denton rolled his eyes up and back to look at his captor. It was Mr. Edwards, the one from the Kroll incident. Edwards smiled hello and released him.

Denton was too indignant to be afraid. His mouth twisted in outrage. "You bastard! Who do you think you are?"

Edwards drew back a fist and sent it smashing into Denton's face.

The next few minutes were surreal. In his entire life, Denton had never been struck. Not once. Ever. It was so beyond his experience, so unfathomable, that his mind could not keep up with the program. It could only jolt from sensation to sensation: the surprising weight of a blow, the immensity of the pain, the meaty thud of fists against his flesh, the jar of impact through his neck and body, the relentlessness of it, going on and on, the mechanical absence of pity. Mentally, he simply gasped from second to second, shocked into stupefaction.

He had probably only been hit six or seven times, but by the time he realized he was on the floor and that the blows had stopped coming it felt like he'd been beaten for hours. He felt very, very far away.

"Help me," someone said gruffly, and Denton was pulled to his feet. They propped him up on one of the chairs in the dining room, leaning him into the shiny mahogany table. Why, he could probably see his own reflection if he looked down. He didn't. He didn't want to see.

He could feel the pain all over now. It was bad. And it was sharper in his ribs when they moved him, like maybe something was broken. His right cheek stung like a sonofabitch. His nose was throbbing. He tried to sniff in, felt a blockage. Blood ran down the back of his throat. He started to cry.

Mr. Edwards sat companionably across from him. "Very good, then, Mr. Wyle. I'll keep this brief. We are taking all your Kobinski material. You will not get it back. You will tell us how you learned of Kobinski and what your interest in him is."

Denton hitched a breath. "I already told you in—"

"You will tell me again, truthfully this time. And you will drop all interest in Kobinski. You will not read, write, or speak about him ever again. You will not publish in any format, even on the Web. If you do, you will be very, very sorry. Understand?"

Denton nodded, tears mingling with blood on his cheeks. He did not feel far away now. No, the world was no bigger than this miserable dining room. "The editor at *Mysterious World* magazine. He k-k-knows all about Kobinski."

Edwards took a small notepad from a pocket, flipped it open. "Name?"

"Jack Lorenz. Their a-a-address is in my files. His phone number is . . ." He slurped up blood from the bottom of his mouth.

"We have it from your phone memory."

"Oh . . . I'm sure he's talked about it to people. I haven't. I mean, I haven't discussed it with my f-f-friends or anything. Except one guy, Dave Banks. He works for Lockheed. And then there's my antiques agent, Fleck, and this r-r-rabbi, Schwartz. . . ."

Denton regurgitated everything, everything and anything he might have said or done, anything he'd ever *considered* saying or doing. Edwards watched him coldly. Occasionally he made a notation, but mostly he just stared, as though this information were valueless. And Denton knew that it mostly was. He was babbling, but he didn't know how to stop. He even told them about Molly Brad and about stealing Schwartz's letter. Everything. Anything they wanted. Anything at all.

"We're done," one of the other men interrupted him.

"Take it all downstairs," Edwards said.

The two men carried out boxes of Denton's work. Denton watched them go, tears making his vision of the travesty mercifully dim. He let out a blubbering sigh.

"What are you going to do now?" Edwards asked, rising.

Denton looked up at him in confusion. "Wha . . ."

"I asked," Edwards said more firmly, "what will you do?"

"I-I-I. Nothing."

"Correct. Will you call the police?"

Denton tried to shake his head, but it hurt. "No."

"Because it would be a waste of time and you'd be sorry."

"I won't c-c-call them."

"If your editor phones tell him you're no longer doing the story and hang up. You will not discuss it any more than that."

" 'Kay."

"And you won't speak about Kobinski again."

"I know."

"Or write about him."

"Or write about him."

Edwards put his hand on Denton's chin, pulled it upward—painfully—so that Denton's eyes overflowed with fresh hot tears. "Because we'll be watching."

"Yeah."

Edwards left. In the hall, Denton could hear the *ding* of the elevator.

For a while he just sat there. Then the phone rang. He lost precious time staring at it, trying to decide if he wanted to answer it or not. He decided he wanted to. It might be someone who'd feel sorry for him, someone to come and tend his wounds. He started for the phone, but he had a dizzy spell as soon as he stood up. Blood gushed from his nose. At the feel of it, the taste and sight of it, he nearly passed out, went white and clammy. He never could stand the sight of blood. He headed for the kitchen and let the blood drip bright and red onto a couple of dirty dishes in the sink. The answering machine clicked on. He heard his cheery message: *Hi! This is Denton. I'm your humble servant, so . . . leave me a message! Beep.*

"Denton, you *asshole*! I can't believe what you've done!"

Jack Lorenz's voice, barely controlled fury. Blood spun lazily in the sediment of a soup bowl.

"You are *so* finished in this industry! Can you understand that, Denton? Can you understand that it's *wrong* to break into private property and *steal* things?"

Denton pulled off a fistful of paper toweling, stuffed it in his face to stop the bleeding, and sank to his knees.

"And don't bother to deny it. How could you be so stupid? They have a fucking *videotape*, Denton, of you prying open that whateveritwas in the library. A video! What were you *thinking*! Did you not *see* the camera or what? What am I saying? That's not even the point."

Denton hobbled on two knees and a hand—the other hand holding toweling to his face—into the living room. He didn't pick up the phone, only fell down beside it, back propped up against the couch.

"I can't believe you did this. You're going to get us sued, and you know we don't have the money for that! I'll be surprised if we're not *ruined*. After all the effort I've put into this magazine. I just—I can't believe you did this to me!"

Denton shivered with cold. He grabbed the silk throw off the couch and put it over his knees.

"So you can anticipate a class action suit against you *personally*—from *us*. But then, you won't need your money anymore, will you, since you'll be *in jail*. Because that little stunt was *a felony*, and I hope they—"

There seemed to be some background discussion going on. Denton pulled the toweling away from his face and looked at it. Bright red blood against the papery white. It reminded him of his entire life—an abortion.

"Hello, Mr. Wyle?" A man's voice. "I'm Gip Bernstein, lawyer for Rabbi Schwartz. He does have an offer to make," officious clearing of throat. "Assuming we get back the property you took, of course, and the monies for the property damage you inflicted . . . well, against my better judgment, he's willing to not press charges. He says you purchased a manuscript in Germany recently, from a private family, the Krolls. He would like that manuscript, Mr. Wyle. If you turn it over to him in the next week he will not prosecute you for burglary. Please call my office at . . ."

The lawyer rattled off his number. Jack came back on the line. There was a bewildered silence in which Denton could hear him breathing.

"Um . . . Denton? Just . . . call me, okay?" Jack sounding confused. Jack thinking that if Schwartz wanted the damn thing that bad, if it was that valuable, maybe the magazine wasn't completely through with Denton after all. Jack had a surprise visit coming from Mr. Edwards. Denton hoped they got along really, really well.

He was humming something in his throat. He heard it—it was "Mandy" by Barry Manilow. He stopped. He sat there while the sun set outside, the light from the window creeping away, making the condo dimmer and dimmer.

He must have fallen asleep. The phone rang again, startling him awake. He almost picked it up, then looked at it with a laugh.

Tee hee. Tee hee hee, he giggled stupidly. What now? His mother had died in a plane crash? Tibet had just succumbed to a gigantic earthquake? His latest lover had tested positive for AIDS? Nukes were headed this way?

The answering machine clicked on. "Denton Wyle? I hope you remember me." The voice was thin and papery, an old man's voice. "I, uh, was a friend of your father's. We met once, overseas. You liked the tattoo on my arm."

Denton grabbed the phone. " 'allo?"

"Is that you, Mr. Wyle?" The caller's voice was wary. Denton didn't exactly sound like himself. His lip had swollen like a water balloon and his jaw had frozen up.

"Yeth. Where arth you?"

A pause. "We can meet if you'd like. I'd like to catch up. And I have something of yours."

"Yeth!"

"Are you sure?" The voice was serious, warning. "You'll have to come to me, I'm afraid. Perhaps you're up for a little vacation?"

Denton thought about it for half a second, but deep thought was really beyond him. Only one word rang in his head, despite everything, or because of everything, or maybe he was just a freaking idiot. Tears rolled down his face, stinging his many cuts. "Yeth."

"Very well. Now listen carefully. . . ."

12

If only there were evil people somewhere insidiously committing evil deeds and it were necessary only to separate them from the rest of us and destroy them. But the line dividing good and evil cuts through the heart of every human being. And who is willing to destroy a piece of his own heart?
—Aleksandr Solzhenitsyn, twenty-first century

12.1. Jill Talcott

"What exactly is the one-minus-one wave?"

"I don't know yet."

"Speculate for me."

"I really couldn't."

"Oh, yes," Agent Calder Farris said with forced cheer, "you could." He flipped his notepad open. "In fact you already have. Shortly after discovering the one-minus-one you jotted down a number of hypotheses including cosmic radiation, the wake of extra dimensions, the modulating wave of space-time . . ."

Jill clenched her jaw. Old notes, probably from one of her desk drawers. They'd gone through her office.

Agent Farris wasn't what Jill had expected. She'd expected the police, not the FBI. She'd expected to be questioned about the explosion, but ignorantly, by men who didn't have a clue about her work. This wasn't like that at all.

"I'm sure you've made a lot of progress since you wrote this, Dr. Talcott."

"I . . . I don't think it's cosmic radiation."

"No."

His eyes—those spooky bizzaro eyes—narrowed at her, as if trying to judge her veracity. He moved on.

"What is the impact of the one-minus-one on matter?"

"It *does* impact matter," she admitted. Her hands twisted the sheet at her chest. "Matter and the one-minus-one are intercoupled, but I don't yet understand the relationship."

He stared.

"Listen, can we back up a minute? I'm not clear on what h—" There was a catch in her throat. She swallowed. "I'd like to know what happened at Smith Hall."

"What was the nature of your experiments?" Farris asked her, face blank.

She looked down at the sheet mounded in her hands, confused. "Well, that's just it. There was nothing that could have . . . We didn't have any chemicals down there. Nothing that should have caused a fire or . . ."

She glanced up. He was watching her, completely unmoved. She realized what bothered her about his eyes. They were so cold and flat they appeared to be those of a blind man, as if he were seeing her with blind eyes or maybe not seeing her at all but feeling her with some alien sixth sense.

"What was the nature of your experiments?"

Why wouldn't he tell her about the explosion? How did he know so much about her work? Why was she all alone in this?

"I'd like to have a lawyer present."

"You don't need a lawyer."

"It's my right, lega—"

"This is not about *your rights*."

Farris didn't shout. In fact, his words were accompanied by a tight smile. But there was an underlying violence in his tone that made her blood turn cold. It hinted at a rage that lurked just below the surface and promised hell on earth should it ever get out. She shrank back on the bed, silent. He went over to the window and looked out, his face averted.

"You see, this is not a criminal case. If you cooperate, in fact, I am prepared to guarantee you immunity from prosecution. Therefore, you don't need a lawyer."

"Prosecution?"

Agent Farris didn't answer. He let her think about it. The room was still; even the hallway sounds were muffled. She twisted the sheet harder.

The outline of his body at the window didn't help. His dark pants and white shirt were starched like a uniform. The body underneath was hard, slab-like, uncompromisingly male. It wasn't a sexual thing, this maleness; it was more a personification of everything aggressive in the gender. His very image spoke of crime and punishment.

Prosecution.

He walked back to his chair and sat, knees spread. "You should understand the situation you're in, Dr. Talcott. On the one hand there's arrest, media coverage, having to face the families of the victims and very likely jail time for manslaughter. I would guess a minimum of ten to twenty."

Yes, she could picture it all, thanks to images in her head from CNN. *The long shot goes down.*

"After all, there *are* twenty-three dead."

Twenty-three. Jesus. But even while part of her collapsed under that burden, was responding to all of this with utter despair, another part, the survivor who had clawed her way out of rural Tennessee, was still swinging.

"There's no proof that my lab had anything to do with this!"

"No? That would be up to a criminal trial to decide. On the other hand . . ." Farris left it dangling.

"On the other hand? What do you mean?"

Farris tried to look helpful. It was like a shark trying to smile. "Dr. Talcott, we believe that you didn't mean to hurt anyone. Unfortunately, these tragedies occur when you don't take the proper precautions. We'd like to make sure it doesn't happen again. Frankly, we're interested in your work, and we're willing to give you an opportunity to pursue that research in a more suitable—and *safer*—environment."

His words rang in the silence that followed like the clanging of a lighthouse bell in a troubled sea. And Jill understood then that her career was not over, that Farris wanted more from her than her head on a platter. She had blown it—*badly* blown it. *But.*

Yes, but. There was always the work, wasn't there? The value of the work. *Reardon would have given his firstborn son.* Had they learned enough about her work that even twenty-three dead did not matter? She looked at Farris and knew that they had. They didn't care about the body count. That thought made her feel both triumphantly vindicated and pretty damn disgusted.

"I don't understand. Are you offering me a job with the FBI?"

Farris hesitated a fraction of a second. "No. That's a cover story for the media. I'm actually with the Department of Defense. Dr. Talcott, let me be blunt. If you cooperate, this situation goes away. The explosion is put down to . . . say, a faulty furnace, and you're off the hook. *If* you cooperate. Now. What was the nature of your experiments? We know you were a student of the late Dr. Henry Ansel of the University of Tennessee. How is your work related to his?"

To buy time, Jill reached a hand to the tissue box next to her bed and spent an inordinate amount of time caring for her nose. The mention of Ansel's name shocked her as nothing had yet done. How the hell did they *know?*

She was frightened . . . but she was also incredibly excited.

"Agent Farris . . . no, it isn't 'Agent,' is it?"

"Lieutenant."

"Lieutenant Farris, you're offering me a job with the Department of Defense, is that correct?"

He looked surprised at her bluntness. "Yes."

"Because I'm getting a mixed message here. Am I a criminal or a desirable recruit?"

"Desirable recruits are not normally facing charges for manslaughter."

"Well, you appear to be interested in me regardless. I'd be happy to consider your offer, but I want it in writing. I'd like details: position, title, salary, who I'd report to, how many people I'd have on my team, and what kind of facilities I'd have for my research. I want to know if I'd be able to publish under my own name and what you'd expect to be held back for security purposes. I want everything to be absolutely clear. Of course, I'll need to interview the people I'd be working with before making any final decisions. Also, I'd like to see something legal outlining the immunity from prosecution that you mentioned. And I—I really *do* want to know what caused that explosion. If the fire department issues a report, I want to see it."

Farris studied her, cheeks sucked in. He managed a patronizing smile. "There's no way we can even begin to discuss such things as salary and facilities until you've been *a lot* more forthcoming. How would we know what we're paying for?"

Jill folded her arms. "I think you know exactly what you're paying for. And if I told you what I know, you wouldn't need me, would you?"

His eyes narrowed. He was not happy. Jill stuck out her chin.

"We're not in the business of stealing research, Dr. Talcott. But we can't just—"

"Lieutenant Farris, I'm an associate professor at the University of Washington and a graduate of the University of Tennessee. That doesn't add up to much. The only thing I have of value is my work. I'm not giving it away without a contract, signed, sealed, and delivered."

Farris considered her coldly for a long time. He was one tough SOB; Jill could see that. But she refused to be afraid of him. Jill the Chill. Her chin went farther up into the air. She stared him down.

He nodded. "We want you on board, Dr. Talcott. I'll see what I can do."

*   *   *

Jill was up out of bed as soon as Farris left. She looked in the closet—no clothes. She looked under her bed—not surprisingly, no clothes. There was nothing in the bathroom except a robe, a thin cotton thing that smelled of bleach. She put it on over her hospital gown and tried to calm down. Where did she think she was going, anyway?

She leaned over the bed, not wanting to lie down again but too weak to stand. She put her head in her arms. Jesus, this was really happening. This was everything she'd always wanted, wasn't it?

Wasn't it?

There was a click as the door opened behind her.

"What?" She straightened up in embarrassment. Why couldn't they leave her alone?

"Dinner, ma'am." An orderly fussed with something in the doorway, holding the heavy door open with a shoe. Jill went to the window, wishing he'd hurry up and leave. She heard the door shut.

"Here we go."

The voice was awfully familiar. Jill turned to see a crop of blond-tipped dark hair as the orderly put the tray on the table.

"Nate!"

He held a finger to his lips. *Shhh.* He came over and hugged her awkwardly, as he'd done at her house. She was nervous when he hugged her, more nervous when he let her go after only a second or two. She worried that he'd felt, well, more of her than he cared to in the thin hospital robe. She wrapped her arms around herself, painfully aware of how skinny she'd become over the past few months.

"Are you all right? God, you were practically dead last night!"

"I'm better. It must have been a twenty-four-hour thing."

He put a palm on her forehead. His fingers were warm. He removed his hand but didn't bother to comment on her temperature one way or the other. For a moment, they just stood there, Jill feeling extremely weird. Suddenly she came to her senses.

"What are you doing here?"

His expression became grim. "Jill, that's the FBI out there. I think they know about our technology."

Jill suppressed a nervous giggle. "Actually, it's the Department of Defense. And yes, they know."

Nate's olive skin lightened a couple of shades. "DoD! Shit! What did you tell them?"

"Well . . . not a lot. Not . . ." She shied away from his eyes. *Not yet.* "Not much."

"God! What're we gonna do? Do they have your equation?"

Jill thought about it, realizing it was very important to know precisely what they had. Because if they did have her equation she didn't have nearly the bargaining chips she thought she did. "I don't know. They have some of my early notes and they know about the one-minus-one." She had a sudden idea. "My briefcase?"

Nate shook his head. "I went to your place. They cleaned it out. Even took the test subjects."

"Damn!" If they had her briefcase they had the equation. But they still needed her; she was sure of it. Most of her written material was raw data, naked numbers. The important stuff, the meaning behind it all, was in her head—and Nate's, of course.

Nate misinterpreted her worried look. He squeezed her hand. "I know. We have to do something. We *can't* let them get this technology."

His reaction seemed childish to Jill. She spoke crossly: "Don't be stupid. In the first place, we don't have a choice. They already have too much—*know* too much. In the second place, we have a responsibility. Who's going to oversee this thing? If it isn't me—well, I mean and you, too, if you want—but if it isn't *us* it'll be somebody else. Do you really want someone else taking credit for our work?"

Nate looked baffled. "Credit?"

"Nate, this is our chance! Think what we can do with *real* funding and *real* facilities."

"But . . . what about the results we got in our dinky little lab with our dinky little radio transmitter? Can you imagine if they put the power of *HAARP* on the negative one pulse? You can't seriously want that!"

His dark eyes were blazing and . . . well, it *was* a daunting thought. *How* daunting made her realize she was more persuaded by Nate's theories on the one-minus-one than she cared to admit.

"They wouldn't do that," she said, without much conviction. "Not until we know for *sure* what it does. I won't *let* them do it."

"Yeah, like they'd let *you* decide."

"If I'm running the program, yes!"

He gave her a look like she was being incredibly naive.

"What other options do we have?" She realized she was getting loud and lowered her voice. "We can't keep the one-minus-one secret forever. We always intended to publish, right? Am I right?"

"That was . . . before we knew what it did," he said, but he didn't sound very sure of himself, either.

"Come on! It's like any other technology—good *and* bad things might come out of it. It all depends on how you use it."

But Nate was staring at her, those beautiful dark eyes just too damn big for his own damn good. "Jill, *please*. I'm not saying this to hurt you, but . . . twenty-three people died in that accident."

She clenched her jaw. *Unfair.*

"Jill?"

"I will *not* take the blame for that until I know exactly what happened! No one will tell me!"

His face softened. "The Seattle police were on the news a little while ago. Before the FBI sent them packing they'd discovered that the explosion was caused by a furnace. It was right next to our lab."

Jill groaned, an agonizing relief stabbing through her. "Oh my god." She collapsed onto the bed. No wonder Farris hadn't told her what really happened. That *bastard*, that cold-eyed SOB, threatening her with prosecution!

Nate came over and knelt beside her, took her hand tenderly. She almost drew back from the touch—it evoked an equal surge of hurt and want, and a nagging fear that he was trying to manipulate her. Her small fingers were icy and robotic in Nate's warm palm.

"Jill, listen to me. The fire department said it was a 'freak accident,' one in a million. There are all kinds of safety valves to prevent that kind of thing and . . ." He sighed. "The negative one pulse *caused* that furnace to blow. I think we both know that."

Jill snatched her hand away. "Goddamn it, we *don't* know that! We *don't* know what happened and couldn't possibly without a thorough investigation!"

Nate's face tightened with anger. "How can you not face what this thing does? Look at how sick you were, for god's sake! All this trouble coming down on our heads? People dead? Come on! Do you really want the government playing around with this thing? Do you want to be personally responsible for another Nagasaki and Hiroshima—or worse? Is that what you really want?"

Just then, the door opened.

*   *   *

It was a lab technician. Nate breathed a sigh of relief. The last thing he needed was to get caught. Whatever Jill said, *he* wasn't ready to tell these goons anything.

The tech backed in with a cart. The top of it was lined with vials of blood in neat, labeled boxes. Nate's skin danced the jitterbug at the sight. *Blech.*

"I'm afraid you'll have to leave." The tech barely glanced at him. "I have to draw blood."

"I was just, um, dropping off a tray." Nate went to the door, nodded at Jill mutely.

"Bye," she said, giving him a reproachful look, a look that said he hadn't had to bring up *Nagasaki.* She started crawling back under the sheets.

Jesus, she looked so small, like a little kid. Head like a mule, though, and ambitious enough to make Napoléon look like a benchwarmer. Nate sighed with a mixture of exasperation and longing and ditched out.

In the hall the two FBI guys who were stationed at her door gave him a once-over. He felt self-conscious, told himself he really hadn't been in there that long and that the thickness of the walls and that slug of a door prevented their conversation from being overheard. He strolled casually down the hall, turned the corner, and went to the elevator. Here he stopped and stared at the elevator button.

Leave. That was simple enough. Would they come looking for him? Probably. But maybe, if he stayed out of sight, they'd give up. After all, if they had Jill—and it looked like they had her all right—they wouldn't need him. He could save his own conscience, and that's all he could do, right? There was nothing he could do about Jill's decisions. Right? If she wanted to go work for the military and build some kind of Death Wave Machine, there was nothing he could do to stop her.

He paced, continuing the debate with Jill in his head, unable to let it—or her—go. Damn it, but the asinine, idiotic thing was, he believed that deep down, she cared. He believed that she cared about those people who had died, that she cared about him. Well, maybe the "caring about him" part was wishful thinking, but she cared about those people, he was pretty sure.

When the lab tech showed up with the blood cart and pressed the button for the elevator, Nate knew exactly what he was going to say to her. He marched around the corner, back down the hall to Jill's room.

One of the FBI guys was reading a magazine. He put it down, gave Nate a hard look.

"Picking up the tray," Nate said, in a jeez-what's-wrong-with-you-people voice, given credence by his anger. He pushed open the door to her room.

Jill was not there. He checked the bathroom, even glanced under the bed. She had vanished.

Of course, that wasn't *necessarily* weird. They could have come for her, sometime in the past, oh, twenty seconds. They could have taken her away to be questioned or for a medical test or something.

He picked up the tray, still loaded with untouched food, and went back into the hall. The FBI guys watched him, standing now, not liking all this traffic at all. Nate kept going, pretending not to notice. At the elevator, the lab tech was just getting in with his cart.

"Hold it." Nate dodged inside.

To avoid the cart, he pushed his way to the back of the car. The door closed. As the car started to move Nate heard something, realized it was the lab tech mumbling. The guy was in front of Nate, white coat, thick dark hair, Caucasian skin. He said something again, low, cleared his throat, glanced back at Nate, a quick, inspecting-a-bug kind of look. He faced the doors again.

Nate's brain almost let it go out of sheer distraction—almost. But something about it stuck in his craw. The guy hadn't been speaking to Nate, which meant he was talking to no one at all, and Nate was pretty sure the words hadn't been English. Neither one of those things made sense.

Nate moved his head a little to one side and studied the lab tech. The guy was wearing something in his ear. It was practically invisible, but the thin flesh-colored wire from it trailed down and disappeared inside his collar. He was talking to someone through a hidden microphone.

Nate's eyes moved to the cart.

It was stainless steel, vaguely resembling a street vendor's cart, about four feet long and three feet high. It was a square bin with a door in the side, presumably leading to shelves and supplies. Nate looked at the elevator buttons. The guy had pressed the button for level C, the third level of the underground parking garage.

Shit.

Nate had about five seconds to think. It was amazing how you can make huge decisions in a window like that when you have no other choice. Because here they were going past floor 2 and their ride would be over in a few seconds, QED.

Nate had brief mental images of himself diving for the emergency button or head-butting the guy in the back. He then had a flash of himself primly setting down the tray on the floor and taking the dull table knife in hand while the guy, who could very well be an expert in every type of combat known to man, watched and wondered what the hell he was doing.

But none of these things would work and Nate's body knew it. While his mind still debated a plan, his hands were already acting on instinct, turning the tray sideways. Dishes, silverware, and food went flying, and in the next instant, while the lab tech's head was in the process of coming around to see what all that noise was, Nate's hands brought the tray up and smashed it, hard, into that dark head of hair.

The sound it made on contact, a substantial *boink*, was embarrassingly loud. The lab tech stood there, upper body turned, staring at Nate with a perturbed, disbelieving look, as though he had done something incredibly inane. Nate stared back. He was aware of the ongoing ringing of the silver dish cover as it spun like a top on the elevator floor. He was aware that he was dead meat. This time he mentally *ordered* his hands to bring the tray back up and conk the man again, and again and again, as many times as necessary, but, paradoxically, they now refused to budge. His arms, and the hands attached to them that still held the tray, had turned as rigid as a GI Joe stuck in the karate chop position.

It felt to him as though the moment stretched out nearly to the point of hysteria, but it couldn't have really because the elevator still hadn't reached the parking garage. Then Nate noticed a growing red stain on the white lapel of the lab tech's jacket, a stain coming from a trickle that originated under that thick, dark hair. Nate looked up to meet the lab tech's eyes, guiltily, but the guy's eyes had rolled up into his head. He crumbled to the floor like a deflating Macy's Thanksgiving Day Parade balloon.

*　　*　　*

The elevator doors opened to level B of the parking garage. It looked quiet. Nate pushed out the blood cart and went running with it down a ramp to his left. As he cleared the roof of the garage he could see the exit up ahead where a driver was paying the attendant in the booth. He made himself slow down. Jesus, the cart was heavy. He had to push hard when the ramp ran out. He rolled it past the booth, earning a brief puzzled look, and out onto the sidewalk.

There was a moment of panic as he tried to orient himself. He was on Madison Street. It was afternoon and there were pedestrians, mostly elderly going in for their doctors' visits or people in surgical greens crossing from one medical building to another. He tried to look like it was perfectly normal for him to be wheeling a cart full of blood vials out here, just taking it next door, la-di-da-di-da.

He turned into a side street and saw the employee parking lot two blocks away. He was shaking. He expected at any moment for the long arm of the law—or whoever might have been with that lab tech guy—to descend, but after what felt like miles he made it to the parking lot unchecked.

Rabbi Handalman was there, waiting in his rental car. Manny's employee parking permit was on the dash. He was napping, head thrown back on the seat, but he woke up when Nate accidentally bumped the car with the cart. He got out, yawning.

"So what? You saw Dr. Talcott? You talked with her?"

"You have to help me." Nate was trying to catch his breath. "And then we have to get out of here *fast*. Where're the keys?"

Handalman handed them over, eyeing the cart. "I don't have to give blood, I hope?"

Nate opened the trunk. "Help me get Jill into the car."

The rabbi made a gesture with his hands, *And that makes sense how?*

Nate motioned, hardly able to believe it himself. "She's in the cart."

                    *   *   *

Jill woke up to find herself lying on an itchy sofa in a stranger's living room with Nate hovering over her. She blinked up at him from behind a fuzzy headache. There was a smell in her nostrils like rubbing alcohol.

"Are you all right?" Nate asked. Over his shoulder peeked the face of a man with slicked-back brown hair, a yarmulke, and an enormous beard.

Jill sat up. Her head throbbed as she moved, but when she sat still and put her head in her hands, the pain went away. "What's going on?"

"Someone tried to kidnap you from the hospital."

"The Mossad," said the stranger, with a slight accent.

Jill raised her head, moving it ver-r-ry slowly, to give Nate a look.

"It could have been the Mossad," Nate agreed. "Or some other foreigners. I'm not sure what language they were speaking, but it sure as hell wasn't English—or Greek, either, for that matter."

"What. Are. You. Talking about?"

"The lab guy, the one who came to draw your blood. He must have drugged you. He put you in his cart and . . ."

A story followed, one that hit the limits of her imagination and then sailed over like a fly ball. Jill gingerly moved her head as Nate talked, rolling it on her neck. But the pain seemed to be gone and the smell in her nostrils was fading. Funnily enough, the last thing she remembered *was* the lab tech sticking a needle in her arm.

She looked around sharply. The only windows were small and high and overlooked the bottom of a fence. They were in a basement apartment. "Nate, where are we?"

"A friend of mine's place."

The bearded man passed her a glass of water. She took a sip. It was all coming back.

Was there really another *government onto the one-minus-one?* It wasn't possible . . . was it?

She felt a thrill, shoved the glass at Nate, and stood up. "We have to go back to the hospital. Nate, I can't believe you did this! What were you thinking *stealing* me like that? What am I, a sack of potatoes? What will they *think!*"

"Jill," Nate said quietly, "will you sit down and listen, please?"

The other guy, the stranger, was watching them both, eyes intelligent and patronizing as hell. Jill couldn't for the life of her see how some third party fit into all this, particularly not a Jewish third party. What was he doing sitting there listening to her and Nate's private conversation? Was he the owner of the house or what?

She sank down slowly, because the look on Nate's face was hard to refuse and because her legs didn't want to hold her up anyway. She had to admit that part of her was secretly relieved to be out of Lieutenant Farris's grasp, even though that didn't make sense. She would have to think this through carefully.

"Jill, this is Rabbi Aharon Handalman."

The man studied her warily, as if she were dangerous. "I wish I could say it was nice to meet you. But I have the feeling none of us has much to be glad about at the moment."

12.2. AHARON HANDALMAN

Aharon had been in worse places. The apartment Nate had brought them to was in the basement of a large old home in a residential neighborhood. The apartment, Aharon could tell right away, was *trayf*, not kosher, probably not even Jewish. He touched nothing. He longed for a cup of tea.

He brought out his briefcase and his heavy binder. The woman, the scientist, kept eyeing him with distaste, as if he were lugging samples, like maybe he was going to sell her new carpeting or life insurance. He knew what it was—he was a religious. Nothing he had to say was anything she wanted to hear. To be honest, he felt the same. But his curiosity, his desire to know more about the weapon, went a long way toward making peace.

He arranged his things on a coffee table the size of a small car and opened the code binder. To prepare himself he closed his eyes and mumbled a prayer over the Scripture. He felt, as he had been feeling lately, like the words had changed into a language he didn't understand. When he opened his eyes, Dr. Talcott was making a face.

"What is this?" she asked Nate. "You don't want me talking to the government, yet you get mixed up with some religious cult?"

"Judaism," Aharon said curtly, "has not been a religious cult for three or four thousand years."

"I ran into Rabbi Handalman at your place."

"My place?"

"I was looking for you," Aharon said.

"Just hear him out, please."

The woman settled back reluctantly and looked at Aharon with a dull challenge in her eyes. As if he couldn't handle that. As if he hadn't run into a hundred like her at the *Aish HaTorah* seminars, people who refuse to believe anything.

"I teach yeshiva in Jerusalem and I study Torah code."

The woman groaned.

"You know something about Torah code?"

"Only that it's silly, and it's been thoroughly disproved."

A flame of irritation burned in his stomach, but Aharon only made a "we'll see" gesture. "Odd that your name should turn up in it then." He turned the binder to a marked page. "I found your name in a group of arrays I've been studying about a man named Yosef Kobinski."

"Kobinski was a Polish physicist," Nate explained. "He wrote a manuscript before he died during the Holocaust. The Mossad is looking for it."

The boy glanced at Aharon for confirmation. Aharon nodded. *Go on.* He'd seen something in Dr. Talcott's face change when the word *physicist* was mentioned.

"Rabbi Handalman showed me some of Kobinski's work. It has mathematical notations in it that—well, it looks to me like he might have been on to your equation."

The woman's forehead knotted with skepticism. "But that's . . . The Holocaust was sixty years ago. That's just not possible!"

"Kobinski was a genius," Aharon told her.

"And you got this from *Bible code*? Really, Nate!"

The boy gave Aharon an apologetic look. "I think you need to see this for yourself. Rabbi?"

On the plane ride over here, thank god, he had thought to copy out the meaningful keywords in English, anticipating just such an encounter. He pushed the list across the coffee table to Dr. Talcott. She leaned forward reluctantly. One fingernail went into her mouth to be chewed as she scanned the list. Her other hand worked at the nub of the sofa. The woman had so much bottled up it could only come out through her hands, Aharon thought.

kobinski—400
auschwitz—200

quantum physics—30
weapon—200
law of good and evil—8
heaven—40
hell—40
equation—26
weapon of obliteration—5
from him the weapon—3
book of torment—30
weapon of torment—5
weapon of terror—4
weapon of evil—4
the great weapon—5
demons—20
weapon loosing demons—4
angels—20
weapon loosing angels—4
Talcott—40
Dr. Jill Talcott—25

If he was not mistaken, he saw a flush of fear on that freckled little face. But—typical!—she went into denial immediately.

"This is ridiculous! Nate, we don't know who this man is or *what* he's trying to do. What if *he's* the Mossad? What if there *is* no Mossad in all this? Who's to say this list of words isn't completely fabricated?"

"You think I'm inventing this?" Aharon huffed.

The boy held up his hand to stop the argument. He was a good boy for a non-Jew; Aharon liked him. It was true, he looked very strange with his hair so weird and that earring in his ear. But he had a good heart. He listened at least, had a brain in his head, maybe.

Nate took the list from the woman, sighed. "Doesn't this strike you as being . . . well, awfully relevant to our research? And how would anyone besides us *know* these phrases were relevant?"

"Those phrases have nothing to do with our research."

" 'Dr. Jill Talcott'? 'Weapon of obliteration'? 'Quantum physics,' 'law of good and evil,' 'equation' . . ."

" 'Angels,' 'demons'? Gee, Nate, I must have missed it the day angels and demons showed up in our lab!"

"I think you're being too literal."

" 'Law of good and evil'? What does *that* mean?"

Nate took a deep breath, looked nervous about what he was going to say. "The one-minus-one. It *is* the law of good and evil."

Dr. Talcott stared at him, her brow troubled but in her eyes . . . something knowing, something shocked. The boy stared right back. There was a profundity in the moment that Aharon didn't really understand, but he leaned forward, his pulse quickening.

"*Yes,*" Nate urged her quietly. "The one-minus-one is in the very fabric of space-time. And we discovered, through our trials, that when we pushed it more toward the 'one' side, there were positive results—life prospered. And when we pushed it toward the 'negative one' side, bad things happened; our virus died; systems broke down."

Dr. Talcott shot an unfriendly look at Aharon, as if she didn't like him listening to their secrets. She was right not to like. He was eating up every word. He was a sponge.

"So let's take the admittedly wild leap of wondering if the crest in the one-minus-one represents the *creative urge* in the universe, the impulse for life and growth. And the trough represents the *destructive urge*, the tendency to decay and chaos."

Dr. Talcott opened her mouth to protest, shut it again. "The law of good and evil." Her voice was ironic, but there was something not quite so mocking in it, too.

"That's right." Nate's young face was serious. "What if . . . *what if* we've discovered a *physical law* of creation and destruction? Remember the mice, how eager they were to procreate under the one pulse? And the virus, too?"

Dr. Talcott nodded tersely.

"What if we've discovered the underlying physical law of life itself, Jill? Not *how* two parents biologically create an offspring, Darwin's law, but *why*— why our universe creates things at all, and why everything must decay back to dust. It's not just about *time*, about the momentum from order to chaos. It's the nature of space-time itself, creation and destruction. And it's not just about life and death, but everything—every little thing—is influenced by either a creative or destructive impulse, good or evil, crest or trough. And they're exactly paired, fifty-fifty."

So blithely a boy could say such a thing, Aharon thought with a stab of pain. That the world could be capable of as much evil as good—it was blasphemous to even suggest it. Yet having been immersed in Kobinski's world, Aharon could no longer deny the strength of evil. And that alone was enough to make his faith tremble like a branch in a heavy wind.

For a moment there was a thick silence, but Dr. Talcott was clearly chewing things over in her head and also, as it happened, was literally chewing on her fingernails again. Such a habit!

"Let's just *say,*" heavy doubt in her voice made it clear she didn't really *believe* this, "that was the case. The crest in the one-minus-one is a creative impulse and the trough a destructive impulse. How does it actually impact us . . . *things*? It seems to me that the impact the one-minus-one has on all matter is to pull everything more toward fifty-fifty."

"That's right!" Nate leaned forward intently. "It's like a moderator. I've been trying to think of examples. . . . For instance, it's not just matter that's affected—not just bananas or even our physical bodies, which are obviously governed by growth and decay. When an event happens in the world—say the signing of a peace treaty—that event has to have a wave pattern, too, doesn't it? After all, it takes place in space-time, where *everything* is energy waves."

"Yeesss . . ." Dr. Talcott agreed reluctantly. "Though an event is probably more like an entire group of waves."

"Fine. So let's see how the one-minus-one would affect an event. Let's take something simple: say you give a homeless person on the street five dollars. That action has a wave pattern and that wave pattern is made up of crests and troughs. So let's say giving the money to a homeless person is eighty-twenty— eighty percent crest or 'good' and twenty percent trough or 'bad.' The good part is obvious—you're doing a kind deed. The bad twenty percent may be because at some level the act is done out of ego or a fear of retribution from God or social guilt."

"Hmmm . . ." Dr. Talcott said, a deep frown between her brow.

"Now that act doesn't *stay* eighty-twenty because it interacts with the one-minus-one. Basically, there are a lot more troughs in the one-minus-one than there are in our eighty-twenty act, right? So the net result would be to 'tame down' the goodness of our act. The resultant interference pattern would be more like seventy-thirty."

"But what, exactly, would that additional ten percent trough *be*?"

"Some negative side effect that we can't predict. Maybe the homeless person uses the money to buy alcohol that further deteriorates his liver, or maybe it keeps him from going to a shelter that night and he winds up getting mugged. But *something* negative will come of it, even if it's minor. We all instinctively know this is how life works. That's why we say 'there's no such thing as a free lunch' or 'there's always a catch,' right?"

The woman smiled despite her face, as Rosa would put it. But she said, "Very philosophical, Nate," and the way she said it, it wasn't a compliment. The boy went on, excitedly talking with his hands.

"On the other hand, take a mostly *negative* act such as a young girl being murdered by a serial killer. The act itself might be ninety-five percent evil or trough. But under the influence of the one-minus-one, it's neutralized a bit. Maybe it brings the victim's family closer together, or maybe the mother of the dead girl starts a support group. *Something* positive comes of it. You know: 'in every cloud there's a silver lining.' "

Dr. Talcott arched an eyebrow. "But—"

"And that's just considering how the event and the one-minus-one interact. In reality, the event also interacts with a billion *other* waves, the waves of all the people involved, of the locations where the action occurred, of the police, and so on. Any of those waves has the power to influence the wave of the original event toward being slightly more negative or more positive. But underlying absolutely everything like . . . like a heartbeat there's the one-minus-one, always operating to moderate it all, to generalize the gross effect of everything back toward fifty-fifty. The law of good and evil. And the metaphysical concept of 'angel' or 'demon' could be just another way of representing the basic idea of crest and trough, the positive and destructive forces."

The woman waited to see if the boy was done or what, her mouth drawn in a line that reminded Aharon of Hannah. He waited, too. Personally, he thought Nate was leaving something large out of the picture—like God. But as the sages say, "if you keep your mouth shut, even a bird can teach you something."

"Your brainstorming is very creative, Nate," Dr. Talcott said slowly. "But we *don't* know that events per se have waves, or that the crests and troughs of the waves would represent what you're implying they do. We've only begun to test the one-minus-one, and we have to be careful not to get carried away."

The boy sank back, looking unfazed by this censure. Aharon supposed he had heard it all before.

"So!" Aharon said. "I think perhaps we should hear what *Kobinski* has to say on the subject, nu?"

"You have that material here? The manuscript Nate was talking about?"

She had definitely heard that part. Aharon gave her what he had, the six notebook pages from Yad Vashem. She went over them, ignoring the Hebrew and turning each page this way and that to examine the mathematical scribbles. Nate peered over her shoulders and several times they pointed things out to each other. She made notes, getting more absorbed. Aharon held his breath, anxious to see what a scientist, especially *this* scientist, would make of Kobinski's work.

He could see the woman's interest regenerating itself along with the color in her cheeks and brightness in her eyes. So angels she didn't get, but numbers, that she understood.

"Is there more?" Dr. Talcott demanded when she'd assimilated all there was. "He mentions two pages of equations. Do you have those?"

Aharon stroked his beard. "As a matter of fact, yes."

"Can I see them?"

"Naturally you may see. But first we have to fly to Poland."

13

They said to Moshe:
Is it because there are no graves in Egypt
that you have taken us out to die in the wilderness?
What is this that you have done to us, bringing us out of Egypt?
Is this not the very word that we spoke to you in Egypt,
saying: Let us alone, that we may serve Egypt!
Indeed, better for us serving Egypt
than our dying in the wilderness!
—Exodus 14:11–12, Everett Fox Translation, *The Five Books of Moses*, 1983

13.1. Nate Andros

Nate hadn't heard word one about Poland until Rabbi Handalman mentioned it to Jill. He hadn't even planned to spring Jill from the hospital. He'd just gone there to talk and events had taken on a life of their own, kind of like a car plummeting over the side of a mountain—a few seconds of spinning wheels on gravel and then *bingo*, every priority you had takes a sudden and dramatic shift.

So here they were. Officially on the lam. But Poland? Go to *Poland*? That was way beyond the scope of things he was willing to consider for his immediate future.

Except . . . Jill was seriously thinking it over. He could see the wheels churning as she ran through the possibilities. Nate waited for her to cleave Handalman in two with one snap of those mighty jaws.

Instead she asked, "How much more of Kobinski's work is in Poland?"

"A complete draft of this manuscript, *The Book of Torment*. Yes, including those two pages of equations. One of Kobinski's followers lives near Auschwitz. I telephoned him already. Unfortunately, he will not send it. We'll have to go to him. Given the state of things, he is probably right not to let it out of his grasp."

Jill fingered the pages absently, like a baby fingering a blankie. Unbelievable. She was seriously considering it.

"Okay. But we have to go right away." She looked at Nate. "Are you going to go?"

"Who . . . me?"

"Yes, *you*, Nate. Will you come?"

"Well . . ." He was trying to figure out what was going on. Why was Jill, who was pissed at him for taking her from the loving arms of the DoD at all, now willing to go to *Poland*?

And then, looking at her, he knew. Jill wasn't agreeing to go because anything he'd said had been compelling. *He* was intrigued by all this Heaven and Hell stuff, good and evil, the things Handalman had found in the code, and how it related to the one-minus-one. Jill, however, would not take a trip to Tacoma for more of that malarkey. No, it was Kobinski's math that had gotten her. And Nate knew her well enough that he could read the tense set of her shoulders, the drawn look on her face, and the faraway, calculating look in her eyes.

She wanted Kobinski's work. She wanted it for herself, for her project. Because, according to these scribbles, Kobinski *had known*. And—*damn*, he knew her so well—she figured if she could get her hands on his manuscript, she could come back to the DoD at her leisure and they would welcome her with open arms, just as she'd figured Chalmers would absolve her once she'd published.

She was still going for it. God help her. God help them all. Especially him, because he was the poor sap who was in love with her.

"Yeah, I'm going," Nate said.

"All right. So how do we go about it?" Jill went into lecture mode. "I say the sooner we leave the better. The DoD will be looking for me. I'll need my passport. It's at home. I don't have my wallet, which means no ATM card. Damn. My wallet was in my briefcase. I can get cash off my credit card, though. It's at home, too. Nate?"

"Huh?"

"Do you think you can get into my house?"

Nate looked at Handalman, who was shaking his head. The rabbi looked at his watch. "They'll know she's missing. If they're not at her house already they soon will be."

"So *go!*" she said, shooing Nate. "Go to my house; get my passport and credit card. The card's in the filing cabinet in the living room and the passport's in the table next to my bed. *Hurry.*"

"Oh. Right." He jumped up.

"And get yours, too," she said as the rabbi handed him the keys to the rental.

"Right."

"And, whatever you do, don't get caught! Don't take any chances!"

Nate gave her one last blank look and headed for the door.

"And get me some clothes!" he heard her yell as he bounded up the stairway.

*   *   *

Nate called his roommate and asked him to rendezvous in an hour with a couple of changes of clothes, his passport, and basic toiletries stuffed in a backpack—and to be as discreet as possible leaving the apartment. He wasn't worried. If anyone could look nonchalant it was his roommate, Mikey. He was a champion loiterer. That accomplished, Nate headed over to Jill's place.

It was the second time that day he'd scoped out her neighborhood in Wallingford. This time he was even more paranoid than before. He saw no cars, no indicators that anyone was inside. Yeah, right. Like they'd advertise the fact.

He had no choice. Besides, what was the worst that could happen? If government agents picked him up he could claim ignorance. What could they do, torture him?

Yeah, they could. They could torture him.

He went around to the back, approaching on the alley. The house seemed dead—no noise, no movement. He had Jill's key, but he'd never tried it in the back door. He put it in the lock—it worked. He let himself in.

Christ, his heart was pounding. *Credit card, passport, clothes. Credit card, passport, clothes.* The thought, as he snuck through the kitchen in his black boots, of digging through Jill's lingerie drawer picking out stuff was . . . Well, it wasn't bad, actually. Made him feel a little bit better about the whole thing.

The house was empty, ominously so. In the hall he picked up the empty garbage bag he'd left on the floor. Two steps more and he was in her bedroom. Passport first—it was still where he'd seen it earlier, in her bedside table. He stuffed it into the pocket of his jeans. Next, the closet. He pulled open the doors and began pulling things off hangers, clothes he recognized, clothes she'd worn often. God, this stuff was awful. Wool vests, button-down shirts, a regular Lands' End catalog all miniature-sized. There was one odd note—a red, silky dress. She'd *never* wear such a thing. It still had a tag. Ever hopeful, he put it in the bag.

He went to the dresser for her pants, selected four pairs. One drawer up was lingerie. He grinned, giddily amused that he was looking at Jill the Chill's underwear. First and *last* time, no doubt. They weren't exactly Frederick's of Hollywood, but they weren't white cotton, either. He picked up a small underwire bra—peach silky fabric with just a hint of lace trim. He felt a stomach-twisting rush, Pavlovian in its predictability. He made himself stuff the bra in the bag. He followed it with a few more handfuls of whatever came into his grasp.

He was rubbing a silky bit of black panties between his fingers when he realized he'd been standing there like that for a couple of minutes. Damn.

Credit card.

Right. He shoved the drawer closed and headed for the living room.

He was trying to recall his sisters' underwear. Not that he ever saw much of it, but it hadn't been white cotton, either. They probably didn't make stuff that plain anymore. So Jill having semihot underwear didn't mean a thing. It didn't, for example, mean that she was a closet nympho. It was probably all she could find. She'd probably bought it with about as much interest as she ordered teriyaki.

Credit card.

Right. Jill kept a filing cabinet and desk in a space between her living room and kitchen. Nate opened the filing cabinet, looking for a credit card file. He found the credit card file, but naturally, there was no credit card in it, only bills. Who would keep a credit card in a filing cabinet? He began going through the top drawer of her little desk and had just wrapped his hand around something that felt suspiciously like a credit card when the front door crashed open with a violent, splintering *crunch.*

*   *   *

Calder Farris was enraged. It wasn't apparent on the outside, not unless you made the mistake of questioning him or getting in his way—which his men didn't. It wasn't obvious as long as his dark glasses were firmly in place. But inside, the demon ran the show, possessing him from fingertip to toenail—and it was Godzilla on a rampage.

An hour ago—and the mere thought made him tremble with fury—an hour ago he'd been on the phone with Dr. Rickman, formulating an offer. Putting together a *fucking job offer.* Dr. Talcott, that tiny, twisted mass of feminine deception, had made him believe she'd cooperate, that she was *panting* to work for the DoD. He could have sworn he'd seen the power lust in her eyes. She'd appeared to have such a practical bent. She seemed to know on which side her bread was buttered and that the government held the biggest, fattest jar of the stuff.

Ohhh, she had made him buy it. *Fuck.* The thought of how he had bought it made him tremble and burn. She'd made him look ridiculous in front of Dr. Rickman. Or he *would* look ridiculous if he had to tell Rickman she was missing. But Calder's plan was to find her and have a little chat, to cram that job offer down her throat before Rickman knew anything about it.

The men he'd had on guard, worthless pricks one and all, had described the platinum blond–tipped youth, gold hoop in his ear, who had gone twice into Talcott's room. Hinkle had ID'd him as Nate Andros, Talcott's grad student. They'd had a picture of him and Calder had shown it around, but it had been old. His hair had been a long, curly mess. No one recognized him and he'd been wearing a hospital uniform, so they'd assumed . . .

There was no excuse. Obviously Andros had been working with the lab tech with the cart. They'd snuck her out in the thing; there was no other explanation.

They'd snuck her out while Calder's men had been scratching their tiny little balls and Calder himself had been on the phone discussing fucking pension plans.

Meanwhile, the Seattle Fire Department's report blamed a furnace. A *furnace*! And he'd called an XL3! Could he *look* any more dickless?

Except that it occurred to Calder that what had happened to that furnace might have been akin to what happened to those birds in Alaska. Only he wasn't going to say that. He wasn't going to risk looking lamebrained again, not without some proof that waves were even remotely involved. He had to know what Talcott had been doing down there. He had to *know*.

And she was going to fill him in, tell him all about it—right after he'd made her luncheon on her invitation to join the happy family in the DoD.

He'd sent Hinkle to Andros's place and other team members to the university. Still others were scouring the hospital and its surrounds. Calder and a Marine named Rice had gone to Talcott's house because Calder figured she was most likely to show up there. She'd need clothes and ID. Calder sent Rice sneaking around the back while he covered the front door himself.

He stood on the stoop and silently removed his glasses, the better to see inside. He drew his gun in his right hand but didn't intend to use it. He wasn't going to shoot the bitch. Not immediately anyway. He noiselessly tried the knob with his left hand—locked. He stepped back and aimed a fury-filled kick just to the right of the doorknob.

And found himself in the open doorway staring at the kid with platinum-tipped hair and the faggy gold hoop in his ear. The kid took one look at him and dropped to the floor in a dead faint.

                              *   *   *

It might have been horrendously stupid, deserving of a mention in one of those "really dumb ways people die" books, but when Nate saw the Fed in the doorway—black suit, spooky eyes, gun, and all—his immediate reaction was to play dead.

Funny, because the reaction was so innate, instinctual really, and he didn't recall reading anything about the Greeks, his ancestors, favoring the techniques of possums in warfare. Trojan horses, yes, maybe even something about Odysseus and sheep. Possums, huh-uh.

But there he was, lying on the floor with his eyes closed, his heart going 10 zillion miles an hour. Then it occurred to him: now what? He'd forgotten that part when he'd fallen to the floor.

Except not all of him had forgotten. His right hand, which was nearly covered by his body, gripped a credit card and something else. His fingertips felt something hard and narrow and plastic. He worked his fingers to scoot the object higher and touched metal.

Scissors. He'd pulled a credit card and a pair of scissors from the drawer. Which meant he could either bribe or stab his adversary. Or he could go into a frenzy and cut up Jill's credit card. *That* would confuse 'em.

"Rice. In here." Deep voice, sounding cruelly satisfied, from about five feet above him. Since the Fed probably wasn't placing a to-go order, that meant there were two of them, one coming in from the back door.

That made Nate move, because there was no way he could get past two of them. He rolled to his left, his right arm coming up fast and hard.

The scene registered clearly the moment he opened his eyes. Above him stood the man he'd seen in the doorway, gun still in his hand. At that precise second, the man was not looking at him but straight ahead at the approach of the second Fed, whom Nate could sense but not see.

It was only for a brief second that the man was looking away. As soon as he saw Nate move in his peripheral vision he looked back down, but by then Nate's hand was already on its course and the scissors connected with flesh.

The man jumped back just as the tip of the scissors connected. It was unfortunate timing—or fortunate, depending on whose side you were on. Nate had swung the scissors hard, and their tips were sharp. They dug through pant material into flesh. When the man jumped back at that same instant, his own movement added a tearing effect. Nate felt, imagined he could almost *hear*, the ripping open of the man's leg in a long gash.

It was repulsive, actually. Damn gross. The man screamed, short and furious. But Nate was already rolling away, toward the front door, then scrambling to his feet. He felt a hand grab his shirt—whether it was the wounded man's hand or his backup's Nate never knew.

His shirt tore, a *real* ripping sound this time; then he was free and heading out the door. Behind him he heard the Fed shout, in a voice dark and furious, "Don't shoot! *Grab* him, you ass!"

Nate ran. It was surreal to be chased down residential streets in the middle of the day. He could hardly even take it seriously, it was so cinematic. Still, his feet moved faster than they ever had in his life. He glanced behind him once and saw that they were *both* chasing him—two guys in suits, one with blood streaming down his pant leg. It never even slowed the guy. His face was hard, set like sculpture. Nate was seriously screwed.

He tried to dodge around, getting things between himself and his pursuers whenever possible. He was afraid they'd shoot him. They might or might not want him dead, but a bullet in the leg would put on the brakes quite nicely.

The thought gave him another surge of adrenaline and he poured on the speed.

*   *   *

Calder Farris was chasing the little pissant, running as if his leg *weren't* practically spurting arterial blood. He did not feel pain; he was too focused to feel pain. He did not even consider using the gun he'd shoved back into its holster when he'd started to run. There was only one thing on his mind, and that was wrapping his hands around that faggy bastard's throat and screaming, *Where is she?*

Rice was fast; he was keeping up. The boy was fast, too, the little cocksucker. Calder motioned for Rice to move around to the side, try to outflank him. Rice took off up a short, steep hill toward an alley.

Then it was Calder and the boy. They had settled into a rhythmic sprint, because you had to when a chase went on this long. Calder's arms, bent at the elbows, pumped at his side. His gun holster was tight to his chest and side, but it still jolted as he ran. He was in excellent shape and he was starting to gain: thirty yards, twenty-five, twenty. He knew approximately where Rice would come out, from off to the right up ahead. He could picture the capture clearly in his mind—the grab, the spin, the tackle, the crunch of the kid's body hitting the ground. The demon inside him was licking its chops. He was looking forward to it enormously.

Then, still twenty yards from the boy, Calder got faint.

The ground began swimming in front of him. Sweat popped out on his upper lip, his ears rang, and his skin went clammy. He hazarded a glance down at his leg and saw that he was leaving great bloody puddles with every step. The sight of it, red on asphalt, and the knowledge of how far he'd already run gushing like that had an immediate psychological impact. He became aware of the pain and of a trembling weakness that wanted badly to come over him.

He *tried* to fight it. He got pissed at himself and tried to run faster. But even so, the figure in front of him was receding—twenty-five yards, twenty-eight, thirty.

In a last desperate effort he pulled his gun from his holster, stopped, and propped it on his arm, prepared to shoot, take his quarry down. But the lucky shit was partially blocked by a tree. Calder hesitated for an instant and the boy dodged around a house, out of sight.

Rice finally showed up, around a house on the other side of the street and down some steps, moving fast, still not winded. Calder, holding his leg, shouted directions, pointed to where Andros had disappeared. Rice went after him.

But Calder knew it was over. The boy was gone, and it was Calder's fault. First for falling for that asinine fainting trick like some green kid and second for underestimating the kid's speed and his own injury. He'd *wanted* to believe the sight of him alone could drop the kid into a dead faint. Hadn't it made him feel great? The big man, the lethal bastard. It had been vanity.

But Calder would not make the same mistake twice. He would find the kid, he promised himself—it was the only way to assuage the demon inside him. He would find the little bastard *and* Talcott. And next time he'd see them dead before he let them escape again.

13.2. jill Talcott

There were footsteps on the stairway. Jill ran to the apartment door and opened it. It was Nate. She was swamped with relief.

"God, what took you so long? I thought something had happened!"

He gave her a dry look. "Gee. What could have happened?"

He pushed past her, arms full. He had a backpack containing his own gear and a garbage bag full of hers. She and Rabbi Handalman, with surprisingly little bickering, had worked out every detail of their plan while Nate was gone and they began implementing it at once—loading her clothes into a suitcase the rabbi had emptied for that purpose.

Jill was talking a mile a minute. "I was about to panic! We only have half an hour to get to Lake Union. I chartered a seaplane. It'll take us up to Vancouver and we can fly out of there. We figured Sea-Tac might be dangerous. Maybe that's paranoid, but better safe than sorry."

"Not paranoid," Rabbi Handalman grunted. "The Mossad came to the hospital, they wouldn't be at the airport?"

Jill looked up for Nate's reaction, but he stood there watching her with an odd, appraising expression. His hands were casually in his pockets as though they had all the time in the world.

"You got my passport, right?" she asked, frowning.

He took a hand from one of the pockets, flashed the passport at her, put it back.

"And yours?"

"Yup."

Satisfied, Jill's mind raced on. "Even flying out of Canada, they'll probably track us eventually."

"Naturally," the rabbi put in. "That's what they *do*."

"*If* they bother to try. We'll have to travel under our own names. It would take too long to get fake ID. The trick will be making it to the airport in Kraków before they do. As long as we can get away from the airport there, we should be fine. No one knows where we're heading."

Handalman shrugged. "They'll figure it out. The question is how long will it take them? *Long enough*, that's all we can hope for."

Everything was packed. Jill checked her watch and grabbed the clothes she'd set aside to put on. She'd taken a shower while Nate was gone and she felt better than she had for days, but she was still in the hospital robe. She started to head for the bathroom to change, but Nate's peculiar silence got through to her at last. She paused. "What happened?"

"What? Did you have a problem?" Rabbi Handalman seconded.

For a moment, it looked like Nate was going to say something. But he was still studying her with that peculiar wary look. He cleared his throat. "Nothing. You said we were in a hurry, Jill. So let's go."

POLAND

Oświęcim—Auschwitz—looked no different from any of the other Polish cities they'd driven through on their way from Kraków. It was charming and modern, well maintained. The main street through town was lined with businesses that had an international flavor. A discreet sign pointed the way to the Auschwitz-Birkenau museum.

"So now it's a national monument." Rabbi Handalman was driving. He snorted sourly. "Polish children come from all over, no doubt, to see what outrage the *Germans* committed during the invasion."

Jill glanced in the rearview mirror at Nate. He was looking at the scenery, quiet and reserved. His head was back on the seat, his eyes brooding. He'd been that way since Seattle.

"This must be hard for you, Rabbi. Coming here." Nate's eyes met hers, briefly, in the rearview mirror as they shifted to Rabbi Handalman.

Handalman shrugged. "It's no one's idea of a picnic." He almost said more, then just shook his head, lips tight.

Nate's eyes shifted back to hers, held. Her hands clenched nervously in her lap as she tried to read him.

On the plane Nate had told them what really happened at her house—a small detail he'd previously left out like *stabbing* Lieutenant Farris. Just the thought of Nate, *her* Nate, and that man she'd met in her hospital room—the man with the soulless eyes—engaged in combat was enough to send her into paroxysms of distress on any number of levels. Nate could easily have been shot! And Farris—god, what a disaster. He was her *recruiter*, for god's sake. How would she ever be able to explain?

She should have gone back to the hospital; she could see that now. She should have told Farris about Kobinski's manuscript and let the DoD track it down. But she'd seen the pages and just . . . well, she hadn't made the best decisions.

Kobinski had her equation. It hadn't been in the pages Handalman had shown her, not in its exact form, but the principle of it had been clearly used in other equations that were there, equations even Jill didn't completely comprehend. Nobody understood what that meant. Nate certainly didn't understand. To know that not only was her equation not original, but that it had been formulated in the 1940s! How could she have gone to Farris and admitted that someone else had gotten there way ahead of her, that everything he wanted was in somebody else's work?

No. No way. She wasn't ready to concede defeat yet, not as long as there was a chance to get that manuscript for herself. It wasn't that she intended to *bury* Kobinski's work. That would be unconscionable. No, but she could *adapt* it. Aharon had translated several pages for them on the plane and, however good the man's math, some of his ideas—for example, the microscopic black hole thing—were clearly looney tunes. That was a good thing. That meant she could still be the one to place the equation in a rational, twenty-first-century framework. After all, she *had* rediscovered the equation after it had been lost for decades, confirmed it, really, using Quey. This didn't have to be a complete catastrophe.

If only she could be alone with Nate so she could explain. She needed his support now, more than ever, when everything they'd worked for was balanced on the head of a pin.

Anatoli Nikiel lived outside of town, down a country road. It was a tiny place surrounded by empty land and woods. The porch light was on. They parked in the long dirt driveway and got out, shivering in the frigid temperatures. The front door opened as they drew near.

Anatoli was impossibly old and fragile. He wore a sweater that looked like the vestigial tatters on a skeleton thanks to its age and his emaciation. He welcomed them inside and took their coats, hardly seeming strong enough for the task. He disappeared to take the garments into a back room.

Jill glanced at Nate. She was so nervous her stomach was quivering. She wanted to slip her hand into his but didn't because that would be incredibly childish, not to mention unwelcome, the way he'd been acting. Then he turned to look at her. There was a new excitement in his eyes now that they were finally here, and a smile of reassurance on his lips. For the first time in a long while, she felt as though they were in this thing together.

"Please, this way," Anatoli said.

He motioned a hand to a short, narrow archway. It looked like something from a gnome's dwelling. They bowed their way through it and on the other side was a miniature parlor and a man standing in the middle of the room. The stranger was blond, tan, preppyish, and someone had beaten the crap out of him. His nose was swollen and there were deep purple bruises on his face.

"Hi. I'm Denton Wyle." He smiled. The smile looked odd on someone who'd been used as a punching bag.

Introductions went all around. There was something a little too smooth about Wyle that Jill disliked immediately. He was friendly enough, but she didn't trust him. Still, it wasn't her house and she couldn't very well ask him to leave. They took chairs that Anatoli dragged into place, including a shaky wooden one brought in from another room.

As soon as they were seated, Jill began. "Rabbi Handalman says you have copies of Yosef Kobsinski's manuscript. I'd like to see it."

Anatoli motioned to Wyle. "*One.* There is only one copy. There it is. Look all you want."

Wyle hesitated. He had a paperbound manuscript about two inches thick in his lap, which he seemed reluctant to give up. After a moment he held it out. She met his eyes as she took it.

"*The Book of Torment,*" he said, with an awe that made her uncomfortable.

What *was* this? Was there a cult around this thing or what? Wyle didn't look like a man who'd be up on his physics. As if reading her mind, he said, "I'm a reporter. I was tracking down the Kobinski manuscript when I met Anatoli."

"You're working on an article about the Holocaust?"

"No, about disappearances."

"I don't understand."

Wyle and Anatoli looked at each other, but neither answered. Jill didn't really care. The manuscript was in her hands and that was the important thing. She didn't care what the rest of these wackos were into. She had problems of her own.

She flipped past the notations she'd already seen in Seattle, past pages of text in Hebrew. She came across two sheets of mathematical equations in a sure, cramped hand and her breath caught in her throat. She got absorbed in it. After a while, she was aware that people around her began talking. She didn't follow the conversation. She got a notepad and pen from a satchel she'd bought at the airport and dived into the math. Nate scooted his chair closer and watched her work.

She was dumbfounded. She became more so as she went along. There was her full equation, right there, and there it was again, embedded in longer sequences she didn't recognize. There were cosines and functions that she remember vaguely from . . . astronomy? She thought she saw glimpses of relativity and theoretical time constructs.

After a while she stopped trying to decipher it and just let herself absorb it like another person might absorb a painting or music. Finally she put the manuscript down carefully on the floor beside her chair, along with her paper and pen. Her hands were shaking so badly she could no longer hold them. Her throat was constricted with emotion.

She'd always known that she was no genius, no child prodigy. But what she had just witnessed was a brain so much greater than her own that it provoked a stabbing pain, a kind of martyr's wound.

The voices of the others buzzed in her ears. Nate placed his hand on the back of her arm, cupping her. The contact brought her down to earth. With some effort she got a grip. It was going to be okay. She might not be in Kobinski's league, but she *had* worked the equation and discovered the one-minus-one all on her own, damn it. She'd fight all the demons of Hell before she'd give up her rights to this thing. Fortunately, these people couldn't have a clue what it was they had. She straightened in her chair, pulling away from Nate.

Wyle was talking to Anatoli. The rabbi had the manuscript on his lap and was studying it, frowning, fingers stroking his beard.

"So," said Handalman, closing the pages carefully. "What do we discuss? Should we discuss, maybe, the weapon?"

13.3. DEΠTOΠ WYLE

"I think a little background is in order first," Anatoli said in his frail, wavering voice. "I was captured close to the Russian border. I was nineteen. The funny thing is, I was born a Jew, but my family was not religious. I even changed my name, but I got picked up anyway, as a Marxist.

"I arrived there a few months after Kobinski, at the end of 1942. It was so cold, you wouldn't believe . . ."

Denton had already heard Anatoli's story. It faded into the background as his mind wandered. He'd arrived only that morning and was in a fugue state: tired, buzzed from painkillers, barely mobile, and giddily excited. *Anatoli had the complete manuscript of* The Book of Torment. He had the Schwartz sections, which, apparently, Schwartz had been happy to send him when Anatoli wrote requesting them. (That stung a little, though of course Schwartz *would* kiss Anatoli's butt. Big-time.) And he had the Kroll manuscript and the Yad Vashem section and lots of other pages no one had ever seen. Unfortunately, it wasn't translated from the Hebrew, so Denton couldn't just chug it down, but he'd managed to get the old man to translate some of it for him verbally. Better still, Anatoli had told him what happened the night Kobinski and his group had made their escape. It was everything he'd hoped for and more— and from a living eyewitness, too. *He had his story!*

Of course, he couldn't publish it. Wouldn't publish it. Anatoli didn't want it published, and if Denton did publish he'd get another visit from Mr. Edwards. But . . . he wasn't going to think about that. Life was long. He had money. He would think of something. The real fly in the ointment was that Anatoli, his lone eyewitness, was more than a few cards shy of a full deck. Heck, the deck was gone and the old man had been left holding the joker.

What Denton hadn't figured out yet was how the others were involved. There was the rabbi—whom Denton couldn't help but take an immediate dislike to vis-à-vis Schwartz. And the other two . . . Nate seemed cool, the sort of guy Denton would get along with usually, but he was protective of the woman. Obviously, he had a big thing for her. For her part (Denton sized her up, since no one was paying attention), she wasn't bad. She had the librarian thing going, could use a serious salon day, but she had a cute figure and sexy freckles. Of course, she was snotty as hell, but that was standard in the brainy type. Ice queen. Nate was nuts if he thought he was getting anything off her.

"Kobinski opened my eyes," Anatoli was saying. "I had been fervent about Marx. Now I became fervent about Yosef Kobinski. I made him teach me; I wouldn't leave him alone." Anatoli's eyes were hazy with memory and more than a little unhinged. "I had some science, you see. It was a favorite of mine in school. But what *he* knew . . . He could have moved Heaven and Earth."

"What *were* his ideas—can you give us a summary?" Dr. Talcott asked.

Anatoli sighed. "A summary. . . . First, he founded everything on the kabbalistic Tree of Life, on the *sephirot*. Kobinski believed that the highest spiritual path was to *balance* your *sephirot*, to come into perfect alignment right down the center of the tree. It is like a stick, he said, which is all crooked. It cannot go through a narrow hole. In the case of the soul, there is also a narrow opening, at the navel, and the soul must be perfectly straight and smooth—without a bend or a bump—to pass through."

"To pass through into what?" Denton asked, his interest picking up.

"To escape the lower five dimensions—the dimensions of good and evil."

"You mean, to escape the cycle of reincarnation? Like achieving nirvana?" Denton had once written an article for *Mysterious World* on past lives.

Anatoli shrugged enigmatically. "In kabbalah it is called *tikkun*, the reclaiming of the sparks."

"Can we get back to the physics part of it?" Dr. Talcott asked impatiently. *Binah*, definitely.

"It is *all* physics." Anatoli's voice trembled.

"Maybe what we've discovered will help," Nate suggested.

He ran the group through an account of their experiments. Denton couldn't follow everything, despite the fact that Nate was obviously simplifying quite a bit. But he followed enough. The physics side of Kobinski's work came into focus with the force of an explosion. It wasn't kabbalah magic at all. . . . Jeez, how could he have been so stupid? It was *math*.

"Yes," Anatoli agreed, excited. "That *is* the law of good and evil. The law of good and evil states that there is a force that influences everything. It tempers both the bad and the good. And the fifth dimension is where these energies interplay. The fifth dimension is vast; it stretches across *all* the multiverse."

"What about the potential for a weapon?" the rabbi asked Anatoli. "Did Kobinski discuss that with you?"

Anatoli opened his mouth to speak and then sat still for several minutes, staring into space. Denton saw the two scientists glance at each other. Dr. Tal-

cott rose to her feet, but Denton had seen Anatoli do this before and motioned her back.

Anatoli began, suddenly, like a skipped record finding a groove. "He did
recognize the danger, but only at the end. At first he wanted to make *certain*
the work would be saved. We spent months—him writing and us burying it
for the future. But after Isaac . . . the rebbe was so brokenhearted, he no longer
trusted humanity to have it. The night he left he made me promise to dig up
the manuscript and destroy it. For many years I couldn't bring myself to come
back here. But twenty years ago I arrived and I have been here ever since.
Many, many nights I broke into the grounds of the camp, trying to remember
where we put the pages. Most nights I would dig and find nothing. But slowly,
as you see, the whole thing has been recovered."

"It's all there," Denton commented, looking jealously at the pages in
Aharon's lap. Trust the rabbi in the group to end up with his grubby hands all
over it.

Anatoli nodded, lip quivery. "The last of it was in the hands of a Nazi
family. Denton bought that for me."

That wasn't quite how it happened, but Denton didn't sweat it.

"But how did Kobinski come up with his equation and the . . . the 'law of
good and evil'?" Dr. Talcott asked. "He didn't have access to the technology
necessary to even *begin* to—"

"Meditation," Anatoli interrupted. "He used to say meditation provides
the insight and physics enables you to make sense of it."

Dr. Talcott was looking at Anatoli like he'd just sprouted horns. "You said
the fifth dimension stretches across *the multiverse*. Did Kobinski have proof
that ours was not the only universe? Mathematical proof?"

Denton thought he knew. "Kobinski mentions a vision in the manuscript.
He saw a whole continuum of universes, which he called Jacob's ladder, and
our universe was in the middle."

"There have been theories that there are other universes," Nate said, leaning
forward eagerly.

"Pure speculation," Dr. Talcott tsked.

Anatoli's voice rose, upset. "There *are* other universes, and they have *different* balances of good and evil. The rebbe said this is where the religious traditions got the idea of 'heavens' and 'hells.' Mystics get visions of these other
universes, or maybe we remember having lived there, down deep in our soul."

Dr. Talcott opened her mouth to protest, but Nate spoke up, his face
alight. "Cool! Think about it, Jill. The one-minus-one we discovered is exactly
matched, crest and trough. But why couldn't there be universes that had different one-minus-one waves, different balances of crests and troughs, creative
and destructive urges?"

Dr. Talcott actually considered it. She spoke slowly, thoughtfully. "Even if there *are* other universes, any other balance of the one-minus-one may be physically impossible. Or such a universe might exist, but it might never have experienced a big bang. Or it may have expanded but not have stars or planets." One eyebrow peaked with interest. "The fifty-fifty balance might be *necessary* to create any meaningful universe."

"No," Anatoli said simply. "There *are* universes with other balances of good and evil. And they have stars and planets *and* intelligent life. Kobinski worked all of that out in his book."

Dr. Talcott glanced at the manuscript. She looked, Denton could swear to god, intimidated! That look told him all he needed to know about the legitimacy of Kobinski's physics. But the rabbi was still hoarding the manuscript in his lap like a freaking Pekingese.

"This is all fascinating," Rabbi Handalman said. "An inexhaustible mine of wisdom, no doubt. But for one moment, if it's not too much trouble, can we get back to *this* universe? Did Reb Kobinski work out the implications of a weapon using this technology? Because the Mossad has some of the manuscript."

Nate nodded, looking worried. "I think I can answer that. At least, I have an idea what could be done with *our* work—"

"*Nate!*" Jill warned.

Nate put a hand on hers in the vee of her lap, which, Denton noticed with a smirk, shut her up quite nicely, since it sent her absolutely rigid.

"Basically, you can use a wave pulse to increase the destructive power of the one-minus-one. If you did that with sufficient energy in an enemy's country it would cause all kinds of terrible things to occur. And the thing is, they wouldn't even know you were doing it. If they didn't know about the technology it would probably just look like they were having a series of unrelated problems and natural disasters."

"Could it be as dangerous as atomics?" the rabbi insisted, eyes piercing.

"I have no idea what the technology could do at really high levels," Nate admitted. "But we're talking about doubling or tripling or quadrupling the destructive tendency in *all matter.*"

The rabbi's mouth tightened into a grimace. Anatoli's eyes were lost in La La Land. Denton himself was intrigued by the concept. It had great scare potential, journalistically speaking. But he wasn't particularly frightened himself. Who would make a weapon like that? How stupid would that be?

"We don't know that it could do anything of the sort," Jill protested, yanking her hand from Nate's with fire in her eyes. "We've only *begun* to examine the potential of the wave."

Everyone ignored her.

"Unfortunately, it might be too late," Nate said. "The Department of Defense knows about the technology, though we're not sure they have the actual equation. And as Rabbi Handalman just mentioned, the Mossad has a few pages of the manuscript, too. All they need are the basic principles, and they could build machines to manipulate the one-minus-one quite easily."

"Um . . . wouldn't the U.S. and Mossad share information?" Denton said, rubbing a bruise on his face. "They're allies, aren't they?"

Aharon snorted. "Ha! The Americans want to remain the big guns on the block. How can they do that if their allies know all their secrets? No, the Americans, if they find this, won't share it in a hurry, and the Mossad, if I know the Mossad, will do whatever they have to do to get a piece of the pie. *Especially* since Kobinski was a Polish Jew. If this technology belongs to any-one, it belongs to Israel."

"Now just one minute," Dr. Talcott said, her face getting very stern. "Let's all give the paranoia a rest for a moment, shall we? Just because—"

From outside came the unmistakable sound of cars pulling into the drive-way. They were going fast, with brakes squealing and the sputtering of gravel. Before the rest of them could move, Anatoli was on his feet.

"This way!" he hissed, "Hurry! *Schnell! Schnell!*"

His panic was infectious. He shoved and pushed, and before Denton could even get his head around the danger, they were out the back door. A flight of steps led down to a bare yard and the yard opened onto a forest. Anatoli picked up a broom from the side of the house and whacked at the porch light, putting it out with a crunch of glass. *"Kommen sie!"*

He raced away. The rest of them glanced around at one another in confusion.

"Nate, this is silly," Dr. Talcott said. Her eyes darted toward the front of the house.

Nate grabbed her hand. "We don't know *who* it is. It might be the guys who tried to kidnap you, and there's no time to hang around and find out!"

Denton agreed wholeheartedly but found he was frozen solid. Rabbi Han-dalman, his face drawn and white as a sheet, ran after Anatoli without a word. There was the sound of car doors slamming, and Denton got a visceral flash of fists pounding into him.

That got him moving. He lurched from the porch in a shuddering start. Once he was in motion he recovered some semblance of grace and found himself running hell-for-high-leather—directly into the woods.

He heard Nate and Dr. Talcott coming behind him.

13.4. Aharon Handalman

It was freezing, absolutely freezing. None of them had coats. The ground was crunchy with frost and ice, but there was, thank god, a moon to light the way.

Aharon was not doing well. His heart was thumping dangerously—not so much from the exercise of sprinting through the woods but from terror. And he was still clutching Kobinski's manuscript—a smoking gun if ever there was one. What could he do with it? He couldn't throw it away—Anatoli had been clear that "they" must never find it.

He passed a chain-link fence. The wire had been cut through and was slightly bent. Aharon reeled backward, shaking his head. He knew what it was—it was the camp. That's why Anatoli lived out here, so he could be close to the grounds. And this, this must be where he went through at night for his digging. There was no way; *nothing on earth*, was going to get Aharon through that fence. Lord God!

But Anatoli hadn't gone through the fence; he was continuing along the perimeter and now he was out of sight. Aharon heaved himself forward. If anything could be worse than being chased through the dark woods in Auschwitz by armed men, it would be being chased *alone*! How had a devout, quiet-loving man like himself ended up in this situation?

He sprinted, his breath rasping in his ears. Anatoli had stopped to wait and Aharon soon caught up with him. Wyle, too. The woman and Nate jogged up last.

"What's the point of this?" Dr. Talcott asked no one in particular. Her breathing was labored.

"Let's keep moving, for god's sake," Aharon urged, through clenched teeth.

Anatoli said nothing, just slipped away with the stealth of a shadow. The rest of them followed.

Calder Farris was livid. Talcott and her little boy toy had made him chase them all the way to *Poland*. What the hell was she doing here? If she thought she could get away from him by the mere act of leaving the country, she had no idea who she was dealing with. Even Rickman had agreed they should follow her—discreetly, of course, which meant him and three other guys with bogus ID. The United States was not here "officially." But he'd still insisted it was an XL3 and so . . . they were here.

But Calder's superiors were not happy. They were running out of patience. And neither was Calder happy to be running through the woods in fucking Auschwitz!

He felt a surge of hate and it kept him warm, kept his legs sprinting despite the thick bandage on his thigh and the uncomfortable pull of his stitches. Around him his agents fell behind, unable to match his muscles or his rage.

Jill spotted the others up ahead. Nate was pulling her on, relentlessly, and she wasn't arguing. She didn't have the breath. She couldn't run like this, was too out of shape and had been too ill too recently. Nate was clinging to her as mindlessly as a man clinging to a suitcase as he runs for a train, and she was getting fed up with it. Was he going to let her think for herself or what? What if the people chasing them were not the Mossad? What if they were DoD? Could she take that chance?

No. Not really. Up until this moment, she hadn't given her alleged abduction in Seattle much thought. But suddenly the idea that the men chasing them might not be American was pretty damn terrifying. For all she knew, men like that might well torture and kill her to get the information. That kind of thing went on all the time in some parts of the world.

Up ahead was a small clearing where lights flickered in the trees. And there, in the glow of the moon, she could see Anatoli, Wyle, and Handalman waiting. She tried to let go of Nate's hand, but he gripped harder.

"What is this?" she asked, her words huffing between breaths. "Why have we stopped?"

Aharon wanted to know himself. He was itching to keep running, terrified of getting caught. Maybe it was the fear, but time had taken on a strange quality. The night felt dreamlike. As he had in Jerusalem, walking the streets, Aharon was more than capable of putting himself here in his ancestors' shoes. Only those shoes were not so old and they smelled of the ovens. Looking at Anatoli, Aharon could almost see the old man's face morph into his younger self, emaciated still, with a shaved head, prisoner's stripes, staring eyes. He could sense the presence of Kobinski.

Anatoli himself gave off this illusion of being back in time. He stood tensed; his eyes were mad. "This is the spot, Rebbe. Three hundred paces north, fifty south. This is it."

"What's he talking about?" Dr. Talcott leaned over to catch her breath.

Aharon felt a cold hand on his neck at Anatoli's words, as if the angel of death were touching him there. He could now see that the glints in the trees were long metallic strips nailed to the bark. Someone had marked this clearing—Anatoli, probably. And if Aharon was not very much mistaken he knew why it had been marked.

Aharon's feet felt pinned to the earth. He had stepped into someone else's nightmare. They were here, at the very spot where Kobinski and his group had made their last stand. And chasing them through the woods were men with guns, maybe dogs.

The blond goy, Wyle, was looking around the place wide-eyed and grinning, his hands out in front of him as if he were in a fun house. "Oh, *man!*" he breathed. So Wyle knew, too.

Dr. Talcott waved her hand at Anatoli. "Hello? What is this place? Why have we stopped?"

"Shhhh!" The old man put a bony finger to his lips. "They'll hear you. Now everyone, we must pray! Fill your hearts with prayer, and *you have to mean it!*"

"Goddamn it, we have to move!" Talcott looked at all of them as if to ask why they weren't doing something. "If we're *going* to run, then let's at least do it properly."

"Shhhht!" Aharon hissed. He'd heard something.

They all froze. There was the rustle of brush, just barely there. Someone was *right behind them.*

Anatoli moved with a speed and ferocity that seemed beyond his years. He snatched the manuscript from Aharon's hand and held it up maniacally.

"Is this what you want? It this what you all want?" he screamed.

As if in slow motion, Aharon saw the old man's arm come up, and then he threw the thing. It spun end over end in the air, its pages ruffling, straight into the heart of the cluster of trees, into the heart of those silver strips.

All Aharon could see was that bright white paper in the moonlight. All he could feel was the need in every part of himself to protect that sacred—and dangerous—knowledge, to keep it safe. The worry and fear of the past few months bore down on him at this one moment. Without a thought he found himself flying in the air, hand outstretched to catch the manuscript.

Jill ran forward knowing that she had to get her hands on that sheaf of paper or die trying. She was so sudden and so ferocious that she pulled Nate, still gripping her hand, right along with her.

Calder had them in his sights. He could see them huddled together, arguing, in a small clearing. He had his gun drawn, but he realized, looking around, that his agents were not with him. They'd fallen behind. He cursed under his breath, was debating whether to step forward on his own, when the old man, a stumbling corpse practically, grabbed something from one of the others and threw it into the air. Calder saw Dr. Talcott run after it. She was heading for the trees! No fucking *way* would he lose her again.

Calder came barreling out from his cover, gun cocked and aimed in his outstretched arms. "Freeze!" he shouted. He was prepared to shoot. Hell, he *wanted* to shoot.

Just then there was a flash, like an explosion, only noiseless, like flash-bulbs, only a million times brighter. Except the color was not just light but something that seemed to echo in his very cells, not a sound but penetrating deeper than any sound he'd ever heard. Calder squinted, cursed, tried to regain his view of the clearing.

In a halo of an afterglow—Calder wasn't sure if the glow was really there or if it was an aftereffect of the flash on his eyes—he saw that several people had disappeared, including Dr. Talcott.

Calder pushed past the old man. "Stop! Stop!" he shouted. He peered into the woods beyond, rubbing at his eyes, but he couldn't see anything thanks to that damn flash, nothing but an eerie bluish glow.

And then there was another flash. This one seemed to come from inside him, as if the explosion originated in the center of his brain. Reality fell apart.

Denton stood to one side of the clearing, hands gripping his poor mistreated ribs, mouth hanging open. *Bam! Bam, bam, bam!* One by one the others had disappeared: the rabbi, Dr. Talcott, Nate, and then some lunatic police guy with a gun.

Anatoli sank to the ground, staring at the blank space, mind fried. And the manuscript was gone. *The manuscript was gone.* From the woods came the sound of men approaching.

"Ah, hell," Denton said.

He felt the strangest sensation, as if he were removed from the scene, observing his own decision-making process. Not that it *was* a decision. No, it was nothing as deliberate as that. Even while part of him screamed that he was crazy, nutso, freaking *insane*, excitement and a slick thrill of destiny, of fate, rocked him into action. It was like that dizzy compulsion some people got in high places. He wanted . . .

He wanted to jump. He giggled nervously.

He took a step, knees shaking, and another, and another, a weird joy bubbling up inside him. And then he was running and the light claimed him.

BOOK TWO

ON JACOB'S LADDER

14

This world is like an antechamber before the World to Come. Prepare yourself in the antechamber before you enter the palace. . . . This good [the Future World] is not given as a reward, but as a direct result of a person's binding himself to good. A person attains that to which he binds himself.

—*Sefer Yetzirah,* pre–sixth century, translation by Aryeh Kaplan, 1990

14.1. Sixty-Forty Denton Wyle

There was no time to be afraid. The pull was so inexorable, so much larger than himself. He was a bug perched on a freight train. There wasn't even a thought of resisting.

He must have shut his eyes. The ground, solid beneath his feet, came as a surprise to him; he hadn't realized it was gone until it was back. Bright sunlight was red against his eyelids, warm on his cheeks. His body felt strangely light. He wobbled, off-balance, put his arms out to steady himself, and opened his eyes.

He half sat, half fell down in surprise. He was in a jungle, a rain-forest eruption of vegetation. The green was so vivid and bright and obscene it hurt his eyes.

Denton was on the side of a slope. About a half mile away was a foaming waterfall that disappeared into the smothering verdure. And flowers! Christ—from where he sat alone he could see a hundred varieties, screaming with color, stinking with perfume. He could *taste* the breath in his mouth—warm and chewy and textured with scent. The world blurred dizzily. He flopped back on the carpeting of grasses and ferns, heart racing madly, and found himself looking up at a deep turquoise sky. Above his head a magenta phallic-shaped fruit dangled on a fuzzy-leafed tree.

It had to be a dream. Had to be.

It wasn't a dream.

The vertigo was manageable, if he moved slowly. He got to his feet.

"*Hello!* Dr. Talcott? Rabbi Handalman? Nate?" His cries were sucked up by the forest. "Molly?" he muttered.

He spent several minutes tromping around the slope but saw nothing, not a trace of an exit anywhere, no microscopic black holes, no shining gateways, and no evidence that any of the others had ever come this way. It was just him and the flowers and a few weird-ass birds. Oh, yeah, and no way back.

Despite the heat he felt a chill and rubbed his arms. Okay. So perhaps jumping through the gateway had not been the most intelligent thing he'd ever done. Where was everyone? Why weren't they here?

What if they weren't here? *At all?* And where the heck was *here?*

He sank down onto the grass, profoundly, devastatingly, afraid.

The sun rose and set three times. They were three of the longest days of Denton's life. He feared, yes, he really feared, that it was his fate to be stuck in this place, this Hawaiian Tropic ad on steroids, and to go stark, raving mad.

The dense, bright jungle seemed completely uninhabited—at least by anything that could talk back. There were plenty of small birds and mammals, some of them exceedingly bizarre. But he was no botanist, or whatever, and he didn't care about the wildlife as long as it couldn't hurt him—which, for all he knew, it could. The smallest thing could be deadly, so he avoided everything. The only thing he wanted to see was another human being, and he didn't. Nor did he see any indication that any had ever been here. There were no telephone poles, no soda cans, no paths, no roads. For Denton, who felt most comfortable in the heart of LA, it was profoundly unnerving.

And it was freaking *hard.* Until he'd found the riverbank, walking through the uncut jungle had been like wading through quicksand. He'd grown sticky from the effort of wrestling with greenery—sweaty and covered with sap. Vines clung to his legs like beseeching lovers. And he kept thinking, in his best bunny impersonation, that he could at any time be done in by a poisonous snake or spider or a man-eating plant or a huge sinkhole. All this mondo vegetation could hide just about anything. *Anything.*

Once he had heard something extremely large crashing around in the distance. Thank god it had been in the distance. He'd promptly gone the other way as fast and as quietly as he could, but his heart had pounded for a good three hours. He wished he hadn't seen *Jurassic Park.*

He knew, of course, that he was actually *on another world.* He had not stepped through time to some prehistoric version of Earth. The vegetation and even the color of the sky were too weird for it to be Earth. And he had certainly not been teleported to an other-dimensional spirit plane. It was far too corporeal and hot and gummy for that.

If he had any sense of adventure or any curiosity about his extraterrestrial journey, it was not making itself known. All he wanted—all that kept him going—was the idea, an obstinate hope, that he *would* run into people. Any kind of people. He couldn't have justified this hope, didn't even try, just ignored any logic to the contrary. The truth was, he could eat fruit from a dozen trees and the water of the river had not yet made him sick. But even so, he would be dead in a couple of months and he knew it. Denton Wyle was not made to live without other people. This place was smothering and absorbing his very identity into its dense silence, and soon he would not exist at all.

He found a riverbank by following the sound of water, and there he stayed. He had an easier time making his way along the relatively clear beaches—they were soil, not sand, and tuffed with mosses. He also moved easier on the second day, and way easier on the third, because his cuts and bruises were improving rapidly. He felt like he could walk for hours and hours, and that was good, because he had no reason to stop. He kept his mind from pressing the panic button with show tunes, sung sotto voce to avoid attracting beasties.

On the third day the river widened and became tumescent. He followed it, the path growing more treacherous, until the water turned white and fell over a precipice. Looking down from the top of that waterfall, Denton saw a valley below. And he cried.

The vista was mind-blowing. Directly below, the river continued its wide course, splitting a world of green lushness in two like a peach. In the distance were purple phantoms that might be mountains. In the foreground was a swath of lower hills, plateaus, and valleys that ran perpendicular to the cliff. And the sky was deep aqua far above and pink at the seams. The light made the world look translucent.

But Denton had seen awesome scenery for three days now, and he'd just as soon chuck it all for a day at Disneyland. What moved him to tears was *smoke*. Below the cliff was a horseshoe-shaped gorge in among the lower hills. It was almost perfectly round—a valley bordered by the high salmon-colored walls of a plateau. At the back of the gorge was another waterfall, sparkling like crystal in the light. And that smaller tributary, which ran to meet the river that Denton had been following, came from the narrow, open end of the horseshoe so that the valley formed a protected little sphere of jungle with the river flowing from it like a tail.

And there were a dozen or so small trails of smoke rising up from the middle of it. *People.*

By the time Denton reached the horseshoe gorge it was almost dark. The sunsets went on forever here, and Denton had made his way, with the speed of a desperate man, through turquoise, pink, orange, red, and purple light, respectively. Finally, with the world around him fading like a bruised grape, he stumbled upon the opening.

There was no mistaking it. It was as remarkable close-up as it had been from afar. The walls of the plateau were steep enough to escape all but the most incessant forms of life—some lichen and a few scraggly climbers. Their salmon color towered over the sea of green. The walls here were shaped like the ends of pichers, rounded to points. The entire opening to the gorge was only about a hundred feet across, half of that taken up by the river that flowed out of the valley like a snake leaving its hole.

It was very pretty. Denton paused for breath, leaning one hand against a tree. He was charmed by the sight, charmed by the happy thought that people would, indeed, pick such a place to live. If there was a creature with a brain in its freaking head anywhere on this entire planet, in fact, this is the spot it would choose to nest. And as he looked around, he found further proof. There was a clearing here, an area *deliberately* cleared of vegetation. Trees had been cut down, long ago, so that only a half-dozen or so large specimens remained upright, almost like totem poles, in the middle of the clearing.

Definitely man-made. Denton straightened up and took a step back to appreciate it, his heart swelling with relief so strong it hurt. He wanted this to work out so badly!

But then, in that fading purple light, he saw something odd about the trees. They looked . . . scarred, their bark all torn up. And even while he was thinking that, he noticed that his hand, the hand that had been leaning on the tree, felt a little odd. Sticky. Even stickier than usual.

He lifted it close to his face and in the fading light saw *blood*.

Denton screamed. It was a short, intense little burst, coming from the gut. It had no sooner come out than he clamped his lips shut. Announcing his presence was the last thing he should do. All the headhunters, the nasty cannibals out there in the forest, were even now pricking up their ears and heading this way. His eyes darted left and right in a panic.

Too late. Maybe it was his imagination—he didn't stay long enough to find out—but he could have sworn he heard movement behind him, back the way he'd come. Denton ran into the gorge.

He crashed along, his fear making him clumsy. There was a path here, and he followed it with feet that kept tripping over each other in their panic. But after a short while, his ears and eyes on constant alert, over the dimming light, over the sounds of his own breath, he slowed and became aware of where he was.

He was on a *path*. Oh, there were definitely people. This was not a path made by animals heading to the river to drink. Huh-uh. This was a virtual road through the jungle. He paused, trying to hear if he was being followed, jogged ahead, paused.

The path was about four feet wide. Overhead, the grape sky had faded to indigo and the stars were coming out, though they were not as crisp and bright as they would be later. The path looked quaint in this light, homey even, like something out of a summer camp he had once been to or seen on TV. He heard nothing around him.

Maybe he was being an idiot. Maybe the torn-up bark on those trees was completely natural, just the way the trees grew, like hairless dogs or any of the zillions of other weird species he'd seen on this planet so far. Or maybe the bark was shredded from some anteaterlike mammal that tunneled for insects. Maybe the "blood" on his hand—he looked at it again in the twilight—was just sap. Maybe *he* was a sap, panicking over nothing. Had he seen body parts? Severed heads hanging from the trees? No. He'd seen some frayed bark and some sticky dark stuff. Heck, with this light, it could be maple syrup.

He lowered his hand and saw the girl.

She was in the trees, sitting on a limb that was level with his chest, watching him. Her legs were folded in a deep squat, her slender hands lightly holding the branch. She might have looked like a wild animal in that pose, if her face were not so wise, if she were not so stunning.

She was *stunning*. His breath left him. He stared. She seemed just as alarmed as he was, for she stared back.

She was, hands down, the most beautiful girl he'd ever seen, as exotic and exquisite as this whole place. Her hair was long, long as her hips, and the soft texture of spun silk. Its color, in this dark light, glowed white, though his mind corrected this estimate to a very light blond. More important, she was *human*. And not only human but *woman*. And not only woman but a swimsuit edition centerfold. He literally shook with joy. Because up until that moment, despite not allowing himself a thought to the contrary, he hadn't really been sure he would find anyone here at all.

And yet . . . as he continued to stare, his eye began to discern the hundred little disparities that his mind had at first glossed over. There and *there* and that and . . . Christ.

She was female all right, at least he thought so, and certainly gorgeous. But she was not human.

Her torso was long and so narrow it looked like stretched taffy. The center of her—with a navel like a dimple—was no wider than his hand. Her hips, covered by a little skirt, were bowl-shaped and wide. Her breasts, if she had any, were covered by her hair. She was probably no taller than he, but even on the branch she gave the impression of freakish height. She was all attenuation. Her limbs were unnaturally slender. Her knees were bent deeply; her toes *gripped* the branch. Her thighs were as long as his arm.

And her face. . . . it was flat and sharply boned. The nose ridge was only slightly raised from her cheeks, the nostrils peaked and flared with alarm. Her eyes were extremely large and slanted upward, her chin delicate and pointed. She reminded him of . . . what? An ethnic and very thin model, vaguely Asian except for her coloring, or . . . yes, drawings he'd seen of fairies.

"Wow." He released a shaky sigh.

Her head snapped to the side as if she heard something; then she melted away before his eyes. She jumped gracefully from her branch to a neighboring one, fading back into the trees.

"Wait! Don't leave!" he called out.

And that was when he realized that he was surrounded.

He must have been more mesmerized by the girl than he'd realized. A crowd was standing around him and he hadn't even heard them coming. His fear returned, more from the sheer unexpectedness of it than anything else. He gave off a brief cry and stood trapped—heart pounding, mouth dry.

His bruises might have faded, but his skittishness from the beating had not.

There were at least thirty of the creatures around him—males, females, and even children. They were quiet, all staring at him with expressions of what he hoped was more perplexity than homicidal rage.

They didn't look like headhunters. They didn't look mean and nasty. But there were still thirty of them and he could be wrong.

They were the same species as the girl, of course. And now that he saw them in all shapes and sizes it was obvious how very unhuman they were. They were tall, a foot or so taller than him on average, and very thin. Even the grown males had tiny waists and boyishly narrow chests and arms. Their faces were all flat, with noses that were mere bumps-and-nostrils. Their eyes were oversize and almond-shaped. Their fingers and toes had a little of the gecko about them. Their hair was long and wild and fair, even the males, and their clothing skimpy and brightly dyed.

And yet they were a good-looking people. Perhaps none of the females in this group were as hot as the one in the tree, but they weren't bad, either. The whole group looked young and healthy and clean, which was a good thing. And they were wearing clothes, which was a plus. They were not wearing *a lot* of clothes, which was even better. Both males and females wore flappy little skirts and fabric arm- and leg bands like bracelets around their arms and legs. And yes, he could see now that they had breasts. The females had, if he was not mistaken, four of them.

One of the males broke the silence by reaching out a hand and poking Denton in the chest, as if to see how solid he was. It hurt.

"Hey!" Denton's heart picked up speed again. "I mean, uh, hi. Nice to meet you."

Sixty or so big, round eyes blinked at him.

"I hope you guys are friendly. I come in peace? Does that mean anything to you? No? Didn't think so. Maybe you have a town around here, huh?" Denton smiled hard. Nothing.

He was afraid. It wasn't as though he wasn't. But, he reassured himself, they didn't *look* dangerous. They weren't carrying weapons or anything. And he could probably take a couple of the guys at a time if he had to, they were so slight. As for that silliness back there about the trees and the blood, well, he already knew *that* was just stupid.

Even so, his every bunny instinct wanted to run away. But his fear of being alone won out. True, these things were not human. But they wore clothes and had campfires. They made paths and had females and, hey, if this was the only scene on the planet, Denton was willing to adapt.

"Here," he said, taking off his watch. It had been a gift from his mother, which meant it was expensive. It was platinum, though at the moment he wished it were flashier. Yellow gold, perhaps, with diamonds.

He held it out to no one in particular. "A gift. Take it."

They looked at it. Denton stood there holding it out, feeling scared *and* foolish.

Then one of the males reached out and took it. He looked it over, mildly curious, then passed it along. It made the rounds.

"Denton," Denton said, pointing to himself. He smiled harder, though his teeth were still chattery.

"Allook saheed," one of the men said.

"Allook saheed!" The words rumbled happily through the group, and then he was being patted and smiled at and offered pieces of fruit that had materialized from nowhere.

Denton Wyle had found a home.

14.2. Denton Wyle

Calder Farris opened his eyes to a nightmare. Somehow, someway, he'd gotten himself into the middle of a battlefield. He wasted only seconds on confusion. His body had been in war before and it took control, shoving away anything irrelevant to survival like, for example, questions about what the fuck he was doing here.

He began panting, heart pumping fresh blood double-time, nerves responding to the fire alarm, all systems go. Stress kills, but bullets kill quicker. The body makes the expedient choice.

It was daylight, but the light was dim from smoke and heavy cloud cover. There was an icy drizzle that struck his face and hands like tiny chips of ice flung hard. It was *freezing*. All around him were the explosions of heavy artillery and the crack of rifles. He saw no one, had no idea where he was in relation to the line, but the sound of bullets whizzing through the air told him he was not anyplace he wanted to be.

He dropped to the frost-crusted earth, began crawling on his belly, stopped. Which way? Was he crawling *toward* the enemy or away from them?

Who was the enemy?

The fact that he knew none of these things caused a moment of panic. He got it under rigid control and began crawling perpendicular to the shots, hoping to work his way out the side of the line. He elbowed his way past a corpse wearing a thick, heavy uniform in a silver color. He paused to look at it, hoping for information. The jacket was well made and was decorated with elaborate insignia he didn't recognize. *At all.* He blinked at it for a moment, stupidly, then grabbed the rifle from the dead man's hands. Long barrel, foreign. He didn't stop to examine it, just kept crawling.

Two massive explosions battered his eardrums and sent earthen projectiles into the air, hitting his back. It was only dirt, but it was moving fast enough to cut. Blood dripped into an eye.

Voices shouted. He didn't recognize the language. He saw shadowy figures moving to his right. The line was advancing. He crawled faster.

The panic was returning, slowly, but with every intent to stay this time. He knew he wasn't dreaming. The smell and sounds of war were too real; the physical sensations of the ground and of his own body, too real. And he had no idea where he was or why. He had just been . . .

Tracking Dr. Talcott through the woods. Had that happened years ago? Had a head injury erased his memory of more recent events, like this war? He hazarded a glance down at himself. If he belonged in this battle, why was he still dressed in civilian clothes? In his black *trench coat*?

He heard movement to his left—the advancing line, close now, and he was right in its path. He looked around desperately and saw a mounded darkness a few feet away that he prayed was a bunker. He reached out to grope its perimeters and slipped inside like a snake. It was a tiny hole and thankfully empty. Troops were creeping up on all sides, stealthy, moving low. He shrank down inside the hole, his breath steaming against the frosted dirt near his face.

Oh god, he was terrified. Absolutely fucking terrified. He felt a rising urge to scream and had to use all of his training to get it under control. His eyes darted, ears strained. He could figure this out, goddamn it. He just needed information.

He picked up two voices nearby, speaking in hushed whispers. Through the smoke, he detected two men crouching together, a flash of silver uniforms, heavy braids on a shoulder. He recognized the scene—it was a commander giving orders for the advance. But he didn't recognize the uniforms or the language. It wasn't the U.S. Army, so he must be behind enemy lines. How the hell had he gotten behind enemy lines?

A freezing current of wind cleared the smoke a little and he saw the two figures clearly. Caucasian, very Caucasian, with white-blond hair. They wore heavy black boots, highly polished, with a square-toed design. Their uniforms were similar to the one on the corpse.

Words wafted to him between explosions. He strained to identify them. Not German. Not Russian. Not Serbian. . . . Not Arabic. Not Chinese.

Fear shot through him then, a whole new level of it, deep and churning in his bowels. He had been fucking trained by the fucking *Pentagon*. Anyone dressed in uniforms of this quality, this organized of an army, this *white* of an army, carrying heavy artillery like this—he should recognize the damn language.

He must have made a sound. The officer's head swiveled toward him, eyes searching the gloom.

Calder panicked. He slipped from the hole and began running. He knew he didn't have a prayer, but it still was a shock when the mortar hit, blasting the earth beneath his feet.

And then he was flying through the air like Superman, mind peculiarly free.

14.3. Seventy-Thirty ȷɪʟʟ Talcott

"Jump!" Jill screamed.

They were not in Poland, not in the snowy woods, not in the dark, but on some red rock plateau in the middle of a hot and sunny desert. That in itself was strange enough, but they were also surrounded by enormous insects. The insects were as large as medium-sized dogs, heads antennaed like ants, and entirely disgusting. Their iridescent eyes mirrored Jill and Nate like a semicircle of fun-house mirrors as they backed toward the edge of the plateau.

Nate followed Jill's glance behind them. It was a good thirty-foot drop to the desert floor and he was already cradling an injured arm. "Are you nuts? We'll break something. We'll break *everything*."

But the insects were advancing, their flanks swinging in, and Jill had no intention of letting those things any closer.

She grabbed Nate's hand and launched herself off the cliff.

"Not that arm!" he screamed in pain as they fell through the air.

*   *   *

They landed hard on the sand—but not that hard.

"What the . . . ?" Nate had even managed to keep his feet, his right arm protectively cupping his left. "Shouldn't we be lunch meat? And weren't we just in snow? You aren't a figment of my imagination, are you?"

"Why can't you be a figment of *my* imagination?"

"Good. It must be you; I'd never say that."

Jill, who had three different kinds of Raid under her sink at home, was busy looking up. The insects had been peeking over the edge of the cliff at them, but now they retreated, presumably coming down the easy way. She took Nate's good arm to get him walking.

"How'd you know we could make that jump?" he asked.

"Can't you feel it? Low gravity." There was a catch of excitement in her voice.

Nate waved his good arm, jumped up, and settled back down with magical sluggishness. "Jesus! I thought I was just light-headed. Jill, what the heck is going on? You don't suppose we could be . . . You don't think we're . . ."

"Dead?"

"That's the word I was looking for, yes."

She shook her head firmly. "Not possible. There *is* no life after death."

"Right," Nate said ironically. "I forgot."

The insects appeared around the bend at the base of the plateau, moving in formation. Jill pulled Nate forward, both of them stumbling over their floating feet.

They found the reason for their reception committee not far away. The plateau was near a colony of the giant insects. The structure was built from the reddish sand, hardened with saliva or water. It was the size of a football field, its walls folding upward in narrowing bands like a wedding cake. Round holes in the walls opened into tunnels. The entire thing had a mathematical precision and, seeing it, Jill thought the creatures must be intelligent. Then she realized that insect nests on Earth had this kind of logic, too—anthills, for example. She'd just never seen one on this scale.

Heads were popping out of the tunnels. Insects dropped down from the structure to approach them, and their vanguard was creeping in. Jill knew she should move instead of standing there staring, but for once in her life she was completely at a loss.

"Uh, I don't think there's a phone in there," Nate said. "Can we go? Not that I want to rush you."

She blinked. The insects were getting close enough that she could see herself in their eyes.

She and Nate backed away. A thousand eyes watched every move. After they'd put some distance between themselves and the colony they turned and began walking away as fast as they could in the resistanceless air. On all sides there was nothing but open desert. The insects, in stealthy movements, followed.

Jill's watch had stopped. Nate didn't have one. They walked for what felt like hours, saying little. There was too much to absorb to try to box it up, make it tidy enough for conversation. Although walking was disturbingly easy, it had to be over a hundred degrees and there was no shade to speak of. Shock kept Jill going. Her neck began to ache from turning to look behind her so often. Their escort fell away, little by little, until the last determined survivor of the regiment stood and watched them go. Long after it had faded from view, Jill couldn't resist turning to look, just to be sure.

It was on one of these insect-checking rounds that she saw it—a sun rising on the far side of the desert. She looked back in front of her, where the sun that had cooked them all day was just starting to set, looked behind her, looked ahead, stopped walking.

A sound escaped her lips then—not so much his name as a sigh.

Nate turned and saw it, too. The second sun looked as though it would be huge. It peeked over the horizon, ripe as a plum, its egg-yolk gold filmed by a shimmering, hazy red.

"For god's sake, Jill. Where *are* we?"

She shook her head mutely. *I don't know.*

For a long while they stood there, marveling at the sunrise until the sun was high enough, and bright enough, to hurt their eyes. And then, finally, she looked at *him*, at poor Nate, and saw what she should have seen earlier, had she not been so lost in her own head. He was holding his left arm and trembling with fatigue. His olive face was pale and drawn with pain.

"God, Nate, I didn't think. Let's take a break."

He didn't argue—a sure sign that he was hurting pretty bad. She pointed the way to a jumble of rocks and hovered, concerned, while he settled himself on a baked dry boulder.

"How is it? We'd better take a look."

He attempted to roll up his sleeve, but it was too tight. He unbuttoned his blue shirt and took some time in removing it. Jill waited, trying not to show her discomfort at the sight and texture of his skin. She squatted at his side and actually missed the sensation of heavy weightedness that normally came with resting. She was hot and sweaty and a deep sense of lethargy was settling into her bones, as if she were coming down with the flu. She noted all of this in a detached way, then noted the detachment. It was dangerous. The shock could undo them even if the terrain didn't. She had to stay alert.

Whatever was wrong with the arm, it wasn't visible from the outside. Blue shirt draped over his knees, Nate held the limb out for examination.

"Can you bend it?"

"Yeah. It's not broken." He touched the muscles tenderly with his fingertips. "It's more like I pulled it. The muscles are really stiff."

She reached out her hand to touch him as well but hesitated. Stupid. *She* wouldn't be able to tell if his muscles were stiff just by feeling them.

"Look at that." Nate pointed to her hand.

On the back of her right hand, aligned in a row, were deep purple bruises. Nate put his injured hand—moving his arm very slowly—into hers. His fingers lined up exactly with the stains. He met her eyes.

"Wild. You don't remember it, do you?"

She shook her head. The feeling of his hand in hers, hot and moist, increased her nauseous sense of heatstroke.

"I had your hand and you went after the manuscript. I tried to pull you back and then—jeez, I thought it was a bomb—I felt this incredible force yanking you away, so I held on as tight as I could. I thought my arm was gonna come out of its socket."

"Why didn't you just let go?"

He shrugged, his eyes not meeting hers. "Dunno. Instinct, I guess."

She extracted her hand and rubbed his moisture from her palm. "We ought to be able to make a sling from your sweatshirt."

He'd removed it miles back and tied it around his waist. She knotted the wrists of the sweatshirt together and it made an adequate support. She caused him some pain getting him into it—awkward as ever at touching him—but he looked relieved when it was done.

Then they both sat numbly.

"What happened, Jill?" Nate started the inevitable conversation with some reluctance.

She looked back the way they'd come, anxiety and excitement roiling in her belly. She'd been thinking about it for hours but wasn't quite ready to share those thoughts.

Nate said, in a half-mocking tone, "Remember that section of Kobinski's manuscript Aharon read to us on the plane? That whole thing about 'microscopic black holes'? You don't suppose . . ."

Jill nodded, completely serious. "What else can we think? What I don't get is this: even if there are subatomic black holes, an idea which we obviously can't completely dismiss since we don't appear to be on Earth anymore, how could something like that transport the two of us and leave us whole and alive?"

Nate thought about it. "Quantum leap?"

Jill chewed on a fingernail. She didn't like the answer but didn't have a better one.

"Or," Nate added, getting into it, "since matter is essentially energy waves in the fifth dimension, maybe our energy waves were what were transferred and we simply 'reprojected' here. Kind of like a *Star Trek* teleporter?"

They looked at each other doubtfully. There was no answer to that, nothing that wasn't embarrassing to even speculate. Neither of them said anything for a while.

"I was thinking. . . ." Jill cleared her throat self-consciously. "I wonder if the black hole—if that's what it was—was discovered through Kobinski's work on the one-minus-one?"

Nate didn't comment.

"The manuscript might be able to tell us. If we had it."

"The manuscript!" Nate looked around, as if they might find it lying on the ground. "You're *sure* it's not here? I mean back there, where we, um, came in?"

"No. It was the first thing I looked for." She shook her head impatiently. "Did you hear what I said, Nate? Using one-minus-one technology, Kobinski figured out how to travel through space-time!"

"He was working on a *lot* of things, from the look of it."

"Yeah, and it's all one-minus-one technology, Nate! Think about it!"

Nate wasn't nearly as excited as she expected him to be. He rubbed a hand through his close-cropped hair, his face unreadable. "What about the others— Rabbi Handalman, Anatoli?"

She shrugged. "Back on Earth probably." She thought of her bruised hand, and it occurred to her: *You'd probably be there, too, Nate, if you had let go.* She gazed up at him in surprise, but he didn't appear to be thinking anything of the sort. He yawned.

"I hate to be a wet blanket, but theorizing isn't going to get us food, water, or shelter, and this place isn't exactly a 7-Eleven. The only thing I've seen which looks remotely edible is those giant bugs, and frankly . . ."

Jill couldn't imagine it, either, but looking at the desert landscape, she thought they were lucky to have the bugs. Water was an even bigger issue. She was already parched.

"Let's go a little further," she suggested. "Maybe we'll find something. Can you walk?"

"Of course." But he gritted his teeth as he got up.

They'd walked a short distance when Nate spoke again. His voice was deliberately casual, as it always was when something was important to him. "Say, do you think there's any chance we can get back home?"

"I don't know," Jill answered, just as casually. She picked up her pace so she wouldn't have to see the look on his face.

The second sun was almost mid-sky when they saw the City. At first it looked like a mirage, unsubstantial as dust swirling above the desert floor. Their steps quickened—his, then hers—but they said nothing, each wanting to spare the other false hopes. Step by step, the phantom took form.

The outline of the City stretched for miles. Nothing led up to it; it was simply there, in the middle of the flat desert plain. There were no freeways leading in or out, no traffic on the streets inside the City or in the air above. There was a low wall around the perimeter that appeared to be made of polished red rock. A break in the wall led onto a smooth, paved street. There was no gate where the road met the sand; it simply terminated in a straight edge at the desert. Inside and outside: two sides of a coin.

The mass of the City was made up of buildings—white high-tech boxes as nondescript as children's blocks. They were all exactly the same shade of white, and there was nothing to distinguish one from another except a variance in height and width. Windows were small and few, dark and blank as shark's eyes. The street grid had an extreme orderliness, as if someone had neatly lined up the buildings, row upon row, with a ruler and plumb line.

The City looked manufactured; it did not look human.

They stopped at the perimeter. Jill had to work to achieve the kind of wariness she knew was appropriate. She had the strangest sense that the City was, simultaneously, both perfectly normal and dismissably unbelievable. Unbelievable because she'd been sure the insects in the desert would be the highest form of life on this planet; it seemed too dry and barren to have created a higher species. Unbelievable, too, in its surreal flatness. Yet there was also something about the City that seemed familiar—familiar enough to get under her guard. And that was dangerous.

"Look at this, Jill. It's as if the red sand had suddenly risen up and . . . *hardened* in a tremendous heat."

She tore her eyes away from the buildings. Nate was trailing his hand along the red perimeter wall. The top of it varied in height from two to four feet, in an irregular, wavy form that was at odds with the straight, orderly lines of the City. As her fingers brushed off its dusting of sand she saw that the wall wasn't rock at all but red glass.

"You're right. I think it *is* hardened sand. That's weird."

Nate went over to the break in the wall, where the street met the desert and abruptly ended. He dug his toe into the sand and then tapped. She didn't need to see it to know that he'd encountered that hard, glassy surface a few inches down, as if the wall had been there, too, and had been cut away.

"It reminds me of *The Wizard of Oz*," Nate said thoughtfully.

"Nate!" Jill cried in warning.

A round metal sphere hurtled toward them, flying down the street of the City. It was two feet in diameter, completely silver, and smooth except for a rectangular opening in one side. It stopped in front of Nate, its opening tilting up and down, regarding him head to foot. He froze.

"Don't move," Jill said in a low voice.

"Don't worry," Nate muttered.

The sphere flew with a zip over to Jill and "sensed" her as well, then zoomed off, disappearing back into the buildings.

"A sentry?" Nate suggested, letting out a relieved breath. "A camera?"

"Maybe."

"Maybe it's gone to sound the alarm."

Jill and Nate looked at each other. *He* looked wary at least. He looked scared. "I really don't like this place, Jill. Maybe we should get out of here."

"They'll have water," she said.

"Yeah." The look on his face admitted defeat.

Jill's mouth dredged up saliva at the thought. She shaded her eyes and regarded the City. But it wasn't water that engendered the kernel of excitement in her belly, small and hard, that created that sense of attraction, of destiny. It was as if the City were calling her, as if she were home.

14.4. THIRTY-SEVENTY AHARON HANDALMAN

> To reign is worth ambition, though in hell:
> Better to reign in hell, than serve in heaven.
> —Satan in *Paradise Lost*, by John Milton, 1667

They were carrying him up crude steps. Aharon could see the pitted stone through the coarse weave of the blanket that covered him, slung as he was like an anchor over a monstrous freak's back. There was no breath and no room to take it in; his soft stomach was crushed against the thing's shoulder even as he shivered violently from a bone-deep chill. God help him, he was about to pass out from the pain! Maybe that would be a mercy.

Doors opened and he was dimly aware that they'd entered a large room. Through the blanket he got blurry glimpses of stone benches and hairy, brutal figures. The room was full of beasts, growling and frothing. His heart slammed in his chest. He could smell them, these . . . *creatures:* smell sweat and, and musk, and some other stink—dark and earthy and pungent as the dead. On top of his terror, the revolting smell was enough to make him sick. He retched, halfheartedly; then the floor rose up to meet him as he was dumped, head cracking on hard stone. The blanket was yanked off. Aharon cringed as howls and animal screams rose in the room.

He didn't want to—god, he didn't want to do this!—but he looked; he *made* himself look. He still prayed for something, anything, that could allow him to believe that this was not real, that it was all a horrible dream, anything that would let him deny everything that had happened since he'd arrived in this terrible place.

He'd awoken, he had no idea how many hours ago, under a tree in a frozen wilderness of sharp, pitiless rocks and sparse, rubbery grass. He was freezing to death in the dark, and the dark went on and on. At first he'd thought he was dead because of the dark and because of the way he was pinned to the ground. There were a few awful minutes when he was sure he was in his grave. But the frigid wind blew over him, shattering that nightmare. He was definitely not underground.

Next he thought he had been wounded, paralyzed by a bullet, and left to die in the woods of Auschwitz. But when the daylight finally came—dim and insubstantial as watered milk—he saw that he was not in Auschwitz. He might have been on the surface of the moon for all the life around him. There was just that one tree, black and twisted, towering overhead, and rocks, painful rocks. After hours of lying there helpless, growing so cold that his limbs went numb, he'd been picked up by these . . . these demonic *things*. They'd shoved him into a cart and jolted him for miles before reaching a crude, nightmarish town—a place so awful, hung with things, *bloody* things, that were so disgusting that he'd kept his eyes squeezed shut even under the blanket. Now he was surrounded by these *animals*. He made himself really look at them, because the truth could be no worse than the terror.

They were like nothing on Earth, but then, he had accepted that fact some time ago. They were loathsome, unclean things—short in height but muscled with great slabs of meat, their necks as thick as their square heads. Their faces bore the hair of beasts even on their temples and noses, making them look like animals. But their bodies were covered with the primitive robes of men. Their hands were wide and their short, thick fingers bowed like an ape's. Strong. Hideous. Demons.

Weapon loosing demons.

Had he, Aharon Handalman, been transported to Hell? And dear God, what had he ever done to deserve this?

He blinked up at the ceiling, eyes wide and dry. He wanted to feel nothing, to not even acknowledge this place, but that was impossible. It was a little warmer here, but he was lying on his back, the worst position for his heart. In his chest it thudded and shuddered like a badly tuned engine. He could hear his own panicked panting, the whistling in his throat of a coward.

Lord, where are You? Where have You sent me? Why me?

A few feet away they were fighting over him, yes, like dogs over a scrap of meat! Sweat dripped down his face, rolled into his ears. Those pictures from Yad Vashem would not leave him alone. He wanted to believe that God would keep him safe, that there was a plan, but his fear was rich as cream and his prayer a frail thing.

He tried to turn his head, made an effort. It took a great deal of effort. He was definitely paralyzed, gunned down by the CIA or Mossad or someone like that. His body was made of immobile steel, hugging the floor. But his neck *would* move, if he strained.

Across the room he saw the beast that was doing most of the speaking. No, you couldn't call it speech; that would be giving them too much credit. It was barking or snarling. A dense black robe hung from its massive shoulders, making its body a squat rectangle. Its face—somewhere between an ape's, a jackal's, and a human's—was flat, impervious, and cruel. Its hair was groomed back from its brow, lips pulled back from its teeth. This animal was snarling at a figure that was seated on a raised platform. The figure . . . it was in a chair of some kind, wooden maybe, and it was taller than the other animals, even sitting down. It wore a blood-purple robe patterned at the neck and hem with gold. Its head was covered by a golden mask that had a short snout, menacing eyes, growling mouth, and golden fangs.

The ferocity of the masked figure, its undeniable position as some kind of leader, sent a fresh wave of mortal dread shuddering through Aharon's body. This wasn't right, that these animals acted like men. It wasn't right! He wouldn't look, wouldn't sully his eyes with such obscenities! He turned his head back to the ceiling, trying to be gentle. It was a bowling ball cranium on a flower stalk neck. The pain! God help him. Oh, god help him!

If this is it, if this is what it comes down to, just kill me and have it done with. Only please, Lord, make it quick. The thought of Hannah and the children being widowed, orphaned, sent despair flooding through him. And still, he could not believe where he was.

Hell. He was in Hell, some abysmal place of punishment. Somehow, that place, that hole that Kobinski had found with his magic or his mathematics, that awful hole in the world near Auschwitz, had brought him here—not to Heaven, not to a fiery chariot like Ezekiel, but straight to a place of abomination.

The very stars should cry out against this outrage to a righteous man!

There came a pounding that reverberated up from the floor. The creatures carried heavy staffs, and it was these they were using now, the entire assembly, pounding the staffs on the floor in a jarring rhythm. Aharon tried to sink farther into the stone.

At any moment these jackals would fall on him and rip him to pieces, and he could almost welcome an end to this nightmare, dear merciful God, if only they would be quick.

Then the room fell silent and he thought he heard . . . he could *swear* he was hearing . . .

Hebrew?

"Are you a Jew?" a voice said, in the Hebrew tongue. The sound was awkward, as though the mouth was not used to forming the words.

Aharon froze, listening.

"Are you a Jew!" the voice demanded, louder.

"Yes," Aharon whispered. He made the effort to turn his head again and look up at the masked figure. It was leaning forward in its thronelike chair, bending toward him.

The creature with the flat face walked into his line of sight, barking angrily. The masked one snarled back. Aharon's neck was screaming, sending shock waves of pain, but he ignored it. His ears sifted the air for clues; he didn't dare breathe.

"Tell me who you are and how you got here," the masked figure snapped. "Do it now."

"Who are you?"

"Answer!"

"Aharon . . . Aharon Handalman. From Jerusalem. I . . . I was . . . I have a wife, Hannah. Children. I'm a rabbi." These words brought fresh tears.

"Stop blubbering if you want to live!"

Aharon did stop. He took deep breaths, swallowed. The fear, no longer having an outlet, sent his body into convulsionlike shivers.

Among the crowd there was a growling rumble. The flat-faced one spoke again, loud over the crowd, and again the masked one snarled back. It went on for some time.

Aharon allowed his neck to release his head, swallowing the pain. Hebrew? Would demons be given the power to speak the Hebrew tongue? Yes, certainly. It was an ancient tongue, the tongue of the chosen people. Had angels not spoken to Jacob? Would not the language be known even in Hell? And yet this answer did not satisfy him. There had been no kindness or sympathy in the voice of the masked creature and yet . . . it was not the voice of a demon, either. Deep inside him, there was a small sparking of hope.

The staves pounded again, insistently. When they fell silent, Aharon heard the slow, heavy fall of footsteps. He cringed but was incapable of moving far. The purple robe appeared in his line of sight, looming over him. He had no choice but to stare up at that hideous face.

"Listen to me carefully, Jew." The voice sounded remote coming from behind the mask. "You must sit up."

Aharon drew in a sharp breath. "Sit? I . . . I cannot. I'm injured."

"You are not *injured.* Gravity is heavier here. Moving is difficult, but it can be done. Sit up or die, your choice."

Had he imagined something human in the voice? Nothing human could be so cruel. Aharon believed the threat completely. If he did not sit up he would die. And yet . . . did that mean that if he could sit he would *live?* He heaved a quivery sigh and tried to gather his strength. The voice said he could move, that he was not paralyzed but only burdened by gravity. The implications of that were too unfathomable to provide any relief, but it did make him try. He strained. It was impossible. Perhaps, if he had been asked when he'd first arrived, before the day of terror and the journey had worn his reserves to nothing, but now . . .

Even as he told himself he couldn't do it, the desire for self-preservation worked miracles. He managed to turn onto one shoulder and press his palms deep into the floor. Grunting like a pig, spittle flying from his lips, he leveraged his upper torso partially off the floor. His arms shook uncontrollably. His heart was going to burst under the strain.

"Now hold it," the voice said.

Aharon didn't, couldn't, answer. He felt veins popping out on his neck. A stab of agony raced from one side of his chest to the other like a warning shot across a bow.

The masked figure turned to the assembly and the crowd shook the roof with their pounding staves.

Without warning, Aharon's elbows collapsed. He slammed to the floor, his left eyebrow splitting on the stone, sending blood into his eyes. He moaned. Was it over? Please, God, let it be over.

The pounding was still reverberating in the room, but the voice spoke again, to him alone this time, urgent and low. "Listen—you must give me something, anything. A wallet, a letter, a watch. Do it quickly."

Aharon opened his eyes. The figure was bending over him, one hand held out. The hand trembled, white and long-fingered . . . and hairless.

Aharon tried to see the eyes behind the mask, but they were buried in shadow. "Who are you?"

"Never mind."

"You're . . . You're human, *nu*?"

No answer.

"Yosef Kobinski?"

The figure gasped in surprise, drew back. There was only that mask and, behind it, what?

"Yes. Now do as I said. Hurry!"

"In the back. Inside my jacket."

The figure reached over him and sought the place—felt the stiffness of the rolled-up manuscript and pulled it free. The bound pages were thrust into the air in triumph as the figure stood. The assembly roared.

Aharon felt paws on his arms and legs. He was being lifted. The terror came back in a rush.

"Reb Kobinski!"

The figure had its back to him, still raising the manuscript for the crowd.

"Reb Kobinski!"

The mask turned. Aharon had the strange idea that those eyes, those human eyes, glared maliciously at him. But he only saw them for a moment before he was carried away.

*   *   *

Aharon was taken to a room that, while dark and smelly, was private. It had a bed that, while rough and scratchy, was still a bed. There was warmth under the covers, filthy as they were. These small comforts, after a day of horrors, were like manna from heaven. Exhausted, he slept.

He was abruptly awoken—shaken from sleep by the paw of one of those creatures. He looked up to see a delicate rodentlike face and intelligent eyes set atop a huge torso and surrounded by a mass of brown fur. The creature bore a torch, its fire thick and low, barely illuminating the dark room. It moved back when Aharon's eyes opened, bowing its head subserviently.

Behind it was the figure in the gold mask, sitting on a chair beside the bed.

Aharon tried to sit up and speak and was reminded that he could not sit up. This had the immediate effect of depressing him, as all that had happened came back and he realized that he was still lost. So it was not over. He lay weighted against the cushions, eyes on the figure, and said nothing.

"That will be all, Tevach. You can go. Make sure no one disturbs us."

The masked figure spoke in Hebrew and the animal grunted something back that sounded like *"My Lord,"* in Hebrew, which Aharon found extremely offensive. The creature shuffled to the door.

When they were alone, the figure took off the mask. Underneath was the face of an old man—but not as old as Aharon had expected. The man in the chair looked fit, muscular, even muscle-bound, like those men in magazines, something that Aharon couldn't help thinking was anathema for a Jew. The old man leaned forward and used both hands to straighten out first one leg, then another, his face lined with pain.

"My joints. They're disintegrating. They weren't built to withstand the gravity on Fiori."

"Fiori?"

"That's the name of this accursed rock. That's what the natives call it. *I* call it Gehenna. And I—I am the king of Gehenna." There was dark irony in his voice.

"It really is Hell?" Aharon asked tremulously.

"One of the many. Charming, isn't it?" The man oozed an aloofness, a cold disdain, that Aharon couldn't understand. He studied the face.

"You're *not* Yosef Kobinski. You must be his son, Isaac, *nu?*"

An expression of outrage flickered in the man's eyes. "I *am* Yosef Kobinski. How did you know about my son? Or about me, for that matter?"

The words were threatening. Aharon chose to ignore the tone. "That? *That* is a long story. But, if you don't mind my saying, you don't look so bad as you should, for a man of one hundred and five."

Kobinski's eyes narrowed. "Two thousand five?"

"Yes."

Kobinski sat contemplating. His eyes were far away, as if he was doing equations in his head. "Einstein showed that gravity bends light. It also bends time. It's been thirty years here, sixty on Earth."

"Even for *thirty* years—how could you survive a place such as this?"

"Did I survive?" Kobinski asked bitterly.

"You never tried to go back?" Aharon asked.

"No."

"You didn't *try*? I can see that Auschwitz was not much of an option. But you must have thought, after some years had passed, that maybe—"

"Be silent," Kobinski commanded, in the voice of a man who expected obedience. He put a hand to his mouth. "You said you were from Jerusalem."

"Yes. Israel is a country now—a Jewish nation. *Eretz Israel*—it exists!" It was a blessing to say this to a Jew who had no idea. But if he was impressed, Kobinski didn't show it.

"However," Aharon added, "just to prepare you—it might not be what you'd expect. There's much secularism—you see it everywhere. You could hardly believe we fought so long for something and, the younger generation especially, they don't have any idea what it means. Not like you and I. At the wall—"

"And Auschwitz?"

"Auschwitz? It's a memorial now. They call it the *Holocaust*. Six million died."

Kobinski's hands on the arms of the chair tightened until his skin was white with the strain. "Six million," he whispered. "And when did it end?"

"Nineteen-forty-five. The Americans and the Russians liberated the camps."

Kobinski looked away, was silent for a moment, then said, "It was only a matter of time. Even we knew that. But it was too late for six million. And too late for . . ."

"Yes?" Aharon frowned. "Listen—isn't it a simple matter of finding the gateway again, the hole thing, and stepping through? You'll come with."

Kobinski didn't even look at him.

"For the love of God! Listen, I'm glad to have found you. God has His reasons, and I suppose He sent me here for this very purpose, but we must go back at once. I don't belong here, and neither do you!"

Kobinski laughed. "For the love of God? You're in the wrong place for that, my friend."

Aharon pressed his lips, growing more irritated at this man, who was not responding as he should to anything Aharon said.

"What do you think?" Kobinski asked, almost sneering. "Do you think it's some kind of magic door that will take you back home? Something out of a fairy tale?"

"Listen—"

"What do you imagine would happen if you found that spot again? If you stood in just the right place and waited?"

"I would return to Earth, naturally!"

"Naturally? Let me tell you what nature dictates: you would stay right here. At best you might get dizzy for a moment, then find your feet planted back on the very same ground on which you were standing."

Aharon scowled at him. "What are you talking?"

"You came here because this is *exactly* where you belong."

"What are you *saying*?" Aharon whispered, angry now. "That thing—that clearing near the camp. It came directly *here*."

Kobinski motioned a hand dismissively, his face bored. "Why should I bother? Men like you never understand. I can see it in your dress, in your eyes. I can hear it in your voice. Israel! You have the nerve to complain to me about *secularism*? About the *younger generation*? Do you have any idea how ridiculous that is in this reality, in *this place*?"

Kobinski pushed hard on the arms of the chair and rose from his seat with a great groan of pain. He stood at his chair resting, hand propped against the back of it.

"Let me tell you about this world. These people, the *Fiore*, they believe . . . it is their religious conviction that they are the *feces of God*. Can you fathom that? Can you fathom their self-loathing? It's the only way they can explain why life is so relentlessly cruel. They eat *each other* because this planet provides almost nothing to sustain them. And you—making it a life-and-death issue to eat or not eat pork! You make me sick." Kobinski growled deep in his throat and spit on the floor. He had taken up some of the native gestures and facial expressions and Aharon was deeply offended.

Who was this man? Surely not Yosef Kobinski, the gentle *tzaddik* Aharon had seen in a photograph, the saintly martyred rebbe who faced down the Nazis! Aharon didn't care what the natives here believed or didn't believe— they were animals. If this place was terrible, then they must deserve it. But he *did* care about getting home.

Aharon made an expression of surrender. "Listen, you're right; I shouldn't complain. We have it good compared to this place, obviously. But tell me— what does *that* have to do with my not getting home?"

Kobinski gave him a brittle smile. "Let me tell you where you are, because it is better that you suffer no illusions. You have met your destiny a little early is all, Aharon Handalman. This is the place where you would have come upon your death. This is your judgment."

Aharon stared at him, too shocked to even be offended. "Why would *I* belong here? You don't even make sense!"

"You went through a hole in space-time that took you into the fifth dimension. Or rather, it *detached* your energy from the lower dimensions of space and time, the physical dimensions. It was detached only for a fraction of a second, but in that fraction of a second your energy, your 'soul,' if you will, went to the place in the fifth dimension *most like you*. Because the fifth dimension is outside of space and time, do you understand? In the fifth dimension, there is no 'here' and 'over there'; there's only one way data is organized, like to like. That is the law. After you went through the hole, your energy was *re-attached* to the physical dimensions. But when it was reattached, you were linked to the *physical* location closest to where your soul had gone in the continuum. And the place where it linked you was here."

Aharon's mouth was hanging open. "You're crazy!"

Kobinski growled. "This world is *gevorah-chochmah*. This is its *physical reality*. It is the embodiment of *you*, Rabbi Handalman. So you see, it's not such an easy matter, 'going home.' You are home."

Aharon was furious. He had never been so angry before in his life. He didn't believe a word, of course, but that this person, whom he had never wronged, should utter such filthy lies and blasphemy!

"Then why are *you* here? Eh?" he demanded. "Reb Kobinski? If that hole does not come directly here, then what about *you*?"

Kobinski's face went so blank it was as if he had put back on the mask. "I? I chose it."

"You are evil to say such things!"

Kobinski shrugged, more an expression than a gesture. "Think what you like. But as for how you *act*—that is another thing. Your behavior endangers me as well as yourself. One of the Fiore, Argeh, he is my enemy. He is also high priest. He would be eating you this night for supper if I hadn't intervened."

Aharon knew of whom he spoke—the Fiore with the flattened face, the one in the square black cassock who had been arguing with Kobinski in that room. "But who do these . . ." he almost said "people," "who do these animals think you are? I am? What did you tell them?"

Kobinski closed his eyes, as if he didn't want to talk about it. "This place is governed by superstition and fear. I told them I came from the heavens and they believed me. I am a messenger from Mahava, their god. Today I told them you were also sent from the heavens, as a messenger for me. To bring me, as it turns out, my manuscript." Kobinski said this last with irony.

"You told them *that*?"

"Would you rather be roasting over a fire?"

"But . . . what am I supposed to do? What can I say? How can this go on?"

"The first thing you must do is build up your strength so that you can move in this atmosphere. Right now you're completely vulnerable. In front of the Fiori, you must appear calm and assured. If you're hysterical, if you show fear, it will go badly for us. As for what to say, the only one who can understand your Hebrew is my servant, Tevach. Say as little to him as possible."

Kobinski eyed him appraisingly. "You're fat. I was starved when I arrived. If I adjusted, so can you. You must eat the food. It is vile, but it will build muscle. You need a great deal of muscle to move in this atmosphere. And remember: if you do not play your role convincingly, you will die. If they don't kill you, I will. I won't let you endanger me. Be warned."

Aharon could only stare, unable to believe Kobinski would treat him in

such a way and still in shock, also, about Kobinski's lies. The man called loudly
for Tevach. The rodent-faced creature scurried into the room, and Kobinski
leaned his weight on the creature's broad shoulders.

"You're going?" Aharon asked. "Wait. Let's forget all this . . . all this craziness for an instant. There's something else."

"I can't help you."

"No, *listen*. There's this whole thing I have to tell you about a weapon.
Your manuscript. I . . . Parts of it have fallen into the wrong hands. That's why
I'm . . ."

He was going to say that's why he was here, but it wasn't, and at this point
he wasn't sure he would have come willingly to such a place even if he'd *known*
he'd find Kobinski. The man was watching him, his face registering something
other than disdain for the first time. He looked alarmed. He turned his face
away.

"—*listen to what I'm saying!*" Aharon pressed, trying to raise himself up.
"They're going to make a weapon, a terrible weapon. It's in the Torah code.
You must return; you must *help*, somehow, to prevent a tragedy!"

Kobinski remained with his face turned from Aharon. He was utterly still. At
last, Aharon thought, at last he had gotten through to the man!

But when Kobinski turned back to look at Aharon, his face was set hard as
a stone. "I knew this would happen if the manuscript was found."

"So? We must *do* something!"

Kobinski shook his head. "The dead cannot go back," he said with flat finality, "and we are the dead."

15

God has framed you differently. Some of you have the power of command, and in the composition of these he has mingled gold, wherefore also they have the greatest honour; others he has made of silver, to be auxiliaries; others again who are to be husbandmen and craftsmen he has composed of brass and iron ... And God proclaims as a first principle to the rulers, and above all else, that there is nothing which should so anxiously guard as of the purity of the race.
—Plato, *The Republic*, fourth century B.C.E., translation by Benjamin Jowett, 1871

The condition of man ... is a condition of war of everyone against everyone.
—Thomas Hobbes, *Leviathan*, 1651

15.1. Forty-Sixty Calder Farris

Pol 137 and his partner, Gyde 332, pulled up beside the armored riot vans. There was no riot in progress. There hadn't been a riot in this city for a hundred years. But there was clearly some state crisis, as witnessed by the gathering of manpower and the presence of a Gold official.

As the two detectives got out of the sedan, Pol 137 saw the cause of the commotion. On the marble walls of the Hall of Justice someone had painted graffiti three feet high:

THERE ARE ALIENS AMONG US.

Below the words was a simple signature rendered in broad swipes: an open circle with a bar across the top.

The wind was subzero this morning, chilling Pol through his thick wool uniform. Even so, it was reading the graffiti that made him shiver. His eyes shifted to Gyde, wondering if he had the same reaction. But what he saw on Gyde's face was patriotic outrage, the appropriate response to effrontery to the state.

The Gold turned his eyes on them, his lips pinched white.

"Chancellor Henk," Gyde addressed him. He snapped his right arm forward, fist clenched, then brought the fist to his left shoulder in a salute. Pol mimicked the gesture.

The chancellor sent a grazing glance over their identification badges. He made them hold the salute longer than was customary, to indicate his displeasure, then nodded at them to relax. "You're the detectives assigned to this case?"

"Yes, Chancellor. I am Gyde 332 and this is Pol 137. He's new to the department, but he has an outstanding battle record."

"The Department of Communications wants an end to this."

"Yes, Chancellor," Gyde replied.

"This kind of thing cannot be tolerated. This is the third defacing. Did you know that?"

"We were briefed."

"And the Department of Monitors has still not caught this terrorist."

"No, Chancellor. But I have the case now. My classmate and I will find him, and we will destroy him."

Gyde, with his straight back, lifted chin, scarred features, and hard eyes, was the embodiment of Silver determination. He knew how to make his superiors feel secure. Chancellor Henk's anger visibly diminished.

Pol watched this shift, studying Gyde's proficiency. He was also fascinated by the Gold. His grooming was immaculate, his yellow hair polished straight back like a helmet. The blue at his temples reflected a soft light, even in the perpetual cloud cover, and his smooth, handsome face was toned and oiled. Pol had never been this close to a Gold in the flesh. He'd only seen them on posters or on the evening telecast. He stored the details mechanically.

Chancellor Henk was used to being stared at and ignored Pol's unnerving blue-white eyes. "Gyde 332, I will accept that as a commitment."

"Chancellor, you have my pledge."

"Good. I'm elevating this degenerate to a state terrorist. You'll receive a memo today. In the meantime, my adjunct has all the information. Good luck. The state rewards service."

"Long live the state!" Gyde saluted again.

The Gold signaled for his driver and pulled away in his long black car. The adjunct stood waiting for Gyde. He was a young Silver, and his face was haughty with the privilege of his position. While Gyde went over the case with him, he sent Pol to survey the site.

Pol went carefully over the broad marble steps leading up to the portico, but they were smooth and clean. In front of the steps was the pedestrian zone, also unremarkable. On the portico itself there were no footprints, no paper or wrappers or smoke butts. Pol took out a small knife and envelope and scraped a sample of black paint from the wall. Up close, the letters were so tall he couldn't read the message, and it helped his concentration not to think about what it said.

He shared a smoke with the monitor commander and questioned him. The Hall of Justice, the state's grandest courthouse, was just off Victory Plaza at the heart of the capital. Monitors walked the district at night, but their route and timetables meant that most buildings, the courthouse included, were left unwatched for ten minutes at a time. The commander believed the message had been left between 0100 and 0140 hours. They had seen no one on the streets, not even someone with a legal curfew pass.

So whoever the terrorist was, Pol wrote in his notebook, he was clever enough to study the monitors' routes and to time his defacement accordingly. There hadn't been an air raid last night, so the streetlights had been on, harsh and glaring, yet he had done his business without being seen. Pol had to wonder who would be so stupid as to risk so much for so little. What could possibly be the motivation? A malcontent. A madman.

The commander's eyes lingered on Pol's face as they talked. The look was only a brief second too long, but Pol felt a stab of concern. Gyde was still talking to the adjunct, so Pol went inside the Hall of Justice and found a service room. It was at the back of the grand foyer. The sign said it was for Golds and Silvers only.

The interior was impressive—high ceilings, marble floors, elegant but cold. Marble columns divided the spaces. Polished metal receptacles reflected nary a thumbprint. An Iron attendant was waiting to assist Pol and to clean up after he had gone. He motioned the slave back and turned to the fountain. He put the tips of his fingers in the flowing water, using the moment to examine his reflection in the mirror. The blue at his temples was intact. His eye color helped to focus attention away from it in any case. His brow was clear and smooth. The small scars hidden inside his hairline just above both ears were not visible. There was a hint of darkness on his cheek, but only if you were looking for it. It would hold until they got back to the office. The commander had been staring at . . . what? Nothing. Often eyes lingered on him, and he never understood how much people could or could not see. He could drive himself mad worrying about it.

The Iron waited with a towel. Pol dried his hands. He was about to leave, but he decided he might as well relieve himself while he was here. There was no one, only the Iron, who was busy wiping down the metal he had splashed at the fountain. The bathrooms back at the Department of Monitors were usually occupied; Pol avoided them.

He turned to the metal receptacles, his back to the room.

He was releasing a stream of urine when he heard the heavy hall door swing open. He hurried to finish and tie up his pants. He thought he not been obvious about his haste, but as he turned, Gyde stepped up to the receptacle beside him, smiling.

"You make me laugh, Pol. Shy as a girl, as if you weren't raised with a few hundred men."

Gyde released his own uncircumcised, slightly hooked penis with exaggerated boldness—or was it pride? A sardonic smile dimpled his aging face.

"I'll be outside," Pol said.

*   *   *

Back at the Department of Monitors, Pol sat at his desk eyeballing the photographs in front of him. Black paint on a white marble wall: THERE ARE ALIENS AMONG US.

Gyde stood up at his desk. "Lunch?"

"I'll be down in a minute."

Gyde's departure opened the floodgates. The massive old room, with its towering cracked ceilings and clanging radiators, held the desks of six other Silver-class detectives. Their occupants followed Gyde to the dining hall as instinctively as they had once followed him into battle.

Pol was relieved to be alone. He opened the case file from the adjunct. The terrorist had left two other messages in graffiti prior to last night's defacement.

THEY ARE HERE. THEY ARE US, said the most recent message.

And the first: WHAT ISN'T THE STATE TELLING US?

That one was stupid. What *was* the state telling them? But the other message struck that mental funny bone just as the alien message had. THEY ARE HERE. THEY ARE US. Pol felt the darkness in his mind quiver responsively, as though disturbed by a neurological aftershock. He did not know what it meant, only that it meant something.

When he reached the dining hall and sat down, Gyde put a finger to his lips to hush his greeting. He motioned his head toward the next table, where a group of Bronze monitors, their rust-colored uniforms tight and foreboding, were having a conversation. An Iron female came to determine his choice of the two menu options today. Pol gave her a quick response, hardly knowing what he'd ordered. He was listening to the Bronzies.

"Where was this?" one of them asked, voice low.

"Saradena. I was stationed there until last week."

"How do you know the corpse was a Silver? You said the head and hands were missing."

"You wouldn't know a Silver when you saw one? He had an old sparring scar on his left thigh, his skin was white, prominent blue veins at his privates, like a statue, and his physique was perfect, a classic warrior. By the blood, he was a Silver."

Pol felt a rush of fear-based adrenaline, but no one was watching him; no one was looking at him at all. Gyde's head was tilted, his eyes half-lidded, listening to the dialogue.

"*I'd* know a Silver," another Bronze agreed, "even with more than that missing! But who would do such a thing? In one of our own cities? Not even in battle!"

"Maybe he did something wrong," a quiet voice said. Pol hazarded a glance. The speaker was a tall Bronze he'd seen before—hulking, mean-looking. His voice was dull with import.

The table went silent. "Doing something wrong" could easily be fatal. It was, in fact, not a very smart thing to even talk about it. The Bronze from Saradena looked around apprehensively. He saw Gyde and Pol watching him and paled. He began carving his steak.

"Not decapitated," Gyde said calmly but loudly. "Not by the state."

Gyde turned back in his chair and lifted the bare ridge above his eyes at Pol, as if to say, *Look how I'm playing these children.*

"That's right," someone at the next table ventured, emboldened now. "If he'd done something wrong he would have disappeared, not been found carved up like that. It must have been a private citizen who did it—a murderer, a lunatic."

Pol slammed his hand down on the table with a painful bang. "Be silent!"

The Bronzies at the next table fell into a mute attentiveness to their food and, after a show of eating, rapidly dispersed back to their cubbyholes.

Pol's plate came. Gyde leaned forward thoughtfully, chin on his hand. He was studying Pol with that damned inscrutable expression. His eyes were a soft sea green at the moment, but if you looked closer you could see the steel in them, the glint of a spear, even when he was relaxed.

Pol had the urge to say something, to justify what he'd just done, something like "they shouldn't talk that way about the state" or "I don't like that kind of talk while I'm eating." But wisely, he said nothing.

"You ever heard about that case?" Gyde asked slowly. "A decapitated Silver? You were in Saradena, weren't you? Before you were assigned here?"

"Briefly. On leave. And no, I never heard of it." The knife was heavy as Pol picked it up to cut his meat.

"You'd get a lot of merits solving a case like that."

Pol shifted his eyes to his partner in a cold, lazy stare. He brought the dripping meat to his mouth. "It's in *Saradena.*"

"I know. Don't they have the luck of the gods."

"Should be some decent merits on our new case."

"Yes," Gyde said, brightening. "He's been elevated to a full-blown state terrorist, our man. I want to solve this one quickly. Let's put a few days on it starting now, drop everything else. After lunch we'll sit down and make a list of all the angles."

After lunch. There was still a long afternoon stretching ahead. Pol felt as though his mind were cracking in two. He really ought to sit through it, but he honestly didn't think he could, and there was that darkening cheek to administer to.

"I thought I'd do some research after lunch. For an hour or two. We should make sure we have all the facts before we lay down a strategy."

Gyde's weathered, hairless forehead pursed into lines like those the tide leaves in sand. "Research?"

"At the Archives."

The lines deepened. Pol felt Gyde's eyes bearing into him, but his partner didn't comment.

Pol managed to catch one of the Silver buses, its thick leather and cranked-up heat a welcome respite from the cold. It dropped him off at the gymnasium on the Silver grounds, the pool and spa visible and empty through the large glass panes. Inside, only a few recuperating wounded, their bare flesh pink from steam, were using the facilities. Outside, a unit of young Silvers, perhaps ten or eleven years old, was practicing hand-to-hand wrestling. Their Iron caretakers waited patiently to one side while Silver instructors gave the lesson. The children wore the woolen one-piece garments that fit them like a second skin. Similar garments were worn under the uniforms of Silvers in battle. Pol had one under his own black detective's uniform. It was one of the many small details that distinguished a Silver from the other classes. Even warmth was a privilege of rank. Not that anyone was ever truly warm in Centalia.

The wrestling lesson was a small knot of activity on the endless gray parade grounds of the Silver compound. The dormitories were on either side, massive and silent in the dim afternoon light. There were few Silvers in residence this month. A big offensive push was going on over at the border with Mesatona, and most of the soldiers were in the field. Only the children and the older ones, like Gyde, reassigned to state jobs, still haunted the grounds. The old Silvers moved up the steps and across the frosty soil like shadows when it got this quiet, their eyes on distant blood-soaked battles they could no longer join.

And then there was Pol.

It began to hail in great icy lumps. He quickened his pace. He had two rooms on the third floor of building fourteen. The rooms were tall and elegant, the furnishings spartan, and there was no lock on the door. He had found a way around that. He went into his bathroom, taking along a small chair, and propped it against the handle. Alone at last.

His craggy face was bleak in the light that came in from the small window. He turned on the overhead. It made him look bloodless. He leaned forward, hands on the sink, staring into the mirror.

He'd been sweating, and he must have touched himself unconsciously. The blue at his temples was smeared.

He turned on the tap, waited for it to run hot. He took a few of the dark paper sheaves stored by the commode and wiped his temples. The light blue makeup, almost the same shade as his eyes, came off, staining black against the rough paper. He wiped again, wetting the paper, making sure he got it all. Then he flushed the paper down the commode. He splashed water on his face and poured it over his short blond hair (there was just a trace of black at the roots; he'd have to dye it again tomorrow night). He stuck his head fully under the spigot, wishing he could disappear in the flow.

Pol 137 was the name of the dead Silver in Saradena whose head and hands were never found.

He soaked a cloth with hot water and wrapped it around his entire face, holding it tight. He sat down on the commode and leaned back, waiting for the heat to soften his skin. With all this shaving, he was getting noticeably raw.

Silvers did not have facial hair or eyebrows.

There are aliens among us.

If only he could remember.

The darkness of the impostor of Pol 137 was more than skin deep, ran deeper than the hair on his face that he shaved or the hair on his head that he dyed. There was a black chasm in his mind, a schism that was torment to try to breach. He probed at that place now, the way a tongue probes at a painful tooth, only because he must, because he was in danger. That place was like a hole in reality. He could, with effort, take himself to the far side of that hole, that schism. And what he glimpsed there had a logic that he wouldn't expect madness to have. And yet the logic of "back there"—that far side of the chasm—was not consistent with the logic of "here," this side. And so it broke down; it all broke down. His memories fractured and fell apart. If he tried too hard and for too long he tottered on the brink of falling permanently into that hole and never coming out.

It was much more functional to not go there. And functional was what mattered. He had to have his wits about him at all times. But still, he knew that schism for what it was: a wound. He'd had a head injury in battle; that was the superficial cause. He had once believed that was all there was to it. Now he wasn't so sure.

The first thing he remembered with certainty was wandering around in the gray blasted plains of a battlefield in utter confusion and terror. That was how Marcus had found him—greedy, slobbery Marcus. The merchant had been driving across the war zone during a ceasefire, his truck full of black-market goods.

Marcus had scooped him up, clamped him with servant's bracelets, and given him an identity: Iron class, Kalim N2. Marcus had thought him a shell-shocked enemy soldier, a free-and-clear profit on the hoof. The greedy bastard had hoped to turn him around quickly—sell him off before he could get back his memory, rebel, make trouble. But first Marcus had to patch him up—or, rather, have his servants patch him up, sew up his wounds, teach him the rudiments of the language, get him over the deep wracking chills and vomiting, the look of utter panic in his eyes.

He remembered Marcus's drab, Bronze class 2 household. Its very meanness, its coarseness, had been a comfort at first. It had offered a routine that calmed the whirlwind in his brain, as if having someone tell him what to do at every moment took the burden off himself. Gradually, the schism in his mind had separated and solidified, and the current reality began to gel. There was a weight on him that felt oppressive, made him weary all the time, but every day he felt his feet settle more and more naturally on the floor, as though he were touching down, like an angel.

But he had reached the point of functionality and then passed it. After a while, the menial labor began to grate. Being given orders lost its comfort factor. He sensed, then *knew*, that he was not born a servant. He saw the uniforms in the street, the beautiful men and women flashing like military diamonds, the posters everywhere of the triumphant, handsome, perfect Silvers—muscular, haughty, glorious, the pride of the state. The more he looked at them, the more he knew what he was, what he must have once been. He'd been a Silver in some foreign state; he'd had wealth, privilege, power over others. Especially that. Especially power. Somehow he'd been wounded in battle and captured by his enemy, but he was still a warrior.

He'd been sure of that in Saradena. Did he still believe it?

The cloth was cooling. He went back to the mirror and unwrapped his face. He examined his skull minutely for the hundredth time, fingertips tripping over the surface to feel the scars. There were the smaller scars hidden in his hairline where he himself had done a little surgery, nipping and tucking his skin back so that his eyes would have that subtle slant of the Centalian Silvers. And at the back of his skull was the scar from his battle injury, so small and insignificant—a crooked line no longer than a single joint of his finger. Underneath it was a bony knot. He probed, as if his fingers could unlock its secrets. He understood how the injury might have torn, shredded, his memories. But what he didn't understand was how it could have caused what he *did* remember to be so completely mad.

Those memories had to be madness; they couldn't be real. He had spent the past few weeks confirming that at the Archives. But there was one thing he *did* trust about those memories: he had been on a mission, a very urgent mission. And whatever else he did, however he survived, ate, worked, dreamed, while his brain healed, it was critical that he remember just what that mission was.

*   *   *

The impassive young Silvers at the entrance to the Archives, straight as ar-rows, sculpted like effigies, did not betray any recognition of him on their faces, though he'd seen this particular one, the one who held his identity card, on many occasions.

"Pol 137." The Silver wrote meticulously in his book. He looked up, meet-ing Pol's eyes for the first time. "Working on another case, Detective?"

"Yes. For the Department of Communications."

Pol took his ID back and went on past.

Stupid. Why had he said that? That Silver had no need to know. He had been flustered at the question. *Keep your mouth shut. Shut!* He had only gotten this far on a damaged brain by saying as little as possible and by never, *never*, asking questions.

There was another checkpoint, the main archivist. Pol had to leave his things here. The archivist copied the documents Pol needed onto a special green paper and wrote down the number of sheets he had been given. When he left, these would be returned for disposal. No papers went in; no papers went out.

Inside the Archives, Pol went to a bank of small lockers and took a key from his pocket. Notes could not be taken from this place, so they were stored here. Even so, Pol knew that anytime the state decided to look at his notes, they would, so he kept them cryptic. He took his archive notebook and his green pages to the massive old tables in the center of the room. From his seat he was visible to the archivists, visible to the armed guards who stood along the balcony. There could be no secrets here, where all secrets were kept.

There wasn't much in his notes. His search for the language he remem-bered had yielded nothing. He had found six different languages in the Archives, two obsolete, the other four still in use in foreign states, but none of them matched the language he'd had in his head when he was picked up. So he still did not even know what state he had come from. He'd been inserting his own private keywords into searches for his cases whenever he could. He hadn't found any references to "United States of America," "United States Army," or any of the other words that rose to the surface of his brain like flotsam from a sunken ship.

He turned to his green pages. According to the lab analysis of the graffiti message, the black paint was a type used in construction. Construction sites were peopled with slave labor—Irons. The terrorist could be an Iron. But if so, he would risk a lot being caught out after curfew. For an Iron such an in-fringement was punishable by death.

He made a list of keywords for the search. *Aliens. Graffiti. State terrorists. Construction sites. Black paint.* He paused. He added: *Washington.* He tore it off and made his way to one of the lower archivists. Her badge identified her as a Bronze 3, a dark-haired beauty. She was all business. She took the list and the copy of the terrorist's signature circle, looked at his ID again, and told him to wait.

While he waited at his table, a hand fell on his shoulder. He managed not to jump. It was Gyde. He slipped into the next chair, looking as nervous as a mouse confronted by a cat.

"I don't like this place," he muttered, eyes darting to the guards. "Why do you come here so much? It's not healthy to be too curious. Someone will notice."

"I don't come here much."

"Find anything?"

"She's looking now."

His partner looked at his watch pointedly. "Just now? How long have you been here?"

"A while." Pol stared at Gyde heavily. Gyde smiled, a slight, unreadable smile, and dropped it.

The archivist brought the information. There were several large folders to sift through, most, if not all, of which, would turn out to be irrelevant. Pol took his list from the top of the stack as the archivist put it down. He glanced at it briefly before balling it into a wad. "Washington"—zero records located.

"Let's get started," Pol said.

15.2. Sixty-Forty Denton Wyle

Denton rolled away from the Sapphian female, breathing hard. He stretched and yawned.

"I bring you food now," she said.

"Thank you," he responded in Sapphian.

She got up, tying her little skirt in place, and left him to bathe with the bowl of warm water she'd brought earlier.

He'd been in the village for, jeez, it had to be a couple of months now, and so far they'd sent a different female every morning. He did a few calisthenics, idly wondering if they considered it an insult to send a repeat and hoping that he wouldn't be stuck doing the very old and the very young eventually out of some bizarre hospitality requirements.

Not that he had to worry anytime soon. There were several thousand Sapphians living in the horseshoe gorge, and lots and lots of them were nubile females. Yes, lots and lots.

Whistling, he walked to the basin. The air was warm and soft on his skin. He splashed some water around on his body and shaved his face with a primitive knife. A sharp, flintlike stone served as the blade. The iron age had evidently not yet put in an appearance. The shaving sucked, but there was no way he was doing a Tom Hanks. The Sapphians didn't grow beards, and he had a hard-enough time fitting in as it was.

He put his own clothes back on. Fitting in was one thing, but wearing those little Sapphian skirts was just not going to happen.

They'd given him his own hut. It was like all the others—a one-room structure made of dried mud with a roof woven from huge rubbery fronds. It was cozy, in a me-Tarzan-you-Jane kind of way. It was *not* a suite at the Ritz. His mother would have a cow or maybe even a whole herd. He wondered if she knew he was missing by now. He wondered if she had penciled ten minutes into her busy routine to shed a freaking tear.

"Your breakfast." The female returned with a wooden bowl of cut fruit and a sticky tapiocalike grain.

"Thank you, Gertrude." He smiled.

The female gave him a typically blank Sapphian smile, her eyes on his cheek, and left.

The Sapphian village was spread throughout the horseshoe gorge, paths connecting clusters of huts, each cluster designed around a center circle. His hut was on the largest community circle, the place where everyone ate the evening meal and enjoyed the subsequent dancing and carousing. It was, you might say, prime real estate. During the afternoon siesta the circle was used for lounging and visiting, and in the mornings it was filled with women and children. The women soaked and dyed the silky husks they used to make clothing, while the young children clambered about like sleek little rats.

It wasn't that Denton disliked children. He didn't have an opinion one way or the other. But these weren't exactly *children*, were they? And anyway, he'd be damned if he was going to spend another morning watching husks turn red. At this early hour, with the Sapphian sky a fresh, light aqua, the men and boys were gathering to form work committees. Denton walked over and joined a group of men.

"*Allook saheed* does not need to work," one of the men said to him, motioning him away oh, so politely.

"I know." Denton smiled. "But I *want* to work."

The man looked surprised, as if Denton had said he'd like to join a chain gang. "If *allook saheed* wishes?"

"Yes, thank you, but I want to work."

The man took Denton to join a group of young males. They greeted him like he was the second coming. He bobbed his head and said hello to each of them in turn, "*Ta zhecta. Ta zhecta. Ta zhecta.*" His neck had grown stiff from all the bobbing. He had probably dislocated a disk or two.

The eight of them headed down a path into the jungle. Denton found himself paired with a young male he'd noticed before. "Hey, John."

The boy looked at him in confusion. "Zhohn?"

"I can't say your name. Can I? What is it?"

The boy rattled off something with at least three *k*'s. Denton had learned basic Sapphian, because there was no way he could live without being able to wheedle. But the names were harder than everyday speech and, anyway, calling them by human names was a small-enough illusion.

"See? I cannot say that. I say 'John,' okay?"

"Zhohn," the boy repeated, looking pleased. "I like this name."

Like all the Sapphians, John was a beautiful creature. His feet were long and thin, inhuman-looking, with those sticky gecko toes. They reminded Denton of angel's feet—except for the dirt and the rough red inner edge where the skin had calloused. John was only now coming into manhood, and he looked like Peter Pan or Puck, the eternal boy. Well, sort of. He might have looked like that if not for a birth defect, a withered right hand. Denton had noticed him before because such things were rare among the Sapphians. It was a surprise that it *was* rare, actually, given that there wasn't a plastic surgeon for a couple of million light-years.

"What are we doing today?" Denton asked him.

"We pick fruit."

"Is that right?" It didn't sound too difficult. Not breathtakingly exciting, either.

"The true way is: I pick. *You* catch." John's eyes twinkled.

"That is how it works, eh?"

"Yes."

"Are you good at picking fruit?"

"So good the fruit comes to me. I don't even climb the tree."

Denton realized he was being teased. And John was looking directly into his eyes. Denton felt ridiculously grateful at being treated like, well, like a person. A lump clogged his throat. "I want to see that."

"You *will* see. I am Mighty John." The boy struck his chest in a machismo gesture. His own use of the fake name made him giggle childishly. Denton laughed, too.

The vista as they walked was a pretty one. They passed a stream where the water sparkled, reflecting the green of the jungle in glints of emeralds. A delicate fernlike moss covered the banks of the stream like lace. They passed a tree that was curved like a woman and had a climbing vine up its length with bright red flowers the size of Denton's head.

Jesus, it was beautiful. It was not LA and never would be. The lump in his throat throbbed.

"Listen, John? Are there other things to see away from here? Maybe . . ." Denton wracked his brain for vocabulary. "Maybe big water? Or other villages? Other people?"

John looked away into the distance as they walked, the smile fading from his face. "Away from here? I have never left the gorge in my life."

"No? Maybe you heard stories?"

"No person leaves the gorge. Never." John's tone indicated that the very idea was inconceivable. His eyes went nervously to the others.

Denton got the idea that this was not a welcome topic of conversation, but he found the whole thing perplexing. The gorge was a gorgeous place, sure. But what kind of a people would not explore their own planet? Out of sheer boredom if nothing else.

"Why, John? Why do people never leave the gorge?"

John turned and met his eyes. He looked frightened and his words were quiet and urgent. "It is not safe. It is very dangerous out there. You must not go out there, friend."

"Oh," Denton said. "Okay."

John had not been bragging by much. Of the eight of them, he was the only one who climbed the trees, the job apparently being his specialty. He chose a *paava* tree first, its trunk smooth and straight and covered with tough, needle-like spines. John wrapped rags around his wrists and feet and mounted the tree, agile as a circus performer.

Denton worked with two of the other males handling a large net. They manipulated it to catch the fruit as John tossed it down. Every few minutes they swooped the contents of the net to the ground and the remaining males gathered the fruit into bundles.

It was a short workday. None of the Sapphians ever worked past noon, the heat of the day. The others coddled him at first. But after a while, they seemed to forget that he was *allook saheed*, and that was all right. It wasn't exactly a day of international thrills and adventure, but it beat the heck out of sitting outside his hut watching his toenails grow. And that was a little bit pathetic.

All morning, as he worked with the net, he kept remembering what John had said: *It is not safe*. He thought of the terrors he'd had those first days before he'd found the gorge, walking alone and wondering what deadly forms of life might exist on this planet. He remembered the large thing he'd heard far away in the jungle and the blood on the trees.

Maybe it wasn't that important to find out if Molly Brad or any of the others had ever been here after all.

*   *   *

Denton tilted back his head, looking at the stars.

The stars on Sapphia were incredibly bright, and there were zillions of them. They formed a mesh across the sky far denser than the star pattern he remembered from home. It was like . . . like looking at downtown New York from the air.

The lump in his throat hurt. It was becoming chronic, that damned lump. It was like bad heartburn, only higher and . . . lumpier. He stopped looking at the stars.

He wished the party would start already. He was sitting on a log in the community circle. The place was crowded with Sapphians, as it was every night. And like every night, the minute he moved close to a log people got up, motioning for him to take their place. On the subway in New York or Paris this would be considered suspicious behavior. But here . . . well, the Sapphians had this generosity thing down cold. Yessiree. He smiled and nodded at people passing by until he thought his head would fall off. "*Ta zhecta. Ta zhecta. Ta zhecta.*"

He was waiting for the good stuff to be broken out—*gancha*, a fermented fruit juice that was sickly sweet but intoxicating enough to justify any insult to the palate. *Gancha* was especially effective at dissolving lumps. But before he could get his hands on some he had to wait through the weekly ritual. Finally one of the older males, his blond hair only lightly dusted with silver, got up and announced the list.

This was a thing they did every seven days; Denton had counted. In a world without Thursday Night Ladies' Night or Monday Night Football, it was nice to have a way to mark your place in time. He had come to think of it as "the Saturday Night Special" and had named the other days of the week accordingly.

The Saturday Night Special went something like this: Someone would stand up and make a brief announcement. Then there would be an hour or so in which the Sapphians cried and yodeled and stomped around and in general acted like the world was coming to an end.

The first time Denton had seen it he'd been really freaked. He'd been sure something catastrophic was going down. But the crying gradually subsided and what followed was the biggest binge of the week, lots of drinking, lots of sex. And he could really go for a trip to Blottosville right about now. But first he had to get through the crying.

There was a female on his right. She sniffed out a few crocodile tears, working herself up to a genuine cry. She was nothing special. Denton tried, but he could not for the life of him remember if she had ever visited him in the mornings or not. That thought made the lump ache.

"*Ta zhecta,*" he said to her. "Are you okay?"

"Yes. It is sad."

He leaned toward her, trying to get her to make eye contact. "Why is it sad? What the man said—it was a list of names, yes?"

She looked as if she didn't understand the question.

"Are they . . . ?" He didn't know the word for "ancestors." "Fathers? Fathers of fathers of fathers? And mothers of mothers of mothers? From a long time ago?"

She looked at his cheek in total bewilderment. "No."

He didn't know how to phrase the question any differently. He kind of figured this ritual was a memorial, a recounting of some tragic communal event—a plague or meteorite or something like that.

"We say good-bye to them now," she said.

"Yes, I see," he said, though he hadn't a frigging clue.

"Do you want to take me to your hut?"

He was annoyed. "No. I want to talk."

"Oh."

She waited. Something about the way she waited made him feel stupid.

"What do you do in the day?"

"I collect grain at the river."

So! Do you do a lot of traveling with that job? How are the benefits?

"Do you have children?"

"I have given birth three times."

She looked young, but he wasn't surprised. As much as he liked the Sapphians' free-for-all attitude toward sex, he had to admit that the abundance of rug rats and pregnant females was a less than attractive result. Sometimes it seemed as though there were more children than adults in the village.

She was still staring at his cheek.

"So. You want to . . . uh . . . go to my hut?"

When Denton returned to the circle a little while later the party had started. He blinked at the nighttime brightness—a combination of starlight and firelight. Before he could take more than three steps, an older female brought him a plate loaded with roasted meat and grain. He thanked her three times, as she kept nodding and bowing at him. He looked at the plate and sighed.

What he really wanted, and badly, was the hard stuff. What he wanted even more was someone sympathetic to drink it with. And the only one who qualified was John. He and John had hung together a lot lately.

He scanned the crowd of Sapphians and saw the boy at the outer edge of the firelight talking to a young female. He headed over there, but by the time he arrived John and the female had taken off down a path into the jungle. Denton followed.

There was not a lot of light on the path. He walked, the plate warm in his hand, feeling a little uneasy. Something rushed toward him from the trees and snatched the plate.

He cried out, stumbling backward. But as the figure darted back into the trees, Denton saw what—or who—it was. It was the girl with the long white-gold hair, the one he'd seen first that night he'd found the village.

"Hey! Wait!" He ran after her.

This girl, he knew for a certainty, had never been sent to his hut in the morning. He knew because he was always disappointed that it wasn't her. There was something wrong with this female. She wasn't accepted in the village. He'd seen her a couple of times, hanging around outside the circle, always in the mornings. She sat up in the trees watching the women and children with an expression of resentment and want. She had reminded him a little of a dog he'd had as a kid, shut out of the house by the servants and sitting at the back door intently, desperate to be let in.

She must have done something to get herself booted, but he didn't know what and, at the moment, he didn't much care.

When he caught up with her she was sitting up in a tree. She looked down at him blandly and ate from the plate, picking up the meat delicately with her fingers.

Denton paused beneath the tree, breathing hard. "What's your name?"

She didn't even look at him.

"Let me think." He tapped his chin. "I will call you . . . Mary. Why do you not eat with the other people, Mary?"

She sighed, her mouth full, but didn't look up from her meal.

His eyes were adjusting to the starlight and he could make her out well enough, done up in shades of blue. God, she was beautiful. Her face . . . He really liked that face.

The Sapphians were not mental giants as a rule. Perhaps it was just the simplicity of their lifestyle and lack of education. After all, what was there to talk about? There was no *Frasier* or *Friends* to discuss, no Howard Stern. And the females . . . Even thinking it made the lump throb, but he had to admit that they were all starting to look alike to him, that making love to them was starting to feel . . . dang . . . it was starting to feel a little like having sex with cute animals.

And that was not a place he wanted to go in his mind. Because if he really went there he might eventually have to stop, and that would suck.

This one's face, though . . . there was something different about her. There was something other than bland cooperation in her eyes; there was sadness, a depth. Or maybe he was just freaking imagining it.

"Will you come down and talk to me, Mary?"

"My name is Eyanna."

He smiled. It was a bit rude, but she was communicating at least. "But 'Mary' is easy for me—"

"*Eyanna.*"

Yes, definitely rude. He grinned. "Okay. Ee-yaah-ña." He said it a couple of times. "Will you come down and talk to me, Eyanna? I won't hurt you."

She laughed, as if to say he couldn't hurt her if he tried.

"You don't think I could catch you, huh? You're probably right. I'm too big to climb trees."

He wracked his brain. He wanted to lure her down, but he didn't have a whole lot on him. He pulled out his wallet. He had plenty of cash, but he didn't think that would interest her. He dug around in one pocket and pulled out some old snapshots.

There was a head shot of an ex-girlfriend, an actress. She was a blonde with big hair, a cute girl. He put the others back.

"This is for you." He held it out.

She didn't come down, but she looked at it. He held it as high as he could and tilted it into the starlight. "A female, you see? Very pretty. Come look."

She finished her food, taking her time. His arm got tired holding up the damned picture, but he thought it was working. She tossed the plate to the ground and slowly, keeping her eyes on him, she began to climb down.

At the base of the tree she stood, watching him, as if telling him with her eyes that she wouldn't put up with any funny business.

He held the picture out to her. "Take it."

She took a step forward and stretched out her long arm. She took the photo, staying as far from him as possible. She stared at it at the front, then the back, then the front again, her eyes wide.

"I want to be your friend." Denton smiled. "Here."

He reached toward her. He only meant to take her wrist and pull her a little farther into the light so she could see the photograph better. But at his movement she was gone, quick as a cat, bounding into the trees.

*　　　*　　　*

It was Wednesday, by Denton's reckoning. He and John and the other males they worked with were at the waterfall having a swim. It was a gorgeous day and the swim was a nice change, but Denton wasn't feeling too happy. The lump in his throat was worse.

Doctor, it hurts when I do that.

So don't do that.

Only he wasn't sure what it was he was doing or how he could stop.

The waterfall was loud this close-up. The Sapphians had brought him to a perfect spot, close to the waterfall but not right beneath it. The water was fast in the middle of the stream, but at the sides there were still pools and some nice big rocks for lounging. He and John were lounging on one right now. The three males were swimming lazily in the water. Denton waved.

"Hey, John?"

"Yes, Denton?"

Denton loved the way John said his name—it sounded like "downtown" and always made him smile.

"I wanted to ask you this for a long time. What does *allook saheed* mean? *Saheed* is God, yes?"

The boy was stretched out on his back, his right hand in the water as if, consciously or unconsciously, he was hiding his deformity. Now he sat up. His right hand came out of the water, and he watched it dripping the wet onto his lap as if giving it some thought.

"Yes. And *allook* is a thing one person gives another person, something nice."

"Like a 'gift' or a 'present'?" Denton tried to explain the English words with pantomime.

"Yes," John said, "that is the way."

Allook saheed. Gift from God. That was nice.

John looked shyly into his eyes. "Do you know . . . I am also called *allook saheed*."

"Yeah? You mean, all Sapphians are *allook saheed*? Gifts from God?" Denton felt a little bit disappointed.

"No, not all." Looking humiliated now, as if it were a big deal to acknowledge it, he held up his withered hand. "But I am called *allook saheed* because of this."

"Oh."

Denton thought he understood. John was unique because of his hand, and Denton was unique also. The Sapphians acknowledged that specialness and that was, you know, kind of a mature way of looking at things. It was like the way some Indian tribes thought insanity was a blessing from God. *Mysterious World* had done an article on that once.

Now that he thought about it, John *was* treated pretty well by the others. He was never teased about his hand or shut out of reindeer games or anything. And he seemed to have as much access to females as any of the other males. That was cool.

He'd never seen the Sapphians mistreat anyone. Except Eyanna.

"Hey, John? There is a female named Eyanna. She is very beautiful. None of the people talk to her and she stays up in the trees."

"Yes, I know that one."

"Why does no one talk to her?"

John looked at the others, as if to see if they were listening. They were not that close and the waterfall was loud. He turned to Denton, folding his long legs in front of him. His face was serious.

"It is best to forget this female, friend."

"Why?"

"Because it is best to follow the ways of the people. The people do not talk to this female or even say her name."

"Why?"

John shook his head. In Sapphian that didn't mean "no" but "you're stubborn" or something like that; it was a mild censor. "Why do you want this female when you can have every other one?"

"Because I can have every other one."

It took John a minute to get it; then he laughed and laughed. He seemed to find this extremely funny. Denton laughed, too, but he didn't drop the subject.

"Why do the people not talk to Eyanna? What did she do?"

John's laughter subsided. He made a reluctant face and moved one leg out to bob his toes in the water. "She is a ghost woman." He made a fake crying face, rubbing at invisible tears in his eyes.

Denton didn't get it at first, but there was only one situation in which he'd ever seen Sapphians cry. "You mean . . . her name was said in the circle and the people cried for her?"

John made the hand gesture for agreement.

"But what are those names? I wanted to ask you for a long time. I thought the names are ones who . . ." Denton pretended to choke himself, falling back as if dead.

When he opened his eyes, John had backed away on the rock, face pale. And the others, the swimmers, were racing toward them in a panic. Jesus, they thought he'd really choked himself.

"I'm sorry," he said to John, deeply embarrassed. "I was playing."

But John looked truly shaken and the others, pulling themselves onto the rock and looking him over carefully, were grim and brusque.

"I'm sorry," Denton said to them. "I was playing. I'm fine. I'm good."

Behind the backs of the others John looked at him with frightened eyes and made the hand gesture for "no," making a face that could only be interpreted as a warning.

And Denton knew that he did not understand anything about these people, not anything at all.

15.3. Seventy-Thirty Jill Talcott

The City was like an unfinished plastic model, like a movie set before the paint and props had been added, before the extras had arrived for the day. Its great scale was more apparent from the inside; its streets marched into the distance, featureless white buildings on both sides growing smaller and smaller until they merged with the horizon. It was absolutely still.

It wasn't that the place felt deserted, Jill thought; it was more like a half-remembered dream of something that had never existed at all.

They had not found water the previous day. The buildings were unlocked, their interiors filled with cubelike rooms, their windows dimmed by a dark film to moderate the strength of the sun. The only contents were a few pieces of molded furniture that did not fit their human proportions. Some of the rooms had wall plates that might be electronic displays and counters with concave indentations that might be sinks. But the wall plates were dark and the holes from which water might conceivably emerge were dry as dust. Exhaustion and the futility of the sameness of building after building had stolen over Nate and Jill as they searched. They'd lain down on the hard floor in one of the rooms and slept.

Jill wasn't sure how much time had passed, but the larger of the two suns was at about three o'clock and they were back on the streets, plodding past building after building in the dazzling heat. A sense of lassitude was making it more and more difficult to go on, and Jill was beginning to become seriously concerned. If they didn't find water soon, they would die.

Beside her, Nate stopped walking. They'd hardly said two words to each other since they'd awoken, sparing their throats. Now he looked pensive.

"I know what's wrong. Jill. . . . All these streets and buildings and there are no advertisements. No billboards, no posters, no *cafés*, no neon signs, no addresses, no *stores* . . . Jesus."

"This is an alien culture. You can't expect it to be like ours." Jill's voice sounded like chalk on a blackboard and felt like it, too.

"Or *sounds*. No music or anything. Even inside the buildings there's no art, no knick knacks, no *mementos*—there's nothing at all."

It was true that there were none of these things. Jill had accepted it the way she'd accepted that the streets were straight and the windows were filmed. But hearing him put it like that, it was pretty unsettling. They hadn't seen a visual representation of *anything* since they'd been here. Not even, now that she thought about it, writing.

"You know what?" Nate said, with another glimmer of realization. "It reminds me of your place."

"What?"

"Yeah. I always thought your place was kind of strange. Now I know why: no photographs or posters on the wall or—"

"It's nothing like my place!" Despite her dry throat, Jill managed to sound plenty forceful. "I *have* a framed poster on my wall. It's from the Louvre."

"You told me it was there when you moved in."

"I could have taken it down!"

"Um, I don't think 'not caring enough to remove it' is exactly artistic sentiment."

"What, exactly, is your point?"

Before Nate could answer, a flying object zipped over their heads with the drone and swoop of a speeding insect. It stopped in mid-air a short distance up the street and landed softly with a vertical maneuver. The object was a vehicle, far larger than the sphere they'd seen at the wall. It was long and narrow, round with a pointed noise, smooth and pale as the buildings. A door opened and a being emerged, stepped into the street lightly, and unfolded to full height.

Jill had the distinct thought—accompanied by more wonder than fear—that she was, honest to god, seeing an intelligent alien species, that she and Nate were perhaps the first human beings ever to do so. The scientist in her was awestruck.

The creature was tall, at least seven-foot, with four long limbs and an upright torso that was papery thin. Its skin was pale and tinged with green. Its eyes were enormous. The rest of its features, including the ears and nose, were mere holes in the skull. The top of its head was a rounded dome sporting a few hard, bristlelike hairs. Its clothes were nondescript, a loose-fitting unitard made of a light-looking fabric the same pale color as the alien's skin. There was something vaguely geeky about it, perhaps because it had a large overbite and its upper teeth stuck out above its weak little chin.

Jill was holding her breath, waiting for the moment of mutual recognition. Nate had put his hand on her arm, just above the elbow, and was gripping her hard. The alien had to see them—it had flown right over them and now it turned in their direction as it circled the car. But its eyes gazed right through them. They were so close, they could see the dark veins under its translucent skin. There was no reaction to their presence. It walked with a hurried, gangly gait into a large building in front of the vehicle and disappeared.

Nate and Jill looked at each other. Nate's eyes were so wide they were almost comical. He looked like he'd just swallowed a bug. Jill almost laughed, from his expression and from a feeling of amazement and disbelief bubbling up inside her, but she couldn't summon the saliva for it.

"Jill, it didn't *see* us."

"How would we know?" She shrugged, smiling.

"Well . . . it would *do* something!"

"No, *you* would do something, Nate. This is an alien species, remember? We have no idea what they would do."

Nate and Jill waited in the street, just in case the alien did do something—send some kind of security force or reemerge with welcome baskets—but nothing came. The City was as silent and blank as ever.

Nate moved first, drawn by male hormones to inspect the vehicle. Jill followed reluctantly. She peered at the building the alien went into for signs of activity, for light. The dark windows looked indistinguishable from all the others they had passed.

"No steering wheel," Nate said, peering into the car. "Looks like a control pad and—" The door hinged open with a pneumatic sound.

"Nate, don't!"

"I didn't! Must be on sensors." He stuck his head inside, pressed his fingers against a hard-looking seat so narrow it looked more suited to a banana split than a human behind. He poked unadvisedly at the control pad.

"Nate, this is all superneato, but we have to have water. Right now."

"Yeah? And where do you propose . . ." Nate began, straightening up.

He stopped, seeing the direction of her gaze. The building's entrance was as unassuming as any other. There was no sign on its front, no writing to indicate its purpose, but it was taller than most of the buildings, at least thirty stories. On the side was a tube that looked like an elevator.

"Um . . ." Nate began doubtfully.

"The power. It's been out in all the buildings we've tried so far. We're not going to find water until we find power."

She didn't need to elaborate. Since the alien entered that particular building there was at least some chance the power might be on in there.

Nate sighed. "What if there are a whole bunch of aliens in there? What if it's a trap?"

"Then it is," Jill replied, heading for the door.

Inside, the layout looked much the same as the other buildings they'd seen—a plain, square lobby with freakishly tall and narrow unmarked doors against the flat wall opposite. In between those doors a long hallway ran straight down the middle of the building. The hallway was also featureless except for more unmarked doors. The elevator at the far end of the lobby was wide open—no doors, just a platform inside a rounded shaft that disappeared straight through the ceiling. The only color was white.

The alien architecture was having a strange effect on Jill's brain. It was so blank it seemed to absorb impressions—the impression, for example, of being in a hypnotic state where one is asked to picture a corridor with doors. This kind of corridor, these doors, would be what Jill's subconscious would conjure up.

"Jill!" Nate was pointing at an oval fixture on the wall. It was emitting light.

Jill's mouth went even drier at the sight. She followed Nate into the hall. The doors, as they had already learned, opened by proximity, even in the buildings without power. Now Nate stepped right up to a door and it slid back silently. She knew he was being brave, stepping into the doorway like that, and she had a bad moment before the door had fully opened.

But there was no one inside; it was just another boxlike room. Nate made a bowing gesture to let her through.

She headed toward a long narrow counter in the corner. It was like the ones they'd seen in other buildings. The counter had a concave depression with holes arranged around in a ring. It reminded her tantalizingly of a drain and spigots.

"Please, please, please, please, please . . ." Nate was muttering as he came up behind her.

The sink operated as soon as she stepped in front of it. Water spouted from the ring of holes around the basin.

Jill was past worrying about whether the water was viable for humans. She stuck her hands in it, making a crude cup, and drank greedily. It tasted wonderful, like good, clean water. Her mouth and throat relaxed into a semblance of soft tissue. When Nate took his turn he stuck his whole head in the sink, his close-cropped hair trickling with errant streams as he drank. Then he tried to roll up his sleeve.

"Do you mind if I wash my arm?" he asked, looking sheepish. "It's still pretty sore."

"Of course not."

His sleeve would not roll up far enough, so he took the shirt off and put his forearm in the basin, splashing the water up onto his bicep and shoulder, face grimacing with pain.

"I just wish the water were hot," Nate said, forcing an uncomfortable smile. "Wait—it's warming up now."

She stepped away, not wanting to stand there watching him, and began moving around the room. The water—both the drinking of it and the relief of having found it—had made her feel a thousand percent better. Her curiosity returned. They were no longer in imminent danger of dying and, by god, if they weren't, she was going to take a damned good look around.

There were two plain chairs with impossibly narrow seats and a long cotlike bed against one wall. The bed was topped with a hard cushion, and it emerged from the wall much like the molded counter. Near the door was a metal plate they'd seen in many of the buildings. It resembled a fuse box cover, but it didn't open—wouldn't budge under her prying fingertips. There were raised designs on the plate that Jill realized—at last—were alien writing. She moved her fingers over it, an expectant smile tilting the corners of her mouth. The characters were like Morse code in their simplicity—horizontal lines and dots in a variety of directions and groupings. She pressed against the writing, trying to get a sense of it through her fingertips. There was a dull *thud* behind the plate.

Jill had eaten dinner in too many college dorms not to recognize that sound. Her stomach growled and her fingers probed the metal surface hungrily for what she knew had to be there. At the bottom the metal folded neatly inward, revealing a drop bin and a thick, solid bar the size of a brick.

"Food," she breathed, picking it up and sniffing it. She spent some minutes trying to unwrap a shiny film until it began to melt to her fingers and she realized it was edible. She was about to try a small bite when Nate came over.

"You got it to work!"

"Wasn't difficult," she said. Like an old pro, she pressed the writing again to get another bar and held it out to him. "Try it."

"Oh, I see. I'm the guinea pig."

"No! I—" She took a hurried bite. The bar crumbled under her teeth. She made a face.

"What's it taste like?"

"Honey, cardboard, and machine oil."

"Yum. My favorite." He took a bite and woofed out his cheeks in disgust. "The good news is we can lubricate a gasket with our breath."

"We shouldn't eat much. Not until we see what it does to our system."

"It's fine. Really. I feel just—" Nate gasped, bent over, contorting in pain. He fell heavily to the floor, face in agony.

Jill blinked at him for a moment, then sank down to the floor, folding her legs to sit next to his prone body. She took another small bite. He opened one eye to see if he'd gotten her.

"That's what I like about you, Nate. Your maturity."

They drew a cache of the bars and made a pack from Jill's sweater, but they couldn't find any way to carry the water. At least they knew where to find it if they needed it.

"What now?" Nate asked as they reentered the lobby.

"I want to try the elevator."

"And, um, why would we want to do that?"

"Because we need a better plan than just walking around. Because this is a relatively tall building. Because if we can get to the roof we might get a strategic view. Any more questions?"

"I liked it better when your mouth was too dry to talk," Nate said, stepping onto the platform beside her.

There was more of the alien script on a panel on the wall. Jill and Nate were debating about what to push when the elevator began to rise of its own accord.

As it ascended to reveal the next floor they could see alien feet waiting, then legs. Nate and Jill backed into the far side of the elevator. Jill sought, and found, Nate's hand. A torso appeared, then those big, buglike eyes. The elevator stopped and the alien stepped onto the platform.

It wasn't the same alien they'd seen in the streets, Jill was sure. It didn't have the same overbite. This one had a tiny mouth that was perfectly flat. But again, it stared right through them without a flicker of interest, then turned to face the panel. Its fingers moved over the panel briefly. The elevator began to descend.

Nate was gripping her hand so tightly it hurt.

"Hello?" Jill ventured, her voice sounding hollow. Nate squeezed, hard. "Ouch!"

She glared at him and he shook his head mutely, pleading.

But the alien had heard something. It looked around the elevator, its eyes grazing right past them. It scanned the ceiling, blinking translucent lids over thick, gooey eyeballs. The elevator stopped on the ground floor. The alien, after taking one final look around, got out.

Nate dived for the control pad, banged on it. The elevator began to rise.

"Jill," Nate hissed, "did you see that? I told you, they can't *see* us!"

His eyes were large and dark—freaked-out eyes. She knew what he was thinking—some weird, supernatural thing, like maybe that they were ghosts after all. She felt a flash of irritation.

"Maybe this species is blind. How would we know?"

"With *those* eyes? That'd be a sorry waste of real estate."

"Anyway, they can *hear* us, at least. Why didn't you want me to speak? We're going to have to make contact sooner or later."

"What if they're dangerous!"

"Why assume they're dangerous?"

He gave her a look like she was being incredibly stupid. "Um . . . because it's a hell of a lot safer than assuming they're not?"

She rolled her eyes, but she had to admit . . . She was just as glad herself that the alien in the elevator hadn't seen them. There was something about those huge eyes and husklike bodies that was not very pleasant at all.

The roof was a flat, dusty surface made of the same stuff as the rest of the City—a dense white material that was difficult to distinguish as either synthetic or stone. Nate looked around the rooftop for more aliens before deigning to get out of the elevator. He walked to the edge.

"So . . . what are we looking for?"

"I don't know yet." Jill studied the street grid. There were no plazas, no circular turnabouts, no variation in the street widths—just endless rows and columns. The air was very clean, startlingly so for a cityscape, which meant they didn't burn fossil fuels. And the planet seemed to have little precipitation. The sky was cloudless.

"Do you think those are power indicators?" Jill asked, pointing to a light on a roof down below.

Nate perked up. "Cool! I don't think that's what they're *for*, but they sure work that way, don't they?"

Every building had a large light at the center of the roof—including their own. The original purpose of the light was probably for communications or rooftop landings. But looking out over the cityscape now, these roof lights were an ideal indication of which buildings had power. They'd been designed to be visible even in this perpetually bright world—shining a determined red. Jill sucked in a breath as the full implications hit her.

They were looking over a city so vast they could not see the far edges of it. And all that they *could* see—all of the buildings surrounding them for blocks and blocks and blocks—was 90 percent dead, turned off, deserted.

"Oh my god. Look at that," Nate muttered.

They were standing in a pocket of red, maybe twenty buildings in all. A few blocks away was a street running north–south that had to be a major artery. The lights on that street were red all the way into the horizon. There was another artery, perpendicular to the first, that was also red down its entire length. Other than this red cross, there were only rare splashes of red dotting the landscape. The rest of the city was dark.

"What happened to them?" Nate asked, his voice faint.

"I don't know."

"Do you think it might have been a disease? It couldn't have been an atomic weapon or a meteor—there's no damage."

"No."

"You'd think war would have left some damage, too, unless they have some pretty funky weapons."

Jill's hands floated to her collarbone and tapped thoughtfully. She didn't reply.

"So what do you think? This place must have had *millions* of inhabitants—where'd they all go?" Nate insisted. She knew he wasn't really asking her; he was just asking.

"I *think* we'll find more clues, if we're patient." Jill sighed. "This could take a while."

The thought was somehow satisfying. Nate shot her a look that she ignored. She was focused on those red patches. "There!" She pointed.

To the east, about a mile away, was a round building in a patch of red. It had a dome shape, incongruous in this square-filled field. Even more interesting was what was next to the dome—an enormous field of antennae.

"Communications," Nate guessed.

"Maybe." Jill squinted to see the antennae better. Something had just crossed her mind, a possibility that, in all the hours they had spent in this place, had so far eluded her. As the idea fully revealed itself in her brain, almost bashfully due to its enormity, she found her mouth dry once more. She understood now her initial feeling of excitement at the wall. There was a moment, standing at the edge of that rooftop, when she completely accepted the City. Not just accepted it but embraced it as her right, as part of her purpose, her destiny.

"Jill!" Nate's voice, eager, broke the moment. He had moved to the other side of the roof and was pointing as excitedly as a kid at a toy shop window.

There, on the southern edge of the city, miles away, was another domed structure. This one looked even larger than the first. Around it was a smooth sea of tarmac. And parked at one end of the tarmac was a planelike craft that, despite its small size from here, had to be enormous close-up.

"It's a spaceship!" Nate crowed. "They have interplanetary travel! Whoo-hoo!"

Jill smiled tentatively.

"Good ol' Earth! Christ, what are we waiting for?" Nate walked toward the elevator.

"Just a second. What about the antennae?" Jill's eyes drifted magnetically back to that other dome.

"What about the *antennae*? What about the *antennae*?"

His voice got her attention. That boyish face of his, so ingeniously expressive, was disbelieving and hopelessly young. "Jill, hello? I don't know about you, but I want to go *home*."

She was used to diagnosing Nate's moods in a rational framework for her experiments. One look told her that arguing with him would take more energy and tact than she could muster. She tried anyway. "But, Nate," she said gently, "we have an entire city to explore."

He folded his arms over his chest. His dark eyes stared at her, daring her to say anything more.

"Okay," she sighed. "All right. We'll check out the airport first."

He grinned. "It's a *space*port."

"Fine. Whatever. I guess it won't hurt." She looked out over the cityscape. "How 'bout we go down that main artery? That'll give us food and water most of the way. It might take us a while. I have a feeling it's even further than it looks."

"Why don't we nab one of those air cars? We can be there in an hour."

"We will *not*. I'm not crazy about flying when the pilot *knows* what he's doing."

"They're probably user-friendly! They probably drive themselves!"

Jill gave him her best freezing look. "And how would you know until you were up in the air and couldn't get down? We'll walk."

"Fine! Have it your way." Nate looked at the distance between them and the spaceport and got into the elevator, a very determined look on his face.

15.4. Thirty-Seventy Aharon Handalman

> At what point do we lose our conscience? Our call to the divine? There are things, maybe they're different for everyone, but there are things . . . and from these experiences no man can return.
> —Yosef Kobinski, *The Book of Torment*, 1943

Everything he had ever held back or held in, everything he had pushed aside, refuted, argued against with Talmudic vigor, these doubts, fears, and shadows, now crowded Aharon's mind. He had been proud and strong in the wind; he had been a mighty oak, a wall, unbreachable, like the walls of Zion. But Kobinski had blown his trumpet and the wall that was Aharon Handalman had come tumbling down.

The weight on his chest, on his limbs, was a mocking presence. It wasn't gravity: Death sat on him there. Satan sat on him; despair and hopelessness and an utter and complete emptiness where once God had dwelled, these things pressed him down. The tent in the wilderness of his heart, where the priest had to remove his shoes, where sacrifices were made, where the living presence of Yahweh shone like a bright and terrible thing, this place was empty. God's spirit had left him.

The Holocaust—what it had done to a man like Yosef Kobinski! And if it had done this to such a learned man, who was Aharon to say, "I will not be bowed"? Who was he to deny that God's chosen had gotten the raw end of the deal? That maybe He *didn't* have a plan? If He knew what He was doing, why had Aharon been given the knowledge of what might happen to Earth and then had his lips sealed forever? To lie here helpless, knowing that his beloved Hannah, his Devorah and Yehuda and Layah, were all in harm's way, waiting to be victims of perhaps the worst weapon ever known to man? And *this* place? This terrible hell: was this really the reward for the faithful? For those who stood tall and said, "No, I will not compromise! I will not fudge on God's teachings? I will not—"

The torch next to his bedside flickered and beckoned. He spent long hours staring at it. Alternately, he sobbed, tears of blood coming from the depths of his soul. He stuffed his mouth, fearing who might come in answer. But no one came. He wanted to die, truly, but what could he do? Try to roll himself out of bed? Crack his head on the floor hoping he could splatter his brains before he passed out? Could he work his arm up to grab the torch, fling it onto the bed he lay in? As much as he wanted to die, burning to death unable to move lacked a certain appeal.

Because if you don't bend you will break; God will teach you, teach you to bend.

He was left alone too long. He messed the bed. That, too, was appropriate! Was a literal symbol of the horror he lived in! Kobinski didn't come. Nothing human came. They cleaned him, these animals, they gave him food and, when he didn't eat it, forced it into his mouth. It was vile, vile, like the gall he drank from his own heart.

Argeh came, the "enemy" Kobinski had mentioned. And where was Kobinski when this thing showed up? Nowhere. Argeh smelled Aharon, screamed at him with barks and growls. As much as Aharon wanted to die, it was not at the hands of this horrible creature. Aharon stared at the torch, terrified, wishing the beast away. Argeh left.

Tevach, the mouse-faced servant of Kobinski, was the only thing that wasn't completely awful. There was something in his eyes, something gentle, that made Aharon look forward, a little, to his visits. And Tevach's visits were no picnic. He came to work Aharon's muscles. He pushed and prodded, flipped Aharon around with iron hands in a way that was most undignified. And as much as he wanted to die, overexercise was *also* not Aharon's idea of a way to go. On Tevach's third visit the urge to complain overcame even his depression and Aharon broke his silence.

"You want to kill me?" Aharon said as Tevach pushed his head toward his knees. It didn't go that way, not even in Earth's gravity. "You keep this up, and you'll get your wish."

Tevach groveled, but a second later he shoved Aharon back on the bed and urged him to do a sit-up. "You must get strong. You must walk. My Lord wishes it."

"Where is 'My Lord'? Why hasn't he come back? Why does he leave me here?"

Tevach only bit his lips nervously, nibbling at them like the mouse he so resembled.

"What does it matter?" Aharon said bitterly. "What does anything matter?"

Tevach dared a glance at Aharon, then looked away. "You are from Mahava. Why sad like Fiori?"

Aharon made a *nu* face. He didn't answer.

Tevach grunted. "Work is good for one who is sad."

"I don't have any work."

Tevach pushed his leg up into the air and ordered Aharon to hold it. He did, with a little more energy than he had previously displayed, thinking, *If I get strong, at least I can get out of this bed and find myself a decent knife to slit my wrists!*

"Work is good," Tevach said when the leg had been lowered.

"I don't have any work!"

They did the other leg.

When Tevach had finished, he wiped Aharon's sweat away with a cool cloth and propped him back on his pillows.

"Is there something I can bring?" he asked, preparing to leave.

Aharon looked at the torch and sighed. He almost didn't say the words; then he almost did, almost didn't. Finally, he decided it wasn't important, one way or the other. What did anything matter anymore?

"Yes, Tevach. Would you ask Kobinski if I could read the manuscript?"

*   *   *

My Lord was so agitated by the Jew's presence in the House of Divine Ordinance, even unseen, even avoided, as he was avoiding it, that he at last told Tevach to order his carriage. He put on fresh robes and Tevach helped him down the stairs, into the creaky conveyance.

Like everything else in this accursed place, the carriage was not working half the time. Between the pressure of gravity and the rocky ground, very little could be kept mobile for long, including, it seemed, his knee joints. He settled back onto the grass-stuffed pillows, breathing deeply, waiting for the excruciating pain to pass. Tevach, beside him, was full of concern.

My Lord had had many servants over the years, but he'd grown close to only a few. There was Decher, the male he'd promoted to captain of his guard (a smaller and quite separate unit from the Gestapo-like priests that Argeh controlled); Erya, a female who acted as nursemaid and caretaker; and Tevach, his constant companion and leaning post. He had learned much about the Fiore, spent the first ten years here putting together theories about them and this planet. The part of him that put together theories had still been linked in some way to the man who had been in Auschwitz, was separate from the man who now survived here at all costs, the king of Gehenna.

What Decher and Erya and Tevach shared was a spark of curiosity, a leaning toward open-mindedness absent in most of their species. Naturally, they had learned to hide it well. To My Lord they had only appeared a little softer at first. It took him time to decipher why, and then he understood. They were souls on the way back up. If Fiori was a lesson about the dangers of *gevorah*, they had learned it, had learned the price of restriction, and were rebounding, maybe slowly, but still rebounding, back toward openness, *chesed*—back toward the center of Jacob's Ladder. They were more advanced than the Jew in that regard.

The planet as a whole, of course, was not going anywhere.

Tevach, the little mouse, was actually strong as an ox and blessed with a rare abundant family, most of them kept from starvation by Tevach's wages. He was timid but bright and had shown a penchant for learning that was impressive. But even with all this, he was still a Fiore and there was an unbreachable gulf between them.

"You are upset by the divine messenger, My Lord," Tevach said, with nervous fawning. "I hope he has not brought bad news?"

My Lord sighed. How could he answer? He shut his eyes as the carriage jolted toward the marketplace.

What would he do with the Jew? In the heat of the moment, he had called him a messenger from Mahava, and no one would expect a messenger to hang around for long. Argeh had seized on Handalman's unexpected appearance in the assembly: *Many years ago we had two such creatures arrive on Fiori; now there is one more. Is this* another *envoy from the heavens?* And My Lord could think of nothing to say except that the stranger had come to deliver a message for him. Argeh had asked, *But is not My Lord in contact with Mahava at all times?* Naturally, My Lord answered, he knew Mahava's *thoughts* as soon as Mahava thought them. But *physical objects* could not be relayed so easily. (The human brain of Kobinski still offered My Lord some advantage, even if his joints were worthless.)

It had been extreme good fortune that the Jew had papers on him, and such a nice, convincing sheaf of them, too. But good fortune of any kind should never be relied upon on Fiori. Still, the assembly had been impressed—it seemed to improve his shaky position with them. Argeh, on the other hand, had not believed a word.

My Lord had struggled with Argeh for thirty years, since he'd first seen that flattened face in his cell, standing behind the old one's—Ehlah's—shoulder. Ehlah had declared My Lord an envoy from Mahava, not because he believed it but because the Fiore had been in one of their typical points of crisis and needed a diversion. My Lord had been set up as that diversion, a new hope— in reality, a puppet icon. Argeh eventually replaced Ehlah as high priest, and he'd been seeking to both use and discredit My Lord ever since. Argeh played the game ruthlessly.

The carriage stopped. Tevach helped him down, taking My Lord's full weight on his rounded shoulders. My Lord was wracked with pain at every step, but he walked into the House of Cleansing upright. Before him the Fiore groveled; behind him they kissed the stones his feet had touched. He moved past the attendants and those waiting in line for a purgative beating, hiding his limp as best he could.

Down long corridors, down flights of stone stairs, and the pain in his knees was the reason he did not come very often anymore. Screams and wracking sobs greeted his ears, bounced off the stone, also the sounds of whipping, the dull thud of stones and wood on flesh, even—there—the sound of breaking bone. It took a great deal to break Fiore bones, hard as iron rods, condensed by gravity. But the priests were quite skilled and they were artisans besides. Torture was one of the few creative outlets on Gehenna.

Outside the door of the special cell waited Gehvis, the physician.

"What do you want?" My Lord snapped, impatient in his pain.

"Apologies for my unworthiness, My Lord, but I fear . . ."

"Hurry and speak."

"We have sustained the evil one for many years, but the end is coming soon." Gehvis was bowing so low, he looked like he was staring at My Lord's knees. My Lord had an urge to kick him.

"I have heard you. Now let me past."

Inside the cell, the attendants hastened to turn up the lamps and back from the room. My Lord turned to the body lying on the table. Tevach helped him lower himself into the single chair. He stared for a long time, sighing deeply.

"And how are we feeling today, Wallick?" he asked softly, in German.

There was a wet sound as the figure made an attempt to lick its lips.

"Water, Tevach."

Tevach fetched a cup and poured a little into Wallick's mouth. It seemed to revive him.

My Lord had come for reassurance, but now that he was here he could see it was a mistake. *Why had he stayed,* Handalman had asked. This was why. He was chained here by the odious mass on the table, by a force even stronger than Fiorian gravity—hatred. But there was something new in his perception of the bruised, broken, and partially skinned carcass in front of him. It felt as though he were looking at it through someone else's eyes, the bearded Jew's no doubt. The sight did not reassure him at all.

He closed his eyes. *For my son, Wallick. For all the others, too, but mostly for my Isaac.*

The Fiore excelled at few things. If you were in a universe where, for example, higher technology existed and beings could shop from planet to planet (which was not the thirty-seventy universe, to be sure), there would be little you would care to export from Fiori. The planet produced few precious metals or gems beyond dribs and drabs of gold. It had no great works of art, only truly hideous religious artifacts. There were no appetizing native dishes. Its inhabitants had never developed enviable learning or skills, and even though they were physically strong, they had so short a life expectancy as to make their value as slave labor questionable. But the Fiore were masters of mutilation. It was intertwined with the very foundation of their culture, their entire cosmological system. Their sacred book told the tale through words and morbid pictures.

There were two forces in the universe: God the good, called *Mahava*, and the evil demon, *Charvah*. Mahava was busy creating wonders, such as the sun and the heavens, but Charvah, a less powerful entity, was spiteful and jealous, so he regularly spit out impurities, sullying Mahava's creation. Mahava's wife, Magehna, had the task of going around sucking up all these impurities, which she would then shit out in a specific corner of the universe where they could be isolated and repurified.

That cesspool was Fiori.

Since nothing divine, no bit of creation, could ever be destroyed, these impurities, these feces that were the Fiore, had to work to repurify themselves and thus be fit to reenter the glorious part of creation when they died. Purification came through fire, pain, humility, mortification.

It was amazing to witness the fact that on a planet where life was already 70 percent evil (that had been Kobinski's estimate shortly after his arrival, based on his gravitational calculations), the inhabitants had built up a culture in which they inflicted further evil upon themselves. Yet what other example did they have? Life beat them down at every opportunity; therefore, it must be divine will that they *be* beaten down. Kobinski had once hypothesized that their propensity for mortification was part of that 70 percent evil. Massive depression, suicidal self-loathing, these were problems reserved for the unfortunate on Earth. Here they were the norm.

Not every Fiori bought into this scheme. There were the rare few, like Tevach, who secretly loathed the torture. But there were also the ones, and they were not so few, who relished it. As for the starving masses, they simply did what they were told, as Catholics fasted. The Fiore were very tough. Wallick was tough also. He had lasted thirty years.

My Lord rubbed his lips with a finger as he looked at his enemy.

That portly, pious little Jew, what did he know about suffering? Yosef Kobinski, he understood, he alone, who had known the greatest goodness, the greatest sweetness, and lost it; who had experienced firsthand the depredations and mockery of life that was the Nazi regime; who had then come to know intimately *this* hell that God created for His beloved creatures. He'd understood God as deeply as perhaps any man had ever understood Him, had seen His face more clearly and more horribly, too, in the kabbalistic way: the black head and the white, the long black locks of hair and the white, evil and good, two heads on one body, destruction and creation. Two faces—and he'd shaken his fist in both of them.

His old companion licked his lips and tried to speak. My Lord leaned forward, waiting, watching the painful struggle.

"*Bitte,*" Wallick said, after much effort. *Please.*

My Lord sat back drolly. Wallick never had been very original.

"Leave me, Tevach," My Lord said.

After Tevach shuffled out, My Lord began to recite Wallick's crimes. The German tongue was an appropriate language for the recitation, appropriately harsh and literal. He spoke softly and calmly, as he always did: *This is what you did to my son.*

Isaac's Story

In 1941, the villagers had come to him, and they'd said, "The old rebbe is dead; it's up to you now. Tell us what to do about these Germans? What should we think? Should we run away or stay put?"

And from the vast wisdom of his learning Kobinski had answered, "Things only get so bad before they get better," and, "The pendulum always swings the other way."

A year later, Anna, queen of his soul, was lying in the ghetto with pneumonia, weakened by her second pregnancy, by the cold, by too little food. She and the fetus died. And still Kobinski put the shawl over his head and said *kaddish,* pouring his mourning out to God and feeling that God shared his bottomless sorrow.

Even in Auschwitz he didn't lose his faith that God knew what He was doing, even there.

There are things.

Who can measure a man's love for his son? Who can define that tenderest moment of the human soul, when it looks on promising youth, youth of one's own face and frame, still dewy with its newness on the earth? Who can fathom the protectiveness a child engenders?

The Christians have this myth: *For God so loved the world that He sent His only begotten son.*

Did God love the world? My Lord wasn't so sure, but at least the Christians had the analogy right, the turnkey idea of it—*giving up one's son.* There couldn't be a greater sacrifice. And he had been tortured, too, this Jesus, and God had sat through it all, barring maybe a little vitriolic thunder and lightning. Yes, the Christians had tapped into something there. What could be more difficult? And there was God, big enough to allow it to happen, just to show how much He loved the world.

Yosef Kobinski wasn't that big.

When had Wallick gotten the idea? My Lord had asked himself that a thousand times. What had *he* done, what had been the fatal sin in his demeanor, that had provoked such a plan? Should he have lain down on his belly earlier? Should he have whimpered and groveled and begged like the others? Would that have kept Isaac alive? Yes. Maybe.

So then you had to ask: how much of his refusal to submit to the horrors of Auschwitz had been true religious faith . . . and how much arrogant pride, a mystic's show-offmanship? These were the sins Kobinski's soul carried, and they were only the start.

Yosef Kobinski had gone on detail one day, marching out of camp with other inmates to unload building materials off a train, heavy boards, rough in the freezing rain. Still, it was light duty compared to what he was usually sentenced to: cleaning latrines. He even said a prayer of gratitude for the reprieve, didn't wonder at it at all—not until that evening when he returned to the barrack to learn that Wallick had taken his son.

That had gotten to him, pierced him through. He'd been shaken, disturbed, unable to pray, unable to write. He wanted to go find the boy, needed it like he needed air, but it was futile. The officers' quarters were in a different part of the camp; he couldn't get close.

The next morning during roll call, Isaac was nowhere to be seen. Afterward, Kobinski dared approach Wallick. *What have you done with my son?*

Wallick studied his face, slyly pleased, reading the measure of the fear there. *I'm taking good care of him,* he said, *very good care.*

That next night Kobinski was sick from worry, feeling, finally, what it meant to be powerless, when Wallick sent for him, brought him into his own little house, sat him in a corner. Made Kobinski watch while he raped his son.

"You raped my son," My Lord whispered to the mass on the table.

The mouth worked, but nothing came out. Years ago, Wallick had accepted that he was in Hell. It fit that older, Germanic mythos, or perhaps the Bavarian Catholic one. When they'd arrived Kobinski had the advantage of foreknowledge; he'd landed on his feet. Wallick had been merely hysterical. So when Kobinski figured out enough of the language to proclaim himself divine, he'd proclaimed Wallick a demon at the same time. Wallick had not even understood what was happening; much less could he defend himself. He believed that he had died that night in the woods and had accepted that he was in the afterlife, being punished, that Kobinski was his tormentor. He used to plead to God for mercy, but he seemed to have given up hope of that.

There are things.

"Except . . . it doesn't even approach the truth to say 'you raped my son.' Does it?"

Wallick's chin tiled down a little. It probably wasn't a nod, but it could be taken as such and My Lord did. Even without Wallick's voice, My Lord knew his lines. They'd had this dialogue many times before, in better days.

"A crime is not a single act. It is a series of indignations to living souls. And you can't *see* the crime, you can't possibly punish it, unless you comprehend each wound at its birth."

I did not . . . I was only acting . . . They told us . . .

"Be quiet now," My Lord said softly, "and feel it: There I was, a man, a father, sitting in a chair. You remember the chair? It was heavy, carved mahogany, an old dining room chair with an upholstered seat. And that first night you made me sit there and you tied my wrists to the arms—the chair had curved arms, remember? And my ankles were tied to the legs. The chair itself you had fastened to the floor earlier with nails.

"It goes hard for you that you nailed down the chair, Wallick. It shows that you understood far more than you admit. You understood that a father would thrash, that he would propel his own body into the path of whatever it was that threatened his son, that no coercion could keep him from doing so. And that first time you tied me I knew then that it would be bad, and I wanted to know what you were doing and where was Isaac. Do you remember what you told me?"

Wallick blinked. His eyes did not look at all well. The left was swollen and red, nearly shut. Curious. One of the advantages of torture on Fiori was the relative lack of microbes. Even they did not flourish here. Be that as it may, there was something in that eye. The other was not swollen, but it ran constantly with mucusy tears.

"You told me that if I didn't cooperate, you'd kill my son. And at that time I didn't know there could be worse things."

Wallick began to gasp, choking. There was some fuss while the attendants were called in. My Lord waited patiently. He did not lose his place in the narrative. As soon as they were alone again, he picked up the hideous thread.

"And then, when I was tied down, you brought him out. That first night, Wallick, how clever you were! That first night, he was still an innocent, still my Isaac. Why, I could see that you'd even been kind, given him food. He was wary, but he had a look on his serious little face, as if to reassure me that things were all right. He was still trying to be strong; can you imagine it? Still trying to be strong for me."

My Lord sighed. People thought it was easy to sin; that was a myth. Handalman, what did he know about sin? It was the hardest thing My Lord had ever done to sit here and go through it, relive it over and over. How blessed it would be to forget! To lay it aside! But if he allowed himself respite, Wallick would also have respite, and that could never be.

"You didn't gag me—another thing against you. You would like me to believe that you were some dumb ruffian, a brute, cruel only by instinct, not by deliberation. But you were cleverer than that. Not gagging me: I have thought it over many times. In the first place, no one would think it so very odd to hear screams coming from your house. True, there was a danger that I might shout something embarrassing, might name the act you were committing, but you knew I wouldn't, didn't you? You *knew*. Because whatever came out of my mouth for your Nazi neighbors to hear, Isaac, my son, would also hear!"

Another sigh. These memories, suckled like demonic children, clawed at his throat and chest. The saner parts of him begged him to put them away. No. It took great will to sin greatly.

"At first I *did* speak, that first night. When you grasped his two wrists in your left hand and forced him over the table . . ."

My Lord described the events of that night with the polish of long practice. This was the way it was when you accused: you had to spell it out. The crime had to be brought into the light, in all its sickening detail, because criminals lived in the dark, believing no one could see. Shame came with the light. But even he was only half listening. His eyes lingered down Wallick's left arm where the flesh had been drawn away in strips. His fingertips were raw and nailless. It made My Lord sick and yet also satisfied, especially when he saw again those muscled white arms stretching Isaac's thin, frail ones up and over the table.

"I said, 'Take me.' I told you to do anything you wanted with me—torture me, rape me, kill me. I would lick your boots; I would clean your messes; I would take any humiliation. But you only smiled."

On the table, Wallick was apparently crying. His chest rode up and down. That mucus in one eye became more watery, and the other eye, red and swollen, spilled burning drops as well. It had been years since Wallick had cried. There was an exhaustion in it, an utter letting go. My Lord recalled what the physician had said. *No,* he thought, *not yet.*

"But that was not the worst thing, what you did to his body. What was worse was what you did to his heart, to his soul. He was *humiliated,* you see. And that's why I couldn't speak, even though you didn't gag me. Because I knew that the only thing that could make it a little better for him was to forget that I was there, to pretend I wasn't watching. So I became silent as the grave. But I remembered. It was thirty days in all that you did this to *my only son,* and I remember every single one. I recorded every move you made."

My Lord sat still for a long time. He was tired and freezing. His own cooling sweat made him shiver. He wanted to go to bed. But he wasn't done yet. He had the worst mile still to go.

"Those thirty nights you are paying for now, Wallick. And the last, the thirty-first, will take you another eternity after this punishment is through. On the thirty-first night you must have thought my pain was dulling or maybe you had just grown tired of your little game. Because when you were done with him that night you took his life. *Took it,* like it were a piece of fruit you could pluck from a tree and discard with a flick of your wrist."

This was the worst of it, the very worst: the last two minutes or so of Isaac Kobinski's life. It had lasted so long, an eternity. Wallick, his large hand covering the boy's nose and mouth, and Isaac . . . he had hardly struggled at all. His beautiful, angelic, magnificent boy, his own David—to die in such a way, *in such a way!* God had spared Abraham. An angel had stopped the raised knife. Who could believe such fairy tales when there had been no mercy for Isaac Kobinski?

"I have tried to imagine a punishment fit for your crimes, Wallick, but even the greatest of the artisans here, even *they* could not come up with anything to match them. I cried then, didn't I? I screamed and begged."

My Lord stopped. There was silence for a time.

"If you think back on it, Wallick, perhaps you can hear again Kobinski's cries. I know I was only a Jew to you, and you had heard so many Jews cry. But it was personal between us, wasn't it? Because when you were finished, you turned to look at me and there was triumph on your face. You knew you had beaten me."

Yes, I knew. Wallick had said it many times over the years. My Lord said it for him now.

"Yes, you knew. And I'll tell you something: I know you did many horrendous things during the war, many things. But what you did to my Isaac—that was what has damned you forever and ever, Wallick. *Forever and ever and ever.*"

Wallick was crying again, and My Lord was so tired. His knees were killing him in this cold, from the stiffness of sitting. He called loudly for Tevach.

16

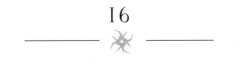

The doctrine of Karma is one in which the whole phenomenal universe as perceived by us is understood to be an effect, corresponding to previous thoughts, speeches, and physical actions of the individual and of all living beings, which are the cause.

—Ashvaghosah, *Buddhacarita,* first century c.e.

16.1. Forty-Sixty Calder Farris

Thick gray clouds covered the sky from horizon to horizon as Pol left the dorm. This morning they were the color of pearls, which meant there might be snow. There had been air-raid sirens in the night and Pol had slept badly. In his dreams he was trying to find a certain file in the Archives that had to do with his mission—the important mission that he couldn't remember. Upon waking, he could almost grasp it, but it slipped away again, leaving him frustrated and angry.

At the Department of Monitors, Gyde was already in. His face was ruddy from his morning trip to the gymnasium. They'd found nothing of significance in the Archives, and Gyde had been resentful about it. If there was one thing you didn't do to an old warrior like Gyde, it was slow him down, not when there were merits to be won.

"Good day to serve the state," Gyde greeted him coolly.

"Good day to serve the state."

Pol turned to his desk and saw a white envelope with the official state seal propped up in the center of it like a birthday present.

"That came for you this morning."

Pol took the envelope and tossed it aside, his fingers cold. He sat down, pulling the case files toward him.

Gyde eased onto the edge of Pol's desk and picked up the envelope. "Department of Health. That would be notification of your annual physical."

Pol kept his face impassive.

Gyde smiled. "How old are you, thirty-eight? Wait till you hit forty. Then they *really* start probing. They expect your bowels to be as fit as your biceps, and may you rest on your trophies if they're not."

Pol changed the subject, "Anything new on the case?"

"Well, we're not going to the scarping Archives."

"No," Pol said lightly. "Sorry about that."

Gyde rubbed his hand against the gray-blond curls of his hair, a glint in his eye. "Someone scared off our friend last night."

"What? Where?"

"He was trying to distribute pamphlets downtown. Only got a handful out before giving up—monitors came across a bag of 'em. They must have been close to the mothered scum, made him dump and run. We should thank the gods. It would have been our heads if those pamphlets had gotten around."

Pol eyes swept Gyde's desk. "Where are they?"

"Lab." Gyde's eyes were heavy and slow on Pol's face. Or maybe it was Pol's imagination. He was aware of the old soldier's almost unconscious use of such tactics to intimidate, like the occasional glint of steel in his eyes. Now Gyde draped an arm around Pol's shoulders, fatherly. "I thought we could check out some construction sites while we wait for them."

Pol smiled and slipped from under Gyde's arm to pick up the envelope. He put it in a pocket. "Excellent idea, classmate. Lead on."

The construction site was downtown, twelve blocks from Victory Square. The foreman, a Bronze 2, snapped to life when they appeared, eager to tell two distinguished Silvers anything they wanted to know.

The black paint was stored with all other construction materials in a chain mail cage that was locked at night. The foreman had never heard of any cages being broken into. Pol made a note to have Research check for incidents citywide.

But the look Gyde gave him, and his own reasoning, said they wouldn't find anything. If no cages had been broken into, then their terrorist was making away with the paint during the day. They could see for themselves that under the watchful eyes of the supervisors an obvious interloper would be noticed. Who, then, had casual access to the materials? Only someone who worked on such a site.

"An Iron's not going to walk off with a can of paint undetected," Gyde said to Pol.

"The Irons take nothing off-site," the foreman assured them. "They're looked over as they leave."

"He could put it into a smaller container," Pol suggested, "something easily smuggled out."

"Unlikely. They're not that smart." Gyde turned back to the foreman. "Besides Irons who else is on a construction site?"

"The foremen are Bronze, as are the architects, masons, and inspectors."

Pol was watching some of the Irons. They were lifting heavy stone blocks with pulleys. Sweaty work. They were suited to it: drab, dark, smelly, hairy.

He didn't see this level of Irons very often. The ones in public service were the nicer ones. Almost a third of these poor animals had some kind of minor deformity—a twisted ear, a split palate, a drooping eye. Mongrels.

Pol clenched his hands at his side. He was *not* one of these.

When they were alone, Pol said, "I don't think we can completely eliminate an Iron. Not yet."

Gyde pursed his lips. "Irons don't read and write. Not this class, anyway. House servants maybe, but not these."

"What if our suspect was a house slave who got demoted? It's possible, particularly since our friend has a problem with authority."

"What would you suggest, my tenacious partner?"

"There." Pol pointed to a long, unattractive apartment building. Clearly Iron housing, it was as modest and institutional as the state produced, painted a leaden gray like the clouds. Gyde's expression was one of contemplated misery.

"We should look while we're here," Pol said flatly. "It might trigger an idea."

Gyde shot him a look that said he felt this was as fertile a use of time as the Archives had been. "I'll give it twenty minutes. You realize we can have Research check for any Iron construction workers in the city who can read and write?"

"We should do that as well." Pol headed for the housing.

What was he looking for? For the thirty-some years that were missing from his brain? He wasn't sure, but he had learned not to ask questions and this was one way of avoiding them. Even though he'd spent time as a household Iron, he really knew little about this class. Instead of asking, he would see for himself. Thoroughness was a good cover for ignorance.

From the look on Gyde's face as they entered the building it occurred to Pol that his partner might know even less about Irons than he did.

The interior smelled putrid. It was the kind of stench Pol had become unaccustomed to in his short time in the privileged world of the Silvers. It smelled of the sweat of despair, the self-loathing of the unwashed. The narrow cement hallways were empty except for bundles of rags here and there that turned out to be children. Some of the apartment doors stood open, and as Gyde and Pol moved silently from floor to floor, Pol could see why. The apartments were tiny boxes, filled with the discarded trash that Irons used as clothes, furniture, or household items and crowded with bodies, even now, when the majority of the Irons were at work.

Pol, who insisted on stepping through the open doors and glancing around, saw no signs of literacy, no signs of any mentality that could calculate, plan, sneak past guards, or formulate obscure theories worth writing on walls. They might as well have been monkeys for all the intelligence he saw. And there was something else that bothered him.

"Children," he said to Gyde with a disapproving tone. They were peering into one apartment where a dark-headed baby was attached to a startled female's breast. Two others, toddler age, were playing listlessly on the floor.

Trick number two in avoiding detection: if you must ask a question, don't phrase it as such; simply open the topic for discussion.

"Disgusting isn't it? They let them breed at will, this class. It's their mortality rate. Can't even procreate right." Gyde, who did not appreciate having to be here in the first place, let his abhorrence fully vent. "I've heard half of 'em are born monsters. Have to kill 'em right out of the womb. Racial garbage. Besides, you know the state—they always need more slaves."

They were four stories up when the air-raid sirens went off: jolting, the way they always were, no matter how many times you heard them. Sometimes Pol heard them even when they weren't there.

"Scarp!" Gyde cursed.

From all sides, Irons flooded the halls. Gyde and Pol were caught in a panicked stampede. There was no time to get out of the building, to search for another shelter. They were trapped in a crowd that pushed through the narrow corridors and stairwells like a tide through a funnel, going down, down, down.

The bombs began to hit as they reached the cellar. Someone lit a lantern.

Pol could feel Gyde next to him, muscles stiff as a ramrod. In the flickering light, the old warrior's eyes were closed: closed against the sight, wishfully closed against the smell, of a hundred terrified Irons, panting, rank, braying, groaning, moaning. The light flickered in and out. The bombs were close. Then they were *very* close. The building shook. Dust was in the air—from the ceiling, walls, corridor, coating Pol's throat.

How easily it could happen: a ceiling collapsed and you were trapped under a ton of rubble. If you were lucky, you died in the first few minutes. If you were not, you lived for days in the crushing dark until done in by your wounds, by starvation and thirst. It happened every day in Centalia. It was as common as rain.

Trapped with a hundred Irons in a cramped basement during a bad air raid—it was a Silver's worst nightmare.

The bombs drew closer and Pol found himself flat on the ground. Through the clogging dust that was the first round of liquefaction of the building he was in, Pol saw a female not far from him. She was huddled over a bundle, her face looking upward plaintively, as though to hold the ceiling in place. The bundle in her arms shifted and stretched. Coverings parted to reveal a young boy—bare from his waist to his toes, struggling against his mother's frightened grip. He was wailing, but Pol's ears were ringing with the sound of the explosions.

They must be hitting next door. The enemy loved to hit construction sites. That was another reason that hardly anyone but Irons worked them and perhaps why the state was so low on slaves.

The boy's right foot was clubbed, a fleshy mass. If the state had let him live they were desperate for warm bodies. The mother felt his struggles, reached down, and gathered his arms around her neck, pulling him to sitting. He was two or three years old. He clung to her, looking at Pol. His thumb went into his mouth. Staring eyes. *Mother.*

Something came surging across the chasm. He had been held like that once, hadn't he? He'd had a mother. She . . . She had left him before he was very old, he was pretty sure, because his memories of her were faint, but he'd had one. In a house, a private home, she had held him in just such a way. And then later there had been a father. Hate flared in his heart. Yes, he was very sure there had been a father.

But the lives of Silvers were dedicated to the state: they didn't have wives, homes, children, mothers, fathers.

He buried his face in his forearms. If this scarping noise didn't stop he would kill someone!

"Get up!" Gyde said. Pol felt a toe in his side, nudging. "What's the matter with you? Are you hurt?"

Pol looked up. The Irons were shuffling from the room. The air raid was over. Gyde wanted out at all costs, was going to leave him here in a minute if he didn't move.

Outside, the air was hazy with dust. Gyde might have upbraided Pol for making him go in that hellish place except for the fact that right in front of them the construction site—where they'd been standing minutes ago—was a smoking pile of beams and steel and the occasional bloody limb of a construction worker.

Gyde looked at the site briefly, rubbed his reddened eyes. "If that scarping terrorist dies before we catch him and I lose my merits . . . !"

The very thought—that the terrorist might die in just such an air raid, that they might never know any more about him, might never solve the case—caused Pol to feel very upset as well.

There are aliens among us.

"Let's wash up and get out of here," Gyde said gruffly. He headed for a spigot on the side of the building.

"The water line might be down. Let's just get back to the station."

Gyde turned the spigot. Water came out. He shot Pol a look and removed his coat. "Come on. We're filthy from that place. I don't want you getting it in the car."

They *were* filthy. The dust darkened the water that sluiced off Gyde's hands. Pol could feel it clogging his pores, coating his hair, even his eyelashes. *Damn.* It must be matting on the blue makeup at his temples.

Gyde rolled up his sleeves, revealing his corded, hairless forearms. He rubbed his hands and face in the stream: "What are you waiting for? Let's go!"

Pol went over to the spigot reluctantly. Put his hands in the flow.

"You're going to get your sleeves wet," Gyde said with exasperation.

Pol shook the water from his fingers, face hard. "It's the smell of blood, too many memories. I just want to get out of here."

To the Citizens of Centalia

Some secrets lead to destruction.

Let it be known then: there are other realities beyond this planet.

I have been in contact with aliens, beings from other worlds. I have been taken to those worlds.

These aliens have advanced technology. If they choose (maybe I should say when they choose. . .) they will take all power from us and enslave us (every citizen . . .).

This is a warning. They are already here. Their spies have infiltrated our society from the lowest levels to the highest ranks of our government. These aliens are in disguise and they are almost impossible to detect. (I know how, but I cannot speak for obvious reasons.)

We must unite, in secret, to save ourselves. Do not trust the State. TRUST NO ONE.

The pamphlet was signed on the back page with the open circle with the bar on top, the "signature" they'd seen on the wall.

Gyde was gleeful. "The more this scum dares, the easier it will be to find him and the more merits we'll get when we bring him down!"

Pol almost said "*if* we bring him down," but he bit it back. Gyde's confidence made him angry. He didn't know why. He wanted to find the terrorist, but that wasn't the same thing as wanting *Gyde* to find him.

"He has access to a copier and supplies. The lab is checking now on the paper. . . ."

Gyde went on. Pol shut him out. He shut out the anger, too, and his own confusion. One thing at a time. When your mind was wounded you had to grasp reality one fistful at a time. He tried to focus on the pamphlet's message. He read it over several times, waiting for it to stick. Suddenly the paper was shaking in his hands.

It took him a moment to realize it. Meanwhile he stood there, shaking. He put the paper down carefully and made his way past Gyde with what he believed was a stony face, heading into the service room down the hall. For once it was empty, thank the gods.

It was his scarping hands. They were trembling, the traitors. He stuck them under his armpits, leaned forward from the waist, squeezing them tight, and his eyes, too.

Their spies have infiltrated our society.

He had opened the letter from the Department of Health. Gyde was right. It was his yearly physical, scheduled for one month hence. No, it was the yearly physical of Pol 137, scheduled for one month hence. Pol 137 would not be showing up.

Had he known about the physicals when he killed the Silver? No. He had thought of many things: of the hair color and the eyes, of removing the head and hands. The Silver had been just what he'd needed. Pol 137 had come to Marcus for some black-market hooch, and he'd mentioned that he was leaving the next day for Centalia and had Marcus ever been there? Kalim N2 had slipped from the house and followed the dashing officer, had later broken into his hotel room and found the letters of commission. He'd been retired from active battle duty, reassigned as monitor, detective class, in Centalia. Kalim had made up his mind instantly. He knew it was dangerous and chances were high that he would be caught. But at the time, he thought he would rather die than remain a servant. Perhaps he had not been thinking clearly after all. Craftily but not clearly.

He had not counted on the physicals. But even if he had thought about them, would it have made any difference? He tried to think back. He remembered wondering if he and Pol 137 were the same blood type.

He wanted to laugh, gripping his stomach. The same blood type! He couldn't even roll up his sleeves or pull out his dick in public! What would they find in his scarping *veins*?

In the cafeteria over lunch, Gyde was still going on about the pamphlet. He puzzled over a copy while eating his soup. " 'I have been in contact with aliens, beings from other worlds,' " he quoted. "What a lunatic."

"Perhaps that's the angle," Pol said. "Can we check records of anyone with known mental disturbances?"

Gyde gave him a peculiar look. "Not much tolerance for that."

Meaning, Pol understood, that mental deviants simply "disappeared." There would be no such records.

"Any other ideas?" Gyde prompted.

"We've eliminated Irons. What if he's higher than a Bronze?"

"Scarp! No Silver or Gold is gong to hang around construction sites. Besides, this sociopath is too sick to be from the upper classes."

Pol didn't respond, but he must have looked unconvinced.

"No Silver or Gold is going to think up scarp like this! When he wrote the other messages I thought he was talking about foreign spies. But aliens from *other planets*? By the blood, what does *that* mean?"

Pol looked at the pamphlet, a reflective finger stroking his lip.

"Who ever heard of such a thing?" Gyde insisted, requiring an answer.

Pol's cold blue eyes looked into Gyde's. He could sense shifting sand under his feet.

"Have you ever heard of such a thing?" Gyde asked.

"No."

"Everyone knows there are only four planets and ours is the only one capable of sustaining life."

The finger stroking Pol's lips faltered.

"You've . . ." Gyde lowered his voice, "you've never heard of Bronzies being taught anything different, have you?" His baffled tone suggested that the state would certainly be capable of teaching the Bronze class something else—anything else—if it was in their best interests to do so.

"Not to my knowledge."

Gyde shook his head in disgust. "It had to come from somewhere. This slag can't be *that* original."

"There was nothing about aliens in the Archives." And now Pol realized how odd that was. The "aliens" search had yielded not one word about extraterrestrials in the Archives, not even a claim from the state that such things didn't exist.

"It came from somewhere." Gyde's eyes glinted with calculation.

The communal library at the dorm was empty. Only a few older Silvers were spending their evening in the lounge through the open archway. Pol scanned the bookcases of state-sanctioned titles and found what he was looking for—a book on astronomy.

He took it to a big leather chair and sat down. The lamp beside him cast a rosy glow. He thumbed through the pages and found a large color chart at the center of the book.

There: the sun and around it in elliptical orbits . . . four planets. Recalia, this planet, was the closest to the sun. Beyond it, cold and lifeless, were three smaller planets. None of the planets had any moons. And around this small solar system was a black encircling dome, affixed with pinpoints of light that were meant to be the stars. And that was all.

In the comfortable library, a fire not all that far away, Pol shivered. *Bullshit*, he thought, a word from his old language. *Bullshit.*

Why would the state teach this? It was wrong, all wrong. He didn't know how he knew this, but he knew. It was part of that embedded knowledge inside him. It was like a strange conviction he had that the sun ought to shine, that he ought to be able to look up and see blue sky, at least once in a while. For the longest time, he had thought the weather was simply terrible, kept waiting for the dense cloud cover to break. Finally he'd asked one of the Irons at Marcus's house, *Is it always like this?* They'd thought he was crazy when he said the sun was visible where he came from, that there were such things as *sunny days*. There was also the certainty that things were *heavier* than they should be. At first, he took it for a symptom of his illness, but after that passed, he still retained a conviction, sometimes when he had to step up onto a bus or pick up something simple, like a pen, that everything weighed more than it was supposed to.

Now this. He stared at the chart for a long time, as if it might trigger something in his brain, something, no matter how small and forgotten, that might enable him to fit the pieces into a reasonable pattern. Instead, the longer he looked at the chart the more that chasm in his brain solidified, deepened, yawned, threatened to suck him down into its icy darkness until at last he snapped the book shut.

In his bathroom he propped the chair against the door and ran the shower. He removed his clothes and stood under the water, the dust of the air raid washing down the drain. He could feel something hard inside him; maybe it was his will or maybe something he couldn't even name, but he felt it shift, break, collapse, and wash away like the dirt down the drain. And for the first time since Marcus had picked him from that battlefield he cried, deep, shuddering wracks, shaking until the warmth softened his muscles to limpness.

16.2. Sixty-Forty Denton Wyle

Denton dreamed of people screaming in the night. When he awoke, the Sapphian village was quiet all around him. He was spooked enough that he got up and stepped out of the hut into the village common. It was quiet. Everything looked peaceful. The large wood bonfire in the center of the circle was low and hot like a bed of coals. He went back to bed.

In the morning he slept late and missed the work crews. The day was long and dull and he could not even find John in the afternoon to shoot the breeze or go for a swim. He looked, too. And asked around. No one had seen him.

That night, at the Saturday Night Special, John's name was among those announced in the circle.

Denton was standing in the crowd when he heard it. He had, in fact, just been scanning the crowd for John, and not for the first time that evening. He froze, his hands folded politely in front of him.

Denton knew it was John's name, John's *real* name. He knew that Sapphians did not often, if ever, share the same name. And John's absence now took on an ominous meaning. He had never seen the boy miss a gathering like this one. Something was majorly wrong.

And then Denton remembered that he did not really know the purpose of the list. He'd tried to find out, but maybe not hard enough, because suddenly the fact that he did not know seemed lazy and horribly, horribly unwise.

Denton scanned the crowd again, as if to change the message his ears had heard. His gaze stopped upon an apparently inconsolable cluster of females—John's mother and sisters. He worked his way over there, trying to keep it together. They were hanging on one another in a kind of ball of limbs and tears. Denton tugged on one, disentangling her with more force than he had intended, but he was upset, damn it. He *made* her look at him. "Where's John?"

She gaped at him with confused hurt, as if he were purposefully being mean. Then she started wailing again and turned back to her family.

Denton would have tried again, but it was hopeless. He put his hands on his hips, feeling very, very unhappy. He was breathing hard. His anger was building. He turned and strode through the crowd, looking for someone who could give him an answer. *Just a simple freaking answer!*

Then he saw one of the young males he and John worked with almost every day. He was standing still, watching Denton approach, looking right at him. Denton felt a twinge of relief and went to him, grabbed his arm. "Do you know what happened to John?"

But the male—Denton had called him Pete—just looked at him, looked *at* him, right the heck into his eyes. Stared, really. After months of the guy looking at his cheek, it was kind of disconcerting. And his eyes . . . they were not nearly as dim and clueless as Denton had always imagined. In fact, they were rather callous eyes. When had that happened?

"John? What h-happened to him?" Denton heard his own voice squeak and realized that he was very badly scared.

Pete slowly smiled. "*Allook saheed.* He will be missed."

Denton worked his way toward the jungle, smiling and nodding at the few Sapphians who paused in their grief to give him his due as he passed. His heart was pulsing. The throb of it joined with the lump in his neck in a blood duet. His palms were wet. He told himself he had to calm down. It seemed very important that he calm down.

He reached the jungle. No one seemed to be watching him. He attempted to slip off into the trees, but it turned into something more like thrashing his way into the trees. It got him away from the circle, though, and that was the point.

He blundered around in the starlit jungle for a while, his limbs jerking, sweat coming out of his body in sheets. He was like a rabbit caught in a net and, like a rabbit, he struggled with every muscle and nerve and, eventually, inevitably, exhausted himself.

Panting, he stopped and listened. He couldn't hear anything. He was alone. It was just him, by himself, going nuts in the nighttime jungle. No one had followed him. No one was coming to get him. He'd gotten a bit lost and it took him ten minutes to find a Sapphian path. It was deserted. He sank down on it, sitting on the packed earth. He had to get a grip.

After all, he didn't know what Pete had meant. He could have meant "*Al-look saheed* [meaning Denton], yes, we will miss John." He hadn't necessarily been referring to John's *allook saheed*ness. The fact that John was also called *allook saheed* didn't necessarily have anything to do with his disappearance anyway. And Denton still did not know what the list meant. Even if something bad had happened to John—death, for example—maybe he had died of natural causes. Maybe there was some kind of superquick virus on this planet, one that he would, by virtue of his Earth genes, be completely immune to. Even if that list did mean people were gone forever or even dead, that didn't mean his name would ever be on it—at least, not anytime soon.

Only it did. His stomach, which was currently a quivering, sickened mass of bunny guts, said so. He had been covering up, pasting over a lot of things that bothered him. There were a lot of things that didn't seem quite right. Like the way that, in their solicitude, the Sapphians never quite left him alone. Or John, he recalled. Even swimming, they had always been surrounded. And there were other things. If he'd been in a movie theater, he would be screaming at the idiot on the screen by now: *Get out of there, you stupid jerk!* But he'd been pasting it over because in real life, unlike the movies, nothing dramatic ever *actually* happened. There never was a bogeyman under the bed, even if it would be kind of cool and dramatic if there were. And, mostly, he'd ignored stuff because he was a *big freaking coward*. Because he didn't have anywhere else to go. Because he needed this all to be true *so badly*!

Yes, he needed it to be true. He was lost. He was so terribly, terribly far from home. And the semblance of belonging helped him to forget. He sniffed, feeling very sorry for himself.

And then he thought . . . it still *might* be okay. He really didn't know for sure that it wasn't. He could be letting his imagination get the best of him. He did that, like that time with Carter and the cat burglar thing. He knew he had a tendency to do that and—

A branch cracked.

Denton got to his feet, all panicked motion. Before he could run, a shape stepped from the trees. It was the girl with the white-gold hair, Eyanna. She watched him warily. She had probably heard him blundering through the trees earlier. *Earth* had probably heard him.

"*Ta zhecta*," he said.

"*Ta zhecta*." She hesitated, wary, then held something toward him. It was the photograph he had given to her. "Yours?" Her face was intent, questioning.

"No. . . . I gave it to you. You keep it."

She frowned at him in frustration. "Yours?" she asked again, more loudly now, holding the photograph up as if he wasn't looking at it properly. "Is she *your* female?"

He hadn't a clue what she was going on about and couldn't care less. The photograph, its subject, the entire history and science of photography, for that matter, was the last thing on his freaking mind right now.

"Yes, she is my female," he answered, more to shut Eyanna up than anything else. And then he remembered what John had said. What had he called Eyanna? A ghost woman? That was right! Her name had been said in the circle—and she was here, looking healthy and, if not happy, certainly alive.

"Eyanna, listen! My friend's name was said in the circle tonight. What does that mean? What happens to these ones?"

Eyanna took a step back ungracefully. A small fearful sound escaped her mouth.

That was not quite the reaction Denton had hoped for. He tried to keep his voice calm. "Eyanna? Please? It is important. Tell me what happens to these ones. No one will tell me."

She looked up at the sky, clicking her teeth anxiously. Her legs quivered as though she desperately wanted to flee. One arm reached back behind her, groping. She found a tree and her fingers dug into it. She squeezed her eyes shut.

Denton suddenly had the conviction, unwelcome as it was, that she was *reliving* something—the way her head was tilted up, the cant of her body. The thought made him turn cold, because whatever it was, it was not a nice happy memory. Oh no. She knew where John had gone all right. She had *been* where John had gone. And it was not a good place at all.

She whispered something. He didn't understand the word.

"What? Eyanna, what did you say?"

"Skalkit!" she said loudly. She opened her eyes. They were wild. "Skalkit! Skalkit!" She looked at him, intense, as if she'd just revealed some big secret.

He wanted to stomp in his frustration. "I don't know this word. *Damn it!* What is *skalkit*?"

She gave the gesture for "no," backing away into the trees.

"*Eyanna, what is skalkit!*"

She stopped, just visible behind the foliage, her eyes huge, but she didn't speak.

Denton took a deep breath. Made himself count to ten. If he wasn't careful he'd scare her away and then he'd never know. He spoke with quiet hysteria. "The ones whose names are said, are they . . ." He pantomimed death again because he had no alternative. This time he grabbed his chest and fell to the ground, doing it in a half-assed way so as not to alarm her. He looked up to see if she had gotten it.

She'd gotten it. He could see on her face that she had. She gave the gesture for "yes." He got up, his heart knocking. Okay. So they were dead. That was bad but he'd already guessed that much.

"But how? What is *skalkit*, Eyanna? How?"

Her face was slack in the starlight, her nostril ridges flared with her rapid breathing. She was traumatized, he could see that, but he didn't care. He didn't give a flying fig what she was feeling, as long as she told him. She *had* to tell him.

She slowly raised her hands. He had no idea what she was doing until her hands reached her shoulders and slowly formed themselves into the semblance of claws. Her lips pulled back, baring her teeth. And she roared.

*   *   *

Three hours later, Denton was on the run. He had managed to pull himself together enough to go back to the village and act like Mr. Happy-go-*allook-saheed*. He had gone to bed early. And then, when all sounds had died away, when he was pretty sure the entire Sapphian race was drunk and dead to the world, he snuck out of his hut and headed for the trees.

He took very little with him—a couple of blankets, which he had done up in a bundle, along with some cooked grain. He could live off the land easily. What he really needed was just to get about a million miles away.

He entered the jungle on a path that he thought led toward the bottom of the horseshoe gorge, the mouth of it, the way out. He hadn't been there since the day he'd arrived and he'd lain in his hut for a good while trying to map it out in his head. He never had been good at directions, but he thought he could pull this off. He *had* to.

He didn't know what the hell kind of animal Eyanna had tried to describe to him, but he knew that he never wanted to see one, hear one, smell one, or even see one on TV. Because now that he had faced the truth, now that he had made the firm decision to go and had given up on the fairy tale—and even on the sex part—this whole *allook saheed* thing seemed more and more like the biggest hunk of mouse bait he had ever seen in his life. What, were they fattening him up like Hansel and Gretel? Was he about to become an Aztecan Blue Plate Special or what?

Not if he had anything to say about it.

He walked down a dark path he thought was the way out of the gorge. He walked for a long time. Too long. He was about to admit that he was going the wrong way when the trees cleared and he got a view of salmon wall. It had to be the opening of the gorge. He increased his pace.

It wasn't that he was *not* afraid. He was. But once he had put some distance between himself and the main circle of huts, he felt better. He would feel better still once he was out of the gorge, but he was not really worried about making it. Maybe it was that old denial, that conviction that nothing serious would *really* happen to him, that the bogeyman would not end up being under the bed when he looked, that he would be scared, maybe even badly, but that in the end he would be fine because he always had been before.

So when the path before him darkened and the shadows resolved themselves into Sapphians, to three or four males, he was legitimately surprised.

He stopped, not even having much of a reaction. Then, in a rush of as much annoyance as fear, he started ahead again, jogging, then running, prepared to plow his way through them and just get the hell out of there. After all, he was bigger than they were by far. Hadn't he once thought he could easily take them if it ever came to that?

He picked up speed, seeing, even as he was running, that there were more than three or four of them there, that there were a lot, maybe a dozen, and probably more behind him, too. But he was still going to run right through them. He was! He would scatter them like bowling pins and . . .

He hit them. They had formed a line across the path. He did take down a couple, the ones right in front. But he went down, too, and before he could get up again, there were hands on him, many hands, and they were stronger than they looked.

He still struggled, an outraged American. He didn't cry out, but there were athletic grunts coming out of his mouth. His feet pedaled over something soft trying to gain traction. They grabbed his legs. Someone was binding his arms, hard, behind his back, and there were no more bobbing heads, no more *allook saheed*, no words at all.

And it wasn't until he was sure, really 100 percent sure, that he was not going to escape, that they had captured him and were not being nice to him at all, that he understood that the bogeyman *had* been under the bed this time.

And he began to scream.

16.3. Seventy-Thirty Jill Talcott

The landing field at the spaceport was enormous—as long as three or four of the City's blocks. In the center sat the dome, looking like the round head of a giant emerging from the earth. And at the edge of the landing field, next to the red glass wall that marked the southern border of the City, was the spaceship.

It had taken them longer to get here than Jill had anticipated. In fact, they'd gotten so hot and tired the night before that they'd camped out in one of the buildings with power on the east–west artery. There were any number of empty rooms to be had, but Nate had wanted them to "stick together" in case "the aliens showed up."

So Nate had slept on the floor next to Jill's narrow bed. She could fit in the alien beds, if she turned on her side. Barely. She'd awakened at one point and lay listening to him breathing for a long time, thinking, *This is what it's like not to be alone in the night.*

It wasn't bad. But she didn't want to come to depend on it.

Nate made a beeline for the spacecraft. It was shaped in the same functional aerodynamic manner as the air cars, but it was huge, larger than a zeppelin, and a deep rusty brown from stem to stern. As they drew closer, Jill realized this was not paint but dust from the red desert sand.

She wasn't all that interested in the thing. The sun was hot, and she couldn't shake a sense of lassitude no matter how often they rested. She yawned, watching Nate walk excitedly up and down its length, then crouch underneath it so he could touch the landing gear. The belly of the ship formed a cavelike roof over his head. He rubbed at the dust—it had been baked into a hard glaze.

"They haven't moved this thing in ages," he said, disappointed.

Jill bit back a plea for him to come out from there. She didn't like seeing him poised under the giant machine like a bug under a giant's foot.

"Wow!" Nate reached up as high as he could to touch the side of the craft.

"Let's go inside," Jill said. A fingernail found its way into her mouth to be chewed. She looked around, feeling exposed on this vast open field, to the rays of the sun, if nothing else.

"Inside the ship?" Nate sounded excited.

"Inside the *building*, Nate, the spaceport."

"But, Jill . . ." He backed up to get a better look, tennis shoes shuffling on the landing field. "This is, like, *a spaceship*."

"Yeah, maybe later, Dr. Who. Come on."

Up close, the round dome was like the shell of some thick-plated insect. There was an alcove into which the main doors were set, and the depth of this alcove—a good ten feet—was the actual width of the spaceport walls. The doors were metal and heavy and had long vertical handles. There were no windows at all.

Nate looked at Jill, eyebrow cocked, and tugged on a handle. The door gave easily—it had been made for a light touch. With a throaty suction noise it opened. Inside was a heavy rubber seal two feet thick.

Nate whistled. "Interesting. I don't suppose that's for air-conditioning, do you?"

Jill shook her head. She felt a tingling excitement in her belly, but she wasn't ready to discuss the idea she'd had on the rooftop with Nate. Not yet.

The power appeared to be out in the building, but as they stepped inside the lights came on. There was the sound of machinery kicking in.

"Could be worse," Jill said. "Power could be off completely."

Nate said nothing, but he looked worried.

The spaceport was nothing like an airport back home. There were no gates, no chairs for waiting relations, no boards announcing departures and arrivals—and certainly there were no travelers. The halls were not all that large, either, as though the building never had been intended to accommodate crowds.

"Next flight to Milwaukee, ten minutes," Nate mocked with a staticky voice spoken through his hand. He looked at Jill with a fake astonished expression: *Did you hear that? Let's go!* She rolled her eyes.

They followed the hallway to the center of the building. There the corridor opened up into a gigantic empty hangar. There was a fifty-foot-wide ledge all around the cavernous dock, and this ledge ended abruptly in a plummeting drop. The space was large enough to accommodate several dozen ships the size of the one on the landing field, but there were no ships at all.

"Where are they?" Nate sounded seriously bummed.

Jill didn't answer. Things were looking worse all the time. The spaceport appeared to be completely defunct.

"Shit, Jill, this place is a tomb."

"There *ought* to be aliens here. The City isn't completely uninhabited."

"I guess when your world is dying it's not a big priority to explore space," he answered bitterly.

"We don't know that their world is dying. Besides, they still have to get around *this* planet."

"Who says? What if this city is all there is?"

Jill tapped a shoulder blade with her fingers, frowning in thought.

"There's still that ship outside," Nate said, with as much doubt as hope. "It *might* be operational."

"The control room's over there. Come on. Let's see what they've got."

The control room powered up when they walked in the door, the screens going from black to green readouts in seconds. Nate's mood perked up a bit at the sight of all those computers. He pulled two of the narrow chairs over to a table and sat in both of them. There was no keyboard. He passed his fingers over the screen experimentally. The alien text shifted under his touch.

"I'm working an alien computer," he said to her in a voice that a boy might use while displaying a prizewinning toad to his mother.

"Yes, I see that, Nate," Jill answered, smiling.

Jill watched him work for a few minutes, then pulled up two chairs of her own. It was time to come clean about what she'd been thinking, but it felt so momentous to say it out loud that a sudden awkwardness gripped her.

"Nate . . . you know those seals we saw just now, on the spaceport door?"

He glanced at her. "Yeah."

"What did they remind you of?"

He stopped messing with the screen and turned to look at her, waiting.

"Like the rubber curtain we had in our lab, Nate! It's insulation. *Wave technology.*"

He didn't look surprised. "Yeah?"

"Well . . . we have to find out! We have to find out if they're using wave technology. Because if they are . . ." She drummed her fingers on the table. It was so important that she explain it well. She made herself take a breath and slow down. "Nate, what if Copernicus had had the opportunity to be rocketed three hundred years into the future, to see the full implications of his ideas?"

Nate lifted an eyebrow, but his face was still guarded. "That would be very cool. Assuming he could understand it."

"Well, that's exactly what *we've* been given! We have a chance to see what the one-minus-one can really do—if it's really as important as we think and how and in what ways it can be used. Think of the possibilities! Kobinski's manuscript—I mean, the manuscript is *nothing*. We're being offered a look at the future—*our* future! We can move our research forward by several hundred years—maybe even more!"

She forced herself to stop, though she could have gone on. Her father had been such a huckster that she, by inclination, hated the very idea of a sales pitch. She waited for Nate to latch on to the concept on his own, had no doubt that he would. After all, hadn't he been by her side for the past two years? Wasn't the one-minus-one as much his baby as hers? But his dark eyes looked troubled. She couldn't read him.

"What we want to know," she said, nodding toward the computers, "is if their space technology uses the one-minus-one wave. Any suggestions on how we do that?"

Nate turned slowly back to the monitor. "Maybe we can find some math."

"Nope. I thought about that. We're used to math being a cross-language tool because most cultures on Earth use the Greek math symbols. But of course, that wouldn't apply here."

"No. You're right. Who knows how they represent the number four?"

"Exactly. But *diagrams* might be helpful. Think you can get into the guts of this thing?"

He was staring blankly at the screen.

"Nate?"

He blinked, sat up straighter. "I can try." His fingers moved over the screen. "I'm pretty blind without knowing the language; all I can do is poke around. But something might come up." Even as distracted as he seemed to be, he couldn't let a line like that go by without comment. He looked at her and waggled his eyebrows. "Heh heh heh."

She let out a snort that was part laughter, part embarrassment. Nate proceeded to poke around for a good long time. Mostly the screens made absolutely no sense to them. After about twenty minutes a diagram appeared.

"What's that?" Jill asked, studying it.

"Looks like a diagram of the spaceport." Nate pointed out the shape of the dome. "It's marked one of the rooms. See? It's blinking."

"Umm," Jill said, not very interested. "Let's see what else we can find."

They found a few other diagrams but nothing that looked like physics, nothing that provided any insight. The day dragged on. Jill was starting to get deeply frustrated, realizing the depth of their ignorance. Here she was with the most amazing technology at her fingertips and she couldn't read a damn word. It was a *Twilight Zone* nightmare, like the episode where the guy who loves to read is left alone at the end of the world with all the books and endless time to read them—but his glasses break.

How were they ever going to be able to learn the language?

The spaceport diagram came up several more times; they ignored it.

Jill groaned, rubbing her eyes. "What we really need is something like Hammurabi's code—a key that would help us decipher their math symbols. Do you think there's any chance they might have developed something like that for their space program?"

Nate started to answer when paper emerged from an unnoticed slot in the computer's side. It slid to the table's surface and another followed. Nate shot Jill a confused look and picked up the page. She studied it over his shoulder.

"Holy shit," Nate breathed. "It's a code breaker!"

"Let me see." Jill was sure he was having her on. She tried to take the page from him but he refused to give it up. They ended up leaning over it together, their heads jockeying for space.

On one side of the page, in very small print, was a simple series of lines. Next to them was a character of the alien script. The lines went from one line to two lines to three, increasing in neat rows.

"Those are their number symbols!" Nate said, putting his finger on the alien script next to the lines. "That's the symbol for 'one,' then 'two,' three, four, five . . . Christ!"

Jill turned the page slightly toward herself. She didn't want to allow herself to hope, forced herself to look at the lines again and again. The computer, meanwhile, continued to print pages. She and Nate pored over them. By the fourth page the ideograms were describing the symbols for addition and subtraction, and from there it grew increasingly complex. It would take days, if not months, to figure out some of the ideograms. But she had no doubt that they *could* decipher them, eventually. The ideograms were very well designed.

"Jill," Nate said, his voice strained, "you asked for it and *it printed it.*"

"You must have pushed something."

"Yeah," Nate snorted, "I knew how to do it all along. I was just holding back." He looked around the room, paranoid, as if expecting an alien Allen Funt to reveal himself.

"Maybe it was an idiot detector," Jill suggested, her heart beating fast. "Like . . . I don't know, a help screen that comes up when you clearly don't know what you're doing."

"I *hope* so." Nate snuck a look under the tables. "Because the thing is, even if the computer understands speech, which is no biggie, how would it be able to understand *our language?*"

"I don't know." Jill felt uneasy herself and then got annoyed for feeling that way. "Look, what are we complaining for? This is the best thing that could have happened. We should be drinking champagne!"

Nate gave her a funny look and got up. He scratched his head. "Well—it *is* incredible luck, even if it's damned weird."

"Absolutely."

He gave her a rough congratulatory hug and moved away before she could return it. "Um—I'll be back. I need to take a quick break."

" 'Kay." Jill smiled at him, already focused on the next ideogram.

She lost track of time after that. She had never been particularly emotional, and her surprise over their discovery was quickly replaced by exaltation, and that was quickly replaced by an unobtrusive satisfaction and a determination to get down to work. She identified the symbols for multiplication and division and the notation for exponentials. Her butt was killing her, straddling these ridiculous banana-split chairs. It was going quite numb. She didn't care. With some impatience she skipped past more ideograms looking for complex equations.

It might be here, she thought. *It just might.* But when she finally did locate what she thought were longer equations, she realized it would take weeks to painfully translate each one, symbol by symbol by symbol. She put the papers aside and got up, stretching her tired back. Nate had not returned, which was strange in itself. She walked back and forth to get the pins and needles out, glanced at the computer.

She dismissed the idea when it first occurred to her, but a moment later it was back. And as silly as it was, it was worth a shot. So she turned to the computer, a bit shamefaced, and began to talk to it.

Nate came in a few minutes later. He snuck up on her and leapt out wearing huge black goggles that covered most of his face. "Booga-booga!"

Jill screamed bloody murder. She lectured him halfheartedly about the dangers of heart attacks or serious injury here, where there were no hospitals, but she could not deflate his good mood or her own.

"I found that blinking room on the spaceport diagram," Nate said, pulling off the goggles. "It's a supply room. *Super*cool. There are all kinds of alien spacesuits, helmets, these sunglasses, I think like pagers or signaling devices—a *ton* of stuff. I have no idea what most of it is. I got a handful of these...." He fished in his pocket, brought out little metal capsules. He shook them. "Thought you might have an idea—"

"Nate?" Jill interrupted.

"Huh?"

She handed him a piece of paper.

It took him a minute. He referred back to the code, where Jill marked down what she'd deciphered of the symbols. He grew serious. "God, Jill, this is your equation."

"I know."

"How did you get this?"

"From the computer." Jill said evasively. "But look at this. . . ." She pointed at the page. "This is an equation for the one-minus-one wave—at least it's supposed to be. But the numbers are wrong."

Nate studied it, eyes narrowed. After a moment he stepped back so abruptly that he banged into the row of tables behind them. The blood drained from his face.

"Nate?" For a moment Jill thought he'd been poisoned or invaded by some alien parasite, that something had happened to him when he'd been out of the room, so extreme was his physical response. But he was staring in horror at the page.

"The equation for the one-minus-one . . ."

"*What?*"

"Don't you see?" He looked up, his eyes feverish. "This wave function assumes a wave with seventy percent crest and thirty percent trough. Kobinski was right, Jill! We're not just on another planet. *We're not even in our own universe anymore.*"

16.4. Thirty-Seventy Aharon Handalman

Kobinski did not show his face again until the first day of Festival. Aharon was seated in a chair when he came in. A nurse was finishing dressing him, putting hard sandals on his still-heavy feet. The Fiorian robe she had given him was smelly and uncomfortable, not to mention a little immodest, since he wore nothing underneath.

Aharon kept his mouth shut at the sight of the golden mask. He had wished so hard for the man's return, now he had nothing to say. He was angry at Kobinski, his host, for leaving him alone and vulnerable for so long. He was in awe of Kobinski, the kabbalist, whose work in the past few days had taken the blasted and empty plain of Aharon's soul and had whispered to it, had started something new growing there. That man, the kabbalist, the mystic, the writer of the manuscript, seemed to have no part of this being before him, and Aharon decided it was better, for his own sanity if for no other reason, to divorce the two here and now. He needed the manuscript like a drowning man needed a life raft. He could not risk being disappointed in its author.

The king of Gehenna waited until the nurse had finished, then sent her and Tevach from the room. He was dressed in a purple robe decorated with gold thread. His belt was hammered gold; his mask sparkled cruelly. But when he took it off, Aharon could see that underneath all that savage finery the human being sweat.

"I should explain what you will see today."

"That would be helpful." Aharon clenched his hands in his lap.

"This is Fiore's largest sacred holiday. There will be idols, speeches, religious trappings. The Fiori religion emphasizes . . ." Kobinski hesitated. ". . . They're extremely stringent against those who question the faith. Their belief system is *absolutely* rigid. After all, that's why they're here."

Aharon said nothing, but he felt a deep repulsion. Dear God, what was he going to have to witness?

"The punishment for heretics is brutal. It will be bloody, even grotesque. You cannot react."

Aharon moved his arm sluggishly to clutch the chair. "Must I go? Why?"

"Because," Kobinski said coolly, "it will benefit me. And I, in turn, am your only chance of survival. I told you my position is tenuous. The sight of you will impress the masses—if you don't do anything stupid. Don't show your emotions. Don't do anything at all. If you can't bear what you're seeing, look down at your lap. Do you understand?"

Aharon nodded. He wanted to refuse, but he knew that wasn't an option.

"In a way, you're quite fortunate to have arrived so close to Festival. It means Argeh has been too busy to bother with you—yet. You learn to milk good fortune for all it's worth on Fiori." Kobinski smiled thinly.

"I have you," Aharon said. "That is the greatest good fortune."

"Is it? We shall see."

They left town by carriage—a crude, heavy thing that made Aharon feel as if he had gone back in time, was riding to a *shetl* in the frozen Polish countryside in the Middle Ages. The coach had small windows cut into the door. There was no glass, and the icy wind howled through. Gravity pinned Aharon to the hard seat. He pressed his hands down on the bench to keep himself upright—a straining, monumental task—as the wheels jarred against the rocky ground. Across from him was Kobinski in his mask, and next to him was Tevach. The Fiore's big dark eyes darted between him and Kobinski, as if trying to figure out their relationship. Not so dumb, that one.

The town consisted of little more than a few large stone buildings, numerous hovels, mud and rocks, filthy beggars. Aharon averted his eyes from the hanging carcasses of meat in the town square—carcasses that looked squat and muscled and horribly familiar. He tried not to think of the food that had been forced on him since he'd been here.

They hadn't gone far when something struck the carriage. There was a hard crash on the door, followed by three or four smaller missiles. My Lord

stiffened and grasped the edge of his seat. Outside, Aharon heard the snarls of
Kobinski's guards who rode into the crowd to find the culprits. The mask revealed nothing.

"Friends of yours?" Aharon asked.

"I told you there were problems. There's been some . . . vandalism to my
images. Organized, it seems."

"Argeh?"

"No." Kobinski paused. "I don't think so."

Tevach was plucking at Kobinski's sleeve repeatedly.

"What *is* it, Tevach?" Kobinski turned to him irritably.

"Forgive me, My Lord, but . . . there . . . there is a prisoner . . . a heretic . . ."

Before the cringing Tevach could get his full sentence out or Kobinski take
the umbrage he was gathering himself to take, the carriage slowed and one of
the guards looked in the window. He addressed Kobinski in the growling Fiorian language.

Which meant, Aharon surmised with profound dread, that they had arrived.

*   *   *

My Lord made his appearance in the official box to the usual fanfare. He was
greeted with cheers, though they were weaker than they had been even last
year. Argeh was present, his own chair a few steps down and to the right of My
Lord's. He turned, a challenge in his eyes. My Lord ignored him.

My Lord waited until the audience was distracted with one of the events;
then he motioned to Tevach to carry Aharon in and place him in the next seat.
As the Fiore caught sight of "the messenger" an electrified tension rushed around
the arena, a kind of mass inhale. Soon everyone was looking at the box, rising
to their feet to see over one another's heads.

Aharon, feeling their stares, began to shake.

"Everything's fine," My Lord said, putting his hand on Aharon's arm.

The gesture was one of domination, and it was meant for the crowd. For
maximum effect he had left Aharon unmasked. Years ago, when he'd first arrived, it had been Ehlah's idea to mask him so that his face would not cause
undue alarm. It worked, but not for that reason. What the Fiore imagined behind the mask was even more awesome than what was really there. But that
dread had worn off. They needed a reminder. And as he'd told Aharon, when
you lived on Fiori you milked good fortune for every drop you could get.

My Lord stood and held up his arms. "You have heard that Mahava sent
me a messenger from Heaven," he spoke loudly. "Today we welcome him to
our festival and show him the depth of our devotion!"

The crowd did not respond with quite the hysterical jubilation he had
hoped for, but there was moderate pounding of staves. My Lord sat down. He
glanced at Argeh, who rose and, without commenting on the visitor or even
looking at him, motioned for the ceremonies to go on.

Aharon spoke low at his side: "Why do you do it? Why do you trick these people into thinking you're some kind of divine being?"

"Be silent," My Lord said. "Unless you want to get us both killed."

He was angry with himself that he had not spent more time preparing Aharon. It would be dangerous if the Jew made a fool of himself today. But he had avoided the mere sight of the man, with his long, proud beard, the *yeshiva* cadence of his voice, those burning, self-righteous eyes—these things triggered too many memories, were too much of an immediate window back to a time and place that was gone and buried. By avoiding Handalman, My Lord was avoiding Kobinski.

Yet the Jew seemed different today, softer. Perhaps it was simply that he wasn't talking so much.

Down in the arena, they brought in the great statues of Mahava and Magehna. Magehna was squatting, in her divine position of elimination, and Mahava was standing imperious, above it all. They looked like Fiore, naturally, though taller and lighter of bone, with the smooth, round features that My Lord had learned to recognize as a standard of beauty. The statues were made from stone, and the great carts that wheeled them groaned under the crushing weight. Around the statues were piled displays of the meager harvest of Fiori: sheaves of their plant staple, *gha,* berries, and newly sacrificed animals, including dressed Fiore carcasses. On Earth, it would have been impossible to conceptualize having every remotely edible thing on the planet in attendance, but here they could manage it, though not easily. Some of the foodstuffs had been brought from around the world, traveling as long as several years to get here. The seas on Fiori were notoriously treacherous and the land endlessly dull and unsustaining. The crowd stood and cheered at the bountiful display.

My Lord, more to keep Aharon calm than anything else, explained the ritual to his guest. He told him the story of Mahava and Magehna, his wife, who shat out Fiore.

Aharon questioned him with a frown, "You told me that you thought the souls who were embodied here were . . ."

"Gevorah/chochmah."

"Yes. I was reading about that in your manuscript."

My Lord was surprised at the mention of the work. He kept forgetting it was here. It was another incongruous bit of the past that didn't fit into the present.

"If the religiously strict of Earth reincarnate here—" Aharon said.

"Not just Earth, from all over the ladder."

"Yes, but some *are* from Earth."

"Probably."

"So how could they worship these idols? If they were so rigid in their faith, wouldn't they worship the One True God here as well?"

My Lord snorted incredulously. "What do you expect? That they'd call Him *Yahweh*? Make him look like a long-bearded human patriarch?"

The Jew looked embarrassed. "No . . . but . . . but there are *two* of them, and one is a female. Shouldn't they *at least* be monotheists?"

"Should? According to whom? Females are extremely valuable on Fiori. The death rate in childbirth is around fifty percent. And Fiore are dependent on each other to live. No one stands alone here—not even God."

My Lord realized the Fiore in the box were looking at them. It made no sense for him to be arguing with his messenger, even if they couldn't understand what he was saying. And then there was Tevach, who *could* understand. . . . Better not talk to Aharon at all.

With the statues in place, Argeh rose and voiced a long prayer over them, exhorting Mahava's mercy on even the most loathsome and worthless parts of His creation. Then he left the box, going down to the arena where they were swearing in fifty new members of the priesthood. It was a coveted position on Fiori. They didn't break their backs cultivating the soil, didn't starve. Only the most fervent applicants made it through the winnowing process. Even My Lord, who, after thirty years, still appreciated the sight of the Fiore but little, was moved by the group's fierce bearing. For the crowd the new priests stripped to the waist and beat themselves with scourges as they chanted in a low guttural that sounded like one continuous growl.

This was mild stuff compared to what was coming. My Lord snuck a look at Aharon to see how he was handling it. The Jew was staring down at his hands, his chest shaking. At first My Lord thought, disgusted, that it was tears, but then he realized it was the strain of being upright, even in the chair. My Lord wondered how long Handalman could hold out and when it might be expedient to have Tevach get him out of here. A heavenly being that slumped to the ground would not impress anyone.

My Lord beckoned to Tevach and the little mouse crept up. My Lord whispered instructions in his ear and Tevach took a seat behind Aharon, used his strong paws on Aharon's shoulders to pin him back in his seat, take off some of the strain. Aharon shot My Lord a grateful glance, then returned his gaze to his hands.

The new priests assisted in the interminable service that followed—prayers of humiliation and the standard exhortations against sin, especially against the houses of ill repute, disobedience to one's superiors or the church, and the eating of one's own children. The crowd sat through it impatiently, waiting for the "good part": the bloodletting.

The arena had been set up days ahead. The devices they called *hechkih* were already in place—large X-shaped structures with pyramid bases that functioned as places to mount bodies for torture and exposure and, eventually, served as roasting stakes as well. In anticipation of the latter their bases had been painted black with a flammable pitch. Now the prisoners were led in, stripped of all but undergarments, faces miserable and petrified. They cowered like the terrified animals that they were . . . all except a group of males who looked around at the crowd defiantly.

Argeh had returned to the box. He gave My Lord a suspiciously smug look before addressing the crowd.

"The Holy Book says that we must be ever diligent in our battle against corruption! We are born corrupt, and unless we redeem ourselves through the necessary toil we die corrupt! We must ruthlessly seek out corruption and excise it from our society. If we do otherwise, the Holy Book tells us that we will sink down into the filth for all eternity!"

My Lord wanted the Jew to hear this. If he heard, he might understand where they truly were—why any lie was justified. He motioned to Tevach and instructed him to whisper a translation of the speech into Handalman's ear. Tevach seemed distracted. He had a desperate look as he gazed into his master's eyes, and My Lord was reminded of the episode this morning—something about one of the heretics. He shook his head in a strong negative to tell Tevach this was not the time, to do as he was told.

"All of the prisoners here today have violated the sanctity of Mahava!" Argeh spit onto the ground, showing his disgust. "They have disobeyed His teachers and His holy pronouncements. Instead of striving to raise themselves up, they have fouled themselves further, and in the process they have fouled us and Fiori. . . ."

My Lord looked at Aharon, who was shaking again. His face was red with the effort of holding himself upright, even with Tevach's help. But his eyelids flickered as Tevach's words registered. My Lord turned his gaze back to the arena, satisfied.

Let him chew on Argeh's mentality for a while. Let him choke on it.

The group of prisoners My Lord had noticed earlier began wrestling with their guards. They had no hope of escape, of course, shackled as they were, but they succeeded in making a scene. The male in charge of the group raised his bound hands in a gesture of command.

"I demand to speak! I ask to be heard!"

My Lord waited for Argeh, with a motion, to order the guards to pull him back in line. Instead, Argeh hesitated, his head cocked thoughtfully to one side.

"I am so moved to let you speak," Argeh said, and he sat down.

Stunned silence. Around the arena, the crowd was absolutely quiet. The high priest? Allow a prisoner to speak? My Lord gripped the arms of his chair, knowing that something was terribly wrong. He recalled the challenging look Argeh had given him earlier. *About me—somehow, this is about me.*

My Lord half stood, but he could not think of an excuse to interrupt. And then the heretic was speaking in a loud and fiery voice.

"My beloved clansmen! I die today because I dared teach a message that differs from the one we have been forced to accept for so long! I dared to ask why we punish one another? Why do we engage in spectacles of terror like this one? Why do we inflict injury on our fellows and ourselves? Can Mahava really want that of us? Our priests tell us that, yes, Mahava wants to grind us into the dirt! But I say no. I say we should ease one another's suffering, not add to it! I say we should work together to scratch our bread from the rock. I say there is room in Mahava for kindness—even for us, even for the Fiore!"

The world shifted beneath My Lord's feet. He was shocked to his soul. He had seen a few Fiore, like Tevach, relax the typical Fiorian temperament in private, but he had never heard one speak so radically and publicly against the norm. He looked at Argeh, marveling that the high priest would let such words be spoken aloud, and in the Festival arena! If there was one heresy Argeh pursued with special venom, it was this one. But Argeh was looking down at the heretic with a shuttered expression. Unfathomable.

"But, my fellow," Argeh said with sickly formality, "how can you believe that we are wrong in our judgment of heavenly will when we have, on our own throne, an envoy from Mahava Himself? Would you deny that *My Lord* knows the ways of our Maker?"

My Lord gripped the arms of his chair. There it was. The knife.

"I do deny it!" the brazen Fiore yelled. "Look at him, all of you! On our throne sits a . . . a creature who claims he is from the heavens! But if he is divine, where is the proof? What good has he done the Fiore since coming here? What good does he do us now? Surely if Mahava sat among us our harvests would succeed; our bellies would not be gnawed with hunger; our women and children would not die in blood and filth."

My Lord rose shakily to his feet. Even the pain in his knees was nothing. "You dare speak to your Lord that way?" he growled, pointing his long, straight arm and pale, hairless hand at the prisoner.

"I do dare it! I say: You do not love us! You do not care for us! And you keep us chained to this evil priest! The pair of you keep us bound to misery and death in the name of Mahava!"

"*Silence!*" Argeh roared. The heretic had gone too far. Argeh motioned to the guards.

My Lord, panicked and sweating, watched the guards beat the Fiore to the ground with their staves. In the crowd there were those, perhaps as many as fifty scattered throughout, who stood and raised an open palm in a gesture of solidarity, hissing their disapproval. Argeh made a quick, angry motion, and the hand raisers ditched from the arena as the guards headed their way.

Argeh looked over his shoulder, his lips curled. "Your orders for the prisoner, My Lord?"

My Lord hesitated. It was not his role to hand down judgments. Argeh had never asked him before. But he knew he had no choice. The entire arena watched.

He made the sign for slaughter across his breast.

The crowd rumbled like an earthquake, though whether in approval or disapproval it was difficult to tell. Then the staffs began to pound in agreement, low, building.

"Kill the heretic!" came the cry.

My Lord quivered with relief, a tidal rush that told him he'd been more terrified than he'd known. He had escaped Argeh's treachery—for now. Thank god one could always count on Fiorian bloodlust at least.

"No!" Aharon called out.

My Lord turned in surprise. Tevach was glaring at him from behind Aharon. The cagey rat had translated the entire thing! He motioned Tevach angrily to get away. For the first time, he felt rage at his servant—could have whipped him had he the weapon at hand.

"Yosef, no," Aharon pleaded, his eyes wet.

My Lord motioned him to desist, looked back toward the crowd, seething. Argeh was watching the three of them with infinite calculation. Worse and worse.

"The sentence?" My Lord prompted the high priest.

Argeh licked his lips in a gesture of faux submission. He turned back to the crowd. "The heretic shall be executed on the last day of Festival!"

My Lord fell back into his chair as his knees gave out. His joints screamed; his heart thudded miserably in his chest. He studied the faces in the crowd. How well known was this heretic? Could he be the source of the sentiment against him, the seed of the vandalism? He must have Decher do a full investigation as soon as possible.

The heretic and his men were led away. One by one the remaining prisoners were charged, led to the *hechkih*, and mounted upon them. There were still interminable hours to go, and My Lord was already exhausted. But one mercy: all eyes in the crowd would be on the bloodletting from now on.

What had possessed him to have Tevach translate for Aharon . . . *in public*? What had he been thinking?

He knew: He had wanted Aharon to understand. He'd wanted the Jew's approbation, and that had made him unwise then, furious with himself now. He was walking a razor's edge on this planet, where the least breeze could be his ruin. He knew, right then, that Aharon would be that breeze. He'd brought with him too much of the past. And the past could not be reconciled with the king of Gehenna.

My Lord motioned Tevach to take the slumping Jew to the carriage.

*   *   *

Aharon fell into a feverish sleep the minute they put him in bed. He was depleted from the nightmarish festival, from the strain of trying to control his body. He had dreams involving bestial Fiore ripping him apart.

When he awoke someone was shaking him. It felt quite late, a sensation that had more to do with the reddened, puffy eyes of Tevach—whose paw was doing the shaking—than the black outside his window. Kobinski was waiting. He was dressed in a simple undyed gown that might have been his bed clothes.

Tevach helped Kobinski into a chair and left the two of them alone. The torch burned sputteringly in its holder on the table, that old familiar torch. It flickered against the old man's lined face when he removed his mask. It was a face that was deeply pained by its very structure, but the expression itself was slack, void of emotion.

He opened his lips, almost spoke, didn't. Aharon could sense that Kobinski was in a very different mood from any he'd shown before. He waited.

"I am as much a prisoner here as you, Aharon. You think I have power; I don't."

Aharon sighed inside. He felt instinctually that he should say nothing; it was that angel pressing its fingers to his lips, *Shhhh*. He didn't say, for example, *That's what the capos said*. He could see, even as Kobinski spoke those words, the guilt in his eyes.

"Argeh uses me to make the populace afraid, like an intimidating dog chained to his side."

Aharon again said nothing, though Kobinski waited for him to speak.

The massive man put his legs out in front of him, trying to straighten his knees, grinding his teeth at the pain.

"Come sit on the bed," Aharon said. "You can stretch your legs."

"I'm fine."

"Come!" Aharon used an irresistible tone that had been his mother's specialty. It was a large bed, and though hard and scratchy from the dried-grass stuffing, it still offered welcome support in the heavy atmosphere. Aharon forced his aching muscles to rally and pushed himself to one side to make more room.

Kobinski shook his head, rubbed at his knees, but a moment later pulled himself upright. He managed to get onto the bed, his legs stretched out, his back propped against the wall. He shivered. Aharon tried to give him his blanket; Kobinski refused.

"The cold is not in the room." Kobinski turned his head, and for a moment Aharon saw the demons that tortured his soul. Then Kobinski turned his gaze to look up at the ceiling, as if the contact had revealed too much.

"I did . . . try. At first. When I first came. I tried to make things better for the Fiore. But . . ." He sought for words. "This place gets inside you. It beats you down. How can you change an entire culture? A way of life, a history, a people, a world? And I had come from Auschwitz, where things were not much better. After a while, you just plod forward, surviving day to day. I was broken when I came here."

He paused. Aharon, feeling that finger on his lips, said nothing. Kobinski was confessing. Aharon did not know why, but he knew enough not to interrupt.

"I could *not* openly defy their Scripture. If I had spoken against their religious views I would have been gone, like that." He wiggled his fingers in lieu of the harder task of snapping them. "I did try to improve some things—agriculture, technology. My education was not so useful. What good is calculus in a world struggling with addition and subtraction? Or chemistry in a place where there are no labs, no manufacturing, no microscopes? But I did try.

"It's this planet, Aharon. Every machine breaks—it's as simple as that. Only the most basic and hardiest devices survive. The soil is rocky and barren, unresponsive to either irrigation or fertilization. The seas are largely uninhabited. Medicine is barbaric and deadlocked in religious superstition." He paused again. "It beats you down. It just beats you down."

He raised a hand, rubbed at his trembling lips.

When it didn't seem like he would continue on his own, Aharon said gently, "Also, maybe, you'd given up before you ever came here, *nu*? You already were not the man you were when you wrote *The Book of Torment*."

Kobinski didn't reply.

"Maybe that's *why* you came here. You had given up hope."

Kobinski gave a bitter laugh. "I hated; that's why I came here. I *wanted* to take us both to Hell, so that night, wrestling with Wallick, I let it fill me. Hate is a form of restriction, too."

Aharon studied Kobinski's face, eyes narrowed in thought. This afternoon, *he* had hated. He'd hated Kobinski for his participation in these atrocities, hated it that a Jew—one of the chosen and particularly one as "chosen" as Yosef Kobinski—could do such things. And how could he when he had *written* . . . when he was the author of this incredible work Aharon was reading? It seemed a double blasphemy.

But now Aharon felt . . . compassion. He had no idea where it had come from. It was such a large compassion, he couldn't even take credit for it. It was as if someone were opening his heart and filling it up.

"What happened to the Nazi? This Wallick?"

Kobinski drew in a breath. His chest rose and fell; again his lips formed words that wanted to come out but were held back at the last moment. Finally he released them. "I told the Fiore he was from *Charvah*, the devil. He . . . he's dead."

"I understand," Aharon said. And he did. He remembered Yad Vashem, remembered the feeling of utter desolation and emptiness he had felt here, in this room, when all of his old ideas had been burnt to the ground.

Kobinski rubbed at his lip, his face trembling with emotion. "He raped my son, Aharon. For thirty nights, he made me watch. Then he killed him in front of me."

A deep groundswell of sympathy and pain rose up between them. Aharon muttered meaningless words, watched the old man fight for control of his emotions, watched as his face went stony again. Seeing the emotion was hard, but seeing that harshness, that disassociation, was worse. Aharon reached out his fingers and touched Kobinski's arm as if by touch he could keep the kabbalist with him.

Kobinski shook like a leaf under the touch. His face did relax a little.

Who am I? Aharon wondered. *Because I, Aharon Handalman, have never been this generous in my life.*

Kobinski wiped his nose. "I don't know why it should, but it's bothered me what he said—the heretic. I couldn't sleep. Because he's right, you know. I don't love the Fiore. I never did."

"The Fiore are hard to love," Aharon agreed.

"Most of them repulse me. But what repulses me more is that this place even exists. *God* repulses me."

Aharon bridled at such a statement, tried to find a way to turn toward something positive. "I've been reading *The Book of Torment*. There's so much wisdom there, Yosef. Perhaps you, too, should look at it again."

"It's pointless, don't you see?"

"Why? You don't think there are places better than this? You don't think good exists?"

"Oh, it exists. But what does that mean to the Fiore? What did it mean for my son? No amount of good can possibly justify the evil."

Aharon sighed. His heart was heavy with the responsibility, the desire, to say the right thing. He thought of the old stories, of how the Israelites, when they conquered an enemy, would kill every living thing, women and children included, burn houses and fields and livestock, leave nothing standing. That was what God had done to Aharon—laid him waste. And Aharon understood it had been the only way that anything truly new could ever take root in his heart. He mourned for Kobinski, who had suffered a similar decimation but who had never found that new seed. His heart had remained barren all these years.

"What the heretic said today, about helping one another—is this sentiment common among the Fiore?" Aharon asked.

"Oh, no."

"And his soul: If I understand your book, when he dies he'll go back toward the middle of the ladder. Is that correct?"

Kobinski latched on to this. "Yes. So you see, death is hardly a punishment for him."

"But what if he needs more time to develop his thoughts? Or to teach others? What if he could help other Fiore, Yosef?"

Kobinski flushed, but he spoke bitterly. "That might happen. And it also might happen that if he had more time here he *would* grow disillusioned in this hellish place. Or he would gain power and become corrupt. This place has a way of twisting everything to a bad end. Don't allow yourself to be fooled by sentiment. This heretic is no messiah, no martyr. He's only a Fiore with a modicum of common sense and perhaps some leadership skills, nothing more."

"*Nu?* Maybe that's all that's required."

"Required for what?"

Aharon sighed. For a long moment he meditated on the question. His arm was strong enough now to reach up and stroke his beard—how his hand had missed that beard! "You know what I felt when he spoke? *Hope.* Just that someone—anyone—could speak of love and charity *here.*"

Kobinski didn't answer, but Aharon could feel his will hardening. He had said the wrong thing, maybe; he was losing him. He knew the issues were not simple. It was not, god forbid he admit this, black-and-white. He changed the subject. "And what will happen to *you*, Yosef? When you die?"

That, too, was the wrong thing to say. Kobinski struggled to sit upright. Aharon put a hand on his arm, but this time the older man shook it off. He shoved his legs off the bed and sat on the edge, breathing hard from the effort.

"I'm sorry," Aharon said. "I cannot imagine what you went through with your son. And who am I to make excuses for God? But that's the point. It doesn't matter whether I—or you—excuse Him or not. It seems to me that in this battle—in this battle you cannot win. You can kick and scream and flail all you want to, but you might as well rage at a storm, *nu? You cannot win.*"

Kobinski got off the bed, placing his weight on his feet with great pain. "The Midrash says God weeps when He loses the heart of one of His beloved. That would have been enough for me, Aharon, to have made Him weep. But the awful thing is, I'm not even sure of that anymore."

17

> ... that has been for me the mystery of Sunday, and it is also the mystery of the world. When I see the horrible back, I am sure the noble face is but a mask. When I see the face but for an instant, I know the back is only a jest. Bad is so bad that we cannot but think good an accident; good is so good that we feel certain that evil could be explained.
>
> —G. K. Chesterton, *The Man Who Was Thursday*, 1908

17.1. Forty-Sixty Calder Farris

Pol got into the office early again, but again, Gyde was there. He was always there; his face was always there when you turned around. But that face was so guileless that surely it was paranoia to think this was anything but the light-footedness of an old warrior.

This morning Gyde was absorbed in a thick case file when Pol entered the room. He put it in his desk drawer—not hastily but immediately. Pol stood at the coatrack, taking his time, hearing Gyde lock the drawer. It could be anything, that file, personnel records on some monitor that had caught Gyde's eye, anything at all.

"Don't get too comfortable," Gyde said pleasantly. "We have a lead—a citizen's report. Some Bronze thinks his neighbor might be the terrorist."

"You want to go now?"

"You have a better idea, classmate?"

On the thirty-minute drive to the Bronze 2 suburb, Pol asked, "What did the report say? Does this neighbor have an ax to grind?"

That glint of steel sparkled in Gyde's eyes. Only Gyde could look pleased with himself and deadly at the same time. "The report mentioned illegal books. I've been thinking—these lunatic ideas our friend writes about had to come from somewhere, and it wasn't from *The Lives of Our Noble Forefathers*."

Pol nodded. That was smart. "Does this suspect work in construction?"

"No. He's an entry-level clerk for the Department of Transportation."

Pol didn't think that sounded promising. He didn't voice this opinion.

"Can I ask you something?" Gyde said, glancing at him as he drove.

"Yes."

"You've been acting a little strange about this case. Not interested?"

Pol smiled coldly. "I *am* interested. I'm very interested."

"Good. You should be. You've got to want merits more than you let on."

Pol looked out the window. If an air-raid siren went off—as they had a tendency to do two or three times a day—he and Gyde would have to abandon the car and find shelter. Pol always thought about that when they had to drive across town, checking the buildings as they went past for structural soundness as though evaluating life insurance policies.

"You haven't mated yet," Gyde said. "After this case you'll have enough merits to qualify. You have to be excited about that."

Pol turned his blue-white eyes to Gyde. It seemed like every day something came out of Gyde's mouth that Pol had never told him. How did he know Pol 137 had never mated?

"Have *you* ever mated?" Pol asked, turning the conversation around.

Gyde hesitated, an odd look on his face. "I have a son."

"A son?"

"They tell you after the birth—if it's healthy or not, if it's been accepted into the class, and its sex. My son is a Silver."

"Congratulations."

Gyde's lined face shone with pleasure. "It's a great thing to do for the state. You'd be proud if it happened to you."

Pol shrugged. He couldn't see what difference it made, knowing that you had a child out there.

"And mating a Silver female," Gyde said in a low rumble. "It's nothing like the Iron whores at the rec hall. Nothing at all."

Silver females were beautiful, it was true. They were plastered on billboards all over the city, just like the males. In their tight battle uniforms they were perfection: cool, marble white, strong, athletic, remote—unobtainable. Pol had learned from the gossip among Marcus's slaves that Silver females were notorious lesbians. The state did not allow them male lovers, not until they were assigned to mate, not even the male equivalents of the sterilized Iron whores the male Silvers were granted.

Pol had no interest in the Iron whores. He had no interest in female Silvers, for that matter. He had bigger problems.

Gyde let out a long sigh. "The Silver I had . . . she was like milk. Like a river of warm milk."

"What happened to her?"

"After the mating I heard she was transferred to the Gefferdon Zone."

For a moment neither commented.

"I saw my son once," Gyde said quietly.

"I thought that wasn't allowed."

Gyde glanced in the rearview mirror, as if to confirm no one was there. "I saw him on the parade grounds three years ago. I knew he'd be about fifteen and I just happened to pass this class of fifteen-year-olds. There was one boy, I swear to the gods he looked exactly like me except for his hair—that was his mother's."

There was an uncharacteristic tension in his voice. Pol turned his face to the window and smiled. It pleased him, seeing a crack in the tough old grindstone. It made him feel more secure somehow. He tried to think of a way to continue it.

"What about you?" he asked. "You've already mated. You're in the highest Silver class, and you're close to retirement. Why are *you* still chasing merits?"

In the distance, air-raid sirens went off. They both fell silent, peering out the window as Gyde let the car roll to a stop. But the tall speakers on either side of the street remained silent. The bombers were not coming this way. Gyde accelerated.

"Have you ever seen the retirement communities for Silvers?" Gyde asked lightly.

Pol hesitated. What was the right answer here? "No."

"Me, neither. In fact, I don't know anyone who has."

"They're down by the Southlands, aren't they?"

"Supposed to be." Gyde looked intently at the road for a moment, both hands on the wheel, as if challenged by conditions. But the traffic was light, the roads clear of ice. "I thought I would have heard more about it, since it's only six months away for me. But I haven't."

"You probably will."

"Yes. I probably will."

For once, Pol knew what to expect. The Bronze 2 suburb was not unlike the one Marcus had lived in, except that he'd had more servants than any of these people would ever have. Marcus had made a lot of money on the black market, but that didn't change his rank, didn't earn him permission to live in bigger or better housing, so his place had been crammed with things and slaves.

The homes were small units, single-bedroom many of them, each abutting onto the next. The front lawns, sporting raggedy snow, were no more than eight feet square. In the streets a few Bronze children played. Unlike the Silvers, Bronzies were allowed to marry. There was some genetic preapproval, but nothing like the scrutiny that went on while mating the upper classes. Once married, a Bronze still had to get a permit for breeding, and generally they received only one such permit in a lifetime.

The children in the street were unremarkable—flat, ruddy faces, black hair. They stopped playing ball to watch the car drive past. There were whispers as they tried to peer inside. Pol could see the words on their lips. *Silvers!* Eager. Then, frightened: *Monitors!*

Within seconds, the children had disappeared.

Pol and Gyde found the address. According to their suspect's file he lived alone and should be at work this time of day. No one answered their knock. They let themselves in with their monitor keys.

Inside, they split up. Pol searched the kitchen while Gyde moved off down the hall. Within minutes Gyde called his name. Pol found him in a small bedroom. Gyde had turned over a narrow mattress and was peering down at a hidden stash with disgust, as though looking at a nest of spiders.

"Illegal books," he said, poking at them. "*Secrets of the State, The Truth about the Races, Questioning Family Law* . . . This Bronze slag is done for."

"I don't see any sign that he's our terrorist."

"Keep looking. If he's not our terrorist he *could* be, reading this scarp."

Pol had no problem being thorough. In fact, he hunted obsessively. He pored over the details of the kitchen, opening every can and looking in every container for signs of black paint, an address, a name, anything. He was hoping he *would* find something—the slightest clue that this guy was who they were looking for or, better yet . . . yes, better yet, a hint that he was not their terrorist but that he *knew* him—was part of some kind of clandestine society of deviants. And Pol would slip this hint—this name, this address, this secret password—into a pocket and not show it to Gyde.

Pol finished the kitchen and was examining the cleaning products under the bathroom sink when he heard the front door open and, a second later, a gunshot. He unholstered his piece, his senses on hyperalert, and ran into the living room. Gyde stood over a prone body, weapon relaxed in his hand. The corpse was that of a Bronze: thin, ruddy-skinned, and prematurely balding. He wore the orange uniform of a clerk. A dark pool was spreading like water on the floor. Pol stared at the blood. He had one of those weird shifts. It was too black, wasn't it? Didn't it spread too fast? He'd seen *lots* of blood when he'd decapitated the Silver, but that had been at night and he'd other things to worry about. Now he remembered—even in the dark, the blood from the neck ran out like wine. . . .

"What's the matter with you?" Gyde asked him, putting away his gun. "Never seen a dead body before? What kind of a warrior are you?"

"What happened?"

"What happened? He walked in."

Pol's tongue played against the back of his teeth. *Don't ask. Don't ask questions like "Are you supposed to just shoot them like that?"* Instead he lit a smoke and passed one to Gyde. "You're sure it was him? The Bronze who lived here?"

"He used a key, didn't he? Besides, I saw a photo in his file this morning. It's him."

"We could have questioned him."

"What for? He didn't do it. You didn't find anything, did you?"

"No."

Gyde's green eyes snapped defensively. "He had illegal books. I'll get ten merits for taking him off the roll."

"Yes. Well done."

Pol took a few more drags, waiting for the weed to calm Gyde. It did. Gyde finished and dropped his smoke in the blood, where it hissed out. He walked back toward the bedroom.

"I'll get the contraband," Pol offered. "Why don't you radio the morgue? It's your kill."

Gyde's eyes narrowed at him, and for a moment Pol thought he saw suspicion in them. But then Gyde grinned in that disarming way of his and winked. He went out to the car, stepping carefully over the body.

*　　　*　　　*

Pol sat in his bathroom at the dorm paging through *The Truth about the Races*. He had once taken the mirror off the wall in here to be sure he wasn't being watched. He found he somehow knew about bugging devices and how to search for them, though he wasn't sure how or where he'd been trained for it. In any event, he'd found nothing. But in the process he had made a hole behind the mirror where he could store a few things—his makeup, hair dye, razors . . . and now the book.

The author discussed at length the physical characteristics of the Gold, Silver, Bronze, and Iron races. Pol didn't find himself in any of them, nothing about a fair-skinned, dark-haired, blue-eyed, round-eyed, eyebrowed, bearded visage. Was the book missing races in other parts of the world, in other states? What about the enemy state, Mesatona? But the book was poorly written, and he couldn't find any definition of its scope. Like everything else in this world, the book painted a picture that was irredeemably polemic, and, to him, it read like a badly imagined lie.

There had to be other races. He couldn't be that much of a freak.

Everyone knew the Irons were damaged genetically and often produced monstrosities, the author wrote. But what was kept hidden by the state was the fact that monstrosities were also born to Silvers and Golds due to overbreeding for certain traits, like the bluest temples. That was why the state instituted the policy of merits. To rise from a Bronze to a Silver or from a Silver to a Gold was a task beyond the reach of most citizens, but when a citizen *did* advance upward by merit the higher race benefited from the fresh blood of one of the best examples of the lower classes.

You could advance from Bronze to Silver or Silver to Gold? Pol reread the paragraph carefully. How could he not have known that? No wonder everyone was so driven to earn merits. It was one of the basic assumptions underlying everything in this society that he had completely missed. He got up, splashed cold water on his face, and stared into the mirror.

He had seen his blue-white eyes scream with rage, as when he had killed the Silver. He had seen them confused and wary, as when he first came to live with Marcus. More recently they had been determined and grim, hard eyes. Now they looked frightened and unsure. Weak. They were weak. The vulnerability shook him deeply.

The genetic inferiority of the Iron race, according to the book, was due to a great calamity that happened at least two thousand years ago. The state had secret evidence of a prior civilization. This earlier culture had invented a weapon of mass destruction, a bomb that could destroy entire cities at one blast and poison the air for centuries. There had been a Great War with these bombs. The richest members of society and the big brass of the military had survived in bunkers underground. The rest of the population had been left outdoors to fend for themselves. Thus were the Gold, Silver, and Iron races born; thus the propensity for deformity among the Irons, their genetic chain contaminated forever by the bombs. The origins of the red-skinned Bronze race, so the author claimed, had been a native people dwelling in this land before the war began. This continent was one of the places least devastated by the war, so the survivors had settled here. Beyond the Southlands the rest of the planet remained uninhabitable. And in that vast desert were monuments that might indicate that this Great War was not even the first of its kind, that the warlike people of this planet might go through this cycle again and again.

Pol could almost see it in the glass like a moving picture. He had heard this story before, hadn't he? Hadn't there been the threat of a war like that where he'd come from? And there was the feeling he always had, too, another of those places where the seams did not meet, that they were missing . . . *things* here, that their technology was behind where it should be, that he was always reaching for devices that didn't exist—such as the small phone he kept imagining to be in his pocket when in reality there were only large ones, like the one on Gyde's desk.

Staring into his own ice-blue eyes in the glass, he was suddenly quite sure that he'd come from a place where these bombs, these weapons of mass destruction, existed. In fact, he felt he had been involved with them in some fundamental way. And he had no idea what to do with that.

He had planned to hide the book behind the mirror. He changed his mind. He tore the pages into small fragments and flushed them down the toilet; then he burned the cover in the sink. He watched as the black ash swirled, carried by the water down the drain.

17.2. SEVENTY-THIRTY JILL TALCOTT

The math code printouts were tucked away in a silver soft pack they'd found at the spaceport. Nate had it on his back, and the oversize bug goggles hung

from the front of his jeans. The metal capsules from the supply room were being bounced in one hand pensively.

He looked like a prop person for a sci-fi film, especially with the blank, silent
buildings filing past as they walked back from the spaceport in the descent of
the smaller sun. Jill had had the prop person thought, anyway—fleetingly. But
her brain was churning from their momentous discovery, and what Nate looked
like, or even an acknowledgment of their surroundings, had a hard time keeping a foothold there.

"Seventy-thirty," she said. "I still . . . I don't know."

"It's not *that* unbelievable. We know we were completely bounced out of
our own space and time. Why not to a whole other universe?"

"But what does it *mean*, to be in a seventy-thirty universe?"

"I have a guess. In our experiments we saw that the crest in the wave cor-
related to a positive force and the trough to a negative one—which you could
call 'good' and 'evil.' If life on Earth is a balance of good and evil—fifty-fifty—
that means *this* planet, and probably the entire universe we're in, seventy percent good or creative impulse and thirty percent evil or destructive impulse."

"It's still hard for me to accept that Earth is fifty percent 'evil,' " Jill debated,
with an impatient shake of her head. "That's certainly not my experience of it.
And will you quit playing with those things? They could be dangerous."

Nate grinned sheepishly and put the metal capsules back in his pocket.
"Why? Things decay and die, don't they? Who is it that said, 'What's not busy
being born is busy dying'?"

"Nixon."

Nate gave a huffing laugh. "Anyway, all you have to do is look at our history. Most of it's been a bloodbath, including the twentieth century. What
about Hitler? Nagasaki? Vietnam? The Khmer Rouge? Bosnia? And it's not
just man—it's nature, too. 'Nature red in tooth and claw'? By all accounts the
dinosaurs had a pretty vicious existence before they were wiped out permanently. In fact, *most* species become extinct."

"That's true, but . . ."

"I know; I know. Our life *seems* cush. But we have a warped perspective.
We happen to live—ha! we *lived*—in a particularly benign place and time on
Earth. But even so, even though modern Americans aren't being overrun by
Huns or living in fear of plague or the Inquisition, are most people living a life
of ease? Hardly. We invent more and more 'stuff' and gadgets and mindless
entertainment, yet everyone *I* know is stressed. People have to put their kids
through sixteen years of expensive education and continue to reeducate themselves as adults. We have to maintain our cars and houses and all our 'stuff,' get
groceries, feed the kids, pay the bills, worry about retirement, yadda, yadda,
yadda. Meanwhile there's the IRS, mental illness, heart disease, AIDS, cancer,

terrorist threats, stock market crashes, and school shoot-outs. Which explains why so many guys drop dead in their fifties from heart attacks. So even we Americans can't escape the law of fifty-fifty."

Jill looked at him in disbelief. "Where do you get this stuff? You're a carefree student."

Nate waggled his eyebrows. "I have six older siblings, remember?"

"Well, *my* life isn't that complicated—*wasn't* that complicated. Back on Earth, I mean. You can make the decision *not* to have life be that complicated."

"Yeah, you can be single and not have kids. But what are you giving up on the flip side? Because I think that's the point. No matter what choices we make to try to make life easy for ourselves, there's always something negative or some *challenge* on the new path. You can't escape it. *That's* the law of good and evil."

Jill grimaced, face set stubbornly. "I don't agree. There is no disadvantage to being childless for me."

"Sure there is. It's just that you, as an individual, don't put much value on the positive aspects of having kids. Nor are you particularly worried about the negative aspects of *not* having kids. But let's look at the issue from a completely dispassionate point of view."

Jill shrugged.

"Okay. So having kids—here's on the good side: nurturing, mentoring, love, having a family around you, passing on your genes—"

Jill snorted. "A: they're not that great as genes go. B: there are too many people on the planet already."

"Fine. That's your opinion. We're just listing pros and cons, remember? On the negative side of having kids there's the loss of personal time and space, the financial burden, the limitations on lifestyle, the 'exasperation factor' of dealing with a child all the time—"

"Exactly."

"So you, personally, are more afraid of the negative stuff than you value the positive stuff. But for someone who gets off on being nurturing or really can't imagine life without a big family, it might be the other way around. But *objectively*, having kids is equal amounts reward and shit factor. In fact, I would say that, as with anything, the bigger the rewards, the bigger the shit factor. That's how fifty-fifty land works. And *not* having kids is equally good and bad. It's just a different set of gotchas."

Jill folded her arms defensively as she walked. "What's negative about not having kids?"

"You don't get all the *good* stuff about having kids for starters, all the nurturing, family stuff. Plus, don't you want someone to take care of you when you're old?"

"If I can't take care of myself, I'd rather not hang around, frankly."

"Really?" Nate gave her an appraising look. "Okay, what about this: I remember my mother talking about my great-aunt. She was a ripe old bitch and Mom said it was because she'd never had kids, never learned how to have patience or put someone other than herself first. Without love in her life she just sort of hardened up. Emotions are like a muscle—use 'em or lose 'em. Kids definitely make you use 'em."

Jill shrugged indifferently, but a knot of pain flared in her chest. He had aimed that barb at her personally, and it was pretty damn cruel.

For a moment she said nothing. Then, because she didn't want him to know how much he'd hurt her, she asked, "I assume this theory of yours has other examples?"

He shrugged, jiggling those capsules around in his hand. "Of course. *Everything* is fifty-fifty. Take flying, for example. Airplanes introduced a fast way to travel to just about anywhere on Earth. That's an amazing benefit compared to what our ancestors had. But it's never that simply good, huh-uh. Now we have all of the great cities, like in Europe, and all the most beautiful islands, like Greece, so packed with tourists that you can't even enjoy them anymore. People hijack planes and use them as weapons or target them with missiles. And the airport scene has gotten increasingly intolerable. There's also the little fact that although planes crash very rarely, when they do, your chances of survival are nil. In fact, that's kind of an interesting point. It's almost like *because* planes crash infrequently when they do it has to be catastrophic, as if the badness of the bad, when it happens, has to be *so* bad that it still balances out all the good."

"But planes are incredibly convenient!"

"Of course. So we invent stuff like that, trying to make life convenient. But there's always stuff that comes with it that we don't like, because nothing can be purely good."

"But how can you deny that life on Earth is a whole lot better now than it was in the Middle Ages? If everything stays fifty-fifty, by law, how would anything ever progress?"

Nate considered it. "But it progresses *because* it's fifty-fifty, because we always try to make things better, but we never actually get there. I mean, that's how evolution works, right? I do see your point, though. Things may be better for us, *overall*, than they were for our cave-dwelling ancestors. It may be that things gradually improve over time, even if it's still fifty-fifty. You know, more like the entire graph shifts upward in tiny increments."

Jill gave an appreciative *hmmm*. It wasn't all that far from Darwin's theory, actually. Species did, overall, improve, but things rarely ever stabilized. There were always new challenges to be overcome, new ways for the species to try to adapt.

"Even so," Nate continued, "nothing comes without a cost. Is life really that much better in the twentieth century than it was in the fourteenth? Yeah, we have modern technology. But with it came the bomb, car and plane crashes, computer hackers, global warming, and TV zombification. What are we missing emotionally now that we no longer live close to the land, raise our own food, or live in extended communities? Modern society may be superior in some ways, but it's highly isolating and remote, from other people, even from our own planet. Nothing comes without a price. That's fifty-fifty."

Despite herself, Jill had to smile at his *cojones*. "Give me a break! You're as much of a TV zombie as anyone, and you wouldn't know how to raise a potato to save your life."

Nate spread out his hand. "Naturally. I'm a product of my culture. So give me another example."

"What about modern medicine?"

Nate didn't even have to think about it. "Uh-huh. Modern medicine is cool, 'specially if you're the one having the heart attack. But overuse of antibiotics has led to immune microbes, blood transfusions give AIDS, our health care system is in crisis, we have a zillion old people hanging on now, like, *forever*, eating up their kids' resource and the government's, and medical technology has allowed us to engineer nifty new plagues like anthrax. . . . I mean, don't you find it incredibly *elegant*? No matter what we do, no matter what we invent to make life easier, there's bound to be a catch in there somewhere. That is so incredibly cool. Scary as hell, but cool."

Jill was taking it as a personal challenge now. She wracked her brain. "Mother Teresa? Gandhi?"

"For every one of them there's a Ted Bundy?" He shook his head, eyes narrowing. "No. Check that. I have a better answer. I was raised Greek Orthodox, right? So look at Jesus Christ. During his lifetime he taught pacifism, equality, charity . . . Yet the religion created in his name caused some of the bloodiest, most ignorant centuries ever. And even Gandhi—a lot of the Pakistani–Indian hostility came out of that whole period."

"Hmmm."

Nate spun to walk backward, facing her. He had the energetic bounce of a twelve-year-old, even in this heat. "Anything else? Come on. You've got more."

Jill threw up her hands. "Nope. You're too smart for me, Socrates."

"Come on!"

"Huh-uh. I'm done."

"Please? Please, please, please?" he wheedled, making a pout face designed to bug the crap out of her.

It was good to see him come back to life again, even if there was a tinge of mania about it. She sighed. "Oh, all right. What about being a big celebrity? You're telling me that life as Nate Andros, physics student, is just as fifty-fifty as, say, being Keanu Reeves?"

Nate made a *psah* gesture. "Keanu Reeves? Are you kidding? Oh, sure, there's the money and the glamour and the chicks, but on the downside you can't go out in public without being mobbed, critics lambaste you, you have to keep in incredible shape and compete with about a thousand up-and-comers who are even more gorgeous than you are, you struggle with egomania, question your own identity, are terrified of growing old, and are pretty much stuck with dating actresses who are even vainer and more screwed up than you are! Jeez, that wasn't even hard."

Jill laughed. "Anyone ever tell you you're a pessimist?"

"Nah, I'm not a pessimist. I still hold out hope for you and me, don't I?"

He abruptly stopped walking backward and looked away after he'd said it, for which Jill was grateful. They walked in silence for a while. It was Jill who broke it, in a very neutral voice.

"It's a clever theory. But I'm not sure how you'd quantify it. And if you can't quantify it, it's not—"

"I know. It's not science. So shoot me." Nate bounced the metal capsules in his hand. "What I don't get is this place, though. At seventy percent good, why is this civilization dying? Shouldn't this be Paradise? It's not consistent."

Jill felt a spark of excitement. "It *is*, though. Remember the mice, what happened when we pushed the one pulse too far? How lethargic they got? It may *take* certain levels of . . . of challenge and stress to make life vital and interesting."

"Well, *I'm* dying of boredom, and I've only been here a few days." Nate yawned hugely and juggled the metal capsules in the air like fruit.

"Quit that!" Jill grabbed one of them and looked at it. It was shaped like an aspirin except it was more slender, and tiny holes perforated the metal in a grid design. "For all you know it's a bomb."

"I think it's something you swallow," Nate said, bringing it up to his face.

"Don't you dare!"

But Nate only sniffed it. "Doesn't smell like anything."

"Those holes remind me of a telephone mouthpiece or a speaker." Jill turned it over in her fingers.

"Really?" Nate held it up to his ears to listen. Then he began to scream.

"Nate, what is it? Nate!"

He was screaming and jerking around, bent over at the waist, head tilted to one side, fingers scrabbling at his ear.

"Oh my god, I knew those things were dangerous! Nate, talk to me!"

"It flew in my fucking *ear*," he screamed.

"Let me see!"

"No!"

He was trying to push a finger into his ear canal, as if he could dig it out.

"Nate, *let me see!*"

He finally stopped his panicked dance, but he remained bent over at the waist, his wounded ear tilted down, panting hard.

Jill put her hand on his arm. "Let me look."

"I don't want to move my head," he said through gritted teeth.

"Does it hurt?"

He was reluctant to say. "No."

"No? What's it feel like?"

He shook his head, gingerly at first, then harder. He remained bent over. "I can't feel it now, but I felt it go in."

"Well, let me see!"

"If I move my head it will just go in more!"

Jill rolled her eyes. "So you're going to hold your head like that for the rest of your life?"

With great reluctance Nate straightened up, an inch at a time, pausing to wait for sensation. When he was almost upright, Jill moved in, placing one hand on his jaw and the other on his hair near his ear.

"I don't see anything."

"Um, that's because it's *in my ear*." He put his fingers at the base of his ear, pressing carefully. "I can't feel it. But, Jill, it's in my *head*. That can't be a good thing."

She didn't know what to say. She couldn't say "we'll get it out" because she had no idea how and there wasn't exactly an emergency room down the street. In fact, she was as alarmed as Nate.

"Let's get back to the main artery and we can find an apartment with power and rest. Okay? Can you make it?" She put her hand on his arm for support.

He didn't answer, but he started walking, cautiously, like an old man. He kept moving his jaw, trying to feel the capsule.

"You're only working it in deeper," she commented.

He stopped doing it.

Nate's arm was over Jill's shoulder and hers was around his waist, helping him along. He didn't seem to be suffering from any specific complaint, could no longer feel the thing in his ear. She realized this, recognized that their contact was completely unnecessary, and held on to him anyway.

It was nice to have an excuse to touch him, to allow herself to be close to him without worrying about what he might think. She liked the way it felt as they walked together, how they fit. She liked that he winced every once in a while so that they could maintain the farce. And she was scared enough about what had actually happened to him to make her reluctant to let go. The fingers of her left hand felt the muscles of his waist working as he walked. His arm over her shoulder was warm and heavy, even in this light gravity.

She was so distracted by these unusual sensations that it took her a while to realize that something was bothering her ears. It had started out as white noise, but they had to be approaching the source, because it grew louder. It sounded like high-pitched feedback, squeaking and squawking.

"What is that?" She grimaced. "It sounds like the feedback from an amplifier or—"

Nate stopped, abruptly. No, not just stopped, he jerked back, detaching them. She turned to look at his face. It had gone pale as milk.

"Nate? What is it? Are you in pain?" She could only think of the thing in his ear, praying to god it wasn't burrowing into his brain or doing something equally gruesome.

"Nate, answer me!"

He shushed her. He was listening, and she realized it was the sound he was responding to. She listened, too. It occurred to her that the squeaking and squawking could only be alien speech. It was being broadcast from someplace nearby. That might have been interesting, if she weren't so worried about Nate falling dead at her feet any second now.

"What do you hear?" he asked her, with emotion held deliberately at bay.

"Um . . . a high-pitched noise. Almost like radio feedback. I was thinking it might be alien speech."

"Oh my god." His forehead went smooth as his brow pulled back in amazement.

"What?"

But with a jolt, she knew what he was going to say. *Knew.* Her heart turned over, then began to race. She waited for him to tell her. He walked forward slowly, like a man in a dream. A smile started first in his dark eyes, then spread to his lips. He titled his head back and crowed.

"Nate?" she asked, smiling herself. "Nate? Is it—"

He grabbed her arms, pulling her close. "My god, Jill! I'm *hearing English.*"

The source of the voice was a metal sheet on a post stuck at the side of the street. It was blank until they approached; then the sheet turned transparent, revealing alien text on a screen.

Jill watched Nate with a mixture of excitement and disbelief. It was difficult to accept he was actually hearing anything other than what she was hearing—that god-awful racket. But if he was acting, it was a helluva performance. He stood at the post, an expression of happy confusion on his face, like someone trying to place a familiar tune.

"What's it saying, Nate?"

"Um. 'Remember your duty, citizens. Report to the fertility clinic today.' "

"What?"

" 'This is not an optional activity. Your identification will be recorded.

Penalties will be enacted on any citizen . . . um . . . not recording sufficient time at the clinic, per Standard 10-39714—something something something. . . .' Then it starts over."

Jill was skeptical. "Fertility clinic? Are you sure?"

"That's what it says."

"And you're *really* hearing it in English?"

"*Yes!*" He gave her a goofy smile. "That thing in my ear—it's a translator!"

She bit her lip, nodded. "Yeah, I got that much. What does it *sound* like though?"

He listened, as if sorting it out. "Like, uh, a very high, weird voice, except I'm actually hearing it form words in English. I mean, it's funky, because it's definitely not a human voice, but I can understand it."

"And your ear doesn't hurt?"

"No." But he didn't look thrilled to be reminded that he had a foreign body in his head. His brow cleared. "What amazing luck."

He touched the metal sheet, and the alien characters shifted. Then his face closed up—she could see it, going from ecstatic to thoughtful to grim. Jill thought he was feeling the magnitude of what had just happened. She felt it, too.

"This changes everything, Nate." Jill began to pace excitedly. "It'll be easy to make contact with the aliens now. *Damn.* As for their technology—I wonder if we can find a computer that will talk to us? Can you imagine? If we can get it to read aloud, we could understand everything! And even barring *that*, after we make contact the aliens could—"

"Jill," Nate said quietly. "That won't be necessary."

She stopped pacing. "Why not?"

"Because I'm *seeing English as well*." His voice was numb.

"What?"

Nate reached out a tentative finger and pressed the screen. The screen changed again to a diagram. He laughed in a strangled voice and backed away from the monitor.

"Nate?"

He was laughing and crying at the same time, could hardly get the words out. "I p-pressed a button labeled . . . 'directions' and g-got a street grid. Our current position—" He doubled over with laughter, his face red. "Our current position is . . . marked: 'You are here.' Oh my god! 'You are here'!"

"Nate, calm down."

Jill didn't—couldn't—believe him. He had to be mistaken. And he was getting hysterical, and it was really scaring her.

She had the metal capsule she'd grabbed from Nate in her pocket and she'd known, from the moment when it had become clear what was going on, what she would do. Without a thought, she brought it out now and looked at it. His eyes widened.

"Jill, no!"

She didn't even have to put the capsule in. As soon as her hand got close to her ear, the capsule slipped through her fingers and into her ear canal as if it were a living thing. It startled her, making her gasp. Her hands clenched at the very unpleasant sensation of the capsule traveling deeper, burrowing. It was all she could do not to scream. Then the movement stopped and she was left with a full, stuffed-up feeling in her ear that gradually began to fade.

Nate was watching her, wide-eyed. "Why did you do that? We have no idea if these things are safe or not, Jill. God*damn* it!"

She gave him a defiant glare and held up a hand. She strained to listen.

At first nothing changed; then she was hearing English. It was weird, like a switch being thrown, as if her brain always *had* been hearing English and she just hadn't recognized it as such. Nate was right, the voice had a high tone, but the words were unmistakable. She felt a rush of joy and terror at it—how simple it was, how cleanly it worked. Now *that* was technology.

"Remember your duty, citizens. Report to the fertility clinic today."

"It works!" She had a hard time keeping her legs under her. She grabbed his shoulder for support and stepped closer to the monitor. Nate pointed to the screen. At first she just saw the incomprehensible alien characters, but from one blink to the next she was seeing English. It was as abrupt and integral as the speech had been, and no matter how her eyes strained, she couldn't see anything *but* English now. Unbelievable. Whatever that capsule was, it was altering the very sensory perceptions of her brain.

Nate pressed a button that was labeled: DIRECTIONS and a map came up. The fertility clinic was a few blocks away, marked in green. And there was a red dot labeled: YOU ARE HERE showing their current position.

"Do you see it?" Nate asked.

Jill nodded dumbly.

Nate barked a laugh. "Explain that, Jill. *Explain that.* This is like some sick freaking *joke*."

"Nate—"

"Isn't it? I mean, what—are we dead after all?"

"We're not dead."

"But this place is like a dreamworld! Everything we say, everything we want, and *snap*, it just happens. I feel like a rat in a maze! I mean this whole empty world, this feeling of being watched . . ." He backed away from the machine, scanning the buildings on either side of them, looking for Alien Funt again or perhaps Joseph Mengele.

Jill tried to remain calm, but her equilibrium was thrown off, too. She remembered how she had asked the computer at the spaceport to locate her equation, the universal wave equation, and based on no more information than that it had printed it out. And the blank emptiness of the City, almost like . . . what had she thought that first day? A movie set.

She shook her head angrily. "No. Why would someone go to the trouble of running us through a maze? This City doesn't exist for our sake, Nate; I mean, it's pretty damn vain for us to think so. 'Any technology sufficiently advanced will seem like magic,' remember?"

"I know that. And I can handle the audio translation and even, though god knows how they do it, the *writing*. But 'You are here'? I mean, is this an alien planet or a shopping mall?"

She swallowed a lump in her throat. "Well . . . 'You are here', means pretty much what it says, doesn't it? Maybe it's just a coincidence."

"Why not 'This is your present location' or something? That's a pretty big coincidence!"

Jill did find it freaky, but she would never admit it. "Well . . . any good translator program uses colloquialisms. Right? So it must be familiar with that particular colloquialism, that's all. We don't have the technology to do this kind of thing, but that doesn't mean it isn't possible."

Her words seemed to be having some effect on Nate. He stopped trying to find hidden cameras in windows and sank down against a wall in a squat, head in his hands. "So why does this place give me such a creepy feeling?" He shuddered.

"You're just not used to it." Jill squatted down next to him.

They were quiet for a minute, but even in English, the alien voice was annoyingly distracting. She thought at the metal plate, telling it to shut up, and was relieved when it paid absolutely no attention to her.

"It really *is* all too easy, Jill. We needed food and water—we found them. What are the odds that the food the aliens eat would be suitable for us? Shelter has been no problem at all. I mean, there just happen to be hundreds of abandoned apartments in this City, unlocked, unguarded in any way."

"Nate—"

"Then there are the aliens, right? Could be dangerous. Could be very dangerous. But not only haven't they threatened us; they *can't see us at all*. Or the spaceport—the power came on when we went in, including all the equipment in the control room. It didn't have to. It clearly isn't being used anymore. You ask the computer for a Hammurabi math code and presto! it gives you one. But even that's not enough." His voice was rising again. "*The same day*, I find a translator in the supply room *and* decide to hang on to it, *and* I hold it to my ear like an idiot. Presto, chango, I can hear alien speech! Then you say—"

"I get your point."

"No, then *you* say maybe we can get the computers to talk to us and *blink*,

I can read the alien script. We now have access to everything, Jill—*absolutely fucking everything.*"

"I know."

"I mean— You've heard of 'too good to be true'? There's never been anything as 'too good to be true' as this. This is the paradigm, the quintessential, the Platonic ideal of 'too good to be true'!"

Jill didn't know what to say. Despite her brave words her stomach was in knots. She was a scientist; she didn't believe in coincidences or fate. And she didn't like it when life looked rigged any more than Nate did.

They both sat there for a moment. Then Jill reached over and gave his arm a big pinch.

"Hey!"

"Feels real to me." She sighed. "We *have* been lucky. But if you're suggesting that someone is watching our every move and pressing buttons . . . I can't buy that any more than I bought it when Christians back on Earth claimed God was doing it."

Nate frowned as a thought crossed his mind. "Haven't we had this conversation before?"

Jill could see he was on to something. She waited. After a moment, his face cleared; his eyes widened. "I know what it is. *Dang!*"

"What?"

He shifted to face her, face avid. "Jill—we're on a seventy-thirty planet!"

She studied him, eyes narrowed. "Go on."

"We were talking about how this place should be a paradise. Well, obviously it's not, but what it *might* be . . ." He took a shaky breath. "What it *might* be is *easy*. Is that possible? That things go the way you'd wish them to *per law of nature*? That there's a much shorter gap between wanting something and having it? That the constant struggle we take as a fundamental part of reality on Earth just doesn't exist here? Maybe it feels so spooky to us because we fifty-fifty folk are used to having to work our butts off for every little thing and here a quarter of the effort gives twice the return. Could that be it?"

Sometimes he amazed her. He had a theoretical instinct that humbled her, though she didn't completely trust it. She preferred plodding, methodical work to brainstorms, but as brainstorms went, his were class A hurricanes.

"If our theory about the one-minus-one wave is correct," she said slowly, "a change in it *would* affect just about everything. The fundamental way things work."

"Remember that conversation we had months ago, about how the crests in the one-minus-one didn't necessarily *manufacture* good things, but it might cause a right-place-at-the-right-time kind of phenomenon? You know, up your random chances of a particular good thing coming to pass? So maybe these translators *weren't* invented for us by some alien maze master. Maybe they were used in the alien's space program way back when. But the luck—*our* luck—was that we found them sooner rather than later or perhaps never at all. We might have spent a lifetime on this planet and never discovered them."

"They're certainly small enough. But, Nate, does it really matter why we've been lucky? The point is, *we can read.* You were right before—now we have access to absolutely everything. All of the alien technology!"

"That's not even the best part," Nate countered, grinning. "The best part is: *we can get home.*"

Jill paused in her elation like a car hitting a bump in the road. "Really? How's that?"

Nate's eyes were dancing. "Don't you see? Because this planet is lucky! Because all we have to do is really want something and we'll get it! And I want— Do you hear me, planet?" he shouted. *"I want to go home!"*

Jill felt a sudden antagonism at his words. Her mind answered back, *I don't.*

But that wasn't true, was it? That wasn't exactly what she felt. She was going back to Earth at some point, obviously, and she was going to be the next Einstein. She just wasn't ready to go home *yet.* There was far too much work to be done right here. How could Nate not see that? What kind of scientist walked away from an opportunity like this one?

Besides, they were in another *universe.* Just because they wanted to go home didn't mean there was a chance in hell of getting there.

"Remember, Nate," she said carefully, "even if this is a seventy-thirty world, that's still not one hundred percent, right? Not *everything* that happens is good, and, as you say, we've been pretty lucky so far."

"Are you saying there's a kickback coming?"

He said it teasingly, but Jill didn't find it funny at all. She shivered.

"Are you cold?" He put his arm around her.

She stood up abruptly and brushed off her pants. "Why don't we get back to the main artery? All this sunlight is deceptive. We have to make ourselves rest, Nate. We can't afford to get overexhausted."

"Right." He slowly got to his feet. The excitement on his face dimmed, responding to the reappearance of "strategic Jill." She felt a perverse relief.

That was what happened when she let down her guard and allowed herself to touch him, as she had while they were walking. It made him think he had the right to have his hands all over her all the time. Talk about dangerous. *Someone* had to retain control here.

"You sure you're all right?" Nate asked.

"I'm great," she said briskly. "Couldn't be better. After all, you said it yourself, Nate: we're in Paradise."

17.3. Sixty-Forty Denton Wyle

Denton Wyle was lost in Paradise and he was in big, big, *big* trouble. His back was up against the rough, scratched-up bark of one of the bloody trees at the mouth of the horseshoe gorge, his hands were tied behind him, and his mouth was gagged. There were four Sapphians with him in a similar predicament. Their captors had mounted them there early this morning and had taken off again without so much as a thank-you or a parting gift of Valium.

Denton wished very much that he had some good drugs or that he'd fought harder with his captors and been knocked unconscious. Unconsciousness from a head injury would be great about now. But . . . no. He was completely awake and fully conscious and apparently was going to be for every long, stinking minute of this.

He worked against his bonds. The tree was fat and his arms were forced around the back—back there where they could do nothing to shield his nice soft belly and throat. The vine around his wrists was supertight, and he couldn't even try to rub the vine against the bark, because he couldn't move that way. His feet were untied, but there was nothing in front of him to kick and bracing them against the trunk and trying to push himself off only killed his arms. He still tried, crying with frustration and pain, until he could try no more.

The *skalkits*, whatever they were, still did not come. After giving up on escape, Denton had plenty of time to relish his fear, for the terror to have its way with him. You would think that you couldn't sustain that level of fear for very long, but yeah, you could. It didn't help that all he had to look at was the other Sapphians. They were visual echoes of his own doom. Their eyes rolled and streamed and their thin bodies trembled. He thought one of the females had wet herself. He wondered briefly what they'd done to be sent here, but he couldn't spare much head room for them because he was too consumed with his own tragic loss.

Except that across from him was a young female who had been one of his morning visitors, an unusually shy, skittish type. She pleaded at him with huge brown eyes. As if *he* could do a freaking thing. As if it weren't her stupid society's fault in the first place.

He could have made his peace with all that free time, but all he could think about was how bad it was going to be, how much it was going to hurt, how terrified he was, how he hated this, how unfair it all was, how he would give everything to be far away, how he couldn't believe this could really be happening to him, Denton Wyle. He cried for himself, great bunny tears. It was so unfair for a nice, white, twenty-first-century guy like him to be treated like this. It just was not right. And the worst thing was, he wouldn't even get a decent funeral in LA with all his friends to mourn him. No one would ever know what had become of him; that was the worst part.

No, screw that. The worst part was going to be the pain.

And just when he was convinced it was never going to happen, it did. He heard them coming through the trees.

Denton thought he'd already been as scared as humanly possible. He'd been wrong. The sound in the trees caused his body to shoot sharp, cold stabs of panicked blood through his veins. His veins ached with the force of it, like getting a tetanus shot. He would have screamed except that he had no breath: his entire respiratory system had gone on strike.

What was coming through the trees was *large*. And eager, too; you could tell. The things, the *skalkits*, were crunching through the brush at an amazing speed. Whatever they were, they had to be enormous to slice through the jungle like that. Denton could hear things cracking and breaking that sounded like tree trunks, not just branches. Those things were freaking bulldozers.

Louder and louder.

He still hadn't breathed, and he could feel his eyes bulging out of their sockets as they stared at the brush. His vision was going red. His entire body strained against his bonds in a completely automatic flight reaction, and he hadn't even seen them yet.

Then two of the things entered the clearing.

His first thought as he saw the *skalkits* was: *Holy freaking cow*. They looked every bit as bad as his most paranoid conjurations. His last shred of hope that this would all turn out to be less of a big deal than it seemed choked and died.

The *skalkits* were slightly bigger than hippos or rhinos. Their skin was gray and leathery, hairless and wrinkled. Their massive limbs were muscled and they moved fast. They had large heads with beady little eyes and huge mouths of sharp, protruding teeth. Two lower mandibles curved upward, resembling tusks, and the rest of the teeth were chaotically arrayed. Their front limbs ended in three massively clawed toes.

Some button marked PREDATOR in the deepest recesses of his reptilian brain was being pushed, hard. Denton finally found his breath and screamed behind the gag. He screamed like a woman. He screamed like a little girl.

The *skalkits* stopped at the edge of the clearing, sniffing the air. One of them raised up on its hind legs, its front claws held a few feet off the ground, nostrils huffing, tongue darting out as if tasting their scent.

There was no doubt that that thing was looking right at him—at him, Denton Wyle. There was something in its eyes, something about as murderous as Denton had ever imagined an animal could look. It was like the look of his old dog, Lucky, when Denton would hold her favorite ball in the air in the backyard and move it around teasingly before throwing it. The *skalkit* was looking at him with the same intensity with which Lucky looked at that ball.

No, like Lucky *would* have looked at that ball had Lucky been a ravenous man-eater instead of an easygoing canine and if the ball had been a blood-engorged hunk of meat. Or a bunny perhaps.

Denton fought his bonds like a wild man. And now that he thought about it, screaming wasn't such a great idea—it was drawing their attention to him—but that didn't mean he could stop. What was coming out of his mouth was completely beyond his control and sounded like one long, "Waaaaaaaaaaaaaaa!"

The other *skalkit*, the one that was not staring at him, approached one of the male Sapphians. Its body was crouched low, almost in a stalking maneuver, but its stealth was a mockery in this case, since its prey not only could see it but also was completely immobile. The *skalkit*'s eyes glittered with anticipation. It seemed to Denton to widen its mouth, to be grinning at its victim.

It stopped close to the male, sniffing him. The Sapphian struggled, looking pathetically vulnerable. The *skalkit* made a single easy swipe with a foreclaw and opened a nice long scratch across the male's chest. It wasn't deep, but it was the first blood of the day and the *skalkits* got very excited about it. The one that had been focused on Denton earlier was now riveted by the blood and let loose a piece of drool that could have filled a bathtub.

"Waaaaaaaa!" Denton screamed.

"Waaaaaaaa!" the Sapphians screamed.

And then, before Denton's eyes, the *skalkit* tilted its head, almost delicately, placed its open jaws on either side of the Sapphian's rib cage, and . . .

Denton stopped screaming. He closed his eyes, trying desperately to pretend that none of this was happening. He couldn't stop up his ears, though, and the sound . . . There was the sound of bone crunching, the high, mortal scream of the Sapphian, ending in a gurgle and bubbling air, a tugging, tearing sound that was indescribable, and then the only sound in the clearing was that of the *skalkits*' chewing.

Denton was sick. He was going to pass out. The blood drained to his feet. His body was covered in sweat, his head swimming. Bile rose and burned at the back of his throat, acidic and sour. His head slumped forward, unable to hold itself up. He saw red stars on his eyelids.

Through ears that were ringing and muffled with cotton he could hear the *skalkits* finishing off the Sapphian. He could hear the ripping of flesh and bark, the *crunch, crunch* of powerful jaws breaking bone. There were no more screams, not from anyone.

Denton cried. The tears were silent and gushing and probably the first real tears he had ever cried in his life. His chin dug into his chest as his head hung. And he knew, with a blackness that was absolute, that he was about to die. It was as if all of his terror had been reduced, like broth being boiled down on a stove, to this: utter weakness, misery, self-pity, despair.

And then he felt something. Something was tugging at his wrists. He moaned, sure for one instant that it was a *skalkit*, but when he opened his eyes he could see both of them snuffling the ground, picking up stray bits of flesh from their first course.

And then he felt something cold. . . . Someone was cutting the vine around his wrists with a knife!

Denton's head cleared instantly. With a renewal of hope, every iota of cowardice and flight instinct in his personality—and Denton had lots—came rushing back. He thrashed, trying to pull apart the weakened vines, but a cool hand on his forearm bid him to stop. It was hard, but it occurred to him that he might get free sooner if he helped the person behind the tree, so he held still.

He waited. What was *taking* them so freaking long? The vine at his wrists was tugged, pulled excruciatingly tight, mashed, and mangled and still he was not free.

He watched the *skalkits*, praying silently at them not to turn his way before he was free. The tree their first victim had been on was wet with blood, as was the ground all around and beneath the tree. If only he had seen this clearing in full daylight, Denton thought, he never would have gone into the gorge. If only he had arrived a few hours earlier, he wouldn't be in this predicament at all.

The ground was pretty much picked clean of any remaining bits of matter, and the *skalkit* who had been watching him earlier lifted its head and looked right at him, its eyes greedy. The other one perked up and strode casually to the next tree, not even pretending stealth this time. The female on the tree tried to kick. But the *skalkit* caught her leg easily in its jaws and tugged, lightly at first, then hard, with a whip of its head. The female's leg came off at the hip joint. Blood sprayed.

Denton gave a yelp and pulled as hard as he could at his wrists. The vines snapped. He would have been gone then, instantly, but the *skalkit* with the greedy eyes was fixated on him, head alert. If he ran, that thing would be on him in two seconds flat.

"Help," he squeaked behind his gag.

There was no answer from behind the tree.

The *skalkit* with the leg dropped what was left of it and went for leg number two. The female on the tree was . . . Well, it was far too real and far too gruesome and Denton couldn't look. He stared at the other *skalkit*, praying for it to look away, even for a second! But it licked its lips and started moving toward Denton, crouched low, coming in for the kill.

Denton reached up his free hand and ripped out his gag. "Help!" he screamed.

There was a whistle, shrill and yodeling.

It was Eyanna. Denton saw her across the clearing, at the edge of the jungle. She uttered a yodeling call, waving her arms. Denton could see, he could *see*, that she was terrified—her eyes were sick with death—but she stood her ground. She yelled and hollered at the *skalkits*, some native chanting thing, jumped up and down.

Denton watched, mouth hanging open. The *skalkits* watched, mouths hanging open. Then they turned, like a maddened pack of paparazzi, drawn by the irresistible bait. Eyanna ran into the jungle. The *skalkits* thundered after her.

Denton watched them go and felt a stab of horror and pity. Poor, dumb girl. She didn't stand a snowball's chance. He was dumbfounded that she would do this for him, had no idea why. He was so struck by pity, in fact, that it took him a moment to realize this was his own personal lotto ticket. His hands were free. The *skalkits* were gone.

There was a brief moment where he thought, *I ought to help the others,* but it was a momentary aberration. He ran.

Denton ran for a long time. He headed away from the gorge and away from where the *skalkits* had chased Eyanna. It was jungle, just rough jungle, and it was hard going, but still he ran. He crashed and tripped and fell a lot, but he always got up again. At first there were noises in the distance: roaring. He didn't hear any more screams, though in truth he tried pretty hard *not* to hear any. And after a while there were no sounds at all.

When he couldn't run anymore he walked. And finally he reached the big river. It was the same river he'd been following when he'd first come to this world. In the distance to his left he could see the enormous waterfall from the top of which he'd seen smoke in the horseshoe gorge. To his right was the purple hint of mountains.

At the river he felt safe because if any *skalkit* came, the two he had met or their relatives, he could go into the river and let himself be carried downstream in the current. That was not without its own problems, since he was a mediocre swimmer, but in comparison to *skalkits* it sounded fine.

His legs gave out and he fell to the riverbank. He began to shake. Bits and snatches of the whole horrible morning came back to him. And the one thing he could not stop seeing, over and over, was not the *skalkit* putting its jaws around the male Sapphian's rib cage or even the detachment of the female's leg. What he could not get out of his mind was the image of himself . . . running.

I left her to die.

It was a very ugly thing, and if he'd been feeling more himself, he might never have let it into his head. But once there, it was tenacious. He felt bad about it. Eyanna had risked her life to save his. Even knowing what the *skalkits* were, even *knowing*, she had come to help him. And in return he had checked her off as dead meat the moment he was free and had run away.

"There's nothing I could have done," he said aloud. "And anyway, it's not like I really know her." And a few minutes later: "Eyanna's fast. She might have gotten away."

And the girl? The one he had made love to? The one who had been tied to the tree just opposite his? How fast could she run tied to that tree? What were her chances?

He lay down on the cool moss. His thoughts were insupportable, so he slept. When he opened his eyes again it was twilight. The stars were dimly visible against a magenta sky. The world around him was empurpled.

He sat up. He hadn't moved an inch from where he'd fallen and his body was stiff and aching. He stood up, stretched, and went over to the river to get himself a drink. He heard a soft noise behind him and whipped around, heart in his throat.

It was Eyanna. She was dirty and exhausted and had some minor scratches but was otherwise unharmed. She plopped down on the moss.

"Eyanna! Sweetie! How did you get away from the *skalkits*?"

"Ran. Hid." Eyanna's face was exhausted, expressionless.

"Well . . . um, I am happy you are okay. You are . . . You are very brave. Thank you." The words ought to have turned his tongue to salt.

She didn't acknowledge his words. Her back straightened determinedly. It was a strange gesture and signaled a change about her, a new solidity and strength. She was no longer the girl who skulked in the trees.

It pushed him away without a word and made him feel his smallness.

17.4. THIRTY-SEVENTY AHARON HANDALMAN

Aharon had enjoyed several quiet days of study with *The Book of Torment*. Well—*enjoyed* was maybe too strong a word. The spiritual work was hard, and the tension in the House of Divine Ordinance was like caged electricity. He sensed that things were occurring beyond his ken, wheels within wheels. He longed to speak with Kobinski, but since the night when he'd laid out his heart the kabbalist had not come again. The last day of Festival was the day after tomorrow and the heretic would be killed. Aharon himself felt like a condemned man, waiting for the powers on this planet to notice him again, to sweep them up in their current. And like a condemned man, he tried to make his peace with God.

He could see the beauty in the system the manuscript laid out: the *sephirot*, the ladder, the idea of balance. It had an intuitive right-feeling about it, and that in itself was disturbing. It was so completely different from his old beliefs, from the black-and-white world of the yeshiva. And although those old beliefs had been torn away from him, the memory still lingered of what it had felt like when they were inviolable. Their inviolability had always been the highest principle in and of itself, had it not? Because once you let things slide a little, then where would it stop?

Now he saw that kind of thinking for what it was: a way to keep his mind closed and frozen. But it was still a struggle to let it go. Such a double-edged sword! He decided to put the matter into God's hands. The manuscript outlined exercises—prayers and meditations—for balancing your *sephirot*. Aharon was willing to admit, at the very least, that he could stand a little more compassion. So he tried the exercises for *chesed*, asking God to fill him with mercy, to fill up his heart.

He remembered the feeling he'd had that night, talking to Kobinski, when his heart had opened up and something greater than himself was pouring compassion through him. He wanted that feeling again. He prayed for *chesed* and he thought of Hannah. He thought of all the times he had been cold and hard because she'd failed his image of what a good Orthodox wife should be. Now it was not these things he remembered, not the times when she'd been obedient or silent. What he remembered was Hannah laughing goofily, like a girl, Hannah smart-cracking or stubborn, even that, yes, sexy rebellious pout, like a Jewish Greta Garbo. In expecting an ideal from her he had missed the opportunity to enjoy what she actually was—a crime and a shame, for both of them.

In response to these thoughts, he felt the blood stir in his chest, the almost physical swelling of his heart. *Fill me with love,* he asked, and he was filled. He had ignored his heart for a long time, he knew, because the tremors of love and compassion were like the quickening of the dead. But miraculously—and he knew a miracle when he saw one—his heart was not so shriveled that it could not rise again.

He heard the door, soft, quiet sounds, and when he opened his eyes Tevach stood by his chair. Aharon had made himself get out of bed for the past two days, fighting his way to the chair and back. His muscles were stiff and painful, but walking was easier.

"Tevach," he said, genuinely glad to see him. "And how is Ko— How is My Lord?"

"He talks to no one." The Fiore's nose twitched like a rodent's. He seemed to push himself to speak. "I came—I came to see the new Scriptures. I wished you would be sleeping."

Aharon wasn't sure he cared for the word *Scriptures*, but he had the manuscript on his lap, and he offered it to Tevach. Tevach gazed down at it in his hands with awe.

"I read a little. The night you came, when My Lord slept."

Aharon was surprised Tevach would admit it, and more surprised that he was able to read Hebrew as well as speak it.

"*He* does not care for the Scripture." Tevach spit on the floor.

"Tevach, My Lord *wrote* it."

Tevach looked confused. "He . . ."

"Long ago."

Tevach gazed at the manuscript with new bewilderment. "I did not understand what I read."

Aharon made a *nu* gesture. "It's not easy. I have a hard time myself."

"Would you teach me?" Tevach cowered, as if expecting to be punished for making such an outrageous request, but his eyes had a mind of their own. They gazed into Aharon's openly.

He felt the answer in his heart. "I'll try to teach you, yes. If you wish."

Tevach looked tremendously pleased. He glanced nervously toward the door. "Would you . . . Would you also please . . . yes? . . . to speak to another Fiore about it? Very important. I could take you tonight."

This was something else entirely. Aharon knew at once that it was a treacherous idea—to leave his room? To speak with other Fiore about something Argeh would consider heresy? And yet the answer was in his heart just as clearly and immediately as the previous answer had been.

"Yes, Tevach. I believe that I would."

Tevach returned long after darkness had fallen. Aharon had spent the time in meditation, struggling with waves of uncertainty and fear. But he felt no better by the time Tevach arrived. The Fiore was carrying one of Kobinski's cloaks and a golden mask.

"This is an old mask he won't miss," Tevach said in response to the look on Aharon's face. "My Lord sleeps now."

"But, Tevach—"

"Fiore can see us in halls." Tevach thrust the disguise at him. "Wear this."

Aharon reluctantly took the things. He'd pictured a short distance to the carriage with almost everyone asleep. Now he was not so sure. But Tevach didn't give him time to change his mind. He helped Aharon into the robe and mask, as he must have helped Kobinski a thousand times; then his hand was around Aharon's waist, supporting him out into the hall.

The guards Kobinski had posted at his door paid no attention to them. They made a show of not looking at Aharon, contemplating the ceiling, the walls, scratching their chins, picking their teeth. It would have been funny if Aharon were not so afraid. He wondered if Kobinski knew how influential his little servant was. They moved through the halls with Aharon's arm slung over Tevach's shoulder, his legs struggling to keep up. They saw no one as they left the House, a blessing for which Aharon gave thanks; then they were out into the icy night.

A carriage was waiting. Inside, Aharon could not make out Tevach's face across from him in the dark. Again his courage failed him. He was suddenly afraid to be alone with this strange beast, defying Kobinski, his only human protector. He was afraid to be back out in the bloody streets, afraid of where he was going. He had agreed to *speak*, god have mercy. What would Argeh do to him if he was caught? Would he die in the arena on one of those black devices?

He closed his eyes and gripped the rough plank seat inside the rocking carriage. Where had that quiet, sure voice gone? He prayed again for *chesed, fill me with love,* but this time fear kept his heart curled tight as a fist.

They didn't travel far. When the carriage stopped they were outside a large building. Its dark stones and craggy lines sent his heart knocking. It was a terrible place; he could feel it—pure evil. Although it was very late, there were guards in front of the door.

"Tevach, what is this?"

"We go see Ahtdeh."

"Ahtdeh?"

"The one from the Festival—you remember. You said, 'No.'"

A terrible understanding filled Aharon. He blanched. "But . . . ! You didn't say . . . ! This is a *prison!*"

"No worry. My Lord comes here all the time."

"I can't!" Aharon shook his head, looking at the awful place. "No. I can't."

Tevach was quiet. The carriage sat in front of the building. The guards stood outside, glancing at them from time to time. They carried torches, and their faces seemed more bestial, more demonic, than any Fiorian faces Aharon had ever seen. He kept shaking his head. Finally he looked at Tevach. The Fiore was staring out the window at nothing, his eyes dry, his mouse-face perfectly defeated. It was a face used to defeat, and that only made Aharon feel guiltier.

But the heretic is going to die! Aharon wanted to shout. *Why should I teach him? It's useless!*

Had he doubted there was a God? Oh ho! And ah ha! He was there all right, and when He wanted to test you, to see if the "big changes" you claimed to be making were all talk or otherwise, He really knew how to stick it to you!

"Yes, Tevach," Aharon sighed. "Okay, yes, all right already, what are we waiting for?"

Tevach helped him from the carriage, led him up the steps of the prison supporting his weight, just as he supported My Lord's. Kobinski must come here often, because the guards didn't question him. They fell to the ground at the sight of the mask and stayed that way until the two of them were inside. Well. Good then. He might actually survive this night.

Inside, the place was lit by torches. The cramped stone corridors, low-ceilinged and filthy, were empty. There were only the sounds of moans and sobs, enough to curdle your blood. Tevach helped him down several flights of stairs and turned into an arched hall so low Aharon had to stoop. It was lined with cells. Aharon kept his eyes on the floor, knowing that he didn't want to see what was in them. The heretic's cell was at the end of the hall, fitted with a heavy door with a grilled window. This cell had guards, two of them, tough Fiorian priests. But the mask was fierce and confident, even if Aharon was not, and Tevach—thank god, who could have guessed the mouse had it in him?—spoke authoritatively and the guards let them inside without any fuss.

"I am clever," Tevach whispered gleefully in the darkened cell. "I told them My Lord wished to question the heretic about the vandalism to his images. Is that not clever?"

"Yes, Tevach," Aharon sighed. *Clever enough to get us killed.*

"Here is Ahtdeh."

As Aharon's eyes adjusted to the light in the cell, he could make out a shape lying in the corner. It looked like a heap of bloodstained rags, but when Tevach went to it and gently turned it over, his paws stroking, soothing low sounds coming from his throat, Aharon recognized the bundle as the Fiore from the arena. The way he looked, he should have been dead, but he was not dead. He responded to Tevach's urgings, gathering himself up slowly from the floor. When he saw Aharon, he stiffened, hate on his face.

Tevach growled and whined in that beast-tongue; then he came over and took the mask away. They looked at each other, Aharon and the heretic, man to man, yes, man to man. If you looked into the heretic's eyes, you knew, without any doubt, that he was a man.

The heretic motioned with his eyes to Tevach, and Aharon had the distinct feeling he had been accepted. He felt his heart stir again with that simple act of trust.

"Teach him the manuscript, Messenger," Tevach said. "I try to, but I understand little."

"How much time do we have?"

"Hours. Till almost morning. I will tell you."

Aharon nodded. He felt the burden of fear and anxiety slip from his shoulders, as if he were someplace safe, though nothing could be further from the truth. He saw clearly the risks these poor creatures were willing to take, and for what? For the truth. For love's sake—they still had faith in the idea of God's love. His heart was moved.

He didn't understand what was happening, why he was really here, or if anything he could do or say would make any difference. But as he began to speak, searching inside his own beginner's understanding for the right words, he knew that none of that mattered. He could only let compassion flow through him and let the consequences fall where they may.

*   *   *

They talked longer than they should have. The heretic was slow but thought deeply. His questions were often basic and sometimes hostile, but he had the true heart of a student. If only Aharon had had such a one among the boys at his yeshiva!

Tevach paced by the door and was literally whining by the time he got Aharon to leave the cell. The guards posted outside did not bother them, but Aharon could feel their eyes pinned to his back as he and Tevach crouched toward the stairs.

Before they had gone up one flight a Fiore was suddenly in front of them, looking at Aharon and bowing up and down from the waist. He spoke rapidly, gestured, and Aharon didn't need to understand the words to know he was being summoned. He froze; Tevach, too. Unfortunately, the wily schemer under his arm had been swallowed up again by the mouse. Aharon had no idea what to do.

"We must go downstairs," Tevach whispered.

"What? Why?"

"We must!"

Down they went. As they moved into the bowels of this vile place, Aharon got the feeling he was descending into a grave and would never climb out again. Every step he took away from the night—if it was even still night outside—away from the relative safety of the carriage was tightening a noose around his neck.

At the bottom of the stairs was a single short hall with a thick door and two guards. And also . . . Argeh. Tevach trembled, his eyes on the ground, useless. Aharon could smell his own stinking sweat. His heart—well, the only good thing that could be said about pain in his chest was that it was going to kill him before Argeh did. Small mercies. He had feared the worst and the worst had come to pass. He had left his room, he had to admit it, with every understanding of the danger. There was no one to blame but himself. The sages say, "He who takes the bread must pay the baker."

The high priest barked something at him, gave him weird sideways glances. Something was happening, but Aharon had no idea what. So he tried silence. Argeh barked again. Aharon gave an imperious gesture with his hand. Argeh gave him a look like he had completely lost his mind but stomped up the stairs, growling to himself.

The other Fiore bowed his head nearly to the floor and backed away also. The two guards followed. Then it was only Aharon and Tevach and that door.

*   *   *

The House of Cleansing was just beginning to stir when My Lord arrived at dawn. A carriage pulled away from the front steps as his carriage pulled up. My Lord frowned at it. Carriages were few and far between on Fiori—they were too expensive to maintain. Then he realized it must be Gehvis, going to fetch medicines. The message from the physician had been urgent and succinct: *He's dying. Come.*

Joints screaming, My Lord made his way into the prison. The pending death of Wallick seemed to have infected the whole place. The guards at the door groveled with even more fear and confusion than usual. Inside, Fiore scattered at his presence. Down the treacherous stony stairs he went, each level colder than the one before. And with every step he cursed Tevach, that ingrate. When My Lord needed him most the Fiore had disappeared, forcing him to rely on Decher. As competent as Decher was as a bodyguard, he made a miserable leaning post, always out of step, hesitant in his support of My Lord's weight.

Halfway down, My Lord ran into Argeh. The priest stiffened on the stairs with a look of puzzlement. My Lord snapped at him, not pleased to see him anywhere near Wallick's cell, especially now, "What is it, Argeh? Why are you here?"

Argeh gawked. Then the strangest look came into his face: a wondrous, dreadful, devious look. My Lord did not know what was going on and it frightened him. He pushed past Argeh abruptly. "My presence is required."

At the bottom of the stairs there were no attendants, no guards, outside Wallick's door. My Lord sighed his frustration. Upset after upset, as if it were not enough to have to deal with what was waiting for him in that room.

"I'll go in alone," he told Decher tersely, and pushed open the door.

Kobinski could smell the presence of death. The cell felt somber and oddly respectful. Wallick's rasping, uneven breath was like a broken machine turning its last few cycles. He had been left completely alone, but he was still alive. My Lord was greatly relieved. That look from Argeh—My Lord had half expected Wallick to be dead already.

My Lord crippled his way to the table and looked down at the devastated mass of tissue. The last time he was here, he'd caught a glimpse of the ruin that could come upon him if he allowed himself to see this situation in just a slightly different way, if he turned his mirror just a touch to the left or right and got another perspective on the two men, two enemies, facing each other over the years in this room. This time, standing here, the mirror was already tilted, and there was nothing he could do to turn it back. He could remember clearly what he'd felt like before, why he had done it, how it had been about justice, how he'd felt he was sacrificing himself for his son's justice. But that rationale now felt as flimsy as—he looked at Wallick—a man's life.

My Lord closed his eyes, willing forth the avenger. *Isaac,* he thought, willing forth his boy's face. But the face had faded a long time ago. All that was left was the hate that had wrapped around that name, and he saw that clearly, too.

"Ko-binski," Wallick said, his tongue small and hard in his mouth, the syllables distorted.

My Lord opened his eyes. Wallick, only one eye visible at all now, was looking up at him. That lone orb was bright and shiny, almost incandescent. He worked his reddened maw to form words out of some memory that it had once been a mouth.

". . . dying," Wallick managed, ". . . I know . . ."

The maw paused to swallow, to gum itself back to someplace capable of speech. *I know.* Know what? That he wasn't already dead and that this wasn't the afterlife? That this had been done to his living flesh? That the god that had judged him was none other than Yosef Kobinski?

"For-give me," Wallick gasped, "as I for-give . . . you."

My Lord bit his tongue, hard, to stop up the outraged tears that came to his eyes.

That single bright eye gazed up at him desperately, as if it could cling to him, force him to relent.

"For-give me . . ." Wallick tried again, "as I for-give . . ." This time, his speech was given a moment of clarity, just for an instant, the words coming out sharply defined. "You, Yosef . . ." Then the eye fixed itself in space and the light inside it faded.

My Lord looked at the face for a long time. Wallick's had once been a handsome face, an Aryan ideal, perfect but cruel. Now it was neither. The body was already stiffening into something objectified, the raw, bloody aspect of it organic and terrible, terrible and cold, like an animal struck and left at the side of the road, like the shanks of meat in the market square.

Surprisingly, My Lord felt no triumph, no satisfaction, no anger, no remorse. As Wallick turned cold, it was as though the spark of life inside him were cooling also; an era was dying, a reason to go on; an entire history as dense and smothering as a blanket was being pulled away. What was underneath it? Rot. Nothing. He felt empty as a husk, except perhaps for resentment at Wallick for dying, for escaping and leaving him alone to face the void.

Forgive me, Wallick had said.

"I can't, you son of a whore," My Lord said softly. "Because if I forgave you, how could I ever forgive myself?"

On his way up from the cell, Decher tucked under his arm, My Lord heard something. There was a murmur bouncing along the stone walls. On this floor, the screams and cries were uncharacteristically absent; only the murmuring voice could be heard.

My Lord paused on the stairs, his knees trembling with pain, his armpit soaking the shoulder of Decher's rough tunic. He was going to ask his servant what—or who—it was, but the look on Decher's face stopped him, so he just listened for a moment, and then he knew.

It was the heretic. Somewhere down that corridor he was being held for execution, and he was talking—perhaps to his followers, perhaps to his fellow prisoners, perhaps to himself—and the whole ward had stopped its sobbing long enough to listen to his words.

His voice, guttural but soothing, swept across the stones like water.

18

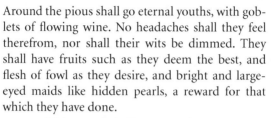

Around the pious shall go eternal youths, with gob-
lets of flowing wine. No headaches shall they feel
therefrom, nor shall their wits be dimmed. They
shall have fruits such as they deem the best, and
flesh of fowl as they desire, and bright and large-
eyed maids like hidden pearls, a reward for that
which they have done.

—Muhammad, *the Koran,* seventh century

18.1. Sixty-Forty Denton Wyle

Sitting on the riverbank under that purple-red twilight sky, Eyanna was so
beautiful and so fierce she looked like a goddess, something beyond human,
beyond Sapphian, beyond the laws of space and time. Denton just sat there
more or less drooling at her, hoping that she had a better opinion of him than
he had of himself at the moment and figuring that she must like him a lot to
have braved the *skalkits* on his behalf.

She brought something out of a pouch she wore under her skirt. It was
that photograph again. She did not try to foist it on him this time but sat with
her long legs propped up, the picture between them. She spoke slowly, as if
she had not spoken much in a very long time.

"I had a man also."

"What do you mean?"

"My man. He wanted only me and I wanted only him. The people didn't
understand that. They didn't understand why we would not go with others.
That is why they sent us to the *skalkits.*"

Denton didn't know what to say. He wasn't big on monogamy himself, but
it was hardly a reason to condemn two lovers to death, especially when one of
them was as beautiful as Eyanna. Then again, maybe that was the point. Her
monogamy must have really pissed the Sapphians off.

"I'm sorry the people did that to you, Eyanna."

"I helped you for her." Eyanna handed him the photograph.

"Oh."

If it was possible, Denton felt even smaller. There was no point in disabus-
ing her of the notion that the woman in the photo was his great love or that by
saving him she had done this woman a favor. And then he thought about how

weird life was. He'd given her that photograph thoughtlessly, on a whim. And if he hadn't, he would just have died a horrible, gruesome death.

He put the photograph back in his wallet. His hands were shaking so hard he could barely accomplish it.

"How can they do it, Eyanna? How can your people send their own to the *skalkits* like that?"

She studied the water, her face subdued. "Everyone agrees because the person being sent away is not them."

"But it *could* be them!"

"No one thinks it will be them."

"Yeah, but someday it will be them."

Eyanna made a gesture of indifference. "No one thinks about this."

Denton thought that was inane. Then he thought about how polite and friendly and helpful everyone was—not just to him but to one another, too. What hypocrites! It was all such a lie!

But it wasn't a lie, he realized. It was a *clue*—or it would have been if he'd been paying attention. No one could be that nice all the time, not unless the alternative was pretty severe. For the Sapphians, it was.

"Do they choose the old and sick mostly, or . . . ?"

Eyanna made the gesture for "maybe." "Yes, this is the way. But also, females have many children. It is known that some of them will go. Mothers choose the ones who will go. Children who are chosen like this are sent as soon as they are grown."

Denton gaped at her, shocked. They bred children for the *skalkits*? Poor John, with his deformed hand. He never had a chance.

"That is terrible! Do they not understand what it's like to die this way?"

Eyanna didn't answer, but Denton knew. The Sapphians didn't *want* to understand.

Eyanna wrapped her long arms around her long legs, huddling. "If we do not feed the *skalkits* they come into the gorge looking for the meat. That is worse."

He could picture it. Oh, yeah. Sitting around the communal circle and hearing them coming through the trees, people running and screaming, being chased through the jungle, *skalkits* tearing through huts, ripping up pathways. . . .

He looked around uneasily. They were sitting on a riverbank. *Skalkits* might come here to drink. Might? Probably. They probably came here to drink. And the swimming option seemed less reassuring than it had a little while ago.

"We will walk," he said, getting to his feet. He pointed toward the mountains. "That way."

She stood up, but her face was troubled. She looked back over her shoulder, toward the gorge.

"Eyanna, we can't live in the gorge. Your people will catch us and they will send us to the *skalkits* again. I can't hide in trees like you."

"*Ta zhecta*," she said, backing away. *Good-bye.*

"Eyanna, *no.*"

She was going to leave him, and then he would be completely alone. It was one thing to find himself outside the gorge with gorgeous, natively savvy Eyanna at his side. It was another to be a defenseless foreigner on his lonesome, with long cold nights and *skalkits* lurking.

"If you go back to the gorge they will catch you, Eyanna, and they will send you to the *skalkits,* and you will not get free again. If you come with me, I will find a place that is safe. I promise."

Eyanna knew what he was saying was true, he could see it in her eyes, but she made the gesture for "no." "I cannot leave the gorge."

"You *can.* I know you are all afraid of—"

"My children are there."

She said it in a quiet, doomed way, and he knew in an instant that, of course, that's exactly what it was. He'd thought Eyanna hung around the village out of some Sapphian fear of the unknown or maybe a desperate need to be near her kind. But now he remembered that the times he had seen her had been in the mornings, when the women and children were in the circle alone. And she had watched from trees with such an intent, longing expression not because she wanted to be part of the group—she was watching *her children.*

Crap. That really sucked. He even knew which ones they were. There were two young girls with hair white-gold like Eyanna's—pretty, shy little things. He whined in frustration, rubbed his eyes. Why did she care anyway? It sounded like Sapphian mothers weren't exactly swelling with maternal instinct as a rule.

Like, for example, *his* mother, who would not only ship him off to the *skalkits* to save her own neck but probably send along his dog and gerbil, too.

No, Eyanna had to be different. *He* had to be stuck with the one Sapphian who was a saint.

"Your children are safe in the village until they are full-grown. You said this."

"Yes."

"So they do not need you now. And if you are there, the people will always remember they are your children and maybe they will send them to the *skalkits.* But if you are not there, Eyanna, if you are not there the people may forget they are yours."

She looked stricken by this logic. He almost felt ashamed for manipulating her, but hey, it was for her own good. She couldn't go on living the way she had been before, and he certainly couldn't.

"Your children are safe in the village. And outside the village," he waved his hand at the surrounding area, "there are *skalkits.* You cannot take them outside. You cannot help them, Eyanna."

Tears filled her eyes. Her golden shoulders heaved.

"And you can always come back," he reminded her. "Anytime."

* * *

Following the riverbank with Eyanna was an exercise in frustration and fear that could have been designed to train Special Ops agents for enemy territory. The ground was uneven and the days, and the walking, were endless. Unlike those first few days on this world, Denton now *knew* what lurked in those trees. He was constantly tense and his eyes grew tired from watching the jungle with every step. Then there was the constant rein he had to keep on Eyanna, who looked more and more reluctant with every mile. Most of the time, she looked like a cat being dragged out for a walk in the rain. He had to keep up a constant barrage of chatter to keep her going.

Only one thing kept *him* going: Eyanna's body gracefully moving ahead of him. And that was its own form of torture. *Damn. Skalkits* or no *skalkits*, he hadn't been this rabidly horny since he was fifteen. It had to be something in the air. That or Eyanna.

"How much further do we go?" she asked one night at their campfire.

"I don't know. Not far."

He said "not far" because that's what she wanted to hear, but the truth was, he had no idea. He was looking for something—a cave, a ravine, anything that looked like it might be safe.

"How did you get away from the *skalkits*, Eyanna? The first time when your people sent you there."

She had been eating a large piece of fruit, but at his question she lost her appetite and put it aside. "My man hid a knife and cut himself free. Then he cut me free also." She played with her toes in the dirt, her face close.

"What . . . What happened to your man?"

"The *skalkit* got him when we ran."

"I'm sorry."

She looked up at him with surprise, as if she did not know what to make of his sympathy.

"Do you not . . ." He felt kind of like a heel for saying it, but he could not go on like this forever. "Do you not miss having a man?"

She stood up to tend the fire. He was starting to recognize her body language. Whenever she tried to avoid a conversation by working, it meant she disagreed or didn't want to talk about it. He supposed Sapphians learned at a young age not to argue.

"Eyanna . . ." he pressed gently. "It is not good for a woman to be without a man."

She poked at the branches. "When my man was taken, I promised there would never be another."

Great. That was annoying. It was also plain stupid, especially for a Sapphian. As far as he had seen, they were all complete sluts and had sex about as often as they ate. Besides, Eyanna being celibate was like the biggest, most perfectly shaped Christmas tree in the lot going unsold. What a waste.

"Your man is gone, Eyanna. That will not help him. And being without a man is not good for you, sweetie."

She looked directly into his eyes through the fire, her hair flickering gold. "I can see you want a woman. But I will never be with you, Denton. Never."

"Oh. Okay." Denton took a bite of fruit. It tasted very sour.

The next day, when it was time to stop for the night, he said, "We should make a small fire. I think the big fires may attract the *skalkits*."

So they made a fire with a handful of twigs. He tried to gauge it right because he really didn't want to completely freeze his balls off. When they lay down to sleep, it was just right—cold but not chattering-teeth cold.

He pretended to try to sleep, then sat up, rubbing his arms. "Eyanna, come over here. If we sleep close to each other it will be warmer."

She hesitated, looking at the pitiful fire as if wishing it would magically grow. But she was cold, too. After a minute she came over. He let her lie closest to the fire and spooned up next to her.

She was stiff, on her guard, but he did nothing further, just lay behind her. After a long time, she slept. He could hear her breathing deepen.

Denton had lain awake for hours the previous night, horny and sullen, and had come up with this plan. But he had only planned this far. He was pleased that he had pulled it off, that she had fallen for the "big fires may attract the *skalkits*" line. But now that he was lying here, pressed against her in the dark, he realized that he should have thought it through a little more carefully. Had he imagined that just the power of being next to him would change her mind? That she would get all sexy in her sleep and turn around and grab him? It wasn't happening.

He could set this up as a routine. They could do this every night and maybe, eventually . . .

But Denton knew it was not going to happen that way. Because it was *this* night, and Denton was already out of patience. He was patience-free. He was also ripe. He had put up with too much crap in the past few days, needed to win too badly. And her tender bottom was pressed against him and he was *right there* and it was so selfish of her to deny him. After all, wasn't he taking care of her? Wasn't he offering her a life better than the one she'd lived as an outcast in the gorge? Didn't she owe him? And what, really, did it cost her to be nice to him? The other Sapphians, all those *allook saheed* groupies, had never given it a second thought. Why was *she* so freaking stingy?

He lay there awake for a long time, all night in fact, thinking up these and plenty of other excuses. He didn't really think he would *do* anything. He was only playing games with himself, making himself miserable. But it was like those days in Zurich when he had debated whether to buy the manuscript. Deep down, in perhaps the only place where Denton was ever really honest with himself, he knew how this night would end, how it was destined to end from the time he'd suggested they make a small fire and she'd agreed.

And so it did. Before dawn he cautiously moved her little skirt aside. Then he rolled on top of her, pinning her down, and he took her.

It felt amazing. It should have felt amazing. But even though he closed his eyes and pretended hard, he was still aware of her struggles. And even though he tried to move in a way that would give her pleasure, even though he'd talked himself into believing she would get into it once he'd started, his movements felt false. She didn't get into it. And when he finished there was a heavy, polluted feeling accompanying the gratification.

He rolled off her. "Wow. I think . . . I was dreaming, Eyanna. I had a dream that we . . . I'm sorry."

She got up and moved away a few feet down the bank and sat, staring at the water. Her chin trembled.

"I was dreaming," he said again. "Wow, that was weird."

Still nothing. He lay back down, looking up at the sky. A fluorescent pink sat at the crack of the horizon, like a box lid being opened on endless treasures. This world was so freaking beautiful that it made him cry sometimes. And right now, he hated it to death.

"Eyanna, I'm sorry. You are so beautiful, and I want you so much. There is only you and I now. We have to help each other."

She stood up and slipped off into the water to wash, leaving him alone with his conscience.

18.2. FORTY-SIXTY CALDER FARRIS

Gyde was having a conversation with someone at the top of the stairs outside their office. It was the Bronze from Saradena, the one who'd been talking about the dead Silver case in the cafeteria.

Pol froze, his hand on the rail at the bottom of the stairs. There was a second when he might have spun around and walked the other way, fled the Department of Monitors and Centalia, and never returned. But Gyde saw him and smiled and Pol's hand went round around the banister and pulled himself upward because it was the most logical thing to do.

"We have an appointment this morning," Gyde said pleasantly.

"What appointment?"

"A banned book expert. A Gold. He's a collector."

"A collector of banned books?"

"He's a *Gold*. He can do what he likes."

"Where did you find him?"

"I have my ways, classmate." Gyde winked.

They drove across town to one of the great old imperial buildings. The Gold had a luxury suite overlooking Gorenten Square, including a balcony with primo seats for state parades. In the elevator Gyde asked, "Have you ever been in the home of a Gold before? No? It's quite a lifestyle. But they're very private, so don't ask a lot of questions."

Don't ask a lot of questions. Pol almost laughed.

It turned out the Gold was an expert in rare books, not banned. And he was not old—perhaps thirty-five. Pol was surprised. All the Golds he'd seen on posters or heard on the radio were old, the councilmen of state, distinguished white-hairs. But of course, there had to be younger Golds as well, didn't there? They didn't reproduce much, the Golds. "To set an example for the lower classes" was the official line. "Because there's only so much room at the top" was no doubt closer to the truth. This Gold's penthouse was the most subtly lavish display of money Pol had ever seen—carpeting like an elaborate mosaic and furniture that was heavy and weighted and black.

And his *wife* . . . The Gold female floated through the room as though her body were made of the same insubstantial stuff as her gown. Her light blue eyes were rimmed with a darker shade that matched her temples, and her white-blond hair was coiled and stiffened into an elaborate headdress. Silver females were trained for combat. This female was different—delicate and soft, rare as an orchid. She appeared briefly to welcome them, then disappeared again like a dream. The book expert himself was not attractive. He had the requisite signs of class—blond hair and rich blue temples—but on a short and fleshy frame. He had bulging eyes.

"How can I serve the state?" Chancellor Tyches asked as they settled down in his library.

Gyde's face was grave with concern. "Have you heard about the state terrorist who's been writing messages on public buildings?"

"I've heard it mentioned." Tyches settled back into his chair. He withdrew a Balsala smoke from a box on his desk and offered them each one. The expensive smoke tasted wonderful.

"His last was a pamphlet." Gyde handed Chancellor Tyches a copy. "There are some curious ideas in it. I was hoping you might recognize his source."

"Ah!" Chancellor Tyches sank back with an expression of complacent arrogance. He scanned the pages. "Mad."

Pol leaned forward. "Do you really think so?"

"Oh, yes."

"Why?"

"I think what we want to know," Gyde interrupted smoothly, "is if you rec-ognize any of the ideas in the pamphlet. I thought he might have gotten them from a banned book."

"What things in particular?"

"I apologize; I'm being unclear. What I find odd is this reference to there being 'aliens' from other planets."

"Um. I see. Yes, that is an odd idea. You know, I really admire the Silver class. Truly, I do."

"Thank you, Chancellor."

"What a tremendous service you do for the state. I admire your . . . sense of glory. It's very dashing. As a young man I even wished *I* could be a warrior."

Tyches and Gyde chuckled gently over the naïveté of this.

"Did you enjoy your upbringing?"

". . . Of course, Chancellor Tyches." Pol had never seen Gyde flustered before. Tyches's eyes moved to Pol.

"Certainly," Pol agreed. There must have been something unexpected in his eyes, for Tyches forgot Pol was inconsequential. Their gaze locked. Pol wanted to look away but feared it would reveal too much. He held it, smiled.

"You must forgive my curiosity, but I so rarely meet Silvers."

"It's our pleasure to tell you anything you like, Chancellor." Gyde had re-covered himself. Now his tone indicated that they would be at the chancel-lor's disposal for hours if that's what he wanted, tell him every intimate detail he might want to know: how they groomed their teeth, what it felt like when they shat.

"Well, never mind." Tyches lost interest. "Let me think."

Gyde smoked his Balsala halfway down and put it out in a dish on the desk. Pol reluctantly put his out as well. He immediately wished he could light another.

"What I tell you does not leave this room," Tyches said slowly. "And it will have to go on your records that you've heard this."

"We are in your hands."

"Very well. There are banned books which theorize that there are . . . other suns and planets, up among the stars."

Pol felt his heart quicken. The Gold was lying. He knew very well, he *knew*, there were other solar systems out there. Apparently the state had decided that Silvers had no need of that knowledge. But the *Golds*, they had been taught the truth about the universe—the truth that he, Pol, also knew.

"Could these books be obtained by a Bronze?" Gyde asked.

"Nooo," Tyches said thoughtfully. "The two books I know of are more . . . technical writings, probably not comprehensible to most people. I have just thought of something else, though. . . ."

He went to a glossy black cabinet and unlocked it with a small key. Inside were neat stacks of thick-papered files. He locked the cabinet again, bringing one of the files back to his desk. He turned over pages of scribbled writing.

"There is a banned book called *Heavenly Mysteries*. Occult-religio trash. It claims there are all sorts of other worlds inhabited by strange creatures, some of them intelligent." Tyches closed the file, satisfied. "I wouldn't be surprised if that was your terrorist's source."

Gyde wrote the title in his notebook. "Do you have any idea where someone might have access to that book?"

"The city of Madamar. That's where the book was found, anyway. Three copies were confiscated years ago."

"Is there any chance we could see the book itself?" Pol asked.

Chancellor Tyches turned his bulging eyes to Pol. There was contempt in them. "That's why the books are *banned*. No one is supposed to read them."

"That's fine, Chancellor Tyches," Gyde said quickly.

"I don't *have* the book. As I said, it's occult-religio trash. But even if I did, I couldn't let you see it."

"We don't need to see it, thank you," Gyde said with humility.

Pol bowed his head apologetically. "I'm sorry. Of course you're right, Chancellor Tyches."

In the car, Gyde's silence was chilling.

"They let us into the Archives to do research for cases," Pol said. "I thought . . ."

"Are you out of your scarping mind? Do you really think they let you see *anything* in the Archives other than what they *want* you to see?"

The words dried up on Pol's tongue. He felt suspended all of a sudden, tricked into taking a false step out over nothingness. He should never have said anything, not one word. He looked out the window.

"By the blood, Pol, sometimes I wonder where you've been all your life!"

Pol studied the passing buildings.

Gyde cleared his throat: "Where *did* you serve?"

"Sachiasus, Ephiphron, Mona Res," Pol regurgitated names from Pol 137's file, keeping his voice even.

"I had friends in Ephiphron. I heard it was cold there."

Pol gave him a glare, a glare that might be read as either "of course it was cold" or "cold—are you crazy?" and certainly meant "get off my scarping back."

The car felt stifling. Pol tried to think. Was Gyde suspicious? If he was, could Pol take him out? Even if he succeeded in killing Gyde and getting away with it, what then? There was still that upcoming physical. He would have to run. Run where?

But Gyde didn't continue to question him. Instead, he began talking about a battle he'd been in, the Great Battle, the Battle of Cross-Plain.

"It was cold *there*, I can tell you. In the morning there were icicles hanging from the guns. It was the worst battle I ever saw, in twenty-five years of combat."

"I've heard about it. What was it like?" Pol didn't give a scarp about the Battle of Cross-Plain, but he was happy to let Gyde talk about himself, fill up the silence.

"I was an assistant to the commander. He made me stick close to him; that's the only reason I survived. Entire units were decimated." Gyde paused. "When we set up trophy we didn't have enough men left to bury the dead. There were corpses stretched out for miles. We had to call a truce to deal with it. For two days we worked side by side with the enemy making bonfires of the bodies. You'd think fighting would have broken out, but there wasn't a single incident. There were too many dead all around us already. We didn't have the stomach for battle."

"It sounds like a great glory."

"It was. I earned a hundred merits for that battle."

Pol stared at him in astonishment. "A *hundred*?"

"There were so few survivors," Gyde said with a roguish wink and a smile.

They drove on quietly for a while. Pol pictured the battle in his mind, or tried to. He hadn't been at that battle, he was sure, though he might have been. It had been fifteen years ago, and he had been old enough to fight if he'd really been a Silver. He didn't think he'd been there, not even on the enemy side. But he did remember being in combat, vaguely. He got a brief impression of a desert and tanks. Desert?

"My best classmate from childhood was wounded," Gyde said casually. "The femur in his right leg was shattered. I visited him in the infirmary. I could see, looking at it, that it would never be right. He wouldn't be able to keep the leg. He knew it, too."

There was something strange in Gyde's voice. Pol turned to look at him.

"I said good-bye to him one day, and the next day when I went back, his bed was empty." Gyde looked in the rearview mirror, then glanced over into his passenger's eyes. "A warrior exists to serve the state, and when he can no longer serve . . ."

Pol understood; at last he understood Gyde's insinuations about Silver retirement. He looked at Gyde's clenched jaw and, with a chill of horror, he knew.

It must be true. If anyone would know such a thing, it would be Gyde.

"The state rewards service," Pol said.

"Long live the state," replied Gyde.

*   *   *

"There are no construction Irons with reading and writing on their profile, at least not working in this city." Gyde ripped the printout from the telex. The results from Research had arrived while they were gone.

"We already agreed; he's not an Iron." Pol leaned against his desk, hands tucked in his pockets in case they started shaking. "He's a Bronze construction worker, most likely a foreman or a guard."

"Who hails from Madamar."

"We'll see. How long will it take to get the results on the Madamar search?"

Gyde was just sealing up the request. He went into the hall and motioned for an Iron runner to take it down to Research.

"I marked it 'urgent,' so the night staff will work on it. It ought to come in over the telex sometime tonight. By tomorrow morning, my friend . . ." Gyde winked. "Come in early."

"I'll take the first bus."

Gyde strolled closer to Pol, getting very close. Gyde was occasionally given to displays of chummy, even paternal affection—a common-enough sight among Silvers. But this felt . . . different. Pol tensed up.

"What about tonight? What are you doing?" Gyde's voice was a murmur.

"The usual. Have dinner, go to bed early. Do you need something done?"

"I was thinking we could go to the gymnasium together. Release some stress. Tomorrow will be a big day."

Pol was momentarily speechless. Gyde's words were seductive, but his smile was contradicted by glittering eyes—it was the smiling welcome of a dagger.

"Come on! I may be an old man, but I can still wrestle a middle-aged buck like you."

"I trained this morning. I'm . . . tired."

"You did not. I never see you at the gymnasium." Gyde wrapped his hand around Pol's bicep. "You have to stay fit, you know. Nothing more deformed than a flabby Silver."

His hand was a shock. It gripped Pol's arm, kneading it. There was something calculated in it, probing, testing. Pol felt a surge of repulsion and terror. He violently yanked his arm away.

He stood to his feet breathing hard, looking into Gyde's half-lidded eyes. All he could see in those eyes was a cool and dangerous mercenary.

"Maybe next week," Pol said stiffly.

"Sure. Sure." Gyde's face relaxed. The moment was over.

It was wrong, all wrong, but there was no way to salvage it. Pol mumbled his good-byes and left.

18.3. Seventy-Thirty Jill Talcott

The fertility clinic was a five-story monster stretching an entire city block. There was nothing remarkable about it other than its size. It was square and nondescript, with the occasional small blank window. It looked no less deserted than every other building in the City.

"Didn't work very well, did it?" Nate commented as they stood on the street looking at it.

"What's that?"

"Fertility."

Jill agreed absently. She hadn't wanted to come here this morning. She'd wanted to go to the antenna field, the one she *still* hadn't gotten to see. But Nate had his heart set on the spaceport, and this had been the only alternative they could agree upon. Now that she was here, though, she was getting a wee bit curious.

"If fertility *is* their problem," she said, "then it must have been a problem for a very long time. Species don't die out overnight."

"They would if they had your libido."

"What!"

He grinned. "I said, 'Let's go inside; it would be neat-o!' "

She glared at him but couldn't stop a laugh. "One of these days, Nate."

"Don't I wish."

Inside, the power was on. Light panels lit a large, plain room with branching hallways. It was possibly a waiting room, though there were only two of the narrow molded chairs—both empty.

"Not expecting a crowd," Nate remarked.

Jill looked around the room, but there was nothing much to see—plain white walls, no signs or directions or anything else. The hallways all looked the same. She tapped her collarbone, pondering which direction would be their best bet.

If fertility *was* the cause of this species' demise, it would be an interesting point for her report. There had to be data somewhere, and with the help of the translator in her ear she might actually be able to read it. What she needed was a computer. She picked a hall and motioned for Nate to follow.

His tennis shoes made little squeaks on the future relative of a linoleum floor. Down each side of the hallway were regularly spaced doors, and at the end was another branching corridor. Jill tried a door on her right and found a small observation room, approximately four feet wide, consisting of a counter and computer facing a thick-paned window. Cautiously she stepped up into it.

The window looked into the neighboring room. This had to be where the "clinical" part of the clinic occurred. There was a bed in there—at least, that's what she assumed it was. It was a large amalgamation of bedding, steel, and what looked like stuffing built up and around. It resembled a nest. Next to the bed was a table with shining metal instruments of ghastly design. A mechanical arm with a needlelike protuberance hung from the ceiling.

Jill's lip curled in fascinated disgust. "Ewww," she said, and then, because that wasn't very scientific, "It doesn't look too appealing, does it?"

"Yeah," Nate breathed a shaky laugh. "If this is their idea of a romantic setting, no wonder they have problems feeling sexy. They need some James Brown and mood lighting in here."

Trying not to think about Nate in the context of James Brown and mood lighting, Jill sat down at the monitor. This was the first computer she'd had access to since they'd tried the translators, and she was anxious to check it out.

"I'll see if I can find some records. They should have data on birthrates, population, things like that."

" 'Kay. I wanna look next door."

He left her alone. In a minute she saw him enter the neighboring room from her peripheral vision. She looked. He picked up one of the instruments on the table, turned, and threatened her with it menacingly. Jill uttered another "ewww" and went back to her screen.

She was disappointed to see that although the words on the monitor were now in English, she still had no idea what she was looking at. There were many terms that were apparently untranslatable and remained in the alien text. She decided to try the speech approach.

"Computer," she said, feeling slightly ridiculous, "show me the birthrates for the past two hundred years."

The computer understood her perfectly. It brought up data, but it was arranged in a graph that could have been designed by Escher. It hurt her brain just looking at it. She squinted at the confusing lines and symbols. The numbers on the screen were incredibly low. If they were really birthrates, they ran in the mere dozens per . . . what? Month? Year? Decade? She was still trying to figure that out when she heard a muffled noise and glanced up.

Nate was being dragged from the clinical room—by an alien.

For a moment Jill was too surprised to respond. Then she got her feet under her and ran out the door. Nate was being pulled down the hall, his wrist gripped tight in the alien's long greenish fingers.

"Come along, citizen!" the alien said. "Do your duty!"

The voice—the first Jill had heard coming from a living alien—sounded right off an old Alvin and the Chipmunks album. And there was something comic about the way the alien was marching Nate along. He looked fragile but stern, like a determined old man. Nate was trying to get away without hurting the thing.

"Hang on a minute. I think you have the wrong—"

"Do your duty!"

Nate glanced over his shoulder at Jill and they exchanged a confused look.

"Hey!" Jill said. "Hello!"

The alien paid her no mind. He stopped at a door and the door opened. Without further ado, the alien shoved Nate inside and the door closed.

From behind the door, Nate let out a bloodcurdling scream.

The situation went from baffling to dead serious in a heartbeat. Jill called his name and went running toward them. The alien, ignoring her, disappeared behind a second door. She hesitated a moment, then went to the door Nate had gone through. She pounded on it, but nothing happened. Nate screamed again. He sounded terrified.

Jill pounded harder, yelling at the door to open, but it wouldn't budge. She ran back to the door the alien had entered and this one opened immediately. Inside was an observation room, just like the one she'd been in. The alien was seated at the computer, his fingers dancing over the screen. He peered through the window into the next room. Jill stepped up to look.

Nate had stopped screaming. He was backed up against the doorway, a horrified look on his face. He was not alone. The bed-nest in this room was occupied by something the likes of which Jill had never seen. It was an alien, or so she thought, but its body was *huge* and grossly fat. It was naked, with a whole row of nipples and a pubis partially hidden by waving legs. Through its rolls of translucent skin Jill could make out bubbles or sacs.

As her eyes grazed over the corpulent mass, pulled by a sickened fascination, she saw that one of the sacs had something in it. She knew at once what it was and thus what the sacs were. They were eggs. Most of them were empty, but this one had a tiny embryo inside. As the mass on the bed shifted, the embryo's face rolled lazily to face Jill. Its large head and eyes looked like any other embryo she had ever seen, but there was something wrong. The thing was frozen in a calcified position. It was dead.

"Oh my god," Jill whispered.

The alien on the bed was a female, the first they'd seen on this planet. And she was horrid. The creature lay quivering, barely alive herself. She slowly turned her enormous filmy eyes to Nate. He pressed back harder against the door, shuddering.

"Nate, can you hear me?" Jill called. He gave no response. She knocked on the glass, but it was hard as a diamond and scarcely gave off a vibration, much less a noise.

Oh god, Jill thought. *Tell me the females don't eat the males on this planet. That would explain their reluctance to breed.*

But the female didn't lunge at Nate—far from it. She looked completely immobile. Next to Jill, the alien at the computer pressed something, sent his high chipmunky voice echoing into the next room.

"Do your duty, citizen! Do your duty!"

"You've got to let him out of there!" Jill demanded loudly. The alien ignored her.

"Hello!" She bent over, waving her hand in front of him to get his attention. But he was focused on the computer screen again.

"Bad!" the alien muttered. He turned those long fingers to a set of controls.

Jill, uncomprehendingly, watched the mechanical arm start to move. Nate backed away, sure it was coming for him, but the arm headed for the female. She made a high squealing cry of panic and protest as it approached. The needle-probe didn't pause but embedded itself into her skin above the dead embryo and sucked it up, sac and all. Jill squeezed her eyes shut, felt her gorge rise. In the next room, Nate screamed and resumed his pounding on the door.

"Do your duty, citizen," the alien said over the intercom, "or I shall report you. Do your duty!"

On the bed, the female weakly *unfolded* in invitation. Nate glanced over his shoulder, pounded on the door more fiercely. The look on his face—Jill couldn't bear it.

And she did *not* like him being alone with that . . . that thing.

She ran back into the hall and pushed at the door to his room, pushed where it went into the wall, trying to get it to slide. Nothing.

"Nate, can you hear me?"

"Jill! Get me out of here!"

"I'm trying, but the door won't budge!"

"Well . . . *make* it!"

Before she could figure out how to do that, the alien stomped into the hall from the observation room. Despite his inhuman features he had a distinctly petulant air. He would have walked right into Jill if she hadn't backed up. He might be able to see Nate, but it appeared he still could not see her. The door opened at his touch.

A terrified Nate stood on the other side.

"Nate!"

"Bad! Move back!" the alien ordered.

Nate dodged around the alien into the hall. The alien, with a mutter, stomped into the room, heading for the nest.

"Are you all right?" Jill asked as Nate grabbed her hand.

"I will be. Let's get out of here!"

Jill resisted his pull. "Wait!"

She couldn't resist a final look into the room. The female was straining as if to get up. She appeared to be choking, her mouth gaping open, her face going from a gray to purple. The frail little alien paced helplessly beside her as if unsure what to do. He kept muttering but seemed unable or unwilling to actually touch her.

Nate tugged Jill again and this time they ran, down the hall, through the waiting room, out into the street, back outside, into the bright, hot sun.

*   *   *

They were quiet as they walked back to the apartment, quiet as they sat on the floor and ate food bars. Jill could tell Nate was feeling the lethargic effect of the planet—he looked tired. She was feeling it herself. And the clinic . . . the clinic had gotten to them both.

"Jill?" he said at last, clearing his throat.

"Yes?"

"I've been thinking about how far away from Earth we are." Nate looked down at his bar, half-eaten. "And I was thinking that . . . You were right. We may never get home."

Jill sighed. "This place has all the technology we could ever need for anything. Including getting home. It may take us a while to find it."

He looked at her, his eyes savage with the purple stain of exhaustion under them. "A while."

"Well. Quite a while, actually." She smiled. "What are you worried about? You're the one who said this place was lucky."

"Not so lucky for the aliens," he muttered, looking back down at his food.

Jill could feel that Nate was really in the thick of it. She tried her cheeriest voice. "Look at the bright side. We have water, food, and shelter, and all of those indefinitely, as far as we can tell. We can set up a more permanent place to live—a home base, if you will. And we could use an air car or two to save time. You'll have fun with that. Perhaps in a few days you can see if you can find one."

He didn't answer.

"I know this is hard, Nate. But the important thing is the *work*. We should be able to take notes on the computer now. Remind me to try that tomorrow morning. Of course, the biggest priority is to learn how they're using wave technology, particularly for things like space travel and energy—maybe even medicine or the production of goods. We really have to go see those antennae tomorrow."

Nate clenched his jaw. She didn't seem to be getting through to him. The clinic *had* been awful, so very alien and heartbreaking, too, in a way. But it wouldn't do for them to brood. She decided to talk about something she'd been holding back, the way a mother might offer a pouting child a new toy.

"Listen, you've been so worried about the government getting the one-minus-one, about how it could be used as a weapon. Well, it's true, there is the potential for a devastating weapon, *if* you pushed the negative one pulse. But what if you pushed the *one* pulse? You could create a climate of benevolence, couldn't you? Imagine the possibilities! Everything you were saying about 'there's always a catch,' well, that might have been true up until now. But if we could increase the crest of the one-minus-one with a one pulse, maybe for the whole world, that wouldn't have to be the case any longer! Think about what that could mean for us, for our entire species. That's why those antennae interest me. Tomorrow we can—"

"Jill, what is *wrong* with you? Are you crazy or just plain stupid?" Nate's eyes were blazing from under a deeply furrowed brow.

She blinked at him, mouth still open to speak.

"What does any of that *matter* now? Suppose we spend the next ten or twenty years researching this place and writing little notebooks full of our findings. *So what?* So those notebooks can lie next to our bones bleaching in the sun? If we can't get home, *none of it matters.* You don't seem to get that. And frankly," a flare of embarrassment stained his cheeks, "frankly, I'm not so sure it wouldn't be the best thing for Earth if we never *did* get home."

"What's *that* supposed to mean?"

"It means . . ." He took a deep breath. "It's exactly like this situation, Jill. All you see is the science, not the human equation, not our predicament. God! Don't you think I know you were planning to work for the DoD? Even after we'd gone to Poland?"

She pressed her lips tight, looked away.

"Even now you can't give it up. Can't you see that whatever this species knows, it hasn't done them any good? Why do you want it so badly?"

He didn't seem to be angry anymore, more genuinely trying to express himself, to plead with her. But that only made his words that much more unbearable. A groundswelling of resentment pulsed inside her.

"I'm a *scientist*, that's why! That's my job. And, as long as we're being honest here, why can't you just do *your* job instead of whining all the time? If we're stuck here, we're stuck here! What do you want me to do about it? Lie down and give up? You're a man, not a boy. Why don't you act like one!"

He laughed. "A man? Really? I didn't think you'd noticed. How am I not being a man? Because I'm *reacting*, for god's sake? You can say that so blithely: 'We're *stuck* here.' That would be fine with you, wouldn't it? You'd be perfectly happy to bury yourself in work *again*. My god, it isn't even the fame, is it? I always thought you were just incredibly ambitious. But there's no chance of fame here. It's just *blind work*. What is that? Escapism, is that what it's about for you? Do you work so you don't have to *feel*?"

She started to protest but didn't know where to begin. His words were so malicious and so unfair.

He stood up, shoving himself back from the table. "Well, I, for one, *don't like this place.* Maybe you're content to spend the rest of your life eating little white food bars and being alone, never seeing your family again, and . . ." There was the angry edge of tears in his voice. "Forget that there's no one to talk to, no TV, no books, no news, no food, no beer, no music, no *anything*— it's so *dead*, Jill. The aliens . . . and this whole place—it's sterile and lifeless and dead! Didn't you see what I saw today? Don't you get it? This place is a tomb!"

Jill was purposefully *not* looking at him, embarrassed by his emotion. She felt nothing but anger, but she was already cooling, had already decided that she wasn't going to give him what he wanted, wasn't going to have a big scene and allow herself to get all upset. It was the stress, she told herself, the effects of the altered one-minus-one on his system.

"I understand that you're homesick," she said in a let's-be-reasonable tone. "But we have no idea what might happen down the road. We may find a way home. We may even be rescued. In the meantime, I see no excuse for wasting this precious opportunity. If you were thinking clearly, you'd feel the same, so I think we should just—"

"Rescued?" he laughed. "By whom?"

"You'll feel better in the morning," she said, with a deep sigh.

Nate, apparently, didn't agree. He got up abruptly and went outside, flinging his chair aside as he went. The door wasn't the kind you could slam, but Jill heard the noise in her head all the same.

Although she'd been tired for hours, Jill couldn't sleep. What she really wanted was to be alone—alone, as in not having to worry about where Nate was or what he was thinking or when he would come in. She wanted a break from all of this, from the burden of the relationship, from feeling like it was her fault that he was here, that she needed to take care of him. But she wasn't going to get a break from that responsibility. More to avoid another argument upon his return than anything else, she bedded down. She could have pulled his mattress farther away from her cot or even put it in another room, but she didn't want to set him off again, so she left it.

She lay down and tried to sleep, but something was growing inside her. She felt a hollowness blooming, despite her determination to ignore it. It was a niggling doubt: What if Nate was right? What if they *couldn't* get home—was it all pointless after all? And would it really be the best thing for Earth if she was lost for good, and the one-minus-one with her?

No. That was Nate's idealistic hogwash. Progress was never bad. Learning, even if it ended up in a notebook next to her bleaching bones, was never for naught. It was her only god. She had to believe in it.

But the hollowness in her belly deepened, quenching her enthusiasm like coals being overwhelmed by dark, filthy water. The images from the clinic wouldn't leave her. The poor female, chained to a bed and no male willing to go near her. How had this society come to that? How could beings who'd had enough of a spark of life to evolve from nothing, from microbes out in that desert, to a highly technological society suddenly lose the drive to reproduce, to live?

Nate came in. The lights went on automatically at his movement. She was lying on her back, and now she wished she'd been facing the wall. She squeezed her eyes shut. She heard him taking off his shoes, quietly, getting ready for bed. She wanted to say she was sorry, but she wasn't sorry and didn't know why she should be. The room was so still. He lay down. It got quieter. The lights went out.

That hollowness reverberated inside her in the silence, like a place where her name should be and wasn't. Then her name appeared. At first she thought it was just in her head, but it was Nate. He had said her name, "*Jill.*" His tone, lingering in her ears, sent a shiver up her spine.

"*Jill.*"

Again. The hollowness, despair, was in his voice, too. It said a lot of things. It said he was sorry about the argument—not as in an apology but as in it didn't matter anymore, not in the face of that overwhelming emptiness. She knew what he needed—human contact. A touch, comfort, something real, something from home, something to ease the chill. She wanted it, too.

She could reach across in the dark and take his hand. She could even imagine herself rolling off the bed in the dark and lying down next to him, putting her head against his chest. She almost did it. But the thought occurred to her: Then what? Where would it lead? Would he kiss her again? And then what? It had been such a long time since she'd been intimate with a man, not since her college days, and even then it had been a disaster. She'd felt sexual desire for Nate, god only knew. But the idea of being naked, vulnerable, *here* in this place—exposing herself so intimately physically and mentally at this precise moment of time? It terrified her.

"Jill," he said again, this time louder, darker, demanding a reply.

She pretended to be asleep. The silence was so uncomfortable that she added a light snore, just to make sure he was convinced, to plug up once and for all the awful stillness.

19

Loved and honoured hadst thou lain
By the dead that nobly fell,
In the underworld again,
Where are throned the kings of hell,
Lordly in that citadel
—*Aeschylus, "The Libation-Bearers,"* 458 B.C., translation
by E. D. A. Morshead

19.1. SEVENTY-THIRTY JILL TALCOTT

When Jill awoke, Nate was gone. She could hardly believe it. She looked around outside the apartment, even outside the building, to confirm. Why would he go *anywhere* without her? That wasn't very smart. Now she had to sit around and wait for him to get back.

Her doubts of the night before had vanished. She was ready to work again, thought it would do them good—do *him* good—if they could get a fresh start on the day, make some progress, keep their minds occupied. She tried to study the pile of printouts from the spaceport, but her mind kept wandering, listening for the sounds of his return.

When he came in an hour or so later, he said he'd gone for a walk, hadn't slept well. His answers were clipped and stiff. Jill was determined to be patient.

"Nate, please don't go off on your own like that, not without telling me."

"You know what?" Nate flashed an icy smile. "You're not my mother, or even my boss for that matter, not here."

Jill stared at him in dismay. "What is the *matter* with you?"

"I know you were awake last night. I mean, how stupid do you think I am?"

Jill was embarrassed. The snore had, perhaps, been overdoing it. "I'm—I'm sorry. I just . . ."

"Whatever." He began folding his blanket in quick jerks.

"What are you doing?"

He didn't answer.

"Nate, *please*. I do . . . I do care about you. It's just that at this moment I think we should stay focused on what's important here."

"You know what? When you say 'we should stay focused on what's important' what you're really saying is 'this is what I *choose* to deal with.' That way, you can sweep everything you can't handle—all that 'unimportant stuff,' like emotions, and *love*, and your *humanity*—under the rug. You know what that leaves you with?"

She blinked at him, speechless.

"It leaves you with a very fat rug!"

Jill was at a loss. She had never seen him like this. His face was harsh with anger and pain. His words were not half as bad as that look on his face.

"Nate . . . I—"

"Forget it. You do what you want. I'm done with it." He stalked out, leaving her alone.

Jill ran to the door of the building and called after him, told him he was being childish, told him he couldn't go off on his own. God only knew what all she said, but she didn't say the *right* thing. Nate disappeared around a corner, never even turning around.

Jill waited at the apartment for several hours. It was a stressful situation, she told herself. It would be for anyone. She tended to forget that Nate had a very large Greek family, friends. He might never see any of them again. Of course he'd be grieving about that.

She tried to understand, to imagine what he was feeling, but it was hard. The truth was, this place did not feel all that bad to her. She rather liked the quietness of it, the feeling of owning the City that its desertion allowed her to have. And there was that sense she'd had from the start of something familiar. She didn't miss all those things Nate missed—TV, radio, even food. Not really, not when she had her work, the potential of the alien technology laid out in front of her. It was about as thrilling an opportunity as any scientist could imagine.

And she wasn't leaving anyone behind. If there was one person in her old life she would have missed, it was Nate, and he was here. Nate was here.

And if Nate were *not* here? Would she like being here then? No, she would not be nearly so okay with this if Nate were not here.

Still, whatever pressure he was under, he was being outrageously unprofessional and irresponsible by going off like that. Something might happen to him out there on his own. How would he get back? How would she know? Would he even *come* back?

Of course he would come back. Of course he would.

The printouts were on her lap. She tried to pull her mind back to them and could not. She sighed. How much time this was all taking! They should be getting work done, not wasting time arguing. But the only thing she could think about at the moment was, How could she get him to forgive her? How could she make it okay?

If they *couldn't* get off the planet it only made sense to allow her relationship with Nate to . . . to develop. He had needs, even here apparently, even on a seventy-thirty world. At the very least he had emotional needs. She should be more sympathetic. For the sake of the mission, if nothing else.

The flat, featureless cubicle of a room was dead, so amazingly empty. Jill had never heard a quiet this deep. She suddenly realized that since Nate had sprung her from the hospital she'd been with him every second. How many hours had that been? Seventy-two? Longer than that. Well over a hundred. At least a week since she'd not known where he was, since he had not been within earshot, if not right beside her.

She *did* desire him; that was not the issue. It was . . . what? Her, her own body, her own self. She was afraid of . . . of not being attractive enough, of being foolish in her intimacy, of being absurd. How could she bear that? Better not to let him get close at all.

And she finally saw that for what it was: a very old defense mechanism. When, she wondered, had she decided she was unlovable? Decided rejection was so inevitable it was better not to try?

"This is ridiculous," she said, standing up. When Nate *deigned* to return they could discuss it like rational human beings. She was willing to . . . to make concessions, even if the mere thought turned her to jelly. Yes. Okay. Yes. Fine!

Until then, she was going to go see those damned antennae!

The walk took several hours. The round dome was smaller than that of the spaceport, but it had the same thick walls. There was the suction sound of a breaking seal as she tugged the doors open. Inside, endless branching corridors were labeled at the top in numbers, probably coordinates. The individual rooms were comprised of enormous panels in rows like bookshelves, panels with millions of tiny light indicators, most of them dark. This was the City's power grid.

The place was empty. She thought about searching for the grid's control room, to try to learn more about their power source, but she didn't want to spend hours in here, not alone. Besides, what had really drawn her was the antennae. She left the building to check out the field next door.

The antenna field was on the power plant's western side. It was the coolest time of day. The larger sun was setting and the smaller was still too low in the sky to broach the skyline. She explored the field in the shadows. It was one vast plain, ten or twelve of the City blocks long and almost as wide. It was also ancient—much, much older than the power planet itself. The antennae rose only about twelve feet from the ground, and up close she realized she was seeing just the tops of them. Most of their bulk had been buried. And not, she was pretty sure, because the ground had been purposefully filled in: they'd been covered by the drifting sands of the planet; they'd been covered by time. Their metal tubing, like the ship she and Nate had seen on the spaceport runway, had fossilized, coated with red dust that had baked hard, layer after layer. Even thin wires jutting from the tops of the antennae had this coating. They looked like lacquered Chinese chopsticks.

Jill fingered them, as if she could tell time by the density of the layers. *Old.* How old? She had no idea. But she had the feeling it was like finding ancient pyramids in the middle of a modern city.

This place was a riddle, but it was not what she'd been hoping for. If this civilization was manipulating the wave, this kind of antenna field might be how they would do it. Had they used this technology long ago? Had they since developed subtler ways of influencing the wave? If so, why hadn't they torn all this down?

She had walked quite a ways into the antenna grid and now she turned around and headed back to the power plant, puzzling things over in her mind. She hadn't noticed the bunker the first time she'd passed it, but this time it caught her eye—a set of concrete steps leading down under the antenna field. She contemplated it, moved closer without much motivation.

The bunker, too, looked like it hadn't been used in years. At the bottom of the stairs was a door. Did she dare? Was there a reason to? She sighed. What she wanted was to go back to the apartment and see if Nate was there. But she was here and it had been a long walk. She might as well get her money's worth.

She went down the steep well of a staircase and felt the air grow chill. The door at the bottom looked heavy and old. It did not open automatically. She put her fingers experimentally into a narrow slot and found a latch. The door sprang inward.

Inside, steep stairs continued down and down. A cool tunnel of a stairwell arched overhead, lit by protruding lights. These were on a dim level of power causing the steps to cast shadows on one another and bleed together. And she was greeted with the smell of old air, surprisingly musty for such a dry planet. She hesitated, glancing behind her, then decided she would just go a little ways.

She began descending, one hand checking her balance against the wall.

The stairs went on and on for a long time. At several points she almost turned around, but in the end she went down the steps because they were there, because the bottom, by definition, had to exist. She felt as though she was descending into the underworld. There was a metallic smell, like the reek of a subway system.

The stairs leveled out, growing narrower and narrower. Then there were no more stairs.

She stepped out into a vast underground complex. It was so cavernous, the distant sides were lost in darkness. It had to be vast because it had been built to house a machine, a machine with long, curving arms that stretched for miles. Its scale reminded her of a superconductor, but it wasn't a superconductor. No, she knew what it was: it was a generator, a wave generator. She had found what she'd been looking for.

She stood and admired it, heart tripping in her chest, appreciating its scale, appreciating its very existence. The antennae were aboveground from here. This machine had originally, she surmised, been built underground, though not nearly as deep as this. It had been built underground to insulate the wave it was generating. The antennae above relayed the resultant pulse.

But this machine was as ancient as the antennae. It was covered with inches of dust and rusted with time. Still, she felt extraordinarily hopeful. This technology would be closer to the world she and Nate could understand, closer to what Earth might be able to accomplish. It lay between where the aliens were now and where the humans were before the one-minus-one. It was the connection, the missing link.

She found a door in one of the curved walls—a door with a handle not very much different from those on Earth. She pulled on it—it gave a little, but it was stuck from neglect. She tugged and tugged, slowly gaining half inch by half inch.

Inside the machine, the corridors were so dark she had to grope her way along. With some trepidation she moved away from the door, unwilling to give up now. She felt chairs and walls and knobby instruments. She thought she could make out a faint glow up ahead, and she stumbled toward it.

The glow, up close, was coming from a screen set in a disarray of wires and switches, a screen that looked very much like a computer or a television screen. There was a button underneath the screen and she touched it. The glow was replaced by a video recording of a man. It wasn't a man exactly, but it was humanoid and closer to her own species than the aliens were. The translator in her ear clicked into action, deciphering his words.

He was explaining the use of the machine. His voice was low-pitched and slow and there was something wrong with him. There was something in his voice, in the wildness of his large, swimmy eyes. But she couldn't quite make out what he was saying about the machine because he was repeating himself. He kept talking about "only wanting to help" and the dead, the dead, the dead.

The screen switched to images of bloody carnage in the desert sun, of red-soaked sand and fragments of limbs and unidentifiable body parts, of a city in ruins, smoldering, parts of it oddly warped and distorted. In one surreal image the camera panned in and Jill could see fingers sticking out of a solid wall like some horrific avant-garde art.

Explosion, Jill thought, her mind and heart sickening. It was the only thing that came to mind. But where was this city and who were these people? Why were these images *here*, in the bowels of this machine, in the subterranean vaults of *this* place?

And then on the screen she saw the wall as the camera panned out into the desert. There—the red glass wavy wall. It was new and sharp and the sand beyond it was seared and blackened and in places sprayed with blood. The wall marked the boundaries of the rubble as if the sand had risen up . . .

. . . *in a giant "splash." As if the City had been set down intact, like the house in* The Wizard of Oz.

The ruined city she was seeing was *this* city or, at least, its predecessor. And the planet where this cataclysm had taken place was *this* planet.

The man was back, his voice rising and falling with emotion. He tried to explain what had gone wrong, but it didn't sound like he really knew. He knew only that they had turned on the machine, they had turned it on, and at first it had all gone well, but then at nine hours, twenty-three minutes, and sixteen seconds after throwing the switch . . .

Idiots! Jill thought, furious. *They made a weapon! They made a negative one pulse machine. And it . . .it . . . it exploded. Or . . . for god's sake!*

Her hands were clammy. She felt dizzy. She was going to pass out; her consciousness was slipping away like quicksilver. It was the musty air in this place, those ghastly images.

She groped around in the dark for a chair, but her hands found nothing. The man was saying that the machine had been shut down and it must never, ever be turned on again, at least not until they had found a way to reverse the effect, to get home. But Jill just kept thinking, *They made a weapon; they made a goddamn weapon!*

The dark was stifling, suffocating, and she wanted out. The slightly restrained hysteria of the man on the tape was getting to her; it was sinking hooks into her that would probably never come out. But if she turned around now and tried to grope her way through the dark toward the door she might not find it in her panic—she might miss the door and spend hours wandering this vast machine in the dark!

She made herself sink to the floor and put her head between her knees. The air in here was so bad, it was like breathing the air of a coffin. But her nausea did slowly fade. As her head cleared, she kept hearing the man repeating over and over, *We only wanted to help,* and those words, and a dozen other hints in his long speech, finally clicked.

Dear God. Oh dear God. This isn't a negative one pulse machine. It wasn't created as a weapon. This machine was made to send a one pulse.

Jill gasped hugely, her head coming up, eyes riveted on the screen. It was true. She had just told Nate about her idea, that they could push the one pulse instead of the negative one, make Earth a living paradise. She thought she would be a god, a legend, an immortal for inventing such a thing, that she would change humanity's lot forever. And this very machine was just that—a "benevolent atmosphere producer"—and the aliens had built it. And it had done *that*.

"Get up now," a voice said.

She looked around, confused. For a moment she thought it was another television speaking. But the source of the voice stepped in front of the monitor and the light of the screen gave it form. It was an alien, a male, one of the tall, pale creatures they'd seen several times on this planet. He switched the button to end the video transmission.

"I am becoming ill on this air," the alien said flatly. "And I cannot leave you alone inside the machine. You must exit at once."

Jill didn't move, too amazed to connect these words with herself.

"Please get up and leave the machine," the alien repeated in a higher pitch, motioning his long fingers.

She stood obediently and began to move back the way she had come. She didn't feel the alien brush past her, but in a few minutes she heard the door up ahead of her open and saw the light of the outer chamber. The alien was at the door, holding it open. She slipped through, anxious to keep her distance from the thing, and she didn't turn around until she was a good twenty feet away. When she did turn, the alien was standing at the machine with his arms at his sides, face blank.

He was tall and stick-thin, as all the males were. It was startling to have those huge gelatinous black eyes actually focused *on* her. He spoke: "The probability is low that you would be able to start the machine, but I prefer that you not enter it again."

"You can see me," Jill said.

"Obviously."

It was spoken in such a dry, factual way that it was almost funny. The weirdness of the situation—actually talking to one of these creatures—suddenly impressed itself on Jill and for a moment pushed everything else from her mind, even the machine.

"Most of the aliens on this planet don't seem to be able to see us. At least, they have not acknowledged us in any way."

"They do not see you because they do not expect you to be there. I, myself, saw you and the male some days ago. I have been analyzing the benefit of contact and had decided against it. It was only to ask you to leave the machine that I spoke."

"What do you mean, they do not expect us to be there?"

He answered patiently, as if talking to a moron, "The brains of most species are designed to interpret energy patterns into three-dimensional solid matter.

If an energy pattern is not anticipated it may be discarded by the filter as random noise."

Jill gave this some thought. She herself was certainly capable of filtering out an awful lot when she was preoccupied, even large expected things, like, say, Dick Chalmers. "But we saw *you*. Are your brains so different from ours?"

The alien did a slow double blink before answering. "Your brain specifically is much like ours. You were in a strange place and therefore were expecting to receive unusual patterns. The same is not true for the ones who live here. I, myself, was able to see you because of the nature of my work. I have been programmed to think about other species. I have diagrams of many species and that is why my brain is familiar with the concept."

"Oh." Jill thought it could take the rest of her life just to understand everything he'd just said.

"However, one thing of interest I have observed while studying you: the male's brain is more different from ours. When you and the male separated I made the calculation to follow you for this reason. I do not understand the brain of the male. You *are* female—this is true?"

"Yes."

"Curious," the alien said flatly.

Despite his choice of vocabulary, there seemed to be no emotion in him, not surprise and not much curiosity. He stood motionless, staring at her, his translucent lids rising and falling over that jelly coating on his eyes. It was a little gross.

"You don't have many females, do you?" Jill tried. "Is that what's wrong with your planet?"

"Wrong?"

"The City is almost deserted."

"You refer to the fact that our species will soon cease to exist. We have come to see this as an inevitability. As machines become obsolete, so do species. I am a postspecies specialist. It is my job to prepare for our extinction, for those who may come."

He said it so matter-of-factly. It was depressing, but Jill couldn't help thinking that if they were expecting someone, there would be space travel, perhaps even rescue. "Who are 'those who may come'?"

"Unknown. The statistics are high that others will come in time. Your appearance was far sooner than predicted. However, I have reached the conclusion that you are not proper recipients. Someday someone will come who will be the appropriate vessels for our legacy."

"Your legacy? You mean your technology? Your knowledge?"

"Yes."

"But I'd like very much to learn what you know!"

"Are you and the male breeders? Can you repopulate this planet?"

"No," she admitted. "Our gene pool couldn't survive without other human beings to breed with."

"Then you can make no use of our legacy. I must go back to work now. Please return to the surface and never go inside the machine again." The alien walked toward the stairs, apparently with every intention of ending contact.

Jill went after him. "Wait! You have space technology. If you can help us get back to our planet, our people would be very interested in your legacy."

The alien stopped and gave this brief consideration. "I have noted your interest in the spaceport. Perhaps you are considering that as a means of transportation. It is impossible. I have detected from your physical makeup that you are from a dark universe. Our intergalactic space travel functionality was shut down four hundred years ago. Our interuniversal was shut down one thousand years ago."

Jill tried to comprehend what he was saying. One thousand years ago they had had the technology to travel between universes. One thousand years ago—but no more. "But . . . if you had the technology once, surely it can be resurrected!"

"*Reinstated* is a more accurate word in your language. At this time most of our power grid has been redirected to our maintenance program. We cannot spare the energy. Also, our space program shutdown program was not designed to be reversible."

Jill felt that news sink in. The spaceport was a bust, just as Nate had feared.

"Furthermore, a species from a dark universe would not be suitable recipients for our legacy."

"What do you mean by 'dark universe'?"

"A 'dark universe' is any universe with a greater than forty percentile negative force. It is difficult to believe, but we once came from one ourselves. Before that." He pointed at the machine and shuddered, his face showing dislike, though Jill couldn't have said how. "But that was over two hundred thousand years ago. We have few records left of what it was like on the dark world."

Jill stared at the machine and back at him. She was struck anew, first by the unbelievable time frame he was talking about, *two hundred thousand years*, then by the picture that was slowly forming in her mind.

"Your people came from a universe like mine? In that . . . that disaster? How? How did that happen?"

"That is not my area of expertise."

"But those *were* your people in there, your ancestors? On the video?"

The alien blinked slowly, processing this. "They were dark people. Yes, they were our progenitors, but many species evolve from lesser things. It is the way of it."

Jill turned and looked at the machine again, hand over her mouth. She had known it was ancient, but two hundred thousand years? Early Egypt had existed only three thousand years ago. The computer had been around for sixty.

"The machine manipulates the one-minus-one . . . I mean, the universal wave?"

"Yes. It was bad technology. This place was left here, never to be touched. I learned of this through the legacy. I repeat my request that you do not go inside the machine again. At this moment, I must return to the surface."

The alien began once again for the stairs. Jill followed him. "Are there records of what the machine did, of what *happened*?"

"Our records are excellent, but you would be wasting your time. It was bad technology."

But what Jill wanted to know, and badly, was why, why it was bad.

Nate was right—he had always been right. If she had remained on Earth she would have gone to work for the DoD and she might well have made a machine just like that one. And maybe what she had seen on that tape would have happened to Earth. There was a branding iron in the pit of her stomach, an anchor in her chest. It was like having a terrible nightmare that one had committed murder only to wake and realize with relief that one had not. Only she wasn't sure if she had really escaped her destiny or not.

By the time they pushed open the bunker door the alien was worn out from the long climb. He was a frail thing, and his body heaved with the effort. He looked even more insubstantial than he had before.

"I must return to my work," he said between gasps. "Good-bye."

"I'm going with you."

As if too depleted to argue with her, the alien only waved his fingers in the air and went to his car.

19.2. Sixty-Forty Denton Wyle

Denton and Eyanna traveled for another three days. After the night of the . . . the incident, he got sick. It was probably some horrible local virus, but he was sick to his stomach, shaky, and the thing in his throat burned like a lump of radioactive coal. And he was afraid that at any moment Eyanna was going to leave him.

Between that and the constant worrying about *skalkits* he was a basket case on two legs. Trying to make himself feel a little better, he bombarded Eyanna with apologies, sticking to the "I was asleep" story. He picked their fruit, made their fire, tried to help her over obstacles (which she wouldn't allow), and in general was the picture of abject misery around her. He did not touch her or sleep close to her again.

At first she would not speak to him. But finally his persistence wore her down. On the morning of the third day she commented with amazement on how big the mountains were now that they were close to them, and he felt reprieved. Maybe, in her own way, Eyanna needed company, too. Even a yellow bellied bunny like him.

On the evening of the seventh day after they'd left Sapphia, Denton and Eyanna found another village. They were at the foothills of the mountains, and there were strange small peaks in the land, like baby mountains or blips on a heart monitor. They were passing one of these abrupt peaks when Eyanna stopped and pointed upward.

There were bright bits of color up there, like the dyes the Sapphians used in their native fabrics. And as Denton squinted he saw movement—tiny people. There was a village at the top of the hill.

Eyanna was nervous about approaching strangers. She also didn't like the looks of the place. "It is a bad place to live," she said with contempt. "Look how far they have to go to get food."

She was right. Even from the valley floor they could see that the top of the peak was rocky and barren. The inhabitants of the village would have to climb up and down a considerable distance to reach the jungle primordial and the food the Sapphians took for granted.

Denton studied the layout, hand shielding his eyes from the sun; then he grinned. "Yes, but that is good, Eyanna! The *skalkits* cannot get up there! That is why they put the village on the hill!"

Eyanna looked unsure, but Denton was convinced he was right. With a little difficulty he talked her into checking out the place. He was tired and sick, and putting an end to their barrel-of-laughs journey sounded just fine.

It was a difficult climb. The hill was not so steep that it couldn't be walked, but it was close. About halfway up, the vegetation gave way almost entirely to rock. Denton had second thoughts as they neared the top. He had already been suckered once on this world. But this was exactly the kind of physical refuge he'd been searching for, and if it came with some people for company who were not playing nun like Eyanna and who also, by the way, didn't hand-feed their members to huge predators, then he'd be one happy camper.

The village at the top of the hill was small and modest. It consisted of no more than thirty huts around a single community circle. They were seen at once and were soon facing about forty or so staring inhabitants.

They were a more ragtag group than the Sapphians—not as elaborately groomed, not as uniformly attractive, and among them were several who looked very old. Denton was happy to see the old people. If he hadn't still been just a teensy bit wary, he would have hugged 'em.

An old male stepped forward. His abundant hair was white and his long, narrow face was wrinkled. He bobbed his head in greeting.

"This place is called Khashta. You are welcome. From where do you come?"

Eyanna looked at the ground. Denton answered, smiling for all he was worth, "We are from Sapphia."

The old man took in Eyanna's fading scratches knowingly. "Be at rest. You will not be harmed here."

Denton believed him. The old man had a sympathetic face and his eyes were warm. He seemed different from the Sapphians. He felt . . . sincere. Denton knew he could be seeing what he wanted to see, *again,* and, certainly, he would keep his guard up, but for the first time in days, things were looking up.

He squeezed Eyanna's hand. "I think this is a good place."

She still looked nervous, but she was a brave girl, god knew. She hesitantly made the Sapphian gesture for "yes."

That night they shared the community meal. There was meat, which they had not had since leaving Sapphia, fruit, grain, and a fermented beverage. Denton nodded and smiled at everyone, ingratiating himself. He decided to forgo the hard stuff until he was more sure of the place, but it warmed the cockles of his heart to know it was there. The old man who had greeted them was named Yulehulha or something like that (Yule, Denton decided). He even offered them hand-rolled cigarettes. Denton passed.

As the night wore on, his relief and gratitude to have found a new place, which he expressed freely to anyone who would listen, was dampened a little. It was not exactly the party atmosphere he'd gotten used to in the gorge. There were a dozen or so attractive young females but not nearly the bounty the Sapphians had. And the licentiousness he had come to appreciate so fully as a perk of this interstellar voyage stuff was not at all apparent. The Khashtans were more subdued, which he supposed was due to trudging up and down the mountain all day carrying food and water, something he himself had to look forward to. Yippee.

He couldn't help but feel a spark of resentment toward the Sapphians.

After the meal, Yule got up. He reached behind his back and produced a small brown egg. He showed it to Denton and Eyanna solemnly.

"*Khashta* means 'place of the egg.' Our people revere the egg because it shows the way of all creation."

Denton smiled and nodded, looking at Eyanna to make sure she was being polite. She was listening quietly.

"All of creation is like this egg when it is conceived inside the mother. The egg has life inside, but it is unformed and soft. As it grows, all that is bad and impure in the egg hardens out to the edges until it becomes the lifeless shell. And all that was good in the egg has become something else."

He cracked the egg with a flick of a fingernail and carefully pulled it apart. In the center was a baby bird, its feathers bright blue. It unfolded its wings and shook them, emitted a sharp *cheep*.

Eyanna smiled radiantly. The old man gave her the baby bird and Eyanna held it on her slender palm, smiling.

"And what kind of 'baby' does this world create?" Denton asked politely. He half expected some native legend about a giant fox or crow or something. But that was not the answer.

"The 'egg' is not just this world, but all of creation, all of the stars, all of the worlds, even the worlds beyond the worlds. And all of creation is still new. Even now, it is only a soft egg inside the womb. But someday, slowly, slowly, the bad will be separated from the good and will harden out to the edges, becoming like the shell. And inside the egg new life will be born."

"But what kind of life?" Denton asked again.

"Sahee," Yule answered. God.

That night in the hut, Denton was wired. Eyanna stood in the doorway looking out at the night as he paced, talking eagerly.

"This is good. We'll be safe here. The people are nice, and I believe them when they say they don't sacrifice to the *skalkits*. They're a little boring maybe, and it'll be hard work, but it is better than getting tied to trees. Don't you think so, Eyanna?"

He wanted her to admit it. In fact, it would be nice if she'd fall at his feet as her savior. More or less. Instead, she just gazed out into the night.

"Don't you think so?"

She turned to look at him. Her eyes were bright with what he thought were happy tears. That was better.

"I could bring my children here," she said in a full voice.

He hesitated, stopping in the middle of the floor. He was a little annoyed. They just got here, for god's sake. What the heck did she want from him? And, anyway, her children were in Sapphia—nice, faraway, never-going-near-there-again Sapphia.

"Maybe. Someday." He started pacing again. "For now, we have a place to live and I think we can be happy here. Especially if . . . if we're nice to each other. Do you not think so, Eyanna?"

She gave him a look that reminded him, oddly, of Dave Banks.

"Eyanna? I mean . . . Come on!"

"Yes, Denton. This is a good place."

He smiled at her, pleased.

The next morning, Eyanna was gone. Denton knew it as soon as he opened his eyes and saw that she was not in the hut. But still, he was not absolutely sure.

He went outside and looked for her around the village, but it was not a big place and it was obvious that she was not there.

Some of the villagers, including Yule, were sitting at the fire in the center of the village and they watched him search without comment. He finally joined them.

"She has left," Yule observed as Denton sat down.

"Yes. She left."

Someone offered him a cup of water. He took it. His stomach growled.

"You will go after her?"

Denton thought about it. He had a hard time even knowing what he felt, much less expressing it. "Eyanna was not my woman. She can do what she likes." He meant it more politely than it sounded, supportive in a women's lib kind of way, but it came out wrong. "She will come back," he amended.

And she might. He thought she intended to. But then, he knew where she was going, and he thought her chances of grabbing those children and getting out of Sapphia alive were only slightly greater than his chances of having a cheeseburger, fries, and milk shake for dinner.

But anyway, he wasn't going after her. She didn't ask him to and it was none of his business. In fact . . . it was a bit harsh maybe, but it was not a totally bad thing that she was gone. He could start with a clean slate now. He would not have to be reminded of . . . of things that had not gone so well between them. And without her here, the Khashtan females might warm up to him and he might not have to live in a perpetual state of frustration. Eyanna was beautiful, but she definitely had some codependency issues.

It was a warm morning, but he suddenly got a bad chill. Yule watched him cough, a wracking, chunky one, and lit up a smoke.

*   *   *

Denton was sick for three days. He felt guilty. He was taking up someone's hut and not helping gather food at all. If he were in Sapphia, he'd be dino meat. But he couldn't help it. His legs were watery and the thing that burned in his throat had expanded into his stomach and bowels. He had a terrible headache and he couldn't catch his breath. It was some native bug, he knew, something horrible, like smallpox or malaria. He lay in his hut wanting to die.

On the third morning, Yule visited him. He felt Denton's head and limbs, made him open his mouth, and looked in his eyes. Then he sat back on his heels.

"This is a sickness of the head," he said.

So much for native medicine, Denton thought.

The old man lit up a weed. "Tonight I make a special drink. With this drink, you can see God. If you take some of this drink with me, you will maybe see what is wrong in your heart."

"No thank you," Denton said.

Yule smiled. "You can stay sick also. It is up to you."

*   *   *

That night, Denton let himself into the old man's hut. It was no different from any of the others in the village on the outside. Inside, the smoke was thick and it had a sharp, bitter taste. Over the fire pit, a pot was boiling. Yule squatted next to it, his long skinny legs folded like a crane's. He wore an undyed tunic. The only other person present was a young male who attended the pot, throwing in dried herbs in pinches and stirring carefully.

It was about what Denton had expected, but he almost chickened out. He had nothing against hallucinogenics. They were all very well and good in the right place and time. But taking major drugs while he was already sick as a dog had little appeal.

Yule was looking at him.

Denton cleared his throat trying to disengage the lump. Damn, it hurt so freaking bad. "Do you truly think this will help?"

"Yes."

"Okay."

Denton's legs were shaky, strengthless. He took a seat on a blanket and propped his back up against the wall, panting.

Words were chanted over the potion; gestures were made in the air. It was all very Carlos Castaneda. Into the potion went the juice of several black spiky fruits. There was more stirring. Steam was coming from the pot now and, along with the smoke, created a miasma in the air. The potion was poured into a cup and it was thick like dirty oil and only slightly greener. Denton got a whiff of it on a breeze—yeasty and bad, like something that had lain in a mausoleum for several weeks.

But somehow it didn't matter anymore. The smoke was settling his stomach, soothing his throat, and making him feel . . . drowsy. Cool. He relaxed into the wall more and more, his limbs heavy. It was the first relief he'd had in days.

The assistant had prepared a blanket for the old man on the opposite side of the fire. Yule lowered himself down and stretched out on his back. When he had arranged himself he raised his torso on one elbow and reached out his hand. The assistant placed the cup in it. Yule muttered a final prayer or incantation and then took a large gulp. He handed the cup back to the assistant and lay down, shutting his eyes. The assistant rose and came over to Denton. Denton watched him approach from the far, far, far side of the moon. And when the hand stretched out to him holding the cup, his own hand reached up and took it.

The stuff in the cup tasted bad—*bad* bad. It was a taste that said, *You really shouldn't drink me.* It was a taste that said, *This stuff is not intended for living things.* With its hideousness it snapped him out of his warm and fuzzy state.

He had to swallow repeatedly to keep it down. He scanned for water, anything, but there was nothing in sight.

Time got indistinct. How long had he been looking for water? He didn't know. But the cup was gone and the assistant was on the other side of the fire. Denton looked at Yule's face. The old man was changing. Denton saw a tremor go through Yule's lean body. He looked *shinier* in the firelight. A veil of sweat had broken out all over his skin. He was absolutely still. Denton could not see him breathing. He appeared dead.

The floor began to spin. Denton crawled onto his back on his blanket. The fabric was rough and scratchy against the skin of his arms. The texture of the ceiling swam, as if covered with insects. The air grew thick and hot.

These were distant facts, lightly noted, as a co-pilot might assimilate the state of certain levers and lights before take-off. Denton closed his eyes and tried to sleep, but that was like trying to fly through the air after being hit by a truck. He had no choice and no control. He was falling. . . .

He was lying pinned to the blanket, deep under, deep, deep under. He had been under for some time. He became aware of someone speaking in the hut, low, mumbling words that seemed meaningful even though he couldn't make them out. He opened his eyes.

He could see nothing. The hut was pitch-black. He could feel the rough texture of the blanket under his stomach and chest, felt its fibrous stamp on his cheek, heard his own breath. He turned over on his back and, just as he did so, saw a figure slipping out the doorway of the hut. The figure was dressed in a strange outfit—bare feet and a woolen shift of the type popularized in Christian paintings. It was shining white. And he knew who the man was, even from the back: Kobinski.

Denton called out his name, but nothing came from his mouth. He wanted to get up, to follow Kobinski, but couldn't move. The fire nearby was smoldering embers. Hadn't it just been dark? Where was everyone? Was he really awake? Had he been dreaming earlier? Had he only dreamed he had seen Kobinski?

He was about to call out for help when a noise came to him, subtle and soft but absolutely the most terrifying sound he had ever heard. He froze, listening. . . . There. A sound like an enormous, heavy snuffle. It was the sound of some extremely large animal scenting the air, and it was right on the other side of the wall.

A *skalkit*. There was a *skalkit* outside the hut. At any moment its jaws would rip through the grass roof, delicately, like peeling tinfoil back from a chicken breast, and Denton would feel its teeth dig into him like ten-inch knives as it grabbed him around his rib cage, swung him up into the air, and bite him in two. He could almost feel the slimy texture of the beast's throat as he went down, suffocating.

He was suffocating. Where was he? He was on the blanket. The *skalkit* was only a few inches away, on the other side of a roof made of freaking fronds. Dare he whisper for help? Dare he move? Denton forced his head to turn and now he could see the old man. The assistant was gone; only the old man was there. He was floating several feet above his blanket, eyes shut utterly to this world, not breathing.

Now the beast was pawing the logs of the wall, high up, nearly at the roof-line. Denton thought he could see the roof shimmy and shake as the enormous nose pushed at it, testing. His heart was racing so fast it hurt. He had never been this terrified in his life—well, yes, he had, when he'd been watching the *skalkits* eat the Sapphians. He had never wanted to be that afraid again and now he was. He was that afraid. To be dead and gone would be better than this. The terror was nauseating. It was unbearable. He could die from this fear alone.

But *he* was creating the terror. He could choose it—he did have that power, didn't he? A rabbit cornered by a dog cannot choose not to be afraid. But a human can choose, can't he? A man can choose.

He closed his eyes.

Kobinski. He was the key to all of this. Denton had almost forgotten that. He had read Kobinski's manuscript but hadn't understood it, not really. It had rolled off his oiled skin like almost everything did. But now he could almost see the binder in front of him, could sense that this was what he needed, that this was what had been burning inside him and what could give him relief.

What had Kobinski said about these other worlds? About going through the light?

The binder opened. And suddenly the hut and the *skalkit* were gone. And Denton was looking at, was *suspended in*, the night sky.

It was breathtaking, so crisp and real. He could see stars by the millions in front of him and then the entire universe filling the dark sky. Its galaxies were mere dots and clouds of dots, their color blazing primarily white but dusted with blue and purple and red, tiny arms spiraling like dancers.

He blinked and everything shifted. Now the universe was far away, no bigger than a harvest moon. And it was not alone. There were hundreds, thousands of universes filling the sky, and then he blinked again and now he could see the ladder. The dazzling wispy balls of light were on a tilted continuum, forming a rectangle in the void. At the right end of the ladder the universes grew increasingly smaller and dimmer until the tip of the continuum was an inky unredeemed blackness. At the left end of the ladder the universes became more increasingly bathed in light until all individual stars were lost from view in a shining brightness.

Jacob's ladder.

Denton cried at its beauty and mystery, at the inconceivable vastness of its scale in time and space. He closed his eyes, unable to bear the sight, and when he opened them again, he saw the kabbalah Tree of Life, the round nodes of the *sephirot* shining. Jacob's ladder was gone and yet it was not. Denton understood that the tree of *sephirot was* the ladder, that it was somehow even bigger than that, that, in a way, it *was* God.

The whole of the vision was too overwhelming, so he tried to look at each *sephirot* in turn. He named each one and its attributes, *chesed, chochmah, binah, gevorah, hod, netzach,* watching them dance before him.

And then he understood.

Chesed, chochmah. He had identified himself immediately when he'd first read those descriptions. He was *chesed, chochmah, netzach,* and this world he had come to—that's what it was, what it was made of, what the people were. He understood. He understood.

Oh god, he understood.

He *was* the Sapphians. He had loathed their shallowness, their falsity, their disloyalty and selfishness, their frivolousness, their cruelty that was even more inexcusable for being thoughtless. . . . And he knew himself for the first time.

You'll find a way to do exactly what you want to do, Dent. You always do.

And, even now, if he had the chance, yes, if he knew for certain that he himself would be spared, he would go back to life in the gorge in an instant. In a freaking *heartbeat.*

There were no words, nor even thought images, for the depth at which he felt this, at which he understood the parallels or how appalling, how accurate, they were, how devastatingly deep they went. There was no expression for how much he loathed himself, or the despair of knowing that there was no escape, that even if he killed himself he could not escape his own soul. These things were *chochmah,* the wisdom that has no form.

And yet they filled the universe. He felt as though his being, his essence, was a tiny candle that could be snuffed out in sheer scale of it. In the scheme of things, in that almost infinite multiverse of the ladder, he was less than insignificant. Relatively speaking, he did not exist. And yet the fact that he did exist seemed to imply some taint in the fabric of that cosmos, some terrible flaw that threatened everything.

He understood now what it meant to look into the face of God, to really see the good and the bad, in all their splendor. For a moment he teetered on the brink of nonexistence. Then Denton's tiny candle puffed out.

19.3. Thirty-Seventy Aharon Handalman

In a few hours the closing ceremonies of the Festival would begin. The heretic would be executed, and whatever was going to happen would happen.

My Lord could not sleep. His brain would not give up the fight but continued to flail about like a man in the sea. He knew meditation techniques to quiet his mind, but it had been years since he'd used them and to do so now felt hypocritical. They called on God. Hadn't he rejected any assistance from God years ago? So the thoughts did their worst to him: Tevach, Aharon, Argeh, the heretic, Wallick, *The Book of Torment.*

Aharon had asked him, *What will happen to you, Yosef? When you die?*

He had not contemplated such a thing before. Oh, he had always been aware that he was damning himself. He had damned himself with great willfullness. But with Wallick gone, the thought of his own death became much more concrete. He had been Job cursing at God. And that had been enough, in his anger and despair; that was the role he had chosen for himself.

Just curse God and die, Job.

So Job's friends had advised him, and there was, in that statement, an implied end, a yearned-for finality.

The trouble was, it was not the end. Certain as the sun rose, even here, pale and distant, he, too, would rise again. And he would not, in his new incarnation, have the benefit of his anger. He would not even recognize the name: *Isaac Kobinski.* Everything came to an end, even our most cherished torments. That was the law. Just as it was the law, also, that nothing ever truly ended. His soul, his energy, would remain on the ladder long after this lifetime's woes had sunk into a past so ancient that the entire life of the multiverse so far was but the first shuddering breath of it.

He might reincarnate in his next life on Gehenna, a tiny Fiore infant, sentenced to this world of rocky hardship without the benefit of his memories to give that life a diabolical purpose. The thought of being sentenced here, with no idea that there were places better than this, with no hope of an education, no deep theological reasons for rejecting God—that was true horror. It was one thing to *choose* rebellion, to have chosen it from a place of high learning, as he had. It was another to wallow in rebellion's hellhole in ignorance.

Aharon was right. You might as well be angry at the phenomenon of photosynthesis. *You cannot win.*

My Lord gazed out over the town. It was nearly dawn and quiet now. But earlier in the night there had been stirrings, shadows in the streets: scuttling mice and scuttling rats, hiding and whispering, making plans. He was seated in the deep recess of a window seat, the cold stone around him cushioned and warmed by a blanket. It was one of the largest windows in the House of Divine Ordinance, and although the glass was not clear by Earth standards, he could see the town below, lit by the conjunction of Gehenna's moons. He turned his head to look at the bed where Erya slept—not for carnal purposes, he couldn't even imagine such with a Fiore, but to provide some warmth for his aching joints. He looked, too, at Tevach, snoring on his mat at the foot of My Lord's bed. *That* little mouse had scuttled out, when he thought My Lord was asleep, and had scuttled back in an hour ago. My Lord had observed both, feigning sleep, and had not said a word.

He could wake either of them, talk, get a massage for the pain, anything to be spared these thoughts. But he didn't wake them and the thoughts marched on. It was as though Wallick had been the black underpinning beneath the decaying tower of his soul and now that underpinning was gone. His soul was poised over the chasm and starting to fall in upon itself and he could not stop it.

For example, what if even Fiori was too good for his detached soul? When he had first discovered the heavens and hells in his physics, he had tried to work out models of what they might be like. He had anticipated heavier gravity; gravity *is gevorah*. And although he really had no idea what the Fiore or the landscape would be like, he had not been wrong about the general principle. He had also imagined a world *worse* than this, a true Gehenna, the far right rungs of Jacob's ladder. He had imagined a world where gravity was so dense that life was nothing more than blobs of flesh attached to the planet's surface like stones. There would be no mobility at all in that world, like the hideous punishment of Dante's ninth circle, where men were buried up to their necks in a lake of ice. And these blobs would congregate like the bubbles in foam or like crystals—how else could they reproduce? And to those who lived in this bubble-mass of base sentience there would be almost nothing redeeming—almost no light and warmth, little food, none of the blessings of family, music, home. It would make Fiori look like Paradise. And God—*Yahweh*—that evasive magician, wouldn't even have to condemn Yosef to such a fate. It was the simple nature of the universe: like to like, like to like, like to like. He could end up there.

My Lord was so lost in thought that he didn't hear the sounds at first. He stiffened as they registered: stealthy footsteps, the creak of the door. There was something altogether too quiet about it—even Tevach sneaking in was not that quiet, and Tevach was asleep on his mat.

Kobinski leaned forward, his knees screaming in protest, to peer around the wall.

A Fiore was sneaking up to his bed. The dark shape raised its arms high—he could see a knife in the furry hands—and plunged it down into the bed-clothes.

My Lord gasped. The sound was covered by a wet *thunk* as the knife made contact. There was a soft cry from the bed. The intruder took a few steps back, arms wide in alarm, the long, bloody dagger in one hand. He made a panicked animal noise and turned to Tevach. As he leaned over the sleeping mouse, the intruder's face fell into the moonlight from the window: it was Sevace, Argeh's bodyguard. Sevace would have seen My Lord in the window, had he turned his head, but he did not. He dropped the blade at Tevach's side and fled. Even brutal Sevace was frightened, murdering a god.

For a few moments My Lord sat stunned. Argeh had finally tried it. It was almost a relief that it was done, that the long years of waiting were over. He moved, painfully, off the window ledge. He could see the shape beneath the covers as he approached the bed. He saw, too, the blood spreading across the skins. *Erya.* He lowered the blanket and saw that she was dead, stabbed through the back into her heart. It had been a quick death at least. He pulled the blanket over her. Tevach still snored, though his twitching limbs indicated disturbed dreams. My Lord picked up the dagger that had been left near his trusted servant's hand.

This is what comes to you, Tevach. This is what happens when you play with treason. Your allegiance with the heretic, your sneaking about, made it simple enough—get rid of me and blame you.

The strategic nature of this thought cleared away his shock.

His guards were slumped in front of the doorway. He checked Decher—his pulse was steady. Perhaps they'd been drugged, but they were alive. He tried to rouse his captain and was rewarded with a groggy growl.

"Get up," My Lord whispered tersely. "Go check on the messenger and make sure he is safe."

Decher reported that Aharon Handalman was sleeping, unharmed, his guards alert and ready. My Lord was not surprised. The night Wallick died he'd seen a certain realization on Argeh's face, though he hadn't known what it meant at the time. The realization was this: as long as there was a mask, who really cared what—or who—was behind it?

Argeh came to My Lord's quarters at the first light of dawn. He was received by Decher and four of My Lord's guards. My Lord could hear the surprised words spoken in the corridor; then Argeh burst into the room. My Lord sat on his bed, waiting. With Argeh was Sevace, his would-be assassin. They both looked at him with horror.

"Why do you burst in on me?" My Lord picked up his mask from a table near the bed and put it on as the guards averted their eyes.

Argeh stood speechless. At the foot of the bed, Tevach snored.

"I apologize . . . My Lord. I only wanted to . . . We had word that you were in danger."

My Lord tilted his head back in the ironic Fiore style, the blankness of the mask giving it a crueler bent. "Your regard touches my heart, Argeh. Good Festival to you. Now leave."

*   *   *

My Lord peered out at the streets anxiously as they approached the arena. His eyes fell on faces, on hands, searching for hints of rebellion. He saw one male Fiore signal another over the crowd. Followers of the heretic?

He leaned back in the seat of the carriage, sighing. The eyes of the Jew were on him.

"I was hoping you would come back to visit me," Aharon said, "and we could talk some more."

My Lord fluttered his fingers in a gesture of indifference. "There is nothing to be said." The depth of that answer did not come through. He tried again. "It has been enough just to see you. Your presence has meant more than you know. It has been a long time since I've seen one of my own."

Aharon inclined his head, accepting the compliment, but he looked a little guilty. "I—I have something to confess. Tevach took me to see the heretic at the prison."

My Lord had already guessed. He had known it the night he had stood there and had heard teachings from *The Book of Torment* echoing through the House of Cleansing.

"You saw Wallick, too," My Lord said tightly. "I don't know what you said to him, but he was quite changed."

Aharon's eyes widened. Two spots of flame appeared on his cheeks. "No. I didn't go into that room, Yosef. I didn't even *look*. Because what's yours is yours. I wanted you to know that. I wanted you to know that I don't judge you, no matter what. I don't have the right."

The hard places in Kobinski ground together as though in agony. It took a moment for My Lord to collect himself. "Thank you," he said simply. He reached into his robe and brought forth a piece of parchment. "You will not be able to stay here after the Festival. I prepared this map for you. It shows the way to a small rural town called Chebia. Tevach's family is there. It is a modest place, but the Fiori are decent. They will help you."

"I thought maybe . . . the gateway. What you said before . . . " Aharon looked embarrassed.

My Lord leaned his head back on the rough seat, studying the Jew's face. It was strange how you could *see chesed*. Like water it softened the lines made by life's bitterness, made the eyes wetter and more open as though they had been flooded. Fiori had done its work on Aharon in a way it had never done for My Lord, in a way he had never allowed it to do. It hurt My Lord to see it, the way hope hurts one who is hopeless, the way the sight of a newborn hurts one who is childless.

"You've changed, Aharon. Perhaps enough to trigger the gateway; I don't know. It takes a significant difference between your own wave and that of the planet to trigger a gateway. But even if you did go through, there is no telling where you would end up. Even if you made it to the fifty-fifty universe, you have to understand that there are thousands of worlds there. The odds of your appearing on Earth are infinitesimal. I'm sorry. Still, I have marked the place on the map also. It is up to you whether you wish to try it someday or not."

Aharon's eyes were bright and somber as this news sank in. He sighed. "I see. I have felt . . . Your book has been a great help to me, Yosef, but I still have much work to do. Maybe you and I could work together? Maybe we could both go to Tevach's family?"

"Time is not a river, Aharon; it's a tapestry. All the threads we've woven over a lifetime create the present. I wish I could go back and change those threads, but I cannot."

Aharon looked baffled.

"There is no time left for me," My Lord clarified.

"Don't say such a thing! You have so much to give. What about your mind, your work?"

My Lord closed his eyes, amazed at how quaint those words sounded. "Believe me when I say that the time for me to be Yosef Kobinski, the teacher and scholar, came and went long ago. Whatever I had to give to the world, it was given in that book. What is left—what is left is between me and God and no one else."

"I can't accept that."

My Lord looked at Aharon and smiled. "If there is one thing you *can* do for me, it is to accept, accept that Kobinski died in Auschwitz. Because that is what truly happened, and that is what I want."

"We have a choice," Aharon insisted, in a soft rabbi's voice. "At each and every moment. *Nu?* You taught me that."

"I understand my choices at this moment very well, Aharon. And if I'm lucky, if God is merciful, I will make the right one."

*   *   *

My Lord scanned the arena, trying to judge how much of the ominous atmosphere was coming from the crowd and how much from his own mind. The closing ceremonies were the highlight of the Festival, so the packed house was not abnormal. But the massed Fiore were agitated, literally on the edges of their seats. The Fiore were capable of ravenous violence, and the threat of it hung above the crowd like a mist. My Lord was leaning forward, upright in his seat, the better to see, and when he noticed Argeh in exactly the same posture an ironic smile came to his lips.

Argeh was sweating as well. Good. Let him sweat.

Behind Argeh, Sevace was outfitted for anything, heavy gloves on his hands, his curved stone blade sharp and ready at his side. When he felt My Lord's gaze he glanced over with unmistakable fear and looked quickly away. My Lord smiled again. Sevace was thinking, perhaps, that he was sure he'd felt the knife go in, that he'd seen the blood . . .

"What is it? Why are there so many guards?" Aharon asked anxiously.

Down in the grisly arena, where the bodies of those who had been mounted on the *hechkih* earlier in the week still hung, Argeh had supplemented the decorative festival troops. Whole companies were arranged near the ground-floor entrances and spread along the walls. They were heavily armed.

"It's the execution of the heretic. Argeh expects trouble," My Lord said quietly. "If things get ugly, you must go immediately. My carriage is in back—take it and leave the city."

"What are you talking? What will happen?"

My Lord held up his hand to stave off the questions. He wiped his face. He turned and pretended to look at the crowd behind them, but instead he looked at Tevach. The little mouse was on hyperalert, his nostrils wide, his eyes darting around the arena. He nodded at someone.

My Lord put his elbow on the arm of his chair, and rested his head in his hand. He was deeply frightened. *I have no power,* said a voice in his head. Another answered, *But I do; I have the power of any man. Even a man who is bound and gagged has this power: to choose who he is. And that is the only power that* really *exists. Any other is illusionary.*

The blare of the opening fanfare.

Kobinski prayed, *Lord, Wallick had no mercy on me, on Isaac, and You did not stop him. I had no mercy on Wallick, and You did not stay my hand. If I have mercy now, will You have mercy on me?*

But he knew the answer: His mercy on others *was* God's mercy on him; by being merciful he *became* mercy. Like to like, like to like, like to like.

In the arena, the opening prayers of the priests were rumbling upward. My Lord forced himself to stand, telling his joints to bear his weight whether they would or no. He slowly made his way across the aisle, down a step. Sevace watched his approach with growing discomfort. He tugged on Argeh's sleeve.

The pushed-in face that turned to him had haunted him for a long time. My Lord whispered in Argeh's ear, "I have been informed of a rebellion."

The priest grunted, unimpressed.

"The heretic's followers are planning to make a march on the House of Cleansing during the execution. They've given up rescuing Ahtdeh—they know the arena will be well guarded. So they're going to storm the House instead—kill the attendants, empty its prisoners in protest."

Now Argeh was interested. His nostrils flared as he sniffed, trying to smell the truth inside the mask. "Where did you hear this?"

My Lord turned to look at Tevach. "My servant. Something frightened him last night. He confessed everything to me this morning."

Argeh growled angrily and whispered orders in Sevace's ear. My Lord made his way painfully back to his seat. He lowered himself into his chair and felt the Jew's hand grip his arm. He put his own hand over Aharon's to feel its warmth. Within minutes, the troops in the arena had filed out to go protect the House of Cleansing, leaving fewer than three dozen guards. My Lord watched for the crowd's reaction. He saw several Fiore stand and stare after the guards, saw others whisper menacingly. Could Argeh really not see it?

But Argeh wasn't watching. Sevace had returned to the box and the two of them were whispering together.

The mind-numbing rituals of the previous days of Festival were thankfully missing on this day. There was only another long exhortation from Argeh. Like any evangelist, he could not resist the opportunity to drum his own obsessions into a packed house. My Lord prayed it would end quickly. He eyed the entrances on the arena floor with trepidation. If the guards returned too soon and said they'd found no attack on the House of Cleansing . . . Argeh droned on.

Finally, just when My Lord was considering acting before the speech ended, it did end. Argeh raised his arms. There was a mild round of staff thumping in the arena. As he dropped his paws, Argeh gave the order: *"Bring in the heretics!"*

Down below, the ragged, bloody group emerged from the prisoners' arch, herded by guards. They had spent days in the House of Cleansing, and they were a pitiable sight. Even Ahtdeh himself—his head was bowed and stiff with gore. Argeh's priests had lavished much loving care on him.

The crowd collectively held its breath, growing far too quiet for a group of Fiore of this size. Around the arena, several Fiore rose to their feet, then several more. It was so still you could hear the armor of the guards clinking as they moved the shuffling prisoners forward.

Argeh looked nervous. He picked up the scroll of the condemned self-consciously and scanned it. My Lord could see his mind working, recalculating his strategy.

"First prisoner! Ahtdeh, son of Hehchah, charged with heresy against Mahava and blasphemy toward our beloved My Lord."

Beloved My Lord. Argeh *was* frightened. And he had changed the order of execution. Normally, he would have saved the big fish for last.

Aharon tightened his grip on My Lord's arm. "Can we *do* something?" he whispered.

"Shhhh," My Lord said.

The guards untied Ahtdeh from the other prisoners and began to lead him—half dragging the weakened body—across the arena to the *hechkih*. My Lord's eyes flickered to Sevace. He stood just behind the high priest, hand poised on the handle of his curved blade, eyes intently scanning the arena. But he was looking for trouble in the wrong direction. Argeh, hands stiff on the lip of the box, was leaning forward, watching the ritual.

My Lord was sweating. It was always freezing on Fiori, but the smooth interior of the mask was misted with perspiration. His head was spinning, yet at the same time he had a remarkable clarity. He felt as if all time and all meaning in his life had swirled together and condensed in this one black hole of a moment. He forced his palms against the arms of his chair and rose again, oblivious to the pain in his knees. He turned, one last time, to gaze upon that human face, upon the beard, the eyes, of a Jew. Aharon felt the gaze, returned it wordlessly but with a profound acceptance that touched My Lord's soul. Still all was silent.

As he had done earlier, My Lord took the few steps across the aisle toward Argeh, his feet pressing hard against the smooth, polished stone. As then, his left foot descended the single stair between them and his left hand went to the back of Argeh's chair to steady himself, to support his knees. Argeh was still cupped toward the arena, his head at the level of My Lord's waist. Four feet from My Lord, Sevace turned, recoiling for a fraction of a moment at My Lord's presence.

My Lord removed from the pocket of his robe the dagger Sevace had dropped at Tevach's side that morning. His hand, cold and numb, did not feel like his own. He pulled the dagger from his robe and plunged it into the center of Argeh's back with a mighty thrust. My Lord's arms were strong from bearing the weight of this world. The dagger went in to the hilt.

The arena was amazingly silent. My Lord felt suspended in time and space until Argeh, expelling his dying breath, arched his back around the knife. Then he fell forward, tipping over the edge of the box and tumbling down to the arena floor. His body landed with a heavy thud and lay still.

There was a collective gasp from the crowd.

Kobinski, standing straddled between two steps, raised his bloody hand in the air, palm open.

"*Free the prisoners!*" he screamed.

For a moment there was nothing; then the multitude of Fiore stood on their feet, roaring hysterically. Kobinski saw concealed weapons appear from under robes, here, there, all over the arena. Others brandished their staffs, yelling. One group near the arena floor vaulted over the balustrade to face the startled guards.

"Yosef!" Aharon cried behind him.

As he turned his head toward the Jew, Kobinski felt a great burst of trembling joy. He felt as though the door of some horrible cell in which he'd been imprisoned had finally swung open, revealing light and warmth. And then he caught a glimpse of a stone blade swinging toward him from the left, heard the *whoosh*, felt the sharp and devastating impact as it cleaved his neck. His head was turning over and over through the air, over and over, and he could feel the movement of the wind against his hair, against his severed throat. The sound of Aharon screaming his name came through the screaming of all the Fiore and then both faded into the void.

The head landed on the arena floor, a few feet from Argeh's dead body. On impact the mask that had belonged to the king of Gehenna dislodged and spun away, revealing the human face of Yosef Kobinski, eyes closed, expression peaceful.

*   *   *

The arena was in utter chaos. Aharon had watched in disbelief as Kobinski murdered Argeh. He'd watched Sevace, intimidated and stunned at first, recover and draw his terrible blade.

If Aharon had moved, if he'd had a weapon, if he'd been fast enough . . . But he hadn't.

He was still staring in horror at Kobinski's headless corpse as Tevach shoved him.

"Go! Get out!" Tevach yelled. The massively built servant had a blade of his own in one hand. He gave Aharon another shove, then gave up on him, throwing himself over the side of the box and pushing through the milling crowd toward the arena floor.

Aharon stood, dazed. Sevace took one step toward him, bloody sword in hand, then paused, suddenly fearful. He changed his mind, leaving Aharon and following Tevach down to join the melee, yelling a cry of pure rage. And still Aharon stood.

Blood ran down the steps behind him and soaked over the edges of his sandals—this made him move at last. He put up the hood on his cloak to hide his face and pulled his weight up the heavy steps by leveraging the backs of stone chairs. He made it out the rear door of the box.

The roaring from the arena intensified now that he was outside. A long, narrow flight of stone stairs led down to the street below. No railing guarded the edge. He saw a few Fiore running from the arena in terror, but none of them looked in his direction. He couldn't take these stairs alone; it wasn't possible. He would plunge over the edge and kill himself. But he took one step, then another, clinging to the smooth stone wall to his left. Somehow he made it to the bottom.

My Lord's carriage was waiting. The driver stood anxiously, alarmed by the sounds of the crowd. He spoke to Aharon, and Aharon realized he couldn't understand or be understood. He wavered uncertainly, with no idea how to proceed; then he remembered what Kobinski had told him.

"Chebia," he said to the driver. He took the parchment from his pocket and showed the driver the map. He looked confused. He glanced again up the stairs toward the box.

Aharon lowered the hood to expose his face. "Chebia," he demanded as the driver drew back in fear. Aharon motioned to the coach, opened the door, and got in.

The sounds from the arena were clearly battle sounds now. Dying screams rent the air. The driver had the look of a dog torn between sticking by its master and fleeing a dangerous situation. Aharon was his excuse to flee. He climbed up to the top of the carriage and, once rolling, moved at top speed. The arena fell away behind them.

*   *   *

Chebia was in the middle of nowhere, a few shacks in a barren wasteland. The community of twenty accepted Aharon without question. Within days, he was working in the field next to Tevach's father, coaxing rocks from the thin, dusty soil.

His new life was a hard one, bitter as gall. He felt like a Jew from ancient times toiling in some distant land—Egypt, perhaps—lost to his people, sold for a slave. But the physical labor freed his mind to reflect on many things, and he was glad to be away from the City. Now he was only a man, a man doing penance, and that . . . well, that was perhaps as it should be.

It was three weeks before any carriage approached the village. The carriage brought Tevach. His family stopped their work to greet him, milling about him with tender-eyed pawing. Tevach seemed glad to see him, coming up and smelling him, rubbing his face against Aharon's arm.

"I thank *Adonai* that you are safe," Tevach said.

Aharon was startled at the use of the Hebrew name. He nodded. "And I you, Tevach. I see you survived the fight at the Festival."

Tevach's nose twitched with excitement. "Argeh's guards won a bloody battle and Ahtdeh is in hiding, but he lives! And there are many followers of Ahtdeh now. All will be well."

Aharon had the feeling that was hopelessly optimistic for Fiori, but he wished it would be so.

Later, after a scanty meal, Tevach took him aside to say good-bye. He handed Aharon the manuscript. "I took it from My Lord's room. It is for you."

Aharon ran his hand over the cover, thinking of Kobinski. He briefly considered giving the work to the little mouse, to Fiori. But with all the trouble it had caused on Earth, he guessed it would be more of a curse than a blessing in the long run. Besides, Tevach and Ahtdeh already understood the heart of it.

"Thank you," he said, swallowing a lump in his throat. He tucked it into his belt.

"My mind thinks often on My Lord," Tevach said, his small face sincere. "He helped free Ahtdeh—did you see?"

"Yes, Tevach. I saw."

"When I thought he would do nothing, he helped us. He showed us God cares, even for the Fiore." Tevach placed his cheek on Aharon's sleeve again, holding it there for a brief moment. When he pulled away, he looked sad. "You stay here?"

Aharon nodded. "I think that's best."

"How long?" Tevach's eyes were bright and curious, curious, still, about where Aharon had come from and where he might go.

Aharon looked over Tevach's head, at the cold wasteland of the farm. He sighed. "That, Tevach, is in God's hands."

20

Follow the Way of Heaven,
And you will succeed without struggling.
You will know the answer,
Without asking the question.
All you need will come to you,
Without being demanded.
You will be fulfilled
Without knowing desire.
The Way of Heaven is like a vast net.
Although its mesh is wide, it catches everything.
—Lao-tzu, *Tao Te Ching*, sixth century B.C.

20.1. FORTY-SIXTY CALDER FARRIS

Pol's room that night was unbearable. He had an attack of paranoia so strong that he found himself jerking open the hallway door and looking out three or four times. No matter how he tried to talk himself out of it, he could not escape the feeling that they were coming for him, that they knew everything. He searched for bugs again, this time not caring what damage he did: wrenching open the pipe under the bathroom sink, prying the mirror off the wall, making his knuckles bleed probing the shower drain. He found only himself, looking back from the glass.

Alien.

His eyes looked haunted. It was no longer a matter of simply being mad or brain-damaged, was it? There were too many things that didn't add up.

He went out and checked the hall again, went back to the mirror.

Who am I?

Gyde wanted to find out. He had felt Pol's arm, which, as far as Pol knew, felt like any other Silver's arm. He had asked him to go to the gymnasium. Bullshit. Gyde had friends from his youth that he trained with every day. That was not a clique Pol ever had or ever would be invited to join. No, Gyde wanted to see him unwrapped, naked, or maybe had just wanted to see what Pol would do at the mere threat of it, how fast he would scramble. And he *had* scrambled.

He grabbed his coat, unable to stay in the room any longer. He did not go to the rec club on the Silver campus. Instead he took a bus downtown where a few mixed nightclubs were open past curfew for those with merit passes.

There had not been an air raid that day and the nightclub crowd was edgy, nervous, and overly loud. Pol recognized a few Bronzies from the Department of Monitors. He sat by himself at the bar and ordered fifty proof.

He was on his second when a young Silver in battalion uniform sidled into a seat beside him. The youth was well made, with a square jaw and lively face.

"Greetings, classmate. Are you a detective?"

"That's right."

"How do you like it—compared to combat, that is?" The boy was eager.

"I like it."

"How much?"

Pol looked down into his drink.

"That was a stupid question. Listen, I heard you're partners with Gyde 332."

"I am."

"By the blood! He was at Cross-Plain, wasn't he? He's a *legend*. I've heard he's got so many merits he's practically—"

"Excuse me." Pol got up and went to a private table. He ordered two more drinks.

From his semihidden seat he could stare with impunity at a Silver female at the end of the bar. She was a beauty and men hovered near her like planets around a sun. Her form was lithe and muscular, her hair soft and limp around her perfect face like silk tassels in an egg-yolk hue. Her eyes turned to his, bright as little fishes.

He tried to feel something for her, but all he felt was emptiness. Had he had a woman, where he came from? He stretched for the memory, but there was only that aching hollow. He took the pamphlet from his pocket and smoothed it out on the table.

It is possible to travel to other worlds. I have done it myself.

*   *   *

Pol had never tried entering the Department of Monitors late at night, but to his surprise, there was no red tape. The doors remained open for late-night arrests and his ID alone did the trick. It was well past midnight.

Up in the office he went directly to the telex, but the results from Research had not yet arrived. While he waited, his eyes kept wandering to Gyde's desk. He tried the top drawer, where Gyde had put that file. It was locked.

The desk, like most things the state made, was heavy, built for maximum functionality and length of life. Its lock was the size of a small mouse and its hasp, Pol knew from his own desk, went deep into the wood and metal. But he found he knew how to pick locks just as he knew how to search for bugs. He took out a pocketknife, the regimental one he'd taken from Pol 137, and began working carefully with the tip inside the keyhole.

He was close to getting it when the telex when off. The loud, clanking noise made him jump. He closed the knife and went over to peer at the paper.

Research had found a match: a Bronze 2 construction foreman originally from Madamar. The name and address were there and it was not far, in the Bronze housing on the west side of the city. Pol put his knife in his pocket and grabbed his coat.

20.2. Sixty-Forty Denton Wyle

By the time Denton reached the horseshoe gorge he'd been walking for six hard days and nights, alone. The journey itself had changed him. He had already done things, and thought things, that were like nothing Denton Wyle had ever done or thought before.

After he'd emerged from his vision of Jacob's ladder, his sickness was gone, as the old man had promised. And he'd had an undeniable certainty about what he had to do. He hadn't liked it, but that was no longer material. So he'd borrowed several knives from the Khashta tribe. One of them he put in his belt. The other he tied with a vine to a long branch, making a rough spear. Then he began the long trek to Sapphia.

He had pressed his pace because he had a gnawing sense that Eyanna was already in trouble. The last night he slept only for a few hours, following the riverbank in the dark. But when he drew close to the entrance of the horseshoe gorge, it was already too late. Through the foliage came the tender grunts of beasts and the muffled cries of Sapphians.

Denton stopped in the jungle, the sounds on his ears turning him cold. How soft they were for what was actually going on, and how ghastly.

His memory of the *skalkits*, of what had happened that morning in the clearing, came back to him in vivid, reeking color. How easily the beasts had consumed the Sapphians, how enormous they were, how intelligent, how strong. When he'd left Khashta he had not even let himself *think* that it might come to this. If Eyanna was there, she was among the victims in the clearning, there was nothing he could do. He could never fight the *skalkits*.

The momentum that had gotten him this far—self-disgust more than anything—deserted him. He was swamped by a sense of futility and insignificance. He would have to turn around and leave. It wasn't like he hadn't tried. Right?

Then he remembered the feeling of someone behind him, cutting his bonds when he'd thought all hope was lost. Eyanna had done it. She had faced the *skalkits*.

He was no less terrified, but he raised his spear up in one shaking hand and the knife in the other. It felt stupid, out of character, like a rag doll wearing armor. Who did he think he was kidding? He couldn't do this. Yet he crept on, step by step. And suddenly he could see the clearing through the trees.

There were two *skalkits*, the same ones that had almost fed upon him, and there were three empty, bloodied trees, the vines hanging down ripped and worn like used dental floss. One of the *skalkits* was tonguing the ground underneath one of the trees. The other was licking a forelimb clean.

Two of the trees were still occupied. On one was a Sapphian boy, barely a man. On the other was Eyanna.

Denton was both genuinely relieved to see her and, shamefully, disapointed. It wasn't too late to save Eyanna. She wasn't, for example, *dead*. That meant he actually had to do this. He took a deep breath, his stomach starting to get seriously upset, and began to edge around the clearing. He would approach her from behind her tree. The *skalkits* wouldn't be able to see him. He would do just what she had done. He'd cut her bonds, keeping himself out of the *skalkits'* sight, and they'd slip away noticed. It could work.

But as he moved, the bunny instinct in his brain had something more to say about it.

What if the *skalkits* smelled him? Or heard? Or what if Eyanna couldn't slip away? What if the *skalkits* went after her? Could Denton do what she had done, draw their attention? No. No freaking way. He didn't have her speed or stealth; it'd be suicide.

He went on.

From the trees behind Eyanna he could see the way her arms were tied. They were red and swollen; the vines were tight. He tucked his spear under his arm to free his hands and slipped out into the clearing. He was a nervous wreck by the time he reached her. His hands were all goosey, and twice the edge of the knife slipped off the rubbery vines. He cut and cut and cut, his ears ringing with the pounding of his own blood. He couldn't see the *skalkits* but he could hear them. They did not seem to be getting any closer. The freaking vines took forever.

And while he cut, Denton did not feel brave. He'd thought that he might, once he was in action, that some latent testosterone might kick in but, no. He was petrified and sweating and nauseous and not remotely manly. He *hated* this.

The vines broke. Eyanna was free.

Denton wanted to turn immediately and flee but he made himself edge around the tree to make sure she was okay. The *skalkits* came into view. One of the *skalkits* was yawning hugely, but one—the smart, evil one—was already looking at his next victim. He was stalking the boy with that intent expression.

The Sapphian was tied to the tree, his head slack on his chest in either unconsciousness or resignation.

For a moment, Denton was mesmerized. Then he remembered that he was, like, in danger, and he turned to look at Eyanna and she was gone. He scanned for her, panicked . . . and saw her white-gold hair like a beacon. She was across the clearing, just inside the trees. She was standing there, watching him, and he thought she must have run when she'd found herself freed, and then had remembered to worry about him and had come back to make sure he got out.

Good old Eyanna. Wasn't she sweet?

He motioned at her to go and started backing away toward the woods himself, quietly, quietly. And for a moment he thought they were actually going to make it. The *skalkits* were full and not paying attention and, anyway, the boy appeared to be next on the menu. They were going to survive this intact, and then all he had to figure out was how to get her. . . .

Eyanna moved into the clearing. She was not leaving. She was *heading for the boy*.

Denton ran through about a million curses in his head. Of course it couldn't have been that easy. Oh, no! He had way too much payback coming for that. Somewhere up there, someone was having a laugh riot.

He ran into the trees, still cursing. He ran for quite aways before he realized what he was doing. He was running away from the clearing. He was abandoning Eyanna.

He stopped, overcome with frustration. He stood there debating with himself. It was the old Denton and the new having it out. The old Denton was adamant, and he had a point. He had already risked a lot to free Eyanna. It was not his fault if she wanted to throw herself back into the frying pan. He was not responsible.

Crap.

He got glimpses of the clearing through the leaves as he snuck back, spear in one hand, knife in the other, and neither one feeling any less ridiculous. He saw the *skalkit* nuzzle the vine that held the unconscious boy's arms, lips drawn back, teeth gnashing. He saw Eyanna creeping toward them from the side of the clearing, completely exposed.

Denton stopped at the edge of the woods, not knowing what to do or if he'd do anything at all. Everything seemed to be happening so slowly. The *skalkit*'s nuzzling loosened the boy and he fell, slumping forward. He was delicately caught and lifted in the *skalkit*'s open mouth. Eyanna, close to the *skalkit* now and still unseen by the monster, darted forward and grabbed one of the boy's arms.

Man. She was a freaking *lunatic*.

The *skalkit* saw Eyanna then, all right. It roared lustfully with a full mouth. Eyanna pulled the boy's arm. The *skalkit* moved its head back. In a minute the two of them were engaged in a full-out tug-of-war. The *skalkit* could have just closed its jaws and crushed the boy, but it apparently didn't want to, because it held him just enough to keep Eyanna from taking him away.

The unusual sounds attracted the attention of the second *skalkit*, who looked up and let out a bellow that was so loud and so enraged that it made every hair on Denton's head stand to attention. But Eyanna didn't seem to hear. She was still playing push-me-pull-me with the boy, and now she was yelling and kicking at the *skalkit*'s front legs. She did not see the other *skalkit* coming. It blindsided her, snatching her right off the ground with a whip of its head.

The *skalkit* had her left arm and shoulder and upper chest in its mouth, and it was not being delicate. Her legs kicked and jerked. She pounded at the *skalkit*'s nose with her fists.

And that was it. Denton found himself plowing out of the trees. He was running across the clearing with his spear raised in one hand and from his mouth came a scream that was only slightly lower in decibel than the *skalkit*'s. He screamed from somewhere deep inside him and it sounded . . . by god, it sounded *pissed*.

For a moment, as he closed the distance between them, he was both in his body and observing himself, stupefied, from someplace high above. Then he reached Eyanna and the *skalkit* and the spear was in his hand so he thrust its as hard as he could into the beast's side. The knife went in, deep. Denton was amazed. He had actually pierced the thing and hurt it. It let out a bellow of pain. He grabbed the spear and pulled. He was afraid the knife would be lost in the *skalkit*'s thick hide but it came out, still secured to the branch. The *skalkit* snarled and dropped Eyanna. It reared back, its front legs coming off the ground, and Denton saw the white flesh of its belly. He thrust the spear again, aiming for the heart.

The *skalkit*'s cry became deeper, more enraged, but it did not fall over or give up. No, it was still very much alive and more dangerous than ever. Gripped only by blind necessity now—kill or be killed—Denton pushed down on the handle of the spear, fishing around inside the *skalkit*, looking for the heart. It was hard. The *skalkit* thrashed. The handle of the spear cracked.

Then something struck him a massive blow from behind. He flew, like a pebble being tossed, and struck the ground. It almost knocked the breath out of him. He gasped and rolled over. Above him the second *skalkit* had discarded the boy and now fully, enthusiastically focused on ripping him to shreds. It waved its clawed feet at him, letting out a growling yelp of lust and greed and rage.

Denton lay there, looking up at the hideous, deadly thing. And he laughed.

Ho ho ho. Ha ha ha ha ha ha ha. He had no idea where it came from. It was not a feeling Denton Wyle had ever had before. But suddenly he felt freaking *great*. He was not afraid. Even with that thing hovering over him, he was not afraid. For the first time in his life he felt free and powerful and so brilliantly, wonderfully pleased with himself.

He, Denton Wyle, was fighting two enormous *skalkit*. And he *loved* it.

"Denton!" Eyanna yelled.

He rolled out of the way just as the *skalkit's* front legs came crashing down to crush him. He bounced to his feet, grabbing the knife from his belt.

Ten feet away, he could see Eyanna looking at him with triumph. She was holding on to the end of the spear. It was still embedded in the *skalkit* and she had managed to find the heart. Blood was spurting from the wound in huge, splattering bursts and the *skalkit* was dying, its eyes half-closed in agony, its jaws frothing blood.

The *skalkit* that was attacking him bellowed and charged. Denton was not afraid, but he was a little disconcerted by its speed. He dodged away, but he was not fast enough and the thing got ahold of his left arm. The teeth burrowed into his flesh and it hurt, but mostly he was just annoyed that it had gotten him. He brought up the knife in his right hand and plunged it again and again into the *skalkit's* head.

Most of the blows glanced off the thick skull and teeth. But the skin was cut and ran blood, and the *skalkit* was surprised by the resistance. It yelped and almost let go. Then it seemed to remember that it was big and Denton very small, and it dug into his arm again with grinding intensity.

It *freaking* hurt. He was eye to eye with the thing and its huge head was ugly and smelly and meaty. A wicked eye glared at him, blindly, cold as the bowels of space, grinding, applying pressure deliberately, about to break his arm.

Denton screamed, full on, leaning into the *skalkit's* face. Then he plunged the knife into the creature's eye, not once, but over and over, even as the thing let go, howling in pain, even as it tried to get away.

He grabbed onto its neck with his bitten and bleeding arm as it raised its head, unwilling to let it escape. It lifted his feet off the ground and still he hung on. Still he plunged the knife into the bloody, gaping eye socket.

The *skalkit* shook its head, hard, trying to shake him loose. He clung tighter. The other eye was rolling and he went for that one, too, taking it out with one hard thrust.

And then the thing whipped him loose.

He landed on the ground again with bruising force. His bitten arm sent shock waves of pain up his shoulder, but he pushed it aside. Nothing was seriously injured. He could still use the arm and he would.

The *skalkit* was staggering around the clearing, both eyes out, blood streaming down. It was letting out blood-curdling sounds and, not far away, the

Sapphians had to be hearing it. Denton was glad. He stood up, the adrenaline pumping through him. Eyanna came to him and hugged him. He could see on her face that something had changed for her, too. She pulled on his arm, wanting to go to the boy, ready to leave.

But he was not ready to let go of it yet. This was the finest moment of his life, damn it, and he would ride it to the end.

"One minute, Eyanna."

He picked up his knife from where it had fallen when he'd been thrown and headed for the blinded *skalkit*.

The boy revived and, beyond cuts and bruises and a bit of trauma, was basically all right. They left him at the clearing to wait for them, and Denton and Eyanna walked into the gorge. Denton carried a heavy load from his good hand.

They saw several Sapphians through the trees as they approached. They quickly disappeared again, faces aghast. But by the time Denton and Eyanna reached the main circle, word had spread and the entire village was huddled there in a tight, silent mass.

Denton and Eyanna stepped into the clearing. They crossed to the central fire. The Sapphians, their eyes huge, backed away.

Denton cast the head of the *skalkit* in front of the bonfire. He was still covered with blood, as Eyanna was. He wanted them to see it.

"This is a *skalkit*. This is the terrible death you send your sons and daughters to every week. I thought you should know."

No one said a word. Some of the Sapphians looked away, at the woods, and the sky, anything.

"And we're taking Eyanna's children."

They were there, in the crowd, clinging to two Sapphian females. Eyanna approached them with a mixture of eagerness and anxiety. Denton knew the girls might be frightened and not want to go. But Eyanna spoke to them softly, kneeling, and within a few minutes she had gotten them to transfer their clinging arms to her. She stood, holding the two of them, one against each shoulder.

Denton looked around at the Sapphians one last time. He saw anger in a few eyes, anger at him. He smiled. "Let's go, Eyanna. This is a terrible place."

He took the youngest child from her and together they walked away from Sapphia.

20.3. Seventy-Thirty Jill Talcott

The alien got into an air car that was parked outside the antenna field and Jill got in as well, her butt poised half in and half out of the narrow seat. As with the elevator, there was hardly any sense of lift. The car glided through the buildings like a whisper of air. Jill watched the streets carefully and only realized after a moment that she was looking for Nate. She didn't see him, but there was no reason that she should. He was probably not in this section of the City at all.

"What do I call you?" she asked, trying to establish some kind of personal contact.

"My designation does not translate. If you find it necessary to address me, you may use 'Cargha.' "

"Cargha. My name is Jill Talcott."

"Yes. I do not find any sense to your name in your language."

"It's just a name. What do you call this planet?"

"Difa-Gor-Das."

He glided the car smoothly to a landing. It was difficult for Jill to judge how far they had come, though she had been paying attention. The City was so mindlessly the same and the air car's speed so much faster than she was accustomed to.

She followed Cargha into a tall building and onto the elevator, which they rode up a dozen floors. They exited into a large room filled with computers and enormous box-shaped machines.

"Are these storage units?" Jill guessed, crossing to one of them.

"Yes. It is the insulation that makes them large. These units are protected against high degrees of radiation. That one stores ten billion data files."

He sat down at a computer, his fingers flowing over the screen. The screen's data changed so rapidly Jill couldn't catch a word of it. He looked as if he were conducting music. His expression was glazed.

Jill pulled a seat closer and sat down. Although it still made her uneasy to be physically close to such a strange being, she was determined to watch him operate the computer. "What are you doing?"

"We estimate that it will be only an additional three-point-four centuries before the planet is completely depopulated. The legacy must be ready by then, so I have no time to waste, even though statistically I will be among the last survivors. That was why I was chosen for this office."

"I see."

Jill found it disturbing how calmly Cargha accepted his species' demise. In fact, now that he was back at work—his fingers flew while he conversed—Cargha seemed willing, even eager, to talk about it.

"Statistically, it is probable that proper recipients will arrive to retrieve the legacy within one million years. However, the legacy will be fully protected for twice that long, two-point-two million years. The chance that proper recipients will find it in that time is ninety-three percent. We are comfortable with that percentile. To get to one hundred percent we would have to protect the legacy for twenty-point-six million years, a time frame outside our capability."

"Even so—two million years! What exactly is in the legacy? Do you have any great masterpieces? Or maybe books by great scientists?"

Cargha contemplated this while his fingers never hesitated. His head tilted to one side as if searching through her mental concepts to find something he could relate to. "I do not understand."

"We have great works of art, for example, paintings of famous historical battles or portraits. . . ."

This was getting no response.

"Okay, what about books? For example, we had a scientist named Charles Darwin who wrote a famous book on the evolution of species. Surely you have similar works. Maybe on wave technology?" she added hopefully.

"The data on evolution of the species is in the legacy files along with all of our other knowledge. But we do not define such things by the individual that discovered them. All citizens provide valuable work in the advancement of our species."

Somehow, that didn't sound very appealing to Jill.

"We do record information about our individuals," Cargha continued. "The legacy includes data on all individuals who have lived in the past one hundred fifty thousand years, which is as long as our records have been one hundred percent accurate. We have partial records before that time, and they have been stored in the legacy even though they are imperfect. For example, the legacy contains the birth designation of each individual, a map of their genetic DNA, their areas of expertise, and links into their specific work in the legacy."

"What kind of work?"

Cargha brought up a file for a male who had been born 603 years ago and had "ceased" 300 years ago. He had been a specialist on the microstructure of minerals. His work on the subject went on for pages and pages—equations and chemical charts—but Jill could see no hint of individuality, of personality.

"This male's work consists of one thousand pages in the mineral database, of which there are six million pages," Cargha said.

Again Jill balked, her mind unable to comprehend those kinds of numbers. Six million pages? On *minerals*? How, in God's name, could it take 6 million pages to describe anything, much less minerals? She squinted at the page in front of her, one page of accomplishments by that 300-year-old male. It was data. Just data.

With a thrill of horror, Jill got a very clear sense of what the legacy contained. Certainly there would be some interesting technology in all of this. How could there not be? But what she had a deeper sense of was the reams and reams and reams and reams of carefully collated and horribly pointless information that no one, and certainly not another species, not the "recipients," was ever going to bother wading through.

Perhaps it was the earlier shock with the machine, perhaps she had already lost her faith in science at some fundamental level, but she suddenly had a paradigm shift. In a moment this intriguing, envy-inducing high-tech culture had become a pure waste that was terrifying in its scale. She felt physically ill.

"Our database is almost complete," Cargha said. "In one hundred years it will be final, except for the last two-point-four hundred years of our existence. But only an estimated twenty members of the species will be living then. At that juncture I will begin making copies of the data. I will make two thousand thirty-three copies of the data in twenty different storage mechanisms, including holistic, digital, optical . . ."

His fingers moved obscenely over the computer screen, his eyes fixed open and staring.

Jill had a flash, seeing herself working, completely focused—just as blindly. What had Nate said to her? That there was no point in collecting the data about this planet if they couldn't get home? If there wasn't a *use* to put it to? And here was this creature, busily working away in his warren on things no one would ever care about while his civilization died all around him. Fiddling while Rome burned. Was that really her?

Dear God.

"Cargha," she said carefully, "I need you to show me the old records on that machine at the antenna field. Right away."

Cargha let out a breath that she could have sworn was a sigh. "If necessary."

"Oh, it is most definitely necessary."

Jill spent hours poring over the computer records of the machine. Fortunately, the translator had an easier time with the information, probably because the concepts were not far off from concepts she knew and understood. And someone from that ancient time had very carefully laid out their theories on what had happened, the way a responsible pharmacist will denote the dangers of a medication. There were detailed constructs using her equation—a fifty-fifty equation; Cargha's ancestors had been from their own universe—that showed a hidden danger that she had never suspected. Cargha's ancestors hadn't suspected it, either, until it was too late.

When she was done, she sat for a long time, thinking. Her fingers rattled on her collarbone while, across the room at his monitor, Cargha's hands danced in front of the monitor in a silent aria. She finally got up and approached him, pulling up one of those banana-split chairs.

"Cargha, I need you to listen to me."

"I am listening," he said, neither looking at her nor stopping in his work.

"No, look at me and *listen*."

His fingers faltered, then stopped. He turned to face her, his blank face giving her the impression that she might as well talk to a wall.

"Nate and I *have* to get back to Earth. We have to warn my people about that machine, because if we don't, what happened to you is very likely going to happen to us."

Cargha blinked at her blandly.

"Now I realize that your space program is shut down, but there has to be another way. We came here through some kind of microscopic black hole. There's got to be a way to reverse it."

"Perhaps." He turned back to his screen, fingers dancing. "There are three million pages on black holes and their function, but that is not my area of expertise."

Jill sighed, picturing herself and Nate going through 3 million pages. "Mine either, pal. But we're going to *make* it our area of expertise."

"I will assist you in locating the relevant data. However, I must continue with my own work."

"If I understand you correctly, you have another three hundred years to do your work. You have time to help us. I'm not sure we can do it without you."

"It is true, I do have a margin of error in my schedule. However, one cannot anticipate all contingencies. For example, I have just realized a need to modify the sentry program."

Something about that rang a bell. Jill sat up straighter. "Are those the round things at the City gate?"

"The sentries function all along the City perimeter. Their function is to prevent the *zerdots* from entering the City and dismantling the legacy."

"*Zerdots?* You mean the big antlike insects out in the desert?"

Cargha considered her vocabulary. "Yes. They are native to this planet. They are sentient, but not a technological species. We have never had a cooperative relationship."

Jill frowned, remembering that morning when they'd arrived at the City, the way the metal sphere had "sensed" her and Nate. "The sentries kill *zerdots?*"

"Yes."

"Do they kill *only zerdots?*"

"That is the anomaly that just came to my attention."

Jill's palms began to sweat. "Could you be a *little* more specific?"

Cargha blinked his gooey double eyelids at her. "Yes. I was examining the sentry program when you interrupted me. For the legacy we took into account the potentiality that the *zerdots* might mutate. The sentries respond to a DNA profile that deviates from our own by greater than one percent and a subject height under four feet."

"But . . . that's so broad! What if the recipients you're expecting are under four feet?"

"The sentries only operate on the borders of the City, where *zerdots* are to be found. The recipients would not come from outside the City. We have a beacon at the spaceport. Also, there is nothing of interest on this planet besides ourselves."

Jill stared at him in amazement. Could his species really be so out of touch with their environment that they couldn't even conceive of a spaceship landing anywhere but in their precious City?

"But *we're* not in any danger, right? Nate and I? Because we're over four feet tall."

Cargha turned back to his screen and ruffled his fingers, examining the sentry code. "That is the anomaly that only now came to my attention. The height check is spatial, not structural. Curious."

"Oh god."

"If a subject over four feet tall were to bend over, or sit down, as you are doing—"

"And how did that come to your attention, just now?" Jill asked, her voice sounding slightly hysterical.

"I received a transmission. One of the sentries shot the male."

20.4. Forty-Sixty Calder Farris

The apartment door was easy. Pol's monitor key worked without a hitch. The hall lights were blaring in the corridor, but it was well before dawn and there was no one awake to see him as he slipped inside.

The apartment was dark and quiet. Pol stood for a moment, listening to hear if he'd wakened the residents. He heard nothing. He turned on a torch.

The apartment was tiny but more dignified than either Marcus's abode or the little box that had belonged to the Bronze with the banned books. It was an older building and had some substance to it—tall ceilings, moldings. A kitchenette was visible off the living/dining room, and there was a short hallway and an open door beyond. Pol entered the bedroom, silent as a snake, and shone the torch on the figure in the bed. The man was asleep, a light wheeze issuing from his throat. He was a singularly unattractive Bronze, Mestido 1123. Pol stepped closer, trained the torchlight on his face, leaned in to look.

No eyebrows, not the slightest hint of stubble. No stubble on the face anywhere, just the rough, flat-nosed, ruddy face of a Bronze. His breath stank of *orin*, a pungent meat. The wheezing in his throat sounded like a leaky pipe.

Pol let him sleep. He wanted confirmation. He searched the kitchenette and found a can of black construction paint and an industrial-sized paintbrush under the sink. He sank back on his heels and looked at it. Gyde would have been so pleased.

Back inside the bedroom, Pol placed a plain chair at the side of the bed and withdrew his gun. He covered Mestido's mouth with his hand. The brown eyes flew open.

"Don't move," Pol said, bringing the eye of the gun into view. "You have a book, *Heavenly Mysteries*."

Mestido's head moved under Pol's hand in a negative. The feeling was most unpleasant, that fleshy mouth. Pol removed his hand slowly, prepared to put it back if Mestido screamed. He didn't.

Pol wiped his hand on his wool uniform trousers. "Yes, you do. Don't lie."

"I've read it, but I don't have it."

Pol waited. The Bronze was a nervous talker and he was petrified. He pushed himself to sitting.

"In Madamar, when I worked at the Department of Surveys. A Bronze I worked with had it. I can give you his name."

"Are you an alien?"

"Me? No! No, of course not!"

"But you've met aliens?"

Mestido looked around, craning his head to peer into the hall. From the fear and bafflement on his face it was clear he didn't know what to think. Pol was obviously a monitor, but was he alone? How much did he know? Pol could feel him working through it in his mind.

"I don't know what you're talking about," Mestido answered innocently.

Pol sent a fist crashing into his face. The blow, coming from behind the torchlight, struck the Bronze without warning, battering his nose. Blood sprang out, blood that was too dark and too runny. It flowed onto Mestido's sour underclothes. Mestido gasped with shock and inhaled it, choking.

"Don't scarp me. Answer me or I'll put a bullet in your head." But Pol was already regretting the blow. There were things he wanted from this scag, things he wanted desperately. He waited while Mestido stuffed sheets against his face, writhing with pain.

"Be good," Pol said, as much to calm himself as Mestido. "Be good."

"I will. I'll tell you anything." Mestido's tone was groveling, but his eyes were hateful.

Pol was glad. He'd been starting to doubt this was the same man who defied the state and risked his life painting graffiti. "You've met aliens?"

"Yes."

"And you've been to their planet?"

"Many times."

"Could you get there again?"

Mestido's brow clouded. His skin appeared dark brown over the bloodied white of the sheet stuffed against his face. He seemed to weigh his answer. "Maybe." He withdrew the sheet and smiled, his teeth stained with blood. "You don't believe me."

"Maybe I do."

Pol took a handkerchief from his pocket. He wiped at his temples, spit on the cloth, wiped again. Mestido, who could not see him very well behind the light of the torch, watched warily.

Pol turned the torch onto his own face, lighting it from below. His other hand trained the gun quite deliberately at Mestido's stomach.

"Am . . . Am *I* an alien?" Pol asked, voice thick.

Mestido's eyes widened. He looked at Pol for a long time, examining his face very carefully.

"I've done surgery on the eyes. They used to be rounder. And if I don't re-move it I have thick hair above the eyes and on my cheeks and chin."

There ought to be stubble by now. When was the last time he'd shaved? Late afternoon? This morning? He couldn't even remember. Scarp, he'd gone out to a nightclub and *he couldn't remember when he last shaved.*

Mestido leaned forward, his face slack with astonishment. "You *are* an alien! I *knew* it! I told them!"

Pol felt elation and terror. In his hand, the gun wavered and pointed off toward nothing. If Mestido had been sharp, he could have taken him. But he was smiling crazily.

"How do you know?" Pol asked, when he could trust his voice.

"I can tell."

"*How do you know?*" Pol screamed.

"Well . . . look at you!" Mestido's eyes wandered up and down. "Turn on the light."

"Shut up," Pol said, but he rose to his feet. There was no window in the bedroom, so he shut the door and turned on the light. There was more blood than he'd thought; the bed was gaudy with it, and Mestido looked like a walk-ing infirmary. But his expression was devious. His wide-set eyes danced crazily.

"I told them you were here, but they didn't believe me. *Now* they'll see!"

"Have you ever seen anyone who looked like me?"

Mestido was grinning, his head going from side to side.

"Answer me! Hair on the face, fair-skinned, blue-eyed. Oh—and my hair, my hair is actually dark, like yours."

"Certainly."

"You've seen others like me?"

Mestido put a finger alongside his bloodied mouth. "When they come," he said, hushing now as though this were a secret, "they can take any form."

"What? But what do they look like on *their* planet? You said you've been there."

"Some of them maybe look like that."

Pol felt the urge to throttle the Bronze. "Do you know any of their language?"

"No."

"Not even *one word*?"

"No. I—"

"What about their planet? What's it like? Do you know the names of any of their cities?"

"I've been telling them. This whole world will be destroyed. Except for me. They promised I'd be safe."

Pol pinched his eyes shut with his fingers. Rage was rising inside of him that was so foul and so overpowering that his body shook with the force of it. "You're a scarping liar," he said blackly.

What was on his face must have been terrifying, for Mestido scrambled farther back on the bed, yelping.

"You're a *scarping liar!*"

"No!"

He had been fooled. This Bronze knew nothing, knew no *real* aliens. He was just a raving lunatic, another piece of shit with a damaged brain. A sob of rage and frustration broke from Pol, and before he knew it he was across the bed. He had Mestido's neck in his hands, choking, choking him. There was a fury in him, a fury that had helped him kill the Silver months ago in Saradena. Lately it had been cowered by fear, but now it was back with terrible abandon. It fused his fingers into the shape of a garrote. He felt as though he could pop the worm's head clean off his neck. Tomorrow didn't exist. Yesterday didn't exist. Only this moment, this revenge. Only his hands and this throat.

Mestido managed one word: "*Green.*"

Pol thought it was *green* anyway. His fingers released. Mestido coughed, wheezing for breath as if his esophagus had been crushed. It was a terrible sound. Pol could already see the skin darkening on his neck. He waited, breathing through his nose like an enraged bull.

"What?"

"Their planet . . . was green."

Something inside Pol's heart broke open. There was a sob low in his chest. *Green.* That was right, wasn't it? This place was all gray: gray sky, gray stone, gray dust, gray bombs, battlefields of soil as icy and gray as the uniforms of the corpses that lay there. Even the plants were sickly pale. But he remembered green.

Mestido was struggling to sit up.

"Show me," Pol said.

*   *   *

It was after dawn when they got to their destination. They'd caught an early-morning bus that carried Irons and low-level Bronzes to a construction project beyond the City line. From their drop-off point it was a mile walk.

To . . . nothing that Pol could see. They had come to a ravine, a V-shaped gorge that might have once been a river but was now only a dark sludge of a stream half-clogged with dirt and ash and other nameless pollutants. The sides of the ravines were overgrown with tenacious brambles. Mestido stopped at the edge of the ravine, arms folded.

"Where?" Pol licked his lips, took out his gun. There was nothing here, but maybe that was the point. The aliens would choose an isolated place, a place where no one would be around, wouldn't they? "Show me."

Mestido started down the sloping bank. Pol followed, moving carefully. The brambles were uniquely configured to latch on to the textured wool of his uniform.

They moved like this for perhaps fifteen minutes before Pol realized Mestido was doubling back, going in a circle. He stopped, freeing his arm and the gun from the vegetation with a jerk. "Stop!"

In front of him, Mestido hesitated, as though considering *not* stopping, but a glance over his shoulder showed him that the gun was still too close.

"Where the hell is it?"

"Here. Somewhere around here." Mestido began walking forward again.

Pol wrenched himself forward quickly, the brambles tearing his clothes. He grabbed the Bronze's arm. "I said *stop!*"

Mestido froze.

"What is this? What are we looking for?"

Mestido turned to look across the ravine. "I saw them land here. It was right here."

Pol's eyes narrowed, trying to read something, anything, on Mestido's face. He didn't look like he was lying, but he didn't look sane, either.

"Tell me what happened."

Mestido rolled his tongue around in his mouth. His throat was swollen where Pol had throttled him, puffing out until his head and neck looked like a ball. "I was looking for ore stone." He kicked at the dirt. "You can sell it on the streets. One day I saw this ship—"

"A *ship?*"

Mestido turned to look over the ravine, motioning with his hand. "A flying craft. It was like a ball and it glowed with light, the whole thing. It hovered above the ravine, lights flashing all over it. Then they came out and—"

"They?"

"The aliens. They looked like gigantic green bugs, but that's just their native form; they can take any shape they want. They had weapons and they took me into the ship and—"

The report of the gun rang out in the ravine, echoing down and back, muffled by the brush.

Mestido dropped to his knees. The brambles hooked on to the flesh of his face, caught in his hair. Dark, runny blood streamed from the back of his shirt. He fell forward, dead. The brambles didn't allow him to reach the ground but held him up at an angle, allowing the blood to pour down his back, making a tunnel to the ground over his right hip.

The gun was still outstretched in Pol's hand as the bugs began to gather at the sticky feast. He stared.

Fool. Stupid, scarping, brain-damaged fool.

"Kalim N2!" The voice came from above, like the voice of God.

Pol operated on instinct, diving into the brambles just as a shot whizzed by. He pulled himself a few difficult feet through the cover, and only when he was sure he was no longer visible did he allow himself to look up.

There was no one at the lip of the ravine. They—or just he; Pol was not yet sure—would be standing back, would not present themselves as a target for his gun.

"I know who you are," Gyde's voice drifted down.

Pol wanted to laugh. Even he did not know that.

"The state wants you alive! They want to question you. I doubt anyone has ever dared what you have dared. Killing a Silver. Taking his identity. That is bad, Kalim. Very, very bad."

Pol was lying as flat as he could in the brambles, ignoring the thorny pain. He found that he was not surprised or angry or afraid. This moment had been coming for a long time. Still, the gun shook with the tremor in his hand. He felt . . . profoundly sad. He wanted to say to Gyde, *You don't understand. They did something to my scarping brain.* But the man at the top of the ravine was not his friend.

"However, I will grant you a mercy since you were my partner. If you come out to me now and surrender your weapon I will give you a clean and swift death right here, right now. Think about it, Kalim. Think hard."

He did. He lay on the frozen ground, shivering. His mind was that of a soldier, whatever his rank or class, and he understood his options. Gyde's mistake had been saying his name. Perhaps Gyde had not been 100 percent sure. Perhaps he had wanted that raised head, that moment of shocked recognition, as final confirmation before shooting Pol dead. Instead, the name had served as warning and Gyde had missed his shot. Now Pol had the opportunity to work his way to the top through the brambles and attempt to trick and overpower Gyde. He was fairly certain Gyde was alone. He would not have offered the "mercy" if he were not alone. Gyde was alone because he wanted all the merits for Pol's capture. Pol's odds of taking him were fifty-fifty. But he did not want to even try.

Father. A voice in Pol's head made the plea. He dismissed it cynically. The man at the top of the ravine was not that, either.

Pol's fingers were stiff as he began removing his uniform. It was snagged in the fibrous spines all around him, making the job more difficult.

"Don't make me come after you." Gyde's voice glittered, dangerous, like his eyes.

Now Gyde would either call backup or work his way into the ravine and attempt the capture alone. Whether he called for backup probably depended on just how many merits he needed to achieve his goal. Pol thought he didn't need many.

The brambles were already working at the skin of his arms and back as Pol raised his hips to pull off his pants. He left the boots on. Their surface would not attract the thorns and they would protect his feet. Last, he removed the woolen undergarment of the Silvers.

"You have a few minutes left, Pol. This is your final chance to surrender. If you do not, I would advise you to use that gun on yourself before they bring you up."

Pol, naked, his clothes discarded on the ground behind him, began worming his way through the brush, heading down, down to the bottom of the ravine.

Gyde understood all the options, too.

"Pol." His voice was softer now. "Do your old classmate a favor and surrender. I told you—a quick death. If you're thinking about escaping, forget it. Even if you did, you would be hunted. You cannot live without a name; you know that. You can't buy food or anything else. And if you're caught on the streets you'll be shot. Surrender to me."

Pol's flesh moved through the brambles more readily than the cloth of his uniform. Still, hooks caught and tiny pieces of him ripped out—here, there—as he moved on his belly over the frozen earth. The pain was stinging, worsening as his own sweat salted the wounds. But the pain inside him overshadowed it like a guillotine over a switchblade.

The brackish, polluted water of the stream came into view.

His hands and arms were in front of him, crawling. At the water's edge he stopped and stared at those bleeding arms, hands. What a tableau they made with the icy ground and filthy water.

"*Pol.*" Gyde's voice a caress.

Pol slipped into the water and let it take him away.

20.5. Seventy-Thirty Jill Talcott

Jill managed to get Cargha to take her to the spaceport in the air car. He had relatively little tolerance for pleading. The tarmac was hot and bright with a mid-sky sun when they landed, and Nate was a tiny figure next to the scale of the ship. He was lying just under its monstrous red-lacquered belly. He wasn't moving.

Jill ran to him, somehow managing to reach him despite the fact that she could hardly breathe. His white T-shirt was burned away over his stomach and underneath was a black-and-red wound about the diameter of a grapefruit, centered in the soft flesh of his belly.

His face was still and utterly white. His long black lashes, two crescents sweetly resting on his cheeks, cut her heart neatly in two.

She dropped to her knees, next to his body, and had the distinct realization that her life was over, that some vital part of herself, one that was far more interesting and important and wonderful than any other part of her, had just been shut down forever. A feeling of pressure, intense and painful and suffocating, built and built inside her. Then she sucked in a gigantic gasp of air and expelled it with a choked wail that turned into racking, heaving sobs. The sobs shook her entire frame, each one coming out so hard, and so fast, that it pushed out the one in front of it violently, like an army of warriors leaving the womb.

Her fingers clutched blindly at his ruined shirt. She could not see for the tears, could not hear for the wails coming out of her mouth. Something had finally broken inside Jill Talcott, and she felt emotion now all right; she felt it all. Too late.

Or maybe not. Someone was touching her arm, some cold—but living— hand, a human hand, Nate.

She tried furiously to clear her eyes. Through veils of salt water and swollen lids, she saw him looking up at her—pale and obviously in pain, but alive all the same and even looking rather amazed at her display.

"*Jill.* Shhhh. It's okay."

She stared at his bloodied stomach in surprise and began ripping back the T-shirt fabric. The laser wound was ugly and wide, but it was not all that deep. She could see what looked like cauterized skin and even muscle. It was a terrible wound, but it was possible that it hadn't penetrated to his internal organs. He might live.

Cargha was standing beside her, watching her with the absorbed, faintly repulsed expression of a scientist studying the mating rituals of weird bugs.

"Point-oh-five-seven millimeters," he said. "That's the depth required to kill a *zerdot*. This cannot be construed as a failure, because it must be statistically impossible that *zerdots* would mutate within the next two-point-two million years to the point where . . ."

Jill tuned him out. Her sobs had subsided to the point where she could almost breathe again, but there was a heaviness deep inside her chest. Nate was rubbing her arm, his teeth gritted tight in pain.

"You know," he told her shakily, "people always wonder what it would be like to be at their own funeral. Well, I guess I just found out. Freaky." Despite his words, there was something new in his eyes—a recognition of what her tears had meant, a question.

"Oh, Nate!"

She collapsed beside him, lying down next to him right there on the asphalt. He turned his head to look at her.

"Hurts like a son of a bitch," he confided.

"Oh, sweetie, I know."

She reached up a hand to stroke his face, that amazingly beautiful face. His expression changed as she touched him; his eyes darkened. She couldn't bear that look in his eyes, never had been able to bear it, but this time, instead of turning away, she turned into it. What freedom, to allow herself to turn into it! She kissed him.

"Nate." She said it for the pleasure of acknowledging that it was really him. His lips were so soft it was like drowning, and his kiss was as sweet as she remembered—god! The nights she had lain awake not wanting to remember! She kissed him with every bit as much intensity and abandon as she had felt in her grief.

When she finally released his mouth he groaned and pushed her away with a quivering laugh. "Jesus. Have you ever tried having a jones *and* a six-inch hole in your abdomen? There's a definite conflict of interest going on down there."

"Oh god, I'm sorry!" She felt herself go red. "Cargha, we need to get Nate inside, *now*. And we'll need painkillers, and antiseptic."

Cargha was still observing them with mild disgust. His lids came down over the goo on his eyes. " 'Painkiller.' Curious idea. It is very much a dark planet concept. We do not require such things. This injury is easily remedied by reassembling the energy of the tissues. There are repair devices in most of the facilities. If you go—"

"You'll take us to the nearest facility in the car. *Now*."

She started to get up, preparing to help Nate to his feet. He stopped her with a hand on her arm. "Jill. Just promise me one thing."

"You're going to be fine," she reassured him, giving him a brave smile. Now that he'd stopped her getting up, her fingers were unable to resist the texture of his hair. "You heard him. And don't forget, this planet is lucky."

"Yeah, tell me about it," Nate said, giving her a smoky look. "But that's not what I meant. Promise me—"

"I don't care about the wave technology," she insisted. "Really, Nate, you've been right about this whole thing. I think we *can* get back to Earth, but when we do—"

"Jill!" he interrupted, impatiently.

"What, Nate?" Her fingers, which found playing with his hair *much* more satisfying than playing with each other, were now exploring the baby soft skin on his neck. How on earth had she resisted this temptation for the past two years? What kind of masochist did that? It was like starving to death in a room laid with a gourmet feast—a gourmet feast that was trying its damnedest to leap down your throat. She must have been mad.

"I want you to *promise*," Nate said, "that as soon as we fix this hole in my stomach, which will hopefully be in the next five minutes, because it really does sting like a bitch, you'll kiss me like that again. In private. For about a year."

"Mmmm," Jill said, feeling herself melt.

Cargha sighed.

BOOK THREE

SYNTHESIS

21

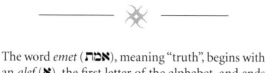

> The word *emet* (אמת), meaning "truth", begins with an *alef* (א), the first letter of the alphabet, and ends with a *tav* (ת), the last letter. Thus, the "end is imbedded in the beginning." This is accomplished through the *mem* (מ), the middle letter of the alphabet." [thesis, antithesis, synthesis]
> —the sage Abulafia, as quoted in *Sefer Yetzirah*,
> pre–sixth century, translation by Aryeh Kaplan, 1990

AUSCHWITZ
LATE OCTOBER

The woods were silent. The only light was the begrudging dregs of a half moon. If there had been activity here recently, men in long coats wandering in and out—scraping bark, studying the ground, taking soil samples—you would not know it now. The trees, silvery gray, slept the long sleep of fibrous things. Nocturnal insects trapped lesser insects; small mammals with night-glow eyes tracked them in turn and had their own deep fear of talons and swooping wings. The higher order of man was absent, leaving the woods to simpler, though not necessarily more innocent, rhythms.

But not for long. Without warning, a miniature sun erupted in the middle of the clearing. It burst into being with a noise like crackling thunder and a flash of light so intense it blinded several of the creatures who chanced to look upon it.

Everything in the vicinity fled. There was only silence as the light faded, growing bluer and bluer, merging with the darkness. The outline of five figures materialized.

Jill blinked into the light, trying to get her bearings. She wasn't dead, at least she didn't think so, and it didn't feel like her legs had replaced her arms or her lungs had turned inside out or anything else of that nature.

She groped around and found a hand—Nate. She grasped it, panicking for a moment with worry. But he squeezed her back, reassuring, whole. Relief made her knees weak. Her feet felt pinned to the ground.

Gravity. It felt so strong—too strong to be Earth? Or was she simply unaccustomed to it?

She closed her eyes against the stinging light and when she reopened them it was better. To her left she could make out the silhouette of Nate, his head turned toward her. Farther away, in a wide circle, were three others. It was like watching a film negative develop. There was . . . yes, the rabbi, on her right, with his full beard, rubbing his eyes. And next was . . . Denton Wyle, tall and slim, his arms held out as if to catch himself, already aware enough to be astonished. And the last . . .

The last figure was farthest from her and she could just make out a well-made masculine shape, tight, heavy clothes. Who . . . ?

"For the love of God, what's happened?" The rabbi found his voice first.

Jill tried to speak and had difficulty moving her mouth. It was as if her brain were trying to reacquaint itself with the engine under its control.

"Rabbi Handalman," she managed, "it's Jill Talcott."

"Dr. Talcott?" came a light male voice. "Is that Nate with you? It's Denton."

"Yup, it's me, Nate."

And still the fifth figure did not speak.

The light had continued to dim, moment by moment, and now Jill could make out Nate's features. He was looking around and then he looked at her and smiled—not a big smile, he was not quite in control of himself enough for that, but it was big in intent. It said, *We did it. We're home.*

She tried to verify that herself, squinting beyond him to make out trees, tall and black against the bluish light. She looked straight up above her and saw a familiar moon. The coldness and the scent of the air penetrated her senses. She breathed it in, her nostrils growing brittle, exhaled to see a plume of mist.

"Is this Earth?" came the rabbi's voice, hopeful, trembling. "It's not possible. . . . Is it?"

"We're back where we started, Rabbi," Nate said. "At least, that was the general idea."

"*You* did this?" Denton sounded delighted.

Jill squeezed Nate's hand, hard. She was staring at the fifth figure across the clearing. At first she had the irrational idea that there'd been some crossed wires in time, that they'd plucked some random stranger out of the ether accidentally. For there he stood, becoming clearer by the moment—a muscular form in heavy dark clothes, close-cropped blond hair, stern, square, craggy face.

The man was staring at *her.* He stood stiffly, arms at his side, face struggling with . . . fear? Confusion? Rage?

Denton found his legs and took a shaky step, going over to the rabbi and grabbing him in a bear hug, to which the rabbi said, "Oooff!"

"Jill? That's not Anatoli. Who is it?" Nate asked in a quiet voice.

His question, at last, triggered a memory, a memory aided by the cold white-blue eyes coming into focus. Only they weren't cold now; they were burning, staring at *her.*

"Oh, god," she muttered.

She saw the same recognition on his face, at the same instant. And then he moved, fluidly, taking a step back and going into a wide stance. Denton and Rabbi Handalman were chatting, oblivious, as the man brought up his hands, revealing the presence of a heavy old-fashioned handgun. He pointed at Jill.

"Freeze!" he screamed, his voice loud and rich with emotion. He aimed the gun from one to another of them as Denton and the rabbi turned to regard him with surprise. "Into a line—move!" He motioned with the gun.

Jill shared a look with Nate—a look of frustration and hopelessness that they had come back all this way only to be captured so easily and so soon. But the four of them did as they were told, moving into a line. Rabbi Handalman was on her right.

"Who is this?" the rabbi demanded. "What's going on?"

Jill shook her head tightly and spoke to the gunman: "It's all right. You're back home now."

"Yeah, take it easy," Denton said soothingly.

Nate was still holding her hand, trying to draw her toward him, behind him, to protect her. She resisted. If this was anyone's battle it was hers.

The man with the gun continued to swing it from one of them to another, staring especially at her and Nate. His widely planted legs were shaking so badly it was a miracle they held him up. The woods were now coming into sharp focus around them and his eyes darted here and there as if trying to get his bearings. In the last of the fading light his face was white, covered with a thin sheen of sweat. He was panicked, Jill realized, completely and utterly out of his head. He might do anything. And for the first time she was genuinely afraid.

"Lieutenant Farris?" she said in a loud, soothing voice. "Are you ill? Could you please lower the gun?"

With great deliberation he straightened his body and pointed the gun, in one extended hand, right at her head. The intention on his face was murderous. And then those white-blue eyes rolled back and Calder Farris collapsed into a dead faint.

*   *   *

They debated what to do with Farris's unconscious body for several minutes. Denton was cold, freezing his ass off cold, and he knew they had to find shelter soon. Nate and Jill wanted to take Farris with them. Apparently, he was an agent with the Department of Defense, someone Jill had met before. Denton wasn't sure why they would want to drag around a man who was out for their blood, but it was certainly possible that if they left him alone he would freeze to death.

The four of them formed a square, carrying the man like pallbearers. Jill's short stature tilted the burden in her direction and Denton had to walk with his knees bent. And he was dressed for ninety-degree weather, so there was nothing between him and the frigid air but a pair of jeans and sandals. All in all, it was excruciatingly uncomfortable, not to mention a nice, sharp dose of fifty-fifty reality. Welcome home!

Yet nothing—not the pain in his knees or the ice forming between his teeth—could touch Denton's elation. They were *back*; they were honest-to-God, no-freaking-way back. He didn't know *how* it had happened, but he figured there was an explanation, technical as hell, and he'd hear it eventually. For now, he was busy calculating all the nifty stuff he was going to be able to do, imminently, like eat ice cream and watch the tube for about a week solid. And then there were, oh, *women*.

At that thought he felt a twinge of conscience. He and Eyanna never had hooked up, and he'd remained celibate the last few months in Khashta. He didn't want to slip back into his old ways now. But he knew that was not going to happen; he would never be that person again. In fact, it would be interesting to find out who he *would* be now that he was back on his home turf.

They took more wrong turns than they needed to. Just about the time all of them were utterly exhausted, they saw lights through the trees. They followed the lights until they saw a tiny house. They paused at the edge of the woods, dropping their burden none too gently.

"This is Anatoli Nikolai's house?" the rabbi prompted, breathing hard. "Does anyone remember?"

"It could be," Nate said, squinting through the darkness.

It had been a long time—for all of them. But Denton had spent more time in the house than any of the others.

"I'll check," he volunteered. He slipped away toward the house and heard someone come after him. He turned to see Nate's dark head. The young man smiled.

"Backup," he whispered.

Denton's heart warmed and he returned the smile. He was back among his own kind and it felt pretty *amazing*. He gave Nate's shoulder a squeeze.

On the right side of the back wall a window was lit up. They crept closer, sticking to the shadows, and peeked inside. It was Anatoli's kitchen. Denton remembered the tiny table and tinier chairs, the stove so old it had a propane tank on the side, the dinged wooden clock on the wall with the painting of the little Polish *Mädchen*.

Sitting at the table, sipping cups of tea, were two men. One was medium-sized, with dark hair and a young, conservative face. The other was a huge guy who could have doubled as a professional wrestler. They both wore plain white button-down shirts, dark pants, and ties. They had crew cuts and there was a mirror-shiny polish on their thick-soled shoes. Nate pulled Denton backward. They exchanged a grim look.

Anatoli? Nate mouthed. Denton nodded.

They made their way around the house, peering into darkened windows. On the second window they tried, something blocked their view—an X shape made by boards nailed to the inside of the frame. Nate peered into one of the openings left by the boards and Denton another. The hall door had been left open a few inches, allowing light into the room. Directly beneath the window was a bed, which appeared to be occupied, but the light and the angle made it impossible to see who or what might be in it.

Still, Denton knew it was Anatoli. He felt a surge of anger. Those goons had better not have hurt the old man.

Nate tugged on his sleeve and the two of them dodged through the shadows back to the others. The big guy was still lying on the ground as heavily as a manikin made out of cement.

"Well?" the rabbi asked.

"It's Anatoli's place all right," Denton answered, "and I think he's in there. But he has company. Two military types are in the house. They have him locked up in one of the bedrooms."

Nate nodded, a little breathless. "They're DoD. I recognize one of the men from Seattle." He looked at Jill. "It's the guy who came to the restaurant looking for me."

Rabbi Handalman tugged at his beard. "Why are they still here? It's been months. Anatoli had only one copy of the manuscript, yes?"

"Actually," Jill said distractedly, "it's only been five days. At least, that's what we were aiming for."

"Cool!" Denton said, having no problem with the concept.

"Five *days*? Five days from what? What are you saying?"

"On Earth it's been only five days since we disappeared." Jill shivered and Nate rubbed his hands up and down her arms. Like Denton, the two of them were dressed only in their own clothes, with no coat or other covering to keep out the cold. "I'd be happy to explain, only first we need to get somewhere warm."

"Five days?" Handalman repeated, sounding wistful. "I left Hannah less than two weeks ago?"

"There's only two of 'em in the house. We might be able to take them." Denton grinned, loving the fact that he actually meant it. Heck, why not? If they could dig up a couple of two-by-fours or even heavy branches, they might have a shot. It was better than freezing.

"No, the last thing we need is to attract attention," Jill said. "We'll have to find someplace else for now. There must be more houses down the road. Or we might find a barn or something."

"We can't carry *him* very far." Aharon pointed out the obvious—the prone and massive guy at their feet.

"Well, we can't leave him," Jill said flatly.

"What if we came back for him? Maybe we'll find a car." Denton suggested.

"What if he wakes up and takes off while we're gone?" Jill shook her head, teeth chattering. "We n-need him. Besides, he knows about the gateway, now, too. N-nate?"

Nate was still rubbing his hands up and down her arms. "Jill's right. Maybe we could take turns carrying him. I'll go first."

Denton hated to be a downer, but he didn't think there was any way Nate was going to be able to carry the guy by himself. *He* would offer; his chances weren't much better. Even the four of them had had difficulty.

Before Nate could even attempt it, the headlights of a car appeared far off down the highway. They watched the car approach, fast at first, then slowing.

"I say we go for it," Denton said.

"We don't even know who it is!" Jill protested.

Denton couldn't care less who it was—they needed that car. But it was going to be gone before he could get to the road at this rate. That was where decision by committee got you. They'd argue about it and it would be gone. But . . . no, the car was slowing. It looked like it was going to pull into Anatoli's house, but it passed it at a good clip, then decelerated quickly. It rolled to a stop at the side of the road, close to the trees, about two hundred yards away. The headlights went out.

"Okay," Denton said cheerfully. "I vote for a carjacking. Anyone with me?"

"I'll go," Aharon grunted. "As long as we don't kill anyone. I draw the line at murder."

Jill nodded. "Nate, go with them. I'll stay here with Farris."

"No, you guys go," Nate told Denton. "I don't want to leave her alone with him."

"But I have his gun." Jill patted her pocket.

Nate didn't answer, but Denton knew he wasn't going to leave her with a death commando like Farris, gun or no gun.

"Let's go, Rabbi," Denton said.

Aharon was trying to keep up with the goy—Wyle—but was still having difficulty assimilating the current situation. In truth, he had a lot of sympathy for the man on the ground back there, even if he was a government agent. It would be easy—yes, it would be nice—to roll his eyes back in his head and check out. Because, look, the brain was only designed to handle so much. And *his* brain—maybe it was due to advanced age, but it had had more surprises than it cared to deal with.

One thing kept him relatively coherent and moving: that if he really was back on Earth, if all this wasn't going to be snatched away from him at any moment, then there was a possibility that he might get home, that his wife and his children were only half a world away. Why, they were within reach of a simple airplane ride. God had given him another chance. Talk about your miracles.

He hurried his steps to keep up with Wyle. Aharon felt amazingly light on his feet, his body practically bouncing after the bone-grinding pressure of Fiori, and his heart was lightening step-by-step as well.

Someone was getting out of the car up ahead, a small figure. He and Denton, well, they weren't exactly quiet. If subtlety had been part of the plan, they were failing miserably. But it was dark outside. The lone figure did not turn in their direction. From what Aharon could make out, there was no one else in the car, either.

He remembered, then, that they had no plan. What were they going to do, talk the person to death? Jump them? Ask nicely if they would mind giving up their car? Aharon didn't like the idea of violence now that he could see the figure was not large and threatening. He intended to say so to Wyle, except they were almost upon this person. And Aharon realized that, yes, Wyle was going to jump the driver. What had happened to this timid young man?

Just before Denton pounced, the figure heard them and turned. It was wearing a sweatshirt with a hood and the face was barely visible in the dim moonlight. It wasn't much, but then, how much does a man need after fifteen years of marriage?

"Hannah!"

He thought he had shouted it, but it came out as a whisper. Her eyes grew large as she stared at him. And then he grabbed her up and she was in his arms.

For a brief moment Aharon held her, felt the soft weight of her pressed tightly to him—*blue jeans?*—his face against this strange cotton hood, his heart pounding with joy and disbelief. And then she was pushing him away, her pretty face scowling.

"Aharon Handalman, where have you been?" She was seriously angry, spoiling for a fight. But as she got her first good look at him, her eyes widened with fear. "Oh, my heavens, Aharon, what *happened?*"

He was wearing a heavy Fiorian robe, which no doubt had its own aroma. And he knew he had changed a great deal physically. He must look an impossible sight, like a ghost maybe. But he wouldn't let her push him away. He cupped her face with his hands, reassuring her with low sounds until she calmed. Only then did he let his own gaze wander up and down.

She was complaining about *him?* Hannah Handalman, a respectable Orthodox *rebbetzin* and mother of three, was wearing blue jeans, white tennis shoes, and a gray hooded sweatshirt. He had never seen anything so wonderful in his life.

She glanced at Wyle and pulled away. "Don't start with me, Aharon. I know, *I know,* what you think. It's terrible that I came, a horrible invasion of your privacy, *your* work, and so on and so on. But what was I supposed to do when the man came to the house and said—"

"Who?" Aharon asked sharply.

"M-Mr. Norowitz," Hannah said nervously. "He told me they'd tracked you here and then lost you. He wanted to know where you were, if I'd heard from you. When I realized you were *missing* . . . that even *they* had no idea where you were . . . what was I to do? I had to come see for myself if I could help or . . . *something.* Aharon!"

Her face looked so stricken and he realized, with a terrible feeling, that her relief at seeing him, and even her anger, had been subsumed by something else—fear of his reprisal. She, his own wife, was afraid of him. What kind of person had he been?

"Hannah." He pulled her to him, realizing anew, from the sensation of her under his hands, how small his wife was, really, how slight, how tender, how brave. "Do you think I could be *angry*? I've never been so glad of anything as I am to see you. How could I feel anything but joy? I love you, Hannah! My precious jewel!"

He kissed her face, her astonished little face. She had that set look in her eyebrows, the look of a wife who knows for certain that an alien has taken over the body of her husband. She snuck a glance at Wyle, as if wondering how Aharon could dare touch her, kiss her like this in front of another person, and a stranger also. It brought him back to his senses a little. He dropped his hands, his fingers brushing the cottony hood now hanging down her back.

"Of course, why you have to dress like a *goyisher teenager* to come look for me is another matter."

He was joking—mostly. But her eyebrow quirked, as if to say, *Ah, there you are!*

And then another thought hit him. "And, while I'm thrilled, light of my life, to see you, and I would be honored to have you share every detail of what's happened with me, my rose of Sharon, my helpmate, frankly, it is a little worrying that you have thrown yourself in the path of danger. After all, we have three children. I'm sure they would be put out to lose their mother. Does Norowitz know you're here? Do you know U.S. agents are just down the road in that house? What are you doing driving a car around in the middle of the woods in the dark of the night, Hannah?"

But she only got that look—that rebellious look—and crooked a devious smile. "Could we get back to the 'I love you' part?"

And then . . . well, what excuse could he possibly have? A rabbi, a man in his forties, and not even alone, and he was behaving like a . . . like a *goyisher* teenager himself, kissing his wife right there and not caring.

"*Rabbi Handalman?*" Denton's voice, loud.

Aharon broke from his wife, cheeks heated. "A man has been away from his wife for three months, what do you expect?"

"Three months?" Hannah asked, confused.

Wyle was jumping up and down. "Hey, I wish you raptures, but could we possibly get out of the cold? I mean, I realize *you're* not exactly cold at the moment, but there's me, Jill, Nate, and an unconscious guy, and we're all turning into Popsicles."

"Oh!" Hannah said, as if remembering something. "My god, Aharon, we have to get you out of here! There are American agents just down the road and the Mossad is here, too."

"Thank you, Hannah. I'm so glad you're up on all this."

*   *   *

Hannah was staying in a tiny hospice in the town of Monowice, a short distance away. By cramming into the car and spreading Farris out over the legs of the three people in the backseat they made it there in one piece. It was the off-season, and they were soon in possession of the entire upstairs of the house, consisting of three guest rooms. The hospice owner was not interested in anything but his TV, and they were able to carry Farris upstairs without being observed.

Jill was exceedingly grateful to be out of the cold. She and Nate quietly shared their amazement over such a benevolent spike of the one pulse as running into Hannah. A coincidence like that might be normal on the seventy-thirty world, but here it was more than they could have hoped for. At least, that was the way Jill figured it. Nate only smiled thoughtfully and kept his opinion to himself.

Upstairs, Hannah bustled around getting them blankets and towels and fussing over all of them with a maternal warmth. Jill liked her at once. She was efficient and outspoken, with a sharp intelligence glittering in her eyes, and she listened to Aharon's suggestions only when it suited her to do so. Despite this, Aharon appeared to be deeply in love. It softened Jill's opinion of him considerably.

They put Farris in the smallest bedroom and left the door cracked open so they could hear if he got up. The rest of them bundled into Hannah's room, sitting on the floor in blankets around the heating duct and sharing a package of fruit cookies. It was the first moment of peace they'd had, and as Jill looked around at the faces she could tell that all of them were in shock to one degree or another. She was having a hard time accepting it herself—that she was really sitting on a hard wooden floor eating packaged Polish cookies. Nate groaned at the taste of sugar on his tongue, focusing his attention on the cookie as if it were the first food he'd ever tasted. But Jill was too anxious to do more than nibble. She kept staring at the marked changes on Denton's face and Aharon's, even Nate's.

Aharon was the most changed. Hannah could not stop staring at him, either. The robe he wore was coarse and rank. He had lost weight and added bulky muscle. Even so, he looked drained and ill-used, as if he'd been on board a Roman galley for three months. Denton, on the other hand, was glowing with a tan, his hair bleached blonder by sunlight. There was a new strength and calm about him. Still, there was a dazed look about his eyes that made Jill think he hadn't transitioned as easily as it appeared.

Nate, if she tried to regard him objectively, had turned from olive to a deep reddish-brown since their days at Udub, and he had lost weight to the point of skinniness. She knew she herself probably looked anorexic. She pulled a strand of her hair forward, studying it. She'd gone nearly platinum from the power of the sun on Difa-Gor-Das. Even her delicate white skin had browned.

"Aharon," Hannah said, "there's no way you could look so different. You said something about three months, but it's only been a couple of weeks. What is going on?"

Aharon looked at the rest of them guiltily. "I'm afraid if I tell you, Hannah, you'll have me locked away, it's so crazy."

"Maybe I'm the crazy one, but at this point I'd believe you if you told me pigs could fly."

Aharon grunted. "Compared to this, Hannah, flying pigs are nothing. So? Should I do the honors, or is there someone here who actually knows what they're talking about?"

Jill took up the challenge and tried to explain to Hannah, in pop science terms, about the black hole. Hannah listened intently but got a feverish half smile on her face, as if she couldn't quite believe it—and couldn't quite not.

"This is what happened to you, Aharon?" she asked her husband incredulously. "You went to some other *world*?"

"On my life, Hannah, that is what happened. I was there for months." Aharon turned to Jill. "So tell me—why has it been only five days here?"

"You were there *three* months," Nate clarified. "We were on Difa-Gor-Das for nine. Time expands along the continuum of universes. During the time we were gone, about six months passed on Earth."

"But it's only been five days, you said?"

Nate looked at Jill for help.

"Let's back up for a minute and explain how we got us back. Nate and I were on a world with highly advanced technology. In fact, they were about two hundred thousand years ahead of Earth—plus or minus a couple of major upheavals."

She and Nate exchanged a look. "We found old data on how to use the black holes, though they themselves had gone beyond needing them centuries ago. To put it as simply as possible, when something goes through a black hole it creates a very distinct energy signature. Using their technology we were able to locate the signature in the fifty-fifty universe that marked our going through the gateway. We were eventually able to isolate each of the five patterns that went through—that would be you. After that it was not difficult to trace where the patterns had gone and to get a lock on you. It's hard to explain, but it's amazing technology—and alarmingly straightforward to manipulate."

"Well, not exactly *straightforward*," Nate said. "It took us seven months."

"Okay, it's not straightforward." Jill smiled. "But it's *possible*, which is amazing enough. Picture yourselves as energy patterns woven into this enormous tapestry. We were able to just . . . cut you out of where you were and *insert* you back into Earth's pattern."

Denton, Aharon, and Hannah were looking at her blankly.

"I still don't get the change in time," Denton said.

"When you reinsert a pattern like that you have to decide *when* as well as *where*," Nate explained. "It's so cool! There's this unbelievably complex energy pattern of life, and when you look at it that way—from the fifth dimension, as energy—you can actually *see* time."

Their faces went from blank to dazed.

"What Nate's trying to say is that we could have brought us back at any time, including at the six months' mark we believed to have actually passed on Earth. But in the end we decided on five days. We wanted it to be long enough since our disappearance that we wouldn't be likely to run into a bunch of cops or agents but not too long, because . . ." She hesitated, looking at Nate. "Well, let's just say that time is of the essence."

"But isn't there some sort of paradox?" Aharon said, waving his hands as he talked. "Are you saying we're here and we're simultaneously somewhere else? Can that be?"

"It can, because the *time* we are in now is not the same time you were in, or we were in, or Denton was in, in the other universes," Nate said. "Space-time is like a sheet. The other universes are entirely separate sheets."

Aharon was rubbing his forehead, trying to get his head around that. Denton just shrugged and grinned.

"Cool. But in that case, why not just bring us back before this whole mess even started?"

Nate got an excited sparkle in his eye. "We thought about it. The problem is we—our *old* selves—existed then. From what we could understand of the alien's notes on the subject, that would not have been a good idea."

"And to be honest," Jill added, "after what we'd seen about the misuse of other aspects of the wave, we wanted to screw around as little as possible with what we didn't understand."

The matter-of-fact way they were talking had Hannah's eyes large as saucers. She turned her head to stare at the changes on Aharon's face as if seeking for confirmation.

"However it happened that you got us back, I can only be grateful," Aharon said, taking his wife's hand.

"Works for me," Denton agreed. "I would have gotten bored out of my skull, being stuck where I was for another forty or fifty years."

"Good," Jill said, feeling relieved. "Because we couldn't send you back, even if we wanted to. We don't have the technology to do it here and, frankly, Nate and I are glad about that."

"Oh, yeah," Nate agreed.

"Maybe we should all describe what happened," Aharon said. "Where we went."

Denton stretched out long legs. "Absolutely. Since you already have us curious about this Difa-Gor-Das, Jill, why don't you guys start?"

*   *   *

Pol 137 woke up on a bed in a warm room. For a long time he tried to pull the fragments of his memory together against the darkness in his mind the way a man in the wind will try to pull together the remnants of a tattered coat.

The door to the room was open several inches, letting in a little light and the sound of voices. Pol had no idea where he was. He listened and listened to the voices, but something about them only made him more afraid. His fear became so acute that it outweighed any possible risk, and he fumbled around and found a lamp near the bed. He turned it on. The room revealed was unfamiliar. But there were a hundred little details, the lacy curtains on the window, the homey checked pillows, a chenille bedspread, a homespun rug on the floor, that hurt his brain.

He was not on the world of Centalia anymore.

This thought was so disturbing that he jumped out of bed. He was fully dressed, wearing some discarded Bronze clothes he had stolen during his days on the road running from Gyde and his monitors. The sight of them, here, seemed all wrong. But his survival skills kicked in and he went on reconnaissance. He went to the door of his room stealthily, prepared to bare his fangs, prepared to fight. There was no one in the hall, but the voices were louder, coming from a room a few doors down. The door to that room was open, like his own. He went back to the lamp by the bed and turned it off. Then he moved down the hall on silent feet, cautious and dangerous.

He reached their door and could not help peering into the lighted room. He moved as far into the shadows as he could, pressing himself against the far wall. He could only see three of them from his vantage point, but one of them was the woman, the blond woman. He stared at her, mesmerized. He took in her face—streaked white-blond hair, brown eyes, brown hair on the ridge above her eyes. Just like his.

He closed his eyes, the pain slicing through his head as though his brain were literally splitting just a little more in two. He was getting a memory of this woman. . . . She was in a bed and he was questioning her. She had looked different then, but even so, he knew her.

And he also knew, with complete certainly, that he had returned to the place from whence he had come. He had returned to the other side of the chasm. Before he had gone to Centalia this had been his world and he had been pursuing *her*. Not the way a man pursues a woman but the way a detective pursues a criminal—the way he had been pursuing the state terrorist.

Had *she* done this to him?

He made himself focus on the words they were speaking, words from his old language. The boy with the woman was describing some city . . . empty buildings . . . two suns. And then another one, the man with all the hair on his face, hair like that on Calder's own cheeks, began to speak of another place— cold . . . darkness . . . heavy gravity . . . some name, Kobinski . . .

The pain in Pol's head grew icier, numbing him, as the torrent of words washed over him largely uncomprehended. It wasn't that he couldn't understand the individual words; it was that they stung like knives and his damaged brain could not keep up, like a man with a limp running for a train. And always the darkness threatened to overwhelm him. But suddenly the accumulation of words reached critical mass and he understood something at least— they were each describing another world they had visited.

Just as he had done.

His pulse skyrocketed and he felt horribly ill. He knew he should continue to listen, to gather evidence. The answers he desperately needed were in that room. But he felt so weak. He could feel blackness crawling up his spine, tugging him under. For a moment he considered trying to escape. There was a stairway not all that far down the hall, and the people in the room would never see him go. But he simply didn't have the strength. It was all he could do to crawl back to the room he had occupied earlier, pull himself onto the bed, and allow his mind to slip away.

*   *   *

Aharon was listening to Denton tell his story with a mild touch of chagrin. The horrors *he* had had to face, and the blond goy had gotten sunshine and gardens and beautiful females? Aharon's pride plucked at him—what would these people *think*? What kind of monster would they take him to be to have gone where he'd gone? And also, despite all the things he had worked through on Fiori, he was confused again. He tried to assimilate what had happened to the others with the new understanding of God he had fought so hard for.

But as Denton continued his story, Aharon did comprehend. The world Denton described was beautiful and even easy, but it was also shallow, without morals or traditions, and cruel from sheer selfishness. Yes, it fit the man, or at least the man he had once been. Like to like. It was the ultimate in free will. If you wanted to head off in a certain direction, no matter how wrong, God would not stop you. You could keep going and going and going until finally you had the good sense to turn around on your own. Or not. Aharon liked it better when he'd believed God had a little more to say about it.

After the stories had been told, the group broke up for a time. Jill and Nate went down the hall to check on Farris and found him sleeping. Hannah made tea. Denton came up to Aharon and gave him a smile that offered friendship. Aharon took it and gave one back.

"Eventually, I'd love to hear everything you can remember about Kobinski," Denton said. "I feel so bad about his death, as if I really knew him."

"I feel bad also. But I think Kobinski's death was a kind of redemption for him, may he rest in peace."

"I hope so, Rabbi."

When they all had cups of steaming tea Jill looked around reluctantly. "I guess it's time to give you the bad news. If everyone is ready. We learned a lot about the wave technology when we were on Difa-Gor-Das," Jill said. "But the main thing we learned is that there really is a danger—the kind of danger, Aharon, that I think you were looking for based on what you found in the code. And there's still every possibility that if my research gets out, mine or Kobinski's, Earth could face a disaster. That's why we had to come back."

"I had a feeling," Aharon said with a sigh, "that this was not over yet."

"It's called a bounce event," Nate said. "It occurs when too much stress is put on the universal wave."

"The universal wave, the law of good and evil, the one-minus-one—they're all the same thing," Jill explained. "The one-minus-one is an integral part of the fabric of space-time. Maybe some of you remember an analogy Einstein made about gravity. He said space-time is like a rubber sheet and the planets are like bowling balls placed on the sheet. Their weight bends the rubber sheet and that's how space-time is bent by gravity. A black hole is a place where gravity is so heavy it punches a hole in space-time."

"Yes, I know," Aharon said from experience.

Jill gave a brief smile. "That happens to protect the integrity of space-time, because it can only stand so much gravitational pressure. The same thing is true of stress put on the universal wave."

"So that's what would happen?" Aharon asked, paling. "Someone might build a machine and tear a hole in space-time?"

Jill nodded. "In a way, yes. If you push the universal wave too far from its natural state it will cause a black hole–like effect. The area that is out of sync with the natural laws ends up *bouncing through* space-time into the fifth dimension."

"It's similar to what happened to us," Nate said. "But in this case instead of an individual bouncing into the fifth dimension, an entire section of the planet's *surface* is bounced."

"Unfortunately," Jill added, "the result is a lot more violent than when we went through the gateway. It's . . . well, it's apocalyptic. And then there's the question of where the bounced section could end up. Depending on the exact state of the stressed wave when the bounce occurs, it could end up in any number of universes, some of them hostile to human life. For example, somewhere where there isn't any oxygen or light. In that case, even if people survived the bounce, they'd die anyway."

Aharon was getting more red-faced by the minute as he looked from her to Nate and back again. "And this could happen? What? To an entire *city*?"

"Um . . ." Nate looked at Jill. "It could be an area smaller than a city—or it could be much larger."

"How much larger?"

Jill bit her lips nervously. "It's impossible to predict. It's so dangerous because there's an effect that happens when you start messing with the universal wave, a kind of echo chamber effect. The wave is so interwoven with everything . . . changes can escalate exponentially within milliseconds, and that is when a bounce is likely to occur. In theory the bounced section could be small or it could be vast. As large as a continent, even. Maybe even bigger than that."

Around the circle everyone was quiet.

"But would anyone be so stupid?" Aharon asked suddenly. "We had nuclear technology for sixty years and we managed not to blow ourselves up. Surely our scientists wouldn't be so dumb."

"We *did* use the atomic bomb," Jill reminded him. "It wasn't until we saw what it could do that we learned to respect the technology. With the wave we may never survive early experimentation. And the thing is, going through a bounce event—well, it happened to the ancestors of the people on Difa-Gor-Das, and I have a feeling there's a good chance of it happening to most cultures that discover the one-minus-one."

"So let's undiscover it," Denton said.

"Yes," Hannah agreed. She sat up, as if collecting herself together. "I have family. I'm sure you all have family. So? What needs to be done?"

"I have to believe . . ." Aharon shook his head thoughtfully. "Maybe God does not interfere as much as I once thought. But I have to believe there was a purpose to my finding the Kobinski codes—to what all of us have been through. We've been permitted to see the danger. There must be something we can do to prevent it."

"We have no choice but to try by any and all means," Nate agreed.

"Absolutely. That's why we're here." Jill didn't say it, but she felt a *personal* sense of responsibility. The looming catastrophe was, in a very real way, *her fault.*

They talked strategy for a while, but exhaustion did them in. Jill yawned, hugely, and it rippled around the room.

"Anyone else ready for some sleep?" Denton was barely able to keep his eyes open.

"Good idea," Nate said, stretching. "I don't think I can stay awake much longer."

"What about him?" Aharon said. "The one in the other room. We should keep watch."

"I'll do it," Hannah said. "After all, *I* only came in from Israel and that was several days ago."

"Hannahleh," Aharon murmured worriedly.

"She is the most bright-eyed," Denton remarked.

"Can you operate the gun?" Jill asked. "Or maybe we can lock him in."

"Lock, yes," Aharon said. "Gun, no. And if you hear any noise from inside the room you scream, loudly."

They all tiptoed out to check Farris. His was a small room under the eaves. The only lock operated from the room interior, so they dragged an armoire out of Hannah's room and down the hall. It completely blocked Farris's door.

"There," Aharon said. "Now no one needs to stay up."

"Don't be silly!" Hannah said in a motherly tone. "What if he gets sick in the night? We can't just leave him in there alone."

"Hannah's right," Jill yawned. "We don't want to kill the man. If he wakes up and needs help, get us up."

"Of course." Hannah nodded.

*   *   *

Hannah wasn't tired. Her mind was so overrun by thoughts and ideas that she'd probably never sleep again. Who would believe a word that was said tonight? No one, that's who, and Israelis, even ones who used to be New Yorkers, were not known to be gullible. Except that her own husband, Aharon Handalman, a man who did not lie and did not kid, was right in the middle of it.

There was a sound behind the door.

Hannah had taken a chair into the hall so she could sit near Farris's door. There was something going on in there. She leaned into the armoire and listened. There was muttering, as though the man was talking in his sleep, and some whimpering.

"*Water.*"

The word, muffled through the door, was low but distinguishable. The man sounded half-asleep. She held her breath, listening.

"*Water.*"

Hadn't they even put a pitcher with some water and a glass in there? She couldn't remember. Or maybe he was so sick he couldn't find the glass. Maybe he would go back to sleep.

"Please," came a low groan.

Hannah drew back from the door and stiffened her spine. She marched down the hall to her own room. From the scant light coming in the window she could make out Aharon's face on the pillow—drawn and troubled. He looked so thin! So white, so exhausted!

She reached out a hand to wake him, but the wife in her couldn't do it, not after all he'd been through. Hesitant, she turned to the man on the pallet on the floor. Denton Wyle was also deeply asleep, lying on his back, arms wide over his head, snoring lightly. Could she wake up a stranger? A strange man in the middle of the night?

She sighed and went back down the hall to the room where Nate and Jill were sleeping. They weren't married, she didn't think, but they were obviously a couple. They had left their door open a little, too, and when she heard nothing she peeked inside. They were so cute together—spooned on the bed, deeply asleep. They were so heavily asleep, in fact, that they looked like they might sink right through the bed—a strange impression.

No, she couldn't bring herself to wake any of them.

She went back to the armoire-blocked door and could hear moaning now, low and pained. Well, for goodness' sake, what if the man was dying? If he was dying, she ought to wake the others. Yes, okay, but what if he *wasn't* dying?

Hannah had nursed sick children through the night plenty of times. You got up, you gave them a drink of water, you listened to their sleepy terrors, soothed their foreheads, maybe gave them some baby aspirin, and that was it. They were back asleep.

She could always scream.

Making up her mind, Hannah went to fetch some aspirin and a glass of water. She placed these on the floor in the hallway and, as quietly as she could, pushed the armoire inch by inch out of the way. When the door was unblocked enough to enter, she paused, aspirin and glass in hand, to listen. She heard another low moan inside the room. She opened the door.

The door swung slowly open. In the light from the hall Pol saw a woman, a dark-haired woman, walk quietly toward the bed. Earlier he had positioned his pillow under the blanket so it would look occupied. Now he made himself wait behind the door until she put down the glass. Then he jumped her.

His hand came over her mouth before she could so much as gasp. She struggled mightily for such a small thing. He clamped his muscles hard around her and dragged her from the room.

He had a plan. It was dangerous. He was outnumbered. But he was not afraid of these people; they were weak. His plan was simple. He was going to escape and take the blond woman with him.

He dragged the dark-haired woman down the hall. He would like to find his gun, too, but unless it was easily spotted there would be no time to search for it. He managed to keep his captive's feet off the ground and mostly her kicks and blows landed silently on his person. His hand blocked his mouth, but she was making sounds in her throat.

The woman he wanted was not in the room he'd spied on earlier, but in a different room down the hall, away from the stairs and freedom. She was lying on a bed, entwined with the boy, asleep.

Something about the scene, that she should have ease and the warmth of another, angered him. He worked his way around the bed and the dark-haired woman's feet connected with the edge of it, making a bang. But it was too late. In one movement he released the dark-haired woman and pulled the warm, sleeping weight of the blonde against his chest. She was too groggy to even struggle. He put one arm around her throat, tight, and the other he wove through her arms and behind her back.

She gasped in a deep breath of pain, fully awake.

"Don't fight or I'll kill you." His arm tightened around her throat to show her how it would be done.

"Denton! Aharon!" The boy was up from the bed, calling for backup. He scrambled under the mattress, and Pol knew he was going for the gun. Good. That meant Pol wouldn't have to waste time looking for it.

He backed toward the door. The boy held the gun on him. *His* gun. The gun of a Silver monitor, detective class. But the woman was between Pol and the gun. The man with the hair on his face came running from down the hall and the dark-haired woman collapsed into his arms.

"Aharon, it's my fault! I heard him ask for water and I thought, instead of waking you—"

"Hush, Hannah. It's all right."

Three of them. There should be four. Where was the fourth? Calder was still several feet from the doorway to the hall—the exit and his escape. The man and woman blocked it. The boy held the gun on him, but from the look on his face Pol knew he wouldn't use it.

"Move," Pol told the couple in the doorway, motioning his head to indicate they should join the boy.

They obeyed. The man said, "So let her go and let's talk, for heaven sake. No one wants to hurt you."

Pol backed toward the door. He looked over his shoulder. The doorway was empty. *Where was the other man?*

"Let her go," the dark-haired boy ordered. He raised the gun, pointing toward Pol's head. Pol smiled. He would never risk it.

"*Nate*," the older man warned, "look, if we wanted to hurt you we would have left you to freeze in the woods. Talk to us."

Pol took a step back, dragging the blonde with him, and now he was in the doorway. He meant to say, *Where's the other man?* He meant to say, *Give me the gun or I'll kill her.* But when the sentences tried to go from his brain to his esophagus, they dissolved into nonsense. That scared him.

The pulse in his arm throbbed against the woman's throat. There was a tangled knot growing in his stomach. He was constantly shocked at how incapacitated he was, kept going to use various functions and found them disabled. He had thought he could do this. He had thought it would be easy. But suddenly he was very confused.

The woman began to make a low, choking sound. Pol heard it, but it didn't completely register. He just needed to take a few more steps, to back into the hallway, and then he would have a shot at the stairs. He pulled her backward.

The dark-haired boy was saying something, his face ugly and panicked. Pol felt his grip on the situation faltering. Why did he look like that? What was wrong?

He made himself go faster, took two steps, backing down the hall. He took a quick look over his shoulder; the way to the stairs looked clear. When he turned his head back around, the three from the room had come into the hall after him, and they were only steps away from him, their faces upset, yelling.

And finally he heard the woman making strangling sounds. *Scarp.* His arm had tightened around her throat. He was choking her.

He loosened his grip just as something struck his kidneys from behind. He registered his mistake—*the fourth man*—even as he doubled over in pain, releasing the woman. He clutched her shirt, then she was gone. His outstretched hands crashed into the floor.

He scrambled to one side, a cry of pain coming from his mouth. The fourth man—the tall blonde—was standing over him holding a broomstick over his head. Pol crawled for the stairs on his knees, hands over his head, prepared for another blow.

The fourth man did not strike again. He lowered the broomstick, his eyes a mix of anger and pity. Pol reached the stairs and paused at the top of them. His eyes moved to the boy—he could fire now. In a minute, the gun would go off and he would be dead.

But the boy didn't fire. He held the gun on Pol, awkwardly. The blond woman was at the boy's side, urging him in a low voice. Pol could no longer decipher the words. He slowly reached back with one knee, finding the first step.

"Don't go," the blond woman said. He understood the words. She took a step toward him, rubbing her throat. Her voice was raw.

He backed down the step, then another. All he really wanted was the woman, but he no longer thought he could take her. If he couldn't take her he would go all the same.

He paused, preparing to turn and run for it. He was braced to move should anyone so much as twitch, but they didn't; they just watched. And he thought; he thought very hard. He struggled, his brain aching with the effort, as if he were pulling up memories cell by cell. He had to ask. He wasn't going to be able to take her, and he couldn't leave without asking just this one thing. He focused on her, only her, willing her to tell him.

"Who. Am. I?"

Her face looked so sad. It made him angry.

"Your name is Lieutenant Calder Farris."

He tried to read her face, to see if she was lying. She had said that name before, but it meant nothing to him. He shook his head.

She nodded, as if acknowledging that it wasn't enough. "You work for the United States government in the Department of Defense in Washington, D.C. You investigate new weapons technology."

He braced his hands on the steps, the words bouncing around his brain like a rubber ball. *Farris. Department of Defense. Weapons.*

He turned and fled down the stairs.

Jill paced for a few minutes in the hallway, her shirt torn, her face still darkened from the pressure Farris had exerted on her neck. She faced the silent group.

"I have to go after him."

"No," Nate said. He raked a hand through his hair. "No way. Huh-uh."

She almost smiled. It was so unlike Nate to try to tell her what to do. "I know it's not logical. But . . . I don't know. My intuition says we can convince Farris."

"Is this the same Farris who almost choked you to death a few minutes ago?" Nate asked sarcastically. He huffed out a breath. "Jesus, Jill, if that's your intuition, I'd say it's a bit rusty."

Jill looked at the others for support. "Farris was in charge of the investigation in Seattle. He's the only one who knows what the DoD has or doesn't have. Obviously he's been traumatized, but I think he can be reached."

"Traumatized?" Nate huffed. "He's bonkers, Jill. That man is *dangerous*."

"I don't think he meant to hurt me," she said doubtfully.

She looked at the others, waiting for a response. Like it or not, they were all in this together.

"Nate's right," Aharon said with something of his old hubris. "The man is dangerous. What if something should happen to you?"

Denton shrugged. "Personally, I think you should follow your gut."

Jill looked at Hannah.

Aharon's wife appeared shocked that she would be asked for her opinion. She hesitated. "I think . . . I think he's more lost than dangerous. He needs help."

Nate groaned.

"I'll need my coat," Jill said, knowing she had no time.

Hannah ran to grab it as Nate came up to her and took her hands. "*Jill.*" His dark eyes were anguished.

"Trust me," she said, touching his cheek. "I'll be back. I love you."

He rolled his eyes and took out his wallet. The thing had traveled to another universe and back again in the pocket of his jeans. He took out a credit card and handed it to her.

"Thanks, sweetie."

Aharon handed her a hundred-dollar bill. "Here. Take it."

"I've got zip," Denton said regretfully, turning out his pockets.

"I'm counting on all of you," she said. She gave Nate one brief kiss and left before she could change her mind.

22

"The intrinsic, extramundane process of *Tikkun*, symbolically described as the birth of God's personality, corresponds to the process of mundane history. The historical process and its innermost soul, the religious act of the Jew, prepare the way for the final restitution of all the scattered and exiled lights and sparks. . . . Every act of man is related to this final task which God has set for his creatures."
—Gershom Scholem,
Major Trends in Jewish Mysticism, 1946

By morning, Hannah's rented car was parked across from a hotel in Auschwitz. Denton's and Nate's knees were crushed in the backseat and Nate felt like hell. He still had the semidazed wonderment of someone contemplating the pain of a knife in the back.

"She'll be all right," Denton said, patting Nate's knee.

"Um, she took off in the middle of the night. On foot. In rural *Poland.* With a hundred dollars, no ID, and my credit card."

"She can handle it. She's a brain."

"I used to think so," Nate said with disgust.

Hannah and Aharon were in the front seat, talking softly together. Nate looked at them to make sure they weren't listening before turning to Denton with a flush.

"We haven't been apart in nine months. I'm acting totally pussy-whipped, aren't I?"

Denton grinned. "Maybe a little."

"It's just that when Jill wants something she can be so . . . *oblivious.* I'm worried about her."

"If it's any help, I think she's right about Farris. I don't think he'll hurt her."

"Gee, I must have imagined that he almost killed her yesterday," Nate said dryly, but he sounded like he wanted to believe it.

"There!" Hannah whispered loudly.

A man and a woman were coming out of the hotel. Nate watched them, wishing he had a closer view. The woman wore a wool hat, navy pea coat, and scarf in the cold, the rest of her clothes ordinary. She was slim and attractive. The man's head was bare. He was speaking to the woman, looked around the street casually, turning to face them.

Denton let out a groan. He sank down in the seat, pulling Nate with him. "I know that guy! He calls himself 'Mr. Smith.' "

"See!" Hannah exclaimed, triumphant. "I told you! Aharon—didn't I say he was Mossad? I told you the Mossad was here."

"Yes, Hannah, and I'm so happy you've been spending your time following such people."

Nate was being crunched in Denton's grip.

"You guys need to look like you're doing something," Denton whispered urgently to Aharon and Hannah. "Look natural."

"It's fine. They're going the other way; he's not even looking," Aharon said dismissively.

Nate sat up cautiously, taking a look for himself. "He's right. They went around the corner."

Denton sat up, looking a bit chagrined. "Sorry. I'm trying not to be a wimp these days; it's just that my body has a very real memory of being pummeled by that guy."

"So he is Mossad?" Nate asked.

"Well, he never actually introduced himself as such, but I think so."

"What about the woman?" Aharon asked Denton. "Did you recognize her?"

"No."

"She's here to make them look like a *couple*," Hannah explained. "She's a *katsa*."

"Yes, thank you, Mata Hari," Aharon said with mock enthusiasm. "So now what?"

"Someone should check into the hotel," Hannah suggested, "pretend to be vacationing. We might be able to overhear them or even get into their room."

Nate nodded. "That's smart. There are four of us. We should spread out. Two can cover these guys and two can take the guys at Anatoli's house."

Aharon shrugged as if to say he couldn't argue. "Fine, someone will check in here. But not *you*, Hannah."

"Who then?" she asked.

"It can't be me," Denton said regretfully. "Smith would recognize me in a heartbeat."

"I'll do it," Nate volunteered.

"Do you speak Hebrew?" Hannah asked.

"Um . . . not last time I checked."

She gave her husband an "I told you so" look.

"Hannah, you're not going in there."

"Not alone . . ." she said leadingly. "It would be more convincing if a husband and wife checked in."

Aharon grunted. "Then that settles it. Look at me!" He ran an open hand to indicate his countenance. "You think they wouldn't be a little suspicious? You think they don't have my picture?"

Hannah studied his face. "You know, I'm looking forward to seeing what you look like under that beard after all these years."

"Hannah, are you *crazy*?" Aharon was aghast.

Nate couldn't stop a smile. *Welcome to my world,* he thought.

*   *   *

It was mid-morning and Pol waited outside the airport in the cold. He stood still, almost like one at attention. But his mind was not at attention. Most of it was shut down. He was functioning with the mindless automation of a mortally wounded soldier crawling away from the enemy's bayonet. He hated this place, with its snow and trees and strange little villages. Even the people did not strike a chord. He did not recognize their language. He was more lost here than he'd ever been in Centalia.

That could overwhelm him if he allowed it to. Instead, he allowed himself a goal: to find the familiar. He had to find Lt. Calder Farris.

Last night he'd followed the road signs toward Kraków because it was the largest name on those signs and must, therefore, be a city of good size. He'd gotten a ride, sitting in the front seat with a farmer who'd had a truck bed full of birds in cages. As they'd approached Kraków, Pol had seen a commercial jet plane in the air. He'd recognized it at once, understood it down to the basic principles of its aerodynamics—wingspan ratios and quantities of fuel—even though he knew very well that this particular type of aircraft did not exist in the world he'd just come from. He'd pushed aside all the ways that wanted to screw with his head. The plane could take him to Washington, D.C. He would ride the devil's tail if it took him to Washington, D.C.

But he could not remember how one got onto the plane. So he'd sat inside the airport until past daybreak, observing the security guards, observing the buying of tickets, taking it in through a heavy filter, discarding everything that wasn't need-to-know.

Need-to-know: He'd need identity papers and money to get on a plane.

Now he waited outside the airport. It was cold, almost as cold as Centalia. After a long time a man got out of a car. He was blond and of the right age and he was alone. Before the man could enter the terminal, Farris approached him.

"Can you tell me which is the road to Budapest?" Pol asked him in his old language.

The man tried to converse with him, pointing toward the city and speaking carefully in English. Pol wore a chilly smile. He grabbed the man's arm and pushed the neck of a bottle in his pocket into the man's side.

"Come with me," Pol said.

The man looked around for help, but no one was paying any attention to them.

"What do you want? Please—"

Pol led the man away, quickly, before he could overcome his surprise. Around the terminal they went, to a place scoped out in advance, a small park.

In the trees, the man grew desperate. His face tightened as images of what Pol might want to do to him crossed his mind. Pol was operating swiftly and with deadly certainty, yet part of him was curious; part of him wished the man would fight back. But it was clear this creature was no warrior. His first instinct was not to fight but to offer money. He did so, pulling out a packet full of bills and the identity papers Pol needed. The man pleaded for his life in Polish and English.

It was time to act. Pol hesitated. He hesitated so long, the man sensed his weakness and tried to run. Before he had taken two steps, Pol brought the bottle from his pocket and down hard on the back of the man's head. The man cried out in surprise and crumpled to the ground, unconscious.

Pol took the man's wallet, passport, and plane tickets. He put the things in his pockets. He stripped the man of his shirt and tie and put them on, taking the man's heavy outer coat as well. He dumped out the contents of the man's bag and put his old clothes in there. He did not think he would need them again, but he did not want them to be found here.

Kneeling down, he wrapped the scarf around the man's throat, pulled it tight, prepared to pull it tighter. And knelt there.

He should kill this man. If the man was left alive, he would be able to describe his attacker. He would be able to give the name on Pol's new identity papers, a name the authorities might otherwise take days to track down. Still, Pol hesitated.

He could not get the images out of his mind, images of the night he killed the Silver, Pol 137, how he had to hack and hack, how the blood had flowed like burgundy wine. Or of Gyde standing over the body of the Bronze rare book owner, putting out his cigarette in the blood.

Sweat dripped down Pol's back inside his new shirt. His hands gripped both ends of the scarf tightly. They shook as if the scarf were alive with a current.

He couldn't do it. He dropped the scarf.

There was a cracking branch behind him. He spun, a snarl on his lips, guilt and fury over his own weakness dogging him.

"Lieutenant Farris?"

The blond woman stepped closer. For a moment he was sure he was hallucinating completely now, his enfeebled senses finally giving in to delusion. But she looked nervous and she looked cold. A glisten of moisture on her red nose testified to her reality.

She looked at the man on the ground, then at him. Pol hated the approval in her eyes. She should be afraid of him. He would make her afraid.

She rubbed her arms to warm herself. "Did you get his passport?"

Pol took it out of his pocket and looked at it.

"Credit cards?"

He handed her the wallet and the tickets. He panicked as the things left his fingers. What the hell was he doing?

It was terrible not to be able to trust oneself, not to fathom the reasoning of one's own limbs. He told himself he was testing her. He was giving her enough rope to hang herself. If she said, or did, one wrong thing, he would break her neck. This time he would lie on top of her, heavy and deadly, and would look in her eyes as he choked the life from her body.

"Paris," she said, reading the tickets. "Where is it you want to go, Lieutenant?" If she was laughing at him, he couldn't see it in her green eyes.

"Washington, D.C.," he heard himself say. He stiffened in horror.

She nodded. "We can get a connection in Paris, but I'll need tickets. It looks like there's enough cash here." She pulled some bills from the wallet. "And we'll need to get me a passport." She looked again at the man on the ground, her face softening. "I'd prefer to steal one without knocking someone out if possible. Maybe in the ladies' rest room? I'm not too good at this kind of thing. You'll have to advise me."

His fists clenched at his thighs to keep them under control. Inside, he was churning like the eye of a storm. He did not understand what was happening. She seemed to be implying that she was going with him. It was a trick. She was milking him.

What was frightening was how horribly tempted he was by the ruse. The idea of help—the mere *idea* of it—filled him with desperate longing. It made him realize how heavy the burden was that he carried, how close he was to complete collapse. But at the same time, he felt enraged. He was a warrior. He would not be nursed, by the blood, and particularly not by *her*.

"Go fuck yourself," he said, pleased to remember the words. His lip curled in a disdain broad enough to fill the seas.

She shied away from the look on his face, licked her lips nervously, but didn't run. She gazed down at the passport again. "You, um, picked a good one. The passport's four years old. The security guards will just assume you had a haircut. Otherwise you match him quite well."

Go to the devil, I said!

"Lieutenant Farris?" she asked cautiously.

"Do what you want," he snarled. He grabbed the papers from her and headed for the airport.

*   *   *

By eight o'clock that evening Mr. and Mrs. Goldman from New Jersey were installed in the small inn's upstairs bedroom—right across from Mr. and Mrs. Dolman, the name Aharon had peeked at in the register as he signed in.

Hannah—that is, Ruth Goldman—had chatted with the innkeeper, a rosy-faced Polish matron, about wanting to be upstairs and wanting something that faced the lovely view in the back, and Mrs. Sochetzchi had given them the room next to the Dolmans. They were the only other guests in the inn.

Hannah had smiled at Aharon triumphantly. And he, Aharon Handalman, had run a hand over his face, as he had been unable to stop doing for the past two hours, still shamed and nauseated by the lack of hair there. He felt like Samson. He felt unmanned. At last, Hannah had managed it.

What on earth was he going to say when they got back to Jerusalem?

Now they were lying on a wooden floor, with only a knotted rag rug between their bodies and the hard surface. Hannah lay on her side facing him, a clear water glass pressed to her ear, its other end on the wall.

Foolishness, Aharon thought again, with a mental snort. Such a thing as a glass against a wall was good for cartoons, maybe, but not for real life. Aharon himself had tried his ear against the wall, but though he could hear murmuring, he could tell nothing that was being said.

"That's not going to work," he said quietly to Hannah, watching her intensely focused face. "We're going to have to make a hole when they go out. Tomorrow I'll buy a drill." He thought about it some more. "Or maybe one of those doctor's things would work—you know what I mean? I could go see the doctor in town about some complaint or other. It's not like I don't have plenty of complaints."

"Shhh!" Hannah said.

He could not believe he was talking about drilling holes and stealing medical apparatus. He could not believe that he, he and his *wife*, were in Auschwitz spying on the Mossad.

On the other hand, after his experiences on Fiori nothing seemed as frightening or as crazy as it ought to. He could even feel *delighted* to be lying on the floor on Earth, spying on the Mossad.

He sighed contentedly, watching his wife. "So what are they saying?" he asked her teasingly.

"They're talking about the Americans," she whispered.

Of course they were. What else would they be talking about?

It was ridiculous. Because right now they were in a life-and-death situation. Not only *their* life and death, the latter of which was extremely likely, but some huge, apocalyptic potentiality, and still he was getting warm thoughts about his wife.

But he'd learned on Fiori that sometimes it served not to think too closely about what you had to do. Better to allow himself to lie here on his side watching Hannah pretending to be able to hear and allow his mind to wander to greener pastures. They were in the hotel, they had gotten in, he and Mrs. Goldman, and that was good enough for tonight. After all, he could hardly drill holes in the wall with their neighbors in the room, even if he had a drill, which he didn't. And if the Mossad was there, in the next room, they weren't out doing anything worse.

"Hannah," he said, his voice soft so as not to be heard in the next room and also a little husky. "This is the first time we are alone, you and me."

"They're arguing about whether or not the woman can get inside the house," she said, her voice conspiratorial.

"Of course they are." Aharon took her small fingers and brought them to his lips.

Hannah flushed, her eyes focusing on him for the first time—finally seeing the kind of mood he was in. She smiled and frowned at the same time, a halfhearted rejection, yet her hand unfurled to close the brief distance to his cheek. She rubbed her fingers over its smoothness. Her eyes ignited playfully.

"I can think of some advantages to those soft, bare cheeks of yours," she whispered.

"Hannah!" he gasped, shifting on the floor. "Are you trying to kill me?"

"Hush!" Her voice went distant again as she strained at the glass. Even he could hear the rising voices, though he still couldn't make out words. Probably because his ears were filled with pounding blood. His fingers reached out of their own volition, smoothing over that crazy sweatshirt of hers.

Hannah's eyes widened. "Aharon, this is important! They're arguing over ways to get her into the house." She made a cease-and-desist motion with her hand.

"Good," Aharon murmured, raising up the hem of her sweatshirt. "You listen for both of us."

*   *   *

Denton approached the back of Anatoli's house, wary of the early-morning sunlight. Hannah had left some of her "spy gear" in the hostel, including a small pair of binoculars. Denton had to chuckle at that, thinking about how crazy she made Aharon.

Just now Denton had seen that the only person who appeared to be awake in the house was the younger of the two agents, or Marines, or whatever they were. The big, hulking one must be asleep. Although the big, hulking one was probably the dimmer bulb of the two, Denton was reassured. He would be watching the house for quite a while today, bundled up like a snowman in every stitch of clothing he could find. But his immediate agenda was to talk to Anatoli.

The younger agent was in the little kitchen sipping coffee. It wasn't far enough away from Anatoli's room for comfort, but then, no room in Anatoli's house was.

Denton slipped up to the window.

He could see better in the thin light of day. The window had been made escape-proof by nailing two two-by-fours in a cross shape on the inside of the window frame. That left gaps for light and air, but nothing bigger than a cat could crawl through. The window itself was indented from the window frame and was not affected by the boards. And it was not locked. It eased up under Denton's fingers—and stuck at about two inches.

"Anatoli?" Denton whispered. "Anatoli!"

A shape loomed up against the glass. Anatoli's bed was just inside the window and when he sat up his face popped into view like that of a ghost. He looked frailer than ever, his wispy hair in a staticky dance around his head, his eyes large and popping, like the eyes of a drowned sailor.

Denton had the feeling the old man was about to scream and put his fingers against his lips urgently. "Shhhhhhh!"

The old man's mouth opened into the shape of a scream, but no sound came out. He blinked at Denton.

"Anatoli, it's me, Denton Wyle!"

The mouth closed. Anatoli's bony fingers crept under the boards and onto the windowsill. Denton looked down at the poor, gnarled things and took off a glove, covering them with his own.

"Denton . . ." Anatoli's eyes were confused.

"Yes. Shhh! We must whisper."

"Is *he* with you? Did he come back with you?"

Anatoli's confusion had melted into a mad fanaticism, his face eager. Denton felt a surge of disappointment and covered it with a smile. "No, Reb Kobinski did not come. But he, uh, sent us back to take care of a few things."

"What things? What did the master say?"

Dang, this was dumb.

"Um, he's afraid that some of his work has gotten out. We have to make sure that isn't the case."

"But . . . I dug up all of the master's work and burned it. I did just as he said!" Anatoli's eyes watered with tears.

"Shhhhh!" Denton soothed. "I know. I know you burned it." But Anatoli had not burned it, thank god. Denton was selfishly glad that he hadn't. "Listen to me, Anatoli. We need to know about the men who are holding you. Do they know about Reb Kobinski? Have they talked about him?"

Anatoli looked upset by the question, befuddled. For a moment, Denton thought this was all hopeless. Anatoli's eyes were like windows into a chaotic whirlwind. But a struggle went on in those eyes and slowly they cleared. Denton could see in the tension clutching that fragile body, knew that Anatoli was fighting hard for this moment of clarity. Denton could have kissed him in gratitude.

"I don't think . . . No, they have never mentioned Reb Kobinski. And I have not spoken his name."

"That's good," Denton said with relief. "Anatoli, that's very good."

"They asked about Dr. Talcott and Nate Andros and . . . and Rabbi Handalman. They did not ask about you."

"That's good, Anatoli; that's just fine. What did they say about what happened in the clearing that night?"

A shudder went through Anatoli as the battle for sanity lost ground in his eyes. "Lights, noise. They keep asking. They ask if I saw . . . if Dr. Talcott had something in her hand, *did* something. I . . . pretend to be crazy." Anatoli smiled a sad, tremulous smile, as if to say, *Who's kidding who?*

"Have you overheard their conversations? Do you know—"

There was only a few seconds' warning. Anatoli stiffened and shoved Denton's hands away. He dropped down onto the bed just as the door to the hall opened. There was no time to run back to the safety of the trees. Denton could only duck down under the window and flatten himself against the side of the house. He looked down and saw his long knees poking out, visible to anyone who might look out the window. He swiveled to tuck them against the wall.

"What the fuck?" he heard a masculine voice inside the room—annoyed.

"What're you trying to do, old man?" came a deeper voice—both men were in the room. "Suicide by hypothermia? It's fucking ten degrees out there."

Denton heard the sound of someone trying to close the window . . . and apparently not succeeding. He froze, waiting.

He should have shut the damn window. Was opening the window even possible from inside the room with those two-by-fours in place? Were the DoD agents figuring that out right about now?

As if confirming his worst fears, he heard one of the men say, very low, "Go check outside."

Denton felt a moment of panic. He very nearly jumped to his feet and took off across the backyard, even though he knew that the men at the window would see him for sure. But he held his ground, trying to think of another option. Then he heard Anatoli's voice, thin and wavery: "Can I have some tea?"

"Let go," came the younger man's voice, quick, impatient.

"But I need some tea!"

And then an exclamation of utter disgust. "Oh, Jesus H. Christ!"

Denton couldn't figure out what had happened at first, only that Anatoli was trying to divert the men—and apparently succeeding.

"Davis! Goddamn it! Pick him up and get him to the bathroom, would ya?"

A smell wafted through the window and hit Denton's nose—acrid and pungent.

Denton grinned, chalking up a couple of points for the old fox. He crept along the side of the wall and around the house where he could make a dash for the trees.

*   *   *

Nate bought a ticket at the gate and entered the large fenced grounds of the Holocaust museum. It was a crisp winter day and the sun was shining. He stood there looking over the original barracks and parade ground, the bare earth frosty in the cold and cleared of anything green. Everything was silent and still. It was a mausoleum that hinted at horrors only because of what one *knew* had happened here. Otherwise, it was just a bunch of crappy-looking old barracks.

But he did know. And the hair stood up on the back of his neck. Jesus, the human race was just *weird* to preserve stuff like this.

The man Nate was following, Mr. Smith, was playing tourist. It wasn't difficult to keep an eye on him as he strolled around the grounds and in and out of barracks. It was a low-key kind of day and there were probably fewer than a dozen tourists around. Nate didn't seem to attract any more attention from Mr. Smith than the rest of them.

Smith headed into a long building that was the museum proper, and after a couple of minutes Nate idled in after him. He was wearing an old parka and a woolen hat. He tried to keep his face mostly averted, afraid that if Smith got a good look at him he would be recognized. The Mossad guy Nate had conked over the head in Seattle might have described him, and if they'd dug into Jill's background they might have his picture and his name.

Mr. Smith strolled among the exhibits, giving Nate time to think. Normally, he would have been quite interested in the exhibits, but today he had other things on his mind.

Jill. Damn her for what she was putting him through. He had never been in love before. It was crazy how it opened a hole inside you. All he could think about was wanting a lifetime with her, some place of their own, cozy evenings of talk and hugging, work they both cared about, nights of exploring each other's bodies with unselfconscious enthusiasm.

It was insane. No wonder so few philosophers tackled the whole mating instinct—it was completely irrational. But man, when it grabbed you . . . Knowing she was out there, in danger, and not going after her was like holding his hand on a chopping block. It was exactly that hard.

The thing that really worried him was that despite Jill's claim that Farris wouldn't hurt her, he was pretty sure she would have gone, danger or no, that she was willing to risk her life because she thought everything was her fault. She'd had that Passover lamb look in her eye. And all he could do was wait to hear if she was alive or dead or what.

Damn, he'd lost sight of Smith. Nate hurried through the museum, but the man was gone. He went outside just in time to see Smith disappear around some buildings on the far side of the camp. Nate ran to catch up. From the side of the crematorium he watched Smith look around and then climb through a hole in the fence.

Nate was pretty sure Smith was going to Anatoli's house. He took his time following, circling around, approaching from the north. The woods beyond the fence were not entirely familiar. He'd only been through them a couple of times and he was no Daniel Boone. But through luck or instinct he reached Anatoli's house the way he'd intended.

He found Denton crouched behind a large group of boulders about where they'd agreed to meet. He had his mittened hands tucked under his armpits for warmth. His face was red from the cold. Nate crouched down beside him and peeked over the boulders through the trees. Smith was there all right. He was four or five hundred yards away at the edge of the woods closest to the camp, watching the house through binoculars. Denton nodded, acknowledging the man's presence.

"Did you talk to Anatoli?" Nate asked in a low voice.

Denton nodded and filled him in. "How do they know about Handalman?" Denton whispered.

"Probably because he and I traveled with Jill."

"Oh, right. That's good. So the DoD probably doesn't know about the manuscript."

"Let's hope."

They crouched there in the cold woods and waited. Hannah had been sure the Mossad agents were going to try to get into the house today, and Mr. Smith's presence indicated something was going down.

It didn't take long for his partner to show up. The woman Nate and Denton had seen with Mr. Smith at the inn soon came walking down the road, hobbling on a broken boot heel. She looked like a refugee from a fashion ad, with a faux leopard coat, tight black leggings, and high black boots. Her hair was as tall as a soufflé and her makeup was discernible at ninety paces.

"Hooker du jour," Denton whispered.

Nate agreed, though he thought she was just tasteful enough to appeal to a couple of alpha males.

"Bet her car broke down," Denton suggested, clearly enjoying this. "And she'll need to use their phone." He used Hannah's binocs on the woman.

Nate thought that likely. He was worried about what the woman had in the large black leather purse she had looped over her shoulder. Although Hannah had been sure the *katsa* and Mr. Smith had been discussing getting into the house, she hadn't managed to hear them say what they planned to do there. Nate hoped they weren't going to bug the place. If they did, they might overhear information about his and Jill's work, and that would be bad.

The woman disappeared around the front of the house. Denton handed the binoculars to Nate for a turn. Nate poked his head up over the boulder to see what Mr. Smith was up to. He was still just inside the edge of the woods, his own binoculars trained on the house. Nate turned in that direction himself.

For a long while he saw nothing in the windows. So long, he became convinced either she wasn't going to be allowed inside the house or whatever business she had would be conducted in front rooms, a possibility he and Denton had discussed. But just as he was about to suggest they move around to the front of the house, a movement in the kitchen window caught his eye.

The *katsa* breezed into the small room, still limping. Hinkle hulked in after her. She appeared to be trying to chat him up, talking gaily, but Hinkle only went to the phone on the wall and picked up the receiver, handed it to her as if to say, *Do it and be gone.*

She had to be playing the part of a dimwit, because she ignored the obvious message and continued to chat on.

Nate's eyes were glued to her, watching for some clue that she was going to put some tiny auditory device on the receiver or anywhere else in the room. Fortunately, Hinkle seemed to be watching her just as closely. Nate almost cheered.

When the woman finally got on the phone, she did a slow turn. Her hands were animated, as if she was in conversation with whoever was on the other end of the line. But something in her face, particularly as her circuit turned her away from Hinkle, indicated she was studying her surroundings quite closely.

As she faced the window, her eyes looked up and straight through the glass. For a pulse, Nate thought she was looking at him, but then he realized that she was looking at Mr. Smith, though she probably could not actually see him from there. The hand that wasn't holding the phone came in front of her, where Hinkle couldn't see it, and she pointed, hard, to her left.

Nate swung the binocs and saw she was pointing to the tiny dining room table. On the table was a large black bag, like an attaché case. Nate's toes curled.

"They have their papers in a briefcase," he said, low, to Denton. "She's spotted it."

Denton put a hand on Nate's shoulder and squeezed in reassurance.

The woman hung up the phone, putting a vapid look back on her face before turning to Hinkle. She started chatting again, but Hinkle took her elbow to escort her out.

She hung back, tugging at her purse. For a moment, Nate thought she was going to bring out a gun. But what she brought out of that voluminous space was a bottle of liquor.

She tried to press it on Hinkle. He shook his head. She tried harder, leaning into him. When Hinkle still wouldn't take it she placed it on the kitchen counter and allowed him to lead her from the room. A few minutes later they heard the almost inaudible sound of a door closing and the *katsa*, still limping, started back down the road.

"Damn!" Nate said. He turned the binocs back to the kitchen window, willing Hinkle to reappear and toss that thing out the window. He didn't. The bottle sat there. "Shit!"

"What is it?" Denton whispered.

Nate realized he'd been hogging the binoculars and Denton hadn't been able to see a thing. He turned them long enough to see Mr. Smith slip back into the woods, toward the hole in the fence and the Holocaust museum, then handed them back.

"He's going. It must be over. She used the phone, just like you said. And then she left him a bottle. Looks like vodka or gin."

Denton didn't look too concerned.

"Don't you see, that would be the perfect way to get a bug in the house!" Nate insisted.

Denton raised the binocs to look at the kitchen. Nate squinted. As far as he could see, there was still no one there.

Denton spoke calmly: "Why put a bug on a bottle of liquor? It's likely to be thrown out in a day or two, whether they drink it or not."

He had a point.

"But why else would she give them liquor?" Nate asked.

Denton lowered the binoculars. "Let's hope Aharon and Hannah find out."

*　　*　　*

Aharon could not believe he was going into the Mossad's *actual rooms*. Well, leave it to Hannah. The woman single-handedly could have brought the Roman Empire to its knees.

He looked around the hall once more—still nothing, not a peep—and put the key into the keyhole. Hannah had gotten the key, filched it from behind the reception desk as easily as if thievery had been mother's milk to her. Aharon shook his head, but he had to admit, he was impressed. The door swung inward.

Could the Mossad have hidden cameras in the room? Infrared sensors? Booby traps? Naturally. That's why Aharon had insisted on being the one to go into the room while Hannah watched downstairs to make sure their quarry didn't return. But now that he'd won that particular battle and was here, it did not seem such a victory.

Thievery had not been mother's milk to Aharon and he wasn't sure where to begin.

He saw nothing of the booby trap ilk, no cameras. He went through the suitcases, trying to put everything back exactly the way he found it, but feeling clumsy about it. Rummaging through ladies' underwear! And beardless rummaging at that. It was not to be believed.

In a drawer of the bureau under a pile of men's pants Aharon found files. This was what he had come for, and though he wanted nothing more than to get out of this room as quickly as possible, he took out the files and sat with them on the floor.

There were half a dozen legal-sized manila folders with elastic bands to hold them closed. The one on top was his.

Aharon hissed in a breath and, fascinated, read someone else's account of him. A photograph of him—a good one, taken outdoors, was in the front of the file. It had been taken without his knowing, apparently in Jerusalem. He was assessed as "fanatically Orthodox."

Aharon looked at the picture of the man he had been and felt a strange tightening sensation behind the eyes. Looking at the photo, he would say that was a hard man, a man who believed he had all the answers, a man who, in fact, knew very little.

He put his own file down and flipped through the others. There was a file each on Dr. Talcott, Nate, and Denton. There was not a file, thankfully, on his wife. The last file was Anatoli's.

Aharon knew that Anatoli had been going under a pseudonym for some time. In Poland he used the name Solkeski, not Nikiel. What frightened Aharon when he opened the file was the first image—a blown-up eight-by-ten photograph of Anatoli's arm. There was a swatch of skin showing where his black wool coat sleeve had been raised, raised by the heavy, meaty hand that had a grip on the arm. The photograph must have been taken when the DoD agents were escorting Anatoli somewhere, Aharon thought. And it must have been taken with a telephoto lens. The numbers on Anatoli's arm were as plain as day.

Aharon flipped the picture forward. Sure enough, there, on the biographical form was a photograph of Anatoli, at least twenty years old, and his real name. The file was thick, including printouts of some of the "pages of testimony" from Yad Vashem that mentioned Kobinski and Anatoli and camp records as well.

Aharon went to stroke his beard and found empty air. He clucked his tongue thoughtfully and rocked a little, the file in his lap.

The Mossad—Norowitz—knew who Anatoli was, that he was Kobinski's closest ally and disciple. Aharon thought about the man who had wiped corned beef juice from his fingers to look at the code binder, the man who had called him so frequently in the last few months.

Rabbi, have you found any more of Kobinski's manuscript?

What would Norowitz do to get his hands on Anatoli? What would he *not* do? But the DoD had Anatoli, at least for the moment. Then again, they'd also had Jill and that had not stopped the Mossad from attempting to kidnap her.

A beep startled Aharon from his cogitation. He scrambled to his feet, running to the window, heart hammering. Then he realized that the sound had not come from outside but from a device on the bureau that looked like an oversize portable phone. It beeped again.

He went over to it and picked it up. It was probably a satellite phone; it was the size of a large old-fashioned receiver, not like the modern cell phones at all. Underneath the buttons for dialing was a two-inch LED screen. There was a message on the screen. Its arrival must have been the source of the beep. It was in Hebrew, something Aharon supposed was encryption enough in most parts of the world. It said:

TONIGHT'S PLAN APPROVED. GODSPEED.

23

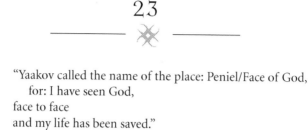

"Yaakov called the name of the place: Peniel/Face of God,
    for: I have seen God,
face to face
and my life has been saved."
Genesis 32:31, Everett Fox, *The Five Books of Moses,* 1995

Calder was crawling across the face of the globe. That's the way it felt. In his mind he was crawling, grasping fistful of earth by fistful of earth, moving one bloodied knee at a time. It was like crawling into his own cerebellum. Every hour, every moment, brought new memories. Few of them were pleasant.

Once, asleep sitting upright in the airplane, he'd had a memory-dream. He remembered himself—Calder Farris—screaming at his *father*. Calder remembered growing up with the hard man, and that he'd been beaten often. In this particular instance he had had enough, and in an unspeakable rage he'd shoved his father against the wall and pounded his face with his fist again and again. Then he had put back his head and howled. He awoke with the woman shaking him, a murmured whine still on his lips.

It occurred to him that the boy in the dream, Calder Farris, himself, had lived with that howl inside him for a long time. That was what had enabled him to do certain things, like almost kill his father and slaughter that Silver male and then cut him up like an animal. Perhaps it was the damage that had happened to his mind, but somewhere along the way he had lost the howl.

He didn't want that rage, but losing it made him weak.

The woman was weakening him, her presence alone. Bringing her had been a mistake. It was hard enough just trying to cope, trying to hold it together against a flood of memories that were as sharp and painful as the pins and needles of an awakening limb.

What did she want from him? Why couldn't she just leave him alone? It felt like his old job, his old life, was being foisted upon him before he was ready. He was *sick*; couldn't she see that? She had tried to talk to him, early on, while they were in an airport restaurant in Poland. She had been talking about some weapons and her words had so disturbed him, had caused such black ripples to burn in his mind, that he had allowed a glass to tumble from his hand and shatter on the floor. She had shut up then.

After they left Poland, he had so much to deal with that he had stopped pretending she was his prisoner. He had even tried to ditch her, but she had stuck to him like glue. She looked at him with such *concern*, asked about his head, gave him pills that eased the pain. He had no idea why she was doing any of it, but he was too confused to resist.

All he could do was try to hold on as information flew at him. Planes, for example. At first they had seemed exotic, almost spooky, even though he had known what they were. But traveling on them, sitting in the cramped seats, feeling annoyed at the quality of the food, even the feeling he got in his ears on landing—these sensations were very familiar.

And the sun—the *sun*! It had been cloudy in Poland, and he hadn't even remembered about the sun until it came out at sunrise on their flight to Paris. He'd stared out the window at it, felt its heat on his face, and known real joy.

It was not that he'd ever *liked* Centalia. He had survived there, nothing more. But once he saw the sun he felt a sense of possessiveness, of happiness, of pride for *this* world. He felt that he was home.

The hardest thing to reconcile was the people. How many people there were in this world, of every shape and size! There was no uniformity at all. And everyone moved without passes, with no one caring where they went, no one taking down their name on a logsheet or asking questions. There was basic security at the airports, but otherwise no one monitored their progress. The disorderliness of it scared him. How could society function with such liberties, with no one in control? How did things keep from simply flying apart?

He was not like them. Watching them, he felt hard and rigid where all around him was turmoil. He was like a stiff log in a churning river. Just as the sun had made him feel that he was home, the people made him doubt he had ever belonged on this world.

By the time they arrived in Paris, he had fallen back in love with chocolate chip cookies. And he was starting to feel that there could be a kind of fascination in the chaos. People-watching in the airport on their long layover, he could almost appreciate the flagrant *willfulness* of the disorder, was enchanted by the magic trick, that all the comings and goings and pairings and teeming could work without any visible means of structure. It was like a toy he remembered—a kaleidoscope. The thing always made amazing patterns no matter which way the random pieces fell.

When they boarded the flight to Washington, D.C., the idea of it, that he would soon be *home*, produced tremendous anxiety. He knew there would be many answers there—and that stepping back into his old life meant he had to be 100 percent. On the plane, the woman sat beside him, as she always did. But she had not tried to speak to him again.

If she was completely stupid she might just follow him right into his superior's office and give herself up. In fact, when they landed in Washington he thought he just might be well enough to grab her arm and make *sure* that was what happened. She had dogged the wounded hunter. Big fun. It was time she learned that he still had teeth.

He was staring at a couple across the aisle and one row up. They were young and attractive, whole and undeformed. Both had pale skin and dark hair. The male had his arm around the female and they were looking into each other's eyes. Some emotion swirled around them that Farris did not quite get. He didn't get it, but he still felt envious.

"Lieutenant Farris?" The woman spoke his name. He turned his eyes to give her a cold look. "Sometimes it helps to talk about things. Would you like to tell me about it? About what happened to you when you went . . . somewhere else?"

He sneered. "I'm not telling *you* anything."

"I understand. You don't trust me. In that case, would you like to hear what happened to me?"

He didn't. He didn't want to talk. But then, she was as good as offering a full confession. And then he recalled that this woman might hold the answers to his own experiences. With all he'd had to deal with on the journey, he'd forgotten why he'd wanted her along in the first place.

"Speak then."

She talked to him with simple words. She explained how they had been in the woods that night and how five of them had gone through a type of black hole. She began to tell a story about the world she had seen. He tried to stay with her, to hear everything without emotion, but it was hard. There was so much to think about, so many directions the mind could turn off, like a freeway with slippery exits, dark eddies pulling him down. *Black hole. And then the battlefield.*

She got to a place in her story that she must have thought important, for she put her hand on his sleeve to focus his attention. He stared down at her hand.

"Lieutenant Farris, did you hear what I said? I was talking about the weapon we learned about on Difa-Gor-Das." She repeated the information about a machine carefully, her eyes locked to his to keep him with her.

He took it in. He was still trying to get his mind around the black hole, but he took this new information in. She carefully explained wave technology and what would result if you tried to manipulate the wave. Fragments of old learning came back to him, enough for him to grasp what she was saying. He even seemed to recall that this, *this,* was what he had wanted from her all that long while ago. She was *revealing secrets,* but she didn't seem disturbed by the fact. She described everything deliberately.

"Don't you see?" she said, her green eyes alight. "The technology I was working on—the technology *you* were looking for—it has to be buried, Lieutenant. Because if it isn't, there is a very real possibility that someone in the government *will* use it, benignly, ignorantly, or otherwise. We can't risk it."

She seemed to want some kind of response from him. She squeezed his arm.

"We don't *have* to be on opposite sides. We've both seen things that have made us realize how precious this world is and how . . ." she sighed, "how responsible we are for our choices. It's not too late, Lieutenant Farris."

It finally dawned on him then what she was doing, why she had come with him, why she had been so concerned about him, so helpful! She was trying to turn him, turn *him*, like some green recruit!

An ugly laugh passed his lips. She had no idea how little he cared about any of it. He felt only numb about what she had told him; he felt nothing at all. He didn't believe her, number one. Number two, he was a soldier, even here, and he would never betray his oaths of loyalty. And, number three, it wasn't even his responsibility to make the kinds of decisions she was talking about. Didn't she understand that? She was trying to manipulate the wrong link in the chain of command.

In fact, he was amazed how little he cared about what she had just told him. He wasn't even angry at the idea that she might be lying or trying to manipulate him. And even as he was thinking so he felt sweat trickle down his face and a hot, burning pain in his abdomen.

"Excuse me," he said, rising quickly.

He barely made it to the bathroom. There was a roaring in his ears and a thickening veil descending across his vision. He locked the door and sank down the wall, his knees jammed up against the sink, and the blackness in his mind swept over him like a blanket.

*   *   *

Ed Hinkle stared out at the dark. It wasn't snowing, but the bare soil outside was crisp as ice and the air hurt when you drew it into your lungs. He was sick to death of Poland.

Still no word today. He'd sent in his report this morning, as usual, and heard nothing back, as usual. He couldn't resist taking a walk in the woods this morning, just to see with his own two eyes that nothing had changed. Nothing had changed.

He wished he knew the test results on the samples from the woods, if the DoD had found any trace of a weapon or not. But he already knew by the way they were treating him that he was eyes and ears and muscle on this case and nothing more. Most of the time he was happy enough to just do his job and be done with it. But in this case he was damned curious. He had been in the woods that night, and he had seen that flash.

He didn't know how much longer he could stay here with that filthy old man without killing him. He was their only witness and he was too mental to tell them jack.

The bottle of Russian vodka on the counter kept drawing Hinkle's eye.

He'd told the broad he didn't want it. He was on assignment, which meant he was on duty twenty-four seven. He wouldn't drink. But the Russian bimbo had insisted on leaving it here, as a gift. He told her he'd just pour it down the drain. She'd laughed and left it anyway.

She hadn't been bad-looking. If it had been any other time . . .

He picked up the bottle. It had the original factory seal—looked just like other bottles of the same or a similar brand he'd seen in the windows in town. Too bad. He had a brief fantasy—wouldn't it be fun if the bimbo had actually been a Russian spy and had put poison in the bottle? Or better yet, Spanish fly, so she could slip in later and ride him raw while her partner stole the goods. He put down the bottle with a laugh.

No such luck. The Russians weren't even on the map these days. Besides, who'd want a bed-wetting old man?

He felt Davis's presence before he saw him. Well, hell, where else would he be? It was a small house.

"Want to play some cards?"

Ed sighed. "Hell, yeah."

They were deep into five card stud, using a huge jar of the old man's pennies for stake, when the distinct noise of slamming car doors caught their attention.

Hinkle and Davis looked at each other and got up to investigate. Hinkle wasn't alarmed at first, but he was on alert. Maybe someone had finally stopped by to see the old fart, maybe someone with an actual dreg or two of information. But he hadn't heard the sound of a motor.

Before they reached the front door he *did* hear a motor—a car starting up. It sounded familiar. He and Davis rushed out the front door to see the faces of two startled youths *in their rental car*. The car backed up, lurching into reverse, and began gunning madly down the driveway.

For a moment, Hinkle was completely dumbfounded. *Some dumb-ass local shits were actually stealing their car.* Stealing the car of the DoD—how unlucky could you get?

Then he and Davis began running after the car—on foot.

From the cover of the woods north of Anatoli's place Nate, Denton, Aharon, and Hannah watched the car lurch down the road and the two men running behind it, guns drawn. The car died and restarted and lurched again just enough to keep Hinkle and his pal from giving up.

"Well, I'd say that's the distraction," Denton commented. He rubbed his hands together as if against the cold, but the truth was, he was far too tense to feel anything as insignificant as weather. His three companions looked a little anxious themselves.

Aharon and Hannah hadn't been able to learn everything about the Mossad's plan, but they had heard bits and pieces and, between the four of them, they'd worked out a basic scenario that made sense. Whether it was the scenario the Mossad had in mind was another matter.

"There they go," Hannah whispered.

From the dark of the woods directly behind Anatoli's house two figures in black emerged and ran for the back door. Hannah and Aharon gave Denton and Nate one last look of support and took off along the edge of the woods. Denton and Nate slipped away for a rendezvous of their own.

The man who sometimes called himself Mr. Smith and his partner, Hadar, quietly let themselves into the house. The back door was locked, but Mr. Smith had a hook that opened it in five seconds. He didn't even have to put the corpse down. Door open, he slipped inside, Hadar behind him.

It was not ideal. The men who had arrived this morning from Czechoslovakia, the ones who were right now out playing cat and mouse with the U.S. agents, could have been in here helping him. And they could have had all the time in the world instead of being rushed—*if* the Americans had consumed the sleeping drug–enhanced vodka. But they hadn't; they were too well trained.

The corpse on his shoulders had not felt heavy when he'd picked it up back at the car, but it was heavy after carrying it a quarter mile through the woods. He let Hadar brush past him and open the door to the old man's room. The lights were out and they left the hall door open in lieu of turning on their torches.

The old man was awake and he sat up, his face, even in the shadows, a grimacing mask of fear. Hadar was fast. She stuffed the gag in his mouth before he could scream and had him up and out of bed in an instant. He didn't even fight the restraints that pinned his arms to his side and his calves together. From the look of the old man, it would be a miracle he'd survive the ordeal.

When Mr. Nikiel was subdued, Hadar lifted him out of the way, arms around his waist, taking him into the hall. The old man was whimpering in his throat.

Alone, Mr. Smith dumped his load on the bed and stripped off the black covering. Inside was one very dead old man of approximately the same age and size as Anatoli Nikiel. The corpse was awkward and the smell and feel unpleasant, but Mr. Smith had done worse things. He tossed the blanket over the corpse. Then he removed a bottle from his pocket and squirted a harsh-smelling liquid on the blanket, the corpse's face and hands, the floor, the bedside table. The highly flammable liquid would dissipate within minutes, so there was no time to linger. He struck a match.

The bed, table, floor, and corpse burst into flame. He went into the hall and took Nikiel from Hadar, wrapped him loosely in the black covering, and hoisted the living weight over his right shoulder. Hadar was already down the hall.

In the kitchen, she had the attaché case in hand, moving it to the table. He gave her a quick hand signal to meet at the rendezvous point—unnecessary but reassuring—and slipped with his burden out the door and toward the woods.

Hadar was alone in the house. She had very little time. She opened the case and grabbed everything inside—not much, as it turned out, just a folder of papers—and stuck it into her black backpack. Then she took a plastic bag from her pocket and deposited into the case an amount of paper ashes that approximated the size and contents of the folder.

The case was shut and put back against the wall where she'd found it. She had a bottle of liquid in her pocket similar to the one Mr. Smith had and she distributed it around the kitchen, particularly on the case and the wall behind it.

The house was already filling with smoke from the fire down the hall when she lit this one. As the flames licked the cabinets she picked up the bottle of vodka from the counter and smashed it on the floor to make sure its contents could not be retrieved and tested. It only fueled the fire. Then, with one last look at the case—it was burning nicely—she went out the back door, careful to lock it.

Aharon was crouched on the far side of the house and he watched the second figure in black dart into the trees. He looked over his shoulder at Hannah. She was at the far end of the wall watching the road. She signaled him, then ran at a crouch to join him. He heard the engine at the same instant—the U.S. agents had recovered the car and were returning.

"Let's go!" she said as she reached him, pushing his back to get him moving. His heart was pumping so hard he had no breath to speak, but his legs obeyed her command. He was *way* too old for this craziness.

As they went around the back of the house, Aharon heard the crackle of fire and saw the flames leap up. He patted the papers inside his coat to reassure himself that they were still there—the papers that he had taken from the attaché case while the Mossad agents were in Anatoli's room. Then Hannah grabbed his hand and they ran.

He felt a surge of victory as they entered the woods, despite all the huffing and puffing. Hannah's trick with the glass had worked after all. And what would the Mossad think, he wondered, when they found that what the U.S. agents had kept in that attaché was a folder filled with old Polish folk tunes?

Mr. Smith had left his car on a deserted maintenance road through the woods that was more of a dirt rut than anything else. When he stepped out of the woods with Anatoli over his shoulder, Denton and Nate were waiting for him.

Denton's breath was visible coming in puffs through the woolen ski mask. He felt a rush of fear and anticipation. Calder Farris's gun was steady in his hand. Smith froze at the sight of them.

"Don't move," Denton said.

Nate slipped around the car and relieved Mr. Smith of his burden, cradling the black sack carefully and setting it on the ground.

"Now hands up." Denton motioned with the gun.

Mr. Smith slowly, almost sarcastically, raised his hands. His eyes glittered pure murder.

Nate fought with the black covering for a few minutes before finding the opening and pushing it down, away from Anatoli's face. Mr. Smith only had eyes for Denton, waiting for him to be distracted by the fumbling. Denton stared straight at him, not distracted at all.

Nate got the black shroud down to Anatoli's feet. The old man looked wild. Denton could hear Nate murmuring to him reassuringly. He loosened the gag, trying to ease the bloated pain on the old man's face.

"Get him into the car and then search Santa Claus here for a weapon," Denton said, trying to disguise his voice. He wanted Nate to hurry. He could see from the tension in Mr. Smith's body that he was going to try something. Smith's eyes said no way was he going to let them get away with this. They said death before capitulation.

Not that Denton was all that worried, but the suspense was killing him.

Nate tried to move Anatoli to the car, unsuccessfully. He kept trying before figuring out that the old man's ankles were bound.

The philosophy-slash-physics student was not very proficient at this, Denton surmised. Nate's movements were nervous and unwise. He should have moved Anatoli farther from Mr. Smith before doing anything more, picking him up and carrying him if necessary. Instead, Nate seemed fixated on getting Anatoli to walk. He crouched down, trying to undo the binding at Anatoli's feet.

"Nate!" Denton called in warning.

Too late. Mr. Smith's foot came out, kicking Nate squarely in the chin with furious force. Denton let off a shot, a shot that came not from panic but from anger. It might even have hit Mr. Smith, except that the man tucked and rolled, disappearing around the front of the car.

The situation, at that instant, was very bad. Nate was sprawled on his back on the ground, out cold. Anatoli was standing bound, black sack at his feet, his mouth open and screeching. And Mr. Smith was out of sight on the other side of the car, no doubt *with a gun*. They hadn't disarmed him. That had been a mistake.

Denton chuckled.

He felt a bizarre sense of ease. It was as if he could see all of the possibilities laid out before him, stretching away from this moment like shining cords of light. He might overcome Mr. Smith, and if he did one band of light would brighten, the rest flickering out, and life would proceed in a certain direction. And if he did not, another path would quicken and spread. He might, within minutes, be lying dead on the ground. Or . . . not. Life, unstoppable, immutable life, would go on either way. It was not concerned with how the pattern turned out any more than it had to deliberate on the design of an individual snowflake.

Denton, however, wanted very much to win.

He did not hear so much as sense Smith approaching, crouching around the right side of the car. Denton shifted, down and to his left, moving around from the trunk to the left side of the car. He was alert, calm but electrified as a live wire. He thought quickly. He could continue to circle the car, risking his life on his power of stealth, hoping that he might be able to sneak up behind Smith even as Smith was trying to sneak up on him.

Or he could do as he was doing now—slip off his shoes and climb up onto the hood.

It was crazy. From his position on top of the car he would be vulnerable. If his feet made a noise, if the metal of the car gave a little, making a tinny denting sound, Smith would know where he was and Denton would be an open, visible target. But if not . . .

Luck was with him. He seemed light as a feather as he mounted the hood. The car took his weight without a sound. As he bellied onto the roof, he got a clear view of Mr. Smith. The man who had beaten him in LA so coldly was crouched near the trunk, gun raised high in his hand, his attention focused as he peered, cautiously, around the end of the car.

Denton's breath misted in front of his eyes, causing the image of the Mossad agent to take on a foggy quality. He aimed his gun.

In a Western, shooting a man in the back was dishonorable. Denton, however, knew he was by far the underdog in this match and had to take his shots where he found them. He also knew he didn't have the skill to wound the man or, like they did in movies, dislodge the gun from his hand with a single shot, leaving him with burning fingers but no permanent damage.

No. That was not real life. The reality was that he was incompetent with a gun and probably should have been dead already. Denton aimed as best he could at the center of Smith's back and fired.

*   *   *

When they landed in Washington, Dr. Talcott was quiet. She had talked herself out, whispering mysteries in his ear like some Lilith for the past several hours. And he had not acknowledged any of them.

As they got off the plane, she looked discouraged and tired. Farris kept tight hold of her arm, pulling her through the terminal and outside. He got them a taxi to his apartment. He'd remembered many things by now, and he was able to give the address to the taxi driver. He even sounded normal when he said it.

When they got there, when they were standing right outside his door, he suddenly couldn't bear to have her see this. He didn't know how he was going to react to what was inside, but he had to do it alone. He thought about tying her up or stashing her somewhere, but he just . . . the truth was, he didn't want to fuck with it. He told her to wait down the hall.

He had to break in, having lost his keys long ago. Inside, he did a quick reconnaissance, but the place was empty. He closed the blinds, locked the door, shoved a chair against it, and turned on the light. He spent a while searching the place for bugs and cameras, but it was halfhearted, satisfying a vague paranoia.

There were no bugs. The doors and windows locked tight. For a moment he marveled at the privacy these things implied. In here as in the streets and airports, Calder Farris was invisible.

The apartment was chilly, sparsely furnished. It was familiar but seemed detached from himself. It stirred nothing inside him.

At length, a box attracted his attention. It was white cardboard and he knew it held the past. He opened it and found pictures—mostly colored, some black-and-white. They were images of Calder Farris, of childhood, his father, high school, a few from Desert Storm and other military experiences. There were not many of them, considering the span of such a life. Farris had not liked being photographed. He stood alone in almost all of them and he always looked the same, staring at the camera with glasses disguising his eyes.

In a muddy, unruly flood, the whole of his previous life came back to him, washing away the bits and pieces of recollection and becoming a solid knowing. He saw it all, not objectively—he was far from objective—but with the rawness of someone who'd had tremendous hope for a thing . . . and was terribly disappointed.

All the way here from Poland he had hoped and had not even known he was hoping—for something warm in this life, for something he could not even define. Maybe he had hoped that for Calder Farris there would be . . . what? A woman, a mate, friends at least—some shelter, some *meaning*, some bright end to all the pain, a haven, a home. And there was nothing.

Dr. Talcott had tried to explain to him about the gateway and how it chose where they went. He had pretended not to believe. But he'd always known that somehow, in Centalia, he had entered the darkest part of his own mind, that

Centalia was a nightmare only he could dream. And maybe that had been part of the madness.

This empty apartment was Calder Farris also. His life had been dedicated to his job and only that, to the government, the United States military. He had believed in it with an angry, brutal faith.

The state rewards service. Long live the state.

*   *   *

"It was a false alarm, sir."

Calder Farris sat at a conference table across from Gen. Franklin Deall. Also in the meeting was Dr. Alan Rickman, the director of the DSO. The two of them were looking at him with incredulity and anger.

"*A false alarm?*" General Deall managed to berate him with that single phrase. "You call an XL3, spend a fortune in Seattle, drag a team of men to *Poland* to chase down this Dr. Talcott, then disappear from all contact for nine days, and now you say it was a *false alarm*? You'd better explain yourself, Lieutenant. And I mean now."

Dr. Rickman was allowing General Deall to run the show, but he was watching with tight-lipped enjoyment. Farris recalled that Rickman had always been a little afraid of him. Rickman had never liked the seedier part of weapon procurement.

"The explosion on the University of Washington campus was due to a faulty furnace," Calder said.

"We *know* that. We have the ever-loving *report*! And at that point Dr. Rickman tried to pull you back and you insisted this was something major."

"That was my judgment call at the time, sir. I was just starting to interrogate Dr. Talcott when she escaped from the hospital. Her escape looked highly suspicious. I thought it was prudent to go after her."

"I have yet to be convinced that anything about this was *prudent*," Deall commented with disgust.

"What happened in Poland?" Dr. Rickman leaned in, his elbows on the table. "The other agents said you were ahead of them in the woods, chasing Dr. Talcott and the others. But they lost them—and you."

"I got ahead of my men without realizing it. I was trying not to lose the quarry. When I reached them they had doubled back toward the concentration camp and a dirt road. They were about to take off in a jeep. I jumped onto the back of it in order to stick with them. That's when I lost my men."

General Deall flipped through the report in front of him. "The other agents made no mention of a vehicle. They said the pursuit took place in deep woods."

"Part of it, yes, but the woods edged the grounds of Auschwitz. I was close enough to the quarry that I managed to stay with them when they doubled back. The other agents must have missed it."

"Why didn't you radio them?"

"I tried at one point, but I was running too fast. And once I was on the jeep I couldn't get to my radio."

"There's *always* time for radio contact, Farris. My god!"

"Yes, sir."

"There was a bright light, according to your men," Rickman interrupted. "An enormous flash. What was that?"

Farris shook his head slowly, face bewildered. "No . . . the suspects had flashlights. Or maybe they saw the headlights on the jeep."

Deall and Rickman exchanged a look.

"Well? What happened once you were on the jeep?"

"It had a hard-shell top and I didn't think they'd seen me. I stood on the back bumper, hanging on to the sides. It took both hands and I couldn't get to my radio. My plan was to wait until we'd reached our destination, then arrest them. I had my gun and I didn't think they were armed. But we drove for miles. It was freezing. My hands grew numb and I was thrown off the jeep on a sharp curve. I struck my head."

Farris recited this stiffly and to the point. He raised his hand to a bandage on his head, where a months-old scar had been carefully reopened that morning.

"I don't remember a lot after that. I walked in the woods for a long time. I finally managed to find a town."

Deall and Rickman were both observing him with suspicion.

"Why didn't you use your radio after you were thrown from the jeep?" Deall demanded.

"I don't know. I don't even think I had it on me. It must have been lost when I was thrown."

"Why didn't you call when you reached a phone?" Rickman asked.

"I think had a concussion. For a while there . . . I wasn't sure who I was or where."

"Have you seen a staff doctor since you've been back?"

"Not yet, sir."

"Well, you'd better!" Deall ordered. "Go directly after this meeting, and have them send me a report."

"Yes, sir."

"You certainly look like you've been through the wringer," Rickman pointed out. He did not say it sympathetically. It was just an observation of fact.

Farris had dyed his hair that morning back to something approximating the color of his roots, but it was still shorter than he'd once worn it. His eyebrows had not completely grown back. His face was haggard. There was nothing he could do about the minor surgery he'd done to slant his eyes.

"What I don't understand is why you now believe this case has nothing of interest when a little more than a week ago you were insisting it was a matter of vital importance to national security."

"I reviewed the case while making my way back here and again last night preparing to make my report. I can see now that I was . . . overzealous. I don't believe Dr. Talcott was working on anything of interest to us. In fact, I believe she is simply . . . a flake, sir."

Ricker raised a patronizing eyebrow. "You might have figured that out earlier, Lieutenant, if you had showed what you were working on to our people. I had several physicists look over the scanty material you'd procured and they were unimpressed. Dr. Everett said that without seeing Dr. Talcott's so-called equation he could only surmise that the simulator results had been rigged and that her brief notes about a 'universal wave' were either delusions of grandeur or an attempt to perpetuate a hoax."

"I don't see how you could be so taken in, Lieutenant. You were trained better than that," Deall said, disappointed.

"I have no excuse except that I'd allowed myself to get too obsessed with my work. It had been a long time since I'd taken a vacation. If you decide to allow me to continue my job, a short leave of absence would probably be in order."

Deall huffed. "Allow you to continue? Do you know how much alarm you caused? Let me tell you, Lieutenant . . . "

The rest of the meeting they lectured him. Farris took it, shoulders straight, hands clasped in front of him on the table. He didn't think they were serious about reassigning him. Calder Farris had not been liked, but he had without doubt been useful over the years. A great emphasis would be put on the results of the doctor's examination, but Farris was not concerned. He knew he could convince a physician, given the very real bump on his skull, that he had met with a mind-altering accident recently.

Deall left the office first, still pissed off. Rickman was slower to gather his things, kept eyeing him. Farris sat, back straight, looking out the window at the sun.

Rickman suddenly leaned forward over the table, staring. That old feeling of being different, of being found out, assaulted Farris. He kept his face impassive.

"Look at me," Rickman said.

Farris did. Rickman gazed at him searchingly from behind John Lennon spectacles.

"My god, Farris, what happened to your eyes?"

Farris clenched his teeth. "I had a little cosmetic surgery. I did it months ago."

The scars were there, behind the ears, should anyone ask him to prove it. It was a strange thing to do, strange enough to go on his record as questionable, but not strange enough to get him committed.

Rickman looked puzzled, his gaze going back and forth between Farris's eyes.

"Did you? Whatever for? But . . . no, that's not it." Rickman's face cleared. "I see. You're wearing colored contacts. They're quite an improvement, if you don't mind my saying so. Make you look more . . . approachable." Rickman flushed, as if embarrassed to have brought up the subject. "Well, good luck with the doctor."

"Thank you, sir."

Before reporting to Medical, Calder stopped at the men's room. A man with a penis remarkably like his own was using the urinal. He finished and left, hardly giving Farris a glance. When he was alone, Calder studied his face in the mirror.

Rickman was right. He wasn't sure when it had happened, but his white-blue eyes, the eyes that had always spooked others, had darkened. They were now a shade resembling the blue of sunlit skies.

24

———————— ✳ ————————

Between the two sides of these divided strands [the
white and black faces of God] is the pathway of ini-
tiation, the middle path, the path of opposites in
harmony. There, all is reconciled and understood.
There, only good triumphs and evil is no longer.
This pathway is that of supreme balance and is
called the last judgment of God.
    —Eliphas Levi, *The Book of Splendours,* 1894

When matter and antimatter collide, they neutralize each other and release enormous energy.
    —Michio Kaku, *Beyond Einstein,* 1987

On the morning of his first day back at Aish HaTorah, Aharon arrived early.
The hallways and office were quiet as he went to work. He gathered up his
binder of code printouts and then Binyamin's. He ripped off the binder covers
and threw them in the trash. He took the two-foot stack of printouts that remained and carried them down the hall to the school office, where he set the
papers on the floor and began to shred them. Feeding them to the machine
was like feeding one's own children to a dragon. But when it was over a huge
burden had been lifted. He gathered up the heaps of shredded waste and went
back down the hall.

Binyamin was inside his office. He was standing over the trash can holding the torn binder covers and wearing a look of sheer panic. His jaw dropped
farther when he saw the confetti in Aharon's arms—and Aharon's bare face.

"Come!" Aharon said. "And bring the matches."

They went down to the back alley. There, to the consternation of the
passersby, Aharon lit the paper scraps. They went up quickly, making a frightening fire against the cobblestones before it faltered into ash.

"I don't get it," Binyamin said, picking at the scraggly hairs on his chin.

"Listen. . . ." Aharon put a hand on the boy's shoulder. Lord, he had missed
even Binyamin! The smell, no; the spirit, yes. "Do you know what I think?"

"No."

"I think that it just might be possible that some of God's secrets, Binyamin, some of them are *supposed* to remain secret."

Binyamin stared at him suspiciously.

Aharon clapped a hand on his shoulder. "Swear to me one thing. Swear not to say the name Kobinski to anyone, not ever."

Binyamin hesitated, then looked at Aharon's beardless chin, at the ashes swirling around on the stones. "If you say so, Rabbi. I swear."

"Good! Now I believe I will attend to some very neglected students, if I even have any left."

When they came for him that afternoon, Aharon went willingly. He was escorted to the office of Shimon Norowitz, a place he had never been invited to before. The man who belonged in that office was a Norowitz he had never seen before, either—hard and angry, an enemy.

Norowitz wanted to know where he had been, what he had found out about Dr. Jill Talcott, and what had happened in Auschwitz.

"Dr. Talcott is an old friend," Aharon said, pretending surprise that Norowitz was interested in his actions. "I heard on the news that she was in trouble, so naturally, I had to go see if I could help."

Norowitz's eyes were like ice. "And you just happened to help that old friend escape the FBI and then, coincidentally, you took her to visit Kobinski's closest follower in Auschwitz."

"No. I had contacted the old man earlier. I wanted to interview him about Kobinski. So when Dr. Talcott needed to get away for a while I decided to kill two birds with one stone and take her with me. It was no big deal."

" 'No big deal'?" Norowitz shouted. He took a deep breath, calming himself down. "I want to know what happened, Rabbi. You shaved. Why?"

Aharon rubbed his cheek. "A bad rash. It happens. Look, about Anatoli, the old man had a terrible memory. It was a wasted trip."

Norowitz's lips were pinched so tight they made a white, bloodless line. "You went to see Talcott because she's in the Kobinski arrays. She's working on something close to Kobinski's research."

"Jill Talcott? In the arrays?" Aharon pretended astonishment. "You know," he shook his head sadly, "I'm beginning to think you can find *any*thing in the code."

Norowitz got up and went to the window, looking out. His hands were fists on the window ledge. Aharon could almost feel sorry for him.

"I can't believe you're going to do this to me," he said, without turning around. "You're going to leave me high and dry. *You*, Rabbi, who came to *me*."

"Look, I can't speak for you, but for me, I think it's time I let Kobinski go. There's only so long a grown man can look for meaning where there is none."

"Ha!" Norowitz turned, eyes blazing. "You won't let go. Oh, no. And I—I won't, either."

"Are you sure that's wise?" Aharon gazed into Norowitz's eyes, for a moment letting his own determination shine through. "The sages say, 'Don't ask a lion to talk. You might not like what he has to say.' "

"Don't patronize me, Rabbi. You know I could have you arrested."

"*Nu?* Well, I can't stop you from wasting your time."

Aharon got up to leave. "I should probably tell you, I may not be staying in Jerusalem. My wife has wanted to move back to New York for some time. To be honest, I think that might not be such a bad idea."

"You won't get away from me like that."

"I wouldn't dream of trying." Aharon paused. ". . . Have you ever considered the possibility that Kobinski was simply a great kabbalist sage, and nothing the state of Israel needs to worry about?"

Norowitz shook his head slowly. "Not on your life."

"Let's hope that it never comes to that, Shimon Norowitz. For you or any of us. Shalom."

*   *   *

Rabbi Schwartz was standing when Denton was ushered into his office in upstate New York. His fingertips were on his desk, his face deeply disapproving.

"Mr. Wyle. Your message this morning took me by surprise. I must say, you have a lot of nerve showing your face here again."

"True, but I thank you for seeing me anyway."

Denton sat in a chair and waited for Schwartz to do likewise. For a moment he hesitated, as though his disdain were much better shown on his feet, but gravity won over and he sat.

"So?"

"I wanted to apologize for that break-in. I guess I had built up some fantasy in my head that we were enemies and that I had a right to use any means at my disposal. I didn't. I'm sorry."

Schwartz made a gesture of disinterest. "You can't get out of this with an apology, Mr. Wyle. I intend to prosecute."

"That's up to you. I just came to drop something off."

Denton pulled a document from his bag. It was a reproduction, 200 pages thick, bound neatly in a blue report cover. He put it on Schwartz's desk.

Schwartz picked it up. He leafed through it once, then again more carefully. The tension in the room changed; Schwartz's entire body language changed. He finally put it down, neatly lining it up with the edge of his desk, his fingers bronze, with long, scholarly nails.

"Where did you get it?"

"It's not important. But it's *The Book of Torment,* in its entirety."

Schwartz picked the manuscript back up and turned a few pages. "It's been doctored."

"All of the math has been removed. And a few other things, here and there. But the majority of it, Kobinski's philosophy, is there."

"Why?"

"Why what? Why was it doctored or why have I given it to you?"

Schwartz pressed his lips together for a long moment, then shook his head. "Never mind. The one question I don't think I should ask, and to the second I already know the answer. You want me not to prosecute and you probably want money, too. Very well. How much?"

"I don't want money," Denton said, rising. "I'd appreciate it if you didn't prosecute, but that's your choice."

Schwartz frowned at him distrustfully, but his eyes kept going back to the manuscript, as if he could hardly keep himself from reading it at once. Denton smiled and went to the door.

"Oh—one thing you should know," Denton added, turning. "You're not the only one who has the manuscript. I've sent about thirty copies of it out so far, to the press mostly. Someone will publish it. It you intend to do it yourself, you'd better get moving."

"Merciful heavens! Why?" Schwartz exclaimed, dumbfounded.

"So that it won't get lost again. So that men can't come and take it from us and hide it forever."

Schwartz paled. Denton knew then that the Mossad had already been there. But the man shook his head. "I'm not sure that's wise, Mr. Wyle. I'm not sure that is at all wise."

"Rabbi, someday we will be put to the test and we will need the wisdom in that book. You're going to have to trust me on that one. But even if you disapprove of what I'm doing, I hope we can be . . ." Denton's smile turned ironic. "Well, not enemies at least. I've had enough of those for a while."

Schwartz touched the manuscript thoughtfully, then rose from his seat. He walked over to the door, his hand extended. Denton placed his own hand out and it was enveloped in what he was surprised to discover was a very warm palm.

"I still think it unlikely anyone but a kabbalist will understand Kobinski. But on the other hand, keeping secrets is like telling a lie—it can be a lot of work and it makes people very upset. I'm tired of keeping this one. You have my thanks for the book and my sincere . . ." he cocked an eyebrow, "nonenmity."

Denton laughed. "There may come a day when I will need more than that. But for now, it'll do."

*   *   *

Jill Talcott was not going to miss her house in Wallingford. The new home she had purchased in Tennessee had been built in 1906 and she loved the southern charm of it. It had a carriage house out back that had been converted into a large home office by the previous owner. It was perfect.

She was not going to miss the University of Washington, either, which was good since she'd been fired. Thank god for Tom Cheever, Dr. Ansel's old dean.

Nate was strapping a moving box with packing tape. He had filled out in the past month, and his hair had gone back to its corkscrew curls. As she gazed at him she did have *one* regret.

"Nate?"

"Hmmm."

She finished wrapping a plate in newspaper and put it in a box. "I still think you should consider staying at Udub until you finish your doctorate. You're chucking away almost two years of work."

"Jeez, woman, how many times do we have to go over this?"

"It's just that I've always believed that a relationship . . . that people shouldn't hold one another back. It's bad enough aligning yourself with an infamously wacky lady scientist. You should at least finish your degree. At the University of Tennessee you'll practically be starting over."

"Jill . . ." Nate sighed and tossed the tape on the counter. He came over and hugged her close. "Will you quit worrying about me? I'm not in a hurry to get my degree. I'm just sorry for *your* sake, that you won't get the recognition that you deserve."

"I don't care about that. But you—"

He silenced her with a kiss. When he broke away he said, with fake sincerity, "Honey, I'd much rather have a boring, humble, mediocre life with you than live without you."

"Nate!"

He grinned. "Besides, in a moment of weakness you promised to marry me. In three days you're going to meet the entire Andros clan, and once that happens you're trapped for life. My mother thinks she's Hera, the goddess of marital bliss. Cross her and you're doomed."

Jill was showing Nate how much she dreaded that prospect when the phone rang. She started to move for it, but Nate wouldn't let her go. "Let the answering machine pick up."

The machine clicked and gave her brief greeting. Then a voice came on, a male voice with a heavy Asian accent.

"Ms. Talcott? Hey, this bag of yours been sitting here for four weeks! You never show up again! Please come pick it up. Oh, this is Teriyaki Madness. Thank you."

Jill and Nate, still entwined, pulled back and stared at each other with a mix of shock and horror. A second later they were racing for his keys and her shoes and anything else they might need before charging out the door.

Teriyaki Madness was five minutes from Jill's house and Nate, driving Jill's car, took the distance with the aplomb of an expectant father. As soon as he pulled into the parking lot, Jill was out of the passenger seat and running. The older man who owned the small restaurant blinked up at her in surprise as she assaulted the counter.

"My briefcase?" she managed to gulp out.

"Oh! Yes, I just call you."

"I know. Is it—"

He brought it out from under the counter. And, yes, it was her trusty beat-up brown leather satchel, bulging with papers like a frog with its throat stuck out.

"Oh my god!"

"You shouldn't leave it here," the man lectured sternly. "Four weeks, it take up all the space under my counter. I keep waiting for you to show up."

"I'm sorry. Just—thanks!"

When she turned around Nate was right behind her. He looked at the bag and looked at her and they both started laughing.

Back in Jill's living room the bag sat between them on the couch like a prodigal child while Jill carefully cataloged the contents.

"The Excel spreads of our experiments on disk . . . a diagram of the way we hooked up our generator . . . the power chart . . . all of my notes about the equation . . . It's all here!"

"Man!" Nate smiled dazedly. "Think of how the DoD stripped this place and went over the university with a fine-tooth comb, and all the time your briefcase was sitting under the counter at a take-out restaurant."

"Calder said they'd never found it. God, I thought for sure it must have burnt up in the lab. I remember now. The last time I came home I was feeling so sick. I stopped to get a bowl of plain rice because I thought it might help my stomach. I must have been so completely out of it."

"What did you say once about the energy pool theory?" Nate mused. " 'The smallest movement, no matter how unintentional, can have the most profound impact on the pattern.' "

Jill sobered. She looked down at a cluster of pages in her hands, deadly pages. The sequences of events and coincidences that had led to their *not* being in the hands of the DoD suddenly seemed so very tenuous, the fate of the world hanging on a gossamer thread . . . and on her absentmindedness.

"You know what kind of sucks, though," Nate groused. "We put ourselves in mortal danger in Poland to keep the Mossad from getting their hands on what the U.S. had, and it turns out they had diddly."

"No, they had the sim and my notes on the one-minus-one. Given what the Mossad knew about Kobinski, I wouldn't have wanted them to have even that much. Plus there was Anatoli."

Anatoli was currently in a retirement home in Tennessee under yet another new name. Not that the most brilliant interrogator in the world could get anything useful out of the old man, but she was glad he was safe all the same.

"Plus, if we hadn't returned to Earth and proven ourselves of no consequence," Jill pointed out, "you could bet that either the U.S. or the Mossad or both would *still* have a tap on that phone. Which means they would have turned up at Teriyaki Madness within an hour after Mr. Lee placed that phone call."

Nate paled. They both looked at the briefcase on the couch between them; then she looked at the phone and he at the front door.

"Jill . . . ?"

"I'll get my jacket and the briefcase. You get your keys."

EPILOGUE

———— ✳ ————

"I don't understand what you want from me," protested Dr. Ernest Namore. He made an effort to sound stern, but he was more than a little flustered.

"I'm trying to be very clear about that." Calder Farris used a low, threatening tone, a tone that promised a world of hurt should it not be obeyed. "Your government wants your research. We're not asking for charity, Dr. Namore. Depending on how valuable we deem your work, there might well be a place for you at the DoD. But first, we need to know specifically what you've got."

Dr. Namore looked down at some papers on his desktop, pushed them around a bit, face worried. He cleared his throat. "I've told you again and again—I've dabbled with some wave mechanics. Routine stuff. I don't know why you keep bothering me."

Farris made a noncommittal sound.

"It's really nowhere near coherent form yet, and I doubt it'll be of any interest to you once it is. I can't be any more straightforward with you than that."

Namore met his eyes boldly. His were lying eyes.

Farris smiled. "Well, then . . . I must have been mistaken."

Outside in his car, Farris used his cell phone to dial the University of Tennessee. Jill was in her office.

"I have one," he said.

"Oh?" He could hear her scrambling for pen and paper.

He gave her the rundown, how he'd overheard Namore talking to a colleague at a conference. The colleague hadn't found Namore's ideas of interest, but Farris had.

"How close do you think he is?"

"His equation is off, but it's in the ballpark."

"Damn. What's he like?"

"Well, he wouldn't give me the time of day," Farris laughed. "Especially when I put on the screws."

"Good for him."

"Let me give you his address." Farris rambled off the numbers.

"Calder?" Jill said when she had taken it down. "Thank you. And . . . be careful, okay?"

"Absolutely. Say hello to that husband of yours for me."

"Ditto." Jill laughed. "Your wife, that is. Take care."

Calder hung up the phone and felt the knot of fear in his stomach dissipate a little. It seemed some days he was more conscious of the danger than others. Some nights he had nightmares about the apocalypse Jill had enabled him to visualize so well. Some nights he lay awake running over in his mind what more he could do, how to structure his work in the DoD to make sure he would always be there when it cropped up, to make sure that it could never get away from him. And some nights he held Cherry as tightly as he could and willed himself to forget.

He remembered Mark Avery saying something about looking at your child and questioning the rightfulness of what they did. Now when Calder held Jason in his arms the fear of what might be tightened its hand around his heart so hard it hurt. Jason was so young. And life was so long and so chaotic. Anything could happen, in time.

He sensed that, of all of them, he was the one who was the most haunted by it. He supposed that penance was his due.

Dr. Namore lived alone, a confirmed bachelor, completely absorbed in his work at UC Davis. When the knock came on the door of his condo, one quiet Tuesday night, he could not imagine who it might be. He opened it to find a blond woman and a dark-haired young man on the stoop.

The woman smiled nervously and held out her hand.

"Good evening, Dr. Namore. I'm Dr. Talcott and this is my husband, Dr. Andros. May we come in?"

About the Author

———— ✻ ————

Jane Jensen grew up in Pennsylvania and the Midwest. She holds a degree in Computer Science and made her fiction debut as the author of computer games. Her mystery series, *Gabriel Knight,* won a cult following. She currently divides her attention between novels and games. *Dante's Equation* is her fourth novel. She lives with her husband and stepdaughter in Seattle.

Printed in the United States
by Baker & Taylor Publisher Services